Tales of Terror

Alfred Hitchcock

Tales of Terror

Edited by
Eleanor Sullivan

Galahad Books   **New York**

Published in 1986 by
Galahad Books
166 Fifth Avenue
New York, New York 10010

Published by arrangement with Davis Publications, Inc.
Manufactured in U.S.A.

10 9 8 7 6 5 4 3 2

Library of Congress Catalog Card Number: 86-80891

ISBN: 0-88365-710-4

ACKNOWLEDGMENTS

Robert W. Alexander for *The Dead Indian* by Robert W. Alexander, © 1969 by H.S.D. Publications, Inc.

Robert Bloch for *A Home Away From Home* by Robert Bloch, © 1961 by H.S.D. Publications, Inc.

Lawrence Block for *The Dettweiler Solution* by Lawrence Block, © 1976 by Davis Publications, Inc.

Gary Brandner for *Bad Actor* by Gary Brandner, © 1973 by H.S.D. Publications, Inc.

Mary Braund for *To the Manner Born* by Mary Braund, © 1972.

Joseph Payne Brennan for *Death of a Derelict* by Joseph Payne Brennan, © 1967 by H.S.D. Publications, Inc.

Michael Brett for *Free Advice, Inc.* by Michael Brett, © 1968 by H.S.D. Publications, Inc.

Bob Bristow for *The Prosperous Judds* by Bob Bristow, © 1964 by H.S.D. Publications, Inc.

William Brittain for *A Private Little War* by William Brittain, © 1976 by Davis Publications, Inc.

Robert Colby for *Death Is a Lonely Lover* by Robert Colby, © 1968 by H.S.D. Publications, Inc.

John Coyne for *A Cabin in the Woods* by John Coyne, © 1976 by Davis Publications, Inc.

Nelson DeMille for *Life or Breath* by Nelson DeMille, © 1976 by Davis Publications, Inc.

Borden Deal for *A Bottle of Wine* by Borden Deal, © 1956 by H.S.D. Publications, Inc.

August Derleth for *The China Cottage* by August Derleth, © 1965 by H.S.D. Publications, Inc.

William Dolan for *The Hard Sell* by William Dolan, © 1967 by H.S.D. Publications, Inc.

Charlotte Edwards for *The Time Before the Crime* by Charlotte Edwards, © 1958.

Hal Ellson for *The Marrow of Justice* by Hal Ellson, © 1963 by Davis Publications, Inc.

Fletcher Flora for *The Witness Was a Lady* by Flora Fletcher, © 1960 by H.S.D. Publications, Inc.

Brian Garfield for *Joe Cutter's Game* by Brian Garfield, © 1976 by Davis Publications, Inc.

James M. Gillmore for *The Real Criminal* by James M. Gillmore, © 1966 by H.S.D. Publications, Inc.

Ron Goulart for *The Tin Ear* by Ron Goulart, © 1966 by H.S.D. Publications, Inc.

Edward D. Hoch for *Another War* by Edward D. Hoch, © 1967 by H.S.D. Publications, Inc.

James Holding for *Career Man* by James Holding, © 1965 by H.S.D. Publications, Inc.

Donald Honig for *Man Bites Dog* by Donald Honig, © 1960 by H.S.D. Publications, Inc.

Richard O. Lewis for *Black Disaster* by Richard O. Lewis, © 1971 by H.S.D. Publications, Inc.

John Lutz for *Have You Ever Seen This Woman?* by John Lutz, © 1976 by Davis Publications, Inc.

Libby MacCall for *The Perfidy of Professor Blake* by Libby MacCall, © 1970 by H.S.D. Publications, Inc.

Barry N. Malzberg for *After the Unfortunate Accident* by Barry N. Malzberg, © 1975.

Margaret B. Maron for *A Very Special Talent* by Margaret B. Maron, © 1970.

Harold Q. Masur for *Pocket Evidence* by Harold Q. Masur, © 1974 by H.S.D. Publications, Inc.

CONTENTS

NEDRA TYRE

Killed by Kindness

John Johnson knew that he must murder his wife. He had to. It was the only decent thing he could do. He owed her that much consideration.

Divorce was out of the question. He had no grounds. Mary was kind and pretty and pleasant company and hadn't ever glanced at another man. Not once in their marriage had she nagged him. She was a marvelous cook and an excellent bridge player. No hostess in town was more popular.

It seemed a pity that he would have to kill her. But he certainly wasn't going to shame her by telling her he was leaving her; not when they'd just celebrated their twentieth anniversary two months before and had congratulated each other on being the happiest married couple in the whole world. With pink champagne, and in front of dozens of admiring friends, they had pledged undying love. They had said they hoped fate would be kind and would allow them to die together. After all that John couldn't just toss Mary aside. Such a trick would be the action of a cad.

Without him Mary would have no life at all. Of course she would have her shop, which had done well since she had opened it, but she wasn't a real career woman. Opening the shop had been a kind of lark when the Greer house, next door to them in a row of town houses, had been put up for sale. No renovation or remodeling had been done except to knock down part of a wall so that the two houses could be connected by a door. The furniture shop was only something to occupy her time, Mary said, while her sweet husband worked. It didn't mean anything to her, though she had a good business sense. John seldom went in the shop. Come to think of it, it was a jumble. It made him a little uneasy; everything in it seemed so crowded and precarious.

Yes, Mary's interest was in him; it wasn't in the shop. She'd have to have something besides the shop to have any meaningful existence.

If he divorced her she'd have no one to take her to concerts and plays. Dinner parties, her favorite recreation, would be out. None of their friends would invite her to come without him. Alone and divorced, she would be shunted into the miserable category of spinsters and widows who had to be invited to lunch instead of dinner.

He couldn't relegate Mary to such a life, though he felt sure that if he asked her for a divorce she'd give him one. She was so acquiescent and accommodating.

No, he wasn't going to humiliate her by asking her for a divorce. She deserved something better from him than that.

If only he hadn't met Lettice on that business trip to Lexington. But how could he regret such a miracle? He had come alive only in the six weeks since he'd known Lettice. Life with Mary was ashes in comparison. Since he'd met Lettice he felt like a blind man who had been given sight. He might have been deaf all his life and was hearing for the first time. And the marvel was that Lettice loved him and was eager to marry him, and free to marry him.

And waiting.

And insisting.

He must concentrate on putting Mary out of the way. Surely a little accident could be arranged without too much trouble. The shop ought to be an ideal place, there in all that crowded junk. Among those heavy marble busts and chandeliers and andirons something from above or below could be used to dispatch his dear Mary to her celestial reward.

"Darling, you must tell your wife," Lettice urged when they next met at their favorite hotel in Lexington. "You've got to arrange for a divorce. You have to. You've got to tell her about us." Lettice's voice was so low and musical that John felt hypnotized.

But how could he tell Mary about Lettice?

John couldn't even rationalize Lettice's appeal to himself.

Instead of Mary's graciousness, Lettice had elegance. Lettice wasn't as pretty or as charming as Mary. But he couldn't resist her. In her presence he was an ardent, masterful lover; in Mary's presence he was a thoughtful, complaisant husband. With Lettice life would always be lived at the highest peak; nothing in his long years with Mary could approach the wonder he had known during his few meetings with Lettice. Lettice was earth, air, fire and water, the four elements; Mary was—no, he couldn't compare them. Anyway, what good was it to set their attractions off against each other?

Then, just as he was about to suggest to Lettice that they go to the bar, he saw Chet Fleming enter the hotel and walk across the lobby toward the desk. What was Chet Fleming doing in Lexington? But then anyone could be anywhere. That was the humiliating risk illicit lovers faced. They might be discovered anywhere, anytime. No place was secure for them. But Chet Fleming was the one person he wanted least to see, and the one who would make the most of encountering John with another woman. That blabbermouth would tell his wife and friends, his doctor, his grocer, his banker, his lawyer. Word would get back to Mary. Her heart would be broken. She deserved better than that.

John cowered beside Lettice. Chet dawdled at the desk. John couldn't be exposed like that any longer, a single glance around and Chet would see him and Lettice. John made an incoherent excuse, then sidled over to the newsstand where he hid behind a magazine until Chet had registered and had taken an elevator upstairs.

Anyway, they had escaped, but only barely.

John couldn't risk cheapening their attachment. He had to do something to make it permanent right away, but at the same time he didn't want to hurt Mary.

Thousands of people in the United States had gotten up that morning who would be dead before nightfall. Why couldn't his dear Mary be among them? Why couldn't she die without having to be murdered?

When John rejoined Lettice and tried to explain his panic, she was composed but concerned and emphatic.

"Darling, this incident only proves what I've been insisting. I said you'd have to tell your wife at once. We can't go on like this. Surely you understand."

"Yes, dear, you're quite right. I'll do something as soon as I can."

"You must do something immediately, darling."

Oddly enough, Mary Johnson was in the same predicament as John Johnson. She had had no intention of falling in love. In fact, she thought she was in love with her husband. How naive she'd been before Kenneth came into her shop that morning asking whether she had a bust of Mozart. Of course she had a bust of Mozart; she had several busts of Mozart, not to mention Bach, Beethoven, Victor Hugo, Balzac, Shakespeare, George Washington and Goethe, in assorted sizes.

He had introduced himself. Customers didn't ordinarily introduce themselves, and she gave him her name in return, and then realized that he was the outstanding interior designer in town.

"Quite frankly," he said, "I wouldn't be caught dead with this bust of Mozart and it will ruin the room, but my client insists on having it. Do you mind if I see what else you have?"

She showed him all over the shop. Later she tried to recall the exact moment when they had fallen in love. He had spent all that first morning there; toward noon he seemed especially attracted to a small back room cluttered and crowded with chests of drawers. He reached for a drawer pull that came off in his hands, then he reached for her.

"What do you think you're doing?" she said. "Goodness, suppose some customers come in."

"Let them browse," he said.

She couldn't believe that it had happened, but it had. Afterward, instead of being lonely when John went out of town on occasional business trips, she yearned for the time when he gave her his antiseptic peck of a kiss and told her he would be gone overnight.

The small back room jammed with the chests of drawers became Mary and Kenneth's discreet rendezvous. They added a chaise longe.

One day a voice reached them there. They had been too engrossed to notice that anyone had approached.

"Mrs. Johnson, where are you? I'd like some service, please."

Mary stumbled out from the dark to greet the customer. She tried to smooth her mussed hair. She knew that her lipstick was smeared.

The customer was Mrs. Bryan, the most accomplished gossip in town. Mrs. Bryan would get word around that Mary Johnson was carrying on scandalously in her shop. John was sure to find out now.

Fortunately, Mrs. Bryan was preoccupied. She was in a Pennsylvania Dutch mood and wanted to see butter molds and dower chests.

It was a lucky escape, as Mary later told Kenneth. Kenneth refused to be reassured.

"I love you deeply," he said. "And honorably. I've reason to know you love me too. I'm damned tired of sneaking around. I'm not going to put up with it any longer. Do you understand? We've got to get married. Tell your husband you want a divorce."

Kenneth kept talking about a divorce, as if a divorce was nothing at all—not harder to arrange than a dental appointment. How could she divorce a man who had been affectionate and kind and faithful for twenty years? How could she snatch happiness from him?

If only John would die. Why couldn't he have a heart attack? Every day thousands of men died from heart attacks. Why couldn't her darling John just drop dead? It would simplify everything.

Even the ringing of the telephone sounded angry, and when Mary answered it Kenneth, at the other end of the line, was in a rage.

"Damn it, Mary, this afternoon was ridiculous. It was insulting. I'm not skulking any more. I'm not hiding behind doors while you grapple around for butter molds to show customers. We've got to be married right away."

"Yes, darling. Do be patient."

"I've already been too patient. I'm not waiting any longer."

She knew that he meant it. If she lost Kenneth life would end for her. She hadn't ever felt this way about John.

Dear John. How could she toss him aside? He was in the prime of life; he could live decades longer. All his existence was centered on her. He lived to give her pleasure. They had no friends except other married people. John would have to lead a solitary life if she left him. He'd be odd man out without her; their friends would invite him to their homes because they were sorry for him. Poor, miserable John was what everyone would call him. He'd be better off dead, they'd say. He would neglect himself; he wouldn't eat regularly; he would have to live alone in some wretched furnished apartment. No, she mustn't condemn him to an existence like that.

Why had this madness with Kenneth started? Why had that foolish woman insisted on having a bust of Mozart in her music room? Why had Kenneth come to her shop in search of it when busts of Mozart were in every second-hand store on Broad Street and at much cheaper prices?

Yet she wouldn't have changed anything. Seconds with Kenneth were worth lifetimes with John.

Only one end was possible. She would have to think of a nice, quick, efficient, unmessy way to get rid of John. And soon.

John had never seen Mary look as lovely as she did that night when he got home from his business trip. For one flicker of a second, life with her seemed enough. Then he thought of Lettice, and the thought stunned him into the belief that no act that brought them together could be criminal. He must get on with what he had to do. He must murder Mary in as gentlemanly a way as possible, and he must do it that very night. Meantime he would enjoy the wonderful dinner Mary had prepared for him. Common politeness demanded it, and anyhow he was ravenous.

Yet he must get on with the murder just as soon as he finished eating. It seemed a little heartless to be contriving a woman's death even as he ate her cheese cake, but he certainly didn't mean to be callous.

He didn't know just how he would murder Mary. Perhaps if he could get her into her shop, there in that corner where all the statuary was, he could manage something.

Mary smiled at him and handed him a cup of coffee.

"I thought you'd need lots of coffee, darling, after such a long drive."

"Yes, dear, I do. Thank you."

Just as he began to sip from his cup he glanced across the table at Mary. Her face had a peculiar expression. John was puzzled by it. They had been so close for so many years that she must be reading his mind. She must know what he was planning. Then she smiled; it was the glorious smile she had bestowed on him ever since their honeymoon. Everything was all right.

"Darling, excuse me for a minute," she said. "I just remembered something in the shop that I must see to. I'll be right back."

She walked quickly out of the dining room and across the hall into the shop.

But she didn't come back right away as she'd promised. If she didn't return soon John's coffee would be cold. He took a sip or two, then decided to go to the shop to see what had delayed her.

She didn't hear him enter. He found her in the middle room where the chandeliers were blazing. Her back was turned toward him and she was sitting on an Empire sofa close to the statues on their stands. She was ambushed by the statues.

Good lord, it was as he had suspected. She had been reading his thoughts. Her shoulders heaved. She was sobbing. She knew that their life together was ending. Then he decided that she might be laughing. Her shoulders would be shaking like that if she were laughing to herself. Whatever she was doing, whether she sobbed or laughed, it was no time for him to speculate on her mood. This was too good a chance to miss. With her head bent over she would be directly in the path of the bust of Victor Hugo or Benjamin Franklin or whoever it was towering above her. John would have to topple it only slightly and it would hit her skull. It needed only the gentlest shove.

He shoved.

It was so simple.

Poor darling girl. Poor Mary.

But it was all for the best and he wouldn't ever blame himself for what he'd done. Still, he was startled that it had been so easy, and it had taken no time at all. He would have tried it weeks before if he had known that it could be done with so little trouble.

John was quite composed. He took one last affectionate glance at Mary and then went back to the dining room. He would drink his coffee and then telephone the doctor. No doubt the doctor would offer to notify the police since it was an accidental death. John wouldn't need to lie about anything except for one slight detail. He would have to say that some movement of Mary's must have caused the bust to fall.

His coffee was still warm. He drank it unhurriedly. He thought of Lettice. He ached for the luxury of telephoning her that their life together was now assured and that after a discreet interval they could be married. But he decided he had better not take any chances. He would delay calling Lettice.

He felt joyful yet calm. He couldn't remember having felt so relaxed. No doubt it came from relief of having done what had to be done. He was even sleepy. He was sleepier than he had ever been. He must lie down on the living room couch. That was more urgent even than telephoning the doctor. But he couldn't wait to get to the couch. He laid his head on the dining table. His arms dangled.

None of Mary and John's friends had any doubt about how the double tragedy had occurred. When they came to think of it, the shop had always been a booby trap, and that night Mary had tripped or stumbled and had toppled the statue onto her head. Then John had found her and grief had overwhelmed him. He realized he couldn't live without Mary, and his desperate sense of loss had driven him to dissolve enough sleeping tablets in his coffee to kill himself.

They all remembered so well how, in the middle of their last anniversary celebration, Mary and John had said they hoped they could die together. They really were the most devoted couple any of them had ever known. You could get sentimental just thinking about Mary and John, and to see them together was an inspiration. In a world of insecurity nothing was so heartening as their deep, steadfast love. It was sweet and touching that they had died on the same night, and exactly as they both had wanted.

JOHN F. SUTER

Just a Minor Offense

They must have come up with their lights cut off, because I didn't know they were there until one of them shone his flash right behind me and said, "All right. What seems to be the trouble?"

He caught me standing there like a knucklehead, with the spring-leaf in my hand, staring at the coins spilling out of the pay phone. There was silver all over the floor of the booth and the shelf under the phone. A coin or two hung pinched in the twisted metal.

I didn't turn around. I figured the flashlight would be right in my eyes, and I didn't want things to be worse than they were going to be. I just stood still, watching his big arm go up and his big hand tighten the light bulb overhead. He crowded into the phone booth, ramming me against the wall while he shut the door. The light came on.

He grunted as though he'd seen what he expected to see. "Jackpot, huh? All right, kid, let's get outside and talk a little."

He opened the door, and the light went out. I started to turn, when his flash came on again.

"Hold it. Don't move or do a thing." He raised his voice. "Andy, take that hamburger out of the bag and bring the bag over here."

In a few seconds, I heard the car door slam and the other cop came up. The one who was keeping me pinned said to his buddy, "Thanks. Junior, here, is gonna clean up his mess for the phone company." He spoke to me. "Turn around. Okay. Now, hand over that hunk of steel. Lay it here."

A big hand came out in front of me, a handkerchief spread across the palm.

I laid the spring-leaf on the handkerchief. My prints would be on the metal. They sure had me cold.

"Look," I said, "I didn't do this. I just came in to phone, and—"

"Sure," he said. His outline was big and bulky against the streetlight. "They never do, not even when you catch 'em red-handed."

"If you'll listen a minute—"

"The only thing I'll listen to is that money jingling in the bag. Get to it."

I'd always been told that you don't argue with cops, and there were two of them, one of them bigger than I am. I closed up and began scooping up the nickels, dimes, and quarters. I took care not to miss any, not even a dime in a far corner, not even the stuff still hanging in the coin box itself.

Finally, I straightened and turned around, passing over the bag.

"All right, officer," I said, as evenly as I could. "I've done what you wanted me to. If you'll listen a minute, I'll tell you something that'll prove I didn't do it."

"You tryin' to tell me I didn't see what I saw?"

The other cop, the one he'd called Andy, cut in. His tone was a little quieter. "Let's give him a minute, Mike. It looks better when we come in with all the angles accounted for. We don't want something flying up and hitting us in the face later."

The big one was quiet for a second. "Okay," he said finally. "Let's hear it."

"It's this way," I said, trying to keep the relief out of my voice. "I've been out with three other guys. I'll give you their names—"

"Later."

"I'd just taken the last one home, and I started across the park, when the car pooped out on me. Right around the bend up there. It's my Dad's car. I can't get it started—acts like there's dirt in the needle-valve. Well, you know what happens if you leave a car on the street, especially in the park. It gets hauled in, and it costs you to bail it out. So I thought I'd better phone Dad, then call Brown's Garage."

"And you didn't have the change, so you thought you'd just help yourself to some—"

This Andy cut in again. "If he'd done that, it might knock out the phone, Mike. Let him finish."

I went on: "When I came in sight of the booth, I thought I saw somebody step out and disappear, but I wasn't sure. And when I got here, it was the way you saw it. The spring-leaf was on the shelf. Like a meathead, I picked it up. Then you came along. And that's it."

The other cop said, "It wouldn't hurt to check out this thing about the car. Only take a few minutes. Which way is it, kid?"

I pointed. "Over that way, half a block. It's a '57 Chevvy."

The big one took me by the arm.

"Let's go."

I walked out to the cruiser with them. They put me in front beside Andy, the driver. Mike got in behind me. As we came out under the streetlight, I saw that he had a sort of blocky face, pitted here and there. His buddy was shorter, thinner, with sandy eyebrows and a sharp nose.

We were over by the Chevvy almost before I got settled. We pulled up alongside. Andy held out a hand. "The keys."

I gave them to him. "To start it, you—"

"I know," he said, slipping from behind the wheel.

He went and turned the starter of the Chevvy over two or three times, then got out and lifted the hood. He flashed his light at the motor for a minute, then closed the hood and came back.

"It's like he says." He returned the keys.

I felt better. I was pretty sure they'd check me, but you can't count on dirt. Sometimes it works loose in a valve when you don't think it can.

Mike cleared his throat. "So how does this let him off the hook?"

Andy drummed on the wheel. "He'd never use that buggy for a getaway the way it is. Incidentally, what's your name, kid?"

"David Carey."

"Your father's name?"

"Samuel E. Carey."

Andy nodded. "The registration was in that name. Let me see your driver's license."

I handed it over. He glanced at it and gave it back. "It checks."

"Sure," I said. "It's on the level, all the way. Look, I've given it to you straight. Why don't you let me go, then hunt for this other guy? I still have to call home, and I'd better phone the garage."

Mike hefted the bag of money. "How do we know you're not in Sergeant Jensen's file on a couple of counts already?"

"I'm not. I've never been in trouble in my life. I'm not wanting to start now."

Andy said, "I'm not out to make it rough for anybody, kid. Neither one of us is. But we'd be pretty poor cops if we didn't take you in. They probably won't do a thing, but they like to be the ones to make the decisions."

"But the car—"

"Don't worry about the car. If you're clean, we'll see you don't get bit for something you couldn't help."

He moved the stick over to *Drive*, and we took off.

We were at the station in less than ten minutes. They took me into a room with several straightback chairs around the walls, a worn hardwood floor, and a cop behind the desk who seemed to match the room. He had thin brown hair and a hatchet face. I found out that he was the night sergeant, Driscoll.

He stared at me poker-faced and pulled out some kind of form, then started asking questions. When he got to my age and I said, "Sixteen," he looked at Mike.

Then he said, "Better call his family and get 'em down here. What's he done?"

"Looks like he smashed a pay phone for the chicken feed. Here." Mike plunked down the bag.

Driscoll's face didn't change a bit. "They won't need a lawyer, then. His old man'll be enough."

Mike picked up the phone. "What's the number, kid?"

I turned to Sergeant Driscoll. "You're going to book me?"

"It has to go on the record, son. They brought you in. I haven't heard it all yet. But whatever comes in here, it goes down on the sheet."

I didn't say anything, trying to figure a way to keep my name clean. Driscoll prodded me again. "If you didn't do it, it can't count against you. You're sixteen. We're not in the habit of blabbing all over town who the kids are who come in here. Now let's get on with this. There's enough other things to keep me more than busy."

Andy, who was standing beside me, dropped a match into an ashtray on the desk. "What's going on?"

"Some kind of fight started five minutes ago," Sergeant Driscoll said, "over near Locust and Third. And some girl's family called in around that same time to say their kid's overdue getting home—not with her friends, not in the hospital. Out parked somewhere, probably." He looked at me. "Her name's Joyce Reynolds. Know her?"

"I know who she is. She's a year ahead of me in school."

"Who's she go with?"

"I hear she goes steady with Herb Blackwood."

He looked at a note pad. "That one hasn't seen her—he says."

Andy asked idly, "Any of these kid gangs breaking and entering tonight?"

"No reports. Well—back to business." He looked at Andy, then at Mike. "Tell me about this one."

In about half an hour, Dad came down. He didn't storm in, like some of the old boys you see on TV, and he didn't come in, hat in hand, to let them walk all over him. He just looked at me, then at Driscoll (the other two had gone back to work) and said, "The officer who called said Dave was caught breaking into a pay phone."

The sergeant tapped the paper with his pen. "That's the way it looks, Mr. Carey. There's some business about your car that might be in his favor."

"What do you want us to do?"

Us.

The sergeant was matter-of-fact. "We'll turn this report over to Sergeant Jensen, of Juvenile, and let him check it out. Right now, we'll release the boy in your custody. I suggest that he come back here tomorrow to talk to Sergeant Jensen."

"He'll be here. What time?"

Driscoll considered. "It'll take a little time. No sense in making him miss school. Say, about four o'clock."

"He'll be here at four. Shall I come too?"

"As you like. Jensen doesn't chew 'em up and spit 'em out in little pieces. Sometimes it works out better when the kid's alone. Why not leave it to him?"

"All right." Dad turned and looked at me. "Well—you don't seem to be the worse for wear. But your mother's liable to say something about the dirt on your knees. How'd that happen?"

I brushed at my pants. It didn't brush off too well. "I guess I got it kneeling in that booth picking up the money."

Driscoll had a faint frown on his face. His voice had a slight rasp. "He wasn't roughed up, if that's what you're getting at." He made a note on the paper in front of him.

Dad seems pretty average sometimes, but he wasn't so average just then. His eyes glinted, and I almost thought his hair bristled. "Nobody *will* bring it up if it's not necessary. But *somebody* will drag it out into the open if it *is* necessary."

He turned back to me. "Now, let's hear about the car, so we can straighten that part out and go home."

In the morning, school was about as usual, but toward the end of lunch period Jack Burton stopped me in the hall. He halfway hung that head of his with the peroxided widow's peak, so that he was looking up, a habit of his. His eyes looked a little worried.

"I'm glad you called me, even if it was awful early in the morning. The cops talked to me, the way you said they would."

I kept up a front of confidence. Better not scare my best witness. "You told 'em straight about what time I left you, I hope? You live right by the park, and they'll be able to figure that I was telling the whole truth about the car and all."

He stuck his thumbs in the corners of his pants pockets. "Sure. We gotta stick together. I know that. Look, Dave, when you let me out, did you see any sign of Joyce Reynolds?"

"Joyce Reynolds? No. How come?"

"She lives the second house from me, remember? She's missing."

"I heard them mention it last night. What's this got to do with you?"

"She was out with Tom Fisher. Mad at Herb Blackwood, I hear, and had this date with Tom, instead. Tom says he brought her home around 12:15, close to the time you let me out. He didn't see her to the door—what a birdbrain!—and he doesn't know whether she got in or not. She didn't. So where'd she get to? The cops asked me, did I see her? I had to tell 'em no."

"Well, I didn't either," I said. "I have enough to do, trying to get out from under this phone business. You'll stick with me?"

He grinned quickly. "Beat the phony rap? I'll do what I can."

"Stick to the truth, that's all. Stick to the truth."

I went down alone to Police Headquarters to see Sergeant Jensen at four o'clock, the time they'd set. Mom tried to get Dad to go along, but he thought it over and said I'd have to learn to face things alone more often now. He'd checked on Jensen and thought I'd get a fair break.

Jensen's office wasn't much more than a desk, three chairs, and a lot of filing cabinets. The sergeant was a short cop, looking something like Franchot Tone, with a good bit of gray in his hair. He seemed sort of good-natured, but when he looked at me with those hazel eyes of his, I felt he'd known me all of my life, that he knew everything about me.

He waved me to a chair beside his desk and sat looking at me without talking for a minute or two. Finally, he decided to open up.

"David Carey. I've never run into you before, Dave."

"It's not my fault that you have this time, Sergeant."

"I wonder how you mean that," he said quietly.

This put me off-balance a little. Getting double meanings out of what I'd said, when I'd hardly opened my mouth.

"All I mean is I've always tried to keep out of things that cause trouble. And here things have turned on me, and I get pulled in for something I didn't do."

"There're a lot of kids breaking and entering these days who aren't getting pulled in. For all we know, you might be a member of one gang we're after. You see?" Jensen fingered some papers. "I have a number of reports on you, Dave. Good reports. That's in your favor. Of course," he said with a little more bite in his tone, "we had a kid in here about three months ago just your age. What they called a 'model boy.' He decided to steal a car and did—but he was caught."

I kept quiet.

"That boy, and these vandals we haven't caught yet, think that they don't amount to anything if they're being normal citizens. If they're not leaders, or something, they have to prove themselves some other way. Maybe that could be you. Could it?"

I tried to figure out what to say.

He studied me. "Dave, if you have anything at all to say about this affair that you haven't told us, I'd advise you to tell us now. It'll make things a lot easier if we decide to carry this further."

"Sergeant, I don't know what you want me to say, but all I can tell you is I didn't do it. It doesn't matter how bad it looks."

He shrugged. "All right." He looked at those papers again. "Against you is the fact that you were caught in a phone booth with the box pried open and money all over the place. You had an automobile spring-leaf in your hand. Your fingerprints were on the metal. *They were also on the phone box*. What about that?"

In spite of myself, I began to sweat some. "I put my hands on the box when they asked me to gather up all the money. Some of it was still in the box. I couldn't help it. Did they mention that?"

He made a note. "No. I'll verify it."

"Did you find any other prints on that spring-leaf?"

"Yes, but they weren't any good. Yours blurred them."

"Isn't that in my favor?"

He compressed his lips briefly. "It could be. It could also be that you just picked up that hunk of steel somewhere, knowing that somebody else's prints would be on it."

"Sergeant," I said, trying to get through to him, "if that's the case, why'd I be fool enough to use the thing barehanded? Why should I want to put my own prints on it?"

His answer was mild. "It doesn't add up. Now—in your favor. Your story about the boys you were out with checks. We talked to them all, and you did just what you said. You did seem to be heading back across the park after you let the Burton kid out."

"And the car—doesn't that help?"

He nodded. "The car. Yes. We called the garage. There was dirt in the needle-valve as you guessed. The officers who brought you in verify that it wouldn't start. All of this, plus good character references, add up in your favor. The question now is, do these things weigh more than our finding you practically in the act?"

"But, Sergeant," I said, "the phone company didn't lose any money. All they have to do is fix the phone. It means a lot to me to keep my name clean. Why don't you give me the benefit of the doubt?"

His eyes became cold all of a sudden. "The phone company helps to pay my salary, the same as everybody else does. Any decisions I make had better be good ones, no matter who's involved."

He just sat there and let me fidget. Finally, he spoke in a mild voice again. "Let's talk about something else for a minute. Do you know a Joyce Reynolds?"

"Some. I see her around school. She's a Senior, I'm a Junior."

"See her last night?"

"No, I hear she's missing."

He looked at me directly again. "Yes. You could have seen her." It was a flat statement, but it sounded almost accusing.

He had me worried. "She lives near Jack Burton," I said, "sure, but I didn't see her last night."

He turned his attention to the tips of his fingers. "What's she like?"

"I don't know too much about her, except in a general way. About five feet four, real black hair, not built quite as much as some—but you might look twice. She's been steadying with Herb Blackwood, but maybe that's over. I hear she was out with Tom Fisher last night."

He said casually, "I understand you're a little interested yourself."

I got sort of hot. Jack Burton must have— "Who says?"

"Somebody."

"Well, you tell somebody he doesn't know what he's talking about! Look, she's a Senior, and Senior girls hardly even look at Junior boys. Besides, she's going steady."

"You go steady?"

"No."

He considered his notes. "You're what? Sixteen? Then it may be understandable that you don't go steady. Run around with three or four other boys, no girls? The way it was last night?"

"Usually."

"But Joyce Reynolds— Did you ever make any passes?"

I felt like squirming, but I sat still. "She's about a year older than I am. Why should I?"

"Why not?"

"I'd seem like a kid to her. Don't you get it?"

He shrugged. "I didn't say she'd reciprocate—though that's not impossible, either."

I imagine he could tell that I was simmering, the way my voice must have sounded. "Sergeant, why're we beating in time to this? What's it got to do with a busted pay phone?"

He was stiff-faced when he answered. "They found Joyce Reynolds' body this morning. In the park, in a crevice under some big rocks. Not too far from that phone booth where they picked you up."

I couldn't say a thing.

"She was strangled and beaten," he went on. "Maybe somebody made a pass and got mad when he didn't get anywhere. Maybe it was somebody she looked on as sort of a kid. Maybe she even laughed at him when he got serious. *How about it?*"

I finally found my voice. "Me? First you say I wreck a pay phone, then you say I killed Joyce Reynolds. What am I supposed to be—a one-man crime wave?"

"It's not so crazy as you might think, boy."

"Me? Why me?" I almost yelled. "How do you know Herb Blackwood wasn't hanging around waiting for her when Tom Fisher brought her home? How do you know Tom even brought her home? How about Jack Burton? All that stuff you said about me you could say it about him—and he lives close to her house. How do you know he didn't walk her over to the park after I left him? What time was she killed, anyway?"

Jensen looked away. "This much I'll give you: we don't know yet."

"Then—"

He stared coldly at me. "I'll tell you what could have happened in your case. Not Fisher's, Blackwood's or Burton's case. Yours. You pick up this girl and drive to the park. You make a pass, but you get nowhere. You get mad and slug her, then you strangle her. You try to hide the body—temporarily, anyway. Then you go to leave—and you can't start the car. You begin to sweat. That car is close to the body. It can tie you to what you've done. So you decide to fake a smash on that pay phone, maybe you even hang around until you're sure of being picked up. This is to fix our attention on you for a minor offense, instead of murder. Who'd be robbing a phone if he'd just committed murder? A neat trick, if somebody doesn't see through it. Now that's the case we can build against you. *Can you prove otherwise?*"

My brain had been busy while he was piling things on. "Sergeant, you'd better be thinking about those others. Listen, if I did what you just said, where'd that spring-leaf come from? The one that was used on the phone?"

"How should I know?"

"If I smashed that phone to draw attention away from Joyce, I'd have to get that hunk of steel in a hurry, wouldn't I? You know how clean they keep the park. Where'd that leaf come from?"

"Out of the trunk of your car. Where else?"

I snorted. "Are you kidding? You take a look in that trunk, the way Dad keeps it. You could eat off the floor. All that're in it are the spare tire, jack, and lug wrench. Chains in the winter, not now."

Jensen looked thoughtful. "What kind of tires have you?"

"Tubeless."

"Okay. With inner tubes, a lot of drivers used to carry a spring-leaf to pry the tire off the rim if they fixed a flat themselves. That doesn't sound likely here."

He shut up and thought. Then he said, "All the same, I'm going to check with your Dad about that spring-leaf. In the meantime, I guess we'd better have you tell me about this Jack Burton."

He pulled some papers over in front of him.

"Where shall I start?" I asked, feeling easier.

He didn't answer. He was staring at two papers lying next to each other. He studied one, then the other. Finally, he looked up.

"You and Jack Burton run around with several other boys quite a bit?"

"That's right."

"Sort of a gang?"

"I wouldn't call it that, Sergeant. You know how that sounds nowadays. Why do you always—"

"Look on the bad side? I'll tell you why, Carey. You don't drive your Dad's car every night. I don't think he'd let you. So, if he keeps the trunk so clean, the spring-leaf wouldn't be in it all the time. Why not? You know—a spring-leaf makes a pretty good jimmy, especially if the end's filed down. I'll have to look at your little toy to see about that. Now, if your gang had been breaking and entering, you'd have a spring-leaf with you on certain nights, all right."

I pointed to the papers on the desk. "I suppose it says so in there."

He tapped them. "Oh, no. It doesn't say a word about that. But one of them says that whoever tried to shove Joyce Reynolds' body under those rocks had to kneel to do it. The other report has a note on it that your father was concerned about some dirt on the knees of your pants when they brought you in last night."

He stood up suddenly. "Now, I wonder if we went out to your house and brought back those pants for the lab to test, would they find the same kind of dirt as that by the rocks?"

I couldn't say a thing. The pants hadn't gone to the cleaner's. And I knew where the dirt on the knees came from.

ROBERT BLOCH

A Home Away from Home

The train was late, and it must have been past nine o'clock when Natalie found herself standing, all alone, on the platform before Hightower Station.

The station itself was obviously closed for the night—it was only a way-stop, really, for there was no town here—and Natalie wasn't quite sure what to do. She had taken it for granted that Dr. Bracegirdle would be on hand to meet her. Before leaving London, she'd sent her uncle a wire giving him the time of her arrival. But since the train had been delayed, perhaps he'd come and gone.

Natalie glanced around uncertainly, then noticed the phonebooth which provided her with a solution. Dr. Bracegirdle's last letter was in her purse, and it contained both his address and his phone-number. She had fumbled through her bag and found it by the time she walked over to the booth.

Ringing him up proved a bit of a problem; there seemed to be an interminable delay before the operator made the connection, and there was a great deal of buzzing on the line. A glimpse of the hills beyond the station, through the glass wall of the booth, suggested the reason for the difficulty. After all, Natalie reminded herself, this was West Country. Conditions might be a bit primitive—

"Hello, hello!"

The woman's voice came over the line, fairly shouting above the din. There was no buzzing noise now, and the sound in the background suggested a babble of voices all intermingled. Natalie bent forward and spoke directly and distinctly into the mouthpiece.

"This is Natalie Rivers," she said. "Is Dr. Bracegirdle there?"

"Whom did you say was calling?"

"Natalie Rivers. I'm his niece."

"His what, Miss?"

"Niece," Natalie repeated. "May I speak to him, please?"

"Just a moment."

There was a pause, during which the sound of voices in the background seemed amplified, and then Natalie heard the resonant masculine tones, so much easier to separate from the indistinct murmuring.

"Dr. Bracegirdle here. My dear Natalie, this is an unexpected pleasure!"

"Unexpected? But I sent you a 'gram from London this afternoon." Natalie checked herself as she realized the slight edge of impatience which had crept into her voice. "Didn't it arrive?"

"I'm afraid service is not of the best around here," Dr. Bracegirdle told her, with an apologetic chuckle. "No, your wire didn't arrive. But apparently you did." He chuckled again. "Where are you, my dear?"

"At Hightower Station."

"Oh, dear. It's in exactly the opposite direction."

"Opposite direction?"

"From Peterby's. They rang me up just before you called. Some silly nonsense about an appendix—probably nothing but an upset stomach. But I promised to stop round directly, just in case."

"Don't tell me they still call you for general practice?"

"Emergencies, my dear. There aren't many physicians in these parts. Fortunately, there aren't many patients either." Dr. Bracegirdle started to chuckle, then sobered. "Look now. You say you're at the station. I'll just send Miss Plummer down to fetch you in the wagon. Have you much luggage?"

"Only my travel-case. The rest is coming with the household goods, by boat."

"Boat?"

"Didn't I mention it when I wrote?"

"Yes, that's right, you did. Well, no matter. Miss Plummer will be along for you directly."

"I'll bc waiting in front of the platform."

"What was that? Speak up, I can hardly hear you."

"I said I'll be waiting in front of the platform."

"Oh." Dr. Bracegirdle chuckled again. "Bit of a party going on here."

"Shan't I be intruding? I mean, since you weren't expecting me—"

"Not at all! They'll be leaving before long. You wait for Plummer."

The phone clicked off and Natalie returned to the platform. In a surprisingly short time, the station-wagon appeared and skidded off the road to halt at the very edge of the tracks. A tall, thin, gray-haired woman, wearing a somewhat rumpled white uniform, emerged and beckoned to Natalie.

"Come along, my dear," she called. "Here, I'll just pop this in back." Scooping up the bag, she tossed it into the rear of the wagon. "Now, in with you—and off we go!"

Scarcely waiting for Natalie to close the door after her, Miss Plummer gunned the motor and the car plunged back onto the road.

The speedometer immediately shot up to seventy, and Natalie flinched. Miss Plummer noticed her agitation at once.

"Sorry," she said. "With Doctor out on call, I can't be away too long."

"Oh yes, the house-guests. He told me."

"Did he now?" Miss Plummer took a sharp turn at a crossroads and the tires screeched in protest, but to no avail. Natalie decided to drown apprehension in conversation.

"What sort of a man is my uncle?" she asked.

"Have you never met him?"

"No. My parents moved to Australia when I was quite young. This is my first trip to England. In fact, it's the first time I've left Canberra."

"Folks with you?"

"They were in a motor smashup two months ago," Natalie said. "Didn't the Doctor tell you?"

"I'm afraid not—you see, I haven't been with him very long." Miss Plummer uttered a short bark and the car swerved wildly across the road. "Motor smashup, eh? Some people have no business behind the wheel. That's what Doctor says."

She turned and peered at Natalie. "I take it you've come to stay, then?"

"Yes, of course. He wrote me when he was appointed my guardian. That's why I was wondering what he might be like. It's so hard to tell from letters." The thin-faced woman nodded silently, but Natalie had an urge to confide. "To tell the truth, I'm just a bit edgy. I mean, I've never met a psychiatrist before."

"Haven't you, now?" Miss Plummer shrugged. "You're quite fortunate. I've seen a few in my time. A bit on the know-it-all side, if you ask me. Though I must say, Dr. Bracegirdle is one of the best. Permissive, you know."

"I understand he has quite a practice."

"There's no lack of patients for *that* sort of thing," Miss Plummer observed. "Particularly amongst the well-to-do. I'd say your uncle has done himself handsomely. The house and all—but you'll see." Once again the wagon whirled into a sickening swerve and sped forward between the imposing gates of a huge driveway which led toward an enormous house set amidst a grove of trees in the distance. Through the shuttered windows Natalie caught sight of a faint beam of light—just enough to help reveal the ornate facade of her uncle's home.

"Oh, dear," she muttered, half to herself.

"What is it?"

"The guests—and it's Saturday night. And here I am, all mussed from travel."

"Don't give it another thought," Miss Plummer assured her. "There's no formality here. That's what Doctor told me when I came. It's a home away from home."

Miss Plummer barked and braked simultaneously, and the station-wagon came to an abrupt stop just behind an imposing black limousine.

"Out with you now!" With brisk efficiency, Miss Plummer lifted the bag from the rear seat and carried it up the steps, beckoning Natalie forward with a nod over her shoulder. She halted at the door and fumbled for a key.

"No sense knocking," she said. "They'd never hear me." As the door swung open her observation was amply confirmed. The background noise which Natalie had noted over the telephone now formed a formidable foreground. She stood there, hesitant, as Miss Plummer swept forward across the threshold.

"Come along, come along!"

Obediently, Natalie entered, and as Miss Plummer shut the door behind her, she blinked with eyes unaccustomed to the brightness of the interior.

She found herself standing in a long, somewhat bare hallway. Directly ahead of her was a large staircase; at an angle between the railing and the wall was a desk and chair. To her left was a dark panelled door—evidently leading to Dr. Bracegirdle's private office, for a small brass plate was affixed to it, bearing his name. To her right was a huge open parlor, its windows heavily curtained and shuttered against the night. It was from here that the sounds of sociability echoed.

Natalie started down the hall toward the stairs. As she did so, she caught a glimpse of the parlor. Fully a dozen guests eddied about a large table, talking and gesturing with the animation of close acquaintance—with one another, and with the contents of the lavish array of bottles gracing the tabletop. A sudden whoop of laughter indicated that at least one guest had abused the Doctor's hospitality.

Natalie passed the entry hastily, so as not to be observed, then glanced behind her to make sure that Miss Plummer was following with her bag. Miss Plummer was indeed following, but her hands were empty. And as Natalie reached the stairs, Miss Plummer shook her head.

"You didn't mean to go up now, did you?" she murmured. "Come in and introduce yourself."

"I thought I might freshen up a bit first."

"Let me go on ahead and get your room in order. Doctor didn't give me notice, you know."

"Really, it's not necessary. I could do with a wash—"

"Doctor should be back any moment now. Do wait for him." Miss Plummer grasped Natalie's arm, and with the same speed and expedition she had bestowed on driving, she steered the girl forward into the lighted room.

"Here's Doctor's niece," she announced. "Miss Natalie Rivers, from Australia."

Several heads turned in Natalie's direction, though Miss Plummer's voice had scarcely penetrated the general conversational din. A short, jolly-looking fat man bobbed toward Natalie, waving a half-empty glass.

"All the way from Australia, eh?" He extended his goblet. "You must be thirsty. Here, take this, I'll get another." And before Natalie could reply, he turned and plunged back into the group around the table.

"Major Hamilton," Miss Plummer whispered. "A dear soul, really. Though I'm afraid he's just a wee bit squiffy."

As Miss Plummer moved away, Natalie glanced uncertainly at the glass in her hand. She was not quite sure where to dispose of it.

"Allow me." A tall, gray-haired and quite distinguished-looking man with a black mustache moved forward and took the stemware from between her fingers.

"Thank you."

"Not at all. I'm afraid you'll have to excuse the Major. The party spirit, you know." He nodded, indicating a woman in extreme décolletage chattering animatedly to a group of three laughing men. "But since it's by way of being a farewell celebration—"

"Ah, there you are!" The short man whom Miss Plummer had identified as Major Hamilton bounced back into orbit around Natalie, a fresh drink in his hand and a fresh smile on his ruddy face. "I'm back again," he announced. "Just like a boomerang, eh?"

He laughed explosively, then paused. "I say, you *do* have boomerangs in Australia? Saw quite a bit of you Aussies at Gallipoli. Of course that was some time ago, before *your* time, I daresay—"

"Please, Major." The tall man smiled at Natalie. There was something reassuring about his presence, and something oddly familiar too. Natalie wondered where she might have seen him before. She watched while he moved over to the Major and removed the drink from his hand.

"Now see here—" the Major sputtered.

"You've had enough, old boy. And it's almost time for you to go."

"One for the road—" The Major glanced around, his hands waving in appeal. "Everyone *else* is drinking!" He made a lunge for his glass, but the tall man evaded him. Smiling at Natalie over his shoulder, he drew the Major to one side and began to mutter to him earnestly in low tones. The Major nodded exaggeratedly, drunkenly.

Natalie looked around the room. Nobody was paying the least attention to her except one elderly woman who sat quite alone on a stool before the piano. She regarded Natalie with a fixed stare that made her feel like an intruder on a gala scene. Natalie turned away hastily and again caught sight of the woman in décolletage. She suddenly remembered her own desire to change her clothing and peered at the doorway, seeking Miss Plummer. But Miss Plummer was nowhere to be seen.

Walking back into the hall, she peered up the staircase.

"Miss Plummer!" she called.

There was no response.

Then from out of the corner of her eye, she noted that the door of the room across the hallway was ajar. In fact, it was opening now, quite rapidly, and as Natalie stared, Miss Plummer came backing out of the room, carrying a pair of scissors in her hand. Before Natalie could call out again and attract her attention, Miss Plummer had scurried off in the other direction.

The people here, Natalie told herself, certainly seemed odd. But wasn't that always the case with people at parties? She crossed before the stairs, meaning to follow Miss Plummer, but found herself halting before the open doorway.

She gazed in curiously at what was obviously her uncle's consultation room. It was a cozy, book-lined study with heavy, leather-covered furniture grouped before the shelves. The psychiatric couch rested in one corner near the wall and near it was a large mahogany desk. The top of the desk was quite bare, save for a cradle telephone, and a thin brown loop snaking out from it.

Something about the loop disturbed Natalie and before she was conscious of her movement she was inside the room looking down at the desk-top and the brown cord from the phone.

And then she realized what had bothered her. The end of the cord had been neatly severed from its connection in the wall.

"Miss Plummer!" Natalie murmured, remembering the pair of scissors she'd seen her holding. *But why would she have cut the phone cord?*

Natalie turned just in time to observe the tall, distinguished-looking man enter the doorway behind her.

"The phone won't be needed," he said, as if he'd read her thoughts. "After all, I *did* tell you it was a farewell celebration." And he gave a little chuckle.

Again Natalie sensed something strangely familiar about him, and this time it came to her. She'd heard the same chuckle over the phone, when she'd called from the station.

"You must be playing a joke!" she exclaimed. "You're Dr. Bracegirdle, aren't you?"

"No, my dear." He shook his head as he moved past her across the room. "It's just that no one expected you. We were about to leave when your call came. So we had to say *some*thing."

There was a moment of silence. Then, "Where *is* my uncle?" Natalie asked at last.

"Over here."

Natalie found herself standing beside the tall man, gazing down at what lay in a space between the couch and the wall. An instant was all she could bear.

"Messy," the tall man nodded. "Of course it was so sudden, the opportunity, I mean. And then they *would* get into the liquor—"

His voice echoed hollowly in the room and Natalie realized the sounds of the party had died away. She glanced up to see them all standing there in the doorway, watching.

Then their ranks parted and Miss Plummer came quickly into the room, wearing an incongruous fur wrap over the rumpled, ill-fitting uniform.

"Oh my!" she gasped. "So you found him!"

Natalie nodded and took a step forward. "You've got to do something," she said. "Please!"

"Of course, you didn't see the others," Miss Plummer said, "since they're upstairs. The Doctor's staff. Gruesome sight."

The men and women had crowded into the room behind Miss Plummer, staring silently.

Natalie turned to them in appeal. "Why, it's the work of a madman!" she cried. "He belongs in an asylum!"

"My dear child," murmured Miss Plummer, as she quickly closed and locked the door and the silent starers moved forward. "This *is* an asylum . . ."

JOSEPH PAYNE BRENNAN

Death of a Derelict

One afternoon in early summer I sat sipping cold sarsaparilla in the Victorian living room of my investigator friend, Lucius Leffing. Shades were drawn against the sun; the room was cool and quiet. Leffing sprawled in his favorite chair.

As I glanced around at the gaslight fixtures, the mahogany furniture, and Leffing's favorite pieces of Victorian pressed glass, I smiled. "I suppose," I said, "that two gentlemen must have sat much like this in somebody's parlor back in the so-called Gay Nineties. If I should hear the clop of horses' hooves outside, it would not surprise me."

Just then the doorbell rang.

Leffing got up reluctantly. "I fear a little reminiscent trip backward into time must be delayed for a more propitious moment. The present seems to be intruding."

I heard conversation at the door and then Leffing ushered in an individual who was not conducive to moods of gentle nostalgia.

He was short, fat and fiftyish with a large-toothed smile which in the dimly lighted room seemed to switch on and off like a neon sign. A suit with a pattern of large checks did nothing to enhance his pot-bellied presence.

Leffing introduced him as Mr. Clarence Morenda and waved him to a chair.

Glancing around, Mr. Morenda favored us with another flashing grin. "Well, well, you gentlemen have got yourselves a cozy little hideaway here." He laughed uproariously.

"Mr. Morenda," Leffing informed me when the storm had subsided, "is manager of the entertainment concession at Frolic Beach. He is here on business."

Mr. Morenda, recalled to the purpose of his visit, scowled portentiously. "Crummy nuisance, that's what it is!" He cleared his throat. "But first you better tell me what this will cost."

"That depends on the particular circumstances, the time consumed, expenses and so on," Leffing told him. "But compensation can be decided later. I do not press my clients."

Mr. Morenda seemed momentarily confused by such an unbusinesslike attitude, but then he shrugged and grinned again. "Okay, Mr. Leffing, I like a man who don't make too much of money."

Leffing nodded. "Quite so. And now, what is your case?"

Morenda's shaggy eyebrows stitched together again. "About a month ago we found a stiff in an alley which runs alongside the Cyclone. Head all bashed in. Couldn't figure out whether he'd fallen off the Cyclone or got slugged. The coroner said he 'came to his death in a manner at present unknown'—or something like that. We'd seen this bum hangin' around for quite a while, but nobody knew his name or anything. They took pictures and then kept him on ice, but nothing turned up so finally they planted him in Potter's."

He paused, took out a large purple handkerchief and wiped the perspiration from his face. "Then a week ago this nutty dame shows up. Claims this stiff was her cousin, Joel Karvey, says he fell off the Cyclone. Claims it was our fault. Now she's gettin' ready to sue us for $100,000!" He snorted. "Imagine that! Why that bum wasn't worth two cents!"

"I appreciate your problem, Mr. Morenda," said Leffing, "but I fear you need an astute attorney, not a private investigator."

Morenda shook his head vigorously. "Those finky shysters! They'd keep the case goin' for five years. I want the suit thrown out before they start chewin' on it. That bum didn't fall at all—he was murdered! If I can prove that, the suit comes apart at the seams."

Leffing winced at the metaphor. "Mr. Morenda, is there any definite evidence to indicate that it was murder—or are you just engaged in wishful thinking?"

"Sure it was murder! The guy's head was all bashed in, but there wasn't another mark on him. If he'd fallen off the Cyclone, he'd be banged up all over."

"Perhaps he landed on his head," I suggested.

Morenda scowled at me impatiently. "It ain't likely. He'd have to take a real swan dive off the top of the Cyclone and drop directly into that little alley. If he fell off, he'd hit at every tier, bang into the railings and bounce around."

"Assuming you are correct," Leffing put in, "why should anyone murder a penniless drifter? Can you suggest a motive?"

Morenda hesitated. "Well, I ain't sure. Maybe somebody thought he had a few bills. You know how it is—they'll cosh you for a quarter these days. Or maybe he got in a fight with some drunk." He spread his hands. "Could be lots of things."

Leffing sat silently for a minute or two. "I will take the case," he said at length. "The motive intrigues me. We cannot at this point, of course, rule out the possibility that the drifter's death was an accident."

After assuring Mr. Morenda that he would start work on the case the next day, Leffing conducted his new client to the door.

"Well, Brennan, what do you think?" he asked as he settled back in his chair.

I set down my sarsaparilla glass. "The whole sordid business looks pretty obvious to me. This female cousin had the drifter murdered and left near the Cyclone so that she could bring a suit against the Frolic Beach. Some rat-trap lawyer is calling the plays for her."

"Well, well, you may already have solved the case!" Leffing replied with a touch of sarcasm. "However, your solution must bear up under investigation. Much remains to be done."

I did not see Leffing again until several days had passed. One evening I stopped in to ask how the case was coming along.

Leffing leaned back in his chair and put his fingertips together. "I am now convinced that the drifter, Joel Karvey, was murdered. I studied the morgue photographs and talked to the coroner, who, incidentally, does not agree with me. I believe Karvey was struck over the head by a lead pipe. The coroner thinks he struck his head against the iron railings which parallel the Cyclone's track along both sides of the structure."

"If Karvey fell," I asked, "wouldn't he have been seen?"

Leffing shook his head. "Quite possibly not. Not if he fell at night. The Cyclone is not too well lighted and the alley in which he was found is dark. There is also the possibility, as the coroner pointed out, that he climbed up on the Cyclone after closing hours—midnight—as a lark, or just to get a view of the harbor lights."

"Highly unlikely!"

"Where murder is suspected, or where $100,000 lawsuits are pending, one cannot dismiss possibilities."

I grunted.

"I can't believe a drifter would be riding around on the Cyclone or climbing up to see the harbor lights. I still think this female cousin had him killed."

"The female cousin," Leffing said, "is a charwoman living in Newbridge, a drab unimaginative creature with no criminal connections that I can discover. She mentioned to someone that the dead drifter was a distant relative; an opportunistic attorney learned the circumstances and descended upon her. He will obviously be rewarded only if he wins the case."

"You are convinced Karvey was murdered?"

"The head wounds indicate assault so far as I can judge from the photographs and autopsy descriptions. What baffles me is the motive. Why should anyone murder such a nondescript beggar?"

I had no further suggestions to offer but the case began to interest me and I made Leffing promise to keep me informed. When I stopped back a week later, he was restless and fretful.

"You have made no progress?"

He stopped pacing the floor and sat down. "The motive, Brennan! The motive! I am now more firmly convinced that the female cousin is innocent, but we have no other suspect."

"How about Morenda himself?"

"He had no reason to kill Karvey."

"Suppose," I said, "Karvey fell off the Cyclone, was found injured, but conscious, and threatened to bring suit? Maybe Morenda finished him off to avoid getting hauled to court."

Leffing frowned. "An unpleasant possibility I must admit I had not entertained. But if Morenda 'finished off' Karvey, as you say, why would he seek help to prove Karvey was murdered? Is he brash enough to risk his own life or freedom in order to nullify a lawsuit?"

I nodded. "I believe he may be bold and callous enough to take the risk. All he wants you to do is establish the fact that Karvey was murdered, in order to end the lawsuit. If he himself is guilty, he must be confident that you can never prove it. Probably he believes he would never be suspected."

"I intend to question him again, in any case," Leffing said. "We will see then what turns up."

"You have learned nothing more at all?" I asked presently.

"Only one minor thing, insignificant perhaps, yet puzzling. Karvey never did any work at the concessions and he was never seen panhandling, yet he always seemed to have a little money—enough for hamburgers, chips, soda and so forth. Morenda hoped to get him arrested for begging and thus get rid of him. He even had the Frolic Beach watchman, Henry Marnault, spy on him at intervals, but Marnault never caught him panhandling."

"He may have been a pickpocket."

"Doubtful. If he picked pockets, he must have been an accomplished professional. He'd never been arrested for anything except vagrancy. A professional of his age—he was about sixty—would certainly have a police record."

"What is your next move?"

"Tomorrow afternoon I am going to make another visit to Frolic Beach. I will see Morenda again and then perhaps just prowl about. Would you care to accompany me?"

Frolic Beach, south of New Haven along the Sound, is a cluster of carnival-like concessions, interspersed with hamburger stands, popcorn palaces, lemonade stalls, and several surprisingly good restaurants.

Early afternoon found Leffing and myself walking down Lavender Street, the main thoroughfare which bisects the beach area. Morenda's office was located in a dingy building behind the merry-go-round.

He glanced up from a sheaf of greasy-looking sales slips as Leffing and I entered. "You got any news for me, Mr. Leffing?"

Leffing shook his head. "Nothing fresh, Mr. Morenda. Can you take time out to stroll about a bit? Perhaps another visit to the scene of the crime might be helpful."

"Sure, sure. But we been there before." He left his sales slips with obvious reluctance to accompany us.

Screaming couples were rocketing about on the Cyclone's track when we arrived. The alley in which Karvey had been found ran along one side of it, a dim, narrow little lane empty except for candy wrappers, bottle caps and a piece of yellowed newspaper.

We followed Leffing inside. He poked about for a time and then stood looking up at the Cyclone. Suddenly he pointed. "A section of the railing up there was recently replaced, Mr. Morenda? Correct?"

Both Morenda and I squinted upward. Most of the iron-pipe railing looked old and rusty, but there was one small section which appeared shiny and bright.

Morenda nodded his head. "Yeah, a piece got loose up there, so we had a new section put in a couple months ago."

"Where was the old piece of railing left?" Leffing asked. "Was it by any chance discarded in this alley?"

Morenda scratched his chin. "Might be. I never paid any attention. You think that bum got bashed with it, Mr. Leffing?"

"I believe it highly possible. That may be why the coroner thinks Karvey fell. The wounds on his head would indicate that that pipe railing caused them, but in my opinion it was the discarded piece, left lying in the alley here, which did the job."

"If we could locate it, we might have fingerprints!" I exclaimed.

"Possibly. But the murderer probably walked a few yards down to the beach and hurled it into the breakers. We would have a herculean task recovering it, and any fingerprints would be scoured off by now."

Morenda shook his head. "You sure got all the answers, Mr. Leffing!" Suddenly he broke into a roar of laughter. "All except the big answer. Who killed Karvey?" He went on laughing like an hysterical hyena.

If Leffing was annoyed, he gave no sign. "You are right, Mr. Morenda," he said quietly when the raucous hee-hawing had subsided. "The big answer still eludes me."

As we walked back toward Morenda's office, Leffing inquired about Henry Marnault, the Frolic Beach watchman.

"We got a real bad worry about fire," Morenda explained. "After midnight, when we close, Henry checks up on all the rides and stands. You know how it is—a smoldering butt could bring down the works."

"That is the extent of Marnault's duties?" Leffing asked.

"His night tour takes about two hours. Then he goes off and doesn't come on again till four the next afternoon. He sweeps my office and does a few odd jobs, but mostly he just drifts around picking up soda bottles and stuff. Sometimes if a stand runs out of change, he'll bring a bill to my office. We don't push Henry. It's hard to get a man for that night tour."

"Where does he live?" Leffing asked.

"Lives in a barn down off the end of Lavender Street. We fixed it up for him and we don't charge any rent. He's got all he needs in there."

Leffing nodded. "Well, we may just have a chat with him, if you've no objection."

"Sure, sure. Leave no stone unturned, as they say, Mr. Leffing!"

We left Morenda and walked down Lavender Street, stopping for a lemonade along the way.

Henry Marnault's barn was situated in a salt meadow off the end of the street. It was not much more than an oversized shack, but the roof looked new and storm windows had been fitted into the front.

We walked around to the rear, but Marnault was not in sight. As we came back around to the front, we noticed someone walking down the near end of Lavender Street. He was hunched over with his head bent down, and for a moment we thought he was searching the road for something he had lost. As he turned in toward the barn, however, we saw that this was his habitual way of walking.

Marnault looked up at us suspiciously out of somewhat bloodshot eyes, but he became friendly enough when Leffing explained his errand.

"Karvey? Yeah, sure. I knew who he was. Mr. Morenda had me watchin' him for a while. We figured he was panhandlin', but I never did catch him at it. Slippery cuss. But I ain't got no information about him. He just hung around, never talked to nobody."

"You think he was murdered?"

Marnault ran a hand through his ragged hair. "Naw. Who'd want to kill him? He wasn't worth killin', a bum like that. But I don't think he *fell* off the Cyclone. I figure he just climbed up there one night and *jumped!*"

"What reason had he for suicide?" Leffing asked.

Marnault tapped his head.

"He was loose up here. Those kind of people get crazy urges like that."

Leffing nodded. "Well, you may be right, Mr. Marnault. You may be right."

He could tell us nothing more. Leffing thanked him and we started back up Lavender Street.

"If Karvey committed suicide," I pointed out, "we are wasting our time."

"Well, there are worse ways of wasting it, Brennan. We have the tang of sea air, and fresh lemonade is just at hand."

Leffing then began a series of inquiries which exasperated me and eventually left me exhausted. He stopped at every stand and stall along Lavender Street and inquired about Karvey. Did they remember him? Did he ever buy food or drink from that particular stand? How did he pay for it?

By the time I fell into my car for the drive back to New Haven, my legs were literally aching. Leffing, apparently immune to fatigue, was in an optimistic mood.

"Well, well, Brennan, I think the case is clearing."

"I can't recall that you learned anything of consequence from the various vendors along Lavender Street."

"You attach no significance to the fact that Karvey invariably paid for his food and drink with coins—usually nickels and dimes?"

"The only significance I attach to it," I replied, "is that he was an elusive and hard-working panhandler."

Leffing would say no more. He began humming an old English music hall ballad. This went on until we arrived back at Autumn Street.

He turned to me as I stopped the car in front of his small house. "Brennan, are you willing to drive me down to Frolic Beach tomorrow morning—about five o'clock?"

I groaned. "Good grief, are we going in pursuit of a murderous milkman?"

He laughed. "I think not, but we must have an early start."

"I'll be right here at five o'clock," I told him.

I knew it would be useless to question him. He loved being both melodramatic and secretive, and I had come to accept the irritating fact that apparently he could not be cured of this deplorable childishness.

I set my alarm for four-thirty and was still sleepy as I stopped in front of seven Autumn Street. It was just beginning to get light. A heavy fog filled the streets.

Moments after I pulled up, a disreputable-looking figure appeared out of nowhere, slouched up to the car and yanked open the door.

I turned in alarm. "What do you want?"

The tramp leered at me. "I want a lift down to Frolic Beach. That's where you're headed, ain't it—Brennan?"

I stared at him for a full half minute before the import of his words came through. "Leffing! You've given me another gray hair!"

He got in the car. "Sorry, Brennan. Did my little disguise take you in?"

I shook my head. "I had no idea you were a master of makeup. Where did you learn the art?"

"In my distant youth I was identified with several amateur theatrical groups. At various times my early stage experience has proved invaluable."

Traffic was light, but the fog slowed us up considerably. Leffing chatted about everything except the case at hand. I remained completely mystified as to the reason for his disguise.

We parked a few blocks from the beginning of Lavender Street. Leffing peered cautiously through the fog. "No more talking, Brennan, and remain close to the buildings. We must not be seen."

We skulked down Lavender Street single file, like a pair of thieves. About halfway down, Leffing nudged me into a doorway.

"We will take our stand here," he whispered.

The light strengthened and the fog lifted a bit as we waited. Suddenly Leffing squeezed my arm and nodded.

Inching out, I looked down Lavender Street. At the far end a shambling figure came into sight. In the fog he looked like a wraith beginning to materialize. He kept his head bent forward and down. Twice, as we watched, he bent swiftly and seemed to pick something out of the street.

This weird behavior was repeated several more times as he approached. When he drew closer, Leffing edged slowly into the street and began to stroll toward him.

I watched, puzzled but fascinated, and now Leffing stooped and appeared to pick up something. He seemed to be entirely oblivious to the figure coming toward him from the other end of the street.

As the other figure slowly emerged from the fog, I finally recognized the features of Henry Marnault, the Frolic Beach watchman. He kept his head bent and his eyes on the ground most of the time, so he did not see the disguised form of Leffing until they were less than a block apart.

He stopped in his tracks and stared. Leffing continued shuffling forward. At intervals he bent to pluck something from the gutters.

Marnault watched him like a man bewitched. He seemed frozen into immobility. When he found his voice, it was high-pitched, frantic, filled with rising hysteria.

"Karvey! Get back! You're dead, you crazy bum, I killed you! Get away from me!"

As Leffing continued toward him, Marnault turned with a scream and began to run down Lavender Street. Leffing straightened up, drew something from a pocket and put it to his lips. The shrill blast of a police whistle cut through the foggy morning air. A moment later a blue-clad figure came pounding from somewhere out of the fog and collared the terrified Marnault.

Leffing called out in his own voice, "Splendid work, Sergeant Corliss! Arrest that man for the murder of Joel Karvey!"

Marnault signed a full confession later in the day, admitting that he had slugged Karvey over the head with a piece of pipe railing found in the alley next to the Cyclone. He had dragged Karvey into the alley, walked to the shore and thrown the murder weapon into the ocean. This had occurred just at daybreak, when the Frolic Beach area was still deserted.

He had killed Karvey, he explained, because Karvey, in spite of repeated threats, had continued to "muscle in" on his territory. Marnault had found that an early-morning inspection of the Frolic Beach streets, gutters and sidewalks almost invariably yielded a modest crop of coins. The area, which was open until midnight, was not well lighted; many coins dropped during the evening remained waiting to be picked up on the following morning. Marnault had averaged enough to pay for his weekly bottle of gin.

Then Karvey had drifted in. One morning Marnault had run into him prowling the gutters in search of coins. The watchman had warned him to leave, but Karvey had remained. Morning after morning Marnault ran into the drifter, and the watchman's daily harvest of coins dwindled ever lower. The amount involved was small, but so was Marnault's salary, and the bottle of gin was important to him. At length his irritation had turned to murderous rage. Finally, one foggy morning, he had waited in the little alley next to the Cyclone, where he had picked up a length of pipe railing. Karvey's coin collecting had come to an abrupt end.

That evening I sat in Leffing's gaslit Victorian living room while he poured a generous portion of his choice, cask-mellowed brandy.

I sampled it with relish. "It certainly was a bizarre murder motive," I commented, "but two things still puzzle me. Why was Marnault so terrified when he saw you approaching in the fog? And how did you figure out the business in the first place?"

Leffing smiled. "Marnault was terrified," he replied, "because I had made up to resemble Karvey. I had studied the morgue pictures, you know. I made up my face to look like his and I had even scoured the secondhand shops to get some rags of clothing which resembled his own. It was a gamble, of course, but it worked."

He set down his glass. "From the beginning the motive interested me. It eluded me for some time. Then I began to speculate as to Karvey's source of money. He never worked and was never seen begging, yet he always seemed to have a few coins. I was still groping in the dark until that day when we went to see Marnault. When I saw him approaching, I immediately tagged him as a 'stooper'—a tramp term for a person who scrounges around looking for coins in the gutters and streets. Marnault had no physical deformity; the bent head and constantly downcast eyes, therefore, could mean only one of two things: atrocious posture arising out of sloth and indifference, or the habitual stance of a confirmed 'stooper.' I was not sure of myself at first, but when I canvassed the stall operators and found that Karvey almost invariably paid for his snacks with small coins, I felt that I had found the motive for his murder."

I shook my head. "It seems unbelievable to me that a man would murder for a few miserable coins snatched out of the gutter!"

Leffing shrugged. "Those 'miserable coins' meant a regular weekly bottle of gin. To a person such as Marnault, alcohol can become pretty important."

A whimsical grin touched his thin face. "Speaking of alcohol, Brennan, would you care for another brandy?"

I held out my glass.

BILL PRONZINI

The Arrowmont Prison Riddle

I first met the man who called himself by the unlikely name of Buckmaster Gilloon in the late summer of 1916, my second year as warden of Arrowmont Prison. There were no living quarters within the old brick walls of the prison, which was situated on a promontory overlooking a small winding river two miles north of Arrowmont Village, so I had rented a cottage in the village proper, not far from a tavern known as Hallahan's Irish Inn. It was in this tavern, and as a result of a mutual passion for Guinness stout and the game of darts, that Gilloon and I became acquainted.

As a man he was every bit as unlikely as his name. He was in his late thirties, short and almost painfully thin; he had a glass eye and a drooping and incongruous Oriental-style mustache, wore English tweeds, gaudy Albert watch chains and plaid Scotch caps, and always carried half a dozen looseleaf notebooks in which he perpetually and secretively jotted things. He was well read and erudite, had a repertoire of bawdy stories to rival any vaudevillian in the country, and never seemed to lack ready cash. He lived in a boarding house in the center of the village and claimed to be a writer for the pulp magazines—*Argosy, Adventure, All-Story Weekly, Munsey's.* Perhaps he was, but he steadfastly refused to discuss any of his fiction, or to divulge his pseudonym or pseudonyms.

He was reticent about divulging any personal information. When personal questions arose, he deftly changed the subject. Since he did not speak with an accent, I took him to be American-born. I was able to learn, from occasional comments and observations, that he had traveled extensively throughout the world.

In my nine decades on this earth I have never encountered a more fascinating or troubling enigma than this man whose path crossed mine for a few short weeks in 1916.

Who and what was Buckmaster Gilloon? Is it possible for one enigma to be attracted and motivated by another enigma? Can that which seems natural and coincidental be the result instead of preternatural forces? These questions have plagued me in the sixty years since Gilloon and I became involved in what appeared to be an utterly enigmatic crime.

It all began on September 26, 1916—the day of the scheduled execution at Arrowmont Prison of a condemned murderer named Arthur Teasdale . . .

Shortly before noon of that day a thunderstorm struck without warning. Rain pelted down incessantly from a black sky, and lightning crackled in low jagged blazes that gave the illusion of striking unseen objects just beyond the prison walls. I was already suffering from nervous tension, as was always the case on the day of an execution, and the storm added to my discomfort. I passed the early afternoon sitting at my desk, staring out the window, listening to the inexorable ticking of my Seth Thomas, wishing the execution was done with and it was eight o'clock, when I was due to meet Gilloon at Hallahan's for Guinness and darts.

At 3:30 the two civilians who had volunteered to act as witnesses to the hanging arrived. I ushered them into a waiting room and asked them to wait until they were summoned. Then I donned a slicker and stopped by the office of Rogers, the chief guard, and asked him to accompany me to the execution shed.

The shed was relatively small, constructed of brick with a tin roof, and sat in a corner of the prison between the textile mill and the iron foundry. It was lighted by lanterns hung from the walls and the rafters and contained only a row of witness chairs and a high permanent gallows at the far end. Attached to the shed's north wall was an annex in which the death cell was located. As was customary, Teasdale had been transported there five days earlier to await due process.

He was a particularly vicious and evil man, Teasdale. He had cold-bloodedly murdered three people during an abortive robbery attempt in the state capital, and had been anything but a model prisoner during his month's confinement at Arrowmont. As a rule I had a certain compassion for those condemned to hang under my jurisdiction, and in two cases I had spoken to the governor in favor of clemency. In Teasdale's case, however, I had conceded that a continuance of his life would serve no good purpose.

When I had visited him the previous night to ask if he wished to see a clergyman or to order anything special for his last meal, he had cursed me and Rogers and the entire prison personnel with an almost maniacal intensity, vowing vengeance on us all from the grave.

I rather expected, as Rogers and I entered the death cell at ten minutes of four, to find Teasdale in much the same state. However, he had fallen instead into an acute melancholia; he lay on his cot with his knees drawn up and his eyes staring blankly at the opposite wall. The two guards assigned to him, Hollowell and Granger (Granger was also the state-appointed hangman), told us he had been like that for several hours. I spoke to him, asking again if he wished to confer with a clergyman. He did not answer, did not move. I inquired if he had any last requests, and if it was his wish to wear a hood for his final walk to the gallows and for the execution. He did not respond.

I took Hollowell aside. "Perhaps it would be better to use the hood," I said. "It will make it easier for all of us."

"Yes, sir."

Rogers and I left the annex, accompanied by Granger, for a final examination of the gallows. The rope had already been hung and the hangman's knot tied.

While Granger made certain they were secure I unlocked the door beneath the platform, which opened into a short passage that ended in a narrow cubicle beneath the trap. The platform had been built eight feet off the floor, so that the death throes of the condemned man would be concealed from the witnesses—a humane gesture which was not observed by all prisons in our state, and for which I was grateful.

After I had made a routine examination of the cubicle, and relocked the door, I mounted the thirteen steps to the platform. The trap beneath the gibbet arm was operated by a lever set into the floor; when Granger threw the lever, the trap would fall open. Once we tried it and reset it, I pronounced everything in readiness and sent Rogers to summon the civilian witnesses and the prison doctor. It was then 4:35 and the execution would take place at precisely five o'clock. I had received a wire from the governor the night before, informing me that there wasn't the remotest chance of a stay being granted.

When Rogers returned with the witnesses and the doctor, we all took chairs in the row arranged some forty feet opposite the gallows. Time passed, tensely; with thunder echoing hollowly outside, a hard rain drumming against the tin roof, and eerie shadows not entirely dispelled by the lanternlight, the moments before that execution were particularly disquieting.

I held my pocket watch open on my knee, and at 4:55 I signaled to the guard at the annex door to call for the prisoner. Three more minutes crept by and then the door reopened and Granger and Hollowell brought Teasdale into the shed.

The three men made a grim procession as they crossed to the gallows steps: Granger in his black hangman's duster, Hollowell in his khaki guard uniform and peaked cap, Teasdale between them in his gray prison clothing and black hood. Teasdale's shoes dragged across the floor—he was stiffly unresisting weight until they reached the steps; then he struggled briefly and Granger and Hollowell were forced to tighten their grip and all but carry him up onto the gallows. Hollowell held him slumped on the trap while Granger solemnly fitted the noose around his neck and drew it taut.

The hands on my watch read five o'clock when, as prescribed by law, Granger intoned, "Have you any last words before the sentence imposed on you is carried out?"

Teasdale said nothing, but his body twisted with a spasm of fear.

Granger looked in my direction and I raised my hand to indicate final sanction. He backed away from Teasdale and rested his hand on the release lever. As he did so, there came from outside a long rolling peal of thunder that seemed to shake the shed roof. A chill touched the nape of my neck and I shifted uneasily in my chair.

Just as the sound of the thunder faded, Granger threw the lever and Hollowell released Teasdale and stepped back. The trap thudded open and the condemned man plummeted downward.

In that same instant I thought I saw a faint silvery glimmer above the opening, but it was so brief that I took it for an optical illusion. My attention was focused on the rope; it danced for a moment under the weight of the body, then pulled taut and became motionless. I let out a soft tired sigh and sat forward while Granger and Hollowell, both of whom were looking away from the open trap, silently counted off the passage of sixty seconds.

When the minute had elapsed, Granger turned and walked to the edge of the trap. If the body hung laxly, he would signal to me so that the prison doctor and I could enter the cubicle and officially pronounce Teasdale deceased; if the body was still thrashing, thus indicating the condemned man's neck had not been broken in the fall—grisly prospect, but I had seen it happen—more time would be allowed to pass. It sounds brutal, I know, but such was the law and it had to be obeyed without question.

But Granger's reaction was so peculiar and so violent that I came immediately to my feet. He flinched as if he had been struck in the stomach and his face twisted into an expression of disbelief. He dropped to his hands and knees at the front of the trap as Hollowell came up beside him and leaned down to peer into the passageway.

"What is it, Granger?" I called. "What's the matter?"

He straightened after a few seconds and pivoted toward me. "You better get up here, Warden Parker," he said. His voice was shrill and tremulous and he clutched at his stomach. "Quick!"

Rogers and I exchanged glances, then ran to the steps, mounted them, and hurried to the trap, the other guards and the prison doctor close behind us. As soon as I looked downward, it was my turn to stare with incredulity, to exclaim against what I saw—and what I did not see.

The hangman's noose at the end of the rope was empty.

Except for the black hood on the ground, the cubicle was empty.

Impossibly, inconceivably, the body of Arthur Teasdale had vanished.

I raced down the gallows steps and fumbled the platform door open with my key. I had the vague desperate hope that Teasdale had somehow slipped the noose and that I would see him lying within, against the door—that small section of the passageway was shrouded in darkness and not quite penetrable from above—but he wasn't there. The passageway, like the cubicle, was deserted.

While I called for a lantern Rogers hoisted up the rope to examine it and the noose. A moment later he announced that it had not been tampered with in any way. When a guard brought the lantern I embarked on a careful search of the area, but there were no loose boards in the walls of the passage or the cubicle, and the floor was of solid concrete. On the floor I discovered a thin sliver of wood about an inch long, which may or may not have been there previously. Aside from that, there was not so much as a strand of hair or a loose thread to be found. And the black hood told me nothing at all.

There simply did not seem to be any way Teasdale—or his remains—could have gotten, or been gotten, out of there.

I stood for a moment, staring at the flickering light from the lantern, listening to the distant rumbling of thunder. *Had* Teasdale died at the end of the hangman's rope? Or had he somehow managed to cheat death? I had seen him fall through the trap with my own eyes, had seen the rope dance and then pull taut with the weight of his body. He *must* have expired, I told myself.

A shiver moved along my back. I found myself remembering Teasdale's threats to wreak vengeance from the grave, and I had the irrational thought that perhaps something otherworldly had been responsible for the phenomenon we had witnessed. Teasdale had, after all, been a malignant individual. Could he have been so evil that he had managed to summon the Powers of Darkness to save him in the instant before death—or to claim him soul *and* body in the instant after it?

I refused to believe it. I am a practical man, not prone to superstition, and it has always been my nature to seek a logical explanation for even the most uncommon occurrence. Arthur Teasdale had disappeared, yes; but it could not be other than an earthly force behind the deed. Which meant that, alive or dead, Teasdale was still somewhere inside the walls of Arrowmont Prison.

I roused myself, left the passageway, and issued instructions for a thorough search of the prison guards. I ordered word sent to the guards in the watchtowers to double their normal vigilance. I noticed that Hollowell wasn't present along with the assembled guards and asked where he had gone. One of the others said he had seen Hollowell hurry out of the shed several minutes earlier.

Frowning, I pondered this information. Had Hollowell intuited something, or even seen something, and gone off unwisely to investigate on his own rather than confide in the rest of us? He had been employed at Arrowmont Prison less than two months, so I knew relatively little about him. I requested that he be found and brought to my office.

When Rogers and Granger and the other guards had departed, I escorted the two civilian witnesses to the administration building, where I asked them to remain until the mystery was explained. As I settled grimly at my desk to await Hollowell and word on the search of the grounds, I expected such an explanation within the hour.

I could not, however, have been more wrong.

The first development came after thirty minutes, and it was nearly as alarming as the disappearance of Teasdale from the gallows cubicle: one of the guards brought the news, ashen-faced, that a body had been discovered behind a stack of lumber in a lean-to between the execution shed and the iron foundry. But it was not the body of Arthur Teasdale!

It was that of Hollowell, stabbed to death with an awl.

I went immediately. As I stood beneath the rain-swept lean-to, looking down at the bloody front of poor Hollowell's uniform, a fresh set of unsettling questions tumbled through my mind. Had he been killed because, as I had first thought, he had either seen or intuited something connected with Teasdale's disappearance? If that was the case, whatever it was had died with him.

Or was it possible that he had himself been involved in the disappearance and been murdered to assure his silence? But how could he have been involved? He had been in my sight the entire time on the gallows platform. He had done nothing suspicious, could not in any way I could conceive have assisted in the deed.

Might his death have been part of Teasdale's vow to destroy us all?

No. My instinct for logic fought for the upper hand.

How could Teasdale have survived the hanging?

How could he have escaped not only the gallows but the execution shed itself?

The only explanation seemed to be that it was not a live Arthur Teasdale who was carrying out his warped revenge, but a dead one who had been embraced and given earthly powers by the Forces of Evil . . .

In order to dispel the dark reflections from my mind, I personally supervised the balance of the search. Tines of lightning split the sky and thunder continued to hammer the roofs as we went from building to building. No corner of the prison compound escaped our scrutiny. No potential hiding place was overlooked. We went so far as to test for the presence of tunnels in the work areas and in the individual cells, although I had instructed just such a search only weeks before as part of my security program.

We found nothing.

Alive or dead, Arthur Teasdale was no longer within the walls of Arrowmont Prison.

I left the prison at ten o'clock that night. There was nothing more to be done, and I was filled with such depression and anxiety that I could not bear to spend another minute there. I had debated contacting the governor, of course, and, wisely or not, had decided against it for the time being. He would think me a lunatic if I requested assistance in a county or statewide search for a man who had for all intents and purposes been hanged at five o'clock that afternoon. If there were no new developments within the next twenty-four hours, I knew I would have no choice but to explain the situation to him. And I had no doubt that such an explanation unaccompanied by Teasdale or Teasdale's remains would cost me my position.

Before leaving, I swore everyone to secrecy, saying that I would have any man's job if he leaked word of the day's events to the press or to the public-at-large. The last thing I wanted was rumor-mongering and a general panic as a result of it. I warned Granger and the other guards who had come in contact with Teasdale to be especially wary and finally left word that I was to be contacted immediately if there were any further developments before morning.

I had up to that time given little thought to my own safety. But when I reached my cottage in the village I found myself imagining menace in every shadow and sound. Relaxation was impossible. After twenty minutes I felt impelled to leave, to seek out a friendly face. I told my housekeeper I would be at Hallahan's Irish Inn if anyone called for me and drove my Packard to the tavern.

The first person I saw upon entering was Buckmaster Gilloon. He was seated alone in a corner booth, writing intently in one of his notebooks, a stein of draught Guinness at his elbow.

Gilloon had always been very secretive about his notebooks and never allowed anyone to glimpse so much as a word of what he put into them. But he was so engrossed when I walked up to the booth that he did not hear me, and I happened to glance down at the open page on which he was writing. There was but a single interrogative sentence on the page, clearly legible in his bold hand. The sentence read:

If a jimbuck stands alone by the sea, on a night when the dark moon sings, how many grains of sand in a single one of his footprints?

That sentence has always haunted me, because I cannot begin to understand its significance. I have no idea what a jimbuck is, except perhaps as a fictional creation, and yet the passage was like none which ever appeared in such periodicals as *Argosy* or *Munsey's*.

Gilloon sensed my presence after a second or two, and he slammed the notebook shut. A ferocious scowl crossed his normally placid features. He said irritably, "Reading over a man's shoulder is a nasty habit, Parker."

"I'm sorry, I didn't mean to pry—"

"I'll thank you to be more respectful of my privacy in the future."

"Yes, of course." I sank wearily into the booth opposite him and called for a Guinness.

Gilloon studied me across the table. "You look haggard, Parker," he said. "What's troubling you?"

"It's . . . nothing."

"Everything is something."

"I'm not at liberty to discuss it."

"Would it have anything to do with the execution at Arrowmont Prison this afternoon?"

I blinked. "Why would you surmise that?"

"Logical assumption," Gilloon said. "You are obviously upset, and yet you are a man who lives quietly and suffers no apparent personal problems. You are warden of Arrowmont Prison and the fact of the execution is public knowledge. You customarily come to the inn at eight o'clock and yet you didn't make your appearance tonight until after eleven."

I said, "I wish I had your mathematical mind, Gilloon."

"Indeed? Why is that?"

"Perhaps then I could find answers where none seem to exist."

"Answers to what?"

A waiter arrived with my Guinness and I took a swallow gratefully.

Gilloon was looking at me with piercing interest. I avoided his one-eyed gaze, knowing I had already said too much. But there was something about Gilloon that demanded confidence. Perhaps he could shed some light on the riddle of Teasdale's disappearance.

"Come now, Parker—answers to what?" he repeated. "Has something happened at the prison?"

And of course I weakened—partly because of frustration and worry, partly because the possibility that I might never learn the secret loomed large and painful. "Yes," I said, "something has happened at the prison. Something incredible, and I mean that literally." I paused to draw a heavy breath. "If I tell you about it, do I have your word that you won't let it go beyond this table?"

"Naturally." Gilloon leaned forward and his good eye glittered with anticipation. "Go on, Parker."

More or less calmly at first, then with increasing agitation as I relived the events, I proceeded to tell Gilloon everything that had transpired at the prison. He listened with attention, not once interrupting. I had never seen him excited prior to that night, but when I had finished, he was fairly squirming. He took off his Scotch cap and ran a hand roughly through his thinning brown hair.

"Fascinating tale," he asked.

"Horrifying would be a more appropriate word."

"That too, yes. No wonder you're upset."

"It simply defies explanation," I said. "And yet there has to be one. I refuse to accept the supernatural implications."

"I wouldn't be so skeptical of the supernatural if I were you, Parker. I've come across a number of things in my travels which could not be satisfactorily explained by man or science."

I stared at him. "Does that mean you believe Teasdale's disappearance was arranged by forces beyond human ken?"

"No, no. I was merely making a considered observation. Have you given me every detail of what happened?"

"I believe so."

"Think it through again—be sure."

Frowning, I reviewed the events once more. And it came to me that I had neglected to mention the brief silvery glimmer which had appeared above the trap in the instant Teasdale plunged through; I had, in fact forgotten all about it. This time I mentioned it to Gilloon.

"Ah," he said.

"Ah? Does it have significance?"

"Perhaps. Can you be more specific about it?"

"I'm afraid not. It was so brief I took it at the time for an optical illusion."

"You saw no other such glimmers?"

"None."

"How far away from the gallows were you sitting?"

"Approximately forty feet."

"Is the shed equipped with electric lights?"

"No—lanterns."

"I see," Gilloon said meditatively. He seized one of his notebooks, opened it, shielded it from my eyes with his left arm, and began to write furiously with his pencil. He wrote without pause for a good three minutes, before I grew both irritated and anxious.

"Gilloon," I said finally, "stop that infernal scribbling and tell me what's on your mind."

He gave no indication of having heard me. His pencil continued to scratch against the paper, filling another page. Except for the movement of his right hand and one side of his mouth gnawing at the edge of his mustache, he was as rigid as a block of stone.

"Damn it, Gilloon!"

But it was another ten seconds before the pencil became motionless. He stared at what he had written and then looked up at me. "Parker," he said, "did Arthur Teasdale have a trade?"

The question took me by surprise. "A trade?"

"Yes. What did he do for a living, if anything?"

"What bearing can that have on what's happened?"

"Perhaps a great deal," Gilloon said.

"He worked in a textile mill."

"And there is a textile mill at the prison, correct?"

"Yes."

"Does it stock quantities of silk?"

"Silk? Yes, on occasion. What—?"

I did not finish what I was about to say, for he had shut me out and resumed writing in his notebook. I repressed an oath of exasperation, took a long draught of Guinness to calm myself, and prepared to demand that he tell me what theory he had devised. Before I could do that, however, Gilloon abruptly closed the notebook, slid out of the booth, and fairly loomed over me.

"I'll need to see the execution shed," he said.

"What for?"

"Corroboration of certain facts."

"But—" I stood up hastily. "You've suspicioned a possible answer, that's clear," I said, "though I can't for the life of me see how, on the basis of the information I've given you. What is it?"

"I must see the execution shed," he said firmly. "I will not voice premature speculations."

It touched my mind that the man was a bit mad. After all, I had only known him for a few weeks, and from the first he had been decidedly eccentric in most respects. Still, I had never had cause to question his mental faculties before this, and the aura of self-assurance and confidence he projected was forceful. Because I needed so desperately to solve the riddle, I couldn't afford *not* to indulge, at least for a while, the one man who might be able to provide it.

"Very well," I said, "I'll take you to the prison."

Rain still fell in black torrents—although without thunder and lightning— when I brought my Packard around the last climbing curve onto the promontory. Lanternlight glowed fuzzily in the prison watchtowers, and the bare brick walls had an unpleasant oily sheen. At this hour of night, in the storm, the place seemed forbidding and shrouded in human despair—an atmosphere I had not previously apprehended during the two years I had been its warden. Strange how a brush with the unknown can alter one's perspective and stir the fears that lie at the bottom of one's soul.

Beside me Gilloon did not speak; he sat perfectly erect, his hands resting on the notebooks on his lap. I parked in the small lot facing the main gates, and after Gilloon had carefully tucked the notebooks inside his slicker we ran through the downpour to the gates. I gestured to the guard, who nodded beneath the hood of his oilskin, allowed us to enter, and then quickly closed the iron halves behind us and returned to the warmth of the gatehouse. I led Gilloon directly across the compound to the execution shed.

The guards I had posted inside seemed edgy and grateful for company. It was colder now, and despite the fact that all the lanterns were lit it also seemed darker and filled with more restless shadows. But the earlier aura of spiritual menace permeated the air, at least to my sensitivities. If Gilloon noticed it, he gave no indication.

He wasted no time crossing to the gallows and climbing the steps to the platform. I followed him to the trap, which still hung open. Gilloon peered into the cubicle, got onto all fours to squint at the rectangular edges of the opening, and then hoisted the hangman's rope and studied the noose. Finally, with surprising agility, he dropped down inside the cubicle, requesting a lantern which I fetched for him, and spent minutes crawling about with his nose to the floor. He located the thin splinter of wood I had noticed earlier, studied it in the lantern glow, and dropped it into the pocket of his tweed coat.

When he came out through the passageway he wore a look mixed of ferocity and satisfaction. "Stand there a minute, will you?" he said. He hurried over to where the witness chairs were arranged, then called, "In which of these chairs were you sitting during the execution?"

"Fourth one from the left."

Gilloon sat in that chair, produced his notebooks, opened one, and bent over it. I waited with mounting agitation while he committed notes on paper. When he glanced up again, the flickering lanternglow gave his face a spectral cast.

He said, "While Granger placed the noose over Teasdale's head Hollowell held the prisoner on the trap—is that correct?"

"It is."

"Stand as Hollowell was standing."

I moved to the edge of the opening, turning slightly quarter profile.

"You're certain that was the exact position?"

"Yes."

"Once the trap had been sprung, what did Hollowell do?"

"Moved a few paces away." I demonstrated.

"Did he avert his eyes from the trap?"

"Yes, he did. So did Granger. That's standard procedure."

"Which direction did he face?"

I frowned. "I'm not quite sure," I said. "My attention was on the trap and the rope."

"You're doing admirably, Parker. After Granger threw the trap lever, did he remain standing beside it?"

"Until he had counted off sixty seconds, yes."

"And then?"

"As I told you, he walked to the trap and looked into the cubicle. Again, that is standard procedure for the hangman. When he saw it was empty he uttered a shocked exclamation, went to his knees, and leaned down to see if Teasdale had somehow slipped the noose and fallen or crawled into the passageway."

"At which part of the opening did he go to his knees? Front, rear, one of the sides?"

"The front. But I don't see—"

"Would you mind illustrating?"

I grumbled but did as he asked. Some thirty seconds passed in silence. Finally I stood and turned, and of course found Gilloon again writing in his notebook. I descended the gallows steps. Gilloon closed the notebook and stood with an air of growing urgency. "Where would Granger be at this hour?" he asked. "Still here at the prison?"

"I doubt it. He came on duty at three and should have gone off again at midnight."

"It's imperative that we find him as soon as possible, Parker. Now that I'm onto the solution of this riddle, there's no time to waste."

"You have solved it?"

"I'm certain I have." He hurried me out of the shed.

I felt dazed as we crossed the rain-soaked compound, yet Gilloon's positiveness had infused in me a similar sense of urgency. We entered the administration building and I led the way to Rogers' office, where we found him preparing to depart for the night. When I asked about Granger, Rogers said that he had signed out some fifty minutes earlier, at midnight.

"Where does he live?" Gilloon asked us.

"In Hainesville, I think."

"We must go there immediately, Parker. And we had better take half a dozen well-armed men with us."

I stared at him. "Do you honestly believe that's necessary?"

"I do," Gilloon said grimly. "If we're fortunate, it will help prevent another murder."

The six-mile drive to the village of Hainesville was charged with tension, made even more acute by the muddy roads and the pelting rain. Gilloon stubbornly refused to comment on the way as to whether he believed Granger to be a culpable or innocent party, or as to whether he expected to find Teasdale—alive or dead—at Granger's home. There would be time enough later for explanations, he said.

Hunched over the wheel of the Packard, conscious of the two heavily armed prison guards in the rear seat and the headlamps of Rogers' car following closely behind, I could not help but wonder if I might be making a prize fool of myself. Suppose I had been wrong in my judgment of Gilloon, and he *was* daft after all? Or a well-meaning fool in his own right? Or worst of all, a hoaxster?

Nevertheless, there was no turning back now. I had long since committed myself. Whatever the outcome, I had placed the fate of my career firmly in the hands of Buckmaster Gilloon.

We entered the outskirts of Hainesville. One of the guards who rode with us lived there, and he directed us down the main street and into a turn just beyond the church. The lane in which Granger lived, he said, was two blocks further up and one block east.

Beside my Gilloon spoke for the first time. "I suggest we park a distance away from Granger's residence, Parker. It won't do to announce our arrival by stopping directly in front."

I nodded. When I made the turn into the lane I took the Packard onto the verge and doused its lights. Rogers' car drifted in behind, headlamps also winking out. A moment later eight of us stood in a tight group in the roadway, huddling inside our slickers as we peered up the lane.

There were four houses in the block, two on each side, spaced widely apart. The pair on our left, behind which stretched open meadowland, were dark. The furthest of the two on the right was also dark, but the closer one showed light in one of the front windows. Thick smoke curled out of its chimney and was swirled into nothingness by the howling wind. A huge oak shaded the front yard. Across the rear, a copse of swaying pine stood silhouetted against the black sky.

The guard who lived in Hainesville said, "That's Granger's place, the one showing light."

We left the road and set out laterally across the grassy flatland to the pines, then through them toward Granger's cottage. From a point behind the house, after issuing instructions for the others to wait there, Gilloon, Rogers, and I made our way downward past an old stone well and through a sodden growth of weeds. The sound of the storm muffled our approach as we proceeded single-file, Gilloon tacitly assuming leadership, along the west side of the house to the lighted window.

Gilloon put his head around the frame for the first cautious look inside. Momentarily he stepped back and motioned me to take his place. When I had moved to where I could peer in, I saw Granger standing relaxed before the fireplace, using a poker to prod a blazing fire not wholly comprised of logs— something else, a blackened lump already burned beyond recognition, was being consumed there. But he was not alone in the room; a second man stood watching him, an expression of concentrated malevolence on his face—and an old hammerless revolver tucked into the waistband of his trousers.

Arthur Teasdale.

I experienced a mixture of relief, rage, and resolve as I moved away to give Rogers his turn. It was obvious that Granger was guilty of complicity in Teasdale's escape—and I had always liked and trusted the man. But I supposed everyone had his price—and I may even have had a fleeting wonder as to what my own might be.

After Rogers had his look, the three of us returned to the back yard, where I told him to prepare the rest of the men for a front-and-rear assault on the cottage. Then Gilloon and I took up a post in the shadows behind the stone well. Now that my faith in *him*, at least, had been vindicated, I felt an enormous gratitude—but this was hardly the time to express it. Or to ask any of the questions that were racing through my mind. We waited in silence.

In less than four minutes all six of my men had surrounded the house. I could not hear it when those at the front broke in, but the men at the back entered the rear door swiftly. Soon the sound of pistol shots rose above the cry of the storm.

Gilloon and I hastened inside. In the parlor we found Granger sitting on the floor beside the hearth, his head buried in his hands. He had not been injured, nor had any of the guards. Teasdale was lying just beyond the entrance to the center hallway. The front of his shirt was bloody, but he had merely suffered a superficial shoulder wound and was cursing like a madman. He would live to hang again, I remember thinking, in the execution shed at Arrowmont Prison.

Sixty minutes later, after Teasdale had been placed under guard in the prison infirmary and a remorsefully silent Granger had been locked in a cell, Rogers and Gilloon and I met in my office. Outside, the rain had slackened to a drizzle.

"Now then, Gilloon," I began sternly, "we owe you a great debt, and I acknowledge it here and now. But explanations are long overdue."

He smiled with the air of a man who has just been through an exhilarating experience. "Of course," he said. "Suppose we begin with Hollowell. You're quite naturally wondering if he was bribed by Teasdale—if he also assisted in the escape. The answer is no: he was an innocent pawn."

"Then why was he killed? Revenge?"

"Not at all. His life was taken—and not at the place where his body was later discovered—so that the escape trick could be worked in the first place. It was one of the primary keys to the plan's success."

"I don't understand," I said. "The escape trick had already been completed when Hollowell was stabbed."

"Ah, but it hadn't," Gilloon said. "Hollowell was murdered *before* the execution, sometime between four and five o'clock."

We stared at him. "Gilloon," I said, "Rogers and I and five other witnesses *saw* Hollowell inside the shed—"

"Did you, Parker? The execution shed is lighted by lanterns. On a dark afternoon, during a thunderstorm, visibility is not reliable. And you were some forty feet from him. You saw an average-sized man wearing a guard's uniform, with a guard's peaked cap drawn down over his forehead—a man you had no reason to assume was not Hollowell. You took his identity for granted."

"I can't dispute the logic of that," I said. "But if you're right that it wasn't Hollowell, who was it?"

"Teasdale, of course."

"Teasdale! For God's sake, man, if Teasdale assumed the identity of Hollowell, whom did we see carried in as Teasdale?"

"No one," Gilloon said.

My mouth fell open, and there was a moment of heavy silence. I broke it finally by exclaiming, "Are you saying we did not see a man hanged at five o'clock yesterday afternoon?"

"Precisely."

"Are you saying we were all victims of some sort of mass hallucination?"

"Certainly not. You saw what you believed to be Arthur Teasdale, just as you saw what you believed to be Hollowell. Again let me remind you: the lighting was poor and you had no reason at the time to suspect deception. But think back, Parker. What actually *did* you see? The shape of a man with a black hood covering his head, supported between two other men. But did you see that figure walk or hear it speak? Did you at any time discern an identifiable part of a human being, such as a hand or an exposed ankle?"

I squeezed my eyes shut for a moment, mentally re-examining the events in the shed. "No," I admitted. "I discerned nothing but the hood and the clothing and the shoes. But I *did* see him struggle at the foot of the gallows, and his body spasm on the trap. How do you explain them?"

"Simply. Like everything else, they were an illusion. At a preconceived time Granger and Teasdale had only to slow their pace and jostle the figure with their own bodies to create the impression that the figure itself was resisting them. Teasdale alone used the same method on the trap."

"If it is your contention that the figure was some sort of dummy, I can't believe it, Gilloon. How could a dummy be made to vanish any more easily than a man?"

"It was not, strictly speaking, a dummy."

"Then what the devil was it?"

Gilloon held up a hand; he appeared to be enjoying himself immensely. "Do you recall my asking if Teasdale had a trade? You responded that he had worked in a textile mill, whereupon I asked if the prison textile mill stocked silk."

"Yes, yes, I recall that."

"Come now, Parker, use your imagination. What is one of the uses of silk—varnished silk?"

"I don't know," I began, but no sooner were the words past my lips than the answer sprang into my mind. "Good Lord—balloons!"

"Exactly."

"The figure we saw was a *balloon*?"

"In effect, yes. It is not difficult to sew and tie off a large piece of silk in the rough shape of a man. When inflated to a malleable rather than a fully expanded state with helium or hydrogen, and seen in poor light from a distance of forty feet or better, while covered by clothing and a hood, and weighted down with a pair of shoes and held tightly by two men—the effect can be maintained."

I gaped.

"The handiwork would have been done by Teasdale in the relative privacy of the death cell. The material was doubtless supplied from the prison textile mill by Granger. Once the sewing and tying had been accomplished, I imagine Granger took the piece out of the prison, varnished it, and returned it later. It need not have been inflated, naturally, until just prior to the execution. As to where the gas was obtained, I would think that there would certainly be a cylinder of hydrogen in the prison foundry."

I nodded.

"In any event, between four and five o'clock, when the three of them were alone in the death annex, Teasdale murdered Hollowell with an awl Granger had given him. Granger then transported Hollowell's body behind the stack of lumber a short distance away and probably also returned the gas cylinder to the foundry. The storm would have provided all the shield necessary, though even without it the risk was one worth taking.

"Once Granger and Teasdale had brought the balloon-figure to the gallows, Granger, as hangman, placed the noose carefully around the head. You told me, Parker, that he was the last to examine the noose. While he was doing so, I expect he inserted into the fibers at the inner bottom that sharp sliver of wood you found in the trap cubicle. When he drew the noose taut, he made sure the sliver touched the balloon's surface so that when the trap was sprung and the balloon plunged downward the splinter would penetrate the silk. The sound of a balloon deflating is negligible; the storm made it more so. The dancing of the rope, of course, was caused by the escaping air.

"During the ensuing sixty seconds, the balloon completely deflated. There was nothing in the cubicle at that point except a bundle of clothing, silk, and shoes. The removal of all but the hood, to complete the trick, was a simple enough matter. You told me how it was done when you mentioned the silvery glimmer you saw above the trap.

"That glimmer was a brief reflection of lanternlight off part of a length of thin wire which had been attached to the clothing and to the balloon. Granger concealed the wire in his hand, and played out most of a seven- or eight-foot coil before he threw the trap lever.

"After he had gone to his knees with his back to the witness chairs, he merely opened the front of his duster, hauled up the bundle, and stowed it back inside the duster. No doubt it made something of a bulge, but the attention was focused on other matters. You did notice, Parker—and it was a helpful clue—that Granger appeared to be holding his stomach as if he were about to be ill. What he was actually doing was clutching the bundle so that it would not fall from beneath his duster. Later he hid the bundle among his belongings and transported it out of the prison when he went off duty. It was that bundle that we saw burning in the fireplace in his cottage."

"But how did *Teasdale* get out of the prison?"

"The most obvious way imaginable," Gilloon said. "He walked out through the front gates."

"What!"

"Yes. Remember, he was wearing a guard's uniform—supplied by Granger— and there was a storm raging. I noticed when we first arrived tonight that the gateman seemed eager to return to his gatehouse, where it was dry. He scarcely looked at you and did not question me. That being the case, it's obvious that he would not have questioned someone who wore the proper uniform and kept his face averted as he gave Hollowell's name. The guards had not yet been alerted and the gateman would have no reason to suspect trickery.

"Once out, I suspect Teasdale simply took Granger's car and drove to Hainesville. When Granger himself came off duty, I would venture to guess that he obtained a ride home with another guard, using some pretext to explain the absence of his own vehicle.

"I did not actually *know*, of course, that we would find Teasdale at Granger's place; I merely made a logical supposition in light of the other facts. Since Granger was the only other man alive who knew how the escape had been worked, I reasoned that an individual of Teasdale's stripe would not care to leave him alive and vulnerable to a confession, no matter what promises he might have made to Granger."

I sat forward.

"If Teasdale managed his actual escape that easily, why did he choose to go through all that trickery with the balloon? Why didn't he just murder Hollowell, with Granger's help, and then leave the prison *prior* to the execution, between four and five?"

"Oh, I suppose he thought that the bizarre circumstances surrounding the disappearance of an apparently hanged man would insure him enough time to get safely clear of this immediate area. If you were confused and baffled, you would not sound an instant alarm, whereas you certainly would have if he had simply disappeared from his cell. Also, I would guess that the prospect of leaving all of you a legacy of mystery and horror afforded him a warped sense of revenge."

"You're a brilliant man," I told him as I sank back in my chair.

Gilloon shrugged. "This kind of puzzle takes logic rather than brilliance, Parker. As I told you earlier tonight, it isn't always wise to discount the supernatural; but in a case where no clear evidence of the supernatural exists, the answer generally lies in some form of illusion. I've encountered a number of seemingly incredible occurrences, some of which were even more baffling than this one and most of which involved illusion. I expect I'll encounter others in the future as well."

"Why do you say that?"

"One almost seems able after a while to divine places where they will occur," he said matter-of-factly, "and therefore to make oneself available to challenge them."

I blinked at him. "Do you mean you *intuited* something like this would happen at Arrowmont Prison? That you have some sort of prevision?"

"Perhaps. Perhaps not. Perhaps I'm nothing more than a pulp writer who enjoys traveling." He gave me a enigmatic smile and got to his feet clutching his notebooks. "I can't speak for you, Parker," he said, "but I seem to have acquired an intense thirst. You wouldn't happen to know where we might obtain a Guinness at this hour, would you?"

One week later, suddenly and without notice, Gilloon left Arrowmont Village. One day he was there, the next he was not. Where he went I do not know: I neither saw him nor heard of or from him again.

Who and what was Buckmaster Gilloon? Is it possible for one enigma to be attracted and motivated by another enigma? Can that which seems natural and coincidental be the result instead of preternatural forces? Perhaps you can understand now why these questions have plagued me in the sixty years since I knew him. And why I am continually haunted by that single passage I read by accident in his notebook, the passage which may hold the key to Buckmaster Gilloon:

If a jimbuck stands alone by the sea, on a night when the dark moon sings, how many grains of sand in a single one of his footprints? . . .

LAWRENCE BLOCK

The Dettweiler Solution

Sometimes you just can't win for losing. Business was so bad over at Dettweiler Bros. Fine Fashions for Men that Seth Dettweiler went on back to the store one Thursday night and poured out a five-gallon can of lead-free gasoline where he figured as it would do the most good. He lit a fresh Philip Morris King Size and balanced it on the edge of the counter so as it would burn for a couple of minutes and then get unbalanced enough to drop into the pool of gasoline. Then he got into an Oldsmobile that was about five days' clear of a repossession notice and drove on home.

You couldn't have had a better fire dropping napalm on a paper mill. Time it was done you could sift those ashes and not find so much as a collar button. It was far and away the most spectacularly total fire Schuyler County had ever seen, so much so that Maybrook Fidelity Insurance would have been a little tentative about settling a claim under ordinary circumstances. But the way things stood there wasn't the slightest suspicion of arson, because what kind of a dimwitted hulk goes and burns down his business establishment a full week after his fire insurance has lapsed?

No fooling.

See, it was Seth's brother Porter who took care of paying bills and such, and a little over a month ago the fire-insurance payment had been due, and Porter looked at the bill and at the bank balance and back and forth for a while and then he put the bill in a drawer. Two weeks later there was a reminder notice, and two weeks after that there was a notice that the grace period had expired and the insurance was no longer in force, and then a week after that there was one pluperfect hell of a bonfire.

Seth and Porter had always got on pretty good. (They took after each other quite a bit, folks said. Especially Porter.) Seth was forty-two years of age, and he had that long Dettweiler face topping a jutting Van Dine jaw. (Their mother was a Van Dine hailing from just the other side of Oak Falls.) Porter was thirty-nine, equipped with the same style face and jaw. They both had black hair that lay flat on their heads like shoe polish put on in slapdash fashion. Seth had more hair left than Porter, in spite of being the older brother by three years. I could describe them in greater detail, right down to scars and warts and sundry

48

distinguishing marks, but it's my guess that you'd enjoy reading all that about as much as I'd enjoy writing it, which is to say less than somewhat. So let's get on with it.

I was saying they got on pretty good, rarely raising their voices one to the other, rarely disagreeing seriously about anything much. Now the fire didn't entirely change the habits of a lifetime but you couldn't honestly say that it did anything to improve their relationship. You'd have to allow that it caused a definite strain.

"What I can't understand," Seth said, "is how anybody who is fool enough to let fire insurance lapse can be an even greater fool by not telling his brother about it. That in a nutshell is what I can't understand."

"What beats *me*," Porter said, "is how the same person who has the nerve to fire a place of business for the insurance also does so without consulting his partner, especially when his partner just happens to be his brother."

"Allus I was trying to do," said Seth, "was save you from the criminal culpability of being an accessory before, to, and after the fact, plus figuring you might be too chickenhearted to go along with it."

"Allus *I* was trying to do," said Porter, "was save you from worrying about financial matters you would be powerless to contend with, plus figuring it would just be an occasion for me to hear further from you on the subject of those bow ties."

"Well, you did buy one powerful lot of bow ties."

"I knew it."

"Something like a Pullman car full of bow ties, and it's not like every man and boy in Schuyler County's been getting this mad passion for bow ties of late."

"I just knew it."

"I wasn't the one brought up the subject, but since you went and mentioned those bow ties—"

"Maybe I should of mentioned the spats," Porter said.

"Oh, I don't want to hear about spats."

"No more than I wanted to hear about bow ties. Did we sell one single damn pair of spats?"

"We did."

"We did?"

"Feller bought one about fifteen months back. Had Maryland plates on his car, as I recall. Said he always wanted spats and didn't know they still made 'em."

"Well, selling one pair out of a gross isn't too bad."

"Now you leave off," Seth said.

"And you leave off of bow ties?"

"I guess."

"Anyway, the bow ties and the spats all burned up in the same damn fire," Porter said.

"You know what they say about ill winds," Seth said. "I guess there's a particle of truth in it, what they say."

While it didn't do the Dettweiler brothers much good to discuss spats and bow ties, it didn't solve their problems to leave off mentioning spats and bow ties. By the time they finished their conversation all they were back to was square one, and the view from that spot wasn't the world's best.

The only solution was bankruptcy, and it didn't look to be all that much of a solution.

"I don't mind going bankrupt," one of the brothers said. (I think it was Seth. Makes no nevermind, actually. Seth, Porter, it's all the same who said it.) "I don't mind going bankrupt, but I sure do hate the thought of being broke."

"Me too," said the other brother. (Porter, probably.)

"I've thought about bankruptcy from time to time."

"Me too."

"But there's a time and a place for bankruptcy."

"Well, the place is all right. No better place for bankruptcy than Schuyler County."

"That's true enough," said Seth. (Unless it was Porter.) "But this is surely not the time. Time to go bankrupt is in good times when you got a lot of money on hand. Only the damnedest kind of fool goes bankrupt when he's stony broke busted and there's a Depression going on."

What they were both thinking on during this conversation was a fellow name of Joe Bob Rathburton who was in the construction business over to the other end of Schuyler County. I myself don't know of a man in this part of the state with enough intelligence to bail out a leaky rowboat who doesn't respect Joe Bob Rathburton to hell and back as a man with good business sense. It was about two years ago that Joe Bob went bankrupt, and he did it the right way. First of all he did it coming off the best year's worth of business he'd ever done in his life. Then what he did was he paid off the car and the house and the boat and put them all in his wife's name. (His wife was Mabel Washburn, but no relation to the Washburns who have the Schuyler County First National Bank. That's another family entirely.)

Once that was done, Joe Bob took out every loan and raised every dollar he possibly could, and he turned all that capital into green folding cash and sealed it in quart Mason jars which he buried out back of an old Kieffer pear tree that's sixty-plus years old and still bears fruit like crazy. And then he declared bankruptcy and sat back in his Mission rocker with a beer and a cigar and a real big-tooth smile.

"If I could think of anything worth doing," Porter Dettweiler said one night, "why, I guess I'd just go ahead and do it."

"Can't argue with that," Seth said.

"But I can't," Porter said.

"Nor I either."

"You might pass that old jug over here for a moment."

"Soon as I pour a tad for myself, if you've no objection."

"None whatsoever," said Porter.

They were over at Porter's place on the evening when this particular conversation occurred. They had taken to spending most of their evenings at Porter's on account of Seth had a wife at home, plus a daughter named Rachel who'd been working at the Ben Franklin store ever since dropping out of the junior college over at Monroe Center. Seth didn't have but the one daughter. Porter had two sons and a daughter, but they were all living with Porter's ex-wife, who had divorced him two years back and moved clear to Georgia. They were living in Valdosta now, as far as Porter knew. Least that was where he sent the check every month.

"Alimony jail," said Porter.

"How's that?"

"What I said was alimony jail. Where you go when you quit paying on your alimony."

"They got a special jug set aside for men don't pay their alimony?"

"Just an expression. I guess they put you into whatever jug's the handiest. All I got to do is quit sendin' Gert her checks and let her have them cart me away. Get my three meals a day and a roof over my head and the whole world could quit nagging me night and day for money I haven't got."

"You could never stand it. Bein' in a jail day in and day out, night in and night out."

"I know it," Porter said unhappily. "There anything left in that there jug, on the subject of jugs?"

"Some. Anyway, you haven't paid Gert a penny in how long? Three months?"

"Call it five."

"And she ain't throwed you in jail yet. Least you haven't got her close to hand so's she can talk money to you."

"Linda Mae givin' you trouble?"

"She did. Keeps a civil tongue since I beat up on her the last time."

"Lord knew what He was doin'," Porter said, "makin' men stronger than women. You ever give any thought to what life would be like if wives could beat up on their husbands instead of the other way around?"

"Now I don't even want to think about that," Seth said.

You'll notice nobody was mentioning spats or bow ties. Even with the jug of corn getting discernibly lighter every time it passed from one set of hands to the other, these two subjects did not come up. Neither did anyone speak of the shortsightedness of failing to keep up fire insurance or the myopia of incinerating a building without ascertaining that such insurance was in force. Tempers had cooled with the ashes of Dettweiler Bros. Fine Fashions for Men, and once again Seth and Porter were on the best of terms.

Which just makes what happened thereafter all the more tragic.

"What I think I got," Porter said, "is no way to turn."

(This wasn't the same evening, but if you put the two evenings side by side under a microscope you'd be hard pressed to tell them apart each from the other. They were at Porter's little house over alongside the tracks of the old spur off the Wyandotte & Southern, which I couldn't tell you the last time there was a train on that spur, and they had their feet up and their shoes off, and there was a jug of corn in the picture. Most of their evenings had come to take on this particular shade.)

"Couldn't get work if I wanted to," Porter said, "which I don't, and if I did I couldn't make enough to matter, and my debts is up to my ears and rising steady."

"It doesn't look to be gettin' better," Seth said. "On the other hand, how can it get worse?"

"I keep thinking the same."

"And?"

"And it keeps getting worse."

"I guess you know what you're talkin' about," Seth said. He scratched his bulldog chin, which hadn't been in the same room with a razor in more than a day or two. "What I been thinkin' about," he said, "is killin' myself."

"You been thinking of that?"

"Sure have."

"I think on it from time to time myself," Porter admitted. "Mostly nights when I can't sleep. It can be a powerful comfort around about three in the morning. You think of all the different ways and the next thing you know you're asleep. Beats the stuffing out of counting sheep jumping fences. You seen one sheep you seen 'em all is always been my thoughts on the subject, whereas there's any number of ways of doing away with yourself."

"I'd take a certain satisfaction in it," Seth said, more or less warming to the subject. "What I'd leave is this note tellin' Linda Mae how her and Rachel'll be taken care of with the insurance, just to get the bitch's hopes up, and then she can find out for her own self that I cashed in that insurance back in January to make the payment on the Oldsmobile. You know it's pure uncut hell gettin' along without an automobile now."

"You don't have to tell me."

"Just put a rope around my neck," said Seth, smothering a hiccup, "and my damn troubles'll be over."

"And mine in the bargain," Porter said.

"By you doin' your own self in?"

"Be no need," Porter said, "if you did *your*self in."

"How you figure that?"

"What I figure is a hundred thousand dollars," Porter said. "Lord love a duck, if I had a hundred thousand dollars I could declare bankruptcy and live like a king!"

Seth looked at him, got up, walked over to him, and took the jug away from him. He took a swig and socked the cork in place, but kept hold of the jug.

"Brother," he said, "I guess you've had enough of this here."

"What makes you say that, brother?"

"Me killin' myself and you gettin' rich, you don't make sense. What you think you're talkin' about, anyhow?"

"Insurance," Porter said. "Insurance, that's what I think I'm talking about. Insurance."

Porter explained the whole thing. It seems there was this life insurance policy their father had taken out on them when they weren't but boys. Face amount of a hundred thousand dollars, double indemnity for accidental death. It was payable to him while they were alive, but upon his death the beneficiary changed. If Porter was to die the money went to Seth. And vice versa.

"And you knew about this all along?"

"Sure did," Porter said.

"And never cashed it in? Not the policy on me and not the policy on you?"

"Couldn't cash 'em in," Porter said. "I guess I woulda if I coulda, but I couldn't so I didn't."

"And you didn't let these here policies lapse?" Seth said. "On account of occasionally a person can be just the least bit absent-minded and forget about keeping a policy in force. That's been known to happen," Seth said, looking off to one side, "in matters relating to fire insurance, for example, and I just thought to mention it."

(I have the feeling he wasn't the only one to worry on that score. You may have had similar thoughts yourself, figuring you know how the story's going to end, what with the insurance not valid and all. Set your mind at rest. If that was the way it had happened I'd never be taking the trouble to write it up for you. I got to select stories with some satisfaction in them if I'm going to stand a chance of selling them to the magazine, and I hope you don't figure I'm sitting here poking away at this typewriter for the sheer physical pleasure of it. If I just want to exercise my fingers I'll send them walking through the Yellow Pages if it's all the same to you.)

"Couldn't let 'em lapse," Porter said. "They're all paid up. What you call twenty-payment life, meaning you pay in it for twenty years and then you got it free and clear. And the way Pa did it, you can't borrow on it or nothing. All you can do is wait and see who dies."

"Well, I'll be."

"Except we don't have to wait to see who dies."

"Why, I guess not. I just guess a man can take matters into his own hands if he's of a mind to."

"He surely can," Porter said.

"Man wants to kill himself, that's what he can go and do."

"No law against it," Porter said.

Now you know and I know that that last is not strictly true. There's a definite no-question law against suicide in our state, and most likely in yours as well. It's harder to make it stand up than a calf with four broken legs, however, and I don't recall that anyone hereabouts was ever prosecuted for it, or likely will be. It does make you wonder some what they had in mind writing that particular law into the books.

"I'll just have another taste of that there corn," Porter said, "and why don't you have a pull on the jug your own self? You have any idea just when you might go and do it?"

"I'm studying on it," Seth said.

"There's a lot to be said for doing something soon as a man's mind's made up on the subject. Not to be hurrying you or anything of the sort, but they say that he who hesitates is last." Porter scratched his chin. "Or some such," he said.

"I just might do it tonight."

"By God," Porter said.

"Get the damn thing over with. Glory Hallelujah and my troubles is over."

"And so is mine," said Porter.

"You'll be in the money then," said Seth, "and I'll be in the boneyard, and both of us is free and clear. You can just buy me a decent funeral and then go bankrupt in style."

"Give you Johnny Millbourne's Number One funeral," Porter promised. "Brassbound casket and all. I mean, price is no object if I'm going bankrupt anyway. Let old Johnny swing for the money."

"You a damn good man, brother."

"You the best man in the world, brother."

The jug passed back and forth a couple more times. At one point Seth announced that he was ready, and he was halfway out the door before he recollected that his car had been repossessed, which interfered with his plans to drive it off a cliff. He came back in and sat down again and had another drink on the strength of it all, and then suddenly he sat forward and stared hard at Porter.

"This policy thing," he said.

"What about it?"

"It's on both of us, is what you said."

"If I said it then must be it's the truth."

"Well then," Seth said, and sat back, arms folded on his chest.

"Well then what?"

"Well then if *you* was to kill yourself, then *I'd* get the money and *you'd* get the funeral."

"I don't see what you're getting at," Porter said slowly.

"Seems to me either one of us can go and do it," Seth said. "And here's the two of us just takin' it for granted that I'm to be the one to go and do it, and I think we should think on that a little more thoroughly."

"Why, being as you're older, Seth."

"What's that to do with anything?"

"Why, you got less years to give up."

"Still be givin' up all that's left. Older or younger don't cut no ice."

Porter thought about it. "After all," he said, "it was your idea."

"That don't cut ice neither. I could mention I got a wife and child."

"I could mention I got a wife and three children."

"Ex-wife."

"All the same."

"Let's face it," Seth said. "Gert and your three don't add up to anything and neither do Linda Mae and Rachel."

"Got to agree," Porter said.

"So."

"One thing. You being the one who put us in the mess, what with firing the store, it just seems you might be the one to get us out of it."

"You bein' the one let the insurance lapse through your own stupidity, you could get us out of this mess through insurance, thus evenin' things up again."

"Now talkin' about stupidity—"

"Yes, talkin' about stupidity—"

"Spats!"

"Bow ties, damn you! *Bow ties!*"

You might have known it would come to that.

Now I've told you Seth and Porter generally got along pretty well, and here's further evidence of it. Confronted by such a stalemate, a good many people would have wrote off the whole affair and decided not to take the suicide route at all. But not even spats and bow ties could deflect Seth and Porter from the road they'd figured out as the most logical to pursue.

So what they did, one of them tossed a coin, and the other one called it while it was in the air, and they let it hit the floor and roll, and I don't recollect whether it was heads or tails, or who tossed and who called—what's significant is that Seth won.

"Well now," Seth said. "I feel I been reprieved. Just let me have that coin. I want to keep it for a luck charm."

"Two out of three."

"We already said once is as good as a million," Seth said, "so you just forget that two-out-of-three business. You got a week like we agreed but if I was you I'd get it over soon as I could."

"I got a week," Porter said.

"You'll get the brassbound casket and everything, and you can have Minnie Lucy Boxwood sing at your funeral if you want. Expense don't matter at all. What's your favorite song?"

"I suppose 'Your Cheatin' Heart.'"

"Minnie Lucy does that real pretty."

"I guess she does."

"Now you be sure and make it accidental," Seth said. "Two hundred thousand dollars goes just about twice as far as one hundred thousand dollars. Won't cost you a thing to make it accidental, just like we talked about it. What I would do is borrow Fritz Chenoweth's half-ton pickup and go up on the old Harburton Road where it takes that curve. Have yourself a belly full of corn and just keep goin' straight when the road doesn't. Lord knows I almost did that myself enough times without tryin'. Had two wheels over the edge less'n a month ago."

"That close?"

"That close."

"I'll be doggone," Porter said.

Thing is, Seth went on home after he failed to convince Porter to do it right away, and that was when things began to fall into the muck. Because Porter started thinking things over. I have a hunch it would have worked about the same way if Porter had won the flip, with Seth thinking things over. They were a whole lot alike, those two. Like two peas in a pot.

What occurred to Porter was would Seth have gone through with it if he lost, and what Porter decided was that he wouldn't. Not that there was any way for him to prove it one way or the other, but when you can't prove something you generally tend to decide on believing in what you want to believe, and Porter Dettweiler was no exception. Seth, he decided, would not have killed himself and didn't never have no intention of killing himself, which meant that for Porter to go through with killing his own self amounted to nothing more than damned foolishness.

Now it's hard to say just when he figured out what to do, but it was in the next two days, because on the third day he went over and borrowed that pickup truck off Fritz Chenoweth. "I got the back all loaded down with a couple sacks of concrete mix and a keg of nails and I don't know what all," Fritz said. "You want to unload it back of my smaller barn if you need the room."

"Oh, that's all right," Porter told him. "I guess I'll just leave it loaded and be grateful for the traction."

"Well, you keep it overnight if you have a mind," Fritz said.

"I just might do that," Porter said, and he went over to Seth's house.

"Let's you and me go for a ride," he told Seth. "Something we was talking about the other night, and I went and got me a new slant on it which the two of us ought to discuss before things go wrong altogether."

"Be right with you," Seth said, "soon as I finish this sandwich."

"Oh, just bring it along."

"I guess," said Seth.

No sooner was the pickup truck backed down and out of the driveway than Porter said, "Now will you just have a look over there, brother."

"How's that?" said Seth, and turned his head obligingly to the right, whereupon Porter gave him a good lick upside the head with a monkey wrench he'd brought along expressly for that purpose. He got him right where you have a soft spot if you're a little baby. (You also have a soft spot there if someone gets you just right with a monkey wrench.) Seth made a little sound which amounted to no more than letting his breath out, and then he went out like an icebox light when you have closed the door on it.

Now as to whether or not Seth was dead at this point I could not honestly tell you, unless I were to make up an answer knowing how slim is the likelihood of anyone presuming to contradict me. But the plain fact is that he might have been dead and he might not and even Seth could not have told you, being at the very least stone-unconscious at the time.

What Porter did was drive up the old Harburton Road, I guess figuring that he might as well stick to as much of the original plan as possible. There's a particular place where the road does a reasonably convincing imitation of a fishhook, and that spot's been described as Schuyler County's best natural brake on the population explosion since they stamped out the typhoid. A whole lot of folks fail to make that curve every year, most of them young ones with plenty of breeding years left in them. Now and then there's a movement to put up a guard rail, but the ecology people are against it so it never gets anywheres.

If you miss that curve, the next land you touch is a good five hundred feet closer to sea level.

So Porter pulls over the side of the road and then he gets out of the car and maneuvers Seth (or Seth's body, whichever the case may have been) so he's behind the wheel. Then he stands alongside the car working the gas pedal with one hand and the steering wheel with the other and putting the fool truck in gear and doing this and that and the other thing so he can run the truck up to the edge and over, and thinking hard every minute about those two hundred thousand pretty green dollars that is destined to make his bankruptcy considerably easier to contend with.

Well, I told you right off that sometimes you can't win for losing, which was the case for Porter and Seth both, and another way of putting it is to say that when everything goes wrong there's nothing goes right. Here's what happened. Porter slipped on a piece of loose gravel while he was pushing, and the truck had to go on its own, and where it went was halfway and no further, with its back wheel hung up on a hunk of tree limb or some such and its two front wheels hanging out over nothing and its motor stalled out deader'n smoked fish.

Porter said himself a whole mess of bad words. Then he wasted considerable time shoving the back of that truck, forgetting it was in gear and not about to budge. Then he remembered and said a few more bad words and put the thing in neutral, which involved a long reach across Seth to get to the floor shift and a lot of coordination to manipulate it and the clutch pedal at the same time. Then Porter got out of the truck and gave the door a slam, and just about then a beat-up old Chevy with Indiana plates pulls up and this fellow leaps out screaming that he's got a tow rope and he'll pull the truck to safety.

You can't hardly blame Porter for the rest of it. He wasn't the type to be great at contingency planning anyhow, and who could allow for something like this? What he did, he gave this great sob and just plain hurled himself at the back of that truck, it being in neutral now, and the truck went sailing like a kite in a tornado, and Porter, well, what he did was follow right along after it. It wasn't part of his plan but he just had himself too much momentum to manage any last-minute change of direction.

According to the fellow from Indiana, who it turned out was a veterinarian from Bloomington, Porter fell far enough to get off a couple of genuinely rank words on the way down. Last words or not, you sure wouldn't go and engrave them on any tombstone.

Speaking of which, he has the last word in tombstones, Vermont granite and all, and his brother Seth has one just like it. They had a double-barrelled funeral, the best Johnny Millbourne had to offer, and they each of them reposed in a brassbound casket, the top-of-the-line model. Minnie Lucy Boxwood sang "Your Cheatin' Heart," which was Porter's favorite song, plus she sang Seth's favorite, which was "Old Buttermilk Sky," plus she also sang free gratis "My Buddy" as a testament to brotherly love.

And Linda Mae and Rachel got themselves two hundred thousand dollars from the insurance company, which is what Gert and her kids in Valdosta, Georgia, also got. And Seth and Porter have an end to their miseries, which was all they really wanted before they got their heads turned around at the idea of all that money.

The only thing funnier than how things don't work out is how they do.

VINCENT McCONNOR

The Whitechapel Wantons

A door opened, the angry sound of rusty hinges echoing through the empty street, but no one heard.

And nobody saw the figure of a girl, briefly visible against a blur of candle-light that revealed a narrow hall with steep wooden stairs.

The girl closed the door and, fumbling with her key in the dark, locked it again. You couldn't be too careful, although, up to now, the Ripper had always killed in the streets. Mostly in dark alleys—some of them not far from here.

She had known all of the girls, Polly Nichols and the others.

The newspaper said that Polly was the second to die.

Hesitating on the top step, peering up and down the silent street, she returned the key to her purse and slipped it into the pocket of her jacket. Now both hands were free for any emergency she might have to face.

The ground-floor shop next door, which did a brisk trade in pickled eels during the day, was shuttered for the night.

Nobody ventured out after dark any more unless it was urgent business. It was the women who were in danger, but men stayed off the streets at night because the police were stopping them to ask who they were and where they were going. If their answers sounded suspicious they were taken in for questioning.

The pubs were suffering. There were still a few regulars every night, but a girl was afraid to speak to a stranger because he might be the Ripper. Nobody knew what he looked like.

She was probably the only one in all of London who had seen his face and she wasn't going to tell the police!

Shivering under her thin summer dress, she clutched the short velvet jacket more securely around her. The air was as sharp as a knife and it was only early October. Another week and she would need to find herself a winter coat from a pushcart in Petticoat Lane.

She glanced at the sky above the low rooftops and chimneys and saw that clouds were shoving across the stars. There was no moon.

As she came down the two splintered steps to the cobbled street, she wondered what name she ought to use tonight.

This week she had been calling herself Annie but somehow that always seemed a bit common. Maybe tonight she would use Violette again. That nice young toff last week had said it suited her when she told him her name was Violette. He had been ever so kind, paid her two whole shillings . . .

Passing a row of dark shops, heading toward the street lamp at the corner, she kept close to the buildings, hurrying her steps as she skirted the mouth of each alley.

London had been choking with smoke and fog each time the Ripper killed. Tonight, at least, there was no fog.

She had decided to tell Cora what she knew and explain about her plan. It couldn't work unless somebody helped her and Cora was her dearest friend now that Polly was dead.

Her plan. She shivered again. She had never thought she would plan to kill anybody. But Polly had been her friend since the first week she had arrived in London. They had met that rainy night near the Haymarket. What a silly innocent she was in those days, fresh from Liverpool. Only three years ago . . .

She had never seen Whitechapel until Polly brought her here, insisting she move in and share her lodgings.

That night last month when the two constables had pounded on the door, waking her from a sound sleep, she couldn't believe what they told her. She had thought Polly was asleep in the other bed. Their questions had frightened her, and when they took her to identify the body she had fainted.

She still lived in Polly's room, but it was getting harder to pay the rent each week. Business was terrible because of the Ripper and it wouldn't get any better as long as he prowled the streets. She never had so much as two shillings in her purse any more—barely enough to buy a scrap of food each day. Something had to be done and the police weren't doing anything.

She reached the street lamp and turned down another dark street.

Last night in the Black Swan one of the girls said the Ripper must be a constable or he would've been caught long ago. Everybody laughed but at the same time they had wondered if the Ripper could be a policeman. Some of them were terribly nasty to a girl, cruel, and insulting. Although there was a new one—Constable Divall—who was ever so nice. In his twenties and not at all bad-looking.

There were so many extra constables on night duty in Whitechapel now that nobody could slip out to do an honest job of burglary any more, afraid they'd be picked up by the police searching the streets for the Ripper. What made it even worse was that some of the constables were not in uniform and those who were traveled in pairs. Though you couldn't blame them—the whole city of London was in a fair panic.

Now she could make out a blur of gaslight at the far end of the narrow street.

Cora should be in the Black Swan by now. It must be past midnight. The empty streets were frightening. At any moment he could appear out of the dark and come lurching toward her.

She had seen his blond hair under a black bowler, his face pale against the high collar of his black coat. She'd glimpsed his eyes when Polly took his arm and, giggling as usual, disappeared into the fog with him. Never to be seen again, at least not alive . . .

Reaching the protective circle of light from the gaslight on the corner, she paused to look in every direction, then darted across the cobbles toward the Black Swan.

A dark shape moved near her feet.

She gasped with fright, then realized it was only Old Cobbie, drunk as a lord, sprawled on the paving stones.

Grasping the wrought-iron handle, she pushed against the heavy oak door and entered the pub.

A candle in a brass lantern guttered above the bar.

Three faces turned to stare. The owner, Tom, behind the bar and two of the regulars, all three with drinks in their fists.

"Evenin', miss!"

"Seen Cora t'night, Tom?"

"Showed up ten minutes ago. She's in the back."

Violette crossed to the bar, sawdust crunching under her thin slippers. "Nobody on the street t'night."

"You girls come rushin' in like the Ripper's after ye."

"Maybe he is! He got Polly, didn't he?" She never stood close to the bar when she ordered a drink because it wasn't ladylike to lean against the polished wood the way men did. "I'll have a mild, please." She brought out her purse, selected a coin from the few she owned, and put it on the bar. "A girl can't make a livin' on these empty streets."

"If Scotland Yard don't soon catch the blighter we'll all be out of business, every bloomin' pub in Whitechapel. Here y'are, me girl." Tom handed her the half-pint and turned back to his cronies.

Violette carried her beer around the corner toward the back, noticing that there was no fire on the hearth to send a flicker of warmth across the smoke-blackened beams of the ceiling. The only light came from a wax-encrusted candle in the mouth of a wine bottle on the table where Cora sat—the only person in the room.

Cora waved, pushing a scarlet feather away from her eye and adjusting her velvet hat more firmly on her black curls. "I thought maybe you wouldn' be comin' out t'night, Annie."

"I had to." She set her beer on the scrubbed wood table and sank onto a bench, facing her friend. "Rent's due t'morrow, so I've got t' earn a bit of money. An' I'm not Annie t'night—I'm Violette."

"Whatever you say, Vi. As I came here I saw nothin' but constables in the streets, strips of rubber nailed t' their boots so the Ripper wouldn' hear 'em comin'."

"I didn't see nobody." She took a first gulp of beer, observing that Cora, as usual, was drinking gin and had been reading something on a crumpled sheet of paper. "I have t' talk to you, luv. About Polly."

"Oh?" Cora held the sheet of paper across the table. "Did you see this?"

As Violette took it she saw that it was a printed leaflet.

"Police 'ave spread these all over Whitechapel!"

Violette held the leaflet close to the candle so that she could read the words.

POLICE NOTICE.

TO THE OCCUPIER.

On the mornings of Friday, 31st,
August, Saturday 8th, and Sunday,
30th of September, 1888, Women were
murdered in or near Whitechapel,
supposed by some one residing
in the immediate neighbourhood.
Should you know of any person
to whom suspicion is attached, you
are earnestly requested to com-
municate at once with the nearest
Police Station.
Metropolitan Police Office,
30th September, 1888

"Someone in the neighborhood?" She looked at Cora. "They're bonkers! He's a toff from the West End." Handing the leaflet back across the table, she asked, "Where'd you get this?"

"Found it under me door this afternoon."

"My landlady must've gotten one but I didn't see the old girl before I came out. Been avoidin' her."

She took another gulp of beer.

"Ivy tol' me last night they're sayin' the Ripper's a famous surgeon from Harley Street! That's why he slices all his victims up so neat!"

"Ivy's a fool. Nobody knows for certain who he is—or, for that matter, how many girls he's done in."

"They're also sayin' the Ripper's a woman."

"The Ripper's a *man!* A real toff."

"Oh?" Cora folded the sheet of paper and tucked it into her purse. "How d' you know what he looks like?"

"That's what I wanted t' tell you."

"What?"

"I've seen him."

"The Ripper?"

"With me own two eyes."

"When?"

"The night he killed Polly. We was in a doorway near Swallow Court, Polly an' me, keepin' out of the cold. She seen him first, comin' down the street, an' went t' meet him—hopin' for a bit of luck, of course! I watched while they talked, standin' close t'gether in the fog, then he offered her his arm like a regular gent an' they turned back, same way he'd come. I thought, of course, they was goin' to a hotel. I had no idea it was the Ripper."

"Did he see you?"

"I never moved out of the doorway."

"But you had a good look at him?"

"I'd recognize him anywhere!"

"Have you told the police?"

"Wouldn' I be the fool t' do that! I ain't told nobody 'til this minute, not even you! An' I'm only tellin' you t'night 'cause I need your help."

Cora stared at her suspiciously. "What sort of help?"

"Well, Polly was my best friend in London. Now you're the only friend I got." She glanced toward the front of the pub to be sure the men at the bar couldn't hear what she was about to say. "The police ain't goin' t' catch the Ripper 'cause they don't know what he looks like. But I do! I've seen him! An' I'm goin' t' get rid of the blighter!"

"Get rid of him?"

"For Polly's sake! Put an end to him—once and for all. That's what I'm goin' t' do. So a girl can be safe on the streets again . . ."

"Then you *are* goin' t' tell the police what he looks like?"

"I wouldn' dare! If the Ripper found out I'd seen him—that I know what he looks like—my life wouldn' be worth a ha'penny! He'd come after me with his bloody knife! You've got t' help me, Cora. I can't do it without you. It'll take the two of us!"

"Do what, Vi? What the devil are you talkin' about?"

"I'm goin' t' kill the Ripper."

"*Kill* him?"

"Of course I have t' find him first, but . . ."

She explained her plan in a rush of words, and then arranged to meet Cora the following afternoon, to search through the nearby docks for a crate. A wooden crate large enough to hold a man's body.

Walking toward the docks late the next afternoon, they discussed the plan over and over, working out exactly what each would have to do.

Cora was dubious at first, but then she was caught up in the excitement of the idea and began to make suggestions of her own.

They located a discarded wooden crate outside one of the warehouses, which they lugged between them back to Violette's lodging. Mrs. Paddick, her land-lady, watched them ease their awkward burden through the narrow hall, past her open kitchen door, with suspicious eyes. "'Ere now! Wot's this?"

Violette winked at Cora as they set the crate down with a hollow thud.

"Cora's helping me put this in the alley, Mrs. Paddick."

"Wotever for?"

"Had t' find a large box for Polly's belongin's."

"The poor girl!"

"I'm sending her clothes an' things to her family in Birmingham. You won't mind if I leave this out in the back for a few days, will you? It's much too heavy t' carry upstairs."

"Leave it here as long as you want. Nobody'll touch it."

"It could be a week or more before I can pack everything."

"Take y'r time, luv. Let me know if there's any way I can 'elp." She moved back into the dark hole of her kitchen. "Stop by when ye finish there an' I'll 'ave a nice hot cup of tea for ye."

"That's ever so kind, Mrs. Paddick!" Cora called after her.

"She's in a right good humor t'day," Violette whispered. "I paid me rent this mornin' so she'll leave us alone. Anyway, the ol' girl's so deaf she never hears nothin' no matter how many times I come in an' out at night."

They carried their wooden box through the open back door and set it down next to the dustbin in the grimy back alley.

Violette raised the hinged lid and let it fall back down the side, then turned the crate over, with Cora's help, so that the open side, out of sight from the door, faced the dustbin.

She demonstrated how Cora could hide inside the crate until she was needed and showed her the barrow that was always propped against the wall next door, behind the eel shop. They would load the crate onto the barrow, push it down the alley to the next street, and in a matter of minutes reach the river. She also pointed to a small ax resting near a stack of firewood that was used in the eel-shop kitchen and showed her where to place the ax beside the back door so she, Vi, would be able to find it in the dark when she brought the Ripper here . . .

They went over the plan several more times in Violette's room after their tea in Mrs. Paddick's kitchen. They stretched out on the two lumpy beds and continued to discuss the plan until they fell asleep.

Later, just before midnight, they went out together.

And for the first time in many weeks they felt safer in the empty streets.

The next day they decided it would be much more practical, as well as cheaper, for both of them if Cora moved in and shared Vi's room.

Mrs. Paddick didn't suspect that she had a new tenant. She was, as Violette had said, extremely deaf and seldom came upstairs unless there was trouble with one of the lodgers.

The two girls saw to it that there was nothing to arouse her suspicions. Even when they brought visitors to their room Mrs. Paddick heard nothing and, from long experience, probably wouldn't have complained if she had.

Violette and Cora went out together each night around midnight and walked through the dark streets and alleys of Whitechapel. But Violette saw no sign of the Ripper.

The entire city of London was in a state of hysteria because any night now the Ripper was expected to kill again. It had been more than a week since the last body was found.

The newspapers printed fresh stories every day.

And, strangely, a deluge of toffs from the West End began to swarm through Whitechapel every night to see the places where Jack had slashed his victims. The pubs began to flourish again and a girl could make several shillings a night. Most of them, like Violette and Cora, took to walking in pairs—like the police—for their own protection.

The two girls went to the Black Swan every night to have a drink and catch up with the day's gossip. With the increase in business even Violette was drinking gin now.

It was crowded and noisy, every table occupied in the back room, where a new barmaid darted back and forth with trays of drinks.

Violette watched the activity, seated at her usual table with Cora, sipping at her glass of gin.

"You think he'll show up t'night?" Cora asked in a whisper.

"T'night or t'morrow night," Violette answered, feeling the warmth from the gin flowing through her body. "Whenever he shows up, we'll be ready for him."

"S'pose he never does come back?"

"He will."

"S'pose all these people keep him away. He might go to another part of London—Chelsea or Soho."

"I think, t'night, we should keep away from the busy streets—stay in the alleys, around Swallow Court, where Polly met him."

"Whatever you say."

"More gin, ladies?"

They looked up to see the blonde barmaid, smiling and eager, her apron splashed with beer.

"Not just now," Violette answered. "We'll be havin' drinks later, with some gents."

"Watch out for the Ripper." The tousled barmaid leaned closer, lowering her voice. "I heard just now, he's left-handed."

"Fancy that!" Cora exclaimed, glancing at her friend. "Left-handed."

"Who said he was?" Violette asked. "I thought nobody ain't ever seen the bloke."

"Gentleman told me it's in the newspaper t'day. Scotland Yard found out from the knife wounds in the last girl's body. Cut her up somethin' 'orrible!"

"A likely story!" Violette scoffed. "How could they tell he's left-handed from that?"

"I wouldn' know, luv. They say the Queen gave orders t' the 'ome Secretary t'day t' catch the Ripper in a hurry so the ladies of London can walk the streets in safety again." She darted away, in response to a summons from another table.

"Ladies?" Cora laughed, the feathers quivering on her hat. "That's us!"

Violette frowned. "Left-handed is he?" She shivered suddenly.

"Drink up, luv!" Cora raised her glass. "We'd better be on our way."

Violette noticed, as they came from the Black Swan, that mist was rising between the damp cobbles and a dirty gray fog was pressing down from overhead. "The Ripper will be out t'night, I know he will . . ."

"If you say so." Cora peered up and down the narrow street but there was nobody in sight.

They turned into the first alley, choking and coughing as their lungs filled with the acrid coal smoke the fog was pushing down from nearby chimneys.

There were lanterns on the stone walls, but their light was so dim that they had to feel their way along. The rough surface dripped with moisture and, within seconds, their fingers were cold and wet. "What a filthy night!" Violette grasped Cora's arm with her hand so they wouldn't become separated. "I almost wish I was home in Liverpool."

"Do you ever think of goin' back, Vi?"

"Not really. I s'pose I could get me old job again, workin' as housemaid."

"You liked that?"

"Cleanin' an' pickin' up? I hated it!" She glimpsed a misty circle of light from a street lamp at the end of the alley. "Here's Swallow Court."

"I don't know this part of Whitechapel."

Violette wiped her damp fingers on her coat. "There's a doorway over there. We can stand out of the fog an' still see the street."

"Where you an' Polly stood that night?"

"That's right." Violette kept close to the building, looking for the remembered doorway. "We knew this street well, Polly an' me. Came here many a night." She glimpsed the dark entrance with its recessed doors through drifting veils of fog. "Here we are!" She led the way under the shallow arch and leaned back against one of the heavy oak doors.

Cora huddled beside her. "The fog's gettin' heavier."

"He'll be here t'night, I know he will." Vi motioned across the street. "You can't see it now but there's another alley over there."

"You really think he'll be out?"

"I'm sure of it!"

"Maybe we shouldn't wait . . ."

Vi turned to face Cora. "You backin' out?"

"No!"

"Do you remember what you have t' do?"

"I remember, Vi. Everything . . ."

"When I see him I'll go straight t' meet him, catch him before he can slip away. You hurry back t' Mrs. Paddick's an' through the downstairs hall t' the alley. Be sure t' put that ax where I showed you, next to the door so I can find it in the dark. Then hide inside the box until I bring him. You'll hear us but don't make a sound. An' don't show y'r face 'til I call you."

"I'm scared, Vi."

"So am I."

"He could kill us."

"We have t' do this. For Polly—for what he did t' her an' all them other poor girls."

"I know we do."

Violette froze. "Here he is!"

"You're sure?"

"It's him. You know what t' do!"

Violette stepped down from the doorway onto the wet cobblestones.

"Be careful, Vi," Cora whispered.

She hurried toward him through the swirling fog. It was the same pale face and the same blond hair under the black bowler. The same coat with the high collar. Tonight he was wearing gray gloves.

He saw her coming toward him and began to smile.

Violette slowed her steps.

"Good evening, miss . . ."

"Evenin' . . ." She listened for Cora's footsteps behind her, but there was no sound of any kind.

"Miserable evening, what?" He continued to smile.

"Yes." He wasn't a bad-looking sort. Nice smile. White teeth under a small mustache. She musn't let him force her into Swallow Court where he had taken Polly.

"It would be much more pleasant inside somewhere, don't you think?"

"I—I've a place near here."

"Could we possibly go there, do you suppose?"

"Why not?"

"Splendid! Can you find your way in this fog?"

"Oh, yes." She trembled as she felt his gloved hand under her arm. The same hand that had killed Polly.

"It's nearby, you say?" He walked beside her, back the way she had come.

"It's a nice room where nobody will bother us. Ever so cozy . . ."

"You're not London-born, are you?"

"How'd you guess?"

"Your accent sounds like Liverpool."

"I'm not sayin' where I'm from."

He laughed. "It doesn't matter."

"We go through here." She turned with him into the side street, avoiding the alley Cora would have taken. This should give Cora time to reach the house ahead of them.

What would happen if Cora got lost in the fog? She had said she didn't know this part of Whitechapel.

Dear God! Don't let that happen . . .

"Have you been in London long?" he asked.

"Long enough t' know my way round."

"I shouldn't wonder!" He laughed again.

They saw only one person, an ancient Chinese, slinking close to the dark shopfronts.

Violette found the house without difficulty, unlocked the door, and motioned for her escort to enter. "We mustn't talk," she whispered. "The landlady lives on this floor an' she's a holy terror." She closed the door behind them and saw that he seemed taller when he removed his bowler. The only light came from a flickering candle in a niche near the stairs. "We go through the back."

"Oh? Why's that?"

"There's another house in the rear. Where I live . . ." She moved ahead of him through the narrow hall, into the shadows. The floorboards creaked underfoot but there was no other sound in the house.

Violette saw that the rear door was closed.

Had Cora gotten here ahead of them? It would be terrible if the street door flew open behind them and Cora came rushing in.

Would she be there in the back, crouched in that crate?

Violette reached the door and saw that the bolt had been pulled back.

Cora was here!

She opened the door and raised her voice as she spoke to warn Cora they had arrived. "Here we are. You go first."

"As you wish." He stepped outside, into the fog again. "I say! It's dark out here."

"Stand still for a minute. 'Til you can see where you are."

"Good idea . . . By the way, you haven't told me your name."

"Violette."

"Violette? I rather like that."

She could see his bare head now, dark against the gray fog. Bending quickly, she felt beside the step until she touched the cold wooden handle of the ax. Lifting it slowly with both hands, she had a sudden aversion to what she was about to do. Never in her life had she done anything like this before. But she had to do it!

"Well, now! Which way do we go?"

The sound of his voice released her.

Violette raised the ax above her head and, with all her strength, crashed the metal head against his skull. Incredibly, as she watched, he dropped out of sight without a sound.

She had done it!

The ax slipped from her hands.

For a moment she didn't move.

The distant moan of a foghorn sounded a warning from the river.

Violette stepped down onto the hard ground and cautiously thrust her right foot out until she touched his body. She gave it a tentative kick. There was no reaction.

Only then did she find her voice. "Cora . . ."

The two girls didn't speak as, side by side, they pushed the awkward barrow through the dark streets.

Everything had worked out as they had planned.

The Ripper was dead and Violette felt no remorse. She had only paid him back for Polly and those other poor girls.

She remembered her grandmother back in Liverpool reading from the Bible. "Eye for eye, tooth for tooth, hand for hand, foot for foot . . ." Her grandmother said it really meant a life for a life.

Jack the Ripper's life for Polly's life! And for all the others.

The only noise was the creaking of the barrow as its wooden wheels bumped over the damp cobbles. No sound came from the crate, which they had covered with an old blanket, or from the silent thing that was stuffed inside.

Jack was in the box! Violette smiled at the thought . . .

She was surprised that he had died so quickly. It took so little to kill a person. She'd had no idea it was that easy.

Cora, beside her, was gasping from the effort it took to push the clumsy barrow through the fog.

Her own breathing, she realized, was becoming more difficult. Each time a wheel stuck, refused to bump over a large cobblestone, they had to lift the barrow clear before they could push on.

The foghorn sounded much louder. They must be getting close to the river. Soon they would reach the old warehouses. After that, and they would see the wharves.

She could smell the river now.

The police would fish his body out of the water, but they would find nothing to tell them who he was. They wouldn't even know he was the Ripper. She had taken all the money from his pockets and stuffed it, uncounted, into her purse. There had been no wallet. And not much money, a few pound notes and some coins.

Also, to her surprise, there had been very little blood. Early tomorrow, before Mrs. Paddick was awake, she must go down to the backyard and clean away any spots.

The barrow struck another cobblestone and wouldn't budge.

"Damn!" Cora exclaimed. "Is it much farther?"

"We're almost at the river. I can smell it." Vi released the wooden handle and circled the barrow to see what was hindering their progress.

Cora followed and bent beside her to peer underneath.

"Wot's all this?"

Cora screamed at the sound of the ominous masculine voice.

Both girls straightened as two uniformed figures appeared out of the fog.

Violette recognized one of the faces. "Constable Divall!"

"Somethin' wrong here, miss?" Divall moved closer, followed by the other constable.

"I'm helpin' me friend move," Violette answered quickly. "An' the bloomin' barrow got stuck."

"Let's see if we can help. Give me a hand, Thompson."

The girls held their breath as the other constable joined Divall to ease the wheel over the obstruction, then watched apprehensively as they lifted the barrow between them and carried it several paces before they set it down again.

"You've got somethin' right heavy here!" Divall turned to look at them again.

"It's me friend's trunk," Violette explained.

"That's right!" Cora managed to say. "Me trunk."

"All her belongin's. She's movin' t' a new lodgin' house. Thanks ever so much, Constable."

"My pleasure, miss." Divall touched his helmet as he continued on with the other constable. "Watch out for the Ripper! He could be out on a night like this."

"We'll be careful."

Cora giggled nervously.

Violette saw now why she hadn't heard the approach of the two constables. They had thin strips of rubber—probably cut from bicycle tires—nailed to their boots. She didn't move until they had faded into the fog.

Cora sighed. "That was awful close."

"He's not a bad-lookin' sort, for a constable. C'mon, luv! Before we're caught again."

They grasped the handle of the barrow and, pushing harder than before, continued on their way. The fear of meeting other policemen strengthened their arms and quickened their steps. And they remained silent, saving their breath, until they found themselves on a wooden dock with the Thames lapping among the pilings underneath.

There were several lighted lanterns at irregular intervals along the side of the large warehouse.

They pushed the barrow to an open space at the edge of the rotting wharf.

Violette pulled the blanket away and, with Cora's help, managed to tip the crate onto the wooden planks of the wharf. Then, grasping the handle together again, they used the barrow as a ram and, pushing with all their might, shoved the crate to the edge. One final violent push and the crate scraped over the side.

It struck the water with a tremendous splash.

The two girls hurried to the edge of the wharf and looked down. In a spill of light from the nearest lantern, they saw circles of waves spreading out from the spot where the crate had entered the water.

They waited, peering down, but it didn't come to the surface again.

Without a word they turned the barrow around and, hurrying now, headed back the way they had come.

The door opened, the sound of rusty hinges muffled by the fog.

Violette came out, closing the door and locking it.

She saw that the fog was much heavier. The street lamp at the distant corner was completely blotted out.

As she came down the steps to the cobbled street she decided that it was a bit late to go back to the Black Swan. Instead she turned toward Swallow Court again. There was nothing to be afraid of there now that the Ripper was dead.

Cora was getting ready for bed when she left. It would have been impossible for her to sleep for another two or three hours—she was much too excited by what she had done . . .

Maybe she would meet a nice young toff from the West End. She couldn't take him back to her lodging because Cora would be asleep there but at least she didn't need to worry about the Ripper any more. He was at the bottom of the Thames.

When she and Cora had reached the back alley at Mrs. Paddick's, the first thing they had done was put the barrow back where it belonged behind the eel shop. Then, in the dark, she had wiped the ax clean and set it in place beside the stack of firewood.

Early tomorrow she would go down and make sure there were no other bloodstains anywhere . . .

When they went upstairs to their room, she had found several dried bloodstains on her skirt. Cold water got rid of them, but she would have to wash the skirt tomorrow . . .

The sound of her heels echoed sharply against the cobbles but that didn't matter now. She didn't care who heard them.

She had taken his money from her purse and, spreading it out on the bed, divided the pound notes and coins equally with Cora. Each of them had ended up with more than three pounds. Three whole pounds!

Aparently he had left his wallet and personal papers at home in case the police picked him up. There was nothing in his pockets that told you who he was . . .

Cora, stretched out on the other bed, had laughed. "Maybe he wasn't the Ripper!"

"Why do you say that?"

"Polly could've gone with another man first—the one you saw—then met the Ripper later."

She had continued folding the pound notes into her purse. "No, he was the Ripper all right. But we'll never know who he was—his name or nothin'."

Of course he was the Ripper! That's why his pockets were empty . . .

She sensed rather than heard that someone was following her.

As she reached the alley that led to Swallow Court she touched the damp plaster wall so she wouldn't lose her way.

The lanterns, hanging from spikes, were like small holes in the fog.

Now she could hear footsteps behind her on the cobblestones.

Maybe this would be a nice gent. Young and pleasant . . .

He was much closer now, almost at her heels.

Violette smiled as she turned to greet him.

A dark figure loomed out of the fog.

She was unable to see his face, only that he was raising an arm as though he was about to lift his hat. His left arm.

Something in his gloved hand caught a glint of light from the nearest lantern.

A knife! In his left hand!

The Ripper was left-handed . . .

Violette tried to scream, but his other gloved hand grasped her throat. She saw the arm swing down and felt the first hard thrust of the knife into her flesh.

ISAK ROMUN

Cora's Raid

The service station attendant opened the hood, looked in at the engine. He reached down with a hand palming a small rubber syringe and applied a quick shot of oil to the alternator.

"Gee, look, sir," the attendant said. "The alternator's shot. It's spraying oil. Once you're back on the road it'll break down in ten, fifteen miles."

The driver, a spare small man, lifted his hands to his chest, soft white palms out, as if pushing away unpleasantness. He had come off the limited-access highway to gas up and had asked the attendant to check under the hood. Bending warily over the car fender now, he peeked into the darkened area below the hood. Adjusting his pince-nez, he looked unseeing at the part pointed out by the attendant. "Oh, dear," he said. "Is there anything you can do?"

"I dunno. I'll check our inventory and see if we have a replacement for it." The attendant turned and went toward a small building over which a sign, black letters on white peeling paint, proclaimed this place to be Moonstreet's Service Station and Garage. He disappeared into a gloomy, dirty car bay, its floor covered with oil-blackened sawdust, and stayed in there out of sight for a moment or two. Then he rejoined his customer outside.

"You're in luck, sir. We have one in stock. Shall I put it in?"

"Oh yes, do, please," said the car owner, his anxiety showing.

The attendant smiled encouragingly. "Don't worry, sir. I'll have your car back exactly the way it was in just a jiffy," he said as he got in to drive the vehicle into the bay. As he did, he reflected on his last statement. He had told this poor dude nothing but the exact truth.

In the bay, he switched off the engine, got out of the car, and pulled down the overhead door, shutting off the customer's view. Looking obliquely out through the small window in the door, the attendant carefully studied the customer now standing by one of the pumps looking forlornly at the garage door behind which his car had disappeared. What the attendant saw was moderate, comfortable prosperity, a man to whom a reasonable sum was worth the price of avoiding imagined discomforts.

The attendant nodded his head decisively, strode over to the car, and flipped up its hood. He reached in and screwed off a battery cap, exposing the cell's acid level. Then he took a cylindrical jar from a shelf, shook out an antacid tablet, broke the tablet into three or four small pieces, and dropped these into the battery cell. He screwed the cap back on securely and turned his attention to the alternator.

Working quickly with a solvent-dampened rag, he wiped the alternator surface clean of its oil and any foreign substance that might have clung to it. Then, after toweling the part of the last dabs of solvent, he took a can of quick-drying paint and brushed black enamel evenly across the alternator surface until it fairly sparkled, just as if it were new. A small, portable fan sped up the drying process. Finished, the attendant looked at his watch. Less than ten minutes had passed since he drove the car into the bay. Time to kill. He sat down, lit a cigarette, took up a magazine with an intriguing centerfold, and, for about the tenth time that day, hungrily surveyed its contents.

A few customers drove in for gas and as the attendant responded reluctantly to the bell summons, he flashed a friendly, confident smile at the small man waiting for his car to emerge from the garage.

"Won't be long now, sir."

"Um, yes, thank you."

At long last, after an hour and fifteen minutes, the attendant put down his magazine, snubbed out the last of many cigarettes, and got into the car. He turned the key in the ignition and heard a low whirr but, as he expected, the engine would not turn over.

He got out, opened the garage door, and beckoned to the customer. "Oh, sir, I'd like you to inspect the job," he said. With that he led the nervous car owner to the engine, indicated the painted alternator, and boasted, "Had a little trouble getting it in. This is a tough engine to work on. But it sure looks nice, don't it?"

The customer was moved to agree that the alternator did, indeed, look nice. However, any elation he might have felt at having his car at last in working order was considerably reduced by the attendant's next words.

"I'm afraid, sir, that you've got a dead battery here," he said and helpfully manipulated a hydrometer in and out of the neutralized cell to lend credence to his statement.

"I suppose this means a new battery," the little man gasped.

"Yes, sir, I think that's what we need," the attendant agreed with a joviality contrasting sharply with the car owner's downcast mood.

"Well, put it in."

The attendant did so, then labored a pencil stub over a sales slip before presenting the little man with a high three-figured bill.

"That includes tax," he said, then put in magnificently, "The boss'll kill me, but I gave you a break on the battery."

The other man took the bill and with unexpected crispness ticked off each item, totaled the figures to his satisfaction, noted the absence of a garage letterhead on the bill, and said, "Yes, everything seems to add up."

He went to his car, opened the door on the passenger side, and slid into the seat. He unlocked the glove compartment with a key that hadn't been on the same ring with the ignition key. From the compartment, he took a handy-talkie, pressed a button, and spoke briefly into the radio's receiver, "This place checks. Come on in."

He reached into the compartment once more and drew from it a pair of dark glasses and a snub-nosed revolver. The former he put on after removing his pince-nez. The latter he pointed negligently at the attendant just as a Volkswagen microbus, tires screeching, pulled into the service station.

Jake Moonstreet sat shivering in the small office of Sheriff Oscar Roche of the county in which the Moonstreet Service Station and Garage was located. Moonstreet was shivering because he was barefoot. As a matter of fact, his only covering was a thin, worn blanket that inadequately covered his large frame, the blanket's nap-free pink surface harmonizing nicely with the flesh peeking through numerous worn spots. Next to him, in a state of identical dishabille, sat his employee, Pat Challoner, also shivering.

Jake was talking to the sheriff whose attention was frequently distracted by sneezing fits brought under control only by the application of a great white handkerchief thrown full into and over the face. Beside the sheriff, a police stenographer was juggling a steno pad upon which a network of meaningless squiggles had been impressed by a usually keen and careful hand, now rendered quivering and slack-wristed by the deep drama of what Jake Moonstreet had related.

Around the walls, straining the capacity of the small office, were a number of uniformed deputies, probably every one the county employed, called in from their patrols to bear testimony first-hand on what would become known as the Moonstreet Ripoff. At any particular moment, one or another of them would be facing toward the wall, wiping eyes suddenly filled with tears, as shoulders shook in the throes of some uncontrollable emotion brought on by the narrative.

"Tell it again, please, Jake," Sheriff Roche begged, motioning toward the stenographer. "I don't think Charlie here got everything."

Jake Moonstreet sighed, shivered a little more, and told his story all over again into the handkerchief face of the sheriff.

"Well, Sheriff," Jake began, "Pat there called me up and told me there was a customer down at the station who wouldn't pay his bill until I come down personal like and talked to him. When Pat told me how much the bill was, I got into my pickup and got right down there. Well, when I got there, I saw a car, a late-model Chevy, and a Volks bus with four guys standing around it, all these guys wearing dark glasses. Pat motioned me into the office where I saw him standing with another guy, also with dark glasses on. As I go through the door, the group around the Volks breaks up. Three of them go into the garage and the other steps behind me and jams a gun in my back.

"'What is this, a holdup?' I say. The guy with the gun almost loses it in my back and I get the idea he wants me to keep moving, so I go into the office. That's when I get a good look at the guy with Pat, a small guy with very clean hands. Uh, I notice that sort of thing in my business."

"That tells you the guy doesn't know thing one about cars. Right, Jake?" one of the deputies asked.

"*That* tells me the guy can use my station's expert help if his car's in trouble," replied Jake loftily.

He went on. "So I get a look at this guy's face, what there is of it not hidden by the glasses, and believe me, fellahs, here's a hard case, a syndicate type."

"Why do you think a syndicate type, Jake?" the sheriff asked.

"I bet they got some racket going, getting all us honest operators outa business so they can set up a chain of ripoff stations," answered Jake, raising his voice somewhat to be heard over the outburst of exuberance that greeted the word "honest."

"Has the syndicate approached you? Offered to buy you out? This is the way they usually operate."

"Well, no, Sheriff. But what else could it be?"

"I don't know, Jake. I really don't know. But go on with your story."

"Anyway, the hard type in the office with Pat says to me, 'Jacob Moonstreet?' I say, 'Yeah.' He says, 'You and your man here, Patrick Challoner, have had a good thing going. Now it's over.'

"So, the guy with the gun in my back steps around and cleans out the register. Puts everything, bills and change, even checks, into a bag with a lock trap. After he snaps the lock on the bag, he gives it to Mr. Hard Face. Just then, another one of them comes in and says, 'All set.' Hard Face asks, 'This place too?' The other guy says, 'Wired.'

"We go out then, and I notice that a guy's car we had in for a tuneup is parked across the road. They had moved it. Also moved was my pickup and Pat's Rambler, which are now in the garage bays. They manhandle Pat and I into the back of the Volks and we drive off aways, Hard Face leading in his Chevy. One guy stays behind hidden in back of an embankment and when he's sure no cars are passing on the road, he pushes down on a detonator he's got and up goes my station. Office, garage, gas pumps, the whole schmeer."

"And now tell us what happened after that," the sheriff urged.

"So, after the explosion, they drive like hell into town, through the business district, and out into that new housing subdivision."

"Warrington Heights," the sheriff clarified. "The place where all the fat bankrolls go to rest up after a hard day in town."

"Yeah, that's it. On the way there, the guy with the gun tells us to undress, like completely. He's got a good argument in his hand, so we do as he tells us. And then they put us out right there in the middle of that Heights place."

"Without a stitch on?" queried the sheriff, busily working his handkerchief again.

"Right. Naked as jaybirds. But you'll catch 'em, won't you, Sheriff?" Jake inquired hopefully. "I gave you their license numbers and I got another lead I didn't tell you before. A clue, like."

"What's that?"

"I think a dame runs the gang. I heard one of the guys mention her name. Cora. He knowed he said something outa school because he clammed up pronto. Maybe this Cora dame was one of them disguised." Jake Moonstreet looked eagerly at the sheriff. "You'll catch 'em, won't you?"

"I dunno," the sheriff said, suddenly sober. "We'll put out a bulletin on the cars and plates. But they'll probably have switched plates or ditched the cars by now."

Besides, the sheriff asked himself, who's the criminal here?

He was remembering the time Jake Moonstreet, some years back, did a job on the Roche family car.

The small man, once in his motel room, pulled his suitcases off the overhead rack, opened them on the room's single bed, and began packing. He packed carefully, slowly, a man who was sure of himself and what he did, and prided himself on the care and deliberation he brought to everything he did, including packing his clothes. He took a snub-nosed revolver from his pocket, hefted it briefly and then tucked it beneath some neatly folded, snow-white T-shirts.

As he went to the dresser for more clothes, he caught himself looking into the wide mirror above. He was mildly surprised to find a small smile of satisfaction creasing his normally stern features, betraying there a softness he usually exposed only to put the enemy off guard. He let the smile widen into a grin. Well, why not? he thought. It was a good operation; well planned, smoothly carried out.

A rap on the door swept the grin from his face.

"Yes. Who is it?"

"Barton, sir."

"Come in, Sergeant. It's open."

The door was pushed in and a tall bulky man wearing dark glasses let himself into the room.

The occupant looked at the newcomer, glanced up at the glasses, and said, "You can take them off, Sergeant. No need to be in uniform now."

The tall man smiled, said briskly, "Right, Lieutenant!" and removed the glasses.

"All taken care of?" the lieutenant asked.

"In the vans and on their way to Sector B. Plates'll be changed en route. They'll be used next week by team 31 for an operation similar to the one we completed today."

"Good. Has the rest of our team departed?"

"Yes, sir, they're on their way. We'll rendezvous with them day after tomorrow at the assembly point. I have a new car outside."

"Fine. I'll pack and we'll be on our way."

"Lieutenant Valore, sir?"

"Yes?"

"What are we going up against next?"

"One of those ghetto superettes. High prices. Extends credit. Interesting accounting practices. We'll meet the research squad tomorrow and hammer out the plan with them before the operations squad arrives the next day. This will be team 17's last action before we shut down for a month with our families."

"There's precious little family life once you're in the Consumer Reaction Army."

The lieutenant turned on Sergeant Barton, his face hard as when earlier, revolver in hand, he had faced Pat Challoner, the service station attendant. "Sergeant," Valore snapped, "you don't think of personal comfort when you're fighting a war."

"Sorry, sir."

"All right. It's tough on all of us but we don't make it easier by grousing about the hardships we knew would be a part of it."

Sergeant Barton, chastened and wishing to change the subject, said, "Of course, sir. Can I help you pack?"

The lieutenant snapped a suitcase shut and replied, "I've just about got it. A few more items." His eye fell on a bottle of Irish whiskey atop the dresser. He also took in Sergeant Barton's embarrassment at being chewed out. "Relax, Barton," the lieutenant said. "Grab a couple of those plastic glasses and pour each of us a good shot of Irish."

When they raised the tumblers, the sergeant asked, "Shall we drink to our families?"

The lieutenant's mouth was a slit of disapproval. "No, the Army," he ordered.

"To CORA, then," said the sergeant.

"To CORA," said the lieutenant.

NELSON DeMILLE

Life or Breath

Martin Wallace stood in a modified parade rest position and gazed out of the twenty-third-floor hospital window. Across the thirty miles of flat suburban sprawl he could see the blazing skyscrapers of Manhattan.

They blinked, twinkled and beckoned to him.

He looked at his watch. Fifteen minutes to nine. Fifteen minutes before he could leave this oppressive room and head for the lights of that enchanted island. He rocked back and forth on the balls of his feet. His reveries were broken by a sound behind him.

He turned and looked down at the form on the bed. The limp arm was tapping the night table to get his attention. He made a slightly annoyed face as their eyes met. Who else but Myra could get herself into a fix like this? But, then, he supposed that the hospital was full of bored suburban housewives who didn't know their capacity for Valium.

He stepped up to the bed. A small green plastic box sat on its stand next to the bed. A clear accordion-type plastic hose led from the box to her throat. The box made a faint, but annoying, pneumatic sound. "Myra, I have to leave, dear. Visiting hours are over. What can I bring you?" He smiled.

She looked petulant. That was her favorite expression. Petulant. In twenty years of marriage, he had labelled every one of her expressions and voice tones.

She made small grunting sounds. She wanted to speak, but nothing came out.

"You just get a good night's rest, Myra. Rest. A nice long rest." He smiled and pulled the respirator hose out of the tracheal adaptor embedded in her throat.

Air rushed into the adaptor and made a wheezing sound. At the same time air blew out of the disconnected hose in a continuous stream. He squeezed the open end of the hose, but it was too late. The alarm went off.

Almost immediately, a big, buxom nurse charged into the room like an enraged mother hen. "Mr. Wallace! Please. I explained to you how to disconnect that. You must squeeze the hose first, before you pull it out, so that the alarm doesn't sound."

"Sorry."

She threw him a look that medical people reserve for naughty lay people. "It's like screaming wolf. You know?"

"Sorry, nurse." He looked her full figure over. Long tresses of chestnut brown hair fell onto her shoulders and framed her pretty German-Irish face. The name tag on her breast read Maureen Hesse.

She made a huff and a puff and turned around. She called back over her shoulder as she left, "Visiting hours are almost over."

"Yes, nurse." He looked down at his wife. She had placed her hand over the gaping rubber tracheal adaptor. With the hole sealed off she was able to speak in weak, aspirating sounds. Martin Wallace preferred this to the high-pitched screech he was used to.

Myra spoke. "Don't forget my magazines." She paused as air rushed into the hole. "And get them to put a different TV in here." She wheezed. "We're paying for it." She opened her mouth and tried to gulp some air. "I want one that works. Call my mother tonight." She tried taking air in through her nose. "And talk to that doctor. I want to know *exactly* how long—"

Martin Wallace gently took his wife's hand away from the tracheal adaptor. Her words faded like a slowing record. The tracheal adaptor wheezed. He began to plug the respirator hose back into her throat.

"Martin! I have more to tell you—you—" Her words were lost as the machine began pumping air back into her lungs.

"You're getting yourself excited, Myra. Now, rest. Rest. Good night." He walked around the bed and left the room.

At the nurses' station, he spotted Dr. Wasserman, the resident physician. He walked over to him. "Excuse me, Doctor."

The young resident looked up from his charts. "Oh, yes. Mr. Wallace. How is your wife doing?"

"Well, that's what I want to ask *you*, Doctor."

"Of course." Dr. Wasserman put on a look of professional concern. "Well, Mr. Wallace, it could be worse. She could be dead."

Martin Wallace did not consider that to be worse. "What's the—how do you call it—prognosis?"

"Well, it's too early to tell, really. You see, Mr. Wallace, when you take a tranquillizer, like Valium, for instance, for extended periods of time, you begin to think you're building up a resistance to it. It seems to have no clout anymore. So instead of taking, let's say, five milligrams at a time, you take maybe twenty, as your wife did. Plus that martini—"

"Manhattan."

"Yes. Whatever. So what happened is that she had a period of anoxic cardiac arrest. In other words, her breathing and heart stopped. Maybe for as long as two minutes. This may lead to residual neurological sequelae—permanent but partial damage to the nervous system."

"Meaning?"

Dr. Wasserman stroked his chin. "It's too early to tell, really."

"Come on, Doctor. What's the *worst* it can be?"

He shrugged. "She can be an invalid for the rest of her life. She may need a home respirator for a while. She may even need occasional renal dialysis.

Frequent cardiac tests. There could be partial muscular paralysis. When you're dealing with the nervous system, you never know. It may take weeks to see what works and what doesn't work anymore. I mean, she was technically dead for a few minutes. How many functions come back is anybody's guess. You understand?"

"Yes."

Martin Wallace glanced back toward his wife's room. He turned back toward the doctor. "How long would she live without the respirator? I mean—you know—when she wants to speak—I'm afraid to keep the hose out too long. I don't want to—"

The doctor moved his hand in a calming gesture. "That shouldn't be a concern. When she has difficulty breathing she signals to you, doesn't she? Or she tells you."

"Yes. Yes, of course. But I was just wondering. You know. If the hose came out in her sleep, maybe."

"That's why the alarm is there, Mr. Wallace. In the event the hose comes out by accident and she can't replace it." He gave him a smile and changed his voice to a paternal scolding tone, even though he was much younger than Mr. Wallace. "You, by the way, must be more careful when you disconnect it. You can't be setting off the alarm every time. It gives the nurses a good workout, but they have enough of that anyway in the Intensive Care Unit." He smiled again. "As long as there is someone in the room or as long as the alarm system is working, there can't be any accident."

Martin Wallace smiled back, although this good news did not make him at all happy. He was asking questions with one thing in mind and the good doctor was answering him with another thing in mind. He'd have to be blunt, "Look, Doctor," he smiled again, "just out of morbid curiosity—O.K.? How long can she live without that respirator?"

Dr. Wasserman shrugged again. "Half an hour, I guess. Probably less. Hard to say. Sometimes a patient can get the voluntary muscles to work hard enough to breathe for hours and hours. But as soon as the patient gets fatigued or sleeps, the involuntary muscles, which should normally control unconscious breathing, can't do the job. I really can't give you a definite answer. But the question is academic, anyway, isn't it? The respirator breathes for her, Mr. Wallace."

"Yes. Of course. But—" He tried to put on an abashed smile. "Just one more question. I worry about these things. I'm an accountant and I have that kind of mind. You know?" He smiled a smile that tried to bespeak professional parallelism. Neurotic complicity between great minds. "I think too much, I suppose. But I was wondering, is—is there any way the alarm system can fail? You know?"

Dr. Wasserman tapped him lightly on his shoulder. "Don't worry, Mr. Wallace. As soon as that hose comes out of the tracheal adaptor and the pumped air meets no resistance, the alarm goes off here in the nurses' station. Now, I know what you're thinking. What if Mrs. Wallace pulls it loose during the night and rolls over on it." He smiled.

That's exactly what Martin Wallace was thinking. He waited, literally breathless.

"Well, it's almost impossible to pull it loose by accident, to begin with. Secondly, she'd have to roll over on it very, very quickly. Otherwise, the alarm would go off. Then she'd have to stay in that position for some time. But you see, as soon as she had difficulty breathing, she'd move or thrash. It's a normal reaction. She's not comatose. The hose, then, would be free of her body and the alarm would sound. But, anyway, in Intensive Care we check the patients regularly. Besides, you have private nurses around the clock."

Martin Wallace tried not to look glum. He nodded. Those nurses were costing him a fortune. Another one of Myra's extravagances. But there was one last glimmer of hope. Dr. Wasserman, however, had anticipated the next question and began answering it.

"And the other thing you're wondering about is the respirator itself. Well, any malfunction in the machine also triggers an alarm. There are several alarms, actually. At least three back-up alarms in that model." The doctor folded his arms and glanced at his watch. "We have a dozen spare respirators standing by. Haven't lost a patient through accident yet." He smiled reassuringly.

"Power failure?" It came out with the wrong intonation. It came out as though he were begging for one.

"I beg your pardon?"

"Power failure. Power failure. You know. Blackout."

"Oh." He laughed. "You *are* a worrier, Mr. Wallace." The doctor's smile faded and his voice became impatient. "We have auxiliary generators, of course. It's the law." He looked pointedly at his watch. "I have to make my rounds. Excuse me."

"Of course."

Martin Wallace stood rooted at the nurses' station for several minutes staring straight ahead.

He walked slowly to the elevator bank. A few overstayed visitors stared wordlessly at the floor indicator. The elevator came and he stepped in. The lights blinked: *22—21—20—19—*

He walked out of the hospital and into the acres of parking lot. A gentle spring breeze blew the scent of newly born flowers across the dark macadam. He walked slowly through the balmy night air as though in a trance. Invalid. Partial paralysis. Home respirator. Renal dialysis.

He had come so close to losing her for good. And now this. What a monumental mess. Myra was hard enough to take when she was well—which was almost never. Twenty years of hypochondria, and never one really good fatal illness. And now this. An invalid.

He walked up to his car and got in. He lit a cigarette and looked out the side window. Three very pretty young girls walked by. They wore jeans and T-shirts. Their long hair fell over their shoulders. Their lithe bodies and lilting voices made his chest heave. He bit his lip in suppressed desire.

Myra. Painted toenails. Painted eyes. Dyed hair. Enough jewelry to drown her in the event she ever decided to jump into the swimming pool she had insisted on having built. Myra. Ridiculous fan magazines and trashy tabloids. Does Jackie O. keep a secret picture of Jack in her snuff box? Is Robert Redford in love with Princess Grace? Who *cares*? Myra. Sitting in front of the idiot box in a crocodilian stupor. Shrieking over a game of Mah-Jongg with her bitchy friends. Sitting for hours baking her skimpy brains under a hair dryer. Myra. Barren of children. Barren of a single original thought in twenty years. Myra and Poopsie. Poopsie and Myra. Of all the dogs on God's earth, he hated poodles more than any other. Myra. Professional shopper. Myra. The last novel she read was *Love Story*. The one before that was *Valley of the Dolls*. The only time she had stirred herself in years was to join a local chapter of the women's liberation movement. The Alice Doesn't Live Here Anymore Chapter. Liberation. What a laugh. Who was freer than that lazy cow? Myra. What a dud. He laughed and slumped over the steering wheel. Tears rolled down his cheeks.

Divorce. Divorce would cost him a fortune. Her death, on the other hand, would put a hundred-thousand-dollar life insurance policy in his pocket.

Martin Wallace pulled the rear view mirror down and looked at himself in the dim light. Not bad for thirty-nine. A few weeks at a health spa. A little sun tan. New clothes. A new hair style. A new life.

He slumped back into the seat of his big, Myra-inspired Cadillac. He pictured the interior of a Porsche or a Jaguar.

He looked up at the tall, bulky, illuminated hospital. Even with his medical insurance, she was costing him two hundred a day. Even flat on her back she was draining him. Her whole life was a study in conspicuous consumption. The quintessential consumer of goods and services. She even consumed more hospital goods and services than the average patient. And she never produced one single thing in her whole life. Not even the thing she was built to produce—a child. Barren. Frigid. Worthless. In his accounting firm she would be called a continuing liability. But a liability which, if liquidated, would become an asset. Liquidated.

He started the car and wheeled out of the parking lot. Within the hour he had parked his car in a midtown garage.

He began walking up Third Avenue. It was a week night, but the streets were alive with people on this first nice spring evening. He walked into P.J. Moriarty's. At the bar were three bachelors from his office—his subordinates of sorts.

They drank there for an hour, then took taxis to each other's favorite East Side pubs. They took taxis all over town. They walked and sang and drank.

They wound up on the West Side and had a late supper at the Act I, overlooking Times Square. Down in the street the Great White Way blazed through their alcoholic haze.

They left the restaurant. To Martin Wallace, there was pure magic in the night air and in the streets of New York, as he gazed out through his clouded eyes at the lights and people swirling around him.

He separated from his friends and walked east on Central Park South and stood in front of the Plaza Hotel, overlooking the park. He fingercombed his hair and straightened his tie. Then he entered the hotel and fulfilled a long-standing recurring dream of checking in.

The marble lobby was an enchanted forest of columns and thick pile rugs. Subdued lights showed little knots of well-dressed people seated in the plush chairs and sofas. An attractive woman seemed to smile at him as the bellboy led him to the elevators.

He awoke and lay bathed in glorious late morning sunlight. He picked up the phone and ordered coffee and mixed rolls and pastry. As an afterthought—he had seen it in a movie—he ordered a pitcher of Bloody Marys.

He put his hands behind his neck and stared at the rich cream-colored ceiling. His mind wandered. On his salary, with no dependents—that is, no Myra—and with no money-sucking house in the suburbs, he reckoned that he could well afford a life style like this. A nice apartment in town. A few wild nights a week like last night. An opera or a little ballet on his easy nights. A Broadway show once in a while. Sunday brunch at the Oyster Bar downstairs. Maybe he would rent a car on weekends and get out to the hinterlands once in a while. Maybe take the train from Pennsylvania Station to the Hamptons or to Belmont Racetrack. Maybe the train from Grand Central Station to the resort hotels in the Catskills or a football game at West Point. Sunday afternoon in Central Park. Saturday in Greenwich Village. A different little restaurant every night. He would have to patronize at least one bar and one restaurant enough to become one of the regulars, though, he reminded himself. He pictured scenes he had seen in movies. The possibilities for life were unlimited in this city. No house, no car, no television, no fan magazines, no Myra. He smiled.

If he had a nice windfall of, say, a hundred thousand dollars to start with, it would be even better. And all this was only a heartbeat away. Just a single heartbeat. But it kept beating, that heart. Thump. Thump. Thump. He could hear his own heart beat heavily in his chest.

He stretched and yawned. He cleared his husky, dry throat and placed a phone call.

A woman answered. "East Park Community Hospital."

"Yes. Intensive Care Unit, please." The phone clicked.

"ICU."

"Yes. Is it still beating?"

"Sir?"

"This is Mr. Wallace. How is my darling wife, please?" He felt reckless this morning.

"Just a moment."

There was a long pause. Martin Wallace prayed.

The voice came back. "Fine, sir. Mrs. Wallace spent a comfortable night. Your private nurse is just bathing her now."

"Swell. Terrific. Thank you." He slammed the phone down and covered his face with the pillow.

There was a knock on the door.

"Come in."

The bus boy entered with a rolling cart. The cart was heaped with all manner of hotel luxury. There was even a complimentary copy of *The New York Times*. Just like in the movies. But the scene paled next to the reality of the telephone call.

He signed for the breakfast and sat down heavily on the bed. He poured a Bloody Mary into a tall glass with a coating of salt on its rim. He downed it in one long gulp.

He opened the paper as he sipped his coffee and scanned it idly. The problems of the world were minuscule compared to his own, but he had developed the defensive habit of eating breakfast behind a newspaper and it was hard to break bad habits. He read, but nothing registered. His mind was elsewhere. Myra. Thump. Thump. Thump. Her heart still beat at the rate of a couple of hundred dollars a day. Thump. Thump. It had been silent for two minutes once, but thanks to the marvels of medical science, it was thumping again. Thump. Thump. Thump. It would thump for how many more years? Twenty? Forty? Sixty?

How do you divorce an invalid, even if you are willing to pay most of your salary for the rest of your life? Why not just disappear, then? That was becoming one of the most popular track sports among men these days. The 100-yard dash into obscurity. But it was a tremendous price to pay. Loss of identity. Loss of friends. Loss of professional credentials. Why should *he* disappear? Why couldn't *she* disappear? "Die! Die, damn you! Die!" The sound of his own voice scared him.

He tossed the paper on the bed. He stared at the open pages for a long second, then picked it up again. There was a lengthy article on the question of medical life-support systems. He read it intently and discovered that he was not alone in wishing that medical science would let the dying die.

He read of cases of brain-dead patients kept alive for months and even years by artificial means. He read of cases similar to Myra's. Overdoses. Strokes. Partially destroyed nervous systems. Human beings snatched from the slashing scythe of the Grim Reaper, but not before suffering permanent life-wrecking infirmities. He read of the burdens of families left with slack-jawed loved ones to care for. Left with staggering medical bills rendered by smiling doctors and hospitals as the price for returning these loved ones to them as vegetables.

But what interested him more was not the horror stories of misguided humanitarianism, but rather the names of individuals and organizations who opposed these extraordinary measures taken to prolong life at any cost.

He nibbled at a big cheese Danish and a smile played across his moving lips.

He took the pass from the girl at the desk and stood in front of the elevator bank. The night was warm, but he wore a tan trench coat buttoned to the neck.

Swarms of visitors waited as the elevators came to collect them and carry them up into the great hospital. Martin Wallace crowded into one of the cars.

He held his brown paper bag at chest level to keep it from being crushed in the press of the crowd.

In the Intensive Care Unit, he stopped at the nurses' station and exchanged a few smiling words with Miss Hesse, then walked into Myra's private room. He nodded to the attractive private nurse he was paying for. "How's she doing, Ellen?" He smiled. She, plus the other two nurses, were costing him a fortune, he reminded himself. He also reminded himself that they were not needed, but Myra had insisted.

The petite young girl smiled at him. "Fine, Mr. Wallace. Getting better every day." She rose. "I'll just leave you two alone." She smiled at both of them and left.

Myra made a weak gesture toward her throat.

Martin Wallace nodded tiredly and reached down and grabbed the hose. He pinched before he pulled and the alarm did not sound. He placed his hand over the tracheal adaptor in her throat and the wheezing stopped.

Myra sucked in a big gulp of air. "I had Ellen call you all last night."

Her voice sounded stronger today, he noticed. It had some of its old screechiness back in it. "Is that so? I must have slept through the phone. Sorry."

She looked at him with expression number three. Suspicion. "I needed my nail polish and manicure kit."

The tone was accusatory. It was supposed to provoke guilt in him, even though it was barely audible and her tonal quality was hard to control. He recognized it, anyway. "Sorry."

What an incredible woman, he thought. Three days ago she was leaning heavily against death's door and today she wants her manicure kit. He stared at her for several seconds. He had an impulse to pour her bottle of skin lotion into the tracheal adaptor and watch her drown. "Sorry, Myra."

"Well, at least I see you remembered something." She pointed to the bag that he had placed on the bed. "Did you—"

He took his hand off the adaptor and air rushed in. Her words faded. "Can't have you off it too long, dear." He plugged the pinched-off hose back in with his other hand and released it. The machine changed pitch and began pumping in air. It was so easy to shut her up that it was almost comical. He could see that she was furious at being cut off. She moved her hand to the hose to pull it out, but he grabbed her wrist. "Really, Myra. That's enough talking for a while."

She tried to pull her wrist free, but he held it easily. Her other hand reached out and she pushed the nurse's call buzzer.

Martin Wallace had enough for one night. He reached inside the paper bag and took out two magazines and threw them on the night table. "I could only find two."

She looked inquisitively at the still-bulging bag.

He didn't acknowledge her questioning eyes.

The private nurse, Ellen, walked in. "Yes?"

Martin Wallace smiled. "I think Mrs. Wallace wants something." He looked down at her. "I really have to go, dear. I'm sorry, Myra, darling. I have an appointment." He looked at Ellen. "Take care of my sweetheart, will you? I'll try to get over tomorrow afternoon. Otherwise I'll see you both tomorrow night." He walked to the door. "Good-bye."

Ellen smiled. "Good-bye, Mr. Wallace."

Myra shot him look number one. Pure malice with a touch of hatred and contempt.

He waved and went into the corridor.

At the elevator bank a chime sounded and a light lit up. He walked over to the open car and stepped in. There were three other early-departing visitors and one orderly. Only the lobby button was lit. Nonchalantly, he pushed *B* for basement.

The elevator stopped in the lobby and the doors slid open. He moved closer to the control panel and out of sight of the guards and reception desks. He frantically hit the *Door Close* button.

The elevator descended to the basement. The elevator doors opened. He stepped into a long, empty corridor. Some of the kitchens were down here and he could smell cooking. He looked around, then walked quickly up to a canvas laundry cart and shucked off his trench coat. He threw it in the cart and buried it with dirty linen. Under the trench coat he wore a white lab jacket.

Still clutching his paper bag, he paced up and down the deserted corridors, examining doors and signs.

At the end of a long, dimly lit corridor he saw it. It was marked *Subbasement. Electrical.* He opened the steel door and descended the narrow metal staircase.

The stairwell emptied into a long, narrow corridor. He walked past the gray painted concrete walls under the harsh glow of evenly spaced naked bulbs that ran the length of the ceiling. He stopped at each of several metal doors, opening each and looking inside.

Finally, he came to a door whose stenciled sign was the announcement of the end of his search: *Electrics Room. Danger. High Voltage.* He went inside and closed the door behind him.

The dimly lit room was medium-sized and crowded with the life stuff of modern buildings. Endless tubes of wire and conduit ran across the ceiling and tracked down the gray walls. On the far side lay two huge diesel generators on raised platforms. Each had a hooded exhaust over it. To the left of the generators sat a rectangular box labelled: *Batteries—Caution: Acid.*

It would take a barrel of dynamite to completely sabotage this room. It would be necessary to blow up both generators, the storage batteries and the external city electricity source.

Every system, however, has its Achilles' heel and he did not have to be an electrical engineer to know what the soft spot in this system was. He had to find it first, though.

He walked slowly around the room. On the rear wall were about thirty black and gray painted metal panels. Plastic label tags hung from each of them. He ran his eyes over each tag.

He smiled when he found what looked like the proper one. Mounted waist high on the wall, it was the size of a deep orange-crate. It was painted a shiny, crackling black. The long switch handle on the side of the door was a sign that said: *Power Sensing and Relay Control Panel.* and *Diesel.* The switch was in the *Automatic* position.

He opened the cabinet door and it made a metallic squeak. Inside the door was a sign that said, *Power Sensing and Relay Control Panel. Disconnect Diesel Junction Connector D-3 Before Servicing.* He would disconnect more than that before he was through. This was it for sure. This was the central distribution point for the sources of the hospital's power. This box decided whether or not the city's power was normal and, if not, it would then activate the diesel generators, drawing on the storage batteries, if necessary. It all came together right here in this box. The Achilles' heel. Remove the box and you removed the whole hospital's energy supply.

From his paper bag, he removed a large number-ten fruit can. The top of the can was covered with aluminum foil. He removed the foil and shoved it into his pants pocket. Inside the can was packed the gunpowder from a box of fifty 12-gauge shotgun shells. It was a small charge by the standards of most bomb makers, but then he did not need much and it had the advantage of using an easily procured and non-traceable explosive.

Also inside the can were a simple wind-up alarm clock and two flashlight batteries attached to a switch. A cluster of the nitroglycerine primers from the shotgun shells was the detonator. The whole thing looked innocuous enough, especially in the foil-covered fruit can. It looked like a container that a doting husband would use to carry homemade cookies to his ailing loved one. Even one of the rare cursory inspections by the hospital guards would have aroused no suspicion.

He put his hand into the can and set the alarm for ten o'clock. He connected the wires with alligator clips. The loud ticking seemed to fill the cryptlike room. He placed the whole thing gently inside the cabinet. He wiped it carefully for prints with a handkerchief and closed the steel door. He wiped the door, also. His face was covered with sweat as he turned from the wall of control panels.

He crossed the room and walked up to the door. From the paper bag he removed a piece of shirt cardboard and taped it to the door. He had wanted to letter the sign ahead of time, but it would be incriminating if by some rare happenstance a guard had wanted to look in the bag. He wrote in large block letters with a marking pen: *God Does Not Want People Kept Alive by Artificial Means. Let the Dying Die with Dignity.* (Signed) *The Committee to End Human Suffering.*

He heard voices outside the door. He stood motionless and breathless as the voices, two males, came abreast of the door. They walked by and he could hear their footsteps retreating down the corridor. He waited.

As he waited, he looked at the sign in the dim light. He smiled. This was enough of a red herring to throw the police off for months. And if by chance they suspected a friend or relative of one of the hospital's current patients, it would make no difference. There were at least thirty people in the Intensive Care Unit whose lives depended on one machine or another. To run down the friends and relatives of each of them would take a very long time. Eventually, they might even get around to asking him to "drop by" for questioning. But so what? There would be a few hundred others, connected with the thirty or so, they would have to question also. Then there would be all the known anti-life-support-systems groups and individuals.

It disturbed him that so many others would die also, but it could not be helped, really. To play with Myra's respirator in the hospital or to see that she had an accident when she returned home was to court life imprisonment. It was no secret to their friends and relatives that he wanted her gone.

To end all the lives hanging on the machines was to scatter the suspicion far and wide. That was the beauty of the thing.

Of course there were some people who only needed the machines for a short while before they could become self-sustaining again. That was a pity. And there were even some operations scheduled at night that would never be completed. That, too, was unfortunate. But Myra had to die and he, Martin Wallace, had to live. The footsteps and voices faded away.

Slowly, he opened the door and slipped into the corridor. He walked quickly to the staircase and walked up from the subbasement into the more brightly lit corridor of the basement. He threw the paper bag into a trash barrel and walked quickly over to the laundry cart near the elevators. He ripped the white coat off and threw it in the cart, then retrieved his own trench coat and slipped it on. He hit the elevator button and waited. He noticed that his knees were shaking as he stood staring up at the floor indicator. His head felt light and his mouth was dry, but his forehead was wet.

He could hear the elevator approach. It stopped and the doors slid open. Four visitors and an orderly stood staring at him silently. He froze. They stared.

He stepped into the car quickly and faced the control panel.

The car stopped automatically in the lobby. The doors slid open.

He turned so as not to face the guard and headed for the main doors. Every step was shaky and he thought his knees might give out and he would topple over. He tried to swallow, but almost choked on the dryness. The doors got bigger and bigger and soon he was pushing on one of them. Through. The foyer. More doors. Push. Outside.

He walked, almost ran, down the path to the parking lot. His hands moved in and out of his coat and pants pockets like fluttering birds. He began tearing at the pockets. Keys. Keys. There. He nearly sprinted the remaining distance to his car.

He pulled at the door handle. It would not budge. Locked. Locked. He took a deep breath and calmed himself slightly. With a hand shaking worse than he could ever imagine, he tried to place the key in the lock. Finally, after a full minute, he got it in and twisted it.

Inside, he had difficulty finding the right key and then could not hold his hand still enough to get it in the ignition. Finally, he steadied himself and put it in. He turned the key and the engine roared to life. The sound made him jump, but then soothed him. He took a long, deep breath and fumbled for a cigarette. Within forty-five minutes he would be sitting in P.J. Moriarty's with his friends.

He threw the big Cadillac into low and shot out of the parking space—directly into the path of a huge delivery van.

"Just take it easy, Mr. Wallace. You're going to be fine. Really."

He blinked his eyes. The voice was familiar. Dr. Wasserman.

The voice spoke again, but to someone else. "It was a simple whiplash. Those headrests don't always do the job. Sometimes they even cause worse injuries if they're not set properly. I suppose you had it set downward for yourself, but it was too low for him. Hit him in the back of the neck. But it's not serious."

A weak voice to his left answered. "Yes. I did most of the driving."

Myra.

Martin Wallace blinked into the overhead light. He tried to move his head, but couldn't. Something was in his mouth and he could not speak. He rolled his eyes downward as far as they would go. He could see a tube. He looked up. On the opposite wall, a television set was mounted on a high shelf. He was in Myra's room. The picture was bad and the sound was lowered so that he could not hear it. It was a commercial for Alpo. A toy poodle was being shown a can of the canine victuals by its mistress.

Another person entered the room. Martin Wallace caught a glimpse of him as he passed by. It was his family physician, Dr. Matirka. Then the face of the floor nurse, Maureen Hesse, came into view for a second, then the profile of the private nurse, Ellen.

Dr. Wasserman spoke to the others. "Whiplash. He's suffered swelling around the basal ganglia and the internal capsule above the base of the brain. Luckily, the reticular activating system was not involved. There is no loss of consciousness. He's conscious and can see and hear us. But everything from the neck down is paralyzed. He can't speak or breathe on his own. That's why I've put the intubation tube into his mouth and through the larynx, instead of into the trachea. We've given him dexamethasone to combat the swelling. The swelling and consequent paralysis didn't begin until we got him in here, so there's almost no period of anoxia. There will be no permanent damage at all once the swelling goes down in a few days."

Dr. Wasserman leaned over him and smiled. "Blink if you understood what I said, Mr. Wallace."

Martin Wallace blinked.

"So you see, as soon as the swelling at the base of the brain goes down in a few days, your nervous system will return to normal and we can take this respirator off. You'll leave here as good as you came in. Blink if you understand."

Martin Wallace blinked through eyes that were becoming misty. A tear rolled down his cheek.

"No need to be upset," said Dr. Matirka. He leaned over the bed. "In fact, I have more good news for you. Myra's breathing is returning to normal. She can get on fine without the respirator for extended periods. We're weaning her away from it a little at a time just to be safe, but I think she can go for at least an hour or two without it. In fact, she's off it now." He chuckled pleasantly and tapped Martin Wallace on the chest, but the paralyzed man felt nothing. Tears streamed down his face.

"Now, now," said Nurse Hesse, a little sternly, "getting upset will make it worse. You'll be fine in a few days. See, we didn't even have to make a tracheotomy opening for the respirator. When the swelling goes down, you can get up and walk out of here."

Ellen leaned over. "It could have been much worse. See, Mrs. Wallace is fine too. You'll both be out of here in a few days."

Only the muscles above his mouth responded to his commands. His eyes blinked furiously and tears streamed down from them. His nose twitched spasmodically and his upper lip quivered. His forehead furrowed. Even his ears wiggled just a bit.

"He does seem quite upset about something, doesn't he?" remarked Ellen.

"He'll be better when he begins to believe us," said Dr. Wasserman.

Martin Wallace fixed his blurry eyes on the television screen. The picture tube said: *Ten O'Clock News.*

Myra spoke. "Turn on *Medical Center* and raise the volume for me, Ellen. I'm not interested in the news."

The lights went out.

Someone said, "Damn it."

There was a short silence.

Dr. Wasserman's voice spoke softly. "Just a second. The auxiliary generators will kick in."

Silence.

"Just a second. They'll be on in just a half second."

Martin Wallace could hear Myra's voice in the dark as he struggled to breathe.

"I'm going to miss part of the show." Petulant.

"Just a second." Dr. Wasserman's voice sounded anxious now. "They'll be on in just a half second."

But Martin Wallace knew they would not be on ever again.

WILLIAM BRITTAIN

A Private Little War

Jake Landis hobbled back into his classroom, hung his cane on the chalk tray, and settled himself onto the tubular steel chair at his desk. With both hands he pulled at his left leg, moving it into as comfortable a position as possible.

The stiff knee, a relic of an automobile accident five years previously, didn't pain him any more. It was just awkward sometimes. But then, a man crowding fifty, with all the dreams of becoming a sports hero or another Fred Astaire behind him, didn't need supple joints to teach freshman history. And besides, the cane added a certain style to his lessons, especially during descriptions of French swordplay or when brandished as a mock threat over the head of some lazy student. Getting up and down stairs was a tedious process, but he was usually able to find a football player to run interference for him and be there to catch him if he was in danger of falling.

He pulled the first batch of test papers from the slow class toward him and began reading: "The Boston Tea Party was wher the coloneal daims planed ther part in the Revelushin." Oh, boy! It was going to be a long two hours until five o'clock.

There was a knock at the classroom door, and Jake looked up. The door opened, and Harvey Cassidy of the math department stuck his head in. "Got a minute, Jake?" he asked.

"Sure. Come on in, Harv. But if it's about math, I'm telling you right now, I always figured you guys worked by magic, not logic. Just apply the right spell, and the volume of a pyramid is yours for the asking."

"At least it's better than reviewing a couple of centuries of man's inhumanity to man," replied Cassidy with a grin. He leaned against one of the student desks, and suddenly the grin disappeared.

"Jake, you've got Alec Whitnine in one of your classes, haven't you?" he asked in a flat voice.

"Sure. Third period. He sits over there by the window. Why?"

"Tell me what you think of him, will you? Never mind the test scores. What's he like as a person?"

Jake considered the question for a moment. "To tell the truth, I don't really know that much about him," he said. "A pretty quiet kid most of the time. About the only time he speaks out is to ask some question designed to embarrass me in front of the class. He's something of a pain in the neck, but not really all that bad. And Mabel Fuchs considers him the darling of her science classes." He adjusted his leg to a more comfortable angle. "Why do you ask?"

Cassidy's gaze was piercing. "Because," said the math teacher, "earlier today, I think Alec Whitnine deliberately tried to kill me."

"What?" Jake's head shook in disbelief. "Alec's a little squirt of a freshman, Harv. You must weigh close to two hundred pounds. He couldn't take you on with anything less than a cannon. And besides, what do you mean you 'think' he tried to kill you? Don't you know?"

Cassidy held up a hand. "Let me tell you what happened. It was seventh period. I'd covered the lesson faster than usual, so I gave the class the last ten minutes to begin their homework. And since the weather's been so hot lately, I had all the windows up as far as they'd go."

"But what's the weather got to do with . . ."

"My room's back in the new wing of the building, remember? The windows there come down to within a couple of feet of the floor. You know how the administration's always warning us to be careful around them. Anyway, the kids were working on their own like a bunch of Einsteins, so I leaned out the window to get a breath of air. My back was to the class, but I didn't figure there'd be any trouble. I heard one or two of 'em walking around the room, but that was all right—they're allowed to get paper or go to the pencil sharpener any time they like."

"Harv, will you get to the point of this cockamamie story?"

"I don't know what it was that made me turn around. But when I did, there was Alec, holding the window pole up over his shoulder like it was a spear. He let it fly just as I turned. The thing missed me by a couple of inches and went right out through the open window. Made an awful clatter when it hit the sidewalk below."

"Look, my students play with the window pole in here too. Either they're Little John fighting Robin Hood or Knights of the Round Table at a jousting tournament."

Cassidy slapped his fist angrily against the top of the wooden desk. "Dammit, this wasn't done in fun! I was kind of off balance leaning out that window, and it's two stories down to the sidewalk. If I hadn't turned at just that moment they'd have been scraping me up with a putty knife!"

"Take it easy, Harv," said Jake soothingly. "All right, Alec was out of line. But he didn't mean any harm. Probably the whole thing scared him a lot more than it did you."

Cassidy shook his head. "With ten years in this business, I figure I can read human reactions as well as the next guy. He wasn't scared. He acted more like he was . . . was . . ."

"Was what?"

"Disappointed," said Cassidy softly.

There was a silence in the room, and the clock clicked off another minute. "Oh, come on," said Jake. "What reason would Alec have to do a thing like that?"

"He got a fifty on a class quiz the other day. First failing mark for him in math all year."

Jake almost laughed out loud. "Now are you going to be scared of any kid you have to fail?"

"I tell you, Alec is—well—different. He's had it in for me since he got the paper back."

"What makes you think so?"

"It's nothing you can put your finger on. Just something I can sense. The way he looks at me. You know how it is. The wise-guy way he phrases his questions. And I'm not the only one who thinks Alec Whitnine is creepy."

"Who else?"

"Manny Shelberg. He's coaching freshman baseball this year. Last week was tryouts, and Alec got cut from the squad. That day, after the practice was over, the kid came into the exercise room to ask Manny to reconsider. Manny was down on the floor looking for one of his contact lenses that had fallen out, and he told Alec to beat it. Five minutes later one of the barbells rolled off its rack when Manny was right beneath it. The way he tells it, if he hadn't done a fast somersault, the thing would have come down on his spine. Have you got any idea how much damage a two-hundred-pound weight falling three feet can do, Jake?"

Jake shrugged. "An accident."

"But there's no way the barbell could have jumped out of the grooves in the rack. Unless it was helped. And Manny remembers he never heard Alec leave the locker room. He could have slipped up on the other side of those racks and . . ."

"And maybe Manny hit the rack with his shoulders while he was crawling around. Maybe a hundred other things. Come on, Harv, you're being silly. You say Alec's got it in for you because of a failing paper. Mabel Fuchs had to flunk him on a few tests, and the two of 'em still get along like a couple of mice in a corn crib. If he's the monster you seem to think, why hasn't he tried anything with her?"

"I don't know, Jake. But from now on I'm going to be on my guard. And I suggest you do the same. That kid'll kill somebody yet. And he'll take the greatest of pleasure in doing it."

Four days later, Alec Whitnine failed his first quiz in Mr. Landis's history class.

At the dismissal bell, Alec chose to remain for what Jake liked to call the inquest. Alec stood before the teacher's desk, a small figure with a vestigial layer of baby fat that made his body resemble an overripe peach. Unlike most of the boys, who wore their hair at collar length and elaborately styled, Alec's was cropped in a short, military manner, one step away from a completely shaved head.

"Mr. Landis," said the boy, "I should have gotten more than a sixty-one on my essay."

Just like that, thought Jake. Shape up, Mr. Landis, and give me the mark I feel I deserve.

"Alec," he began, "you did a fine job on your analysis of the Stamp Act, but the question did say to discuss three causes of the American Revolution. You completely left out the other two."

"I thought, Mr. Landis, that an in-depth discussion of a single cause would be more to your liking." The boy's voice dripped syrupy sarcasm.

"Well, you thought wrong. The question was quite clear."

"Another four points would be sufficient," said the boy. "Simply a passing mark."

It wasn't a request; it was a command. Jake hadn't been talked to that way since boot camp. "You'd better leave, Alec," he said firmly.

Alec merely hunched his shoulders and stared at the floor.

"Look, young fella," the teacher went on. "In about thirty seconds a class of students will be coming through that door. And unless you're out of here by then, they're going to meet you flying low in the opposite direction off the toe of my shoe. Clear?" Jake grinned to make a joke of the threat.

The expression on Alec's face changed, and Jake felt as if he'd been drenched with a pail of ice water. The concentrated malevolence in the young eyes was something all his years of teaching hadn't prepared him for. The boy's twisted features were fanatic—almost inhuman. In the face of this naked hatred, sweat began trickling down Jake's neck, and suddenly Cassidy's story about Alec's attempt to kill him seemed all too possible.

Without a word, Alec pivoted and stalked out of the room.

Jake got through the rest of the day, both ashamed and afraid of the thoughts going through his brain. Alec had to be like all the other students, probably angrier at himself for failing than at the teacher, and yet the awful menace of that single moment before the boy had left made Jake's skin crawl every time he thought about it.

The dismissal bell finally rang, and five minutes later Jake was at work on his homework corrections. He worked his way through the papers in record time and was halfway finished with the last one when he heard the sound out in the hall.

A door opening.

It couldn't be a custodian. Cal Stettner had finished cleaning this section of the building more than an hour ago.

"Hello!" Jake called.

No answer.

Jake hauled himself to his feet, gripped the cane, and hobbled out into the hall. It was empty. He peered around the corner.

The hydraulic device on the door to the boys' lavatory was slowly pulling it closed.

Jake walked into the lavatory, his shoes making shuffling noises on the white tile floor. Nothing. Whoever it was must have been leaving when the teacher had heard him. And it was clear that the unknown person didn't want to be discovered.

As Jake went out into the hall again, the silence was an almost solid thing, broken only by the gentle hissing of air as the lavatory door closed.

And then something else.

A soft, guarded sound of steps on the stairwell beyond Jake's room. He lurched to the top step.

"Who's there?" he called. "Come on, speak up. You know students aren't allowed to walk around the building after school." He looked downward, wishing he could see beyond the landing.

From the floor below came a single low whistle that lasted less than a second.

"Games, huh?" Jake snorted. "O.K., let's find out who in blazes you are."

Bracing himself with the cane, he set his left foot slowly and laboriously down onto the first step and gripped the railing tightly as he brought his right foot down beside it. That's one, he thought. Only twenty-three more to go. He'd never catch the kid, of course, but with a little perseverance, maybe he could chase whoever it was out of the building.

Two steps.

Three.

And then, on the fourth step, as he leaned forward to shift his weight to the cane, its tip squirted off the flat surface as if the rubber tip had grown wheels. Overbalanced, Jake instinctively thrust out his injured leg, but it skidded and slid as if the stairs had turned to ice.

He was falling! He crashed down on one hip, and pain streaked along his side. He gripped at the steps, but all friction between his hands and the terrazzo surface seemed to have vanished. As he rolled over and over, trying to protect his face with his arms, he was aware of a strange odor, musky and somewhat sweet.

Then he tumbled heavily to the landing, banging the side of his head against the radiator.

For a moment he was dazed, and flashes of bright light danced before his eyes. Then, ignoring his pounding head and ringing ears, he gingerly moved first his arms and then his good leg. Finally, the stiff leg, which ached dully but seemed to be in reasonably good condition.

A series of jerky movements brought him to his feet, and he looked upward at the dozen steps down which he had fallen. Lucky, he thought to himself. A broken arm or leg was a distinct possibility from a fall like that, a snapped neck or spine not completely out of the question. What could have caused . . .

He rubbed the thumb and forefinger of his left hand together, feeling a slimy something against his fingertips. Then he brought the hand to his nose and sniffed.

Soap!

Both his palms were covered with the slippery liquid soap used in the school lavatories. One shoe also had traces of the stuff, as did the tip of his cane. Wiping it off with a handkerchief, Jake torturously made his way back up the stairs until he reached the fourth from the top.

The surface of the step had been liberally coated with the soap.

The noises outside his room had been deliberate. He'd been lured into the hall by someone who was bent on killing him.

Someone?

Alec Whitnine?

At home that evening, soaking his aches in a steaming tub, Jake pondered the problem of how to handle the situation with Alec. Tell someone? But who? He remembered how he'd scoffed at Harv Cassidy's story just last week. No, he couldn't mention it to anyone at school.

The police? They'd want proof, and he had no proof. Just a step with soap on it, which could be looked on as accidental, and the expression on a boy's face. But how, Mr. Landis, do you go about getting a facial expression into police records?

And yet a potential murder victim couldn't be expected to wait idly by to give his prospective killer a second chance.

The following day, Jake used his free period to look up Alec Whitnine's record in the guidance office. Not much there. Alec's mother had been dead for ten years, and Alec lived with his father on Derby Avenue. The old man had to be loaded to afford a house in that section. Alec's grade school had been Chindale Park, the newest and best in the whole district. Average marks through the first six years, with only a few D's and F's.

Seventh grade had been a different matter. The low marks became more numerous, with three F's in English alone. Jake smiled. It took more than a cute smile and a polite manner to impress old Sadie Treska. The absentee card for that year showed a total of twenty-five days Alec had been absent.

The teacher thumbed back through the earlier cards. Strange. In all his first six years put together, Alec had only been absent seventeen days. And it couldn't have been a major illness or an accident. The days were too widely spaced for that.

Eighth grade showed much the same pattern. Lower marks and increased absences. But the teacher, Bob Hausermann, had added some comments of his own.

10/17—"Alec's a loner. Quiet. Perhaps too quiet for his own good."

1/29—"Usually a peaceful boy. But sometimes becomes belligerent with classmates at little or no provocation."

2/27—"Moody and unapproachable since midyear marks."

The final comment, dated 4/15, had been heavily crossed out. Jake peered closely at the network of lines on the back of the report card. The first letter was, he thought, a T.

Finally he was able to make out more letters. "To—y Ale- tri— -o . . ."

And then Jake had it.

"Today Alec tried to . . ." There was no more. And Bob Hausermann had done his best to see that no one would read the message.

Jake ducked into an unused guidance office. He picked up the telephone on the desk and dialed the extension for the Chindale Park School. He asked to speak to Mr. Hausermann and listened to a three-minute lecture from the secretary about phoning a teacher during classes. Jake was finally able to convince her of the importance of the call, and she grudgingly got the eighth grade teacher on the line.

"Hi, Jake! Say, I haven't seen much of you this year. Why don't we . . ."

"Listen, Bob, I've got no time for the niceties. Give me a fast rundown on Alec Whitnine, a kid you had last year. I've been reviewing his record. I'm particularly interested in your last comment—the one you crossed out. Do you remember it?"

A long silence. Then: "Yeah, Jake. I remember it. But now that the records are open to the parents, I'm not sure I want to get my head handed to me by . . ."

"Bob, this is me—Jake. Nothing you tell me will go any further. That's a promise. Now give."

"The kid's got problems, Jake. The father's a big bull of a man. Expects his kid to produce just the way all those companies he owns are supposed to. I can't prove it, but I think that during the last year or so he attended here, Alec got slapped around when he brought home low marks. Any time he had a bad time with a test, he'd be out the next day or two. And when he came back, there were the bruises. I saw them."

"Well, that's a start on what I need. But about the report card and your comment . . ."

"Jake, I'll call you a liar if you tell another soul. But I'm sure Alec Whitnine tried to kill me. Don't laugh. It's true."

"I'm not laughing, Bob. How'd it happen?"

"We were getting an assembly program ready. Alec had a lead part. Y'know, that kid's really something. He can mimic anybody. I caught him in front of the class one day doing me, and I couldn't get mad because he was really good."

"What's that got to do with . . ."

"I'm getting to that. Three days before the show, I caught Alec cheating on a grammar test. I took the part away from him. The next day he was absent. I guess you can figure out why."

"His father again?"

"Sure. Anyway, the day he came back I had a practice after school. Naturally Alec wasn't included. I was on the stage, talking to the cast. I finished what I was saying and moved to the front of the stage to hop down to the floor. Just when I moved, a curtain counterweight fell and caved in two boards right where I'd been standing. Later on, when I'd gotten myself and the kids calmed down, I looked at the rope on the weight. It'd been cut. And a janitor told me he thought he'd seen Alec sneaking around in the loft above the stage. Naturally he denied it. There wasn't any real action I could take, but I did start to put a note on his report card. Then I got to thinking of what the legal consequences might be, and I thought better of it."

Slowly Jake settled the telephone receiver onto its cradle, his mind spinning from what he'd just heard. Bob Hausermann . . . Manny Shelberg . . . Harv Cassidy . . . and now his own "accident" on the stairs. Alec Whitnine, it seemed, was prepared to kill whenever the prospect of failure arose.

No, that wasn't really true. His science teacher, Mabel Fuchs, hadn't had any trouble. And Sadie Treska, back in seventh grade, had noticed nothing unusual.

And then Jake understood the pattern.

Until Bob Hausermann in eighth grade, Alec had had only women teachers. And there'd been no trouble. Even now, the boy couldn't consider women among his victims.

But men! When men attacked Alec's image of himself and caused dire consequences at home, the attack had to be repulsed. In the surest and most permanent way possible.

Murder.

Jake wondered whether Alec looked upon all men as surrogate fathers who were there only to punish him unfairly. Or perhaps there was something in his twisted code of honor that made women immune from retaliation, regardless of the provocation. Whatever the case, it was clear that Alec was carrying on his own private little war against any male teacher who implied that he wasn't measuring up to some nebulous standard the boy had set for himself.

But it was done so cleverly that only those attacked even knew that the war existed. And they couldn't do anything about it.

The bell rang for the beginning of the next period.

That evening, Jake deliberately waited until seven o'clock to telephone the Whitnine house. He wanted to be sure to talk to Mr. Whitnine, and he decided that if Alec answered he'd hang up and try again.

"Sam Whitnine here." The voice sounded as if it was coming from inside a bass drum. "Who's calling?"

"My name's Landis," Jake began.

"Landis? Oh, yes. Alec's teacher. What can I do for you, Mr. Landis?"

In for a penny, in for a pound, thought Jake. Taking a deep breath, he poured out the whole story. Events, comments, suspicions. All he left out were the names of the other teachers involved. "So I think your boy's in trouble," he concluded, "and frankly, Mr. Whitnine, I don't know how to handle it."

He leaned back in his chair and waited for the blast. You don't tell a parent point-blank that his child has homicidal tendencies and expect to escape unscarred. What, he wondered, would he be threatened with first? Dismissal? A lawsuit?

"Mr. Landis," said the deep voice, "I must say you make a mighty convincing case. Matter of fact, I've been noticing some things about Alec I'm not too happy about either. I wonder if you'd do me the favor of dropping by sometime so we can discuss what's to be done?"

Jake stared at the phone in disbelief.

"Would tonight be O.K.?" he asked.

"Fine. Alec's out to a movie or something. In about an hour, say?"

The Whitnine house was a colonial with a fieldstone facade, and it looked big enough to park the Hindenberg zeppelin. Jake limped up the brick steps and rang the bell. A little metal box beside the door showed a red light, and Mr. Whitnine's voice came from it.

"That you, Landis?"

"It's me, Mr. Whitnine."

"The door's unlocked. Come on in. I'm in my study, just to the right beyond the living room."

Jake opened the door and stepped inside. The living room, about the size of a basketball court, was done in pseudo-Japanese with low chairs and tables, bamboolike wallpaper, an exotic chandelier right out of Fu Manchu, and even a samurai sword hung in its sheath on the far wall.

Jake looked about. There were two tiny lights on, but they didn't begin to dispel the shadows. Then, at the far end of the room, he noticed a brighter glow.

He made his way across a rug deep enough to drown in and finally reached the open door to Mr. Whitnine's study. It was a Civil War buff's dream, filled with relics that ranged from cap-and-ball pistols to canteens and Confederate flags. And in the center, at a flat desk that Lincoln himself might well have used, sat Samuel Whitnine.

His lined face seemed sculpted from marble, and the set of his mouth indicated that here was a man who stood for no nonsense. His arms were outstretched on the desk, and his hands were pressed flat against its surface. In spite of the warmth of the evening he wore a wool robe of brilliant colors whch seemed to accentuate the man's aggressiveness.

Jake stepped into the room. He coughed gently, preparing to speak.

But then the cane slipped from shaking fingers, and he struggled to retain mental control over himself. His mind refused to accept what his eyes told him had to be true:

The teacup on the corner of the desk, with no liquid in it but only a thick layer of white powder at its bottom.

The man's staring eyes and uncanny lack of movement.

The thin layer of dust on his sleeves and the backs of his hands.

And finally—horribly—the single strand of spider web that extended from one corner of his half-open mouth down to the edge of the desk.

Alec Whitnine's private little war had claimed its first and most logical victim.

"Welcome to my house, Mr. Landis." The booming voice behind him was the same one the teacher had heard on the telephone an hour earlier.

"*That kid's really something,*" Bob Hausermann had told him. "*He can mimic anybody.*"

There was a metallic slithering sound as the samurai sword was removed from its sheath.

And Jake Landis, helpless without the cane now lying on the floor, bowed his head and waited for Alec Whitnine to claim his second victory.

JOHN LUTZ

Have You Ever Seen This Woman?

David Hastings awoke slowly, painfully, not really wanting to lose the oblivion of sleep. As he opened his eyes to slits he raised a hand gingerly to his throbbing head and touched his fingertips to just below his hairline. His hand came away with blood on it, and his eyes opened all the way.

He was in the bedroom, he realized, lying on his back on the made bed. Every beat of his heart echoed with pain in his head. It was morning, judging by the softly angled rays of light filtering through the curtains, the bark of a faraway dog, the distant clanging of a trash can. Hastings' mind was blank to everything but an unexplainable dread, a terrible fact just beyond consciousness that he knew he would soon have to face.

With great effort Hastings raised himself and supported his upper body on the bed with his elbows. Summoning even more strength, he twisted and sat on the edge of the mattress, noticing that his white shirtfront was covered with scarlet-brown splotches. He saw, too, that there were several stains on his wrinkled checked sport coat and his tie. Hastings stood, took a few heavy steps, and leaned on his dresser to look at himself in the mirror.

Vacant, frightened eyes stared out of a face stained with blood from a long deep gash high on his forehead. There was another deep cut on his left cheekbone. Quickly, Hastings turned away from the mirror. He was hot, his body suddenly burning. He peeled off his coat and tie and hung them in the closet, then he unbuttoned the top two buttons on his shirt.

The door to the living room was half open. For a reason he couldn't fathom Hastings knew he didn't want to go through that door, but he also knew he must. He began moving toward the door with uneven groping steps, realizing for the first time that he was wearing only one shoe. As he pushed the door all the way open and stepped into the living room he shuddered, his disbelieving eyes narrowed.

There were slivers of clear glass scattered over the dark green carpet, as if a crystal bomb had exploded in the room. Hastings' left shoe was lying on its side, still tied, near the armchair. On the other side of the room, where the shattered pieces of crystal were the heaviest, the carpet was soaked by a huge reddish stain. And in the center of that stain, near the television with its wildly rolling and distorted silent picture, lay the still, the unbelievably still body of Agnes.

In horrible fascination Hastings extended his outstretched hands before him, as if pushing something away, and stepped slowly over and gazed down at his dead wife.

Agnes' nightgown was torn and wrapped about her neck and shoulders. Her face, framed in a tangle of auburn hair, was completely crusted with dried blood, and the head had been unmercifully battered, unmercifully and brutally mutilated.

Hastings' breathing was abnormally loud, like steam hissing in the small room. He began backing away from the body, cutting his stockinged foot on a piece of broken crystal. Then he slumped down and sat on the floor, his back against the wall. His mind was a revolving, horror-filled maze, a jumble of terrible puzzle pieces that would not fit together no matter how they were turned. With dazed eyes he looked slowly about the living room, and he knew then where the shattered crystal had come from.

The swan. The glass swan that Agnes' mother had sent them from Mexico last summer. Probably it was a typical tourist item, but Agnes had liked it and placed it on the bookcase in the living room. Hastings had also rather liked the swan. It seemed to be made of a very delicate clear crystal that had a prismlike effect so the shapes and colors reflected within the rounded body and long graceful neck were dismembered and twisted to fit the graceful lines of the sculpting. And now it had been used . . . for this.

Hastings closed his eyes and rested the back of his head against the living room wall, and with a pain that was both physical and mental he began trying to recreate in his mind the horror of last night.

He remembered parking his car in front of his small brick home on Lime Avenue, he remembered that clearly enough. He had worked late at the office and hadn't left until almost nine o'clock.

The house was lighted, the glow of the living room swag-lamp shining through the drawn drapes. Hastings walked up the winding cement path onto the porch and turned the doorknob. But the front door was locked. That hadn't seemed normal to Hastings. Agnes seldom locked doors of any kind. He drew his house key from his pocket, unlocked the front door and entered the house.

Here Hastings bowed his head and rested it painfully on his drawn-up knees. He didn't want to remember the rest—his mind recoiled from it. But he made himself fit the pieces together.

Agnes had been at the opposite end of the living room, near the turned-on television set, and she was struggling with a man, a tall man dressed in dark clothes, a man who had his gloved hand pressed to Agnes' mouth.

What had the man looked like? His features were blurred—as if he had a nylon stocking pulled down over his face.

The man saw Hastings and was motionless for a second, then he felled Agnes with a chopping blow across the back of her neck and came at Hastings.

The man was bigger than Hastings, and stronger, so the struggle didn't last long. Hastings remembered being shoved back toward the bedroom door, remembered seeing the man's gloved fingers curl around the natural handle of the crystal swan's neck. And then the swan smashed into his head. The man pushed him violently against the closed bedroom door, breaking the latch and springing it open as Hastings staggered back into the bedroom. Again the swan smashed into his head, and Hastings fell backward across the bed. He remembered feeling the welcome softness of the mattress before losing consciousness.

Hastings raised his head from his knees and looked at the bedroom doorframe, at the splintered wood near the latch. Then he looked again, for just a second, at the still body of his wife.

After knocking him unconscious, Hastings thought, the man must have gone back into the living room and continued his attack on Agnes. Somehow Hastings knew that the object was rape from the beginning. Agnes must have regained consciousness, must have begun to fight or scream, or attempted to run, and the man with the stockinged face must have used the swan to beat her to the silence and submissiveness of death.

Slowly Hastings raised himself to his feet and stood unsteadily, leaning against the wall. Then he made his way into the bathroom and splashed cold water on his face. For a long time he stood slumped over the washbasin, watching the red tinted water swirl counterclockwise down the drain. When he was finally ready, he went back into the bedroom and picked up the phone.

The police converged on Hastings' house in great numbers, photographing, dusting for fingerprints, examining, discussing. And then Agnes was taken away by two men in white uniforms, and Hastings was left with a Lieutenant Sam Newell, a crewcut heavy-browed man who had been personally assigned to the case. Hastings' neighbor and good friend Philip Barrett also remained in the house after all the other policemen but Newell had departed. The three men sat in the living room drinking coffee that Barrett had been thoughtful enough to brew.

Agnes' murder had occurred in Plainton, the community in which they lived, a scant few miles from the city, and while the larger and more efficient Metropolitan Police Department would give some assistance, solving the crime was the responsibility only of the Plainton Police Department, for everything had happened within their jurisdiction. A murder investigation was not the sort of task Lieutenant Newell undertook very often.

"How old was Agnes, Mr. Hastings?" he asked, flipping the leather cover of his notebook.

"Thirty-six, the same as me," Hastings replied, watching Newell make quick jabbing motions at his notepaper with a short pencil.

"And did she have any enemies that you knew of?"

"Agnes was well liked by everyone," Phil Barrett said in a sad voice. "It's impossible to believe this has happened."

Lieutenant Newell glared at him over the rim of his coffee cup. "If you don't mind, Mr. Barrett, we'll get to your statement in the course of the investigation."

Barrett said nothing, raising his own steaming coffee cup to his lips as if he hadn't heard the lieutenant.

"Phil's right," Hastings said. "Agnes didn't have any enemies that I knew of."

"Somebody didn't like her," Newell said. "That swan was shattered into such small pieces we couldn't fit it together." He made a short notation in his book. "Understand now, Mr. Hastings, this next question is simply part of the routine. Did your wife Agnes have any . . . extramarital affairs? Had you heard any rumors of her running around?"

Hastings couldn't keep the agitation out of his voice. "We were happily married, Lieutenant."

"You know what they say about who's the last to know," Newell said. He glanced at Phil Barrett.

"Agnes wasn't the type to go out on her husband," Barrett said.

"What kind of activities was she interested in?" Newell asked.

"As I told you," Hastings said, "we never had any children. Agnes contented herself pretty much with staying home, watching TV, and she worked hard keeping the house neat." He looked around at the blood-stained disarray of the living room and put his head down.

Lieutenant Newell flipped his leather notebook shut and stood slowly, betraying what he was, a policeman with sore feet. "In all honesty there's not much here to work with. The description of the man you struggled with—tall, average weight, dark clothes, stocking mask—it's a phantom. We'll be in touch with you, Mr. Hastings, and I'll let you know about the coroner's report on your wife." He nodded. "I'm sorry," he said and left.

"Don't pay too much attention to his questions, Dave," Phil Barrett told Hastings when they were alone. "They're routine."

"I don't mind the questions," Hastings said, "if they'll help catch Agnes' killer."

Barrett stood and drained the last of his coffee. "Why don't you go in and get some rest?" he said. "I'll clean this place up—the police said it'd be O.K."

Hastings nodded, feeling suddenly as tired as he'd ever felt. "That's nice of you, Phil."

Barrett shrugged. "Listen," he said in a concerned voice, "if you'd rather spend tonight at our place, Myra and I would be glad to have you . . . ."

"Thanks anyway," Hastings said, "but with a shower and some sleep I think I can face things here." He rose to go to the bedroom, and the hurt and anger seemed to rise with him. "Dammit, Phil! Why would anybody want to kill Agnes? Why did this maniac have to choose her for a victim?"

"Who knows?" Barrett said in a sympathetic voice. "He might have just seen her somewhere and followed her to find out where she lived. I guess the husband of any victim would be asking himself the same questions you are."

"I guess so," Hastings said wearily. He touched the bandage on his forehead over the wound that the police surgeon had stitched, as if to assure himself of its reality, and, sidestepping the broken glass, he walked from the living room.

The next afternoon Lieutenant Newell telephoned Hastings to inform him of the coroner's report. Agnes had been sexually molested. Newell then asked Hastings about any men who had expressed interest in Agnes, any rejected suitors. But Hastings could think of no one. He and Agnes had been married fourteen years. The murderer might have been a psycho, Newell speculated, a maniac who had chosen Agnes by chance out of millions without even knowing her name and struck her as lightning might strike. He assured Hastings that the police would keep working on the case and hung up . . .

A week passed, and as far as Hastings was concerned the Plainton Police Department wasn't working hard enough. They had come up with nothing.

The desire to see Agnes' killer apprehended had grown in Hastings, causing him agonizing days and sleepless nights. And the feeling persisted that there was something he should know, something that skirted the outer edges of his mind and that, try as he may, he could never grasp.

Hastings began to telephone Lieutenant Newell regularly, asking him about progress on the case, about what the Plainton Police Department was doing to bring about progress. But there was never any news. He always got a polite brush-off. He came to realize that the Plainton Police Department had finished digging, that they would never apprehend Agnes' killer.

It was then Hastings decided to take action himself. Lying awake nights he worked out a general plan of investigation. The first thing he did was to go next door and talk to his neighbor, Phil Barrett. Here Hastings possessed an advantage over the police, for he knew that Barrett would talk to him confidentially and with complete honesty.

Barrett was in his long narrow back yard, spraying his rose bushes. As Hastings approached him he stooped to spread the aerosol mist on the bottom side of some perforated leaves and smiled up at Hastings.

"Morning, Dave."

Hastings stood, watching some of the spray drift up and past him.

"Haven't seen you," Barrett said. "How are you getting along?"

Hastings smiled and shrugged.

Barrett straightened and wiped his hands on the paint-stained trousers he was wearing. "Have the police found out anything?"

"No," Hastings said, "and it looks now like they won't. That's what I wanted to talk to you about, Phil. I need some honest answers to some questions."

Barrett looked at him with a vague puzzled frown. "I wouldn't lie to you, Dave."

"Not unless you thought you were doing me a favor," Hastings said. "I want to know about Agnes."

Barrett grinned and shook his head. "She was your wife. You know more about her than I do."

"But you might have heard some things. Things a woman's husband wouldn't hear." The breeze mussed Hastings' combed brown hair, causing a lock to fall over the red scar on his forehead. "Did you hear anything, Phil?"

The aerosol can hissed as Barrett loosed some spray in the general direction of one of his rose bushes, then he stood staring at the ground. "I heard a few things, Dave. They didn't mean anything, they were none of my business."

"They're my business now," Hastings said quietly.

Barrett continued to stare at the newly mowed grass for a while before speaking. "I heard she'd been seen a few places around town," he said, "restaurants, taverns, places like that. That's all I heard . . ."

"Seen with men?" Hastings asked, holding back the sudden flow of anger and disbelief that he should have expected.

"Yes, Dave." Barrett raised his head to look Hastings in the eye. "With men, different men, but like I said all I ever heard was second or third hand. It could be that none of it was true, just the kind of loose talk that sometimes follows an attractive woman."

"Did you believe what you heard?" Hastings asked.

Barrett looked at him with an agonized expression as he squinted into the sun. "That's not a fair question, Dave. I didn't know whether to believe the stories or not. You know how Agnes was—she just didn't seem the type."

No, Hastings thought, by all outward appearances Agnes wasn't the type. Auburn-haired, dark-eyed Agnes, slender, pretty in her plain dress or modest slacks, smiling as she worked about the house . . .

"I'm sorry, Dave."

Hastings felt sick. Lately someone was always sorry for him. He nodded to Barrett, said his thanks and walked back to his empty house.

The bottle of bourbon he'd bought a month ago was in the kitchen cupboard above the sink, still over half full. He got it down, sat at the table and poured himself a drink. He couldn't imagine Agnes having affairs with other men. That was another side of her that he couldn't believe existed. But there had been stories, rumors that had never reached his ears. It could be that they were false, and yet who knew what happened on the dark side of a person's mind?

Hastings stood and replaced the bottle in the cupboard, setting the empty glass in the sink. Then he went into the living room and began to rummage through the desk drawers for a clear and recent photograph of Agnes. Finally he settled on one, a color snapshot of his dead wife wearing a pink blouse, staring out of the photo directly at the camera with a tender and somewhat embarrassed smile.

As Hastings slipped the photo into his wallet he found its exact duplicate, another print, behind his identification card. He slid the second photo in the cellophane pocket on top of the first.

That evening he began. He shaved for the first time that day, put on a suit, and drove toward town.

The first place he stopped was on the outskirts of the city, a lounge and restaurant named Tony's. He went to the bar and showed the bartender Agnes' photograph.

"Do you recognize her?" Hastings asked. "Have you ever seen this woman in the past few months?"

"You the police?" the bartender asked.

"No," Hastings said, "I'm her husband."

The bartender looked at Hastings, then squinted at the photograph. He shook his head. He hadn't seen her, he told Hastings. At least if he had he couldn't recall. There were a lot of women who came in here with men. There were a lot who came in alone and left with men. It was impossible to remember them all.

Hastings thanked the bartender, bought him a beer and left.

He drove to three more places, and none of the people there remembered Agnes. Though at a place called The Lion's Mane a red-vested bartender had stared at Hastings in a peculiar fashion as if he were about to say something, then a customer had called him away.

Hastings' last stop was at The Purple Bottle on Wilton Avenue. The bartender was a round-faced man with a mustache who reminded Hastings of somebody. He approached Hastings and smiled at him.

"Bourbon and water," Hastings said. He was sitting toward the end of the long bar, away from the other customers, and when the bartender returned with his drink he opened his wallet and showed him the photograph.

"Do you recognize her?" he asked. "Do you remember ever seeing her in here?"

The round-faced bartender set the glass on a coaster and stared down at the snapshot.

"She's pretty," he said, "but I don't ever remember her coming in here. Of course, I could have forgotten." He turned and beckoned to a younger bartender who was working at the other end of the bar, a slender young man with long black hair.

"Billy," he asked the young bartender, "have you ever seen this woman?"

Billy stared at the photograph curiously, then looked at Hastings.

"No," he said, "but I think I remember the picture."

Hastings' hand began to tremble as he raised his glass to his lips.

"Sure," Billy said, "somebody came in here—must have been about a month ago—showed me a photograph and asked me if I'd seen the girl."

"Are you positive?" Hastings asked.

"I don't know. I seen her picture before somewhere."

"Could it have been the newspapers?" Hastings asked.

Billy's lean face brightened. "Maybe. Maybe the paper. Why? She do something?

"No," Hastings said, "nothing."

The round-faced bartender's eyes moved to convey a look to his companion, and the younger bartender moved away toward the other end of the bar.

Hastings left without finishing his drink and drove home.

He shut his front door behind him and stood leaning against it, breathing as if he'd been running hard. The nerve of that young punk, saying he'd seen Agnes' picture before! The nerve of him!

Hastings wiped his forehead, got undressed and took a shower. Wearing pajamas and a bathrobe, he walked into the kitchen to prepare something to eat. He couldn't get the young bartender's words out of his mind, the sincere expression in the eyes.

There was nothing in the refrigerator, only frozen food that would have to thaw, and Hastings was hungry. He decided to get dressed and go out someplace to eat, someplace that stayed open late. He would treat himself to a steak dinner and forget about the rest of the evening. Slamming the refrigerator door shut, he turned and walked into the bedroom.

He dressed in dark slacks and a white shirt, then walked to the closet and absently pulled out his checked sport coat, not realizing until after he'd put it on that it was the one he'd worn the night of the murder. It was still wrinkled and blood-spattered. Unconsciously he slipped his hand into the right side pocket, and his body stiffened as if a thrown switch had sent electricity through him.

Hastings withdrew his hand from the pocket, staring at it as if it belonged to someone else. Clutched firmly in his grip was the graceful head and jaggedly broken neck of the glass swan.

He stood staring at the crystal head, felt the heft of the smooth glass in his hand. He remembered now. *He had to remember!* He had been in that tavern before, asking the young bartender about Agnes. Lately she had been cold to him, and Hastings had heard the rumors about her and had simply wanted to check. And no one had recognized the photograph—in the half dozen likely places he'd gone to that night no one had recognized the photograph.

Still, that hadn't been enough for Hastings. He had gone home at nine that evening after his inquiries at the various night spots, and he had tried to force her to make love. Agnes had refused his advances and he had confronted her with the ugly rumors he had been unable to substantiate. She had said he was crazy, that they were only rumors and he could believe them if he liked. Then she had screamed that she no longer loved him, that she wanted a divorce. He had grabbed her then, and she had struggled. He could see her now as he pushed her toward the bedroom, her slender hand closing on the crystal swan neck.

Then she had struck him twice, brutally, on the head.

Hastings shuddered as he remembered his rage, as he remembered wresting the swan from Agnes and smashing it against her head until she was dead, walking her about the living room in a grotesque dance, striking her over and over until her face and head were a horrible bloody mass among glittering pieces of broken crystal.

And then . . .

He refused to remember what had happened then. He remembered only stumbling to the bedroom, kicking open the door, falling dizzily onto the mattress.

Hastings stood in trembling horror, staring down at what he'd pulled from his pocket. Then, as if a sudden soothing hand had passed over him, he stopped trembling.

He walked into the kitchen and laid the neck and head of the broken swan in the sink. Trancelike, he opened a drawer and brought out a metal meat-tenderizer mallet. Then rhythmically he brought the mallet down again and again, shattering what was left of the swan into tiny crystals that he washed down the drain in a swirl of water. After replacing the mallet in the drawer, he opened the cupboard above the sink and got down the bottle of bourbon. With a low and clumsy rhythm, he walked back into the bedroom.

He awoke slowly, painfully, not really wanting to lose the oblivion of sleep. It was morning, judging by the softly angled rays of light filtering through the curtains, the bark of a faraway dog, the distant clanging of a trash can. He struggled to a sitting position on the edge of the mattress, knocking the empty bottle onto the floor. Too much to drink last night, he told himself reproachfully, wondering why he had been so foolish. Looking down at his wrinkled and blood-stained sport coat, he remembered it was the one he'd been wearing the night of Agnes' murder.

Drawing a deep breath, he stood. He peeled off the sport coat and hung it in the closet, then he removed the rest of his clothes and stumbled into the bathroom to shower.

After a breakfast of eggs and toast, he picked up the telephone and called Lieutenant Newell to see if there was any news on Agnes' case. There was none, the lieutenant said in an officially sympathetic voice. He assured Hastings that the Plainton Police Department had done everything possible.

Hastings thanked him and hung up.

That evening he drove into the city and at random chose a neon-lighted tavern. Benny's was the name of the place. Hastings stared straight ahead as he walked across the parking lot, entered and sat at the bar. When the bartender came he ordered a beer and as his drink was set before him he withdrew his wallet and showed the bartender the picture of Agnes.

"Has she ever been in here?" he asked. "Have you ever seen this woman?"

BRIAN GARFIELD

Joe Cutter's Game

Myerson looked up from the desk. "Hello, Ross."

Ross shut the door. "Where's Joe?"

"Late. As usual."

As far as Ross remembered there'd been only one time when Joe Cutter had been late arriving in this office and that had been the result of a bomb scare that had grounded everything for three hours at Templehof. Myerson's acidulous remark had been a cheap shot. But then that was Myerson.

Myerson pretended to read a report in a manila file. The silence began to rag Ross' nerves. "What's the flap?"

"We'll wait for Joe." Myerson didn't look up from the file.

The room was stale with Myerson's illegal Havana smoke. It was a room that always unnerved Ross because Myerson's varied indeterminate functions were that of hatchet man. Any audience with him might turn out to be one's last: fall into disfavor with anyone on the Fourth Floor and one could have a can tied to one's tail at any time, Civil Service or no Civil Service; and as very junior staff Ross had no illusions about his right to tenure.

But Myerson didn't seem to be in a savage mood right now. The rudeness was all right—that was what passed for amiability with Myerson.

Finally Joe Cutter walked in, lean and dark with his actorish good looks and the cold eyes that concealed his spectacular shrewdness.

"You're late."

"O.K." Joe Cutter glanced at Ross and tossed his travel coat across a chair. No hat; Cutter seldom wore a hat.

Myerson folded the file shut. "That's all you've got to say to me?"

"Would you like a note from my mother explaining my tardiness?"

"Your sarcasms seldom amuse me, Joe."

"Then don't provoke them. We were in the holding pattern over Dulles International." Cutter sat down. "What's on?"

"We have a signal from Arbuckle." Myerson tapped the file with a fingertip.

"Where's Arbuckle?"

"East Africa. You really ought to try and keep up on the postings in your own department, Joe." Myerson lit a cigar, making a smug ritualistic show of it.

Cutter's amused glance bounced off Ross. Myerson, puffing smoke, said, "In Dar-es-Salaam."

Ross' impatience burst its confines. "What's the flap, then?"

"I do wish you'd learn not to repeat yourself, Ross. And it distresses me that you're the only drone in this department who doesn't realize that words like 'flap' became obsolete long ago."

Cutter said, "If you're through amusing yourself maybe you could answer Ross' question."

Myerson squinted through the smoke and after a moment evidently decided not to be affronted. "As you may know, affairs in Tanzania remain sensitive. The balance is precarious between our influence and that of the Chinese. It would require only a slight upheaval to tip the bal—"

"Can't you spare us the tiresome diplomatic summaries and get down to it?"

"Contain your childish eagerness, Joe."

"I assumed you hadn't summoned me all the way from Belgrade to chew the rag about Tanzanian politics."

Ross marveled that their sparring always seemed to produce satisfactory results in the end. Their antipathy wasn't an act—the mutual contempt was genuine enough.

Along the Fourth Floor they called Cutter "007"—he was one of the last of the adventurers, the ones who'd come into the game for excitement and challenge back in the days when you could still tell the good guys from the bad guys. Myerson naturally regarded him as a hopeless romantic, incurable sentimental-ist, obsolete relic.

And Cutter held Myerson in equal scorn: saw Myerson as a pale slug gone soft where he sat and soft where he did his thinking—clever enough of course but comfortable in his bureaucratic web. Cutter detested comfortable people.

On the surface they were equally cold but Ross knew the difference: Myer-son's coldness was genuine and Cutter's was not. The bitterness between them masked a mutual respect neither of them would admit on pain of torture. Myerson was without peer as a strategist and Cutter was equally brilliant as a tactician in the field and Myerson knew that or he wouldn't have kept assigning Joe Cutter to the toughest ones.

And me?

Leonard Ross is just along for the ride to hold everybody's coat.

But Ross didn't mind. He'd never have a better pair of teachers. And despite all Cutter's efforts to keep him at a rigid distance Ross liked him. If you knew you had Cutter at your back you never had to worry about what might be creeping up on you.

Myerson reopened the file. He selected a photograph and held it up on display. "Recognize the woman?"

To Ross it was only a badly focused black-and-white of a thin woman with attractive and vaguely Oriental features, age indeterminate. But Cutter said immediately, "Marie Lapautre."

"Indeed."

Ross leaned forward for a closer look. It was the first time he'd seen a likeness of the dragon lady, whose reputation in the shadow world was something like that of John Wesley Hardin in the days of the gunslingers.

"The signal from Arbuckle reports she's been seen in the lobby of the Kilimanjaro in Dar. Buying a picture postcard," Myerson added drily.

"Could be she's out for a good time," Cutter said. "Spending some of the blood money on travel like any other well-heeled tourist. She's never worked that part of the world, you know."

"Which is precisely why Peking might select her if they had a sensitive job to be done there."

"That's all you've got? Just the one sighting? No confirmation from Arbuckle, no evidence of a caper in progress?"

"Joe, if we wait for evidence it could arrive in a pine box. We'd prefer not to have that sort of confirmation." The cigar had grown a substantial ash and Myerson tapped it into the big glass tray. "The triumvirate in Dar is fairly balanced. The President—Nyerere—is a confirmed neutralist and an honest one. I'm explaining this for your benefit, Ross, since it's not your usual territory. Of Nyerere's two partners in leadership one leans toward the West and the other toward the Communists. The tension keeps things in equilibrium and it's produced good results over a span of years. We have every reason to wish that the status remain quo. That's both the official line and the under-the-counter reality."

Ross was perfectly well aware of all that but Myerson enjoyed exposition and it would have annoyed him to be interrupted by a junior. An annoyed Myerson was something Ross preferred not to have to deal with. Cutter could get away with insulting Myerson because Cutter knew he was not expendable.

"The Chinese are not as charitable as we are toward neutralists," Myerson went on. "Particularly in view of the Russian meddling in Angola. The Chinese have been discussing the idea of increasing their own influence in Africa. I have that confirmed in recent signals from Hong Kong station. Add to this background the presence of Marie Lapautre in Dar-es-Salaam and I believe we must face the likelihood of an explosive event. Possibly you can forecast the nature of it as well as I can?"

It was an obvious challenge and Ross was pleased to see Cutter rise to meet it without effort: "Assuming you're right, I'd guess Lapautre's job would be to assassinate one of the three leaders."

"Which one?"

"The one who leans toward the Communists."

Ross said, "What?"

Cutter said, "The assassination would look like an American plot."

Myerson, his head obscured in a gray cloud, said, "It would take no more than that to tilt the balance over toward the East."

"Deal and double deal," Cutter said under his breath.

Myerson said, "You two are booked on the afternoon flight by way of Zurich. The assignment is to prevent Lapautre from embarrassing us."

"All right." That was the sum of Cutter's response. He asked no questions; he turned toward the door.

Ross said, "Wait one. Why not warn the Tanzanians? Wouldn't that get us off the hook if anything did happen?"

"Hardly," Myerson said. "It would make it worse. Don't explain it to him, Joe—let him reason it out for himself. It should be a useful exercise for him. On your way now—you've hardly time to make your plane."

By the time they were belted into their seats he thought he had it worked out. "If we threw them a warning and then the assassination actually took place later, it would look like we'd done it ourselves and tried to alibi it in advance. Is that what Myerson meant?"

"Go to the head of the class." Cutter fed him the sliver of a smile. "Things are touchy—there's an excess of suspicion of *auslanders* over there—they're xenophobes, you can't tell them things for their own good. Our only option is to neutralize the dragon lady without anyone knowing about it."

"Can we pin down exactly what we mean by that word 'neutralize'?"

"I'll put it this way," Cutter said. "Have you ever killed a woman, Ross?"

"No. Nor a man for that matter."

"Neither have I. And I intend to keep it that way. I've got enough on my conscience."

"Then how can we possibly handle it? We can't just ask her to go away."

"Let's see how things size up first." Cutter tipped his head back against the paper antimacassar and closed his eyes.

It was obvious from Cutter's complacency that he had a scheme in mind. If he hadn't he'd have made more of a show of arrogant confidence.

The flight was interminable. They had to change planes in Zurich and from there it was another nine hours. Ross tried to sleep but he'd never been able to relax on airplanes. He spent the hours trying to predict Cutter's plan. How did you deal with an assassin who had never been known to botch an assignment?

He reviewed what he knew about Marie Lapautre—fact, rumor and legend garnered from various briefings and shop-talk along the corridors in Langley.

French father, Vietnamese mother. Born 1934 on a plantation west of Saigon. Served as a sniper in the Viet Minh forces at Dienbienphu. Ran with the Cong in the late 1960s with assignments ranging from commando infiltration to assassinations of village leaders and then South Vietnamese officials. Seconded to Peking in 1969 for specialized terrorist instruction. Detached from the Viet Cong, inducted into the Chinese Army and assigned to the Seventh Bureau—a rare honor. Seconded as training cadre to the Japanese Red Army. It was rumored Lapautre had planned the tactics for the bombings of Tel Aviv Airport. During the past few years Lapautre's name had come across Ross' desk at least five times in reports dealing with unsolved assassinations in Laos, Syria, Turkey, Libya and West Germany.

Marie Lapautre's weapon was the rifle. Four of the five unsolved assassinations had been effected with long-range fire from Kashkalnikov sniper rifles—the model known to be Lapautre's choice.

Lapautre was forty-two years old, five feet four, one hundred and five pounds, black hair and eyes, mottled burn scar on back of right hand. Spoke five languages including English. Ate red meat barely cooked when the choice was open. She lived between jobs in a seventeenth-century villa on the Italian Riviera—a home she had bought with funds reportedly acquired from hire-contract jobs as a free-lance. Three of the five suspected assassinations had been bounty jobs and the other two had been unpaid because she still held a commission in Peking's Seventh Bureau.

That was the sum of Ross' knowledge and it told him nothing except that Lapautre was a professional with a preference for the 7.62-mm. Kashkalnikov and the reputation for never missing a score. By implication it told him one other thing: if Lapautre became aware of the fact that two Americans were moving in to prevent her from completing her present assignment then she would not hesitate to kill them and she naturally would kill them with proficient dispatch.

He was having trouble keeping his eyes open by the time they checked into the New Africa Hotel. It had been built by the Germans when Tanganyika had been one of the Kaiser's colonies and it had been rebuilt by Africans to encourage business travel; it was comfortable enough and Cutter had picked it because it was within easy walking distance along the harborfront to the Kilimanjaro where Lapautre had been spotted. Also, unlike the Hiltonized Kilimanjaro, the New Africa emulated the middle-class businessmen's hotels of Europe and one didn't need to waste energy trying to look like a tourist.

The change in time zones was bewildering; it was the same time of afternoon in Dar as it had been at Dulles Airport when they'd boarded the 747 but to Ross it was the wee hours of the morning and he stumbled groggily when he went along with Cutter to the shabby export office that housed the front organization for Arbuckle's soporific East Africa station.

It wasn't as steamy as he'd anticipated. A fresh breeze came off the water and he had to concede he'd never seen a more beautiful harbor, ringed by palm-shaded beaches and colorful expensive houses on the slopes. Some of the older buildings bespoke a dusty Mexican sort of poverty but the city was more modern and energetic than anything he'd expected to find near the Equator on the shore of the Indian Ocean. There were jams of hooting traffic on the main boulevards; on the sidewalks business-suited pedestrians mingled with turbaned Arabs and dark-eyed Asians and black Africans in proud tribal costumes. Here and there a 4x4 lorry growled by with a squad of armed soldiers in it but they all seemed bound for some innocent destination and there was no police-state tension on the streets. There was a proliferation of cubbyhole curio shops selling African carvings and cloth but the main shop windows were well dressed out with sophisticated displays of Euorpean fashions. It occurred to Ross after they reached Arbuckle's office that he hadn't been accosted by a single beggar.

Arbuckle was a tall man, thin and bald and somewhat nervous; inescapably he was known in the Agency as Fatty. He had one item to add to the information Myerson had already provided: Lapautre was still in Dar.

"We've been keeping her under informal surveillance. She's in four-eleven at the Kilimanjaro but she takes most of her dinners in the dining room at the New Africa. They've got better steaks. Watch out you don't bump into her there. She knows your face, I suppose."

"She's probably seen dossiers on me," Cutter said. "I doubt she'd know Ross by sight."

Ross said, "Sometimes it pays to be unimportant."

"Hang on to that thought," Cutter told him. When they left the office he added, "You'd better go back to the room and catch up on your jet-lag."

"What about you?"

"Chores and snooping. Department of dirty tricks and all that. Catch you for breakfast—seven o'clock."

"You going to tell me what the program is?"

He saw Cutter wince. "I see no point discussing anything at all with you until you've had sixteen hours' sleep."

"Don't *you* ever sleep?"

"When I haven't got anything better to do."

Ross watched him walk away under the palms.

He came famished down to the second-floor dining room and found Cutter there nibbling on a mango. The breakfast layout was a fabulous array of fruits and juices and breads and coldcuts. He heaped a plate full and began to devour it unabashedly.

The room wasn't crowded but there was a sprinkling of businessmen from Europe and the Far East, African officials, tourist couples, a table of Englishmen who probably were engineers on hire to Tanzanian industries, a trio of overweight Americans in safari costumes that appeared to have been tailored in Hollywood. Cutter said mildly, "I picked the table at random," by which he meant that it probably wasn't bugged.

Ross said, "Then we're free to discuss sensitive state secrets."

"Do you have to talk in alliterative sibilants at this hour of the morning?" Cutter tasted his coffee and made a face. "You'd think they could make it better. After all, they grow the stuff here." He put the cup down. "All right. We've got to play her cagy and careful. If anything blows loose there won't be any cavalry to rescue us."

"Us?"

"Did you think you were here just to feed me straight lines, Ross? It's a two-man job. Actually it's a six-man job but the two of us have got to carry it."

"Wonderful. Should I start practicing my quick-draw?"

"If you'd stop asking droll questions we'd get along a little faster."

"All right. Proceed, my general."

"First the backgrounding. We're jumping to a number of conclusions based on flimsy evidence but it can't be helped." Cutter ticked them off on his fingers. "We assume, one, that she's here on a job and not just to take pictures of elephants. Two, that it's a Seventh Bureau assignment. Three, that the job is to assassinate somebody. Four, that the target is a government leader here. We don't know the timetable so we have to assume. Five, that it could happen at any moment. Therefore we must act immediately. Are you with me so far?"

"So far, sure."

"We assume, six, that the local Chinese station is unaware of her mission."

"Why do we assume that?"

"Because they're bugging her room."

Ross gawked at him.

Cutter made a show of patience.

"I didn't waste the night sleeping."

"All right, you went through the dragon lady's room, you found a bug. But how do you know it's a Chinese bug?"

"Because I found not one bug but three. One was ours—up-to-date equipment and I checked it out with Arbuckle. Had to get him out of bed, he wasn't happy but he admitted it's our bug. The second was American-made but obsolescent. Presumably the Tanzanian secret service placed it there. We sold a batch of that model to them some years back. The third mike was made in Sinkiang Province, one of those square little numbers they must have shown you in tech briefings back in school. Satisfied?"

"O.K. No Soviet agent worth his vodka would stoop to using a bug of Chinese manufacture, so that leaves the Chinese. So the local Chinese station is bugging her room and that means they don't know why she's here. Go on."

"They're bugging her because she's been known to free-lance. Naturally they're nervous. They want to find out who she's working for and who she's gunning for. Peking hasn't told them because of interservice rivalry and need-to-know and all that nonsense—they're paranoid by definition, the Seventh Bureau never tells anybody anything. They feel a secret has the best chance of remaining a secret only so long as the number of people who know it is kept to a minimum. The thing is, Ross, as far as the local Chinese are concerned she could just as easily be down here on a job for Warsaw or East Berlin or London or Washington or some Arab oil sheik. They just don't know—so they're keeping an eye on her."

"Go on."

"Now the Tanzanians are bugging her as well and they don't bug just any tourist who checks into a first-class hotel. That means they know who she is. They're not sure enough to take action but they're suspicious. So whatever we do we handle it very quietly. We don't make waves that might splash up against the presidential palace. That's another reason we can't have a termination-with-extreme-prejudice on the record of this caper. When we leave here we leave everything exactly as we found it. That's the cardinal rule. Corpses don't figure in the equation—not Lapautre's corpse and certainly not yours or mine."

"I'll vote for that."

"More assumptions. We assume, seven, that Lapautre isn't a hip-shooter. If she were she wouldn't have lasted this long. She's careful, she finds out what the situation is before she steps into it. We can use that caution of hers. And finally—crucially—we assume, eight, that she's not very well versed in surveillance technology."

"We do? How?"

"She's never been an intelligence gatherer. Her experience is in violence. She's a basic sort of creature—a carnivore. I don't see her as a scientific whiz. She uses an old-fashioned sniper rifle because she's comfortable with it—she's not an experimenter. She'd know the rudiments of electronic eavesdropping but when it comes to sophisticated devices I doubt she's got much interest. Apparently she either doesn't know her room is bugged or knows it but doesn't care. Either way it indicates the whole area is outside her field of interest. Likely there are types of equipment she doesn't even know about."

"Types like for instance?"

"Parabolic reflectors. Long-range directionals."

"Those are hardly ultrasophisticated. They date back to World War Two."

"But not in the Indochinese jungles. They wouldn't be a normal part of her experience."

"Does it matter?"

"I'm not briefing you just to listen to the sound of my dulcet voice, Ross. The local Chinese station is equipped with parabolics and directionals."

"Now I begin to get the idea." Ross felt overstuffed. Forewarned by Cutter's reaction he eschewed the coffee and pushed his chair back.

Cutter said, "Good breakfast?"

"Best I ever ate."

"You've got to memorize your lines now and play the part perfectly the first time out. You're well fed and you look spry enough but are you awake?"

"Go ahead. I'm awake," Ross said dismally . . .

According to plan Ross made the phone call at nine in the morning from a coin telephone in the cable office. A clerk answered and Ross asked to be connected to extension four-eleven. It rang three times and was picked up: the woman's voice was low and smoky. "*Oui?*"

"Two hundred thousand dollars, deposited to a Swiss account." That was the opening line because it was unlikely she'd hang up until she found out what it was about. "Are you interested?"

"Is this a crank?"

"Not a crank, Mademoiselle, but clearly one does not mention names or details on an open telephone line. I think we should arrange a meeting. It's an urgent matter."

Beside him Joe Cutter watched without expression. Ross gripped the receiver with a palm gone damp and clammy.

"Are you speaking for yourself, M'sieur?"

"I represent certain principals." Because she wouldn't deal directly with anyone fool enough to act as his own front man. Ross said, "You've been waiting to hear from me, *n'est-ce-pas?*" That was for the benefit of those who were bugging her phone; he went on quickly before she could deny it: "At noon today I'll be on the beach just north of the fishing village at the head of the bay. I'll be wearing a white shirt, short sleeves, khaki trousers and white plimsolls. I'll be alone and of course without weapons." He had to swallow quickly.

The line seemed dead for a while but he resisted the urge to test it. Finally the woman spoke. "Perhaps."

Click.

"Perhaps," he repeated for Cutter's benefit and Cutter shrugged—in any case there was nothing they could do about it now. He would have to be on the beach at noon and hope she showed.

Driving north in the rent-a-car he said to Cutter, "She didn't sound enthusiastic. I doubt she'll come."

"She'll come."

"What makes you so confident?"

"Without phone calls like that she wouldn't be able to maintain her standard of living. She can't afford to turn down an offer of two hundred thousand American. She'll come."

"Armed to the teeth, no doubt," Ross muttered.

"No. She's a pro. A pro never carries a gun when he doesn't have to—a gun can get you in too much trouble if it's discovered. But she's probably capable of dismantling you by hand in any one of a dozen methods so try not to provoke her suspicions until we've sprung the trap."

"You have a way of being incredibly comforting sometimes, you know that?"

"You're green, Ross, and you have a tendency to be flip when you shouldn't be. This isn't a matter for frivolous heroics. You're not without courage and it's silly to pretend otherwise. But it's a mistake to treat this kind of thing with childish bravado. There's a serious risk of ending up in the surf face-down if you don't treat the woman with all the caution in the world. Your job's simple and straightforward and there's nothing funny about it—just keep her interested and steer her to the right place. And remember your lines, for God's sake."

They parked the car on the verge of the road and walked through the palms to the edge of the water. The beach was a narrow white strip of perfect sand curving away in a crescent. At the far end was a scatter of thatched huts and a few sagging docks to which was tethered a small fleet of primitive catamaran fishing boats. It was pleasantly warm and the air was surprisingly clear and dry. Two small black children ran up and down the distant sand laughing; their voices carried weakly to Ross' ears. The half mile of beach between was empty of visible life. A tourist-poster scene, Ross thought, but a feeling of menace put the taste of brass on his tongue.

A few small wretched boats floated at anchor and farther out on the open water a pair of junks drifted south with the mild wind in their square sails. A dazzling white sport fisherman with a flying bridge rode the swells in a lazy figure-eight pattern about four hundred yards offshore; two men in floppy white hats sat in the stern chairs, trolling their lines. A few miles out toward the horizon a tramp prowled northward, following the coast, steaming from port to port—Tanga next, then Mombasa, and so forth. And there was a faint spiral of smoke even farther out—probably the Zanzibar ferry.

Cutter put his back to the ocean and spoke in a voice calculated to reach no farther than Ross' ears. "Spot them?"

Ross was searching the beach, running his glance along the belt of palms that shaded the sand. "Not a soul. Maybe they didn't get the hint."

"The sport fisherman, Ross. Use your head. They've got telescopes and long-range microphones focused on this beach right now and if I were facing them they'd hear every word I'm saying."

That was why they'd given it three hours lead-time after making the phone call. To give the Chinese time to get in position to monitor the meet. In a way Ross felt relieved; at least they'd taken the bait. It remained to be seen whether the dragon lady would prove equally gullible.

He turned to say something to Cutter but found he was alone at the edge of the trees: Cutter had disappeared without a sound. Discomfited, Ross began to walk along the beach toward the village, kicking sand with his toes. He put his hands in his pockets and then thought better of that and took them out again so that it was obvious they were empty. He twisted his wrist to look at his watch and found it was eleven fifty-five. He walked to the middle of the crescent of sand and stood there looking inland, trying to ignore the fishing boat a quarter of a mile behind him, trying to talk himself out of the acute feeling that a rifle's telescopic crosshairs were centered between his shoulder blades. He discovered that his back muscles had gone tense against an awaited bullet.

He started walking around in an aimless little circle, spurred by the vague theory that they'd have a harder time hitting a moving target. He realized how ridiculous it was: they had no reason to take potshots at him—they'd be curious, not murderous—but he was no longer in a state of mind where logic was the ruling factor.

He heard the putt-putt of an engine and turned with casual curiosity and watched a little outboard come in sight around the headland and beat its way forward, its bow slapping the water. Then he looked away, looked back up into the palm trees wondering when the woman would show up. He did a slow take and turned on his heel again and watched the outboard come straight toward him.

It was the dragon lady and she was alone at the tiller. She ran the boat up onto the beach, tipped the engine up across the transom, jumped overside and came nimbly ashore. She dragged the boat forward and then turned to look at Ross across the intervening fifty yards of sand. He tried to meet her stare without cringing. Her eyes left him and began to explore the trees and she made a thorough job of it before she stirred, coming toward him with lithe graceful strides.

She was not a big woman but there was nothing fragile or petite about the way she held herself. The unlined face was harder than the photograph had suggested; it was something in the eyes, as if her pupils were chipped out of brittle obsidian stone. She wore an *ao dai*, the simple form-fitting dress of Indochina; it was painted to her skin and there was no possibility she could have concealed any sort of weapon under it. Perhaps she wore it for that reason.

Ross didn't move; he let her come to him. It was in his instructions.

"Well then, M'sieur."

"The money," he began, and then he stopped, tongue-tied.

He'd forgotten his lines.

The obsidian eyes drilled into him. "*Oui?*"

In the corner of his vision he saw the white sport boat bobbing on a swell. Somehow it galvanized him. He cleared his throat. "The money's already on deposit and we have the receipt. If you do the job you'll be given both the receipt and the number of the account. Two hundred thousand in American dollars. That works out to something over half a million Swiss francs at the current rate."

Her lip curled a bit—an exquisitely subtle expression. "I would need a bit more information than that, M'sieur."

"The name of the target, of course. The deadline date by which the assignment must be completed. More than that you don't get." He kept his face straight and feverishly rehearsed the rest of his lines.

"But of course there is one item you've left out," she said.

"I don't think there is, Mlle. Lapautre."

"I must know the nature of my employers."

"Not included in the price of your ticket, I'm afraid."

"Then we have wasted our morning, both of us."

"For two hundred thousand dollars we expected a higher class of discretion than you seemed inclined to exercise." It was a line Cutter had drilled into him and it went against his usual mode of expression but Cutter had insisted on the precise wording. And it was amazing the way she responded: as if Cutter had somehow written her dialogue as well as Ross'. His predictions had been uncanny.

She said, "Discretion costs a little more, M'sieur, especially if it concerns those whom I might regard as my natural enemies."

"Capitalists, you mean."

"You *are* American?"

"I am," Ross said. "That's not to say my principals are Americans." *The thing is, Ross, you want to keep her talking, you don't want to close the door and send her skittering away. And at the same time you don't want to get her mad at you. String her along, get her curiosity whetted. She'll insist on having more information. Stretch it out. Stall her. Edge her away. Don't give her the name of the target until she's in position.*

Casually he put his hands in his pockets and turned away from her and strolled very slowly toward the palms. He didn't look back to see if she was following him. He spoke in a normal tone so that she'd have trouble hearing him if she let him get too far ahead of her. "My principals are willing to discuss the matter more directly with you if you agree to take the job on. Not a face-to-face meeting of course, none of us could afford that. But they'll speak to you on safe lines. Coin telephones at both ends—I'm sure you know the drill, you're not an amateur." The words tasted sour on his tongue: if anyone in this game was an amateur it was himself.

But it was working. She was trailing along, moving as casually as he was. He threw his head back and stared at the sky. "The target isn't a difficult one. The security measures aren't severe."

"But he's an important one. A visible figure. Otherwise the price would not be so high," she said. It was something Cutter hadn't forecast and Ross wasn't quite sure how to answer it.

So he made no reply at all. He kept drifting toward the palms, moving in aimless half circles. After a moment he said, "Of course you weren't followed here?" It was in the script.

"Why do you think I chose to come by open boat, M'sieur? No one followed me. Can you say the same?"

Position.

He turned and watched her move alongside. She had, as Cutter had predicted, followed his lead. It was Indochinese courtesy, inbred and unconscious—the residue of a servile upbringing.

She stood beside him now a few feet to his right; like Ross she was facing the palm trees.

Ross dropped his voice and spoke without turning his head; there was no possibility the microphones would hear him. "Don't speak for a moment now. Look slightly to your right—the palm tree with the thick bole."

He stepped back a pace as he spoke. He watched her head turn slowly. Saw her stiffen when she spotted Cutter, indistinct in the shadows. Cutter stirred then and it was enough to make the sun ripple along the barrel of his rifle.

In the same guarded low voice Ross said, "It's a Mannlicher bolt action with high-speed ammunition. Hollowpoint bullets and a 'scope sight calibrated to anything up to eight hundred yards. You wouldn't stand a chance if you tried to run for it." He kept stepping back because he didn't want her close enough to him to jump him and use him for a shield. Yet he had to stay within voice range of her because if he lifted his tone or turned his head more than a quarter-inch the finely focused directional mike on the sport fisherman would pick up his words immediately.

He saw her shoulders drop half an inch and felt the beginnings of a swell of triumph. *If she doesn't break for it in the first five seconds she won't break at all. She's a pro, Ross, remember that. A pro doesn't fight the drop. Not when it's dead clear to her what the situation is.*

"You're in a box, Mlle. Lapautre, and you've only got one way to get out of it alive. Are you listening to me?"

"Certainly."

"Don't try to figure anything out because it would take you too long and there are parts of it you'll never know. We're playing out a charade, that's all you need to keep in mind. If you play your part as required, nobody gets hurt."

"What is it you want, then?"

Her cool aplomb amazed him even though Cutter had told him to expect it. Again: *She's a pro.* She had sized up the situation and that was that.

Cutter was motionless in the shadows, too far away for Lapautre to recognize his features; because of the angle he was hidden from the view of those on board the sport fisherman. All they'd be able to tell was that Ross and Marie Lapautre were having a conversation in tones too low for their eavesdropping equipment to record. They'd be frustrated and angry but there wouldn't be anything they could do about it. They'd hang on station hoping to pick up scraps of words that they could later edit together and make some sense out of.

Ross answered her, *sotto voce.* "I want you to obey my instructions. In a moment I'm going to step around in front of you and face you. The man in the trees will keep his rifle aimed at you at all times. If you make any sudden move he'll kill you. But he's too far away to hear us unless we speak up. I'm going to start talking to you in a loud voice. The things I say may not make much sense to you. I don't care what you say by way of response. But whatever it is I want you to say it very softly so that nobody hears your answers. And I want you to look as if you're agreeing with whatever proposition I make to you. Understand?"

"No," she said. "I do not understand but I'll do as you wish."

"That's good enough. Take it easy now."

Then he stepped off to the left and made a careful circle around her, keeping his distance, looking as casual as he knew how. He stopped when he was facing her from her port bow: off to the right he could see the sport fisherman and if he turned his head to the left he could see Cutter. She would have to cross fifteen feet of sand to interpose Ross between herself and the rifle and she knew there wouldn't be time for that. She didn't speak: she only watched Ross.

He cleared his throat and spoke as if in continuation of a conversation already begun. He enunciated the words clearly, mindful of the shotgun microphone that was focused on his lips from four hundred yards offshore.

"Then we've got a deal. I'm glad you agreed to take it on—you're the best in the business, I think everyone knows that."

Her lip curled again, ever so slightly; she murmured in confounding amusement, "And just what is it I'm supposed to have agreed to, M'sieur?"

Ross nodded vigorously. "Exactly. When you talk to my principals you'll realize immediately that their accents are Russian—Ukrainian to be precise— but I hope that won't deter you from putting your best effort into the assignment."

"This is absurd." But she kept her voice down when she said it.

"That's right," Ross said cheerfully. "There will be no official Soviet record of the transaction. If they're confronted with any accusation, naturally they'll deny it and the world will have only your word to the contrary. I needn't remind you what your word would be worth on the open market—a woman of your reputation? So you can see that it's in your own best interests to keep absolutely silent about the matter."

"This is pointless. Who can possibly benefit from this ridiculous performance?"

"I think they'll find that acceptable," Ross said. "Now then, to get down to the matter at hand."

He saw her eyes flick briefly toward the palms. He didn't look over his shoulder; he knew Cutter was still there. He went on in his overconfident voice:

"The target must be taken out within the next twelve days because that's the deadline for a particular international maneuver the details of which needn't concern you. The target is here in Dar-es-Salaam, so you should have plenty of time to set up the assassination. Do you recognize the name Chiang Hsien?"

She laughed then. She actually laughed. "Incredible."

He forced himself to smile. "Yes. The chief of the China station in Dar. Now there's just one more detail."

"Is that all? Thank goodness for that."

Ross nodded pleasantly. "Yes, that's right. You must make it appear that the assassination is the work of Americans. I'd suggest, for example, that you use an American rifle. I leave the other details in your hands, but the circumstantial evidence must be crystal clear that the assassination was the result of an American plot against the Chinese people's representative in East Africa."

The woman rolled her eyes expressively. "Is that all?"

Ross smiled again. "If you still want confirmation I'll arrange for the telephone contact between you and my principals. In the meantime the receipt and the account number on the Swiss bank will be delivered to your hotel. As soon as we receive confirmation of the death of Chiang Hsien, we'll issue instructions to the bank to transfer ownership of the numbered account and honor your applications for withdrawals. I think that covers everything. It's been pleasant doing business with you, Mlle. Lapautre." With a courtly bow Ross turned briskly on his heel and marched away toward the trees without looking back.

He entered the palms about forty feet to Cutter's right and kept going until he was certain he was out of sight of the lenses on the sport fishing boat. Then he curled behind a tree and had his look around.

Cutter was still there, holding the rifle and looking menacing; Cutter winked at him.

The woman was walking back down the beach toward her open boat. The junks had disappeared past the point of land to the south; the catamarans were still tied up on the water by the village; the coastal steamer was plowing north, the ferryboat's smoke had disappeared, the sport fisherman was still figure-eighting on the water but now the two white-hatted men in the stern were packing up their rods and getting out of their swivel chairs.

Ross stood without moving for a stretching interval while the dragon lady pushed her boat out into the surf, climbed over the gunwale, made her way aft and hooked the outboard engine over the transom. She yanked the cord several times until it sputtered into life and then she went chugging out in a wide circle toward the open water, angling to starboard to clear the headland at the end of the bay.

When she'd gone a couple of hundred yards Cutter came through the trees slinging his rifle. "Beautiful job, Ross. You didn't miff a line."

"What happens now."

"Watch."

The sport fisherman was moving now, its engines whining, planing the water—collision course. Near the headland it intercepted Marie Lapautre's little boat. She tried to turn away but the big white boat leaped ahead of her and skidded athwart her course.

"That skipper knows how to handle her," Cutter commented.

With no choice in the matter the woman allowed her boat to be drawn alongside by a long-armed man with a boathook. One of the white-hatted men came along the deck and gave Marie Lapautre a hand aboard.

The last Ross saw of them, the two boats, one towing the other, were disappearing around the headland.

Cutter walked him back to the car. "They'll milk her, of course. But they won't believe a word of it. They've got the evidence on tape—how can she deny it? They wouldn't buy the truth in a thousand years and it's all she's got to offer."

"I feel queasy as hell, Joe. You know what they're going to do to her after they squeeze her dry."

"It'll happen a long way from here and nobody will ever know about it."

"And that makes it right?"

"No. It adds another load to what we've already got on our consciences. You may survive this but if she does she'll never get another job. They'll never trust her again."

They got into the car. Cutter tossed the rifle in the back seat; they'd drop it off at Arbuckle's office to go back into the safe.

Ross said, "It hasn't solved a thing." He gave Cutter a petulant look. "They'll send somebody to take her place. Next week or next month."

"Maybe yes, maybe no. If they do we'll have to deal with it when it happens. You may as well get used to it, Ross. You play one game, you finish it, you add up the score and then you start the next game. That's all there is to it—and that's the fun of it."

Ross stared at him. "I guess it is," he said reluctantly.

He turned the key. Cutter smiled briefly. The starter meshed and Ross put it in gear. He said with sudden savagery, "But it's not all that much fun for the loser, is it?" And fishtailed the car angrily out into the road.

JOHN COYNE

A Cabin in the Woods

Michael remembered clearly the first piece of fungus: a thin, irregular patch twelve inches wide, grayish, like the color of candle grease, growing on the new pine wall of the bathroom. He reached up gingerly to touch it. The crust was lumpy and the edges serrated. He pulled the resinous flesh from the wood, like removing a scab, tossed the fungus into the waste can and finished shaving.

He had come up from the city late the night before, driving the last few hours through the mountain roads in heavy fog and rain and arriving at his new cabin in the woods after midnight. It was his first trip to the lake that spring.

Michael had come early in the week to work, bringing with him the galleys of his latest novel. He needed to spend several more days making corrections. It was the only task of writing that he really enjoyed, the final step when the book was still part of him. Once it appeared between covers, it belonged to others.

He was in no hurry to read the galleys. That could be done at leisure over the next few days. Barbara wasn't arriving until Friday and their guests weren't due until Saturday morning. It was a weekend they had planned for several months to celebrate the completion of the new house.

So while shaving that first morning at the cabin, Michael found himself relaxed and smiling. He was pleased about the house. It was bigger and more attractive than even the blueprints had suggested.

It had been designed by a young architect from the nearby village. Local carpenters had built it, using lumber cut from the pine and oak and walnut woods behind the lake. They had left the lumber rough-hewed and unfinished.

The cabin was built into the side of the mountain, with a spectacular view of the lake. Only a few trees had been cut to accommodate the construction; so from a distance, and through the trees, the building looked like a large boulder that had been unearthed and tumbled into the sun to dry.

"I want the ambience *rustic*," Barbara explained to the architect. "A sense of the *wilderness*." She whispered the words, as if to suggest the mysterious.

"Don't make it too austere," Michael instructed. "I don't want the feeling we're camping out. This is a cabin we want to escape to from the city; we want some conveniences. I want a place that can sleep eight or ten if need be." He paced the small office of the architect as he listed his requirements, banging his new boots on the wooden floor. Michael liked the authoritative sound, the suggestion to this kid that here was someone who knew what he wanted out of life.

"And cozy!" Barbara leaned forward to catch the architect's attention. She had a round pretty face with saucer-sized blue eyes. She flirted with the young man to make her point. "And a stone fireplace the length of one wall. We may want to come up here with our friends during skiing season." She beamed.

The architect looked from one to the other and said nothing.

"He's not one of your great talkers, is he?" Barbara remarked as they left the village.

"That's the way of these mountain people. They come cheap and they give you a full day's work. It's O.K. with me. I'd rather deal with locals than someone from the city."

Still, the cabin cost $10,000 more than Michael had expected. The price of supplies, he was told, had tripled. However, they had landscaped the lawn to the lake and put in a gravel drive to the county road. Michael said he wanted only to turn the key and find the place livable. "I'm no handyman," he had told the architect.

While the second home in the mountains was costly, Michael was no longer worried about money. When he had finished the new novel and submitted it to the publisher it was picked up immediately with an advance of $50,000, more than he had made on any of his other books. The next week it had sold to the movies for $200,000, and a percentage of the gross. Then just before driving to the mountains, his agent telephoned with the news that the paperback rights had gone for half a million.

"Everything I touch is turning to gold," Michael bragged to Barbara. "I told you I'd make it big."

What he did not tell Barbara was that this was his worst book, written only to make money. He had used all the clichés of plot and situation and it had paid off.

He finished dressing and made plans for the day. The station wagon was still packed with bags of groceries. The night before he had been too tired after the drive to do more than build a fire and pour himself a drink. Then, carrying his drink, he had toured through the empty rooms—his boots echoing on the oak floors—and admired the craftsmanship of the mountain carpenters. The cabin was sturdy and well built; the joints fit together like giant Lincoln logs.

The three bedrooms of the house were upstairs in the back and they were connected by an open walk that overlooked the living room, which was the height and width of the front of the cabin. The facade was nearly all windows, long panels that reached the roof.

One full wall was Barbara's stone fireplace, made from boulders quarried in the mountains and trucked to the lake site. The foundation was made from the same rocks. As Barbara bragged to friends with newly acquired chauvinism, "All that's not from the mountains are the kitchen appliances and ourselves."

Michael moved the station wagon behind the house and unpacked the groceries, carrying the bundles in through the back door and stacking the bags on the butcher-block table. He filled the refrigerator first with perishables and the several bottles of white wine he planned to have evenings with his meals. His own special present to himself at the success of his book.

Packing the refrigerator gave Michael a sense of belonging. With that simple chore, he had taken possession of the place and the cabin felt like home.

He had thought of leaving the staples until Barbara arrived—she would have her own notion of where everything should go—but after the satisfaction of filling the refrigerator, Michael decided to put the staples away, beginning with the liquor.

He carried the box into the living room and knelt down behind the bar and opened the cabinet doors. Inside, growing along the two empty plain wooden shelves, was gray fungus. It grew thick, covering the whole interior of the cabinet, and the discovery frightened Michael, like finding an abnormality.

"My God!" A shiver ran along his spine.

He filled several of the empty grocery bags with the fungus. It pulled easily off the shelves and was removed in minutes. Then he scrubbed the hard pine boards with soap and water and put away the bottles of liquor.

It was the dampness of the house, he guessed, that had caused the growth. The house had stood empty and without heat since it had been finished. He knew fungus grew rapidly in damp weather, but still the spread of the candle-gray patch was alarming.

He returned to the kitchen and apprehensively opened the knotty pint cupboards over the counter. The insides were clean, with the smell about them of sawdust. He ran his hand across the shelves and picked up shavings. Michael closed the door and sighed.

Barbara had given him a list of chores to do in the house before the weekend. The beds in the guest rooms should be made, the windows needed washing, and the whole house, from top to bottom, had to be swept. Also, the living room rug had arrived and was rolled up in the corner. It had to be put down and vacuumed.

First, however, Michael decided to have breakfast. On Sundays in the city he always made breakfast, grand ones of Eggs Doremus, crepes, or Swedish pancakes with lingonberry. Lately Barbara had begun to invite friends over for brunch. His cooking had become well known among their friends and his editor had suggested that he might write a cookbook about Sunday breakfasts.

Michael unpacked the skillet, and turning on the front burner melted a slice of butter into the pan. He took a bottle of white wine, one of the inexpensive California Chablis, uncorked it, and added a half cup to the skillet. The butter and wine sizzled over the flame and the rich smell made Michael hungry.

He broke two eggs into the skillet, seasoned them with salt and pepper, and then searched the shopping bags for cayenne, but Barbara hadn't packed the spices. He could do without but made a mental note to pick up cayenne and more spices when he drove to the village later that morning.

Michael moved easily around the kitchen, enjoying the space to maneuver. In their apartment in the city, only one of them could cook at a time. Here, they had put in two stoves and two sinks, and enough counter space for both to work at once.

Michael glanced at the eggs. The whites were nearly firm. He took the toaster and plugged it in, noticing with satisfaction that the electrical outlets worked. That was one less problem to worry about. He dropped two pieces of bread into the toaster and then, going back to the bar, took the vodka, opened a can of tomato juice, and made himself a Bloody Mary.

He was working quickly now, sure of the kitchen. He cut the flame under the skillet, crumbled Roquefort cheese and sprinkled it on the eggs; then he buttered the toast and unpacked a dish and silverware. He smiled, pleased. He was going to enjoy cooking in this kitchen.

Perhaps, he thought, he should move full time to the mountains. He could write more, he knew, if he lived by the lake, away from interruptions and distractions. He fantasized a moment. He could see himself going down on cool, misty mornings to the lake. He could smell the pine trees and the water as he crossed the flat lake to bass-fish before sunup. He could see the boat gracefully arching through the calm water as behind it a small wave rippled to the shore. He sipped the Bloody Mary and let the pleasant thought relax him.

Then he remembered the eggs and he slipped them from the skillet onto the buttered toast, and carrying the plate and his drink walked out onto the oak deck. The deck was a dozen feet wide and built along the length of the east wall to catch the early morning sun. It was Barbara's idea that they could have breakfast on the deck.

The sun had cleared the mountains and touched the house. It had dried the puddles of rain water and warmed the deck so Michael was comfortable in shirt sleeves.

They had not yet purchased deck furniture, so he perched himself on the wide banister and finished the eggs. He could see the length of the front lawn from where he sat. It sloped gracefully down to the shore and the new pier.

The pier he had built himself during the winter. One weekend he had come up to the village, bought 300 feet of lumber, hired two men from a construction firm, and driven out to the lake in four-wheel-drive jeeps. Along the shore of the lake they found twelve sassafras trees that they cut and trimmed and pulled across the ice to Michael's property. They chopped holes in the thick ice and sledgehammered the poles into place to make the foundation. Then they cut two-by-eights into four-foot lengths and nailed them between the poles to make the pier.

Michael's hands blistered and his back ached for a week, but he was proud of his hard labor, and proud, too, of the pier which went forty feet into the water and could easily handle his two boats.

At first he could not see the pier because a late morning mist clung to the shore. It rolled against the bank like a range of low clouds. But as he sat finishing his eggs and drink, the rising sun burned away the mist and the thin slice of pier jutting into the mountain lake came slowly into view like a strange gothic phenomenon.

"What the . . ."

Michael stood abruptly and the dish and his drink tumbled off the railing. He peered down, confused. The whole length of the pier was covered with gray fungus. He looked around for more fungus, expecting to see it everywhere. He scanned the landscaped lawn, the pine trees which grew thick to the edge of his property. He spun about and ran the length of the oak deck, leaned over the railing and searched the high rear wall of the cabin. He glanced at the trash heap of construction materials left by the builders. No sign of more mold.

Next he ran into the house and taking the steps two at a time raced to the second floor. He turned into the bathroom and flipped on the light. No fungus grew on the pine wall. He turned immediately and ran downstairs, boots stomping on the wooden stairs, and opened the cabinet doors below the bar. The bottles of liquor were stacked as he had arranged them.

Michael calmed down, gained control. He kept walking, however, through the house, opening closet doors, checking cabinets. He went again to the kitchen and looked through all the cupboards. He opened the basement door and peered into the dark downstairs. The basement has been left unfinished, a damp cellar. Still no fungus.

When he was satisfied there was no fungus in the house, he left the cabin and walked across the lawn to the tool shed and found a shovel. He began where the pier touched the shore, scraping away the fungus and dumping the growth into the water, where it plopped and floated away. He shoveled quickly. The flat tenacious flesh of the fungus ripped easily off the wood. It was oddly exhilarating work. In a matter of minutes he had cleaned the length of the pier.

He stuck the shovel into the turf and went again to the house where he found a mop and bucket, poured detergent into the bucket, filled it with hot water, and returned to the pier to mop the planks. The pier sparkled in the morning sun.

Then Michael locked the cabin, backed the station wagon out of the drive, and drove into the village.

The village was only a few streets where the interstate crossed the mountains. It had grown up on both sides of a white river, and adjacent to railroad tracks. The tracks were now defunct and the river polluted. The few buildings were weather weary and old. The only new construction was the service station at the interstate, and a few drive-ins. When Barbara first saw the town, she wouldn't let him stop.

But the hills and valleys beyond the place were spectacular and unspoiled and when they found five acres of woods overlooking the lake they decided that in spite of the town, they'd buy.

"I looked down at the pier and the whole goddamn thing was covered with fungus. It's a gray color, like someone's puke." Michael paced the architect's office. He had already told the young man about the fungus in the bathroom and beneath the bar. And without saying so, implied it was the architect's fault.

"I'm not a biologist." The young man spoke carefully. He was unnerved by Michael. The man had barged into his office shouting about fungus. It had taken him several minutes to comprehend what the problem was.

"You're from these hills. You grew up here, right? You should know about fungus. What's all this mountain folklore we keep hearing about?" Michael quit pacing and sat down across from the architect. He was suddenly tired. The anxiety and anger over the fungus had worn him out. "That's a new house out there. I sunk $50,000 into it and you can't tell me why there's fungus growing on the bathroom walls? Goddammit! What kind of wood did you use?"

"The lumber was green, true, but I told you we'd have problems. It was your idea to build the place with pine off your land. Well, pine needs time to dry. Still . . ." The architect shook his head. The growth of fungus confused him. He had never heard of such a thing. But the man might be exaggerating. He glanced at Michael.

Michael was short and plump with a round, soft face, and brown eyes that kept widening with alarm. He wore new Levi pants and jacket, and cowboy boots that gave him an extra inch of height. Around his neck he had fastened a blue bandanna into an ascot. He looked, the architect thought, slightly ridiculous.

"Who knows about this fungus?" Michael asked. He had taken out another blue bandanna to wipe the sweat off his face. In his exasperated state, the sweat poured.

"I guess someone at the college . . ."

"And you don't think it's any of your concern? You stuck me for $10,000 over the original estimate and now that you've got your money, you don't give a damn."

"I told you before we started construction that we'd get hit by inflation. We could have held the costs close to that first estimate if your wife hadn't wanted all the custom cabinets, those wardrobes, and items like bathroom fixtures from Italy . . ."

Michael waved away the architect's explanation. He was mad at the kid for not solving the problem of the fungus. "Where's this college?" he asked.

"Brailey. It's across the mountain."

"How many miles?" Michael stood. He had his car keys out and was spinning them impatiently.

"Maybe thirty, but these are mountain roads. It will take an hour's drive. Why not telephone? You're welcome to use my phone." He pushed the telephone across the desk.

Michael fidgeted with his keys. He didn't want to let the architect do him any favors, but he also didn't want to spend the morning driving through the mountains.

"O.K. You might be right." He sat down again and, picking up the receiver, dialed information.

It took him several calls and the help of the college switchboard operator before he reached a Doctor Clyde Bessey, an associate professor at the state university. Dr. Bessey had a thin, raspy voice, as if someone had a hand to his throat. He said he was a mycologist in the Department of Plant Pathology.

"Do you know anything about fungus?" Michael asked.

"Why, yes." The doctor spoke carefully, as if his words were under examination. "Mycology is the study of fungi."

"Then you're the person I want," Michael replied quickly. Then, without asking if the man had time, he described the events of the morning.

"*Peniophora gigantea*," Doctor Bessey replied.

"What?"

"The species of fungi you've described sounds like *Peniophora gigantea*. It's more commonly called resin fungus. A rather dull-colored species that spreads out like a crust on the wood. You say the edges are serrated?"

"And it's lumpy . . ."

"Rightly so! *Peniophora gigantea*. Sometimes laymen mistake this species of crust fungi for a resinous secretion of the conifer."

"Does it grow like that? That fast?"

"No, what you've described is odd." He sounded thoughtful. "Fungi won't grow that extensively, unless, of course, a house has been abandoned. And certainly not that fast. We did have a damp winter and spring, still . . . you said the cabin was built with green lumber?"

"Yes, I'm afraid so." Michael glanced at the architect.

"Still . . ."

"Well, how in the hell do I stop it?" Michael was sharp, because the laborious manner of the professor was irritating.

"I don't know exactly what to tell you. Your situation sounds a bit unusual. Fungi doesn't grow as rapidly as you've described. In laboratory conditions, we've had fungus cover the surface of a three-inch-wide culture dish in two days. But that's ideal conditions. Without competition from other fungi or bacteria. But, generally speaking, fungi does thrive better than any other organism on earth." He said that with a flourish of pride.

"Doctor, I'm sure this is all just wonderful, but it doesn't help me, you see. I'm infested with the crap!"

"Yes, of course . . . If you don't mind, I'd like to drive over and take some cultures. I'll be able to tell more once I've had the opportunity to study some samples."

"You can have all you want."

"You've cleaned up the fungi, I presume . . ."

"With soap and water."

"Well, that should destroy any mycelium, but then we never can be sure. One germinating spore and the process begins again. Rather amazing, actually."

"Let's hope you're wrong. It's a $50,000 house."

"Oh, I'm sure there's no permanent problem, just a biological phenomenon. Fungi are harmless, really, when they're kept in control. Your home will suffer no lasting effects." He sounded confident.

"Maybe you're right." Michael was cautious. Still, Doctor Bessey had eased his mind. Michael hung up feeling better.

"Do you mind if I make another call?" he asked the architect. "Our phone hasn't been installed at the cabin . . ." The young man gestured for Michael to go ahead. Actually, he wasn't that bad, Michael thought, dialing Barbara in the city.

"I'm sure it's nothing serious," Barbara said when Michael told her about the fungus. "The wet weather and all . . ." Her mind was elsewhere, planning for the weekend. "Did you have time to make the beds?"

"The whole pier was covered, like a tropical jungle. *Peniophora gigantea* . . . that's what the mycologist called it."

"The who?"

"Dr. Bessey. He studies fungi."

"Well, if it's that well known, then it can't be any problem . . . Have you had a chance to wash the windows? Perhaps I should come up earlier . . ."

"Don't worry about getting the cabin clean. I'll do that!" Michael snapped at her. He was upset that she hadn't responded. Barbara had a frustrating habit of not caring about a household problem unless it affected her directly. "I'll clean the windows, make the beds, and sweep the goddamn floors once I get rid of this fungus!"

"And the rugs . . ."

"And the rugs!"

"Michael dear, there's no need to be upset with me. I have nothing to do with your fungus."

"Yes, dear, but you wanted the place built from our lumber, our *green* lumber."

"And you said it would make the place look more authentic."

"The lumber's green!"

"I don't see where that's my fault!"

"It might mean that we'll have to live with this goddamn fungus!" Michael knew he was being unreasonable, but he couldn't stop himself. He was mad at her for not taking the fungus seriously.

"I'm sure you'll think of something," Barbara pampered him and then dismissed the whole issue. "You'll remember the windows . . . ?"

She sounded like a recording.

Before leaving the village, Michael went to the general store and shopped for the week. He did not want to leave the lake again for errands. He bought Windex, the spices Barbara had forgotten, a new mop, a second broom. He bought two five-gallon cans of gas for the boats and more fishing tackle. He bought a box of lures; good, he was told by the store owner, for mountain lakes. He picked up a minnow box, a fish net and a filet knife. He would need them if he planned to do any serious fishing.

But he understood himself enough to realize also that this impulse buying was only a compensation for the upsetting morning. Now that he had the money, he spent it quickly, filling the station wagon like a sled with toys. And driving back to the cabin, his good mood returned.

He would not clean the cabin that morning, he decided, nor would he make the beds. Instead, he'd take out the flat-bottom boat and fish for bass in the small lagoon of the lake. And he'd panfry the catch that evening for dinner. He'd just have the fish and some fresh vegetables, asparagus or sliced cucumbers, and a bottle of the Pinot Noir.

Michael pictured himself on the deck frying the bass. The cloud of smoke from the coals drifting off into the trees, the late sun catching the glass of wine, the pale yellow color like tarnished gold. He'd cover the fish a moment, stop to sip the wine, and look out over the lake as the trees darkened on the other shore and a mist formed. He'd get a thick ski sweater and put it on. When the darkness spread up the lawn to the house, he'd be the last object visible, moving on the deck like a lingering shadow.

Michael turned the station wagon off the county road and onto his drive and the crunch of gravel under the wheels snapped him from his daydream. He touched the accelerator and the big car spun over the loose stones. On that side of the property the trees grew thick and close and kept the house from view until Michael had swung the car into the parking space and stopped. Then he saw the fungus, a wide spread growing across the rock foundation like prehistoric ivy.

He ran from the car to the wall and grabbed the fungus. The mold tore away in large chunks. With both hands, frantically, he kept ripping away. Now it was wet and clammy, like the soft underbelly of fish.

Michael left the fungus on the ground, left his new fishing tackle and other supplies in the car, and ran into the house. He pulled open the cabinet doors. The gray growth had spread again across the two shelves. It covered the liquor, grew thick among the bottles like cobwebs.

In the bathroom upstairs the patch of mold was the width of the wall. It stretched from floor to ceiling and had crept around the mirror, grown into the wash bowl, and smothered the toilet. He reached out and pulled a dozen inches away in his fingers. The waxy flesh of the fungus clung to his hand. Michael fell back exhausted against the bathroom door and wiped the sweat off his face with his sleeve.

It was hot in the cabin. Michael took off his jacket and pulled off the blue bandanna ascot, then he started on the bathroom fungus. He filled five paper bags with fungus and dumped them into the trash heap behind the house. He went to the bar and removed the liquor and scraped the shelves clean again. He took the fungus to the trash pile and going back to the car got one of the cans of gas, poured it on the fungus, and started a blaze.

The wet fungus produced a heavy fog and a nasty odor, like the burning of manure. Michael watched it burn with pleasure, but when he returned to the kitchen to put away the supplies, he found that the fungus had spread, was growing extensively in all the cupboards and beneath the sink. It even lined the insides of the oven and grew up the back of the refrigerator.

Michael needed to stand on a kitchen chair to reach the fungus that grew at the rear of the cupboards, but he had learned now how to rip the mold away in large pieces, like pulling off old, wet wallpaper. Still, it took him longer; the fungus was more extensive and nestled in all the corners of the custom-made cupboards.

He went outside and found the wheelbarrow and carted away the fungus, dumping it into the fire behind the house. The gray smoke billowed into the trees. The mountain air stank. He swept the kitchen clean and washed the cupboards, the bathroom, and the cabinets beneath the bar. It was late afternoon when he had the house finally in order and he went upstairs and flopped into bed, feeling as if he hadn't slept in weeks.

He woke after seven o'clock. It was still daylight, but the sun was low in the sky and the bedroom was shaded by trees and dark.

He had been deeply asleep and came awake slowly so it was several minutes before he remembered where he was and what had happened. When he did remember, he realized at the same time that the fungus would have returned, that it was growing again in the bathroom, beneath the bar, and in all the cupboards of the kitchen.

But he did not know that now the fungus had spread further and was growing along the green pine walls of the bedroom, had spread over the bare oak floors, and even started down the stairs, like an organic carpet. Michael sat up and swung his bare feet off the bed and onto the floor. His feet touched the lumpy wet fungus. It was as if he had been swimming in the lake and had tried to stand on the mucky bottom. His toes dug into the slime.

He shoveled the fungus off the floor and threw it out the bedroom window. The shovel tore into the rough-hewed floor, caught between the planks, and he had ruined the floor when he was done. He took a rake from the shed and used it to pull the fungus off the walls. He cleaned the bathroom again and shoveled the fungus off the stairs. Repeatedly, he filled the wheelbarrow and dumped it outside. The fire burned steadily.

It took Michael three hours to clean the cabin and only when he was done, resting in the kitchen, sitting at the butcher-block table and drinking a bottle of beer, did he first see the fungus seeping under the cellar door. It grew rapidly before his eyes, twisting and turning, slipping across the tile floor like a snake. Michael grabbed the shovel and cut through the fungus at the door. The dismembered end continued across the tile with a life of its own.

He jerked open the cellar door to beat back the growth, but the gray fungus had filled the cellar, was jammed against the door, and when he opened the door it smothered him in an avalanche of mold.

Now it was everywhere. The cupboards burst open and the fungus flopped out and onto the counter. A tide of it pushed aside the food and shoved cans to the floor.

In the living room it grew along the rock fireplace and tumbled down the stairs. It spread across the floor, came up between the cracks in the oak floors. It grew around the tables and chairs and covered all the furniture with a gray dustcover of mold. It oozed from the center of the rolled-up rug, like pus from a sore. There was fungus on the ceiling, crawling towards the peak of the cabin. It was under foot. Michael slipped and slid as he ran from the house.

The fungus crawled along the rock foundation. It filled the deck, and under its weight the wooden supports gave way and the deck crashed to the ground. The pier again was covered and the gray mold came off the wood and across the new lawn, ripping the sod as it moved. It raced towards Michael like a tide.

Michael got the other can of gas from the station wagon. He went inside the house again and poured gas through the living room, splashing it against the wooden stairs, the pine walls. He ran into the kitchen and threw gas in a long, yellow spray at the cupboards, emptying the last of the can on the butcher-block table. When he dropped the can to the floor it sank into the thick fungus with a thud.

He was breathless, panting. His fingers shook and fumbled as he found matches, struck and tossed them at the gas-soaked mold. Flame roared up, ate away at the fungus, caught hold of the pine and oak and walnut with a blaze. In the living room he tossed matches into the liquor cabinet and set fire to the bar. He lit up the stairs and the flame ran along the steps. He tore through the fungus covering the furniture and ignited the couch.

The fungus had grown deep and billowy. It was as if Michael was trying to stand on top of a deflating parachute. He kept slipping and falling as the lumpy surface changed directions and expanded. The floor was a sea of mold. The front door was almost blocked from view. Gray smoke began to choke him. He tumbled towards the door and fungus swelled under foot and knocked him aside.

Michael found the shovel and used it to rip through the layers of wet mold. He cut a path, like digging a trench, to the outside. He ran for the station wagon. The fungus had reached the parking space and lapped at the wheels of the car.

Behind him the cabin blazed. Flames reached the shingled roof and leaped up the frame siding. The house burned like a bonfire. He spun the car around. The wheels slid over the slick mold like the car was caught on a field of ice, but he kept the station wagon on the gravel and tromped on the gas. The car fishtailed down the drive and onto the safety of the county road. Michael drove for his life.

"It's a total loss?" Barbara asked again, still confused by Michael's tale. Her blue saucer eyes looked puzzled.

Michael nodded. "In the rearview mirror I could see most of it in flames. I didn't have the courage to go back and check." He spoke with a new honesty and sense of awe.

"But to burn down our own home! Wasn't there some other way . . . ?" She stared at Michael. It was unbelievable. He had arrived at the apartment after midnight, trembling and incoherent. She had wanted to call a doctor, but he raged and struck her when she said he needed to help. She cowed in the corner of the couch, shaking, as he paced the room and told her about the fungus and the fire.

"I tried to keep cleaning it with soap and water, but it kept . . ." He began to cry, deep, chest-rending sobs. She went quickly to him and smothered him against her breasts. She could smell the smoke in his hair, the bitter smell of wood that had smoldered in the rain.

"A smoke?" Barbara suggested. "It will calm you down." She rolled them a joint. Her hands were trembling with excitement. It was the first time in years that he had hit her, and the blow had both frightened and excited her. Her skin tingled.

They passed the joint back and forth as they sat huddled on the couch, like two lone survivors. Michael, again, and in great detail, told about the fungus, and why he had to burn the cabin.

"I know you were absolutely right," Barbara kept saying to reassure him, but in the back of her mind, growing like a cancer, was her doubt. To stop her own suspicious thoughts and his now insistent explanations, she interrupted, "Darling . . ." And she reached to unbutton his shirt.

They did not make it to the bedroom. Michael slipped his hands inside her blouse, then he pulled her to the floor and took his revenge and defeat out on her. It was brief and violent and cathartic.

Michael held her tenderly, arms wrapped around her, hugging her to him. He turned her head and kissed her eyes. It was all right, she whispered. He was home and safe and she would take care of him.

Yes, Michael thought, everything was all right. He was home in the city and they would forget the mountains and the second home on the lake. He had his writing and he had her, and that was all that mattered. And then his lips touched the candle-gray fungus that grew in a thin, irregular patch more than twelve inches wide across her breasts like a bra.

EDWARD WELLEN

The Long Arm of El Jefe

Soon the presses of *Libertad* would roll and the blazing words of Juan Vallejo, leader in exile of all those opposing El Jefe, would bring new life to butchered trees. In his eagerness to stop the presses, Enrique Saenz made his fatal slip. He let Juan Vallejo see into his soul.

They had been talking about money and power. Vallejo had repeated to Saenz the theme of his lead editorial.

"The millons of dollars Uncle Sap pours out in foreign aid to our homeland go into the Dictator's pockets and those of his family and friends."

That was when Saenz burst out in raw self-interest. "Does that not tell you, Juan, it is well to be among El Jefe's friends?"

Vallejo looked at Saenz with the beginning of a smile, as though believing Saenz to be joking. The smile aborted. The tapping of typewriters and the stutter of the teletype in the crowded office outside Vallejo's swelled to meet the silence. Vallejo sank deeper in his chair as if an enormous weariness weighed upon him.

"So. It is painful to find out that someone I had thought my friend is my enemy's friend. Or do you deny it?"

Saenz shook his head. His throat tightened. He had not meant to admit the truth of Vallejo's charge just yet, but maybe it was just as well. It would never become less hard to soften Vallejo up and now he would not have to hint at the offer El Jefe had commissioned him to make. He stroked his silken beard.

"One millon dollars in a secret Swiss or Bahamas account. You do not have to become a friend, merely cease to be an enemy. You do not have to support El Jefe, merely stop your attacks on him."

"Thank you, Enrique."

The sincerity in Vallejo's voice brought a cynical smile from Saenz.

"Yes, Enrique, it is worth a million to hear that. It tells me what I've been hoping all these years to hear—that your friend the Dictator is worried. He is right to worry. A change is in the wind."

Saenz's eyes fell to the polished rock paperweight on Vallejo's desk. Saenz knew the story of that rock. Vallejo had told him many times. The rock was all that remained to Vallejo of his homeland. In the days when Vallejo had printed his daily paper in the capital, someone in the up-and-coming party had flung it through the window of the composing room. Vallejo had polished it and put it to use as a paperweight. Shortly after, El Jefe had seized full control of the country and forced Vallejo to flee to New York. Now it was a symbol of the homeland, of Vallejo's own rocklike resolve to drive the Dictator from power.

Saenz pointed to the rock. "Juan, you are like that rock, a reminder of a lost cause. You have sentimental value, true, but otherwise you are worthless. What people want is bread, not a stone."

Vallejo sat taller.

"Freedom is bread for the spirit."

"Words! Freedom is a commodity like any other. Even the high-minded Juan Vallejo sells it, doesn't he? What else is this sheet of yours but—" Saenz picked up a desk copy of *Libertad* and weighed it in his hand "—two ounces of your brand of freedom?"

Vallejo's eyes narrowed. " 'Words,' you say. Let us try to use the words that fit this case. You have sold out to the man you call El Jefe. Or have you always been in his pay? Ah, I can see now! Your mission from the first has been to win me over, or at least to remove my sting. Go back to your Dictator and tell him you have failed. That is the worst punishment I can wish you, the best payment for your treachery. You have betrayed our friendship and you have abused my hospitality. I must ask you to leave. *Now.*"

Saenz pulled together the tatters of his self-image. "Before I leave this sacred soil let me give you one word of warning. El Jefe's arm is long. It reaches far. The fingers of his hand will squeeze you lifeless—if you are lucky. If you are *un*lucky, his hand will snatch you back to the homeland, where you will find out for yourself whether there are indeed the torture cells you have written about."

Vallejo's finger poised over the intercom. "I too am a dictator. Before I dictate a new lead editorial is there anything you care to add? Any more threats? Or bribes? Both make very good copy."

Saenz filled with panic. Not only had he failed to neutralize Vallejo, he had provided Vallejo with more ammunition.

He picked up the rock.

Vallejo sat slumped forward, his face on the desk, his blood soaking through sheets of copy paper.

Saenz found himself foolishly wiping his hands on the paper instead of polishing the rock of fingerprints. But even that would have been useless. The only way out was through the editorial room and he would be the last to have been seen alive with Vallejo.

His only hope was to get out of the country before the police could arrest him. Once he set foot on his own soil he would turn from fugitive to hero. El Jefe might publicly deplore the killing of Juan Vallejo but privately he would reward Juan Vallejo's killer.

Saenz strode out through the editorial room. He held his pace down, though the urge to run was strong. Reporters and copy editors stopped what they were doing and stared at him. Had they heard the loud voices, the blow, the silence? Was there blood or its smell on him?

Their features and expressions were imprinted sharply on Saenz's mind, just as his were imprinted on theirs. They had seen him here often. They knew his name. When the alarm went out the police would have a make.

Once out in the corridor, he quickened his step. He punched the elevator button, but, remembering the old elevator's agonizing slowness, he took the stairs down to the street. A wise move. A hue and cry rose and swelled behind him.

Outside, he hailed a cab and gave his address. His heart beat faster and faster as the cab crawled the twenty blocks to his apartment. Every siren he heard spoke his name.

He had only to pick up his passport and his bank book, then draw out the balance El Jefe had fattened, but even this needed time, and the traffic was robbing him of time. Two blocks short of his address he told the cabby to stop, paid him, and got out.

Another wise move. Not only was it faster on foot, but when he stopped at his corner to scout the street ahead he spotted two men in plainclothes in a car across from his doorway. A stakeout.

Saenz hurried over to the next street and approached the apartment from the back. He could climb to his window by way of the fire escape. But the stakeout might include the apartment itself. Hugging the alley wall, he counted up to his window and kept his eyes on it. He watched for nearly five minutes, then he saw it. A curtain twitched, sending a chill through him.

Vallejo must have weighed more importantly than he had realized for the police to have moved so fast and so thoroughly. Had they sealed off the city as well? At the very least he had better get out of the neighborhood. He would have to go without his passport, but that would not matter at the other end and he would not need it at this end if he booked a seat on a flight to Puerto Rico. From there he could find passage by sea or air the rest of the way home. He had to leave his bank balance behind, but he had his credit cards . . .

He stopped short.

A credit economy worked fine—as long as you felt free to use the name on your credit card. But if the alarm had already gone out, if the clerks had his name on their list, if the police stood alert at all the terminals . . .

He could not flash his credit cards. He would need cash. But where could he borrow some?

He stopped again. He knew where to go.

Raquel kept her door on the chain. Her small face stared out at him. He did not like the look in her eyes. Or the tone of her voice.

"Don't give me 'darling.' You have some nerve coming here. I just now heard it on the radio."

He tried a smile. He had thought to borrow a razor from her to shave off the beard she had often told him lent machismo. He felt sure enough of himself without it, and without it he would be less likely to draw the notice of the police. But now he would be content to leave at once with whatever ready money Raquel could scrape together.

"Let me in. I don't know what you heard, but I'm sure I can explain."

Raquel's look softened, but she did not unchain the door.

"Are you going to keep me waiting out here?"

"Juan was a good man. I don't want to call the police, but I will if you don't go."

As he stepped back a pace to ram the door, it shut in his face. The dead bolt shot into place. He heard her walk away—and then silence. Suppose she were calling the police?

If Raquel's door closed to him, all other doors would be closed too. Cash was out. He would have to chance his credit.

He caught a cab to Kennedy Airport. Paying the cabby took the last of his folding money. He did not risk the ticket counters but joined the crowd watching the planes take off and land.

He looked surreptitiously for signs of unusual scrutinizing of passengers on their way to board flights. Just when he began to breathe easier he saw a pair of plainclothesmen examine the papers of a bearded man of his build.

He grimaced. Escape by plane was impossible. He would find the same barriers at bus and train terminals. He was trapped on alien soil.

Then it hit him—there was one place, in the heart of Manhattan, that offered sanctuary, promised asylum.

He mixed in with a group leaving the terminal building and enviously watched them board a chartered bus. He did not have enough change for the ride back, even on a regular bus. Not willing to run the risk of stiffing a cabdriver, he eyed the hazy glow in the west. It would be a long walk back to Manhattan.

He had to keep to the highway to avoid getting lost. The broken shoulders were hard on his feet. After a few miles he stopped at a diner for coffee. He lingered over the empty cup, finally forcing himself back out onto the expressway. Outside, his eyes lit on the cars in the parking area. He cased them, one by one, and finally found one with keys in the ignition. His heart racing, he pulled out into Manhattan-bound traffic.

After a few miles, he pulled over to see what else he had lucked into. In the glove compartment he found an electric shaver that plugged into the cigarette-lighter socket. Quickly he shaved off his beard.

Shortly after he crossed the bridge to Manhattan he ditched the car. Its number must be on the police band by now and it would be a fine thing to be picked up for driving a stolen car. He made a last-minute search of the car and found riches. In the corner under the dash a magnet held a coin container. He pocketed the three dollars' worth of quarters. Now, if the place had closed for the day, he had enough to see him safely through the night. All he needed now was a weapon in case someone should get in his way. He took a jackhandle out of the trunk and stuck it in his waistband under his jacket.

He would not have to wait till morning. As he approached the consulate its lights shone. Behind the windows figures hurried back and forth in a play of shadows.

The police would hardly dare cross that threshold uninvited, so the activity inside would not be a police search for Juan Vallejo's killer. Vallejo's death would no doubt be the catalyst but the activity would be strictly consular business. The information officer would be fielding reporters' questions about the slaying of El Jefe's foe and the communications officer would be handling messages between home, Washington, and the United Nations.

Saenz suddenly knew the assassin's glory, the feeling that he had changed history—whether for better or worse did not matter. He convinced himself that instead of striking out at Vallejo in panic he had struck out of patriotism. The result was the same.

He looked and listened, then approached the consulate with caution. Voices in a hidden doorway froze him.

"Think that Saenz guy will show up here?"

"No, we're wasting our time. He'd be a fool to."

Saenz curled his lip. What arrogance! The police were the fools if they believed they could keep him from getting through to safe soil.

He backed up and went hunting. A lone policeman—one his size—patrolling a deserted area was his prey.

He walked eight blocks north and east before he saw a man of his slight build in uniform. Saenz approached him. Close to, the man proved to be an auxiliary policeman, a civilian who gave up a few of his nights to help man the streets. Saenz asked directions to an address uptown and when the man turned to point the way Saenz whipped out the jackhandle and cracked the man over the back of the head.

The door opened and the consulate guard stared at the uniform. Saenz tried to push inside before the men staked out in the street realized he was not one of them. The guard stopped him.

"I'm sorry, this is not U.S. territory. You can't come in."

"Yes, I can, you idiot. I'm no Yanqui cop. Don't you know me?"

The guard's eyes flickered in uncertain recognition. A man appeared at the door behind him. "Who's there? What does he want?"

The guard stepped aside and Saenz moved in and shut the door.

Safe!

The other man frowned at him. "Officer, I hope you realize your intrusion is most irregular. You are infringing on our sovereignty."

In the light Saenz remembered the man as an underling he had bypassed in his visits to the consulate for instructions from El Jefe. Saenz had even more importance now, and no time to waste giving explanations to this man.

"Take me to the consul."

"I am the consul now."

Saenz stared. El Jefe *could* be capricious at times, elevating or destroying a man on a whim. "I'm Enrique Saenz," he said. "I claim sanctuary. I wish to send a message to El Jefe."

The new consul's face turned to stone. "Saenz," he said. "Haven't you read the papers or listened to the news? You will have to deliver the message to El Jefe yourself—and El Jefe is dead. Your killing of Juan Vallejo set off the coup that has been so long in the making. This consulate, like the homeland, is in the hands of your enemies."

JACK RITCHIE

Kid Cardula

It's just about time for me to close down the gym for the night when this tall stranger comes up to me.

He wears a black hat, black suit, black shoes, black topcoat, and he carries a zipper bag.

His eyes are black too. "I understand that you manage boxers?"

I shrug. "I had a few good boys in my time."

Sure, I had a few good boys, but never *real* good. The best I ever done was with Chappie Strauss. He was listed as number ten in the lightweight division by *Ring Magazine*. Once. And I had to pick my fights careful to get him that far. Then he meets Galanio, which is a catastrophe, and he loses his next four fights too before I decide it's time to retire him.

"I would like you to manage me," the stranger says. "I plan to enter the fight ring."

I look him over. He seems well built and I put his weight at around one-ninety. Height maybe six foot one. But he looks pale, like his face hasn't seen the sun for some time. And there is also the question of his age. It's hard to pin-point, but he's no kid.

"How old are you?" I ask.

He shifts a little. "What is the ideal age for a boxer?"

"Mister," I say, "in this state it's illegal for any man over forty to even step into the ring."

"I'm thirty," he says fast. "I'll see that you get a birth certificate to verify that."

I smile a little. "Look, man, at thirty in this game, you're just about over the hill. Not starting."

His eyes glitter a little. "But I am strong. Incredibly strong."

I stretch the smile to a grin. "Like the poet says, you got the strength of ten because your heart is pure?"

He nods. "I do literally have the strength of ten, though not for that reason. As a matter of fact, realizing that I possessed this tremendous strength, it finally occurred to me that I might as well capitalize on it. Legitimately."

He puts down the zipper bag and walks over to where to set of barbells is laying on the mat and does a fast clean and jerk like he was handling a baby's rattle.

I don't know how many pounds is on that bar, weight lifting not being my field. But I remember seeing Wisniewski working with those weights a couple of hours ago and he grunts and sweats and Wisniewski is a heavyweight with a couple of state lifting titles to his credit.

I'm a little impressed, but still not interested. "So you're strong. Maybe I can give you the names of a few of the weightmen who work out here. They got some kind of a club."

He glares, at which he seems good. "There is no money in weight lifting and I need a great deal of money." He sighs. "The subject of money never really entered my mind until recently. I simply dipped into my capital when necessary and then suddenly I woke one evening to discover that I was broke."

I look him over again. His clothes look expensive, but a touch shabby, like they been worn too long and maybe slept in.

"I do read the newspapers," he says, "including the sports pages, and I see that there is a fortune to be made in the prize ring with a minimum of effort." He indicates the zipper bag. "Before I ran completely out of money, I bought boxing trunks and shoes. I will have to borrow the boxing gloves."

I raise an eyebrow. "You mean you want to step into the ring with somebody right now?"

"Precisely."

I look down the gym floor. By now the place is empty except for Alfie Bogan.

Alfie Bogan is a good kid and a hard worker. He's got a fair punch and high hopes for the ring. So far he's won all six of his fights, three by knockouts and three by decisions. But I can't see what's in his future. He just don't have enough to get to the top.

All right, I think to myself. Why not give the gentleman in black a tryout and get this over with so I can get to bed, which is a cot in my office.

I call Alfie over and say, "This here nice man wants to step into the ring with you for a couple of rounds."

It's O.K. with Alfie, so the stranger disappears into the locker room and comes back wearing black trunks.

I fit him with gloves and he and Alfie climb into the ring and go to the opposite corners.

I take the wrapper off a new cigar, strike the gong, and start lighting up.

Alfie comes charging out of his corner, the way he always does, and meets the stranger three-quarters of the way across the ring. He throws a right and a left hook, which the stranger shrugs off. Then the stranger flicks out his left. You don't really see it, you just know it happened. It connects with Alfie's chin and Alfie hits the canvas on his back and stays there. I mean he's out.

I notice that my match is burning my fingers and quick blow it out. Then I climb into the ring to look at Alfie. He's still breathing, but he won't be awake for a while.

When you been in the fight game as long as I have, you don't need no long study to rate a fighter. Just that one left—and even the *sound* of it connecting—has got my heart beating a little faster.

I look around the gym for somebody to replace Alfie, but like I said before, it's empty. I lick my lips. "Kid, what about your right hand? Is it anywhere near as good as your left?"

"Actually my right hand is the better of the two."

I begin to sweat with the possibilities. "Kid, I'm impressed by your punch. I'll admit that. But the fight game is more than just punching. Can you *take* a punch too?"

He smiles thin—like a kid wearing new braces. "Of course. Please hit me."

Why not? I think. I might as well find out right now if he can take a punch. I take the glove off Alfie's right hand and slip into it.

In my day—which was thirty years ago—I had a pretty good right and I think I still got most of it. So I haul off and give it all I got. Right on the button of his chin.

And then I hop around the ring with tears in my eyes because I think I just busted my hand, but the stranger is still standing there with that narrow smile on his face and his hair not even mussed.

Alfie comes back into this world while I'm checking my hand and am relieved to discover that it ain't broken after all.

He groans and staggers to his feet, ready to start all over again. "A lucky punch." The boy is all heart, but no brains.

"No more tonight, Alfie," I say. "Some other time." I send him off to the showers and take the stranger into my office. "What's your name?"

"I am known as Cardula."

Cardula? Probably Puerto Rican, I guess. He's got a little accent. "All right," I say, "from now on you're Kid Cardula. Call me Manny." I light my cigar. "Kid, I just *may* be able to make something out of you. But first, let's get off on the right foot by making everything legal. First thing tomorrow morning we see my lawyer and he'll draw up papers which make us business associates."

Kid Cardula looks uneasy. "Unfortunately, I can't make it tomorrow morning. Or the afternoon. For that matter, I can't make it *any* morning or afternoon?"

I frown. "Why not?"

"I suffer from what may be termed photophobia."

"What the hell is photophobia?"

"I simply cannot endure sunlight."

"You break out in a rash or something?"

"Quite a bit more than a rash."

I chew my cigar. "Does this photophobia hurt your fighting any?"

"Not at all. Actually I regard it as responsible for my strength. However, all of my matches will have to be scheduled for evenings."

"Not much sweat there. Damn near all matches today are in the evening anyway." I think a little while. "Kid, I don't think we need to mention this photophobia to the State Medical Commission. I don't know how they stand on the subject and it's better we take no chances. This photophobia isn't catching, is it?"

"Not in the usual sense." He smiles wide this time, and I see why he's been smiling tight before. He's got these two outsize upper teeth, one on each side of his mouth. Personally, if I had teeth like that, I'd have them pulled, whether they got cavities or not.

He clears his throat. "Manny, would it be at all possible for me to get an advance on my future earnings?"

Ordinarily, if anybody I just meet for the first time asks me for money, I tell him to go to hell. But with Kid Cardula and his future, I think I can make an exception. "Sure, Kid," I say. "I guess you're a little short on eating money?"

"I am not particularly concerned about eating money," the Kid says. "But my landlord threatens to evict me if I don't pay the rent."

The next morning at around eleven I get a phone call from Hanahan. It's about the McCardle-Jabloncic main event on Saturday night's card at the arena.

McCardle is Hanahan's pride and joy. He's a heavyweight, got some style and speed, and he's young. Hanahan is bringing him along careful, picking and choosing. Maybe McCardle isn't exactly championship material, but he should get in a few big money fights before it's time to retire.

"Manny," Hanahan says, "we got a little trouble with the Saturday night card. Jabloncic showed up at the weigh-ins with a virus, so he got scratched. I need somebody to fill in. You got anybody around there who'll fit the role?"

Jabloncic has 18 wins and 10 losses, which record don't look too bad on paper, except that it don't mention that he got six of them losses—all by knockouts—in a row after his eighteenth win. So I know exactly what type of fighter Hanahan wants as a substitute for Jabloncic.

I think a little. Off hand, there are three or four veterans who hang around the gym and could use the money and don't mind the beating.

And then I remember Kid Cardula.

Ordinarily when you got a new boy, you bring him up slow, like three-round preliminaries. But with Kid Cardula I feel I got something that can't wait and we might as well take some shortcuts.

I speak into the phone. "Well, off hand, Hanahan, I can't think of anybody except this new face that just come to me last night. Kid Cardula, I think he calls himself."

"Never heard of him. What's his win-lose?"

"I don't know. He's some kind of foreign fighter. Puerto Rico, I think. I don't have his records yet."

Hanahan is cautious. "You ever seen him fight?"

"Well, I put him in the ring here for just a few seconds to see if he has anything. His left is fair, but I never seen him use his right hand once. Don't even know if he has one."

Hanahan is interested. "Anything else?"

"He came in here wearing a shabby suit and gave me a sob story about being down and out. He's thirty-five if he's a day. I'll swear to that."

Hanahan is pleased. "Well, all right. But I don't want anybody *too* easy. Can he stand up for a couple of rounds?"

"Hanahan, I can't guarantee anything, but I'll try the best I can."

That evening, when Kid Cardula shows up at the gym, I quick rush him to my lawyer and then to the weighin and physical under the arena, where I also sign papers which gives us ten percent of the night's gross.

I provide Kid Cardula with a robe which has got no lettering on the back yet, but it's black, his favorite color, and we go out into the arena.

McCardle is a local boy, which means he's got a following. Half his neighborhood is at the arena and it ain't really a bad house. Not like the old days, but good enough.

We set up shop inside the ring and when the bell rings, McCardle makes the sign of the cross and dances out of his corner.

But Kid Cardula don't move an inch. He turns to me, and his face looks scared. "Does McCardle *have* to do that?"

"Do what?" I ask. "Now look, Kid, this is no time to get stage fright. Get out there and fight."

The Kid peeks back over his shoulder where the referee and McCardle are waiting for him in the center of the ring. Then he takes a deep breath, turns, and glides out of our corner.

His left whips out, makes the connection with McCardle's jaw, and it's all over. Just like that. McCardle is lying there in the same pose as Alfie Bogan last night.

Even the referee is stunned and wastes a few seconds getting around to the count, not that it really matters. The bout is wrapped up in nineteen seconds, including the count.

There's some booing. Not because anybody thinks that McCardle threw the fight, but because everything went so quick with the wrong man winning and the fans figure they didn't get enough time for the price of their tickets.

When we're back in the dressing room, the first person who comes storming in is Hanahan, his face beet red. He glares at Kid Cardula and then drags me to a corner. "What the hell are you doing to me, Manny?"

I am innocence. "Hanahan, I swear that was the luckiest punch I ever seen in my life."

"You're damn right it was a lucky punch. We'll have the re-match as soon as I can book the arena again."

"Re-match?" I rub my chin. "Maybe so, Hanahan, but in this event I feel that I got to protect the Kid's interests. It's like a sacred trust. So for the re-match, we make his cut of the gate sixty percent instead of ten, right?"

Hanahan is fit to explode, but he's got this black spot on his fighter's record and the sooner he gets if off, the better. So by the time we finish yelling at each other, we decide to split the purse fifty-fifty, which is about what I expect anyway.

A couple of nights later when I close up the gym and go to my office, I find the

Kid sitting there watching the late show on my portable TV set. It's one of them Dracula pictures and he turns to another channel when I enter.

I nod. "Never could stand them vampire pictures myself either. Even in a movie, I like logic, and they ain't got no logic."

"No logic?"

"Right. Like when you start off with one vampire and he goes out and drinks somebody's blood and that turns his victim into a vampire too, right?" So now there's *two* vampires. A week later, they both get hungry and go out and feed on two victims. Now you got *four* vampires. A week later them four vampires go out to feed and now you got *eight* vampires."

"Ah, yes," Kid Cardula says. "And at the end of twenty-one weeks, one would logically expect to have a total of 1,048,576 vampires?"

"About that. And at the end of thirty weeks or so, everybody on the face of the earth is a vampire, and a week later all of them starve to death because they got no food supply any more."

Kid Cardula smiles, showing them big teeth. "You've got a head on your shoulders, Manny. However, suppose that these fictitious vampires, realizing that draining *all* of the blood from their victims will turn them into vampires and thereby competitors, exercise a certain restraint instead? Suppose they simply take a sip, so to speak, from one person and a sip from the next, leaving their victims with just a slight anemia and lassitude for a few days, but otherwise none the worse for wear?"

I nod, turn down the TV volume, and get back to the fight business. "Now, Kid, I know that you'll be able to put McCardle away again in a few seconds, but we got to remember that fighting is also show biz. People don't pay good money for long to see twenty-second fights. We got to give the customers a performance that lasts a while. So when we meet McCardle again, I want you to carry him for a few rounds. Don't hit too hard. Make the match look even until say the fifth round and *then* put him away."

I light a cigar. "If we look too good, Kid, we'll have trouble getting opponents later and we got to think about the future. A string of knockouts is fine, Kid, but don't make them look too easy."

In the weeks which follow while we're waiting for the McCardle re-match, I can't get the Kid to do any training at all—no road work and he won't even consider shadow boxing in front of a mirror.

So I leave it at that, not wanting to tamper with something that might be perfect. Also he won't give me his address. I suppose he's just got pride and don't want me to see the dump in which he lives. And he's got no phone. But he shows up at the gym every other night or so, just in case there's something concerning him.

The second McCardle fight comes and we take it in stride. The Kid carries McCardle for four rounds, but still making the bouts look good, and then in the fifth round he puts McCardle away with a short fast right.

In the days which follow, we don't have any particular trouble signing up more fights because we'll take any bout which comes our way. With Kid Cardula, I know I don't have to nurse him along. Also, we decide on the strategy of letting the Kid get himself knocked down two, maybe three, times per fight. With this maneuver, we establish that while the Kid can hit, he ain't so good at taking a punch. Consequently every manager who's got a pug with a punch figures that his boy has got a good chance of putting the Kid away.

We get seven bouts in the next year, all of which the Kid wins by knockouts, of course, and we're drawing attention from other parts of the country.

Now that some money is beginning to come in, I expect the Kid to brighten up a little, which he does for about six months, but then I notice that he's starting to brood about something. I try to get him to tell me about it, but he just shakes his head.

Also, now that he's getting publicity, he begins to attract the broads. They really go for his type. He's polite to them and all that, and even asks them their addresses, but as far as I know he never follows up or pays them a visit.

One morning after we'd just won our tenth fight—a nine-round knockout over Irv Watson, who was on the way down, but still a draw—and I am sitting in my office dreaming about the day soon when I sell the gym or at least hire somebody to manage it, when there's a knock at the door.

The dame which enters and stands there looking scared is about your average height and weight, with average looks, and wearing good clothes. She's got black hair and a nose that's more than it should be. In all, nothing to get excited about.

She swallows hard. "Is this where I can find Mr. Kid Cardula?"

"He drops in every now and then," I say. "But it's not a schedule. I never know when he'll turn up."

"Would you have his address?"

"No. He likes to keep that a secret."

She looks lost for a few seconds and then decides to tell me what brought her here. "About two weeks ago I drove out of state to see my aunt Harriet and when I came back, I got a late start and it got dark before I could make it home. I'm really not at all good with directions and it had been raining. I turned and turned, hoping that I'd find a road that looked familiar. Somehow I got on this muddy road and my car skidded right into a ditch. And I just couldn't get the car out. Finally I gave up and sat there, waiting for some car to pass, but there was no traffic at all. I couldn't even see a farmhouse light. I guess I finally fell asleep. I had the strangest dream, but I can't remember now exactly what it was, and when I woke, there was this tall distinguished-looking man standing beside the open door of my car and staring down at me. He gave me quite a start at first, but I recovered and asked him if he'd give me a lift to someplace where I could get to a phone and call my father and have him send someone out to pick me up. His car was parked on the road and he drove me to a crossroads where there was a gas station open."

I notice that she's got what look like two big mosquito bites on one side of her throat.

She goes on. "Anyway, while I was making the phone call, he drove away before I could thank him or get his name. But I kept thinking about . . ." She blushed. "Then last night while I was watching the late news, there were things about sports and a picture of Kid Cardula appeared on the TV screen, and immediately I knew that this must be the stranger who had driven me to the gas station. So I asked around and somebody told me that you were his manager and gave me the address of your gym. And I just thought I'd drop in and thank him in person."

I nod. "I'll pass the thanks on to the Kid next time I see him."

She still stands there thinking, and suddenly she brightens again. "Also I wanted to return something to him. A money clip. With one thousand dollars in it. It was found beside my car when the tow truck went to pull it out of the ditch."

Sure, I think. Some nice honest tow truck driver finds a thousand bucks on the ground and he doesn't put it in his own pocket. But I nod again. "So give me the thousand and I'll see that the Kid gets it."

She laughs a little. "Unfortunately I forgot to bring the money and the clip with me." She opens her purse and takes out a ball-point pen and some paper. "My name is Carrington. Daphne Carrington. I'll write the directions on how to get to our place. It's a bit complicated. We call it Carrington Eyrie. Perhaps you've heard of it? It was featured in *Stately Home and Formal Garden Magazine* last year. Mr. Cardula will have to come in person, of course. So that he can identify the clip."

When Kid Cardula drops in the next evening, I tell him about Daphne Carrington and give him the slip of paper she left.

The Kid frowns. "I didn't lose a thousand dollars. Besides, I never use a money clip."

I grin. "I thought not. But still she's willing to ante up a thousand bucks to meet you. Is any part of her story true?"

"Well . . . I *did* drive her to that filling station after I . . . after I found her asleep in the car."

"I didn't know you owned a car."

"I bought it last week. There are some places just too far to fly."

"What model is it?"

"A 1974 Volkswagen. The motor's in good condition, but the body needs a little work." He sits on the corner of my desk, his eyes thoughtful. "*She* was driving a Lincoln Continental."

"Don't worry about it, Kid. Pretty soon you'll be driving Lincoln Continentals too."

We begin spacing out our fights now. No bum-of-the-month stuff. Mostly because we're getting better quality opponents and also because it needs time and publicity to build up the interest and the big gates.

We win a couple more fights, which get television coverage, and the Kid should be happy, but he's still brooding.

And then one night he shows up in my office and he makes an announcement. "Manny, I'm getting married."

I'm a little astounded, but I see no threat. Lots of fighters are married. "Who's the lucky lady?"

"Daphne Carrington."

I think a while before the name connects. "You mean *that* Daphne Carrington?"

He nods.

I stare at him. "I hope you don't take this wrong, Kid, but the dame ain't exactly Raquel Welch, even in the face department."

His chin gets stubborn. "She has a tremendous personality."

That I doubt too. "Kid," I say, "be honest with yourself. She just ain't your type."

"She soon will be."

Suddenly the nub of the situation seems to flash into my mind and I'm shocked. "Kid, you're not marrying this dame for her money, are you?"

He blushes, or looks like he tried to. "Why not? It's been done before."

"But, Kid, you don't *have* to marry anybody for their money. You're going to have money of your own soon. Big money. Millions."

He looks away. "Manny, I have been getting letters from my relatives and many concerned friends. But especially relatives. It seems that they have heard or been told about my ring appearances. And they all point out—rather strongly—that for a man with my background, it is unthinkable that I should be appearing in a prize ring."

He still didn't look at me. "I have been thinking this over for a long time, Manny, and I am afraid they are right. I shouldn't be a boxer. Certainly not a professional. All of my family and all of my friends strongly disapprove. And, Manny, one must have one's own self-respect and the approval of one's peers if one wants to achieve any happiness in this world."

"Peers?" I say. "You mean like royalty? You a count or something? You got blue blood in your veins?"

"Occasionally." He sighs. "My relatives have even begun a collection to save me from destitution. But I cannot accept charity from relatives."

"But you don't mind marrying a dame for her money?"

"My dear Manny," he says. "Marrying a woman for her money is as good a reason as any. Besides, it will enable me to quit the fight game."

We argue and argue and I beg him to think it over for a while, telling him what all that ring money could mean to him—and me.

Finally he seems to give in a little, and when he leaves, he at least promises to think it over for a while.

About a week passes. I don't hear from him and I'm a nervous wreck. Finally, at around ten-thirty one evening, Alfie Bogan comes into my office with an envelope.

Right away I get the feeling that the envelope should have a black border. My fingers tremble when I open it and read the note from Kid Cardula.

Dear Manny:

   I sincerely regret the way things have turned out, but I am determined to quit the ring. I know that you pinned a great deal of hope on my future and I am certain that, under different circumstances, we would have made those millions you talked about.

But goodbye and good luck. I have, however, decided not to leave you empty-handed.

> Best wishes,
> Kid Cardula.

Not leave me empty-handed? Did he enclose a nice little check? I shake the envelope, but nothing comes out. What the hell did he mean he wouldn't leave me empty-handed?

I glare at Alfie Bogan, who's still standing there.

He grins. "Hit me."

I stare. Somehow Alfie looks different. He has these two big mosquito bites on his throat and these two long upper teeth, which I swear I never seen before.

"Hit me," he says again.

May I shouldn't do it, but it's been a long hard week of disappointments. So I let him have it with all I got.

And break my hand.

But I'm smiling when the doc puts on the cast.

I got me a replacement for Kid Cardula.

Career Man

Cardone looked at the tapestry. His eyes sharpened, his thin lips tightened. And he thought to himself, You never know. You really don't. Here I am in a little Hindu shop thousands of miles from home in the middle of this dust bowl called India, and all of a sudden I may be looking at the biggest heist of my entire career.

It was characteristic of Cardone that he used the word "career" in his thoughts to cover the twenty-two years of his life that had started, inauspiciously enough, with muggings and petty burglaries, had proceeded to various grand larcenies committed while armed, and had ultimately ensconced him as a leading practitioner in that most respectable of criminal specialties, bank robbery. Cardone had no scruples, moral or ethical. He was proud of his record, so he called it a "career." It did not signify that his last caper, the robbery of a bank in a small Colorado town, had so nearly ended in his apprehension by the police that he had decided an extended trip abroad might provide a beneficial cooling-off period.

Aside from the slight change in the expression of his eyes and lips, no sign of his emotions showed as he stared through the glass at The Pride of India. Mr. Ganeshi Lall, standing at his shoulder, intoned proudly in excellent English, "There are eighteen thousand jewels embroidered on that tapestry, sir. Emeralds, rubies, diamonds and sapphires, of course, as well as most of the semi-precious stones to be found in India. The tapestry was manufactured in our establishment, the gems sewn into the fabric by our own workmen. Fifty thousand working hours were involved. It demonstrates the fine craftsmanship of Ganeshi Lall & Son."

Cardone nodded, impressed. "It does, indeed," he said. The six-by-eight-foot tapestry was literally encrusted with gems. "How much is it worth?"

"One million dollars. At least it is insured for that, you understand. When it was displayed at the World's Fair . . ."

Cardone interrupted him. "And you have it hanging here in plain sight, protected only by this glass case, almost inviting larceny?"

Mr. Lall smiled. "Of course," he said. "It is a great attraction for tourists, naturally. But it is quite safe, please. A very complicated American burglar alarm safeguards it."

Cardone already knew that. The gold leaf of the burglar alarm laced the protective glass through which they gazed at the tapestry, but it was nice to have Mr. Lall, the owner of The Pride of India, admit it so readily. With a slight turn of his head, Cardone discovered where the connecting wires entered the room.

A score of other tourists had joined them now before The Pride of India. Mr. Lall was busy answering questions from awe-stricken gapers. Cardone, fumbling in his jacket pocket for a cigarette, drifted to the edge of the crowd, sauntered peacefully over to inspect a jade Buddha five yards away. As he withdrew the cigarette from his pocket, it escaped his fingers and fell to the floor near the base of the carved Buddha. Cardone leaned to pick it up. With one swift, beautifully disguised movement, he used the little tool he had brought from his pocket with the cigarette to sever cleanly the burglar alarm wires that disappeared through the baseboard behind the statue.

It began on the veranda of Lauries Hotel the afternoon before.

Recently arrived in Agra by plane from Bombay, along with thirty other American tourists who wanted to see the Taj Mahal, Cardone registered at the hotel desk, washed up in his room, and was taking the first grateful sip of a cool gin sling on the veranda before dinner, when he felt eyes upon him. That curious sixth sense, so often developed in persons outside the law, warned him that someone had him under observation. He glanced around to locate the observer. All the little nerve ends in his wary body were erect and seeking.

The squatting dhoti-clad sellers of ivory, brass and marble curios who, with their wares, occupied most of the veranda space near him, were paying no attention to him. His fellow tourists, mostly female, chattered like temple monkeys around him, but a quick survey assured him that none was regarding him. Then he turned his head slightly toward the doorway of the hotel bar and encountered, with an impact almost physical, the eyes that were watching him.

They belonged to a tall, massively built Hindu with brush-cut hair above a square brown solid face. He stood behind a pillar of the porch to Cardone's right, down three steps on the gravel driveway that bordered the veranda. Dressed in western clothes, his expression was open and candid, and the watching eyes were unusually dark, even for a Hindu. Then Cardone forgot the man's appearance in speculation as to why he was so intensely interested in an American tourist—a perfect stranger, but also, it must be admitted, a slightly hot bank robber at home.

When the Hindu realized Cardone was aware of his scrutiny, he smiled and approached, slipping up the three steps to the veranda gracefully, despite his bulk. "Mr. Cardone?" he asked politely.

Cardone was startled. The guy knew his name. He set his drink down on the table very slowly. "That's me," he admitted coolly. "What can I do for you?" Maybe the fellow had looked over his shoulder when he registered.

"I am Mirajkar Dass," the man introduced himself with a little bow. "Driver and guide. Would the gentleman permit me to show him the Taj Mahal and other Agra sights while in our city? Please?"

Cardone thought Mirajkar's eyes were signaling him, but he didn't know what. "I'm with a tour," he said brusquely, indicating the vociferous group nearby. "We're taken care of, thanks."

"A private guide, sir," the man insisted gently, "is much more satisfactory. I have a very nice American car, and I speak English very good."

"I'm with a tour, buddy. We got a guide, and we see the sights in buses. Thanks just the same."

Mirajkar refused to be brushed off. "I've always admired your work, Mr. Cardone," he said softly.

For an instant, Cardone froze in his chair, oblivious of the chattering tourists around him. Then he looked up at the tall Hindu and nodded reluctantly. "Don't bother me now," he said, "but maybe you've got something with this private guide thing. Come to my room after dinner and we'll talk it over, okay?"

"Okay," Mirajkar agreed instantly, a warm light of pleasure appearing momentarily in his dark eyes. "After dinner, sir." He unobtrusively withdrew to the driveway to take up his stand beside the porch pillar once more.

Does he know my room number too? Cardone wondered uneasily. He took a gulp of his gin sling, his thoughts running oddly on the fact that he really would enjoy seeing Agra on his own with his own guide, rather than in the company of all the tour members.

After having chicken curry for dinner that was so hot it put to shame the Mexican seasoning Cardone had sampled at home, he lit a cigarette and strolled to his room at the end of the hotel's ground floor colonnade. The flickering electric bulbs along the arcade threw their light only a few feet to either side, where it was hungrily swallowed up by the pitch darkness of the hotel's gardens. Cardone was an easy target to anyone concealed in that darkness, he was aware, but although he was small in stature and physically unimpressive, Cardone did not lack courage. His "career" testified to that. He was calm and unhurried in his walk to his room; he even stopped once to take a long savoring breath of the dust-and-dung-scented air. The hand that inserted his key in the door was quite steady.

As the door opened under his hand, he felt a presence materialize behind him. When he switched on the light and turned to close the door, the Hindu was already inside the room.

Cardone, without preamble, said, "How'd you know my name?"

Mirajkar shrugged. "A college classmate of mine was your guide in Bombay last week. He telephoned me you were coming here."

The big Hindu was a college man, it seemed. Cardone automatically fought against a feeling of inferiority that usually assailed him when talking to college graduates. Cardone himself hadn't finished the eighth grade. But why should Mirajkar's pal telephone him that Cardone was coming to Agra? Just to tout him onto a possible customer for his guide's services? Not likely. Then why?

Pressing for information, Cardone asked, "Why did he do that?"

"Telephone me you were coming? Because he thought you were the right man to help us with a little project we have here in Agra."

"Wait a minute, buster. What's that mean?"

"He recognized you."

"How could he do that?"

"He was in America getting his Master's degree several years ago, at the University of Colorado. He saw your photograph in the newspapers."

"Me? He saw my picture in the papers? He was wrong. This is all a big fat mistake. Sorry, buddy."

"No, Mr. Cardone. He remembered the picture very well. You were being questioned in a bank robbery case in Boulder. Everybody thought you were guilty, but nothing tangible could be proved."

"You're so right it couldn't. I'm not completely stupid," he said, "even if I didn't go to college."

"You are a very skillful thief," Mirajkar said with an apologetic gesture of his hands that seemed to disassociate him from the blunt statement. "My friend knew that. That's why he telephoned me."

"I haven't made a score of any kind in India," Cardone hastened to defend himself.

"Of course. That is what I have to offer you, sir, the opportunity to make a wonderful score by helping us."

Cardone breathed out cigarette smoke, relieved. "So sit down," he invited, waving his hand. "I'll turn on the air conditioning."

What could be worth stealing in this jerk town?

As though reading his mind, Mirajkar said in his pleasant baritone, "The Pride of India. It is here in Agra. And it is easily accessible to one of your experience."

"What's The Pride of India?" Cardone asked.

The Hindu told him in some detail.

"A tapestry!" Cardone protested when he had finished. "Six feet by eight! What if it's covered with ice? We'd never be able to move it out of Agra once we had it. It's too big."

"Permit me, Mr. Cardone. My friend and I have given a great deal of thought to that. It is another reason why you can be of such help to us."

"Goody," Cardone said sardonically.

"Yes. When you have stolen the tapestry, we will cut the best of the precious stones from the fabric. They are all unset, and not so very large as to be easily recognizable except in India."

"Well, that's an idea," Cardone said. "Then what?"

"Then you smuggle them out of India in your luggage when you go home. With due caution, you realize cash for them in America. I am sure you have connections there to accommodate you in a matter of this kind?"

"I know a few people," Cardone admitted cautiously. He was beginning to feel his heartbeats quicken a little. "What's this Pride of India likely to split out at?"

"We estimate a minimum of a million and a quarter rupees."

"What's that in dollars?"

"Almost a quarter of a million." Mirajkar allowed this succulent figure to hang in the air between them for a moment before he continued. "The tapestry is insured for five million rupees, Mr. Cardone, but that is the estimated value of the tapestry as it is. If we remove the jewels and accept a fifty to seventy-five percent loss on their true value, by reason of having to dispose of them surreptitiously, we should still realize a quarter of a million dollars."

Cardone said, "That's important sugar. Split three ways, eh?"

"Split two ways. Half for you, half for us. After all, you will do most of the work."

"That's for sure. Otherwise you'd never proposition me."

"Does it sound attractive to you?"

"It has possibilities. What did you say your name is?"

"Mirajkar Dass."

"I'll call you Dass," Cardone said. "That other name's a laugh."

Mirajkar bowed, smiling. "As you wish, sir. The Pride of India hangs behind a glass case in the shop of Ganeshi Lall & Son on Mahatma Gandhi Road, right near this hotel. Almost every American tourist who comes to Agra goes into the shop to see it."

"How hard will the store be to crack?"

"Not difficult for you. No night guards are left, if that is what you mean, and you are good with locks, we have heard."

Cardone was modest. "Not too bad," he said.

"But there are burglar alarms. That is mainly why we need you. You must have had a wide experience with them?"

Cardone grinned. "I'm the best little alarm-gimmicker in the business. But I want to see the layout before we try anything."

"Good," Mirajkar said. "Tomorrow you can see it without suspicion. All your group will probably see it. As your private guide, I will take you there when there is a good crowd. You can look at the door locks and the burglar alarm arrangements, perhaps prepare things for an attempt tomorrow night?"

"We'll see. Anyway, you're hired as my guide and driver."

"I shall try to give satisfactory service."

"Yeah, but wait a minute. You're going too fast, Dass. You say I'm going to take these jewels to America, fence them for cash, then send you your share. Is that right?"

"That is right."

"You'll trust me to take the stuff and send your cut?"

"We must, Mr. Cardone. It is all we can do. We cannot gimmick (is that the word you used?) the burglar alarms at Lall's without you. Even if we could, we could not dispose of the gems in India. They are known here. When the tapestry is stolen, the announcement of its theft will alert every jeweler in India. So we *must* trust you. You can see the point. No?"

"What makes you think I won't keep the whole bundle for myself once I get to America?"

Mirajkar said seriously, "There is honor among thieves, is there not?"

Cardone nodded solemnly, then he probed a little deeper. "What is it with you two guys, Dass, that you're getting into the heist racket? You're both college men, aren't you? You got brains. You got good jobs as guides . . ."

Mirajkar interrupted him indignantly. "Good jobs! There are no good jobs in India. We are guides and chauffeurs to tourists, that is all! And we must have a college education to be eligible even for that!

"Most of our income is in tips from rich Americans and, forgive me, most of you are not generous. We will not live like this for the rest of our lives. We are educated men, worthy of more dignified treatment, and we shall get it when we have a quarter million rupees apiece." The soft eyes blazed and the big hands clenched in unmistakable earnestness.

"Okay, okay, Dass," said Cardone, feeling infinitely better about his own abbreviated education. "Don't make a production of it, pal. I see what you mean." He lit another cigarette and offered the Hindu one. They smoked in companionable silence for a time. Cardone's mind was busy. At last he said to Mirajkar, "Tell me about this alarm system."

That's how it happened that Cardone visited the shop of Ganeshi Lall the next afternoon. Before he left it, he thoroughly nullified the system of burglar alarms that protected The Pride of India. Lall's boast of a very complicated American burglar alarm proved, upon expert inspection, to have been a major over-assessment of an almost primitive arrangement. Inconspicuously and skillfully, therefore, during the ostensible tourist shopping in the Lall showroom, Cardone had arranged that The Pride of India's alarm system, when switched on at closing time that night, would appear as efficient as usual but would fail to function. Even the door alarms, meant to alert the police in their headquarters a block away in case of any attempt to enter Lall's shop, were put out of commission with an ease that Cardone found laughable.

When he entered Mirajkar's automobile, waiting for him on the dusty drive before Lall's emporium, he was still chuckling. To the anxious question in Dass' eyes, he answered, "It was a breeze, Dass. We'll be able to lift the rug tonight without even working up a sweat."

Mirajkar put his car in gear and pulled away from Lall's. "We will now visit the tomb of Akbar the Great at Sikandra," he said in his best guide's voice, then added in his own, "You like the tapestry?"

"Terrific, Dass."

"You believe the project worthwhile, then." The car rattled and shook as Mirajkar guided it northward toward the Delhi Gate. "How long do you estimate it will take you to steal the tapestry tonight, sir?"

Cardone said blandly, "Portal to portal, not more than five minutes. I'll be inside the ship in two, have the tapestry out of its frame in two more, and be back outside in one more. Five minutes, Dass. I've already done all the hard work."

Mirajkar nodded, excitement gripping him. "My friend in Bombay was right. You are a professional, Mr. Cardone. I respect you for it."

"It don't pay to get mixed up with amateurs," Cardone said. He felt expansive, sure of success. He basked a little in the Hindu's admiration.

"Five minutes," Mirajkar repeated. "Then we can do it on our way to the Taj Mahal tonight and never be missed. There is full moon tonight, and all tourists must see the Taj by moonlight. Your tour members will go on their bus. I shall drive you. But we will stop for five minutes at Lall's on the way, you understand. We will leave the hotel when your tour does, and arrive at the Taj at the same time. Five minutes we can spare easily by taking a shortcut. You see?"

"Okay, you're the doctor. That sounds like enough of an alibi for me, but I want to be sure of a safe place to cut the ice out of the rug, and a foolproof way to smuggle the loose stones out of India."

"Both are easily supplied," Mirajkar said. "We will cut the gems from the tapestry at the Taj itself, immediately after we steal the tapestry."

"At the Taj?" Cardone had already viewed the magnificent tomb of Mumtaz Mahal by sunrise that morning. "You're nuts! It's a public place. It'll be dark. We'll be surrounded by romantic tourists."

"I have a key to one of the minarets, Mr. Cardone, molded long ago in the hope of future usefulness. The minarets have been closed to the public for years. Many people used to commit suicide by casting themselves down from them, inspired by the romantic love and tragic end of Shahjahan and Mumtaz, no doubt. So we shall be very private at the top of a minaret, with no interruptions."

"Light?"

"Moonlight will serve, sir. Full moon tonight, as I said."

"What about the smuggling bit?"

"All planned, Mr. Cardone. I estimate the gems we shall cut from the tapestry will be fairly bulky, even though we take merely the better ones. Perhaps a two-quart measure might hold them. Do you agree?"

"So?"

"I have prepared three wooden carvings for you to take home from India as souvenirs. They are carvings of the three wives of Lord Shiva, the Destroyer—Parvati, the goddess of domestic happiness; Durga, the goddess of power; Kali, the goddess of blood and war."

"Never mind the theology, Dass," said Cardone. "What about the carvings?"

"These statues are common tourst souvenirs, turned out by the hundreds here, but our three are slightly different. They are hollow, with a screw-on base for each that cunningly fits into a crease in the fold of each lady's garment. I guarantee the joint to be undetectable by any customs official. The jewels will be placed inside the three carvings, stuffed in solidly and packed with cotton." Mirajkar smiled, turning his head to look at Cardone in the back seat. "Good?"

"Okay," said Cardone. "Where are they?"

"Under the lap rob beside you, sir."

Cardone examined the carvings. "Pretty clever, Dass. These ought to do it." He lit a cigarette. "What happens to the rug after we've cut off the ice?"

"It stays in the minaret of the Taj. No one ever goes there now."

That seemed to cover it. Cardone leaned back in his seat as they passed the lunatic asylum on the Sikandra road and relaxed. The eyes of his body saw mango, neem, tamarind and acacia trees march by, enlivened by flitting mynah birds, crows, flocks of green parrots, and vultures perched patiently on gnarled limbs, waiting for something to die; but the eyes of his mind beheld only double handfuls of diamonds, rubies, emeralds and sapphires. Cardone touched absently with a forefinger the bulge under his arm where his gun lay, and looking at the back of Mirajkar's head, his thin lips curved in what passed with him for a smile.

That night, it all went like clockwork. Waving gaily to the busload of his fellow tourists as they started out from the hotel at nine o'clock, Cardone and his driver-guide, Mirajkar, were already parking the car in the wide parking lot before the Taj gate by the time the bus arrived. No one suspected that they had stopped for five minutes before the darkened shop of Ganeshi Lall, and that The Pride of India was now in Mirajkar's car. No one thought anything of the fact that Mirajkar, as a private guide who knew the foibles of tourists extremely well, was carrying an automobile lap robe over his arm when they left the car, in case his "gentleman" might want to sit for a while on the damp grass, or a marble pool coping, and contemplate in awed silence the most magnificent tomb in the world. No one missed them when Cardone and Mirajkar wandered slowly down the cypress-lined mall past the silent fountains before the Taj, loudly admiring its ethereal beauty in the moonlight, and disappeared.

The blinking oil lamps carried by the Taj Mahal guards cast weird shadows inside the soaring arch of the entrance and on the marble platform nearby, where daytime tourists obtained their mosque slippers to prevent their infidel feet from violating the sanctity of the tomb.

The minaret to which Mirajkar had a key was on the northeast corner of the enormous platform, behind the Taj. Its slender finger pointed to the sky directly above the river bank. They approached it carefully in the moonlight from the side, avoiding the front entrance of the Taj entirely.

Mirajkar fumbled in the shadowed side of the galleried obelisk to get the small iron door open. Cardone looked upward. At the top of the minaret, he saw the open, pillared gallery that crowned it. Then he looked sidelong toward the entrance of the Taj, now out of sight, where the nearest guard would be, noting with satisfaction that it was almost a hundred yards away. He whispered, nevertheless, when he spoke to Mirajkar.

"This is real privacy, Dass. You couldn't have done better."

"Thanks. I think it will serve well enough."

The door came open with a loud rasp of metal against marble which Mirajkar ignored calmly. "No one could possibly hear it," he explained when Cardone inadvertently winced.

They entered the narrow door at the foot of the minaret. "Go on up," the Hindu told Cardone. He shifted the rug over his arm to a more comfortable position. "To the top."

"Okay. Need any help with the tapestry? It must weigh a hundred pounds."

"No, thanks, sir. I can manage it." Mirajkar patted the concealing lap robe fondly.

Cardone began to climb the narrow spiral stairway of marble inside the minaret. He counted the steps almost unconsciously, and was surprised when the total came to a hundred and sixty-four. He was puffing when he emerged into the small circular chamber at the top. Between the graceful columns that walled the gallery, he could see the moonlit Jumna River below him curving away across the plain to the north; to the west were the clustered lights and houses of Agra, huddled around the massive dark walls of the Fort; to the south the huge, moon-bright domes of the Taj Mahal were almost on a level with his eyes. The view was breathtaking.

Cardone gave it only a quick glance, however. He turned as Mirajkar labored up out of the dark stairwell behind him. "Bring it over where we can see, Dass. Put the rug down on the floor here in the moonlight and we'll start to operate." He laughed. "Got your fingernail scissors?"

Mirajkar nodded. He put the lap robe, and what it concealed, carefully down on the floor without unfolding it. "I have them in my pocket. It shouldn't take us long." He reached into his jacket pocket.

Cardone said, "Might as well give me the car keys too."

"The car keys?" Mirajkar looked at Cardone in surprise.

"Yeah," said Cardone, his voice amused. "You won't be needing them any more. I will, however."

The Hindu drew in his breath with a faint hiss. Instead of manicure scissors with which to cut the gems free of the tapestry, Cardone held in his hand a gun fitted with a silencer. It was pointing unwaveringly at Mirajkar's heart.

"But, Mr. Cardone, we are partners in this!" The guide ran out of words and was silent, his eyes glinting big in the moonlight.

"We *were* partners, Dass. But who needs you now?"

The tall Hindu looked briefly toward the dark stairwell. He said nothing.

"Too late to scram," Cardone said. "You understand why I have to kill you, don't you?"

"No. You could get to America and merely keep all the proceeds from the jewels yourself. Why kill me?"

"Because I can take it from here without your help. As a professional, I wouldn't want to leave an eyewitness to a heist of mine behind me, would I?"

"I suppose not. You said it does not pay to get mixed up with amateurs."

"You got it now, pal, and you're an amateur." Cardone laughed softly. "I've got to hand it to you, though, for lining this caper up—right down to the hollow carvings I can use to smuggle the ice out."

"They aren't here," Mirajkar reminded him.

"They're in the car, and that's where I'm going after I cut the stuff off the rug. Let's have the keys, buddy boy."

Slowly Mirajkar handed them over. "If you shoot me, someone will hear you. You will be trapped in this tower."

"I cased the minaret before we came up. It's too far away, especially with this." He touched the silencer on his pistol barrel.

"My friend in Bombay will know you killed me."

"I'll take that chance. What's he know, anyhow? Nothing. I'll be in Paris before he even knows you're dead."

"Paris?"

"Or someplace else. You don't think I'd go back home with this loot, do you? I'm hot there right now."

"You promised to, and send us our share."

"Yeah, that's right. Honor among thieves, wasn't it? Even if you're a college man, Dass, your I.Q. is for the birds. I'm flying out of here tomorrow morning for somewhere, and I'll leave your car right in its regular place in front of the hotel. Nobody will even know you're dead, sucker. They'll be worrying about The Pride of India being gone. No time to wonder about a missing native guide."

"I see," said Mirajkar slowly. "You shoot me. You cut the jewels off the tapestry there," he nodded toward the lap robe, "go out and put them into the carvings, drive my car back to the hotel and leave Agra tomorrow."

"That's about it. You got any better ideas?"

"Yes. Let me help you cut the jewels off before you shoot me. It will save valuable time for you. The Taj grounds close at ten o'clock, you know. You may not finish the job in time alone."

Cardone cast a quick glance at his wristwatch. "I'll make it, Dass. Don't worry." His finger tightened on the trigger of the gun. Mirajkar stood motionless.

"Goodby, sucker," Cardone said. "No hard feelings." He pulled the trigger.

The Hindu leaned slowly over toward the lap robe on the floor. When he straightened up again, he held the robe loosely in his hand. There was nothing on the floor where it had been.

"The Pride of India is not here, Cardone," he said. His tone contained the barest suggestion of contempt. "You have made what you call a big fat mistake."

Cardone hardly heard him. He was looking accusingly at the gun in his hand, genuine shock in eyes. "What is this?" he said unbelievingly. He pointed the barrel at Dass and pulled the trigger six times in rapid succession. The clicks of the hammer falling on empty chambers were like small deprecatory sounds like a man makes with his tongue and teeth when he is overwhelmingly frustrated.

"Yesterday," said Mirajkar, "I was one of the drivers that brought your party from the airport to the hotel. I also helped to distribute your luggage to the proper rooms. I placed your bag in your room, sir, while you were registering. It had your name on it, so I took a quick glance inside and found your gun. Knowing I might have dealings with you later, if fortune favored me, I took the liberty of removing the cartridge—just in case." He smiled in the moonlight, his teeth appearing big and white in the dark face. "It seems I was wise to do so."

Cardone grunted. "This was before you braced me on the veranda?"

"Certainly."

"I take it back, Dass. You're no amateur."

Mirajkar bowed. "Thank you. From you, it is a compliment."

"Where's The Pride of India? Still in the car?"

"Yes. I thought it could do no harm to take precautions, so I slipped it out from under the lap robe just as we left."

"You're pretty sharp, Dass. I'll give you that. You've played this whole thing pretty cool for a foreigner. So now we start over, is that it?"

"Not quite, Mr. Cardone. As you so admirably phrased it, who needs you now? You stole The Pride of India for me, handling the burglar alarm systems very professionally. To my shame, I know nothing about electricity."

"Yeah, I know. You're just an amateur."

"Exactly, sir. But now that The Pride of India is in my hands, your usefulness ends, I fear."

"How do you figure? You still can't dispose of those jewels off the tapestry without me, pal. You said yourself it was impossible in India."

"Quite true."

"So?" Cardone tried to sound more confident than he felt. He fiddled with the empty gun in his hand, damning himself for a fool for not checking it when he'd strapped the holster on that morning. "You'll be needing me to fence the stuff for you. Right?"

"Not right. I never intended to cut the gems from the tapestry, Mr. Cardone."

The American suddenly felt trapped. Too many surprises were coming at him all at once. He raised his eyebrows. "Then why the hollowed-out statues and all that jazz?"

"Merely additional touches to assure you of my good faith."

"Good faith!" Cardone laughed with a high, hysterical giggle.

"Let me explain, sir. My friend in Bombay who told me about you is in reality my cousin. He is the son of my uncle who works for the insurance company that insures The Pride of India for five million rupees."

Cardone's shoulders slumped.

"When The Pride of India is reported stolen, the insurance company will generously pay a ten percent reward for its return, with no questions asked. I happen to know that, because my uncle's company paid that amount on a previous occasion." Mirajkar coughed.

"For the return of The Pride of India? It's been heisted before?"

"Once before; this is the second time. Without undue pride I may tell you, sir, that on both occasions the theft was arranged by me."

"You collected the reward before?"

Mirajkar bowed.

"And will collect it again this time?"

"Yes. A quarter of a million rupees for my cousin and me."

"I'm sorry—sorry I called you an amateur."

The Hindu shrugged. "My cousin does the difficult part—selecting professional help for us from among his tourist groups in Bombay, as he selected you, Mr. Cardone. Of course, we must pay a small percentage to my uncle with the insurance company for his cooperation."

Cardone thought, Amateurs! But this time he didn't speak it aloud.

Mirajkar said, "It is too bad you underestimated us, sir. But take comfort, you will die in the most beautiful tourist attraction in the world." Curiously enough, Mirajkar's voice held a note of genuine emotion when he spoke of the Taj.

"Die?"

"What else can you expect? You yourself said it is unprofessional to leave a living witness behind you."

That's when Cardone gave up hope. He reversed the gun in his hand and hurled it savagely at the Hindu's head, but with a negligent lifting of the lap robe in his hand, the Hindu caught the gun in its woolen folds. It dropped harmlessly to the floor with a small metallic crash.

Mirajkar reached then for the American. There was no escape for the smaller man. The Hindu towered over him. His arms were like steel ropes around Cardone's body. He forced Cardone toward the pillars of the tiny gallery.

"You will be a suicide, sir," he said into Cardone's ear with amusement. "I shall tell the authorities when they find you that, as your guide and driver for the past two days, I have heard you speaking with deep despair of an unrequited love—the great love of your life. I shall tell them you came away from America to try to get over this passion of yours for another man's wife, but that your emotions must have overcome you when you saw by moonlight the ineffable beauty of the Taj Mahal where lie the remains of history's most romantic couple. And alas, while I waited for you, at your request, in the gardens below, you must have done as so many star-crossed lovers have done before you: leaped to your death from a minaret gallery. I may even raise the alarm over your absence at closing time myself." He forced Cardone to look downward over the gallery's edge. "As your official guide, sir, I can inform you that the distance you will fall is exactly one hundred sixty-two and a quarter feet."

Cardone struggled helplessly in the big Hindu's grip. Mirajkar casually offered the crowning insult by holding Cardone with only one hand while his other dipped into Cardone's pocket for the car keys only recently surrendered to him.

"It will be readily explained," he continued to speak remorselessly, "how you could gain entrance to a locked minaret to stage your act of self-destruction. Were you not a professional burglar? One of the best? A criminal to whom opening a little door like this would be merest child's play? I bid you goodbye, Mr. Cardone. And our deepest thanks for your professional assistance."

Almost negligently, he brought the edge of one stiffened hand against Cardone's Adam's apple, effectively paralyzing his vocal chords, choking off the shout for help that was bubbling in the American's throat. Then he quickly pushed Cardone over the gallery's edge between two of the columns.

Falling, Cardone saw the black-and-white marble squares of the Taj Mahal platform rushing up to meet him like a pinwheeling, demented chess board. He made no sound. He was voiceless. But he was conscious, for a split second before his shattered body became a dark blot on the moon-washed marble, of an obscure sense of satisfaction that it had taken a college man to best him in his chosen profession.

LIBBY MacCALL

The Perfidy of Professor Blake

To begin with, the whole thing was out of character, the Morrisons being the kind of people who always told the truth, no matter how unpalatable. They never cut corners on income tax returns—not even quite legitimate corners. Once, Mr. Morrison, who had forgotten to brake at a stop sign, had to appear in court and pay a ten-dollar fine. Once, Mrs. Morrison had an interview with a cop: her cleaning woman, arrested for shoplifting, had given Mrs. Morrison's name as a character reference. These incidents left them quite shaken.

Yes, the Morrisons were law-abiding people. Oh, they knew about the other kind. They'd had experience with dishonest persons. Plenty of it. When they first fell in love with archeology, they'd been incredibly gullible. In Mexico they'd bought a "guaranteed" pre-Columbian statuette. Back home in Riverview, New Jersey, their friend and new neighbor, Professor Blake, smiled tolerantly and pointed out the telltale marks of factory mass production. He hoped they hadn't been badly taken.

They had, by just how much they never told. Before their next trip—this time to Italy—they read and studied books he loaned them. They returned triumphant, proud owners of an Etruscan bowl. Professor Blake, again wearing that superior smile the initiate reserves for the tyro, showed them a photograph of the original (property of the archeological museum in Ravenna) and patiently pointed out the discrepancies between the real vase and their cleverly crafted copy. At least, this fake was an expert one, handmade by a master of the counterfeiter's art.

The Morrisons' enthusiasm for archeology was entirely due to the influence of the neighbor. When Professor Blake moved into the house next door, he began, belatedly, to learn gardening. The Morrisons contributed cuttings and good advice. In return, they were invited to view some of the professor's color slides. Egyptian tombs and the temples of Southern India were a revelation to the Morrisons who, if they thought of them at all, thought of ancient civilizations as something kids studied in school. Their new friend brought the ruined buildings to life, peopling them with a colorful cast of characters: three-dimensional men and women who had servant problems and marital arguments. Mr. Morrison was fascinated by the Romans' advanced engineering techniques. Mrs. Morrison, easily able to contain her enthusiasm for drains, was enchanted by the jewelry and statuettes of semiprecious stone in the professor's collection.

That summer the Morrisons went to Mexico instead of making their usual visit to the Iowa relatives. Professor Blake helped them plan the trip, supplying introductions to friends and colleagues that enabled them to visit sites where actual digging was going on. That did it. They were hooked.

Their children, all grown, were doing well. There was no reason the Morrisons shouldn't spend their money on travel to distant places.

"Why," demanded their eldest, "are you suddenly ruin-happy? Go play shuffleboard in Florida. You might break a hip, wandering around those sites."

Mr. Morrison smiled the tolerant smile he reserved for generation-gap arguments and pressed the button on his new carousel slide projector. Onto the screen flashed a picture of a temple, precariously perched atop a steep flight of steps.

"That's why," he said. "That's a stiff climb. There are two hundred of those steps. But the view from the top—fantastic!"

"How do you get up there?"

"Walk, naturally," Mrs. Morrison said.

Her son stared at the screen, verified that each of the steps was a good two feet high, looked back at his mother's short legs and portly midsection. "That's a physical impossibility," he said.

"No, dear. It's easy. The guides get behind and boost." She giggled. "Try not to think about it, dear, since it seems to distress you."

That spring they stopped in Athens for a few relaxing days between excavations. Now that Mr. Morrison was retired, there was no longer any need to rush madly from site to site. They taxied up to the Acropolis and settled down, hand in hand, on a huge block of stone in their favorite spot near the Temple of Athena.

"I never really believe this air," Mrs. Morrison said softly. "It makes me drunk, like champagne. We're so high, up here, I feel I could reach up and touch the sky."

Mr. Morrison squeezed her hand. "Don't do it," he said. "It might be dangerous."

"Dangerous?"

"Athena or Mercury might just reach down . . ."

"And I'd find myself jerked up to the ultimate heights?"

"Right. So don't do it. I'm not quite ready to let you join the gods on Mount Olympus."

"Mr. Mor-rees-sohn, is it not?" The fat gentleman confronting them was even shorter and more rotund than Mrs. Morrison. His smile glittered with gold. "You do not remember me!" His voice overflowed with sorrow. "I, who have sell you the most beautiful handwoven skirts in all of Greece without charge for the postage. All the way to Keokuk!"

"I'm afraid our minds were far away," Mrs. Morrison said. "Of course we remember you, Mr. Scopas."

"I have follow you." Mr. Scopas lowered his voice to a whisper, though no one was nearby. "I have close up my shop in order to do so. The matter is not one to be discuss within four walls." He turned to peer behind him, the back of his short neck bristling with suspicion. "These days, one is never safe."

"I told you this morning, we don't need a beautiful handmade carpet. You can skip the dramatics, man. A better offer won't change our minds," Mr. Morrison growled.

"Ah! It is no matter of a carpet. I speak now of a priceless object. Because you came to my shop from Professor Blake, I know you can appreciate it."

Mrs. Morrison shaded her eyes against the golden glitter of his teeth in the late-afternoon sunshine. "What sort of priceless object?"

"You know of the persecution of the royal family by the Junta? They have been force to hide. One—a second cousin of the King!—is an old customer. In order to eat, he must sell an item from his collection of antiquities. A tragedy!"

The little man was overacting. The Morrisons felt a strong inclination to laugh. "Lucky he's got things to sell," Mr. Morrison said.

The Greek sighed, a sigh so gusty it ruffled Mrs. Morrison's hair. "It is a tragedy that this magnificent Greek antiquity must leave Greece. But this man has children. So he parts from this precious ring. It is from Crete, where it was found in the Palace of Minos."

"And how can we be sure it's not a copy?"

"But no! This is real, made by a master craftsman, two thousands years before Christ! Think of it! You will present it to a museum, where your countrymen may look upon it and read, 'Generous gift from the collection of Mr. and Mrs. Mor-rees-sohn'! You will be a benefactor of the public."

"Okay. No charge for looking, is there?" Mr. Morrison was not ordinarily impolite, but he was anxious to terminate this idiotic conversation, though he feared it was already too late to recapture his shattered euphoria.

"Not here! You do not imagine I would carry it with me? We make an appointment. You come to my home and then I show, and you have opportunity to study it careful and verify the truth of my story. Here is my address. I am at home until nine in the morning. I do not suggest the nighttime. It is unsafe in the narrow streets of the Old City these days, with this vicious curdog of a Junta we have now . . ."

"What kind of guarantee do I get?" Mr. Morrison interrupted.

"Nothing in writing," the Greek said hastily. "It would not be safe, not for me nor for my client." He raised a pudgy hand. "I give my word of honor!"

"Not good enough. Sorry. I need a written guarantee from a recognized antique dealer."

"Impossible! Surely you know I would not cheat a friend of Professor Blake."

"Let's assume it's real. How do I get it through customs, with no bill of sale? Antiques come in duty-free only if you can prove they're real."

"A ring, it is so easy to slip through the customs."

"Smuggle it in? You must be crazy."

"You are making big mistake," Mr. Scopas said. "It is too bad. I had thought you more courageous."

"It's no use, Scopas. You can't needle me. Find yourself another customer."

With one last enormous sigh, the Greek gentleman turned his back and departed, slipping and sliding over the rough stones in his shiny pointed shoes.

Mrs. Morrison laughed comfortably. "There was a time when we'd have fallen for a crazy story like that. We were inexperienced then."

"If," Mr. Morrison said, "he weren't such an obnoxious little creep, I'd have taken him up on it. I'd like to have a look. It is just barely possible he's telling the truth."

"We promised Professor Blake we'd never buy another artifact except through a reputable dealer," Mrs. Morrison said. "Besides, Scopas' apartment is sure to be full of fleas."

"Right! Just the thought of it makes me itch." Mr. Morrison pointed to a place between his shoulder blades which his wife obligingly scratched for him. "Whew! That's better. Let's try a few more shots in this light. Okay?"

"We must have a hundred slides of the Parthenon from here."

"Not one of them does it justice. Stay right where you are."

Unlike Mr. Scopas, his feet were sure on the uneven ground as he moved into position. Not for nothing had Mr. Morrison been a member of the mountain-climbing club in his undergraduate days. Mrs. Morrison, with a resigned shrug, arranged her red sweater over her shoulders. One of her wifely duties was to be equipped at all times with a touch of red, to serve as a spot of color against gray stone or green mountain. She owned, besides the sweater, a red pocketbook, a red raincoat, and a vast red straw shade hat. She looked terrible in red.

Next morning, following a restless night, Mr. Morrison woke early. In the other bed his wife slept on. He knew there'd be no going back to sleep for him. Might as well go and have a look at Scopas' ring—with no idea of buying, of course, but just for the fun of calling his bluff. He dressed quietly and slipped out.

He covered the distance rapidly, consulting his map of the city from time to time. Though a short man, only a couple of inches taller than his wife, he was thin and wiry. It wasn't fair, she had complained only last night. He ate far more than she did. He had no right to his slim figure while she suffered a steadily increasing girth. He had laughed and ordered more dessert for both of them. The layers of pastry were thin as tissue paper and oozed butter, honey, and other high-calorie, cholesterol-laden undesirables. "We'll walk it off tomorrow," he had said. It made no difference to him that his wife's figure did not show off a frock to good advantage. Besides, when hungry, she was cross, and that did matter. Nothing else upset her equanimity.

The home of Mr. Scopas was in a most unsavory neighborhood. The stench from the gutter was thoroughly uncivilized. Handkerchief to nose, Mr. Morrison sprinted up the four flights of stairs and knocked.

"Who is it?" came a whisper through the door.

"Morrison! Let me in!" he shouted, trying unsuccessfully to breathe in air without smelling it.

"Shhhhh!" The door opened, a pudgy, hairy hand reached out, clutched his sleeve, and drew him in. Scopas closed and locked the door. "So you come after all? Good! My wife sleeps. Come, we go in the kitchen."

They tiptoed down a narrow dark hall. In the kitchen, Scopas opened a battered tin box and took out several half-eaten loaves of bread. From behind them, he produced the end of a final loaf, green with mold. "Good hiding place, no?" His fat fingers fumbled in the moldy remnant. "Ah! I have it!" He wiped the ring on a grimy rag, no less unsavory than the moldy bread, then handed it to Mr. Morrison, who received it without enthusiasm and carried it to the narrow dirty window.

The ring consisted of a circular piece of some semiprecious stone—chalcedony, probably—set in silver and carved. It was hard to see clearly. Deciding to sacrifice his handkerchief to the cause of archeology, Mr. Morrison scrubbed a clean spot on the window pane. Now he could see the carving. It was a seated monkey, the figure distorted to fit the circular shape of the stone. Yes, both style and subject were quite typical of the Mid-Minoan period. An excited feeling began to grow in him. Surely nobody would go to this kind of trouble to create a fake. Would they? With an effort, he assumed an expression of doubt.

"Not bad," he said. "Not bad at all for a copy."

"You know it is no copy," Mr. Scopas replied with quiet assurance. "It is yours for fifty thousand drachmas."

Mr. Morrison did a rapid calculation. He had enough traveler's checks—he and Mrs. Morrison between them—so that he could pay Scopas and still finish the trip as planned. Just barely. If they were careful.

"It's worth much more than that," he said aloud. "*If* it's real . . ."

"But you will not pay more," Mr. Scopas replied with disarming candor. "The owner can live on the sum for a long time, perhaps until the Junta is overthrown and his family return to power."

Still uncertain—after all, he had been stung before—Mr. Morrison continued to hesitate.

"I hear my wife," Mr. Scopas hissed. "Better she not see you. Pay me and go.

Five minutes later, the signed traveler's checks were in the soiled fat hands of Mr. Scopas, and Mr. Morrison was hastening back to his hotel, the ring on the little finger of his left hand. He had put it on backward; all that showed was a narrow band of silver, the carved stone safely hidden in the palm of his hand. Now what? he thought. He couldn't wander around Greece with a clenched fist for the next two weeks. Nor did he care to admit his folly to his wife—not until Professor Blake had verified its authenticity. It must be hidden, not only from customs inspectors, but from Mrs. Morrison—an infinitely more difficult assignment. Where did people hide jewelry? Only diamonds were small enough to be pushed into a tube of toothpaste. There was no false bottom to the heel of his shoe. What did he own that was safe from Mrs. Morrison's tidying fingers? Ah, he had it! Shoe polish. By mutual consent, she was the laundress of drip-dries during their travels, while he attended to shoes. But what to do with the ring until he could arrange an unobserved session with his shoe-polishing kit? He was still seeking the answer to this problem when he reached his room to find that Mrs. Morrison had solved it for him. Her bed was empty and on the pillow reposed a note, stating that she had gone to the hairdresser. She hoped he had enjoyed his walk.

Using the handle of his toothbrush, he scooped polish from the kit, inserted the ring into the hole, replaced the paste, packed it down neatly, and washed the brown stains from his improvised tool. All that now remained was to present a cool and casual air to the customs and passport inspectors. Could he do it? He considered racing back to Scopas, shoe-kit in hand, to return the ring and retrieve his money and his integrity. But he rejected this thought even as it came to him. Too late for that. He shrugged, shoved the whole matter into the back of his mind, and went in search of a morning newspaper.

It was lunchtime when Mrs. Morrison returned, demanding to know how he liked the new hairdo the Greek operator had contrived. He did his best to be satisfactory. It looked just like the old one to him, but he had been a husband too long to say so. As soon as possible, he changed the subject.

"Let's go cash some of your traveler's checks," he said. "Mine are all gone."

Mrs. Morrison looked startled. "So are mine. I haven't one left."

"All of them? Impossible! You haven't paid for a thing since we left!"

"Not a thing . . . except the wonderful surprise I bought for your birthday, dear. Now don't ask questions. It was a lot of money, I know. But when you see it, you'll say it was worth it."

He tried vainly to remember what he'd admired during the last few weeks. That chess set in Ankara, maybe?

"It better be. Nothing for it, we'll have to cut the trip short." He laughed. "Never mind. It'll be nice to get home. Seems to me you've been talking about the grandchildren a lot lately."

"You're right. I start worrying that they'll forget me. Let's count up our cash and see how many days we've got left."

Mr. Morrison kept his bills in his wallet, his coins in his pants pocket. He counted it all carefully, while Mrs. Morrison was adding up the money in her pocketbook. The total was discouragingly small.

"That'll take care of the hotel bill and a taxi to the airport," he said. "Good thing we already have our return tickets. If all the flights are sold out, we may get pretty hungry."

Mrs. Morrison yanked open a dresser drawer. "Oh, I'm not finished counting, dear," she said. "There's some money in my brown antelope bag, the one you bought for me in Bologna. And there must be something in my little white evening bag—from that little shop next to the hump-backed bridge in Venice, remember?"

"Women!" But Mr. Morrison smiled as he said it, for the total when collected at last, was respectable. A call to Air Olympia brought good news: a cancellation had just come in. There would be no problem about changing the reservations to an early-morning flight. Since this was their last night, they decided to splurge by going out to dinner at the Grande Bretagne.

"Pack first, dinner afterward," Mrs. Morrison said. "When we get back, we'll be full of good food and good wine and we won't want to be bothered."

They returned quite late after dinner. Mr. Morrison, having unlocked the door to their room, stepped aside to let his wife go first. She advanced into the room and then, with a small startled shriek, backed out again, treading rather heavily on Mr. Morrison's toe.

"Ouch! What the devil's the matter with you?" he shouted.

"There's a man . . . a man in there! Oh, dear, do be careful . . ."

Pushing her aside, Mr. Morrison catapulted himself into the room, just in time to see a foot disappear over the balcony railing. He ran out and looked over. A dim figure was running down the street. No use shouting; no one else in sight. He turned back into the room, which was a shambles.

"Oh, no!" Mrs. Morrison wailed. "All that packing to do over again!"

"Never mind the packing! What's he stolen?"

Mr. Morrison began rapidly to sort out their belongings. The shoe-polishing kit lay under a heap of tumbled sweaters. He contrived to drop it and in stooping to pick it up again, knocked it under the bed. He took his time about retrieving it and rose reassured. He'd managed a good look and ascertained that the smooth surface of the polish was undisturbed. If, as he was beginning to suspect, the thief had been after the ring, he'd been interrupted in time.

When at last all their belongings had been sorted out and repacked, they compared notes and decided that nothing was missing.

"He was probably looking for money," Mrs. Morrison said.

"Man, did he ever come to the wrong shop!" They laughed inordinately. Mr. Morrison felt his tension draining away. Again he wished he'd never got himself into this. He did not have the temperament for operations outside the law.

By the time they descended from the plane at Kennedy Airport, Mr. Morrison, though his heart was pounding, felt relatively calm—at least, calmer than he had expected to feel. He had lived through the coming hour so many times in imagination, nothing could be so bad as some of his fantasies.

The customs inspector was not one of the friendly sort. He poked and peered. "What's that?" he demanded, pouncing on a white powder in the bottom of Mrs. Morrison's carry-on.

She smiled disarmingly. "Soap flakes," she explained. "The box leaks. Isn't it a mess?"

The inspector glared. He wet his finger, dipped it in the powder, smelled it, tasted. Then he smiled too. "It *is* soap." He seemed surprised. "Okay. Close 'em up."

When they were safely out of hearing, Mrs. Morrison whispered, "Did he suspect me of smuggling in heroin? Surely no smuggler would be so careless as to spill it around loose!"

Her husband, who did not trust his voice, made no reply. Tomorrow, he was thinking, he would make some excuse to get out of the house alone and pay a call on Professor Blake.

As it turned out, no excuse was needed. Struggling to relaunch her household, Mrs. Morrison ignored him. He skulked next door with the ring.

"Scopas!" Professor Blake shouted subsequently. "That crook?" He covered his eyes with his hand. "Oh no! When I gave you the address, I warned you. His shop is okay for handwoven stuff I said. But nothing valuable."

"Well, take a look and let me know the worst."

The professor took the ring and inspected it carefully. He whistled softly between his teeth. Mr. Morrison, annoyed to find that he was holding his breath, let it out with an explosive sound.

"Well?" he demanded.

"Can't be sure . . . yet." Professor Blake wrapped the ring carefully in his handkerchief before tucking it into his pocket. "Let you know in a few days."

Mr. Morrison went home to lunch.

"Where've you been?" Mrs. Morrison asked.

His weary mind went blank. He could think of no reasonable story. Fed up with the strain of keeping secrets from his wife, he blurted out the whole tale. At the end, Mrs. Morrison got up and ran out of the room. In a moment she was back, hand outstretched. In the palm lay a ring, chalcedony set in silver. What Mr. Morrison said then was not language a respectable middle-aged man customarily uses to address the wife of his bosom.

"I don't blame you," she said, when at last he ran down, having exhausted his limited stock of obscenities. "I deserve it. But you're just as bad."

"When did you go to see Scopas?" Mr. Morrison asked.

"It must have been just after you left. We probably missed each other by only a few minutes. When I woke up, you were gone, so I rushed through my dressing and got to his place a few minutes before nine. I pretended I'd been to the hairdresser. I knew you wouldn't know the difference!"

"Where did you hide the ring, to get it past customs?"

"Here." She held out her left hand. "I told you I cut myself peeling an orange, but that wasn't true. This was just to hide the ring." She ripped off the strip bandage from the middle finger, revealing the undamaged skin beneath. "I can take it off now, you know. When I first brought the ring back to the hotel, I put it in my box of soap flakes. I thought of leaving it there, but at the last minute I changed my mind. Can you imagine how I'd have felt if I hadn't—when the customs officer got so nosy about the spilled soap in my carry-on?" She stood up. "Well, I might as well take this over to Professor Blake."

"Why bother? Just admit it: we got taken again, dear."

She set her jaw in an unaccustomed stubborn line. "I'm a pretty good judge of old jewelry by now. This looks real to me. The ring you bought is counterfeit. Mine's not."

"That's ridiculous! If Scopas is dealing in these fakes, he's got a dozen of 'em, all alike, one for every idiot that comes along."

"Maybe so. But I bet you he had a real one to begin with, to copy. Probably he ran out of fakes, so he sold me the original. Say! Maybe he did it by mistake! Oh, I hope so. Can you imagine his face when he realizes . . . ?"

Her giggle and his booming laugh filled the room. Then, abruptly, he stopped. "You know, you might be right? I mean, about his having an authentic ring for copying. That's got to be it. And he sold it to me, because he knew darn well I'd be able to tell the difference." Suddenly he let out a shout. "Hey! How thick-headed can we be? That last night at the hotel . . . Scopas sent that guy to go through our baggage. He wasn't after money. He wanted that ring back!"

"Of course! It's a good thing we left in such a hurry. Heaven knows what he'd have tried next. Well, I'm taking this to Professor Blake, right this minute. We'll see who knows best."

It was several days before the professor summoned them.

"I have wonderful news." He beamed. "Scopas isn't quite as much of a crook as we thought. He actually sold you a fine specimen. Even taking into account the other ring—which is a fake, of course—you got a bargain. It's worth three times what you paid for the pair of them. I suggest you present this valuable antiquity to the museum." He placed one of the rings, which now rested on a bed of black velvet, on the coffee table. The other, he handed to Mrs. Morrison. "Wear it as a souvenir," he said.

Watching his wife slip the ring on her finger. Mr. Morrison grinned. "Wow! What a relief!" he said. "I don't like being made a fool of. Knew darn well that ring was the real thing."

His wife glared at him. "*This* is the ring you bought," she cried, holding out her hand. "It's easy to see the difference. This would never have fooled me!"

Together they turned on the professor. "Well?" Mr. Morrison added, "Mine was the real one, wasn't it?" as his wife shrilled, "Tell him he was the one who got cheated."

Professor Blake shook his head and smiled a benevolent smile. "Dear friends," he said, "during the tests, we put the two rings side by side. I haven't the slightest idea which is which. It doesn't matter. When you present the ring to the museum, a card will be printed to read, 'Gift of Mr. and Mrs. Morrison.' Congratulations to you both!"

For a moment the Morrisons sat in silence, glowering alternately at him and at each other.

"I don't believe you," Mrs. Morrison said at last. "You know which is which. You just don't want to tell us."

"You old devil! You did it on purpose!" Mr. Morrison cried.

The professor shook his head. "That would be most unethical. How can you suggest such a thing?" The lines of his face were stern. But Mr. Morrison could have sworn that he saw the suggestion of a twinkle in the professor's eyes.

HENRY SLESAR

Sea Change

From the day Jane Brissom gave her the invitation, from the moment the travel folders were in her hand, Margo Wheeler underwent a pronounced transformation. Her students, the indifferent, mopheaded teen-agers who yawned their way through her lectures on English Grammar, noticed it first. They smiled more. They kidded with her after class. They seemed to recognize that she was almost as young as they were, and just as interested in getting some kicks out of life. When she was tired, wearied by teachers' conferences, bored with grading papers and untying the snarled word-knots of her students' compositions, she would lean back, say the magic words, and feel herself restored. A month in Europe! Two weeks on a transatlantic liner, and a month abroad! Was there anyone else so happy?

Maybe Jane Brissom, Margo thought, but she doubted it. At forty-five, a matchstick of a woman with watery eyes, random features, and a pitted complexion, Jane Brissom needed more than a vacation to make her happy. Margo couldn't resist the small, secret smile when she thought of Jane, although it was cruel, and rank ingratitude on her part.

Two nights before the sailing, she went to Jane's apartment and found her in the helpless confusion of packing.

"Look at this mess. Just look at it!" Jane said in anguish. "It's like an old clothes sale. I just don't see *what* I'm going to wear."

"Why, you have some very nice things," Margo said. "I always thought your clothes had such . . . taste." She wrinkled her small, pretty face. "Of course, if you hadn't loaned me that money, you could have gone out and bought a whole new wardrobe. I feel like such a *stinker*, Janey."

"Please, Margo, I *want* you to come along. It wouldn't be any fun all by myself. You're doing me a favor, really."

"Some favor," Margo laughed. Then she whistled as Jane picked up a glittering, bib-style necklace from the bureau and placed it forlornly against the flat, protruding bones of her chest. The necklace, with strings of multi-faceted stones, was a fire in the dim room. "Oh, Janey," Margo breathed, "what a hunk of jewelry!"

"Yes," Jane said sadly. "It was the only thing of Mother's I didn't sell after she died."

"Is it real? Are those real diamonds?"

"Oh, they're real, all right. The last time it was appraised I was told it would cost eleven or twelve thousand to replace. It might be worth even more now." She lowered the necklace, and with its borrowed light gone from her face, she seemed older and more haggard than ever.

"Could I try it, Janey? Just for a minute?" She took it in her hands.

In the mirror, the flashing fire around her throat, Margo looked at herself with exultation.

"Oh, it's beautiful! You've just *got* to take it with you, Janey. I mean, if you think it'll be safe . . ."

Janey smiled. "I've never had any occasion to wear the darned thing, so safe or not, I'm taking it. Besides, I've got my protection." She reached into a suitcase and produced a clumsy, black-handled revolver, holding it as casually as a shoe.

"Janey! You mean you're taking a gun along?"

"Don't make a fuss about it. We've had this old gun in the house ever since I was a little girl. It's just another part of the inheritance, that's all."

"Is it loaded?"

"Of course it's loaded. And don't think I won't use it if some *man*—" She flushed, and put the gun back into the suitcase. "Never mind about the gun, it's only sensible for two women traveling alone to have protection. And from what I've heard about Paris—" She snapped the suitcase shut. "Well, I'm ready for them."

Margo smothered a giggle.

The idea didn't come to Margo until morning. She thought she had dreamed it at first, but it was a waking, fully-conscious dream. She was so excited that she telephoned Jane at eight-thirty, and extracted a sleepy invitation to come over.

The older woman was still in her nightdress, a cotton bag that encased her thin body from neck to ankle.

"It's an inspiration!" Margo said. "That's what it is!"

"What is?"

Margo sat on the bed and curled her shapely legs beneath her. "Look, let's face it, Janey. We just won't have any fun at *all* on this trip if we don't—well, you know—meet people. *Men*. And you know as well as I do that there's nothing deadlier than two schoolteachers on a cruise—"

"I don't know anything of the kind," Jane said stiffly.

"But everybody *laughs* at that sort of thing, it's an old joke. The mousy schoolmarms on their sabbatical—"

"Well, I suppose there's something to that."

"But that's what I mean, Janey. Why do we *have* to be what we are? Why do we have to be schoolteachers? Why couldn't we pretend we're the kind of people who *belong* on a luxury liner, first-class passengers and everything? Why, the necklace alone—"

"Don't forget, it's only *one* necklace. We couldn't very well take turns, could we?"

Margo lowered her voice.

"Janey, what if *one* of us pretended to be rich? I mean *really* rich. With that necklace, who would doubt it?"

"One of us?"

"It has to be only *one*, don't you see? As you said, there's only one necklace. But more important, the *other* one could be sort of a—servant. A maid, you know. Then there wouldn't be any *doubt* about how rich we were. One of us, anyway."

Jane walked over to her.

"Are you really serious? You mean we should pretend to be some kind of heiress and servant? For the whole trip?"

"Wouldn't it be *marvelous*? Can't you see the *impression* we'd make? We'd have every man on board in the palm of our hands! Who knows?" she tittered. "We might even meet a *real* millionaire!"

Jane folded her arms. "And who gets to play Cinderella? No, never mind, let me guess."

"Why, *you* do, of course, silly. You didn't think I was suggesting that *I* be the one? It'll be fun, really. I'll be your lady-in-waiting, and you can be very, very *grand* in your umpteen-thousand-dollar necklace—"

The older woman smiled. "You know, I really think you mean it, Margo."

"Of course I do!"

"Well, I wouldn't think of it. It just wouldn't be fair."

Margo chewed her polished thumbnail.

"All right, then!" she said brightly. "We can do it another way. We can take turns!"

"Turns?"

"Of course! We're going *both* ways by ship. We have *two* cruises, don't we? You can be the millionairess one way, and I can be her the other!" She hugged herself joyfully. "Oh, Janey, wouldn't that be fantastic? You're just *bound* to meet some fine, wonderful *man*."

The word was like a bullet. It made Jane Brissom spin about, but she wasn't injured; she was suddenly radiant with a hope that had been suppressed for a lifetime.

Ten minutes later, they tossed a coin and Margo Wheeler won the Europe-bound trip.

They called the ship a Queen, and when Margo first saw its imperious bow and regal funnels, she felt as if in the presence of majesty. Jane was more practical; she took charge of luggage, tickets, and tips, and even before they boarded, they were playing their parts: Margo, the spoiled rich girl, accustomed to red carpets; Jane, the servant, rolling it before her.

In the stateroom, Margo produced a surprise, a bottle of champagne, and Jane rang the steward's button to ask for glasses. The steward was a wiry cockney with a wise, handsome face and bright, merry eyes, and he guessed their relationship at once. He poured Margo's drink for her gallantly, and gave Jane a companionable servant-to-servant wink on his way out.

"To Europe!" Margo said, lifting her glass.

"To you, madam," Jane said respectfully. Then they giggled like the school-girls they taught.

There was a "welcome aboard" party the first night out. Margo wore a powder-blue gown with a low neckline, ideal for the real glory of her attire. Jane put it around her neck herself, touching the diamond-encrusted strands lovingly.

"How does it look?" Margo asked, twirling before the mirror. "Does it look as good as I think it does?"

"It's lovely," Jane said flatly.

"But I feel so *awful*. I mean, wearing *your* necklace—"

"A bargain's a bargain," Jane said. Then she put on a severe black dress with cuffs and collar. The mirror image was depressing, but she smiled gamely. "I *look* like a servant, don't I?"

"You look *fine*, Janey."

"Yes," the older woman said.

The party was slow in starting, the passengers diffident with each other. Then the band played with determination, and the drinks began to flow, and the dancing started, and with the suddenness of a popping cork, the festivities were under way. At their center, glittering, gleaming, dazzling with inner and outer radiance, was Margo Wheeler. From the sidelines, Jane watched her necklace sparkle in and out among the dancing couples, watched Margo tango with one man and meringue with another, saw her laughing with a gold-braided officer and sharing a drink with a bold-eyed man in evening dress.

At eleven-thirty she danced by Jane's table and waved. "Hi, Jane," she said gaily. "Listen, would you be a dear and get my stole?"

"Your stole?"

"You know, the one with the sequins. I'm going for a walk on deck."

"Oh," Jane said. "Yes, of course, miss," she added.

Jane left the party at twelve; Margo didn't return to the stateroom until two. She made just enough noise to wake Jane, then she apologized.

"It's all right," Jane said. "Did you have fun?"

"Did you see *him*?" Margo said. "Oh, Janey, he's a dream. His name is Gordon Baylor, and he's in investments or something. Listen, would you mind very much if I changed dining room tables? He's asked me to. You wouldn't mind, would you?"

"Why should I?" Jane said dryly. "I'm only your servant."

"Oh, I wish *you* could meet someone, Janey. That would make everything perfect." She sighed happily, and started to get ready for bed. Just before she turned out the light, she said, "Oh, would you mind doing me a favor, Janey? That blue knit suit of mine got awful rumpled in packing. Would you iron it for me?"

"All right," Jane Brissom said.

Margo didn't see Jane until late the next morning; she had risen early and gone out on deck. Margo was strolling with Gordon Baylor when she spotted Jane in conversation with the room steward. The little cockney bowed and moved off as they neared.

"Good morning, Jane," Margo said coolly. "Gordon, this is my maid, Jane."

The man with the bold eyes nodded indifferently and looked away. "Let's go on forward," he told Margo. "The captain's an old friend of mine; I'll introduce you."

"That would be lovely. Oh, Jane," Margo said casually, "you won't forget about ironing that suit? And be sure that my black formal is ready for tonight, won't you?"

"Yes, miss," Jane said, in a choked voice.

They moved off together, but their voices carried on the ocean breeze. "She's a gem," Margo was saying. "She's been with me for years."

In the deck chair, Jane sipped her bouillon and grimaced.

That afternoon, Margo returned to the cabin for a change of clothes, and found Jane writing a letter. She told her the exciting news: the captain was having a small party in his quarters that night. Jane became flustered, and worried over her clothes, until Margo said, "Oh, but you're not invited, Jane. I mean, I'm awfully sorry, but you *couldn't* be, really."

"Not invited?"

"Well, it's only a small party, and I couldn't very well ask my—well, my maid, could I?"

"No," Jane said bitterly. "I guess you couldn't."

There was no doubt that Margo Wheeler was having the time of her life. She found a wellspring of small talk and coquetry that she never knew she possessed; she seemed to catch fire each night from the glittering necklace that never left her throat. Gordon Baylor was getting interested; she knew he was intrigued, awed by her obvious wealth, impressed by the maid who jumped at her every command. And Margo made her jump; she didn't miss an opportunity. When Jane began to mutter and complain, she'd remind her that her turn would come on the return trip; but Jane, whose conquests amounted to nothing more than servant-to-servant conversations with the cockney steward, grew lonelier, more bitter, and more miserable with every hour of the voyage.

On the fourth night, when Margo staggered into the stateroom at one-thirty, intoxicated by champagne and her own success, Jane was waiting up with folded arms.

"All right," she said coldly. "I've had enough."

"What's that?"

"I'm sick and tired of playing servant, Margo."

The younger woman blinked, and touched the diamond strands. "But it's just two more days. Two more days and we'll be in Le Havre—"

"I don't care! I'm not having any *fun*. I'm not meeting anyone—"

"But the return trip—"

"I don't *care* about the return trip. I want this farce over now. There are half a dozen nice men I could have met if they didn't think I was your housemaid."

Margo only half-stifled a tipsy giggle. "Really, Janey? You really think that's true?"

"What do you mean by that?"

"Oh, for heaven's sake!" Margo said, flinging her stole to the bed. "You think it would make that much difference? Honestly, Janey, sometimes I think you have no sense at all! You wouldn't have a *chance* with a decent man, servant or not. So you might as well face the truth."

Jane gasped. "How can you talk to me like that?"

"It's true, isn't it? You've got as much chance to get a man interested in you as—as—" She floundered for a simile, and then dropped onto the bed. "I'm tired," she sighed. "Let's talk about it tomorrow."

She was asleep almost at once, fully clothed, the diamond necklace still coruscating around her neck. Even the hateful glare of her roommate's eyes didn't disturb her peaceful slumber.

"I'll show you," Jane Brissom whispered. "I'll show you, damn you!"

In the morning, Margo apologized. "Gosh, Janey, I don't know what came over me. I guess I was drunk; that's all there is to it. Let's not let it spoil things, huh? It's only two more days—"

"Very well, Margo, we'll forget it."

"You're sure you're not angry?"

"No, of course not," Jane said.

"There's a party in the main ballroom tonight. For everyone. You'll be there, won't you?"

"I'll see," Jane said, not looking at her.

Jane didn't attend the party. She sat up in the stateroom until it was over. When Margo waltzed in at three, still giggling over the evening's hilarity, her lipstick smudged and her gown rumpled, Jane was sitting quietly in the armchair near the porthole, looking out at the turgid sea with a strange air of tranquility.

"You should have been there!" Margo said breathlessly. "Jane, it was absolute heaven. We danced under the stars . . ."

"I'm glad you enjoyed it."

"Gordon wants me to meet him in Paris. He knows all about it; he's been there umpteen times—"

"Am I to be your servant in Paris, too?"

"Of course not!" Margo tittered. Then she set her face in a pout. "You're not still angry with me, are you? About those silly things I said last night?"

"They weren't silly," Jane said coldly. "They were true."

"Oh no, Janey—"

"They were true, Margo. I can't get a man. I never could. Not the way you can, with lipstick, and a permanent, and some pretty jewelry. It's harder for me." She stood up, and held out her hand. "I'll take the necklace now, Margo."

"Take it?" Margo looked bewildered, and touched the diamond strands protectively. "But we still have another day to go, Janey. There's the big farewell party tomorrow night—"

"You can do without it. I need it now."

"But what for? Janey, you're not going to tell anyone about—well, about our arrangement?"

"I don't intend to spoil your fun. I simply want the necklace. There's something I want to do with it."

Margo stared at her, and then laughed brassily.

"You *are* going to wear it! You think you can *still* get some man interested, don't you?"

"Give me the necklace, Margo."

"I won't!" Margo shouted, stepping backward and stamping her foot. "What good can it do you now?"

"That's not your affair. It's my necklace and I want it back."

"I won't give it back!" Margo's voice rose toward hysteria. "It's mine until we reach Le Havre. That was the agreement. It's mine! It's mine!"

Jane's unlovely hands became fists. She shivered, as if cold. Then she turned to her bunk, and lifted the pillow. She brought out the awkward, black-handled revolver; her grip on the butt was insecure, but the wavering muzzle was trained in Margo's direction.

Margo didn't believe it for a moment. She sat down limply on her bunk, and stared incredulously at the dark, menacing hole of the weapon.

"For heaven's sake, Janey," she whispered, "put that awful thing down."

"I want my necklace, Margo."

"You're crazy! You're absolutely crazy, Janey! You could—kill me by accident—"

"It wouldn't have to be an accident," Jane said with loathing. "I could kill you gladly, Margo, believe me!" Her anger made her hand shake, and Margo cowered against the wall.

"Please, Janey, you don't know what you're doing—"

The older woman took a step forward; Margo shrieked and leaped from the bunk toward the wall. Her hand slapped at the steward's call button, and she punched it vigorously, over and over. Then she whirled to face her roommate, and there was more fury than fear in her eyes.

"I'll have you locked up!" she screamed. "I'll have them put you away!"

Jane hesitated, turning uncertainly toward the door. In another moment they heard footsteps and a genteel knock.

"Steward, ladies!" said the cheery voice.

Margo smiled triumphantly, called, "Come in!"

The door opened, and the wiry cockney steward entered. Jane lowered the revolver sadly, and stared blankly at the porthole. Outside, the sea rolled by silently.

The steward glanced between them, and the merriment went out of his face. "What is this? What's going on?"

He went to Janey and took the gun from her limp hand.

"You fool," he said hoarsely. "You want to wake the whole ship?"

"She wouldn't give it to me," Jane said weakly. "I tried to make her give it to me—"

The steward smiled thinly. "I'm sure the lady will be reasonable." He turned to Margo. "Won't you, lady? You won't make trouble for us, will you?"

"Trouble?" Margo said. "What are you talking about?"

The steward came closer, his manner more obsequious than ever. His arms shot out, and his large hands locked on Margo Wheeler's throat. She made no sound, and hardly struggled. She looked toward Jane with round, terrified eyes, but Jane only watched with quiet interest. Margo made one last rally for freedom from the ever-tightening grasp, but it was too late. Without air, there was no strength. Then, without air, there was no life. She closed her eyes and died.

The steward lowered her lifeless body slowly to the cabin bunk. When he straightened up, he looked at Jane and clucked.

"Would have been better my way," he said. "If you'd just swiped the bloody thing." He shrugged his neat shoulders. "Well, this way there won't be any complaints. I'll get a trunk or a laundry bag, and over the side . . ."

"The necklace," Jane said dreamily.

"Ah, yes, the necklace. Your mistress's pretty necklace." He bent down and unhooked it, held it up to the light. "We'll have a good time in Paris on this, ducks, see if we don't." He put it in his pocket, and went to the door. "I'll be back in five minutes. Good job, old girl. We working people got to stick together."

He pinched her cheek before going out.

DONALD OLSON

The Blue Tambourine

In the shabbiest precinct of a city so long tainted by economic blight that he is even denied the companionship of his own image in the grime-crusted windows of its vacant buildings, Willie de Garde stoops to snatch a starving cat from a dark doorway, pops it into the sack he carries for this purpose, and then hurries on, for the night air is sharp, winter close at hand. A cold fog shortens the streets and makes pretty but useless golden roses of the street lights.

The young man cradles his furry prize tightly against his chest, as if to revive it by contact with his own strong young heart, and his steps quicken as he approaches an old brick building whose facade still bears faint traces of a gaudy elegance. It is a theater called the Oriental Garden, the only theater in town which has made no concessions to the changing habits of its patrons, and consequently has lost all but a special few. It has not modernized its marquee, nor improved its lighting nor installed retractable seats or refreshment stands, and it continues to show movies consistently lacking in appeal to the general public.

The almost total darkness does not confuse Willie, who knows his way around and can find his usual seat with no other guide than a few spots of orange light where mandarin-colored bulbs glow eerily beneath plaster bas-reliefs of Chinese maidens wearing kimonos that are now chipped and paintless. Overhead, a similarly despoiled jet-black dragon with only one red bulb of an eye holds in its teeth a huge black and crimson Chinese lantern.

Those who still patronize the Oriental Garden seek something other than entertainment: a place to sleep, a place to hide, a place to hope for one of those exceedingly rare occasions when some black-sheep cousin of Eros might lead to a nearby seat a figure whose needs, communicated by signals as universally understood by the initiated as the Morse code is by the fraternity of wireless operators, might correspond to one's own.

Occasionally one might see, it's true, a white-skinned leg extended at a grotesque angle, and a spider-like hand creeping and crawling from ankle to thigh, but it is more often to the solitary passions that the Oriental Garden caters. It is a popular refuge, for instance, of lonely drunks who stumble into the orchestra to sleep off a binge after offering rumbling, gratuitous criticisms of whatever story is unfolding above them on the tarnished silver screen.

Like these others, Willie de Garde comes to the Oriental Garden for a purpose, and no sooner is he seated than his eyes peer through the gloom as anxiously as a seaman's through coastal fog until, perhaps from nearby, perhaps from the other side of the theater, he hears the jingle of the blue tambourine, a sound which violates the silence no more harshly than a discreet cough, and which is repeated at intervals until he has found his way to Mrs. Rainfyre's side.

Without the sound of the blue tambourine she might never be located, for she dresses always in black from head to foot, in garments as out of fashion as her face, a face rather like those that peer out of pre-Renaissance paintings, a Margaritone or a Cavallini, a somber, slant-eyed face as ravaged by time as the plaster faces of the Chinese maidens on the frieze above their heads.

"*Buona sera*, Poet," she greets him as he slips into the seat beside her. "What have you brought me?"

"A choice ingredient for your witch's brew. Another cat."

As usual, she ignores this little dig, just as she drops no hint of what she does with the creatures he brings to her. Nor does he ever ask. It's none of his business.

As he drags the unprotesting cat out of his sack, Mrs. Rainfyre settles her black umbrella against the farther seat and deftly plunges the animal deep into her own black leather shopping bag.

"Quick!" he whispers, for having fulfilled his part of the bargain he is eager for the customary payment; his eyes begin to water and his lips to burn as she rummages in yet another bag as if for some trifle requiring much fishing about to locate.

"*Ecce!*" she murmurs as a figure looms dimly beside them in the aisle, groping blindly along the dark, narrow row of empty seats.

"He can't see! Hurry."

"Ah, *pronto, pronto*," she hisses, mimicking his urgency as her yellow fingers fasten upon the glimmering hypodermic, while the other hand grips his already bared arm pumping up the vein and finally puncturing it with a deft thrust of the needle.

As she puts away her instrument she engages in familiar small talk to which he scarcely listens. "How goes the poem? Soon finished?"

His body droops limply against the seat. "Soon . . ."

"Ah? But not *too* soon, one hopes."

He is so little aware of her now that he misses the faint note of alarm in her voice. "You have other—customers," he murmurs.

She strokes his thigh with an impersonal touch, cold and sexless. "You are my favorite, *care*."

As soon as she departs, carrying her bags, her umbrella, and her blue tambourine, he too drifts out into a foggy drizzle in which the golden roses on their iron stems appear to expand and throb above him, and as he passes through squalid alleys, his mind in a state of swiftly laddering exaltation, a cascade of brilliant images floods his brain so that he fears it will explode before he reaches his own room and can transfer them onto paper. He moves very quickly now.

This creative mood is sustained for an unusually long period, and he is not aware of its passing until one garish dusk as he stands at the window of his room and watches the sun, like a mad arsonist lighting fires in the windows of buildings across the street, while the sky above this conflagration grows purple with news of an approaching storm.

Being above all else a poet, Willie de Garde seeks no logical explanation for the way in which Mrs. Rainfyre manages to be in the Oriental Garden whenever he has something—a cat, a puppy, a rat, a bird—to exchange for her ministrations; he is happy to grant to her occult powers of divination, in spite of having seen her on the street one day, all in black and carrying her usual luggage, stooping to crush a wad of bills into the grubby hand of a dwarf, who thereupon whispered something in her ear which sent her scurrying off in another direction. Apparently, Mrs. Rainfyre paid a whole brigade of street creatures to keep her informed of the desires and movements of her clientele.

When next he creeps into his seat at the Oriental Garden, Willie is shaking with something besides the craving of his burning nerves, for this time he harbors the secret of betrayal, the giddying knowledge that this will be the last time the odious harpy stabs him full of dreams, for the poem is almost finished and he will spend a vagabond winter in the South. He speeds merrily toward the jingle of the blue tambourine.

"*Buona sera,* Poet."

Her perfume is as offensive and rank as the stench of brimstone in the halls of heaven. "Hurry!" he pleads. "I need it!"

She doesn't move. "Ah, Poet, we all have special needs tonight."

"Shoot me! Shoot me!"

"Slowly, Poet. Tonight you must pay for my merchandise."

He jabs at the bag in which she has deposited the gray squirrel he brought her. "I've paid, beldame!"

She jiggles a note of laughter out of the blue tambourine. "These pets you bring me—you think *they* pay for what you get?"

"Give it to me!"

"Will you pay?"

"I'll steal a lion from the zoo in broad daylight! But give—"

"Look. Empty." She opens the black bag and he plunges his hand deep inside, drawing it out damp and trembling.

"I must have it! Now!"

"So you will, *care*, so you will. We're going to leave this place together and go where you will be given what you crave—in return for a small service," she whispers.

They leave the theater and she leads him through a twist of streets and alleys to a tenement in an even more desolate part of town. In a filthy vestibule a dozen rusty mailboxes hang empty and unlabeled on the leprous wall. A bulb glimmers at the top of a long flight of steps.

A flight above this ill-fit landing they stop outside a door upon whose frosted pane has originally been painted in black letters the words:

RAINFYRE
PHOTOGRAPHER

However, the second word has been unskillfully scratched out and underneath has been inscribed the word ESCHATOLOGIST. Mrs. Rainfyre pauses to let him read this before taking a key from her pocket and letting him in.

In a room as dismal as the Oriental Garden, a man sits quietly reading at a cluttered table. He looks as if he had been glued together out of miscellaneous pieces of chalk and string, for there is a curious incompatibility about his features; nothing seems to match. His glasses are so thick they give the illusion that his eyes are actually inside the lenses instead of behind them, rather like monstrous green buttons laminated in plastic spheres. The top of his head is covered by a cap made from a woman's silk stocking; the lobes of his ears sprout grizzled white whiskers. Willie scarcely notices any of this, so fascinated is he by the man's right arm, which ends in a flipper instead of a hand, an elongated tapering paddle of tissue and skin. The left hand is normal, although extraordinarily tiny and delicate, like a girl's.

"My husband," gravely announces Mrs. Rainfyre.

His voice is a passionate squeak. "Honored, dear boy. I know you well already, I feel." A nod toward his wife. "Forgive my not offering my hand, but, as you see . . ." and he deliberately waves the grotesque flipper in Willie's face, at the same time laughing with a sound like breaking glass. "A congenital inconvenience, most distressing at such a time."

"A crucial time," adds Mrs. Rainfyre darkly.

Willie feels faint. "I need—" he starts to say, and Mrs. Rainfyre, leaving her husband to help the youth to a chair, hurries into another room, returning with a hypodermic wrapped in gauze. She no longer has the blue tambourine. Willie tenses his arm, but she merely lays the instrument on the table.

"Yes," purrs Rainfyre. "You need your—medicine. Of course. The inconstant muse must be enticed, mustn't she? I can't tell you how thrilled Mrs. Rainfyre and I have been to have been permitted to play the role, so to speak, of patrons of the arts in the life of so gifted a young man."

In the silence following this remark there comes from behind an inner door the distinct sound of the blue tambourine. Rainfyre smiles at his wife. She consults a clock on the wall. "You had best tell him what you must, and quickly. It grows late."

Rainfyre gets up and circles the table, thumping its surface with that obscene flap of flesh, while with his good hand he removes his glasses and massages his eyes.

"Mrs. Rainfyre is right, Mr. de Garde, and though I deplore the necessity of offering so abbreviated an explanation of what we're going to do I have no wish to conceal from you the reason for which we require your services. At this very moment I am engaged in the most important experiment of my career, an experiment that will crown years of prodigious labor and research. Research, I might add, financed solely by the commercial enterprise of Mrs. Rainfyre, and the demand for that commodity which she has been abundantly able to supply."

Again, from behind the door, comes the jingle of the blue tambourine, and Rainfyre smiles and says, "Once we pass through that door there can be no turning back. I tell you now, young friend, you are under no duress, nor will you be coerced into taking part in the experiment for which we require your assistance—provided you leave at once and never come near this place again. But hear me! Mrs. Rainfyre will make no further visits to a certain tawdry cinema where you have so liberally availed yourself of her services. You will never see Mrs. Rainfyre again. You must employ some new device to woo your muse, or find some other agency. Which will not be easy, for this service of Mrs. Rainfyre's is seldom extended on such generous terms. Am I not right?"

Willie's head droops forward onto his folded arms, his body racked by the savage pangs of his addiction. The poem . . . the poem . . . so near completion . . . if only . . . if only . . .

"Many poets have paid a higher price than you shall be made to pay," whispers Rainfyre, as if reading his mind. "You are the reincarnation of Poe. The shade of Baudelaire. The ghost of Verlaine. An artist to your soul. Your work is your life, as is mine. Upon fulfilling your part of this little business you will be given what you and your muse crave, and as a bonus—hear this—the very instrument of your pleasure in an exquisite velvet-lined case, and with a sufficient amount of that commodity of Mrs. Rainfyre's as will make you a king of dreams, and your muse a slave."

To Willie de Garde, writhing in misery, it sounds like the promise of heaven. He nods his agreement.

Rainfyre vanishes on his tiny feet into another room of the flat, and Willie raises his head and stares at the glittering receptacle of his anodyne, which Mrs. Rainfyre, sensing his intention, snatches quickly out of his reach. Then she removes a locket from inside the collar of her dress and hands it to him. Through the mist that stings his eyes he sees the picture of a young girl of not more than nine or ten, with luminous dark eyes and massive ringlets.

"Our daughter, Poet. She died less than a month after her father took that picture. A drunken motorist ran her down in the street, crushed her little dancing legs. When they carried her to us in the house where we lived she was—"

"Still alive!" Rainfyre comes back into the room, wheeling before him on a squeaky-castored tripod a bulky crepe-covered object. "She lay for hours, broken, helpless, dying so very slowly. Near midnight she raised her little hand and weakly beckoned me. I looked into those eyes which had been rigid as stones with pain and saw such radiance she might have become an angel before death. Her eyes seemed to light the room and she said in a strong, clear voice: 'Papa, papa, make them hurry. It's so pretty!' "

Behind his glasses Rainfyre's eyes expand like soap bubbles, seem sure to burst. "*It's so pretty!* Her precise words, Mr. de Garde. A moment later she was dead."

Raindrops tap against the black-curtained windows like the fingers of beggar children pleading to be let in. No one moves.

Rainfyre removes the shroud from the object and reveals an enormous camera of apparently antique vintage but fitted with innumerable shiny devices as terrifying as those that menace the waiting patient trapped in the dentist's chair.

Taking from his pocket three small pieces of stiff white paper, he lays them before the poet, who examines them gingerly, trembling. He sees nothing but over-exposed snapshots, dull on one side, glossy on the other, with vague bluish streaks on the glossy side.

"These, Mr. de Garde, are photographs of the last optical images in the brain of a dying guinea pig, one of the expendable creatures you so kindly procured for us. They're of no interest. I erred in the calculation of perceivable light ray intensity."

Again, behind the door, the jingle of the blue tambourine. There is a look of mild urgency in the smile that crosses Mrs. Rainfyre's face; her husband continues speaking, however, with no sign of haste.

"This, you observe, is a camera, with many sophisticated refinements. For several years I was a professional photographer. Now, as you may have read on the door, I am an eschatologist, an explorer of those ethereal regions my colleagues have heretofore ignored, although essentially it involves the same problems of timing and lighting. To oversimplify further, my boy, there is an instant between life and death when one is neither wholly out of this life nor entirely within the other. After the death of my beloved child, and with nothing but her deathbed cry to inspire me, I devoted myself to the exploration of that mystical borderland, and finally—yes, with this very camera!—devised a means of recording in black and white a picture of that afterworld whose radiant beauty illuminated my dying angel's face. With the brains of the animals you have procured for us I have mastered the enormous technical problems, and now—*now*, Mr. de Garde . . ."

Willie de Garde scarcely listens to this madness, so acutely painful are the symptoms of his body's deprivation. "Please! Give me . . . give me . . . "

"Yes, yes, soon, my boy. Very soon. Now come, observe."

Rainfyre takes the poet's arm and leads him to the door, pushes it quietly open. In the middle of a smaller room, a young girl sits on a straight-backed chair in a soft pool of light. She has long red hair and skin almost as white as the simple dress she wears. In her hands she holds the blue tambourine and she smiles with infinite sweetness as she gently taps it with her fingertips. She is totally blind, and sits stiffly, as if posed.

Though there was no perceptible sound as the door opened, she turns toward them. "Mr. Rainfyre?"

"Are you fatigued, child?"

"Oh, no. I've been listening to the rain and answering it with the blue tambourine. As long as I do that the rain won't turn to snow."

"Are you warm enough?"

"Yes."

"It won't be long," he promises. "We're nearly ready to take the picture."

Rainfyre motions Willie back into the other room and shuts the door behind them.

"You have glimpsed the rarest of treasures, Mr. de Garde—*total innocence*. A privilege, even for a poet. Our search for such perfect, pristine innocence makes a tale in itself, but we haven't time to entertain you with it now. Suffice to say it was most exhaustive and ended where it began—in this very building. She lives alone in a hole of a room on the floor above us, where she sits in the dark crocheting fancywork in exquisite designs, which she tries to sell by hawking them from door to door. If anyone deserves heaven, that child does."

The sight of the girl and the knowledge of what this madman plans to do with her momentarily distract Willie from his own misery. He starts to protest, but Rainfyre hushes him with a threatening movement of the unformed hand.

"Don't distress yourself, my boy. The animals you brought to us died painlessly, and so will she." His magnified eyes roll upward in reluctant submissiveness to fate. "One would prefer to employ the brain of some hideous sinner, quite naturally. Alas, this is precluded by certain insurmountable technical problems. If you will pardon me for once again oversimplifying, and not to sound too flippant, one would need a most sophisticated flash device to take photographs of hell. So we had to skip that idea. And we needed, you must see, someone of unimpeachable purity in order to take pictures of heaven."

By now Mrs. Rainfyre is becoming quite agitated. She starts plucking at her husband's sleeve and casting urgent glances at the clock, but he goes on just as imperturbably. "Don't ask me to explain how the actual process works—a matter of electrical impulses flowing between the child's brain and the internal mechanism of this specially adapted camera. She thinks it's merely another picture. I've used her as a model for conventional photos on several occasions in order to dispel any qualms she might feel. She is patient and indefatigable. A saint. Her passing will be swift and humane, and at the last quick pulse of life the marvelously sensitive eye of this camera will register the visual image that flashes instantaneously across the optical nerves of her brain on the very threshold of the infinite."

Willie listens to all this with mounting nausea, while out of the corner of his eye he never loses sight of that fascinating steel instrument in Mrs. Rainfyre's hand. Loathing and revulsion serve only to quicken the burning appetite that has drawn him to this lunatic's room. He fights to keep alert.

"You are wondering precisely what you shall have to do?" says Rainfyre. "As you can see, I'm somewhat handicapped by this." He waves the flipper. "And I'm also afflicted with a coronary weakness that forbids undue exertion. Nor is my wife strong in anything but spirit. We must therefore rely on you, my young friend, to dispose of the—er—remains. You must carry the girl's body in a laundry bag down all these stairs to the alley. No one will see you, and once you've got to the river . . . You understand."

As he speaks, the photographer has been deftly, with his one good hand, rolling up Willie de Garde's sleeve, while Mrs. Rainfyre circles the table, the needle poised and ready.

"When you've completed your little errand you might wish to come back here and Mrs. Rainfyre will make you a lovely cup of tea. Yes. We might have a little celebration, just the three of us, and you could read us your poem. Wouldn't that be nice?"

Now he is opening the door into the inner room and Willie sees the girl in white playing happily with the blue tambourine, and then Rainfyre begins wheeling his terrible machine toward the door, pushing it along with the help of his tapering, fish-like flipper.

Willie's eyes are on the glittering shaft of the needle, but just as Mrs. Rainfyre extends it toward his naked arm he cries out and tears away from her grasp. Without realizing he is doing so, he snatches up the three photographs from the table as he lunges toward the door.

Mrs. Rainfyre shrieks. An unlikely roar comes from the puny photographer.

Down, down, down the rickety steps he flies, crashing from wall to wall, bursting through the door and into the deserted street.

Breathless, he runs like a wild man through dark canyons of vacant buildings, big white crystals of snow settling upon his eyes and cheeks and lips like icy moths, and no matter how far and fast he runs he still hears in his head the mad jingling of the blue tambourine.

Near the end of the street a gust of wind tears the small white photographs out of his hand. He claws at the air to retrieve them, and thinks he has, but when he reaches the river and opens his fist he holds nothing but a handful of snowflakes.

WILLIAM P. McGIVERN

Graveyard Shift

The *Call-Bulletin*'s first deadline was at nine o'clock in the morning and by eight fifty-five everyone in the long brightly lighted city room was working under the insistent pressure of time.

Sam Terrell didn't look up from the typewriter when the phone rang; he finished the item for his column, then lifted the receiver.

The voice in his ear said, "I've got something for you."

"Who's this?"

"It doesn't matter, Sam. What matters is I got something for you on Caldwell, our lily-white reform candidate." The tipster's inflection was heavily ironic. Terrell's interest picked up; with elections two weeks off, anything on Caldwell had a priority value.

"I'm sorry, but this connection is bad," Terrell said. "Could I call you back?"

"I'm at the drugstore, so calling back wouldn't tell you much. Be content with the tip, Sam. Don't worry about me. Now: you know Eden Myles?"

Terrell did, slightly; she was a singer, the friend of a minor hoodlum named Frankie Chance.

"Well, she's been huddling with Richard Caldwell for the last month or so. Five or six times, all on the quiet. But somebody saw her easing into his hotel suite. You run this down and you got a story."

Terrell reached for his cigarettes. He was tall and nervous, and when he was working he usually looked angry. "Anybody else know about this?"

"Just you and me. Good luck, Sam."

"Wait a minute," Terrell said, but the phone was dead. He put the receiver down. Rich Caldwell and Eden Myles—an incongruous combination. Caldwell was the high-minded idealist, called to politics by duty and conscience. Eden Myles was a small-time tramp. Singer, hostess, model, all of it small time. Even Frankie Chance was small time.

"Ollie," Terrell said to the frail old man whose desk was beside his, "what do you think of Rich Caldwell? Someone was just trying to peddle a story on him."

"Caldwell's given up a highly profitable law practice to run for mayor of this benighted town," Ollie Wheeler said. "And he's got about as much political savvy as a sophisticated girl scout. Men like Ike Cellars, Mayor Ticknor—do you think they'll let this piece of cake fall into somebody else's fingers?"

"You're a cynic."

"You mean I've the capacity to see what's under my nose."

Terrell smiled, leaned back in his chair and lit a cigarette. Eden Myles and Rich Caldwell . . . The pressure had eased now that the first edition was in. Reporters and editors drifted down the long room toward the lavatory or water coolers. From his corner Terrell had a view of the rewrite section, the copy wheel, and managing editor Mike Karsh's huge, glass-walled office, which dominated both arms of the L-shaped city room. He had been a part of the city room's madness for eight years, and then Mike Karsh had called him in to tell him he would take over Kehoe's column when the old man retired to his farm to raise chickens. Karsh had been at his desk, beautifully groomed as always.

"It's a small piece of blank paper on page three," Karsh had said, glancing up at him with sudden intensity. "But multiply that space a half million times—our circulation as of this morning—and you've got a piece of paper big enough to sky-write on. I want you to do a good job. I think you will. You've learned this raunchy trade of ours pretty well."

"Most of it from you, Mike."

There had always been this strong bond between them.

Now Terrell glanced over his shoulder toward Karsh's glass-walled office and thought that he still felt a copy boy's hero worship for the man. He would have liked to get his opinion on the tip he had just received, but Karsh was in conference.

Terrell picked up his hat and coat, left word at the switchboard that he was going out, and cabbed across town to the Vanderbilt Hotel.

Caldwell's campaign headquarters were on the third floor, in an ornate ballroom. A dozen or so college girls sat at card tables distributing campaign leaflets, lapel buttons and automobile stickers to anyone who wanted them.

A blown-up photograph of Caldwell was at both ends of the room, smiling self-consciously down on his busy, cashmere-sweatered volunteer workers. He was a handsome man, forty-five or forty-seven, with even features, a good jaw, and mild, intelligent eyes. They should have tried for a better picture, Terrell thought—something more informal and engaging. But Caldwell's advisors were all dedicated amateurs. They scorned tricks. They were so sold on Caldwell that they didn't bother selling him to the people.

One of the girls came over to him with a button for his lapel, but Terrell told her no thanks. He gave her his name and asked for Caldwell.

"Mr. Caldwell's tied up in a meeting right now, but please don't go away. I know Mr. Sarnac will want to see you. He handles the press for us."

She hurried off, her ponytail bobbing with excitement.

In a few seconds a small man wearing a gray sack suit and rimless glasses came through a door at the end of the room, and hurried toward Terrell. They introduced themselves, and Sarnac escorted Terrell to his office.

"What can I do for you, Mr. Terrell? Sit down, please." He indicated a straight-backed chair.

Terrell ignored the chair. "What I want," he said, "is to see Caldwell."

"Fine. Of course." That he was handling the press with care was evident in his manner. "I don't see why that can't be arranged. He's a busy man, but—"

"How do you fit into this setup?" Terrell asked abruptly.

Sarnac seemed somewhat flustered by the question. "Me? Why, I'm Mr. Caldwell's press secretary."

"Are you on a regular salary?"

"No, I'm on leave from Union College where I teach." Sarnac looked puzzled now. "But I thought you wanted to talk about Mr. Caldwell."

"Perhaps I was being irrelevant," Terrell said. There had been nothing accidental in his approach; he wanted Sarnac off balance. "Now, tell me about Eden Myles. I know she's been seeing Caldwell. But I'd like the rest of the story."

Sarnac looked stricken. "I haven't the faintest notion where you came across such an absurd rumor, but I can assure you it's completely false."

Terrell nodded thoughtfully; then he said, "You told me I could get together with Caldwell."

Sarnac hesitated. "Yes." Again he hesitated. "Just a minute."

He left the office and it was a good five minutes before he returned. Caldwell followed in his wake. In addition to resembling the big campaign picture, Caldwell looked a bit like a bank teller or the high-minded agent in a life insurance advertisement.

Nervously, Sarnac introduced Terrell to Caldwell and then made himself scarce—quite obviously by prearrangement.

"Mr. Terrell," Caldwell said, "would you mind telling me where you heard this story? Sarnac just informed me about it and—"

"I would mind very much. However, since it's not true, what difference does it make?"

Caldwell was visibly disturbed; his face was white and there were tiny blisters of perspiration on his upper lip. "This is a very serious matter," he said. "Could I talk to you off the record?"

"No," Terrell said. "I'm not a bartender or a cab driver. I don't listen to gossip for the fun of it. I'm a reporter. What I hear I use. What you're saying is that you'll tell the truth, but only if I don't use it in my column. Isn't that your proposition?"

"I didn't mean it that way," Caldwell said. "You don't seem to want to discuss this. There's really nothing to be gained fighting about it."

"I'll tell you what." Terrell smiled slightly. "You convince me I'll get a better story by waiting a few days—then we'll stop fighting."

"Yes, I can do that," Caldwell said, something simple and honest and stubborn projecting from the man when he spoke. "I'll give you everything, all the details. Then you'll see that the important story is still in the making. Sit down, please." Caldwell cleared his throat and glanced at the door behind Terrell. Then he said, "Eden Myles called us six weeks ago. She had information concerning the incumbent administration, Mayor Ticknor and Ike Cellars. She wanted us to have it. Sarnac arranged a meeting between her and myself, in a suite at the Armbruster Hotel. Since then I have had five more conferences."

"Have you been meeting her alone?"

"Every time Eden Myles has talked to me there have been witnesses present—men and women of unimpeachable reputation. Also, every conversation between us has been recorded on tape."

"Does Eden want money for her information?"

"No. I gather it's revenge she's after. I understand that she's had a split with her steady friend, a man by the name of Frankie Chance. He works for Ike Cellars. Eden wants to pay them off."

"And what sort of information is she producing? Anything good?"

"Not at first. But recently she's been giving us more significant information. That Ike Cellars runs the rackets in town, that Ticknor has been re-elected for years by fraudulent registration in the river wards. That there's graft in high places."

Terrell got to his feet. "We've made a deal. If this girl comes up with evidence, I'll be surprised. But I'll be glad to use it. And here's a bit of free advice: Watch out for booby traps."

"We can manage, thanks."

Terrell hesitated at the door. He said bluntly to Caldwell, "What are you going to get out of all this?"

"I want to live in a clean city. To put it negatively, I don't want to live under an Ike Cellars–Mayor Shaw Ticknor axis, with the moral deterioration they've brought to our community. I don't want my children, and the children of others, to grow up sneering at conventional virtues and tolerating the fact that honesty and hard work mean nothing at all in the management of our public affairs."

"You won't start any arguments with those ideas," Terrell said. "I imagine you're all for displaying the flag on the Fourth of July and keeping marijuana out of the public schools."

Caldwell smiled. "Exactly."

The Gray Gates Development where Eden Myles lived was new and elegant and expensive. Terrell rapped on Eden Myles' door. It was opened by a blonde girl wearing brief white summer shorts and a man-styled yellow shirt. She smiled up at him.

"You want Eden, I imagine. My name is Connie Blacker. I just checked in last night." She was beautifully tanned, and her hair was bleached lightly from the sun.

"And when will Eden be back?" Terrell asked her.

"I don't know. She left while I was still in bed."

It was then that they heard the clatter of high heels in the outside hall. Connie said, "Here she is now."

Eden Myles stopped outside the apartment door, made her way slowly into the foyer, staring at Terrell.

"Hello, Eden," he said.

"What do you want, Sam?" She glanced at Connie, suspicion sharpening her eyes. "What's he snooping around here for?"

Connie said, "I was under the impression you were friends."

"Newspapermen are a notch below cops in my form book." She stood tall and angry, her flat model's figure framed effectively in the doorway. "Well, what do you want, Sam?"

"Why are you seeing Caldwell, Eden? That's what I stopped to check on."

Eden stared at him, and then she said, "Would you go now? I've got things to do."

Terrell shrugged. "Okay, Eden, if that's the way you want it." He studied her for a second or so, and then shook his head slowly. "I don't get it," he said. "You're a handsome woman, very elegant, very lovely. When Ike Cellars finds out that you've been indiscreet, you won't enjoy looking at yourself in mirrors anymore. Has that occurred to you?"

She looked suddenly weary and beaten; all of her careful grooming couldn't conceal the fear in her face. "I'm sorry," she said. "Can't we play the scene over with a little less volume?"

"Let's try," he said.

"I've been talking to Caldwell," Eden said. She sat down on a huge yellow ottoman and crossed her slender legs at the ankles. "I wanted to pay off Frankie Chance because he—well, there's no point going into that. It was a stupid thing to do—I know that. But after I got started it seemed the right thing to do. Caldwell's an honest man, and he's big and gentle and straight. I really fell for the guy. In a funny way, I respect him and I want him to respect me. I can't say I'm not afraid of what Ike Cellars will do. But I'm going ahead with it. He can't stop me, Sam."

"Tell me this, Eden," Terrell said, "do you have anything specific and serious to tag the opposition with? Gossip and guesses, you know, aren't going to hurt Cellars or Ticknor."

"I've got things that will hurt them."

"What?"

"It's for Caldwell. What he does with it is up to him."

Terrell was silent for a few seconds. Then he said, "Well, I wish you both luck. You deserve a medal, Eden. You may never get it, but you deserve it anyhow."

Terrell smiled at Connie, left and rode down to the lobby feeling depressed and irritable. The whole business stank. Dramatic revelations inspired first by vengeance, then a growing sense of duty and virtue. Eden's act was a scriptwriter's dream, preposterously pat.

But who was being cast as the fall guy?

Terrell cabbed back to the paper and ate lunch at his desk while he worked out the first draft of his next day's column. When he had it in shape he called Mike Karsh to get his reaction on the Caldwell story. Karsh didn't go for Eden Myles' tale of revenge and suddenly burgeoning conscience, but he did think that Terrell was onto something good.

That evening Terrell called Connie Blacker and tried futilely to get her to go out to dinner with him. He ended up grabbing something to eat at a diner and then headed for the *Call-Bulletin*.

At ten-thirty the newspaper's lobby was dark, and Terrell had to rap on the heavy plate-glass doors to raise a watchman. This was the slow, graveyard stretch; the next edition, the Night Extra, wouldn't go in until one o'clock in the morning.

The skeleton crew was sitting at the long city desk with coffee before them and cigarettes burning away in ashtrays at their elbows. The big lights above the clock drew a circle of brightness around the men at the city desk and police speaker.

Bill Mooney, an old city hall reporter, was in charge of this shift. "Want some coffee, Sam?" he asked. "Prince here made it. It's what they hired him for, I guess."

Prince was a healthy-looking young man with a degree in journalism from the University of Iowa. Mooney did not mind his youth, but he was in no hurry to forgive him for that degree in journalism. "I'll get you a cup, Mr. Terrell," Prince said.

"Never mind. I'll pass."

Ollie Wheeler, Terrell saw, was sitting just outside the cone of light that fell on the city desk. He wore an overcoat, and had his feet propped up on a wastebasket.

Mooney said to Prince, "Keep your eye on the radio for a while and don't let anything slip by. Fires are indicated by the ringing of a bell and a strong smell of wood smoke. I'm going to the john."

Just as he disappeared into the shadows, the police speaker sounded. The announcer's flat voice directed the street sergeant from the Sixteenth District to an address on Manor Lane. A few seconds later he directed an ambulance to the same address.

Prince said, "It's rugged being treated like a stuttering cretin around here."

Terrell held up his hand. "Just a second."

Wheeler walked over to the city desk, a little frown on his lean old face. He bent forward to put his ear beside the police speaker. "Did he say two-twenty-four Manor Lane?"

"I believe so," said Terrell.

In the silence that followed, Prince said, "Mooney thinks it's indecent that I didn't start as a copy boy. He's got the idea that college . . ."

"For God's sake, keep quiet," Wheeler said. "They've sent an ambulance out to two-twenty-four Manor Lane. That's where Richard Caldwell lives."

"Go get Mooney," Terrell said to Prince. "Ollie, you better give the Sixteenth a ring and see if they can tell us anything yet." He picked up a telephone directory, then remembered that the house on Manor Lane belonged to one of Caldwell's friends who was now in Europe. Caldwell lived in the suburbs and used the town house when late speeches or meetings kept him in the city.

"Ollie, what's the name of Caldwell's friend—the one who owns the house on Manor Lane?"

"Just a second." Ollie waved for silence; he was connected with the Sixteenth. "Sarge, this is Ollie Wheeler at the *Call-Bulletin*. Say, what's happening? We just heard you sent an ambulance over to Rich Caldwell's house. Wait, hold on—just a hint, Sarge, for old time's sake. Sure, I'll hang on." He covered the phone with his hand and looked up at Terrell. "Scared little bastard. But it sounds big, Sam. What did you want? Oh yeah. Sims is the name of the guy who owns the house on Manor Lane. J. Bellamy Sims."

"That's it." Terrell flipped through the directory, found the number and dialed it quickly. A voice said cautiously, "Hello?"

"Who's this?" Terrell said. "I want to talk with Rich Caldwell."

"You can't—" There was silence on the line. Then: "Who is this?"

"This is Sam Terrell. *Call-Bulletin.* Where's Caldwell?"

"Look, I can't talk to you. You got to see the detectives."

"Wait!" Terrell yelled the word. "Is this a cop?"

"This is Paddy Coglan from the Sixteenth."

"Don't hang up! Don't. Are you all alone there? Just give me a lead, Paddy. What is it?"

"I was coming down the Lane when I saw a guy run out of Caldwell's front door." Coglan's voice was low and tense. "I chased him and lost him. So I came back to Caldwell's. The door was open, lights on in the front room. He's—" Coglan drew a sharp breath. "The Captain's here, Sam. Better get over." The connection was broken.

Terrell put the phone down and glanced at Ollie Wheeler who was still talking to the house sergeant at the Sixteenth. "Thanks, thanks a lot, Sarge," he said, getting to his feet. "Sure, sure. Thanks." He hung up and looked at Terrell. "Mooney had better call Karsh, and get some rewrite men and photographers on the way in. There's a dead girl over at Caldwell's. And Caldwell is dead drunk."

"Who's the girl? Eden Myles?"

"Head of the class, Sam. Eden Myles it is. Or was. Caldwell just strangled her."

Manor Lane was one of the select addresses in the city; the homes were small, old and expensive.

Terrell paid off his cab and walked over to a patrolman standing beside an ambulance. He recognized him and said, "Hello, Jimmy. They take her out yet?"

"Hi, Sam. No, not yet. Captain Stanko just got here. With one of your boys. The lab men are still working. It's brutal, I guess."

Terrell walked by a couple of squad cars and up the stone steps of Caldwell's home, nodded to the patrolman on duty and went inside. He turned from the foyer into the living room, where he saw shirt-sleeved lab technicians taking photographs and measurements.

The *Call-Bulletin*'s district reporter, a balding man named Nelson, was on the phone talking in a low urgent voice. Terrell nodded to him, then drifted into a quiet corner and lit a cigarette.

Eden Myles lay sprawled in the middle of the room, and Richard Caldwell sat slumped in a deep chair with his head bent forward at an awkward angle; he was breathing noisily and raggedly, and every now and then an inarticulate little moan sounded deep in his throat. Captain Stanko, in command of the Sixteenth, was shaking his shoulder with a big red hand, and a police surgeon was peering into his eyes. The room was a shambles. Lab men moved around upended chairs with efficient speed. Terrell saw Paddy Coglan, the uniformed cop whom he had spoken to from the *Call-Bulletin*. Coglan was a small man, stockily built, with kinky gray hair and a round, red face. His eyes were switching around the room, as if seeking a place to rest.

"We can take her now," one of the lab men said to Captain Stanko, and Evans, the homicide detective, turned and looked thoughtfully at the body of the dead girl.

She hadn't died prettily, Terrell thought. The model, the singer, proud of her lean, elegant body and dramatic good looks—that was all over. She had fought hard; her dress was torn across the front revealing her starkly white shoulders. One of her slippers was off and a stocking had been pulled loose from its garter clip.

"Take her out," Captain Stanko said.

The *Call-Bulletin*'s reporter was winding up his story in a discreetly lowered voice. Terrell turned a bit to listen to Nelson. "Yes, that's all I've got," Nelson was saying. "What? Yes, Caldwell's got some scratches on his face. Look, I'll talk to Stanko when I can—yes, sure."

"Just a second," Terrell said. "What about the man who ran out of here? Did you give him that?"

Nelson looked at him blankly. "First I heard about it. What do you mean? A prowler?"

"Prowler?" It was Captain Stanko speaking. He turned toward them, repeating the word in a cold, belligerent voice. He was a big man with a face like a block of dark wood, and his eyes were angry and suspicious as he stared from Nelson to Terrell. "Let me give you hot shots some advice. Don't start dreaming up angles. You'll get the story from my report."

Nelson put the phone he was holding back into its cradle. "I'm not inventing anything, Captain. I'm waiting for your report."

Stanko glanced at Terrell. "That suit you? Or do you want us to rush things up for your special benefit?"

The room had become very quiet.

"I'm not inventing things," Terrell said. "A man was seen running out of this house tonight. After the girl was heard screaming. That's part of the story, Captain."

Stanko studied him for a few seconds with no expression at all on his face. "Who saw him?"

"Your beat cop." Terrell glanced toward the patrolman. "Paddy, didn't you tell the captain what you told me on the phone?"

Coglan's face was brick red. "What do you mean, Sam?"

The silence in the room suddenly became oppressive and ominous; Terrell felt a little chill go through his body. Would they really try to get away with this? he wondered. Would they try anything so raw? "You know what I mean, Paddy," he said, watching the little man's shifting eyes. "You told me fifteen minutes ago that you saw a man run out of this house. You chased him and lost him. Are you changing your story now?"

Coglan's eyes slid past Terrell and focused on a spot just beside his shoulder. "I told you you'd better talk to the detectives. I remember telling you that, Sam. I was pretty jolted, finding her dead. Maybe you misunderstood me or got it mixed up."

"Sure, you got it mixed up," Stanko said, in a hard, derisive voice.

Terrell didn't take his eyes from Paddy Coglan's flushed and unhappy face. "Once more, Paddy; you didn't see a man run out of here?"

Stanko said, "He told you 'no' once."

Terrell hesitated, not sure of his next move. He knew Stanko by reputation, a cold, unemotional man with a blind and compulsive loyalty to the administration. What were his orders? To make certain that Caldwell was tagged with the girl's murder? To eliminate other suspects?

Terrell made up his mind. He said, "Captain, I'm using what Coglan told me. I don't know what he saw; but I know damn well what he *told* me he saw. And that's going into the paper."

"And your paper is heading for trouble," Stanko said. "Paddy's tried to set you straight. He may have been confused, or you may have misunderstood him."

"We'll print all of that, too," Terrell said, in a tone heavy with sarcasm. "He's been a cop for twenty years, but the sight of a body sends him into a state of incoherent shock. Readers will find that intriguing."

"Sam," Coglan said plaintively, "there's no reason—"

"Shut up!" Stanko yelled at him. "Print what you want, snoop. Now get out of here."

"We'll print all the versions," Terrell said. "Coglan's first account and Coglan's second account. Something for every edition. And when do we get the definitive official report? When the Mayor and Ike Cellars decide just how it should be shaded and tinted for public consumption?"

"Get out of here. Get out of here before I throw you out. You're a trouble-maker, that's all. And, by God, I'd like to beat some manners and sense into you."

Terrell said, "I don't want trouble, Captain, I just want the truth. But those words mean the same thing tonight." He tossed him a salute, walked out of the room.

From Caldwell's house Terrell went looking for a telephone. He found an all-night drugstore six blocks away, and called the paper. Wheeler was writing the first running story. Terrell gave him everything he had learned from Coglan and then headed for the Sixteenth.

There was an air of pressure and excitement in the old mid-town station house. This was where the preliminary hearing would be held; a magistrate was on his way to the Sixteenth now, and Caldwell had already been slated for murder and taken upstairs to the detective's bureau for additional questioning.

The atmosphere was carnival, Terrell realized, glancing around the smoky room. He wondered what poor, blindfolded justice would do, hampered slightly by a gun in her back.

Richard Caldwell was held for the Grand Jury without bail by a magistrate named Seaworth, who listened to Patrolman Coglan's testimony without taking his eyes from the prisoner's face.

The little patrolman, Coglan, stared at the floor as he gave his testimony. He told of hearing a scream and going directly into Caldwell's home. The front door was ajar and he found Caldwell in a dazed condition with the dead girl lying on the floor. He did not mention seeing anyone else in or near the house.

It went faster then. The police surgeon testified that Caldwell had been drinking. A lab technician gave the findings of his section. Caldwell made no statement and his attorney waived cross-examination.

Magistrate Seaworth banged his gavel and gave his verdict.

And that was the end of act one, Terrell thought, as he watched Caldwell being led by the police toward the cell block. There was no expression on Caldwell's face; he stared straight ahead, his eyes were like those of a man on a rack.

Someone shouted, "Get out of my way!" in a high, raging voice and began to fight through the crowd toward Caldwell. Magistrate Seaworth banged his gavel as a man shoved forward and swung a looping blow at Caldwell's face. The blow landed, cutting Caldwell's lip, and then a patrolman caught the man from behind and locked his arms to his sides.

Terrell recognized him as flashbulbs began exploding on all sides of the room. Frankie Chance. Eden Myles' friend.

Chance was tall and slim with wavy black hair and deep brown eyes that were soft as a child's. He was struggling like a maniac against the big cop who was holding him.

"You killed her!" he screamed. "Because she wouldn't let you touch her, because you're not even half a man! When they strap you in the chair . . ."

"Take that man out of here!" Seaworth shouted. "This is a courtroom, not a—" He sputtered as he groped for words.

Terrell eased himself through the crowd and reached the public phone in the hallway. He called Wheeler and gave him a few paragraphs of atmosphere, including Frankie Chance's attack on Caldwell. When he finished, Wheeler said, "That's very juicy. Now here's a message for you. Karsh wants you to come in. There's been some confusion about that prowler Paddy Coglan did or did not see. The Superintendent called Karsh about it, and so did Stanko—they both said you'd gone off half-cocked. Also there've been certain implications that Coglan might have been loaded. Williams says he has a reputation as a rummy."

"So what happened?" Terrell said.

"Karsh killed the prowler angle just before we locked up," Wheeler said. "He wants to talk to you."

Terrell sighed and rubbed his forehead. "Well, there goes Caldwell's loophole," he said. "They've turned it into a noose." The disgust he felt was evident in his voice. "Tell Karsh I'm on my way," he said, and dropped the phone back onto its hook.

Karsh sat down at his desk, twisted a cigarette into his holder, and then looked up at Terrell. "Well, it's a frame, eh?" he said. "Raw, clumsy and transparent. But effective. There's a lesson in that. If you want a man out of the way hit him with a meat cleaver, and go on about your business. Sit down, Sam."

"What do we do now?"

"We're going to save Richard Caldwell's neck. This is about the biggest story I've ever been near—and I want it. I want it all. Now let's go back a bit. Tell me just what Coglan told you, his first version, that is."

Terrell gave Karsh a detailed account of what he had heard and seen so far. And then he asked, "I may be out of line, but why in God's name didn't you use my story?"

"Because I don't want to waste ammunition on jerks like Coglan and Stanko. I want to know who paid the killer—and I want the killer. That's the big story, boy. It may turn this sovereign state upside down and shake a thousand grafters loose from their snug little perches—and among those thousands we may find Ike Cellars, and our beloved, corn-fed Mayor."

Terrell knew that Caldwell had a chance with the paper fighting for him. "We'll be on the side of the angels this time, Mike," he said.

"Don't kid yourself," Karsh said sharply. "I want the story for sensible, selfish reasons. I don't give a damn about public morality. As for you, your job is to find a killer. So get with it. But keep me posted, and take it nice and slow." He brushed Terrell's arm with the back of his hand. "I don't really care if they hang Caldwell, but I'd hate to lose you. Let's get to work."

Terrell went downstairs and found a cab to drive him to Gray Gates. He hoped to talk to Connie before anyone else did.

When she answered her door he knew that she had heard the news; he could sense the fear in her voice.

"When did you get the news?" he said quietly.

"A friend of Eden's—" She moistened her lips. "A friend of Eden's called me."

"Were the police here?"

"Yes, a detective. He said he needed to know who should be notified. I gave him her mother's address. A reporter and a photographer were here a little later. They wanted snapshots of Eden, pictures of me, pictures of the apartment."

"That wasn't very pleasant, I guess."

"I couldn't think about anything but her." She began pacing restlessly, taking quick drags on the cigarette. "Eden knew so much, she worked so hard—and suddenly it's all over. Snuffed out. You know, she got me a job singing at the Mansions. I can't stand any room in the apartment. Everything is full of her things. Dresses, shoes—"

"Take it easy," Terrell said.

"I shouldn't be completely surprised that this has happened."

"No? Why not?"

"She was frightened by something." Connie sat down on the edge of the sofa. She wore pajamas and a blue robe, and looked very tired and very miserable. "I do know it was connected with a job she was doing. Tonight a man came here to talk to her. She was frightened. And she didn't want to go with him. But he insisted."

"Who was the man?"

"You're asking me to break the eleventh commandment," she said. "Keep thy mouth shut."

Terrell hesitated a second. "Take this on faith if you can," he said. "The man who killed Eden is walking free. An innocent man has been charged with—"

"You want the story, sure. That's your job. You'll get a raise and a pat on the back from your boss. Should I stick my neck out to make you look good?"

"Forget about me, for God's sake." Terrell sat down beside her and said, "An innocent man may die—that's why you've got to stick your neck out. Anyhow, you'll be protected. If you trust me, I'll see to it."

The phone began to ring and she started nervously and guiltily. She crossed the room quickly and raised the receiver to her lips.

Terrell lit a cigarette and watched her eyes; something changed in them as she stood listening. "Yes . . . yes," she said, and listened for a few more seconds. Then she said, "Yes, all right. I understand." She put the phone down slowly. Her face was very pale.

"Who was that?" Terrell said.

"A friend of mine."

Terrell took one of her hands. "Ice cold," he said. "What did he say? To shut up? To keep quiet?"

"Maybe," she said, pulling her hand free. "Why don't you go to the police yourself? They're paid to hunt killers. I'm paid to sing in a club."

"And I'll bet you're in for a raise pretty soon," Terrell said quietly.

She looked quickly at him, her expression guilty and defiant. "Don't bother needling me. I'm scared. Do you expect me to be ashamed of that?"

"I might feel the same if I were in your shoes," Terrell said. "I'm not sure. I wasn't needling you. I'm just a reporter at work. If you change your mind, you can always get me through the paper. Will you remember that?"

"It's no use," she said.

"Remember Caldwell then," he said, getting to his feet. "He's facing the loss of his career, reputation, his family, everything—even his life. And he's no more guilty than you are. Remember him while you're singing college songs to bald-headed drunks in Ike Cellars' joint."

"Why don't you leave me alone?" She was very nearly in tears.

Terrell sighed and picked up his hat. "You can reach me at the paper if you need me."

At nine-thirty in the morning, Terrell rapped on the door of an old-fashioned frame house in a poor and dreary section of the city.

The door was opened by a woman with graying hair and eyes that were large and anxious behind rimless glasses. "Yes?" she said, drying her hands on a pale blue apron. "Yes, what is it?"

"My name is Terrell, Mrs. Coglan, Sam Terrell. I'm a reporter with the *Call-Bulletin.*"

"You want to see my husband, I suppose, but he's not here. He's taken a trip."

"Yes, I know," Terrell said. "I stopped at his district first and Sergeant McManus told me Paddy had decided to use up some of his leave time."

"He wants to take what he's got coming before he retires," Mrs. Coglan said. "You know his pension's coming up in a few weeks."

"That's smart," Terrell said, smiling at her. "No point in giving the time back to the city."

"That's what I said to him."

"But you can help me out just as well as Paddy," Terrell said. "That's why I came by. We're doing a round-up of the Caldwell story in next Sunday's edition, and I want to use a piece on Paddy—a picture, a little biographical stuff, that sort of thing."

"I could find a picture of him."

Terrell took off his hat and followed her into the neat, plainly furnished living room that smelled faintly of floor polish.

"Just sit yourself down," she said. "And don't mind how things look. I haven't given the front rooms a lick yet."

"When did Paddy leave, by the way?" Terrell asked casually.

"Yesterday morning, around eight, I think it was. He'd been planning the trip for a long time. There was nothing sudden about it."

"Sure," Terrell said.

"Some people might think it funny him leaving just after testifying against Mr. Caldwell."

"He won't be needed until the Grand Jury hearing. No reason for him to give up his trip. Where did he go?"

"Well, he's visiting some relatives out in Indiana. Two of his sisters live there." Mrs. Coglan rubbed her hands briskly on her apron. "Well, I'll get you some pictures to look at."

"Is there any way I could get in touch with Paddy?" Terrell asked her. "That is, if I need to check an item or a date with him?"

"Well, he's driving," Mrs. Coglan said, looking at a spot on the wall. "He'll just meander along, taking his time. I don't see how you could, Mr. Terrell."

"It doesn't matter."

"I'll get the pictures now. You can take your pick."

When she went up the stairs Terrell stood and glanced around the room. His nerves assured him he was on the right track; his body was tight with tension. Paddy Coglan had been told to clear out. To stay away until after elections. His lie had destroyed Caldwell's only hope. And now he was gone safely away from Caldwell's lawyers or suspicious newspapermen.

The room told him nothing; it was tidy and unrevealing. He hardly knew what he was expecting—a letter or post card perhaps with a return address on it. He looked through the shelves beside the imitation fireplace, moving the dozen-odd books.

Terrell sat down as he heard Mrs. Coglan descending the stairs. "Well, here we are now," she said. She carried a bulky cardboard box which Terrell helped her place on the coffee table. "I've always kept everything," she said. "Newspaper clippings, transfer orders, letters from the pension officers. And here are the pictures. You should find something in that bunch."

"I'm sure I can." He sat on the sofa and began turning over snapshots of Paddy Coglan.

"He worked hard, if I do say so," Mrs. Coglan murmured, studying the photographs with a softened expression. "He'll take a drink. But as God is my judge, it was his only fault. He never, well—you know, had his hand out for favors, or anything like that. Just the drink."

"It's no crime to take a little nip now and then."

"I suppose not. But a man on a beat is different. Captain Stanko said— Oh, I shouldn't be bothering you with my chatter."

"Not at all. But could I use your phone? I have to check in to the desk."

"Just like a policeman," Mrs. Coglan said, shaking her head. "Always checking in. The phone is in the dining room."

Terrell followed her into the dining room and she turned on the overhead lights. The phone was on the sideboard.

Terrell dialed the Weather Bureau's information service, which gave a recorded weather report every fifteen seconds. He nodded and said, "Okay, okay, I'll check that, too."

Mrs. Coglan said, "I'll just be in the kitchen, if you want me," and left the room.

He smiled at her, and went on talking into the phone. When he heard her footsteps fade away, he turned quickly to a small table a few feet from the sideboard. There was a small stack of mail on a metal tray and with the receiver held between his jaw and shoulder, he went through it quickly. Finally, he came on it, an envelope postmarked the day before with the name "P. Coglan" written in the upper left-hand corner. The letter was addressed to Mrs. P. Coglan and the return address was the Riley Hotel, Beach City, New Jersey.

Terrell put the letters back on the tray, hung up the phone and strolled back into the living room. He made a selection of pictures, and was ready to leave when Mrs. Coglan came in to ask him if he would like a cup of coffee.

"Open up, Paddy," Terrell said, as he rapped on the hotel room door. "This is Sam Terrell. I want to talk to you."

The knob turned slowly, and the door swung back a few inches. Coglan stared up at him, his eyes shifting and his lips trying to work themselves into a smile. "Well, Sam boy," he said, laughing a bit. "You could knock me over with a feather. I needed a rest, and I ducked over here all by myself." He rubbed his mouth with the back of his hand. "That's all I wanted, some place where I could have a drink in private without scandalizing the neighbors." He smelled of whiskey, and he needed a shave.

"Can I come in?"

"Why sure, Sam."

Coglan moved away from the door and Terrell walked inside and took off his hat.

"You want a drink, Sam?"

"No, thanks."

Coglan smiled at Terrell. "Well, how come you're over this way?"

"You know why I'm here, Paddy. Me or somebody else—what difference does it make?"

"Yeah," Coglan said, in a gentle, whispering voice. "Yeah." He smiled again, blinking his eyes rapidly. "Somebody had to come, I guess."

"Because you lied, and an innocent man may die for it." Terrell sat down and took out his cigarettes. "You can't live with a thing like that. There's not enough booze in the world to give you a night's sleep."

"They had too much on me," Coglan said. "Too many times playing around with the booze instead of minding my work. And Stanko said he'd toss me out unless I lied. Unless I said I didn't see the man who ran out of Caldwell's. He said it was hush-hush business—that I'd understand later and that sort of thing. I didn't believe him. But I pretended I did. Even to myself." Coglan wet his lips and walked over to the bureau. "Sure you won't have a nip?"

"No thanks, Paddy. You go ahead."

"So I lied to you, to everybody, including the judge," Coglan said, measuring out his drink slowly and carefully. "I finish my twenty-five years in two months. Then my pension comes through. I want it, Sam, not for me, but for my wife. We never had kids, you know, but with the pension we could go out to California where her youngest sister is living. They've got a big family, lots of young ones. And that's what my wife's been thinking about all these years. You know how women are. It changes them not to have babies. It hurts them. And she wanted to be near those youngsters. So I was scared. Not of being slugged or shot. But of being out on my can, without a dime. Do you understand, Sam?"

"I think so," Terrell said.

"I was never a bad cop," Coglan said slowly. "I was just no good. There's a difference. You got to be lucky to prove you're any good. Did you ever think of that?"

"Sure," Terrell said. "But you're getting your chance. What happened the night Eden Myles was murdered?"

"I heard her scream," Coglan said in a weary, hopeless voice. "I had just turned the corner from Regent Square into Manor Lane. Well, I ran up to Caldwell's door and just then it was jerked open, and out came this big guy. I got a good look at him, Sam. He was surprised and he just stood there for a second. He was big, with thick black hair and a wide, tough face. A gorilla, Sam. Wearing a trenchcoat. No hat, so I could see a deep scar on his forehead. Then he pushed past me and ran across the street, angling toward those shadows from the wall around the church. You see how it was?"

"I see. So you lost him. Then you came back to Caldwell's?"

"That's right. The door was open. Caldwell was lying in a chair out cold, and she was dead on the floor. Her face was all swollen and blue. I called the district and Stanko answered the phone. He just told me to sit tight, and hung up." Coglan finished the drink and ran his tongue around his lips. "Then you called, and I gave you a line on what happened. When Stanko showed up he told me to forget all about the big man I saw running out of the house. So I lied. But sitting over here in this crummy joint I realized I couldn't stick it out."

Watching Coglan pour himself another drink, Terrell was touched by a deep, inarticulate pity.

"So what do I do?" Coglan said.

"You can give me the true story, and we'll run it," Terrell said. "That will take the heat off Caldwell, and put it where it belongs. But the cops who take orders from the Hall will boot you off the force as a liar and a drunk. And they'll hound you off any other job you try to get in the city. And they'll stop your pension."

Coglan stared at his empty glass. "You put it pretty hard, Sam."

"We're telling each other the truth, that's all." Terrell glanced at his watch. "Does anybody know you're here?"

"Just my wife. Stanko said get out of town for ten days and stay quiet."

"Okay, you just sit tight. I'll call you tonight—around eight-thirty. I'll tell you where to go then. Everything will be arranged for you. We'll put what you've told me on tape, and then let it fly." Terrell hesitated, looking down at Coglan. He said, "Have you got your gun?"

"Sure, I don't travel without it."

"Good." Terrell stood and walked to the door. "I'll call you at eight-thirty."

"Sure, Sam." Coglan smiled and put out his hand. "I'll be waiting. I've got nowhere to go . . ."

Terrell was back at the paper by five that afternoon, but Ollie told him Karsh was at the track. Finally, at seven, Terrell reached Karsh at home and told him about his visit with Coglan.

"Oh, brother," Karsh said softly. "Get over here fast, Sam. We've got our story now. Get moving . . ."

Karsh sat down in a leather chair before the fireplace. "Let's have it all in order," he said, glancing up at Terrell.

Terrell told him what he had learned from Paddy Coglan and when he finished Karsh looked at his watch. "Eight-fifteen," he said.

For a few seconds he was silent, frowning at the backs of his hands. Then he said, "Paddy Coglan is a ticking bomb, Sam. When he explodes the whole blazing city may go up in smoke. We'd better get him over here. Let's see, there's a train from Beach City around nine. Tell him to catch it. You can spend tonight getting his story and we'll cut loose tomorrow morning."

"How are you going to play it?"

"Straight, absolutely straight." Karsh stood and looked at his watch. "Get Coglan now. I'll fix us a couple of drinks."

The circuits to Beach City were loaded, the operator told Terrell, but she promised to call him back in a few minutes.

Karsh came back with two whiskies and soda and gave one to Terrell.

The phone began to ring.

"Get it," Karsh said.

The operator said, "I have your party now, just one moment." There was a click, and then a voice said, "The Riley Hotel, reservations."

"I'd like to talk to Patrick Coglan, please."

"Yes, sir." There was a silence, and then: "Who's calling, please?"

"Sam Terrell with the *Call-Bulletin*."

"Yes, just a moment."

Terrell heard a murmuring sound in the background, and then another voice came on the line. "Terrell? This is Tim Moran, Homicide. What did you want to see Coglan about?"

Terrell felt a chill go through him. "It's a personal matter, Tim. What's up?"

"Sorry to give it to you this way, but he shot himself about half an hour ago. Was he sick, or anything like that?"

Terrell covered the receiver and looked at Karsh. "Coglan's dead, suicide. I'd better get over there."

"See what they've got to say first."

Terrell uncovered the receiver and said, "I don't know if he was sick, Tim. Can you tell me what happened?"

"All right. He was found by a maid about eight o'clock. He shot himself with his own gun. In the left temple. The doc thinks he might have been dead a couple of hours though. Some shooting galleries across the street covered the shot."

"Did he leave any note?"

"We didn't find anything. What did you want him for, Sam? You were over this morning, I know."

"I was doing a piece on him," Terrell said. "Profile of an average cop, that sort of thing."

"Well, how did he seem when you talked to him? Depressed? Worried? Anything like that?"

"No, he seemed fine. Thanks, Tim." Terrell put the phone down slowly and looked at Karsh. "In the left temple, seven-thirty or earlier, no note. That's it, Mike."

"You should have got his story on paper. You should have taken a statement from him and had it witnessed and notarized." Karsh threw his cigarette into the fireplace, rose and began pacing the room. "Or you should have used a dicta-phone."

"I'll remember next time."

The next morning at nine-thirty Terrell walked into the crowded lobby of the Clayton Hotel, which was an informal gathering place for Ike Cellars and his assistants.

Terrell didn't see Cellars in the lobby, but he noticed a number of his men standing around, portly, substantial types for the most part, studying racing forms, or chatting with one another in an atmosphere of money, cigar smoke and a very special and formidable kind of privilege. Terrell went into the barber shop and settled himself in Nick Baron's chair. Nick was a voluble and intelligent little man, and one of Terrell's best sources. Every tip he heard went straight to Terrell's desk, installments against a debt he could never adequately repay. For Terrell had helped to save Nick's daughter when the child was dying of a rare blood disease; through his column he had alerted blood-donor services throughout the country, and enough of the girl's blood type was found to keep her alive for months. And during that time the disease responded to a new combination of antibiotics, and the girl's life was saved.

"How's it going, Mr. Terrell?" he said, putting a towel around his neck. "You look like you could use a facial, a little tone-up, eh?"

"No, I'm just a bit hung. How about using that vibrator on my throbbing skull."

Terrell had seen two of Cellars' men in the shop, but he knew the sound of the vibrator would cover his conversation with Nick. He and Nick had used this arrangement in the past. Nick switched on the vibrator and began massaging Terrell's forehead with his fingertips.

"I'm going to describe a man to you," Terrell said. "Tell me if he's been around."

"Sure, sure," Nick said, raising his voice slightly. "I bet him to win. Courage, that's what I got."

"He's big, black-haired, with a scarred forehead. Tough-looking gorilla. Have you seen him?"

"Well, I don't know."

Terrell saw the perspiration on Nick's upper lip and he realized that the little barber was frightened. "That's okay, forget I asked."

"No—he was in here two days ago with Ike. That's all I know. Want me to ask around?"

"Absolutely not. Forget it."

"Whatever you say."

Terrell glanced at his watch. "That's enough. I've got to be going."

He paid Nick, tipped him a quarter and slipped into his topcoat. He was turning toward the street entrance, when a man's voice said, "Sam, boy, just a second."

He looked around and saw that one of Cellars' men, Big Manny Knowles, was smiling at him from the doorway that led to the lobby. Big Manny was a sheepish giant, with small, near-sighted eyes, and an expression that usually registered something just short of bewilderment. He strolled toward Terrell, and dropped a hand gently on his arm. "Ike wants to see you, Sam," he said. "Let's don't keep him waiting. You know how busy he is."

"I worry about it a lot," Terrell said. "All right, let's enter the presence."

Cellars was standing at the cigar stand, leafing through a magazine, a healthy-looking man with a dark brown skin and hair as lustrous and beautiful as old silver. He wore a light gray flannel suit, a luxurious, well-cut garment, and a camel's hair coat with slash pockets and hand-stitched lapels. On either side of him were big, purposeful-looking men.

"Good to see you, boy," Cellars said, smiling, putting out a wide, soft hand. "Here's what I wanted to see you about. We've got some really terrific pictures from the circus. You know, our big day with the kids: You know, eh, Sam?"

"Yes, I know," Terrell said. Each year Cellars sponsored a well-publicized outing for a group of the city's orphans. They were fed lavishly, entertained at the circus, and photographed extensively with Cellars, Mayor Ticknor, and other civic dignitaries.

"This year was the greatest," Cellars said, chuckling in a deep, confident voice. "Ben, let's have those pictures."

Ben Noble, his press agent, said, "Right off the griddle, Ike," and put a thick manilla envelope into Cellars' outstretched hand. "Get a look, Sam." Cellars removed a dozen or so glossy prints. "How about that kid with the lion tamer?"

"It's great," Terrell said. "Moving."

"I'll have my girl send you the material you need," Cellars said.

Terrell smiled slightly. "I'll bet you've got enough material to fill my column for the next two weeks. Until after elections anyway."

"That's right," Cellars said, nodding slowly. "I hope you don't think I'm being heavy, Sam. But fill your space with something sweet. You'll find that's a good tip."

"Maybe I should take a vacation for a couple of weeks," Terrell said. "Would that be a good idea?"

"Good's a funny word," Cellars said, watching him carefully. "I don't use good and bad. I use smart and dumb."

One of the big men beside him shifted restlessly. "I think he looks run-down, Ike. Maybe a vacation would be smart."

"Maybe," Cellars said.

"You two have a nice act," Terrell said. "Like an organ grinder and a monkey. Why don't you send him around the lobby with a cap and a tin cup, Ike?"

Cellars shoved the folder of pictures roughly into Terrell's stomach. "Don't be funny with me, snoop." The power of the man was suddenly naked in his face; Terrell could see the sadistic needs in his eyes, and in the turn of his cold, thick lips. "You take these pictures. And you look at them every day, and you remember what I been telling you."

Terrell's mouth was dry, and he knew that his forehead was damp with perspiration. But he let the pictures drop from his hands to the floor. "My space is booked for the next two weeks," he said. "I don't have a paragraph to spare."

Terrell stopped for coffee in a drugstore opposite the Clayton. He sat with the coffee until his fingers were steady, and then went out and hailed a cab. He had decided to see Sarnac; Caldwell and the reform ticket must have something damaging to use against Cellars. Otherwise Ike wouldn't have made such an obvious and stupid play.

The atmosphere of Rich Caldwell's campaign headquarters had changed drastically since his visit forty-eight hours ago. Then the mood had been one of missionary enthusiasm. Now the big room was almost empty, and the bunting and pictures seemed woefully incongruous against the dispirited silence.

A young girl escorted Terrell to Sarnac's office. Sarnac was pale and nervous.

"Please sit down," he said. "There's so much to be done, and at the same time there's nothing to do. Nothing, nothing—" He clenched his fists. "Nothing that will help. Nothing at all."

"What have you been doing?"

Sarnac removed his glasses and pressed the tips of his fingers against his closed eyes. "We've hired a firm of private detectives. They're checking every-thing—Eden Myles' background and that patrolman—what's his name—Cog-lan, who shot himself. They're going over all the testimony for loopholes. The National Committee has offered us a blank check—they believe in Mr. Cald-well. Money, TV time, their best writers, best investigators, anything they've got."

"Well, to be as cynical as hell, he's their baby. They can't dump him. That would hurt the ticket from one end of the country to the other. Have you talked to Caldwell today?"

"Yes, early this morning. He still has no idea what happened. He believes he was struck down from behind. The police obviously don't agree."

"They've got their story all wrapped up," Terrell said. "Paddy Coglan is dead, but his evidence at the preliminary hearing is a matter of record and admissible in court. Caldwell doesn't have a prayer as things stand. As a loyal friend, all you can do is tidy up his affairs and comfort his widow."

"Does his helplessness give you any satisfaction?" Sarnac was angered and disturbed by Terrell's tone. "Are you pleased that the life of an innocent man is in jeopardy?"

"I want to make a deal with you," Terrell said. "But you've got nothing to bargain with. I want that understood. It will save hedging and double-talk. I think Caldwell was framed. I'm not going to tell you why I think so. But I'm going to try to prove it. I want what you've got on Ike Cellars. On the present administration, up to and including Mayor Ticknor."

"Now just a minute, please." Sarnac looked confused and excited. "I can't agree to those terms. I can't give you information without knowing what to expect in return. You've got to consider my position."

"That doesn't interest me at all. I want what you've got on Ike Cellars. I want the information that he's afraid of. I'm offering one thing in exchange for it—a chance to keep Caldwell out of the electric chair."

"You think Caldwell was framed?" Sarnac said. His hands were shaking. "Is that a guess, Terrell?"

"I know he was framed," Terrell said quietly. "Understand? I *know* it. He could have hurt someone important so he was stopped dead in his tracks. Stepped on. Smashed. Now are you going to tell me who he was about to hurt? And how? Frankly, I don't see what you've got to lose. We're after the same thing for different reasons. I want the story, you want Caldwell cleared. Why shouldn't we work together?"

"I don't know," he said. "All right, all right." His voice rose sharply; Terrell had stood and turned to the door. "Sit down. But for the love of God and truth don't deceive us, Terrell. Don't offer us hope if none exists."

"I'm offering you a chance, which depends on what you tell me. So let's get with it."

"If Caldwell had been elected, Ike Cellars and Mayor Ticknor would have gone to jail for life. Along with dozens of smaller thieves in the administration." Sarnac's voice strengthened as he went on. "That's what they feared. That's why they've committed murder to keep him from office."

"That's a good, husky charge," Terrell said. "Now for details. How were you going to do this?"

"I'll make it as clear as I can. First, let me tell you that our Municipal Parking Authority is one of the neatest civic swindles you'll ever come across. And the public's indifference to it has cost the community—the public itself—millions of dollars."

"Okay, I'm shocked. How does it work? And how do you tie Cellars and Ticknor to it?"

"I'll try to explain." Sarnac stood and came around his desk, frowning thoughtfully.

"The Parking Authority was established by City Council at the request of Mayor Ticknor," Sarnac said, in a careful, precise voice. He paused, as if giving Terrell time to take notes, and then continued, "This was about four years ago, shortly after the present administration had been returned to office. Mayor Ticknor was supported by dozens of experts in traffic management and city planning. Their arguments were clear and logical. More cars are being licensed each month. Parking space is contracting steadily. Traffic problems can only worsen unless drastic and imaginative steps are taken. And so the Authority was created, with broad powers to pass laws, condemn property, build traffic arterials, and so forth. On paper all these proposals look fine."

"But they weren't put into effect."

"That's putting it too simply. Let me give you an example from our files. Three years and six months ago it was announced that a parking drome would be built at Ninth and Morrison. This was just one unit in the overall plan, of course. But we'll take Ninth and Morrison to simplify things. That's a slum neighborhood, fairly close to the center-city shopping and business districts. A logical place to provide parking space, close to the main north-south boulevards, and well integrated into the master circulation system. The architects approved the site, and got to work on plans. The Authority stepped in to confiscate the land. Next the buildings were torn down, the ground cleared away, and it appeared that a certain amount of traffic relief was on the way."

Sarnac paused and sighed. "Well, that's step one. As you know, there is no parking drome at Ninth and Morrison. Here's what happened. The architects submitted a new recommendation. Ninth and Morrison wasn't the best spot after all. Twelfth and Fitzgibbons was much more logical, it seemed. This didn't dismay the Authority. Not a bit. They okayed the new recommendation, and scrapped the plans for Ninth and Morrison. They sold the land at cost— apparently losing nothing on the deal."

"But where's the swindle?" Terrell asked him.

"First, they write off the legal expenses of acquiring title to the land. And secondly, they write off the costs of clearing the ground, wrecking the buildings and so forth. These costs are absorbed in their operating expenses. Thus the land becomes a magnificent bargain. You see, there's a vast difference between land with homes and shops on it, and land that is physically and legally clear of all encumbrances. A private firm might spend years, for instance, merely trying to acquire title to the land—but the Authority can set a price and take possession."

"And Ike Cellars snapped up these bits of property?" Terrell said.

"Cellars, Ticknor and others, all operating under various disguises. They've gobbled up acre after acre of our most important center-city property—using the Authority as their price-fixer and enforcer. And here's another angle. The firms that did ninety-eight percent of this work were Acme Construction and Bell Wreckers—firms that no one knew anything about four years ago. They've blossomed overnight into two of the biggest outfits in the state—solely on contracts they've received from the Parking Authority. The legitimate, or should I say established, companies have never had a chance on Authority jobs."

"Why didn't they gripe?"

"They have, but it's done them no good at all. Dan Bridewell, for instance, has fought them on every contract. He's been in business here forty-five years, but he's never gotten a dime's worth of work from the Authority."

"Can you prove all this?"

"If Caldwell is elected, yes. Our auditors could make out a criminal case in twenty-four hours. And that's why Caldwell was stopped."

"We're back where we started," Terrell said wearily. "In the area of rumor, gossip, what-have-you."

"Every word I've told you is true," Sarnac said.

"But you can't prove it—not in time," Terrell said. "Look: who owns those companies you mentioned? Acme Construction and Bell Wreckers?"

"Again, we don't know. But we'd know the day after Caldwell took over the Mayor's office."

"Okay, okay," Terrell said. "Where did you get this story? Eden Myles?"

"No. A clerk in the Property Tax Office came to us with the lead."

"Did you get anything significant from Eden Myles?"

Sarnac shook his head. "No, just a few rather small odds and ends."

"That's the most interesting thing you've told me."

"I don't understand," Sarnac said.

Terrell got to his feet. "Well, it doesn't matter." It had occurred to him that Eden Myles had probably been framed, too; she hadn't been killed for informing, she had been killed to incriminate Caldwell. It was a chilling and terrible thought.

"What can we do?" Sarnac said, in a desperate rising voice.

"If I find out, I'll let you know," Terrell said. "That's a promise."

After leaving Sarnac, Terrell phoned Gray Gates and asked for Connie Blacker, but learned that she had left Eden Myles' apartment the day before. She had given the Beverly Hotel as a forwarding address, but the desk clerk there told him she wasn't in.

"Do you know when she'll be back?"

"Is this by any chance—" The clerk's small laugh telegraphed the joke. "Is this by any chance, *Mr*. Chance?"

"Yes, that's right," Terrell said. "Why? Is there a message?"

"She'll be in around two o'clock, Mr. Chance. She's at the city morgue now, I believe—she asked me for directions, you see."

"Thanks very much."

Terrell took a cab to the morgue. He glanced into the general offices, which were separated from the waiting rooms by a high, wooden counter. Clerks were busy at typewriters and filing cabinets. One of them was talking to Connie Blacker, pointing to a line on the blank she was studying. She was nodding her blonde head slowly. The clerk seemed eager to help, and it was obvious why, Terrell thought. She wore a simple black suit and a short tweed coat, but with her figure and legs she might as well have been wearing a bikini.

Terrell wondered if Frankie Chance had moved into her life. It figured; his girl was downstairs with the iceboxes and running water and he would need a replacement. Connie might just fit. She was young, lovely and manageable. Everything required for the job, including a strong stomach. He sighed, wondering why in hell he felt so bitter about it.

She would be busy for a while, he knew, completing the arrangements to send Eden's body home. He drifted down the wide corridor. As he turned back toward the general offices he ran into a cleaning woman he had known when the morgue had been his beat, a big and cheerful colored woman who had worked in the morgue for the past thirty years. He was pleased to see Martha. They talked for a few minutes and then she said, "You coming back to work here, Mr. Terrell?"

"No, Martha. I'm waiting to talk to a person who's signing the forms on Eden Myles."

"Wasn't that a shame? That poor thing, so pretty and all. What do you suppose is the matter with that Mr. Caldwell? You think he went crazy or something?"

"I don't know, Martha."

"But why did he have to do it? She's so pretty. And expecting a little baby. That made it worse, if you ask me."

Terrell's expression didn't change. He lit a cigarette, and said, "It's a damn shame. But how did you know she was pregnant? That's supposed to be a secret."

"Oh, oh." Martha put a hand over her mouth. "I've done it again, Mr. Terrell."

"It's nothing serious."

"I heard one of the doctors talking the night she was brought in. I didn't know it was to be kept quiet. You won't say I told you, will you?"

"Of course not, Martha."

Terrell walked back down the corridor, covering ground with long strides. In the Coroner's reception room, Terrell told the secretary he wanted to see Dr. Graham, who was the city's chief coroner. She smiled mechanically at him, spoke into an intercom telephone, and then nodded at the door behind her. "Go right in, Mr. Terrell."

Dr. Graham, a tall man with a long, thin nose, came around his desk and extended a big, but seemingly boneless hand. "We don't see you around much these days, Sam," he said. "Too busy being an important columnist, eh?"

Terrell smiled. "It's a nuisance keeping the space filled every day. It's like an extra mouth to feed."

"What can we do for you?"

"I'd like to look at the report on Eden Myles."

"That's all been in the papers, Sam."

"I know, but I'm running down an angle. I'd like to see the report."

"I read the autopsy report to the press," Dr. Graham said, rather irritably. "You think I've left out something?"

"You left out the fact that she was pregnant," Terrell said. "I'm wondering if you left out anything else."

Dr. Graham fumbled through his pockets and finally brought out cigarettes. His face had become white. "What kind of a bluff do you think you're running?"

"Now, now," Terrell said patiently. "I know she was pregnant, Doctor. I want to know how far gone she was. I want to see the report."

"No, that's impossible. We don't pass out autopsy reports anymore. It involves too much clerical help."

Terrell swore in disgust. Then he said, "I'm going over to the Hall and get a court order to pry that autopsy out of you. And I'll bring back a photographer with me. And the character on our front page with the rosy, embarrassed look won't be me, Doc."

Dr. Graham sighed heavily and sat down behind his desk. "I don't want trouble. I don't want to be in the middle. As God is my judge I've done nothing wrong. The girl's condition had no bearing on her health or Caldwell's guilt."

"She was pregnant then. How many months?"

Dr. Graham sighed again. "Almost three months."

"Why didn't you give it to the papers?"

"Captain Stanko said—" Dr. Graham took a handkerchief from his pocket and wiped the damp hollows under his eyes. "Well, he said there was no point in blackening the girl's name."

"The old softie," Terrell said. "This girl has been traveling with hoodlums since she was about twelve, but Stanko doesn't want her reputation besmirched. Come on, Doc, try again."

"The case is open and shut," Dr. Graham said in a hurried, pleading voice. "The girl's a martyr now. Sweet kid, innocent victim, that sort of thing. Why not leave it that way? Why worry about messy details? Caldwell killed her—that's what counts."

"Well, maybe Stanko's got a point," Terrell said. "Don't worry about me broadcasting any family secrets."

"We'll just forget it then?" Dr. Graham said, smiling nervously.

"Sure. Why bother the public with details. So long and thanks, Doc."

In the tiled lobby Terrell looked into the reception room and saw that Connie Blacker was collecting her gloves and purse from the counter, smiling a thank-you at the clerk. He didn't know how to use the information about Eden Myles; he couldn't fit it into the rest of his theory.

Connie pulled open the glass door of the reception room and Terrell walked toward her. "Hello there. All through in there?"

"Yes, I'm through."

"Can I buy you some lunch?"

"No, I have a date."

"With Frankie Chance at two o'clock. But couldn't you be a little late? I'd like to talk to you."

"I'm sorry. I don't have time."

She started past him but he caught her arm.

"Let me go!" Her eyes were mutinous and angry. "Do you want me to start screaming?"

"I want you to start talking," he said. "Who was the man who came to Eden's apartment the night she was murdered? What job did he want her to do? Why was she afraid?"

"Let me go. I don't know anything."

"You're lying, Connie. You can save the life of an innocent man. You can put Eden's murderer in the death house where he belongs. But if you keep quiet nothing will happen."

"Nothing will happen to me," she said tensely.

"And how about Eden?" Terrell's voice sharpened with anger. "You've signed the forms and off she goes by fast freight. Is that the end of it? Have you gone downstairs to look at her? She's lying like a piece of frozen meat with a name tag tied to her ankle. Like something in a butcher shop. Only they kill animals a bit more humanely."

"Stop it, stop it." She turned away, tears starting in her eyes.

Terrell released her arm. "Okay, I'll stop." In his heart he couldn't blame her; why should she risk her life to help him. "I'll drop you at your hotel."

At his desk Terrell typed out an item for his column. He described Eden Myles' killer, the big man with the thick, black hair and scarred forehead, and suggested that the police were looking for him in connection with the Caldwell case. For several minutes he sat frowning and staring at what he had written. This was risky business. Karsh wasn't in or he would have asked his advice. As it was, this had to be his baby. He called a copy boy and gave him the item as an insert for his column; it would be squeezed in in time for the next edition, the two star, and be on the streets around four o'clock. And after that there would be an eruption in the Hall.

Karsh was waiting at Terrell's desk the next morning, looking fresh and handsome in a Chesterfield overcoat with a white silk muffler knotted about his throat. "Why didn't you tell me you were going to toss a grenade?" he asked Terrell. "I might have put my fingers in my ears."

"You heard repercussions?"

"Yes, Jack Duggan, our distinguished superintendent of cops, called me about it. I told him you'd talk to him this morning. Now listen to me." He glanced about the busy room, then looked back at Terrell. "Play it safe. You know about that gorilla who was seen leaving Caldwell's. You're the only one who does. If that gets around you'll become a lousy insurance risk." He patted Terrell's shoulder, in a clumsy and awkward gesture. "You're the staff for my declining years. Remember that, and don't be a damn fool."

"Sure, don't worry." Terrell was touched by Karsh's concern. Without his customary cynicism, Karsh seemed defenseless and vulnerable. He likes me, Terrell thought, and that embarrassed him.

"Don't let them trick you into popping off what you know," Karsh said. "Tell 'em you printed some talk, without checking it."

Jack Duggan was seated at his desk, a large, solidly built man with bold, direct eyes. He wore a uniform with golden epaulettes.

"Sit down, Sam," he said. "This item of yours—" He fingered a clipping on his desk. "It's a strange business. You describe a man in detail, and say we're looking for him in connection with the Caldwell case. Did you make that up? Or what?"

"I gather then the item isn't accurate," Terrell said.

"We aren't looking for anybody," Duggan said. "Let's don't be cute with each other. The Mayor raised hell with this. I know you're a good newspaperman. You don't print gossip or guesses. So it figures that someone gave you the item—someone you trusted. We want to know who it was."

"You and the Mayor, that is."

"That's it. Don't bother reading anything into his interest. He's within his rights. Your item indicates we don't have a complete case against Caldwell. Or that there might be something unexplained and mysterious about it. Neither conclusion is justifiable. The person who peddled this story to you is—a vicious, deliberate troublemaker. And we want to know who it is."

"The tip came in anonymously."

"I wouldn't advise you to stick to that," Duggan said. "This time we aren't interested in anything cute or cryptic. We want the truth."

"So do I," Terrell said. "Supposing we trade."

"What do you mean by that?"

Terrell hesitated, frowning slightly. Duggan was personally honest, Terrell was sure. But Terrell also knew that Duggan was a victim of something that might be called moral inertia; he was honest to a point and beyond that he was neutral.

"I'm waiting," Duggan said. "Who gave you the story?"

Before Terrell could answer, the door opened and Mayor Shaw Ticknor sauntered into the room. Ticknor was grinning widely and scratching the inside of his leg. The grin disappeared when he saw Terrell, but he continued to scratch his leg. "Well, you're the culprit I've been looking for. I hope for your sake you don't mind the taste of crow. Jack, did you put our position to Sam?"

"We were just discussing it," Duggan said.

"There's nothing to discuss," Ticknor said easily. "Not a damn thing." He strolled across the room toward Terrell, smiling again, a tall angular man with shaggy, iron gray hair and big features that looked as if they had been hacked roughly from coarse red rock. The voters seemed to be amused by his calculated oafishness, for they had returned him to office four times running. But he was a man who loved dirty stories, all-night poker games and sadistic practical jokes. He was also a thief on a large scale, and the ruthless enemy of anyone who stood in his path.

"Now let's get squared away," Ticknor said, still smiling at Terrell. "I guess Duggan's made our point by now—long-winded as he is. Somebody peddled you a bum story. The least you can do is print a retraction. Just a line or two. And then tell me where you got the story from."

"That's all, eh?"

"I hope you're not being sarcastic," Ticknor said, and he wasn't smiling any more. "I've been mayor of this city for twelve years, Sam, and I'm not letting you throw mud at my work and my reputation. There's nothing wrong here—but you're trying to stir up dirt. Well, you'll find that doesn't pay off here. Not in my city."

Terrell glanced at his watch. "That all you have to say?"

"Now listen to me," Ticknor said slowly, holding his temper. "I want to know where you got that phony story about a man with a scarred forehead. I'm going to get it, Sam. Or you'll wish you'd never crossed me."

"I'm double-parked," Terrell said casually, "so you'll have to excuse me. I don't want to get in real trouble." He glanced for a second at Duggan, who was staring at the backs of his hands, an expression of shame and anger on his face. Then he walked to the door.

When Terrell returned to the paper it was almost ten o'clock; the second edition was nearing its deadline and tension was building through the long room. Everyone was conscious of the big clock above the city desk. Karsh waved to him from his office, and Terrell crossed the floor and joined him in that soundproofed command post.

"Don't tell me," Karsh said. "His Honor just hung up." He shook his head. "Corn-fed ass."

"They're worried sick," Terrell said. "Even Duggan. I've never seen them this way before, Mike."

"More bad news is on the way." There was a gleam of devil's humor in Karsh's eyes. "Paddy Coglan's wife came in a while ago. She's waiting upstairs to tell you her story. It's a beaut, a fat, cream-fed beaut. Come on."

Mrs. Coglan was waiting for them in an empty office on the ninth floor. She stood awkwardly when they entered and began plucking at the skirt of her rusty black dress. Terrell could see that she had been weeping.

Karsh said, "Please sit down, Mrs. Coglan, and tell Sam what you've just been telling me."

"They asked me to come in yesterday, to the Hall," Mrs. Coglan said. "And they hemmed and hawed, but finally they came out with it. I could have the pension if I said that Paddy was of unsound mind for the past while. They said it would make the difference. Taking his own life might disqualify him, they said. But if it could be proven he had been upset, crazy so to speak, for some little time, then they thought it would be all right."

"She told them she'd think it over," Karsh said.

"Why do they want to say the poor man was insane? Isn't it enough he's dead?" She clenched her work-worn hands and her lips began to tremble. "Why must they ruin his name? Make him a figure of ridicule?"

"Your husband saw something the night Eden Myles was murdered," Terrell said. "Or someone. That version may be brought forward yet. But it can be discounted if you testify he had been acting oddly. Lunatics aren't very good witnesses."

"How long did they give you?" Karsh asked her.

"Until tomorrow morning."

"If you don't hear from me before then, stall them," Karsh said. "You can be down with the flu, if necessary. We're working on a story that yours is part of. Terrell is putting it together. We won't cut loose until we get everything. Okay?"

She said yes and smiled uncertainly.

Terrell took her to the door. "Paddy would like what you're doing," he said.

"Yes, he was a good man, a good man. Thank you, Mr. Terrell."

Terrell spent the rest of the morning studying clippings on the Municipal Parking Authority. It was a tedious business. He even read the Act itself, straining his eyes over the small print.

Finally he collected the pages of notes he had made, and went upstairs to the financial section, which was one of the long arms of the city room, between Karsh's office and the Sunday departments. The financial editor, Bill Moss, was speaking on the phone, but he smiled and waved Terrell to the chair beside his desk.

Moss wound up his call in a hurry, hung up and smiled at Terrell. "Want a tip on the market? Buy low, sell high." Moss was a handsome man with graying hair and dark, alert eyes. "What can I do for you, Sam?"

"I'll remember that—buy low, sell high. Bill, our Municipal Parking Authority has begun to fascinate me. Mind if I ask you a few questions?"

"Go right ahead."

"Well, I've just read through the Act. Isn't it a pretty loose setup?"

"I would say so, yes. That isn't too unusual, though."

Terrell smiled faintly. "Here's another point I'm curious about. Most of the Parking Authority contracts went to two firms—Acme Construction and Bell Wreckers. I'd like some dope on those outfits—everything you can turn up."

Moss made a note of the firm names, and said, "I'll put somebody on it. I assume you're in a hurry."

"Sorry, but I am. I'll have lunch and drop back. Okay?"

"I'll try to have the information for you then."

At two o'clock Terrell was back at Bill Moss' desk.

"Here's your information," Moss said, tapping a neat stack of folders with his pencil. "I can probably give you a synopsis faster than you can dig it out for yourself. To start with, and I imagine this is one thing you wanted to know, both companies are legitimate. But there is something queer about them. For one thing, I'm not satisfied by their statements of ownership. I'll explain that in a minute. And secondly, they've been too lucky. Starting from scratch, they've mushroomed into huge organizations, with all of their work coming from the Authority."

"How about their ownership? You said something was odd there."

"Well, they list four or five men as owners. I know a couple of them, and well—" Moss shrugged lightly. "These men, in my opinion, don't have the brains and backing to have pulled these companies into shape."

"They're figureheads, you'd say."

"That would be my guess."

"How do I find the real owners then?"

"That's a tough one. The arrangements may be verbal and you can't very well examine or analyze a verbal contract."

"Well, thanks a lot."

Moss nodded. "Let me know what else you find out. I'm always interested in larceny."

"Me, too," Terrell said. "Particularly grand larceny."

At his own desk, Terrell sat for a while smoking and mulling over what he had learned from Moss. Finally, he picked up his phone and dialed the downtown office of Dan Bridewell's firm. One of the state's largest contractors, old man Bridewell had started as a bricklayer and worked his way to the presidency of the company. He had come a long way, but he had fought for every foot of it.

"Yes? Who's this?" It was Bridewell's voice, high, sharp and irritable. "Terrell? With the paper?"

"That's right, Mr. Bridewell. Sam Terrell. I'm doing a piece on the Parking Authority, and I've come across a point or two I'd like to check with you."

"I'll save you some time, Terrell. The Parking Authority won't give me a contract—they prefer dealing with fly-by-nights. I use the wrong kind of bath soap, or I don't vote right. I've said all this a dozen times, and it's all on the record."

"I want to ask you about Bell Wreckers and Acme Construction—the firms who do the Authority jobs. Do you know the men who own these companies?"

"You'd better go down to the Hall and ask that question, son. They must know. But they never told me. I've got work to do now. Goodbye." The receiver clicked in Terrell's ear.

Terrell smiled and put his phone back in place. For another fifteen minutes he sat at his desk, staring out at the activity and tension that radiated from the city desk and copy wheel. There was only one way to get the information he wanted; he had to make a deal. He picked up the phone and called Superintendent Duggan's office. He mentioned a trade to Duggan and arranged to meet him in five minutes at the north annex to the Hall.

The Superintendent was waiting when Terrell arrived, his face ruddy but rather anxious under the gold-embossed peak of his cap. They fell into step and walked toward Seventeenth Street, moving at a leisurely pace through the crowded mall.

"Do we trade even?" Terrell said. "I help you, you help me?"

"Let's try it."

Terrell put a cigarette in his mouth, hesitating; Karsh's words had come back to him: "*You know about that gorilla . . . if that gets around you'll become a lousy insurance risk.*" Could he trust Duggan? That was the gamble. He said, "I talked to Paddy Coglan over in Beach City."

Duggan stared at him. "The day he shot himself?"

"That's right. He described the man he saw running out of Caldwell's house. That's the description I used in my column. The man I described was in town huddling with Ike Cellars a few days before he murdered Eden Myles."

They walked along in silence.

"You happen to know," Terrell said, "who owns Bell Wreckers and Acme Construction?"

"That should be on record some place."

"The owners of the records are dummies," Terrell said. "I want to know who they're fronting for."

"I can put some pressure on," Duggan said. "I'll get the information."

"I need it by tonight. Can I call you at home?"

"That soon, eh? Well, I'll do my best. Around eight?"

"Eight o'clock it is. So long now."

Terrell watched Duggan as he shouldered his way through the hurrying crowds, a big military figure, a picture of power and precision. And what was he thinking? Terrell wondered. How to weasel out of this challenge? Whether to take his information to Ticknor and Cellars, and close his eyes to what would happen?

Terrell was wryly amused at his academic attitude—because there was nothing academic about his position. If Duggan let him down, he wouldn't have a prayer.

At eight sharp Terrell dialed Duggan's home. Duggan answered. "Who's this?"

"Terrell. Well?"

"I've got what you wanted," Duggan said. "And I've got a load of trouble for myself. I picked up two of those dummy owners, and put them through the wringer. Ticknor heard about it and blew his stack. When the Council meets tomorrow I'll be suspended. A nice pay-off, isn't it?"

"Well, you're a cop, not an ostrich," Terrell said. "Incidentally, who owns those companies?"

"It jolted me. I've been on the inside for years and I wouldn't have guessed it. Ike Cellars is a half-owner and that figures. But the other half-owner is old Dan Bridewell. Can you figure that?"

"Are you sure? Dead sure?"

"Christ, give me credit for being able to handle a routine investigation," Duggan said wearily.

"Sorry. For what it's worth, you've got friends in our shop. You may look pretty good in our story."

"Thirty-five years in the business and our Huckleberry Capone of a mayor can break me for doing ten minutes of honest work. It's nice, isn't it?"

"Very. But don't quit. Make them fire you."

"I've already done that."

Terrell hung up and began to dress. Bridewell—that was a sleeper. The posturing puritan, the do-gooder, the angry denouncer of mobs and grafters—in thick with Ike Cellars!

As he was about to leave, the phone rang, and he scooped it up irritably and said, "Hello? Terrell."

"You told me to remember the name," she said.

He recognized Connie Blacker's voice. "I'm glad you did. What can I do for you?"

"I want to see you. I've . . . well, changed my mind."

"Where are you?"

"I'm at the club, The Mansions. Could you come over and have a drink with me?"

She didn't sound right, he thought. Scared maybe. Or worried.

"How about nine or nine-thirty?" he asked.

"That's perfect. It's between my numbers. Please don't let me down."

Terrell looked at the phone and raised an eyebrow. She sounded very odd indeed. "Don't worry," he said. "I'll be there."

Terrell drove to The Mansions, Ike Cellars' big and brilliant nightclub in center-city. The headwaiter, Miguel, greeted him cordially and sent a message back to Connie Blacker with a busboy.

The busboy returned and told him Miss Blacker was waiting in her dressing room. Terrell nodded a so-long to Miguel and crossed the floor to the corridor that led to the entertainers' quarters. She was waiting for him at the door of her room.

"I'm glad you could make it." she said.

"You sounded pretty urgent."

"Come in, please. It's cluttered, but there's a spare chair and an extra ashtray."

"Men have lived and died with a lot less," Terrell said. She was nervous as hell about something, he realized. Shaking in her boots. "How's your job coming along?"

"Pretty well. I'm about one notch above a cigarette girl. I do a chorus with the band in the closing number—and I have a little stooge routine with the MC." She smiled rather quickly. "Please sit down."

"You'll get along," he said. "Places like this always need icing." She wore a ribbon in her short, yellow hair, and her skin was like a young girl's, flawless and clean without makeup. Her costume gave her figure an assist it didn't really need. But Terrell had an illogical feeling that she didn't belong in Ike Cellars' elaborately camouflaged clip joint. She was decorative certainly, but she was more than that. She belonged in a home that smelled of clean babies and a pot roast for Sunday dinner, with maybe a log fire and martinis thrown in. But he could be wrong.

"Why did you want to see me?"

She glanced at the door. "If I told you something you could use—what would I get out of it?"

"The usual tawdry things," he said wearily. "Peace of mind, self-respect, an easy conscience. It's a good trade."

She sat down slowly, watching him now. "Nothing else?"

"You mean something clean and idealistic—like cash?"

She crossed her legs and moved her foot about in a quick circle. "That's it," she said. She glanced toward the door again, and Terrell saw her hands were gripping the edges of the chair.

"I think we might make a deal," he said. "But I'll need an idea of what you've got."

She leaned toward him suddenly. "Get out of here," she said, in a breathless, desperate voice. "Get out fast."

Terrell stood quickly, but the door was already opening and he realized that he was too late. Frankie Chance came into the room, his deceptively gentle brown eyes alight with anger and excitement. Behind him was one of Ike Cellars' bodyguards, a tall, wide man named Briggs.

"I told you not to bother her," Frankie said.

"She wasn't complaining," Terrell said.

Frankie glanced at her. "Soft-hearted, doesn't want to finger you, that's all. But I know the story. You had a few drinks, Sam, and you began to get ideas."

"This is pretty stupid—even for you," Terrell said.

"Two things Ike won't stand for are drunks and guys who molest his girls." Briggs put a huge hand on Terrell's arm. "We'll just escort you to your car."

"Thanks for nothing," Terrell said. He tried to pull his arm free but Briggs' hand was as firm as a concrete cast. He looked at Connie then, but she turned away from him. "Nice going," he said.

Briggs led him through the doorway, and glanced at Frankie Chance. "Back way?"

"Sure," Frankie said, taking Terrell's free arm. "It doesn't look good dragging drunks across the dance floor."

They took Terrell through the kitchen and out to the parking lot in the rear which was used for overflow business. Now it was empty and quite dark. An attendant came out of the shadows and flipped his cigarette aside. He seemed to know what was expected of him.

Briggs pushed Terrell against a brick wall, and the attendant and Chance held his arms.

"Sam, you've been a nuisance," Frankie said.

Briggs opened a flask then and splashed whiskey over Terrell's face and shirt front. "Shame to waste it," he muttered. Then he hit Terrell in the stomach with his free hand, bringing the punch up with a kind of lazy power. Frankie and the attendant tightened their grips as Terrell pitched forward, gagging against the pain spreading from his loins to his throat. Briggs hit him a dozen times, methodically and thoughtfully, and then paused and took a pull at the flask he held in his left hand.

"Take him home," Frankie said to the attendant. "We don't want him cluttering up the alley."

Terrell lay on the sofa in his apartment, breathing with infinite care against a frightening pain that moved up and down his body with the rise and fall of his chest.

He wasn't aware of dozing off, but suddenly a chill went through him and he sat up shaking his head and staring about the dimly lit room. The illuminated hands of his wrist watch stood at two-thirty. He had been asleep an hour or more. What had wakened him?

Then it came again, a soft tap on the door. Terrell got stiffly to his feet, pressing one hand against the pain in his side. He crossed the room, and stood beside the door with his back to the wall. "Who's that?" he said.

"It's me—Connie."

Terrell put the burglar chain on, and opened the door a few inches. She was alone, looking young and pale and frightened.

"What do you want?"

"I was worried. Can't I come in for just a minute, please? I want to explain."

"I'll bet your story's cute," Terrell said. But he was interested. He unhooked the burglar chain. "Come on in." When she slipped past him he closed the door and bolted it and then limped back to the sofa.

"You're hurt," she said. She came up behind him and touched his arm. "Can I get you anything?"

"You've helped enough. Any more help from you and I'll need a complete set of new parts."

"I'm terribly sorry. They made me call you. You—you'd better sit down. You look sick."

"Stop fussing," he said foolishly.

"Well, you stop acting like an idiot." She turned him toward the sofa. He tried to pull away from her but the strength was flowing out of him in giddy waves. "Cut it out," he said. He was on his back then and she was adjusting a pillow under his head.

"They made me do it," she said. "Can't you believe that?"

"Sure, that's how concentration camps got built. People were made to do it."

"They said they just wanted to talk to you. Frankie said you wouldn't see him. So he told me to call you and arrange a date. I—I shouldn't have done it. I wouldn't have if I'd known they were going to hurt you. Would you like some coffee?"

"I don't need anything. All right, coffee then." He knew she wouldn't be able to find things, so he decided to get up and help. But instead he went to sleep. He didn't wake until she shook his shoulders gently and said, "Here's your coffee, Sam."

He had been asleep half an hour, and the rest had revived him considerably. The apartment smelled pleasantly of coffee and cigarette smoke, and Connie was sitting in a chair beside the sofa.

"Do you feel any better?" she asked him.

"I'm all right, I guess." He sipped the coffee and looked around for a cigarette.

"Here," she said.

He took one, accepted a light from hers, and nodded his thanks.

"You should go to bed," she said. "I've put out your pajamas and turned back the covers."

"That's fine."

Terrell stood and limped into his bedroom, aware of her following close behind him. He slipped out of his suitcoat and let it drop to the floor, but the shirt was another matter; he could barely raise his hands to his collar.

Without a word, she stepped forward, and facing him, she took off his tie and unbuttoned his shirt. Her nearness felt good; it was warm and soothing. She said something in a little whisper when she saw the bruises along his ribs. Her lips began to tremble. "They might have killed you," she said.

"A small price for a good story," he said. "That was our class motto. Martyrs in the cause of fearless reporting. A fine, clean way to go, don't you think?"

"Lie down and stop it. Should I call a doctor or something?"

"No, I don't think so. Nothing's broken. It will wear away in a day or so."

"Why are you putting yourself on the spot? Isn't there someone who could help you?"

"Sure," he said, "you for one. But you said no."

"It wouldn't do any good. You can't change things."

"Maybe, maybe not. But I can change into my pajamas, if you'll excuse me."

"Yes, certainly."

Terrell got under the covers a few minutes later and let his body sink into the soft warmth of the bed. A knock sounded gently on the door, and he said, "Come in."

She had her coat over her arm. "I'm going now," she said. "Anything else I could get for you?"

"I don't think so."

She came to the side of the bed and looked down at him with a grave little frown. "I made fresh coffee. All you have to do is turn up the burner when you want it."

"Okay, thanks." They looked at each other for a few seconds in silence. She was very pale and her short yellow hair shadowed her face.

"I'd better go."

"So long, Connie. And thanks again."

But she stood watching him and made no move to leave. Finally she sat on the edge of the bed and looked down at the tips of her brown pumps. "I'm running out of small talk," she said. "I thought—don't you want me to stay?"

"Just like that?" he said.

"Sure—just like that." She spoke almost flippantly, but a tide of color was moving up in her pale cheeks.

She started to rise but he caught her arm. "Why do you want to stay? A tender breast for the wounded warrior? Something like that?"

"I don't know. I didn't figure it out." She looked at him and the light from the bedlamp glinted on the tears in her eyes. "You made me feel cheap and useless, that's all. I wanted to do something for you, something I could do—" She shook her head quickly. "It doesn't make sense. I'm sorry."

"It was a very decent impulse." He was oddly touched and grateful and that made him feel awkward. "Would you like a cigarette? Something to drink?"

She shook her head again. "No, I've got to go."

Terrell took one of her hands. He didn't want to hurt her any more than he had already, but he couldn't find the words to express his feelings. "Couldn't we forget the bitterness?" he said.

"Can you do that?"

He touched her cheek and then the smoothness of her throat. When she turned and smiled uncertainly at him, Terrell felt very lucky and just a bit humble. "We'll try," he said . . .

The ringing phone woke him much later. He got up on his elbow and switched on the bedside lamp. The room was dark but lines of soft, gray dawn framed the drawn blinds. He lifted the phone and the operator said, "Mr. Terrell?"

"That's right."

"One moment. Beach City is calling."

Terrell swung his legs over the side of the bed and lit a cigarette. Then he looked over his shoulder and saw that she was watching him with a sleepy little smile. "Sorry," he said.

"And I was having such an elegant dream."

"Close your eyes and pick up where you left off. It's still early."

She snuggled into the pillow, her face small and pale in the frame of her tousled blonde hair.

The receiver clicked in Terrell's ear, and a voice he knew said, "Sam? Sam Terrell? This is Tim Moran, Beach City homicide. Sorry about the time."

"Never mind. What's up?"

"That little cop who shot himself over here, you remember? Coglan? Well, I don't think he did. I don't want to say more now, but if you come over here I'll give you the story."

"There's no traffic. I can make it in two hours."

"Fine. I called you because I just got a brush-off from your police department. They want that suicide tag to stick."

"Who'd you talk to?"

"A cop named Stanko."

"That figures. I'll see you in two hours, Tim. And thanks."

Terrell put the receiver down and said, "I've got to shave and get rolling. You try to sleep."

"You must go?"

"Yes, it's important."

She sat up smiling and pressed her cheek against his arm. "I wanted to help you," she said. "And it was the other way around."

"It was much more than that," he said. "I'll tell you about it when I get back. In loving detail."

"Sam . . ."

"Yes?"

"I want to help you. I want to tell you what happened that night at Eden's."

He was silent a moment, watching her. Then he said, "Does anybody know you came here last night?"

"I don't think so. Why?"

"Listen to me: if I let you help, will you promise me not to stick your nose out of this apartment? And to keep that door locked until I get back? And promise not to let anyone in, up to and including the Angel Gabriel?"

"Yes, I promise." She was smiling. He cared about her, and that made what had already happened much more important. "Ike Cellars came to the apartment that night. He wanted Eden to do a job for him."

"And that job was?"

"To help frame Mr. Caldwell."

"Are you sure of this?"

"I was in the bedroom. I heard it."

It was nine o'clock when Terrell pulled into the parking area reserved for police and press at the Beach City courthouse. He had already relayed Connie's story to Karsh, and the presses were ready to run. He needed Tim Moran's story, but he had everything else; the why and how of the frame around Caldwell, the Parking Authority mess, everything. And it was Connie's eyewitness account that tied it all together.

Terrell went up to Moran's office on the second floor. Moran was in his shirtsleeves, his tie loose, his collar open, and he looked gray with exhaustion. But his eyes were narrow and sharp with a hunter's excitement.

"Well, you made pretty good time," he said. "Sit down, Sam. I'll tell you what I've got. Then I think you can tell me something. Is that fair enough?"

"Sure," Terrell said.

Moran picked up a glossy print from his desk and handed it to Terrell. "There's the mug who shot Paddy Coglan. Know him?"

Terrell studied the dark face, the low, scarred forehead, the bold, angry eyes. He shook his head slowly. "I don't know him. Where did you get the picture?"

"You know something about him though, Sam. I saw your expression."

"This could be the guy Coglan saw leaving Caldwell's." At Moran's puzzled frown he said, "I'll sketch it in for you, don't worry. But tell me the rest of your story. Where did you get this picture?"

"It's a weird thing, Sam. As odd as I ever ran into in this business. We wrote Coglan off as suicide, you know. Well, two days after his death I got a call here in my office. It was from a guy who'd been registered at the hotel at the same time as Coglan. He was on the same floor, just a room away, and he heard the shot. He looked out into the corridor and saw a man closing Coglan's door. He saw only the man's back. But he was able to describe his overcoat, the color of his hair and general build."

"Why did he wait two days to speak up?"

"He was plain scared. But his conscience obviously bothered him a bit. I took the description to the hotel, and talked to the bellhops, elevator men and desk clerks. They'd seen this man, all right. He'd been in the lobby in the afternoon and right after suppertime. And an elevator operator remembered taking him to the floor above Coglan's. Then I played a long hunch. You know there are quite a few sidewalk photographers working this area, so I rounded them up and looked at the shots they'd taken the day that Paddy Coglan was shot. That's how we got this picture. The photographer remembered the guy. He thought the big boy looked like a fighter or a wrestler, someone who might be flattered by a picture of himself. But it didn't go. Our guy stopped and glared at the photographer and then walked off fast." Moran grinned without humor. "I like to think of what that did to his nerves. Anyway, we sent the print to Washington, and they traced it. He's Nicholas Rammersky, alias Nick Rammer, age forty-two, with two convictions and a record of minor stuff stretching back twenty years. He's a paid killer. And I want to know who paid him to kill Paddy Coglan."

"I said I'd fill you in," Terrell said. "I had everything but Rammersky's name when I came over. It goes this way . . ."

Twenty minutes later Moran came to the door with Terrell. He said, "Rammersky will burn for murder of the girl or the cop. Either way, I'm not particular. He can't hide after your story breaks. And neither can those other crums in your backyard . . ."

Terrell drove back through heavy traffic and reached the city shortly after two-thirty. He parked in front of his apartment, and checked the time as he went up the stairs. They would need a couple of hours to get the story organized. By working fast they could make the three-star final at four-thirty. The editions establishing Caldwell's innocence would hit the city like sledgehammers.

Terrell unlocked the door and said, "Hey!"

There was no answer, no stir of life in the apartment. He stood with his hat in his hand, feeling the grin stiffen on his lips. For several seconds he waited, and then he closed the door and walked slowly through the little apartment. Empty. The blinds were still drawn, and the bed was unmade. There was the light fragrance of her perfume in the air. But that was all.

He lit a cigarette and looked around the living room, a frown touching his face. She didn't have any reason to risk her neck, he thought. Why shouldn't she clear out? But he was surprised, Terrell realized sadly. He would have bet anything that she'd stick.

It was then, as he was putting his cigarette out, that he saw the note on the telephone table. He picked it up, feeling the leaden disappointment moving in him. It was written in pencil, in a neat and careful hand: "Maybe I picked sides in too much of a hurry. I'm trying to be sensible now. Forgive me for backing out. Give me that much of a break."

Terrell stared around the room, shaking his head like a weary fighter. Without her testimony much of his story fell apart. The Rammersky part was intact, but that only proved that Coglan was murdered; it wouldn't help Caldwell. Not in time.

He sat down and called the paper, but Karsh wasn't in. His secretary told him he was at the game. The Game. Terrell had forgotten; Dartmouth was playing and Karsh was there with a party of friends. It irritated Terrell; a game, any game, seemed silly and insignificant while Caldwell was in jail, and the truth couldn't be told . . .

Terrell stood and looked around, frowning again; something was wrong. The unmade bed—that was wrong. She wouldn't leave without tidying up. Terrell looked at the note he had dropped on the coffee table. That was genuine. His heart was beating faster. He was suddenly hoping that she *had* walked out on him. That she had left of her own free will.

He sat down and dialed her hotel. When the clerk answered Terrell said, "Is Connie Blacker there?"

"She's checked out, sir."

"When was this?"

"Let me see—that was around ten this morning."

"Did she leave a forwarding address?"

"Just a second—no, I'm afraid not."

"Was she alone?"

"Sir, I can't tie up this phone indefinitely, I—"

"Was she alone?" Terrell repeated sharply.

"No, sir—there were friends with her. Two gentlemen."

"Was Frankie Chance there?"

"There's a call waiting, sir. If you could stop by—"

Terrell put the phone down and picked up his hat. He went downstairs to get a cab.

At the hotel, the desk clerk described the men who had been with Connie: one was large, with dark skin and hair and the other was sharply dressed, with light hair and thin features. The big man sounded like Briggs, Cellars' bodyguard.

Terrell went outside and stopped on the busy sidewalk, wondering what to do next. He was caught between two fears, the first that she had walked out on him, and the second that she had been picked up by Ike Cellars' hoodlums. The first fear was selfish, but the other thing was a matter for the police or FBI—but he had no proof beside his illogical conviction that she wouldn't have run out on him.

Terrell went back to his apartment and called Karsh, but the maid told him everyone was still at the football game. Karsh's son was in with a group of friends, she said, and everybody was coming back after the game for a buffet dinner and some drinks.

Terrell paced up and down the apartment, smoking one cigarette after the other. Finally, he turned decisively and scooped up the telephone. Superintendent Duggan wasn't in his office, his secretary said; he could be reached at home if it were important. Terrell broke the connection and dialed Duggan's home number.

Duggan's wife answered, and said just a minute, she'd tell Jack, and then Duggan was on the phone, speaking in a soft, worried voice. "Sam, it's been a wild day. I guess you've heard all about it."

"I haven't heard anything. I've been working. I want to report the kidnapping of a girl named Connie Blacker who worked for Ike Cellars."

Duggan paused, and Terrell heard his heavy breathing. "Why come to me?" he said at last. "It's a Federal charge."

"Aren't you interested? Did Ike Cellars dampen your flaming official zeal?"

"Who the hell do you think you're talking to?" Duggan said, in an angry, rising voice. "I've been kicked around all day, and I'm sick of it. The Council didn't suspend me—but only by three votes. Ticknor told me off like I was a rookie cop he'd caught drunk on a beat. I'm not taking any more of it—from you or anybody else."

"You're going to take a lot more," Terrell said. "Ticknor can scare up three more votes, don't worry. And after that you're through—another ex-cop whining that he got squeezed out by political pressure. But if you find that girl you've got a chance."

Duggan said, "What do you mean? What's she got to do with me?"

Terrell was aware of the quickened interest in his voice; then suddenly he realized that he'd been beaten on this story from the start: Paddy Coglan, Connie—someone was always ahead of him.

"I don't understand," Duggan said. "What did you say her name was?"

"I forget," Terrell said. "Smith or something like that."

"Why the cute stuff? I asked you a question. What's the girl's name? What's she got on Ticknor and Cellars?"

"Nothing at all," Terrell said. "I was dreaming."

"You sound wide awake to me."

"It's a trick I learned in college. Take it easy." Terrell put the phone down on Duggan's protesting voice, and picked up his hat and coat. Duggan wouldn't help. No one would help. She was trouble, and the smart boys would want no part of her. A pillow over her face, the pressure of a finger on her throat—that was the best thing all around. So the smart boys would figure it. But there was still a chance, Terrell knew. He had enough to print now. Enough to blow a loud whistle on Cellars.

When Terrell reached Karsh's apartment it was late in the afternoon, and the early winter darkness had dropped over the city. The crowd was back from the game and a party was under way.

"Where's Mr. Karsh?" Terrell asked the maid.

"He's talking on the long distance in his bedroom, Mr. Terrell. Can I bring you a drink or something to eat?"

"No, thanks. I'll forage."

Karsh's son and a half dozen of what obviously were his friends had grouped themselves about the massive record player, the young men in dark flannels and white buck shoes, the girls smooth and sweet in tweeds and cashmeres.

At the opposite end of the room Karsh's mistress and an assortment of friends and sycophants were standing in front of the well-stocked bar. To each his own, Terrell thought, as he went over to get a drink. But he felt sorry for Karsh, who seemed to make sense only at work. There he operated with brilliant precision, keeping every department of the paper under meticulous supervision. But the rest of his life was chaos. His marriage had ended in divorce several years ago and he had been bled white by his wife's lawyers. He had never been close to his children—a son and daughter—and saw very little of them now; the girl had married and moved to the west coast, and the son was a smooth and expensive youngster who dropped in at the office occasionally to discuss his financial needs.

Terrell's thoughts turned from Karsh to Connie. It was now after six: Connie had been gone since ten that morning. Eight full hours. Anything could have happened to her in that time—anything might have been done to her.

The bedroom door opened and Karsh walked out. He was fairly drunk, Terrell guessed.

He wore a superbly cut gray flannel suit with a Dartmouth pennant in the lapel, and was groomed to glossy perfection. "Let's have a drink, for God's sake," he said.

Terrell crossed the silent room and took Karsh's arm. "Mike," he said, "listen to me. Will you please?"

"Sam, old boy, glad to see you. Did you meet my son? He's ashamed of me, but he's a good kid in spite of that—or because of it, I should say."

"Mike, listen," Terrell said. "The girl is gone. The witness. Cellars has her."

But Karsh was lost to him. "Old college songs, Sam, that's the spirit of the evening. There's one from ole U. of Peiping—" He laughed as an ad-lib struck him. "The University of Peiping Tom, actually."

Karsh's son joined them and said easily, "Dad, we've got to peel off. I didn't get a chance to tell you during the game, but we're driving up to Skyport tonight." Young Karsh was tall, dark and his manners were impeccably casual.

"That's all right," Karsh said. He smiled and patted the boy's shoulder. "Sorry you have to be on your way. I missed a briefing, I guess. I thought this was to be a real holiday. Well, have a nightcap anyway. And a bite of something to eat. Make your friends live it up a bit."

When Karsh turned back to Terrell his manner had changed; the boozy good fellowship was gone, and his eyes were empty and cold. "I go on kidding myself," he said. "Thinking there's something besides work. But there's nothing." He shook his head quickly. "The girl is gone, eh? When did this happen?"

"Around ten this morning."

"How important is she to your story?"

"She's it. But I can start without her."

"Are you sure Cellars picked her up? She worked for him, you said. Maybe she's still working for him."

"No, she's on the level. I know, Mike."

"It's a question of how far we can trust her. She may have walked out on you—keep that in mind. Scribbled a note and walked out. There's no proof that Cellars grabbed her. Is there, Sam?"

Terrell hesitated, frowning faintly at Karsh. "How did you know she left a note?" he said.

"Clairvoyance, pure and simple. They all leave notes. Now look. Wait for me in my bedroom while I make another call. I'll put the call through out here and say good-bye to the boy. Then we'll go to work. Could you get everything together in two or three hours? For the Night Extra?"

"I'm ready now," Terrell said.

"Good." Karsh winked at him and walked briskly to a telephone on a table beside the record player.

The room was noisy with talk and music. When the connection was made and Karsh was speaking, Terrell turned and walked into Karsh's bedroom. He closed the door behind him and leaned against it, hearing the hard, laboring stroke of his heart. The music from the living room poured around him, but he was aware only of the reactions of his body; the beat of his heart, the tight, cold feeling in his stomach, and then something in his mouth that was like an essence of fear and betrayal and death.

The extension telephone was on a table beside Karsh's long, wide bed—just a foot or so from Terrell's hand. He looked down at the smooth, black receiver, and a little shudder went through him.

But Terrell's hand moved slowly, almost of its own volition, raising the receiver to his ear. He heard music first, a noisy background sound from the record player, and then he heard Karsh's voice, sharp and hard over the music, and insistent to the point of desperation.

"—it can't be covered up, Ike. I'm telling you, it's impossible. Be reasonable, man."

The music beat strongly in Terrell's ear, a pulsing rhythm that matched the quick beat of his heart. And then he heard Ike Cellars' voice, bigger than Karsh's, thick with convulsive anger.

"Don't tell me anything, understand! You keep it out of your paper."

"But Terrell's got everything."

"You keep it from being printed then. That's your job. Don't worry about anything else."

"Just a minute—hold on a second." Karsh's cry was desperate and futile; the connection was already broken.

Terrell heard Karsh's ragged breathing for an instant before he put the receiver quietly back into its cradle. He stood perfectly still, rubbing his hands on the sides of his trousers.

When he heard the knob turn, he put a cigarette quickly between his lips and raised his hands to cup the flame of his lighter. The door swung open and Karsh walked into the room, his manner brisk and business-like. "I'm squared away now," he said. "Tell me what you've got, Sam."

Terrell couldn't make himself turn and face Karsh. He stood in profile to him, almost physically sick with a blend of shame and anger and pity.

"Well?" Karsh said. His tone was puzzled. "I asked you a question, Sam. What've we got? Provable stuff we can back up with witnesses and written evidence?"

Terrell turned at last and stared at Karsh. The silence stretched out until Karsh made a worried little gesture with his hand, and said, "What's the matter, Sam? I'm just asking you what we can use."

"Why not ask Ike Cellars?" Terrell said, softly. "From the weather to classified ads—he's the boy to ask. Isn't that right, Mike?" His voice rose suddenly in anger. "Well? Isn't that right?"

"What the hell are you talking about?" Karsh's puzzled smile was a good effort, but his face had turned clammy and white.

Terrell said bitterly, "Don't lie and squirm. Spare me that. You knew the girl wrote a note. How? How did you know that?"

"I told you—"

Terrell pointed to the extension telephone. Karsh's voice trembled and then he wet his lips and stared at Terrell in silence.

"I heard you talking to Cellars," Terrell said.

"Listen to me—you've got to understand."

"Understand what? That you're working for him? I know that now."

Karsh took a step toward him and raised his hands in a clumsy and incongruous gesture of supplication. "Sam, I was trying to save you—you've got to believe me. From the moment you talked to Coglan and got his story about the prowler—from then on you were slated for the morgue."

"I brought you the whole story," Terrell said. "You could have smashed them to bits with it. But you killed it. We'd wait until we had it all, you said, the drama and the color, the whole thing in one piece, like a beautiful symphony." Terrell's voice became savage and ugly. "But you were lying. I had the guts of the story the first night, but you threw it out. Threw away Caldwell's only chance. Then I traced down Paddy Coglan, and got the truth from him, a scared, drunken little cop hiding in a cheap flea trap in Beach City. But he was dead before his testimony could do any good. Then Mrs. Coglan came in with her story, and you buried that too. More lies. Wait till we have it all, the drunks singing Faust, the symphony of news." Terrell pounded a fist into his palm.

"I fell for it like any prize fool. But I was too close to you, Mike. I believed in you. You taught me this business. For a dozen years you were my model—I even tried to dress like you when I was a copy boy."

"Sam, listen for God's sake."

"Then the girl talked," Terrell said bitterly. "And we had them cold. But you squealed to Cellars again, and now she's gone. Where?" Terrell caught him by the lapels of his expensive suit and shook him with all of his strength. "Where is she? What have they done with her?"

"I don't know—I don't know."

Terrell let him go and Karsh turned away and sat down slowly and wearily on the side of the bed. His face had gone slack, and he was breathing with a definite physical effort, like a man in pain. "I needed money, I always needed money." The travesty of a smile twisted his lips. "The pleas of the absconding bank teller, the defense of a kid who snatches a purse. You'd think I could come up with something more original." He sighed and a little shudder went through his body. "Gambling, alimony, that little fop of mine outside—they suck money out of me every minute of the day and night. Cellars offered to chip in a few years back. At first it was simple. Kill a divorce story, ease up on some characters in trouble with the tax people—favors I could do with a pencil or a telephone call. But I got in too deep. I couldn't pay him back." Karsh looked up at Terrell, his eyes pleading for understanding. "Then the Caldwell story broke. You stumbled on the truth, and Cellars expected me to keep it out of the paper. If it was just my job at stake I might have told him to go to hell. I don't know. But it was your life, Sam. Cellars wanted to kill you. I convinced him it would be smarter to kill the story. So we played you for a fool. Everything you dug up went back to Cellars—and nothing went into the paper. But you're alive, remember that, *I saved your life*. Maybe you don't believe me." Karsh tried to smile, but his face was a mask of despair.

"Where's the girl now?" Terrell said.

"I don't know. I swear it." Karsh got slowly to his feet and moistened his dry lips. "Is she important to you?"

"What difference does that make? She's important to herself. She's a hundred-pound girl who got in trouble with hoodlums because she was willing to tell the truth."

"She won't be hurt, Sam. She'll be all right."

"Is Paddy Coglan all right? Do you want the girl's death on your conscience too? Where is she?"

"I don't know, I don't know."

Terrell turned to the door.

"Wait, Sam, wait. Please."

Terrell looked back and saw the tears trembling in Karsh's eyes. But nothing could touch him any more. He walked out and slammed the door on Karsh's entreating voice.

Terrell stopped at a bar near Karsh's place, and drank two double whiskies, but the liquor failed to dissolve the sickening coldness in his stomach.

The story would break, of course. Nothing could stop it now. When Rammersky was picked up for Coglan's murder, he would talk—he wouldn't go to the chair and leave Cellars in the clear. And when Cellars fell he would drag old man Bridewell and Mayor Ticknor with him.

Terrell didn't need a newspaper to print his story. He could give it to Sarnac, and the national committee of Caldwell's party would splash it across the country.

But would that help Connie? No. He needed something that would stampede Cellars tonight; that would be sure to take his mind off everything but survival.

"Another one?" the bartender asked him.

"Yes, thanks." An idea had occurred to Terrell. There was something cruel and destructive in it that appealed to his need for reprisal. He walked to the phone booth at the end of the room and looked up the number of the Weston Hotel, where Frankie Chance had an apartment.

The hotel operator connected him with Frankie's room and after a few rings Frankie Chance said, "Hello?"

"Frankie? This is Sam Terrell. I'd like to see you in a few minutes. Can I come over?"

"You feeling unhappy about the beating you took the other night?"

"Live and learn," Terrell said. He began to smile, but his eyes were cold and hard. "This is another matter. I want to tell you who killed your girl. I'll be over in five minutes."

"You dirty, filthy scum, I'll—"

Terrell laughed shortly and dropped the receiver onto the hook.

At the Weston Hotel, he walked through the crowded lobby, took the elevator to Frankie Chance's floor. He went along a clean, warm corridor to the apartment and rapped lightly with the back of his knuckles. Frankie pulled the door open and said, "Come in, snoop. I prayed you'd come. I swear to God, I prayed." His hand was in the pocket of a gaudy dressing robe and Terrell knew he was holding a gun.

"There's no point in being mad, Frankie," he said. "I'm not here to needle you. I'm here to do you a favor."

Chance closed the door and took the gun from his pocket. "Don't stall," he said. "What are you trying to tell me, Sam?"

Terrell sat on the arm of a chair, smiling faintly. "I could do this leisurely, but I never got my kicks pulling wings off flies. Your girl was murdered on orders from Ike Cellars. A thug named Nick Rammersky did the job. That's it, Frankie. The guy you work for, the big boy who tosses you your bones—he had Eden killed."

"Shut up!" Frankie said softly. "You already said too much."

"Ask yourself one question, Frankie. Would I come here without proof?"

Chance stared at him for seconds, digesting this, and then he sat down slowly on the edge of the bed. "Proof—what kind of proof you got?"

"It's an interesting and devious story," Terrell said casually. "Eden Myles was peddling a few innocuous facts to Richard Caldwell. You follow me? Or do words like 'innocuous' tax you, Frankie?"

"You keep talking, or I'm going to beat it out of you," Frankie said.

"She was peddling them on orders. You were probably in on it that far, Frankie. And Eden thought it was as simple as that, too—get Caldwell's ear, give him a few bum tips. Wheels within wheels, a bit of standard political flimflam. But she didn't see the end of the script," Terrell said, watching Frankie's hot dark eyes. "Ike planned to have her killed in Caldwell's home— and frame Caldwell for her murder. Cellars had no animus against your girl, Frankie, but she could have been troublesome later. So that's the story. Rammersky came in the back door and knocked Caldwell out. Then he strangled Eden and left."

"You mentioned proof." His voice trembled. "Where is it?"

"First, Rammersky was seen bolting away from Caldwell's by a little cop named Paddy Coglan. Secondly, Connie Blacker heard Cellars explaining the phony deal to Eden. You know Connie, Frankie. You know she's straight."

"She's a square, an oddball," Frankie said, but a tide of angry color was moving up in his smooth brown cheeks. "What'd she tell you?"

"She was at Eden's apartment the night Eden was killed. Staying there as Eden's guest. Cellars arrived about ten-thirty, and told Eden she had to put on an act at Caldwell's that night. Get him drinking, and then start screaming and pretend that she'd been attacked and so forth. And as an added precaution, Cellars went on, one of his men would come in the back way and knock Caldwell unconscious, make it look as if he and Eden had struggled around a bit till he fell and hit his head. Cellars' man would disappear—leaving Eden alone to face the aroused neighbors and eventually the police. Eden would testify that Caldwell had become abusive, and had attacked her. This, Cellars assured her, was all she had to do or say. Connie heard this conversation, and talked to your girl when she came into the bedroom to change. Eden was frightened. She thought the whole deal was raw. She didn't know just how raw it was going to be."

"They didn't have to kill her," Frankie said. Tears were starting in his eyes. "She never hurt anybody. She was kind to everybody. We were together for five years and she never looked at another guy. We were going to buy a six-flat over in Eastport next year. Live in one flat, and live off the rent from the others. It was what she wanted. Something solid."

"Did you know she was pregnant?" Terrell asked quietly.

Frankie began to pound the foot of the bed with the flat of his hand, gently at first, but the blows fell harder and harder. "She wanted it. I didn't. I was scared. For her."

"What were your plans for the kid?" Contempt put an edge to Terrell's voice. "A job running numbers, or maybe selling programs and peanuts in a burlesque joint? Then take him back to Sicily to show the old folks how well you'd done in free, democratic America. Were those your dreams, you bastard?"

Frankie seemed hopelessly confused; he opened and closed his mouth but he couldn't manage anything but incoherent grunts.

"Beautiful dreams," Terrell said. "Then Cellars put his foot down, and there's nothing left but a grease mark on the floor."

"I got to ask some questions around," Frankie said, forming the words slowly and laboriously. "I'll find out the truth."

He dropped his robe on the floor and took down a raglan topcoat from the dressing room alcove. "Nobody ever talked to me the way you did," he said. "So I'll see you again, don't worry." He transferred the gun to the pocket of his topcoat.

"Wait a minute," Terrell said wearily. "Don't be a sucker, Frankie. You start after Cellars or Rammersky and you'll get your head blown off."

"Sure," Frankie said. "They're tough guys."

"I've been steaming you up for personal reasons."

Frankie turned and looked at him then. "What kind of personal reasons?"

"Cellars picked up Connie Blacker. She came to my apartment last night and that's where he found her this morning. I wanted him to start worrying so hard about his own skin that he'd forget her. I thought you were the boy to worry him."

"You're brainy. Using me to save her hide."

"It's no good, Frankie."

"Why not? I'll worry him plenty. And if I get my head blown off, what difference does it make? You'll have your girl. I'm a nothing to you. A bastard, wasn't it? The kind of slug who'd raise a kid to run numbers or work in a burlesque joint." Frankie was smiling but he sounded very much like a child trying not to weep. "Wasn't that you talking a few seconds ago?"

"I shouldn't have," Terrell said.

"You don't know me. You don't know Eden. But we're tramps to you. Isn't that right?"

"For Christ's sake, stop being so emotional."

"I think I'm going to die tonight." Frankie shrugged lightly. "That's why I'm talking like an oddball. It's important. You think she was a tramp, eh?"

"I think she loved you," Terrell said. "She wanted to have your baby. She was no tramp."

Frankie nodded slowly. "That's a logical way to look at it. It's funny that what you thought of her should matter to me. But you may be the last guy I'll ever talk to about her. So it makes a difference."

"You're selling yourself a deal," Terrell said. "You'll die all right. You'll be hit by a truck wandering around talking nonsense."

"No, it won't be that way," Frankie said. His hand turned the knob slowly and the door opened an inch or so. "You bought yourself an address," he said. "Bancroft's Nursing Home, on Madden Boulevard near the city line."

"What's that?"

"It's where Ike sent the little blonde," Frankie said. "You should know how close you came to not getting it. So long now." He opened the door and slipped quickly into the corridor.

Terrell listened to his heels clicking sharply toward the elevators, and then he picked up the phone.

He got the police board, but it took him almost five minutes to get through to Duggan. Finally Duggan's voice cracked in his ear. "Yes? Who is this?"

"Sam Terrell. Listen, I've got an address I want you to take down."

"Sam, you must live under a rock. Don't you know the whole goddamn city is upside down? We picked up a hoodlum named Rammersky who tells us he strangled Eden Myles. Caldwell's clear."

"The Bancroft Nursing Home," Terrell said, raising his voice over Duggan's. "There's a girl being held there. Connie Blacker."

"Wait a minute," Duggan said. "We already got that tip. The Bancroft Nursing Home. Hang on."

"What are you talking about?" Terrell yelled, but Duggan was off the line.

He returned a full minute later, and said, "I just checked with Radio. A couple of cars are on their way to pick her up."

"Where did you get the tip?"

"Mike Karsh called about ten minutes ago. Told us the girl was being held against her will, that she was an important witness against Ike Cellars."

"When will you know if she's all right?"

"When the cars report to Radio. Sam, I'm busy as hell."

"I'll call you back," Terrell said, and put the phone slowly back in place. He sat on the bed and lit a cigarette. Mike Karsh . . . He shook his head, completely bewildered.

Five minutes passed. He called Duggan again, and was another couple of minutes getting through to him. Then he said, "Have you got the girl?" His voice was high, and he could feel the uneven lurch of his heart.

"Yes. They've taken her over to St. Anne de Beaupre's and made three arrests at the Bancroft Home. It's a phony joint."

Terrell's hand tightened on the phone. "What's the matter with her?"

"Christ, I don't know," Duggan said impatiently. "She's in bad shape. That's all they told me."

Terrell said to the nurse in the accident ward at St. Anne de Beaupre's hospital, "Connie Blacker. How is she?"

"Admitted," the nurse said. She looked up at him and smiled quickly. "Hello, Sam. You're a stranger. She's under oxygen, I think. She was having some kind of respiratory trouble. What's the matter? You look pretty rocky yourself."

"Nothing," Terrell said. "Where is she?"

"Just down the hall. In Emergency."

"Thanks," Terrell said, and turned into the wide white corridor. He knew his way around every hospital in the city; he had sipped coffee in this one, and kidded with the nurses while waiting for an accident victim to die.

Now it was all different. A tall, balding doctor came out of the emergency ward, and Terrell caught his arm. "The girl they just brought in," he said. "How is she?"

"Not too good. You're a friend of hers?"

"That's right, I'm a friend."

The doctor removed his glasses and polished them on his clean white smock. "She was injected with considerably too much morphine," he said. "That was sometime this morning, I gather. Then she spent the day in a tank—the treatment for violents, you know. Wet sheets from head to foot. She's completely disoriented now. Out of sheer fright, I'd say. And the morphine has affected her respiratory center."

"Will she be all right?"

"I don't know. I'd say yes, with some qualifications. We're giving her oxygen, and an antidote for the morphine. She's had the raw material for a lifetime of nightmares packed into a very short period of time—that will give her trouble. She'll need help."

"Yes, sure," Terrell said. "When can I see her?"

"Not for a couple of hours anyway. You can leave a message if you like."

"Thanks, I'll give a phone number to the desk."

As Terrell entered the reception room the door opposite him opened and a *Call-Bulletin* photographer named Ricky Carboni came in with his bulky camera.

"Sam, boy," he said, "how goes it?" Ricky was an old-timer, a big, balding man with dark eyes and a warm smile. "Where's the girl?"

"You mean Connie Blacker?"

"Yeah, how is she? Ready to be immortalized?"

"She's in no shape for pictures, Ricky. Not for a couple of hours."

"Karsh said to get a picture—regardless or irregardless."

"Karsh? What the hell is going on, Ricky?"

"Don't ask me. Karsh just tore the Night Extra into tiny scraps. Everything's out except the want ads. And the whole damn daytime staff is back putting a new edition together. I thought you were working when I saw you. Well, I'm going to find the poker game. Take it easy."

"Sure," Terrell said.

He went outside and a patrolman said, "We're riding in, Sam. Need a lift?"

"Thanks, I'm going back to the shop." He was in no hurry to see Karsh. But he had to see him. One more time . . .

The lights were on in the city room, and the atmosphere was one of hectic tension. Normally the Night Extra was put to bed by a staff of three. But now everyone was in; Williams handling the city desk, Tuckerman hunched massively beside the police speaker, and all of the top writers and reporters from the daytime shifts.

Karsh stood directly behind Williams, one foot propped up on a chair, talking urgently and imperatively to Ollie Wheeler.

Terrell dropped his coat over a chair and walked toward Karsh and Wheeler.

Karsh turned, a quick, easy smile lighting his face. "You're just in time, Sam. I want you on the main story—every detail in chronological order. Don't waste time on the Parking Authority—just mention it as if the readers knew all. They will when they read Ollie's piece. He's doing a special story."

"I'll get started, Mike," Ollie said.

"Yes, get with it." Karsh was still looking at Terrell, but his manner was business-like and impersonal. "Bridewell issued a statement half an hour ago—owned up to all his crimes, including not curbing his dog several years back. The mayor can't last much longer than it takes city council to get in session. They're licked, Sam."

"And I'm supposed to write the big, hot story," Terrell said. He lit a cigarette and flipped the match aside. "The works, eh? All stops out?"

"Certainly."

"And how do I handle you?" Terrell asked him coldly. "How do we tint and shade the image of Mike Karsh? Are you portrayed with an arm around Ike Cellars' shoulder, and a hand reaching for the public trough?"

Karsh winced slightly. "No metaphors, please. Never oversell a good story. Play my part for what it's worth. No cover-ups—but don't get off on a tangent. Caldwell was framed. Here's how and why. Bang that home."

Tuckerman looked up then and covered his phone with a huge hand. "Mike," he said. There was an unmistakable significance in his tone and as Karsh turned to him, a silence settled around the immediate area of the city desk.

"What's up?"

"Ike Cellars," Tuckerman said. "For you."

Karsh smiled complacently, and began to screw a cigarette into his holder. He glanced at the clock above him, and said, "I expected to hear from him before this." He touched Terrell's arm. "Now look; you get on an extension and take down our talk. This may be good." He waved to the switchboard operator sitting behind the police speaker. "Nell, put Tuckerman's call through to me here and hook in one of these front desks. All right, Sam. Ready?"

Terrell said, "Yes, let it fly." He sat down and put on earphones.

Karsh picked up a phone and leaned against the city desk. "What's up, Ike?" he said. His voice was almost respectful, but an ironical smile twisted his lips. He winked down at Terrell, and he seemed completely strong and confident. "Something wrong?"

"I hope you're not being cute." Terrell heard the suppressed anger in Cellars' voice. "Photographers from your paper are hanging around my house. They say you sent 'em."

"That's right," Karsh said. "You're going to look nice on page one."

"I pay you to keep me out of the paper. You cross me, and you're through."

"What do you want me to keep out? That you paid a killer to strangle Eden Myles? That you framed Richard Caldwell to keep the city in your own pocket?"

Cellars said softly, "I'll settle with you, don't worry."

Karsh began to laugh. "You're heading for the front page of our next edition. Murderer, perjurer, pickpocket, pimp—have I forgotten anything?"

"Just your good sense, Mike." And Cellars broke the connection.

"Okay, okay, let's get going," Karsh said, putting the phone down and slapping his hands.

Terrell worked slowly at first, getting his lead down right. He had clips on Eden Myles and Cellars and Caldwell sent up from the morgue, and a bit later called the detective division in the Hall for background on Rammersky's arrest, and a direct quote from his confession. A detective he knew well filled him in and said, "A big night, eh, Sam? We got another dead one, you know. Frankie Chance."

Terrell took the cigarette from his mouth. "What happened?" An illogical sadness welled in him.

"It happened out near Cellars' home," the detective said. "One of Ike's bodyguards got him. There's more to it, but I can't give it to you now. Maybe in a half-hour or so."

"Sure," Terrell said. He told Karsh about Frankie Chance, but Karsh said, "Never mind him. We'll run something about it on page six. Don't clutter up your pieces with the bit players."

"Okay. Here's the lead then."

Karsh scanned it quickly, a little grin on his lips. "This is okay. Fine."

Terrell went on working, and Karsh took the pages as they came from the typewriter and handed them on to Williams, who proofed them and funneled them to the copy wheel.

The minutes ticked away.

Terrell finished his last paragraph and took the paper from his machine. "This does it," he said. A copy boy took the page up to the desk where Williams was standing waiting for it. Terrell looked around for Karsh but didn't see him. He went up to the city desk.

Tuckerman said, "A call came in for you from St. Anne's. A doctor there says to tell you that you can come and see the girl. She's asked for you." Tuckerman grinned amiably. "Connie Blacker, a long-legged blonde. A real dish. You're lucky."

"Yeah, sure," Terrell said. He was staring about the crowded, noisy room. "Where's Karsh?"

Tuckerman twisted his big body around in his chair. There was a small frown on his long, placid face. "He wouldn't go out," he said. "Not alone. Not tonight."

A copy boy said tentatively, "I saw Mr. Karsh at the elevators a few minutes ago."

"Was he dressed for the street?" Tuckerman asked.

"Yes, he had his coat and hat. I met him when I was coming up with coffee."

Tuckerman swore softly. "He's crazy." He was reaching for the phone when it began to ring. He picked it up, listened for a few seconds, and then let out his breath slowly. "Sure, Mike." Tuckerman turned and handed the phone to Terrell. "Karsh. For you."

Terrell took the receiver and said, "Where the devil are you?"

"Just across the street. Lindy's. That all-night dope den that sells us our coffee and reefers. It's the first time I've been in here. God! A foul smell of—"

"Mike, call a cab and go home," Terrell said. "Or come back here and we'll have a few drinks." Terrell glanced around the desk. "Everybody's in the mood."

"It sounds fine," Karsh said. "But not tonight, Sam. I've got a date."

"Where? With who?"

"I don't know. It's a face behind a windshield. That's all I saw. I'll know more about him later."

"You damn fool," Terrell said. He covered the receiver and spoke quickly and softly to Tuckerman. "Karsh is in Lindy's. Get a squad over there. I'll try to keep him on the line." Tuckerman grabbed a phone and Williams stood and stared at the clock above his head. They were still four minutes from deadline.

"Mike?" Terrell said. "You still there?"

"Sure."

"Don't go outside. Sit in that booth. You hear?"

"Sure, you're yelling like a fishwife," Karsh said. "But you listen to me. Remember what I taught you about the newspaper business, will you?" Karsh's voice trembled slightly, and then he recovered himself and said quickly, "Will you do that? Remember what I taught you on the job? And forget everything else? Everything I did?"

"Of course, Mike. Of course. But sit still. We're coming—" Terrell stared at the phone in his hand. The connection was broken.

"A squad is on the way," Tuckerman said.

"Sam, come here!" Ollie Wheeler called. He was at the big, floor-to-ceiling window staring down at the street. Terrell went to Wheeler's side, jarred by the urgency in his voice. Tuckerman and Williams came up behind him.

The street below them was dark except for a patch of light that fell on the shining pavement from the all-night restaurant.

Terrell saw Karsh standing in that square of brilliance, his figure square and blocky, his face shadowed by the brim of his homburg.

A car swung into the street a half block away and came toward Karsh with its lights turned off; it rolled silently through the darkness, angling toward him. The car picked up speed suddenly and shot past Karsh. When it was gone, swaying on its springs at the next intersection, Karsh lay in the gutter, looking small and unreal.

For an instant Terrell didn't realize what had happened; he thought Karsh had thrown himself out of the car's path. It wasn't until he saw the fragments of glass gleaming on the sidewalk that he knew Karsh was dead; the bullet that killed him had also smashed the window in the restaurant.

Terrell turned and sat down wearily at a desk. Karsh didn't have to . . . This was the thought running through his mind. Except to prove—to prove what? That he was Mike Karsh. That he could make the gesture. The Night Extra was a writ of habeas corpus for Caldwell, an epitaph for Mike Karsh.

Ollie Wheeler said, "I'd like to get drunk tonight. Anyone interested?"

"Sure," Williams muttered. "Why not?"

The tears stung Terrell's eyes. Later he would go out to the hospital to see Connie and that would be all right. But now he hurt all over.

Above him the illuminated second hand made its last circuit before deadline and the loud, warning bell rang shrilly. Everyone looked up at the clock. The forms were locked up, the presses were ready to start rolling. The Night Extra was just about in.

BORDEN DEAL

A Bottle of Wine

T he Judge sat in a chair where he could see the door entering into the hall from outside. He was waiting. His wife had phoned fifteen minutes ago and he knew that in any minute up to the next ten he would see her again. He sat stiffly, rigidly, as though he were sitting behind his bench downtown, and his mind was as frozen and hard as his face.

The judge was a big man. His heavy frame gave majesty to his grave demeanor and his craggy, lined face forbade human approach. His hair was white, not full-white but grizzled with the crow's-wing black it had once been. It was not whiter than it had been the day he had married the woman he was waiting for now.

The house was silent around him. It was a two-story, white clapboard, set back from the street in old trees. It was comfortable and worn, like the chair he was sitting in, the upholstery faded, the cloth fringing over the round of wood at the sides. It was a house that had been here in this land for a long time for it had been built and furnished by his father, the old judge.

He heard the sound of a motor. He did not move, but there was a hardening in him. His mind followed the motor to a stop beside the house, listened to the click of heels on the porch, felt the unhesitating turn of the doorknob. I knew she would come back, he thought. I knew I would see her one more time. Just once.

The door was open, then, and she was looking at him. "Hello Judge," she said.

He listened to her voice carefully. It was not strained. It was not her bright, careless voice either. It was just a carrier for the noncommittal words.

"Hello, Grace," he said, wondering how his own voice sounded. He couldn't tell. He watched for its effect in her face but he could see none. It wore the bright, varnished look she took to bridge parties and wives' committees, as though her features, her expression, her eyes, had been sprayed with the fixing preparation she used on her hair.

Now at last, he thought, I know for a truth that you are a bitch. I've suspected it almost all the years of our marriage. But now I know. And a vain one too . . . she couldn't go away forever without all the expensive clothing in the closets upstairs. Vain and practical, torturing a man for a few bright rags of shaped cloth.

"I came to get my clothes," she said, the voice still as neutral as sunshine. "I hope you don't mind."

"Then you're going," he said. "You're really going, after all."

She moved toward him, put a foot on the first riser of the stair. "Of course," she said. "You've known. You've known for a week now." She stopped watching him. Then she went on. "I'll get them. It won't take me long and then . . ."

"Your friend," he said. "Where is he? Waiting in a motel somewhere?"

She did not stop this time. She dropped the neutral, emotionless words down the stairs almost carelessly. "He's waiting in the car. I needed someone to help with the luggage."

He was alone again now. I didn't think she'd do that, he told himself painfully. He stood up, lifting the tail of the light linen coat he wore even in the summer heat, and took the .38 pistol from his hip pocket. He looked at it thoughtfully for a moment. Then he put it back into his hip pocket and walked to the door.

When he opened it the outside heat blasted at him, slapping him in the face like a hand. Even the big trees did not stop it. He thought of the sun baking on the concrete streets downtown and felt the sweat start on his forehead in tiny beads.

He went to the end of the porch and looked at the young man sitting in the car. The man's face turned toward him in sudden startlement and The Judge saw clinically that he was very good-looking and probably younger than Grace.

He walked down the steps and leaned on the window-rim of the car, looking in.

"I'm Grace's husband," he said unnecessarily. "You must be Wallace."

He studied the wariness in the young, smooth face, waited patiently until it went away, until Wallace decided there was no danger of violence or harsh words. It must have taken some doing, The Judge thought, for him to come out here in the first place.

"Come on in the house and wait," he said. "This heat will kill you, sitting out here in the car."

The young man hesitated, then opened the door on his side and got out. He was rangy and tanned and beside The Judge's harsh grayness he looked very young. Grace picked well, The Judge thought ungrudgingly. I wonder if he has money, too. Yes, he must have money.

Wallace came around the front of the car toward The Judge, his eyes studying The Judge's face. "I'm sorry, sir," he said. "I didn't want to come . . ."

"But Grace must have someone to help with the luggage," The Judge said gently. "You can't expect a lady to wrestle luggage in this heat. And I'm an old man . . ."

He took Wallace's arm and urged him toward the house, talking about the thick walls that insulated against the sun, how pleasant the house always was in the summertime even though it was hard to heat in winter. He mentioned how thin the walls of modern homes are now, as thin as cracker boxes, and how it takes air-conditioning to make them livable this far south.

"But they keep on building them that way," he said thoughtfully. "Sometimes I think there's nothing as bullheaded and grasping as the building industry. Nothing at all."

They were in the living room now, without the young man having to talk under the casual flow of The Judge's words, and it was cooler here. The Judge could feel the momentary sweat evaporating, aerating his shirt under the linen coat, and for a moment he chilled until his body adjusted to the changed condition. "Sit down," he said. "I'll be back in a moment."

He went into the kitchen, leaving Wallace alone. He stood at the back stairs before going down into the cellar, listening, but he could hear nothing of her movements. The cellar was cool, too, and dark, and he had to grope for the light cord dangling somewhere in the middle of the space. He found it, then he went unerringly to the shelf he sought, feeling far back for the bottle in the wicker basket.

He looked at it, the tactile touch of dust and cobwebs on his hands. For ten years it had lain here, gathering dust, waiting in just the way The Judge had waited previously, upstairs. Except that this bottle could not wait long enough. Not now.

He turned out the light and groped blindly toward the steps, finding them at last with his seeking feet and then letting them lift him toward light again. He paused in the kitchen for full-bellied glasses and a corkscrew and put his shoulder against the door into the living room. He turned and let the door slide shut behind him, seeing Wallace again, still standing uncertainly in the middle of the room. Like a deer, The Judge thought, feeling the wind for danger. Young and rangy and quick to run away and very beautiful in the youngness.

"Sit down, man," he said. He smiled. "I know Grace. It'll be a while before she's ready to use you." He motioned with the bottle. "I thought we'd have a little sherry while we waited."

The young man did not move but The Judge ignored him while his old, wrinkled hands deftly set and twisted the corkscrew, lifting the rotten cork with one easy movement as he grasped the bottle between his knees.

He eased into his comfortable leather chair and looked up to see that the young man had not yet relaxed. "Wallace," he said. "This is a small town. I've lived here all my life, and my father and grandfather before me. I've been a lawyer here, and a judge. I've been The Judge for a long time." He stopped, looking down at the sherry bottle for a moment.

"I know this town," he said thoughtfully. "I know the South. I could shoot you and get off scot-free. You made yourself fair game the first time you put your arms around my wife. You may not have known that, since you're not local. But you couldn't find twelve men among our ten thousand who'd convict a husband for shooting his wife's lover. That's not the law, you understand—that's just the way it is."

Wallace did not move, but The Judge could feel the tightening against danger in him. He was afraid now, very afraid. I'm a terrifying old man, he thought with a touch of sadness. I never knew I'd live to a terrifying old age.

"For a long time I believed I would kill you," he said, "if I ever laid eyes on you for one instant. I love my wife. I'm an old man with a young wife and I love her with the foolishness that the young never know. They know delirium, they know passion, they know desire. But they never know the wondrous foolishness of an old man in love for the first time." He shook his head.

"No, the young never know. They never understand."

He lifted his head. "So I was sure I'd shoot you." He stopped, brooding for a moment. He sighed, as though the remembering were a burden, too. "But I'm a law man, a lawyer and a judge. I've never believed in violence, seeing how it breeds hate and more violence, judging the results of violence every day in my court."

He leaned and carefully lifted the old bottle with both hands. He tilted it and poured lightly into his own glass, just a splash to give himself the floating bits of cork, then poured the young man's glass full. He finished filling his own.

"Sit down," he said mildly. "This is very good wine. You'll never taste the like again."

Wallace moved then, jerkily as a marionette, and sat. He lifted the glass and The Judge knew he wanted to gulp courage and assurance from the glass. He filled his mouth and then he stopped, tasting the old smooth richness of the wine, and a look of surprise crossed his face.

"Yes," The Judge said. "It *is* good. It's very old. We were saving it for our twenty-fifth wedding anniversary."

Wallace stopped in the act of lifting the glass to his lips again. There was shock on his face.

"Go ahead," The Judge said. "Drink it." His lips twisted. "There'll be no better time than now."

He leaned back in his chair, cradling the full-bellied coldness of the glass in both his palms. He swirled the liquid thoughtfully, looking down into the hypnotic topaz swirl.

"When Grace and I were married," he said, "we went to France for our honeymoon. It was . . . one of her conditions. She had never traveled, and she wanted to. We crossed over into Spain, and when we returned, we brought this bottle of rare old amontillado with us. Grace smuggled it through customs with the bottle taped to her body. We felt that a touch of illicitness was necessary and desirable. We planned to open it on our twenty-fifth wedding aniversary. We have saved it until now. Saved it for ten years."

Wallace lifted his glass again. He gulped this time, then he involuntarily sipped, tasting the autumn smoothness of the wine, savoring the last few drops in his glass.

The Judge leaned to pour again. "Drink it slowly," he said. "It deserves to be appreciated. I have waited ten years to taste our illicit wine, and expected to wait for fifteen more. But it is right that we should drink it now, waiting for Grace. Don't you feel that it's right?"

"Sir," Wallace said. "I shouldn't have come. I know that now and I'm . . ."

The Judge moved a hand. "I'm glad you did, Wally. I needed someone to talk to . . . and who better than the man she loves now? Who in the wide South would listen with more attention? And talk is a necessity of age . . . for talk is all that is left."

He stopped again, and there was silence in the room. He looked at the bottle and it was half-empty. Half-gone. The wine was bright and warm in him and he felt comfortable, sitting in his accustomed leather chair. There was still silence upstairs. It would take her a long time to pack with care, he thought. And Grace would pack that way—efficient as she was. We have time for a bottle of wine, he thought. Plenty of time.

"I was fifty years old when I met Grace," he said. "And, incredibly enough, I had never been in love, I don't know why. I had dated and danced and even kissed, though that was not as prevalent in my time as now. But—I had never loved."

He stopped, frowning into his glass. He looked at Wallace, saw his glass was still supplied, and went on. His voice rolled soft and slow in the still, cool air, Wallace sitting forward in his chair listening, and The Judge knew that he was no longer afraid.

"Grace was my secretary," he said. "She was young and very efficient and as beautiful as dawn and old brandy. I didn't know her folks, for she was new-people in town. But within a week I had fallen in love with her. Before Grace I would have said that such a thing was impossible.

"But Grace was very smart, as well as beautiful. She knew the usual relationship between a confirmed old bachelor and his secretary. She wasn't having any of that." He paused, adding the new words carefully. "I didn't know at the time that she was sleeping with a young clerk who worked down the hall. Of course, even if I had known, I don't think it would have mattered to me then."

He saw the shock in Wallace's face, saw him start to rise. "I don't want to listen to . . ." Wallace said stiffly.

He waved him down. "She's not like that any more," The Judge said. "She's changed and learned in ten years. God, *how* she's changed and learned. And she was never a slut."

There was silence again while he thought, remembered. Wallace sat back in his chair now, his momentary anger quelled, waiting for The Judge to continue. The Judge drank thoughtfully, tastefully, from his glass of old wine.

"It was pretty bad for me," he said. "I loved her. I lusted after her. I was old and incredible and crazy. I wanted her any way I could take her. And she was bright and efficient in fending me off. I groveled, almost, in her tracks for one willing smile from her lips. I gave her raises in pay and paid vacations." He paused, sighing. "It went on for a year that way. A full year—an interminably long time, to me."

He took the bottle again and lifted it to the light and watched the amber liquid sparkle. Then he poured the glasses full again and listened up the stairs. This time he heard a thump and a rustle.

"It won't be long now," he said, "before she's ready. You see, she knew what she wanted. Marriage. To me . . . fifty years old. But there was money, not much money but enough, and the good name. She was new in town, and I never knew where her family came from. She'll never tell you. I doubt if she even knows herself any longer. Women can forget at will things like origins and birthdays.

"Age? It didn't matter. I doubt if she ever saw me as a man, with passion in my body. I was The Judge, I was Carter, I was Cartersville. She loved me, not for me but for the freedom from her past. And I loved her though she had no pity for my love."

He frowned. "I didn't know this then, understand. I learned it slowly and painfully over the years and she will still deny every word of it. I won't tell you how we agreed to marry . . . it was an afternoon in my office that I still don't like to remember and certainly not discuss. She waited a full year, moving her womanness before me every day, and then she ruthlessly closed her bargain."

He saw Wallace watching him. "You find it hard to believe, don't you?"

The young man's voice was uncertain. "It's difficult . . ."

"Yes," The Judge cut in. "She *is* different now. She was desperate then, you understand. She was twenty-five, and that clerk is still a clerk. She knew then he would always be a clerk. She's not desperate any more. She hasn't been desperate for a long time."

"But you had ten years," Wallace said, his voice brave in the silence. "You think of her now with bitterness and anger but you had ten years."

"Bitterness?" The Judge said. He smiled. "Anger? She made her bargain and she fulfilled it. She was mine, all mine and all the time, and I did not share her with anybody, not for years. She gave me the love my old heart and body wanted, in full measure and running over. She even gave me a son . . . "

Wallace moved in surprise. It was apparent that this fact was something Grace hadn't told him.

"You didn't know she had a son? Yes. His name is Bobby. He's away at school now. I wanted a son and we had one, though she insisted on a Caesarean. Just one. And now I am sixty, and she is going away."

"I do love her," Wallace said. "You may not be able to understand it or believe it, but I love her like I—"

"Of course," The Judge said. "Grace is all woman, and she can use all of it. I knew that you loved her. And you're not the first." He stopped again and looked at the bottle. This time Wallace handed him his glass without waiting for an invitation.

"There's just enough for one more," The Judge said. "She should be through by then. Drink it slowly, for there's no other wine like this. No other wine at all."

He poured gracefully, ceremoniously, his dark, craggy face stooped over the glasses. They were both leaning forward watching the topaz richness flow in a live stream, then pool into beauty again in the glasses.

The Judge sat back and lifted his glass. "She began to drift about two years ago," he said. "I was fifty-eight then. I saw it coming and there was no way of stopping it. I knew it would come to this when she found the right one. I have been waiting for you, Wally." He looked at him over the rim of his glass. "I wonder what it is you have that she wants, Wally. I wonder."

Wallace was watching him, holding his glass still. His handsome face was as still as his hands, watching the old Judge, not knowing exactly what to say. And so he said nothing, waiting for The Judge to go on.

"And I believe I know," The Judge said. He laughed, a startling sound in the hushed, cool room. "It's youth, Wally. She wants the youngness of you, just as I wanted her youngness a long time ago. How old are you, Wally? She's thirty-five."

Wally moved. The Judge knew his words had touched him, stirred him. "I love her, sir. You know that. I love her. Whatever I've got, I'll give her. Youth or money or . . ."

"Yes," The Judge said softly. "Yes, I know you do. I know you will."

Wally straightened his young body. "I'm glad I came now," he said. "I'm glad I talked to you. I was afraid. Any man would be, in a situation like this. Not physically, but of a scene. Now that I've seen your reasonableness, your intelligent approach . . ."

The Judge listened critically to the young, fumbling words. The fast-drunk wine was strong in Wallace. The Judge did not feel it at all. "You don't have to say it," he said. "I know what you mean. You're trying to say that we needed to drink a bottle of old wine between us." He lifted his glass and swallowed. "Drink up. There's just a taste of it left. Just a taste of illicit wine, after ten years."

Wallace lifted the glass and drank. While he did it, The Judge shifted his weight off the .38 in his hip pocket. He shot Wallace in the head as he put his glass down, empty. There was a momentary surprise on Wallace's face at the impact of the bullet, a shocked surprise as he looked at The Judge, and saw, and slumped forward on the old, worn rug between the two friendly chairs.

The Judge was surprised, too. He hadn't believed he was going to do it until the last moment, until he saw the last drop of old wine disappear down the young man's throat.

The single shot echoed wildly, reverberatingly, in the old house. The sound filled the house like the cry of a baby, and he knew that Grace had heard. He rose and picked up the wine bottle in his left hand, still holding the gun with the other.

He moved toward the stairs, hearing the sudden hysterical flurry of her footsteps in the hall. He looked up into her downward-peering face, white and stricken. Even in the dimness of the stairwell he could see the harsh stricken lines there. *Yes*, he thought. *Now you're thirty-five.*

"Judge!" she cried, her voice almost a scream. The polish was gone now, the hard sleekness in which she wrapped herself. "Judge! What did you do!"

"Grace," he said. "We killed the bottle of old wine we were saving. We killed it between us."

He dropped the warm pistol, then, from his right hand. It thudded on the floor. He watched her eyes for a moment. Then he turned away toward the telephone in the hall.

As he made the call, he still held the bottle in his other hand. It was empty now, and ordinary; just old glass, without the magic of old wine within it.

DONALD HONIG

Man Bites Dog

The place to begin a newspaper career, they said, is in the small town. There, they said, I would learn all the basic concepts: how real news is made, what makes a newspaper run, its unbending devotion to its readers, its ethics, and so on.

So, determined to be a student of my profession, I was anxious to begin.

Just to illustrate how we are all exposed to the reckless indiscrimination of chance twenty-four hours a day, I landed my first job purely by accident. And what a fortunate accident it was to become. (I was to learn later that in the newspaper business any accident is fortunate.) I happened to display my typewriter in the bus depot of a small town (which I would prefer to leave unidentified, for certain ethical reasons which will make their appearance shortly). My typewriter was observed by a gentleman who was many things in one, publisher, editor and staff of the local paper and who had the small, shrewd gray eyes that we associate with eminent newspapermen whoever they are. He assumed from my typewriter that I was a literate, aspiring person who knew how to spell in at least one language. And so was I discovered and hired.

We marched out of the bus depot and the editor, whose name was Mr. Cyril Flagg, took me right up to the office which was over a supermarket. It was a rather small office, with two desks and chairs, worn-out linoleum, faded wallpaper, a few pots of disconsolate and generally unwatered geraniums, a flood of excited-looking paper all over the place, and overall the very scent of thrill and fever, the pulse and the heartbeat of the newspaper world.

"This is it," Mr. Flagg said, unbuttoning his shirt collar and letting his tie-knot slide down. He looked like a real newspaperman.

"It's wonderful," I said.

"The other fellow disappeared," Mr. Flagg said laconically.

"Who?"

"Your predecessor."

"You mean he left?"

"Oh, he left all right. No question about that. But nobody seems to know where or why." He held up a copy of *The Dash*, dated several weeks previous. The headline read: ASSOCIATE EDITOR DISAPPEARS. He put it back down. "It sold out the whole edition. Best story we've had here in months. Disappearance stories never fail to intrigue people. Something morbid in their blood."

"Maybe he'll still turn up," I said.

"'Tisn't likely," Mr. Flagg said. "When a person disappears around here, he disappears permanently."

I didn't like the sound of that. Mr. Flagg did not appear to be lamenting in the least the disappearance of his former employee. It gave me a very odd feeling.

"What's your name anyway?" Mr. Flagg asked.

"Gerber," I said. "Andrew Gerber."

"Do you understand the relationship between yourself and your newspaper, Gerber?" he asked. "It is a relationship more sacred than that of doctor and patient. The dissemination of news, that which interests and influences the minds of people, is the highest calling. We must always provide fodder for public consumption and never divulge our sources. Do you understand that, Gerber?" he asked sternly.

"Yes, sir," I said.

"There is a code of ethics. Once you begin here you're sworn to it. It's an oath."

"I understand," I said.

"Good," he said. We shook hands.

Within a few days I was comfortably ensconced in my job. From my desk I could see the main street and I was able to watch all the happenings and all the comings and goings in town. This would have been an ideal situation except that nothing ever happened and very little either came or went. It was a somnolent little town, with only the merest ripples of animation.

I was beginning to wonder, after a few yawning weeks, what this town needed a newspaper for. Outside of the man who wound the clocks and the tavern that wound the man, there seemed need for little else. With patient fidelity *The Dash* reported births and deaths and anniversaries and other nostalgic events. Sometimes weeks went by with neither a birth nor a demise; that's how disinterested in the tides of history these people were.

But Mr. Flagg was unfailingly absorbed, as though he expected a few ax killings and floods and plagues every day. Sometimes, to fill up space, I had to write descriptions of sunsets, or go over to the school and interview the children about such controversial topics as Christmas and ice cream and bicycles.

One day, however, a crisis came. There was absolutely nothing to put on the front page. Everything in town had come to a standstill. Even the weather had remained unchanged for weeks. I sat at my desk and stared grievously at the indestructible immobility outside. I despaired of seeing a paper getting out that week. The sacrosanct tradition of never missing an issue certainly seemed in jeopardy. It was the most tragic moment of my life, up to that time.

I turned to Mr. Flagg, who was sitting at his desk dipping his pen into his inkwell and throwing patterns of inkspots onto the green blotter. I mentioned the impasse we had struck.

"Is that so?" he said, making his spots.

"Yes, sir," I said gravely.

"We'll have to do something then," he said, going on with his spots, apparently fascinated by them.

"Has this ever happened before?" I asked.

"Frequently," he said. "This very thing cropped up several weeks before your arrival. We were saved then by your predecessor's disappearance."

Again I had that odd, uneasy feeling.

"Now we must face the new emergency," Mr. Flagg said.

"What do we do?" I asked.

"We employ our imaginations. We cease being analytical and become creative. Let's see now," he said thoughtfully, cupping his chin and staring at the wall. "We could demand that a certain corpse be exhumed and an autopsy performed. But no, I think we used that one a few years ago."

I thought he was being unduly facetious. Then he got up and walked over to the far wall and removed from its nails a shotgun which I had hitherto regarded as some harmless and senile relic. He blew a cloud of dust from the barrel. Then he examined the breech, with satisfaction. Then he stepped over to the desk and from a drawer took out a few surly-looking shells, rattling them in his hand. He split the shotgun and inserted several shells and closed the gun up again. Then he looked at me.

"Put on your hat," he said.

I did that, and followed him out of the office. We went down the back steps and got into Mr. Flagg's car. Then we drove from town, Mr. Flagg and I and the shotgun. We drove along an old dirt road until we saw a man walking.

"Ah," Mr. Flagg said with pleasure. "Old Jim." He stopped the car and took the shotgun and got out. I followed. He looked at me, his shrewd, gray newspaperman's eyes severe, uncompromising. "Do you remember you oath, Gerber?" he asked.

"Yes, sir," I said.

Then we went on. Old Jim was walking toward us. He waved when he saw us, giving a senile cackle.

"Doing some hunting, Cyril?" he asked Mr. Flagg.

"Yes," Mr. Flagg said grimly. "And in a good cause too." Whereupon he lifted the rifle, pointed it at Old Jim, squinted carefully down the barrel, and fired. There was a terrific explosion. When the smoke had gone and I had sufficiently recovered my faculties, I gathered courage and went over to Old Jim. He was lying in a peaceful heap in the road, his chest still smoking. My horror may well be imagined.

"All right," Mr. Flagg said calmly, blowing through puckered lips on the end of the barrel. "There's your story. Make your lead, 'Jim Penn murdered by person or persons unknown.' Make some notes."

Being a hired person, and seeing the smoking shotgun in his hands, I was obliged to comply, moving with haste. I took out my pad and pencil and began writing, although I could scarcely hold the pencil.

"It's a good story," Mr. Flagg said, discharging the empty shell. He put the shotgun back in the car and came back with his camera. He took several pictures. "All right," he said. "Tonight you'll go and interview the family. I'll write an editorial. Gosh, it's warm out today."

Murder on the dirt road. It made a thumping good story. It brought people out of their various lethargies. Excitedly they talked about it. We filled one whole issue with the story and the interviews, and the next issue with the story of the funeral and the next two issues with the investigation, and after that we had some editorial indignation left over to fill one more issue. Mr. Flagg said that perhaps we ought to accuse someone of the murder and cover the trial, but decided against it.

"We got five issues out of it," he said. "I'm satisfied. See, Gerber? Sometimes you have to improvise. The public must be served. Someday you'll have your own paper. I hope you'll remember and appreciate what I'm teaching you here."

Needless to say I was living in a state of cold, perpetual horror those weeks. I dared not face people. Directly after work every evening I fled straight home with my coat collar up around my face, my conscience chafing with screeching noises. I realized then that something evil had befallen my predecessor and I began to fear for my own life. So in order to avoid another impasse, which could have meant my own sacrifice upon the altar of *The Dash*, I worked with added vigor in trying to collect news, and through it all was becoming a good newspaperman which, after all, was the most important thing.

But then, a few months later, we struck another impasse, even more formidable than the previous one had been. Blank white pages leered at us from all over the office. I sat and watched Mr. Flagg, waiting. A cold, harrowing chill kept coming and going along my spine. I was terrified, but fascinated.

For several hours he sat in stolid contemplation. I realized that he might very well be having my own disposal under consideration. Once or twice he glanced at me and I could feel my image passing coldly through his imagination. His shrewd gray eyes were filled with deep meditation.

He made a sudden gesture and I leaped up.

"Why, Gerber," he said, "what's the matter?"

"Nothing," I said, embarrassed, feeling the springy little palpitations in my heart.

"I was getting up to leave," he said.

"So early?" I asked.

"Yes, I'm going to go and look for something for *The Dash*. We need something."

He went out and I slumped back down in the chair. I was in a dangerous situation, I realized. The only thing in my favor was the fact that he had so recently disposed of one of his editors, and that if another one were to disappear at this time it might not arouse the interest of his subscribers.

But I could never foretell how his mind was going to work. I was going to have to be on the alert from now on.

The next morning found the crisis still extant. Mr. Flagg, after a half hour's silent meditation, rose, put on his hat and beckoned to me. Like a robot, cold and hypnotized, I followed. We went downstairs. We got into the car. For about half hour we drove through the quiet streets, back and forth, up and down. He had left the shotgun on the wall, so it was going to be different this time.

Then we saw a woman crossing on a side street. Mr. Flagg tore down the block at top speed and got her perfectly. She flew legs-upward into the air as if she had been shoveled, turned over once, and landed comfortably on top of a well manicured hedge. I whirled in the seat and looked back.

"Well?" Mr. Flagg asked.

"She's moving," I said.

"Well, it'll do. Got your lead? 'Hit-and-run driver strikes down woman.' We'll blame it on a teenager and heap some abuse on the Safety Council. Also we'll accuse the Bureau of Licenses of accepting bribes and licensing incompetent drivers. Got it?"

"Yes, sir."

"Good, I'll drop you off at the next corner and you can scoot back and interview her. Make sure you spell her name right."

That story kept us going for two weeks and eased some of the pressure. We had to retract about the bribes of course, but did it in a way as to cast even more suspicion. Mr. Flagg was quite pleased and I was relieved, for the immediate threat to my life had been removed.

One day Mr. Flagg asked how I was enjoying my apprenticeship.

"Very much," I said.

"Have you learned much?" he asked.

"Yes," I said. "A great deal." He gave me a rather searching, uneasy stare. Then I knew that Mr. Flagg had become as afraid of me as I was of him.

That evening I stayed late at the office and began going back through the files. Some of the stories were appalling, but I couldn't help but be fascinated. I found one, dated back several years, about the "Mad Arsonist" who had burned down the school and the hospital. Another time someone had unlocked the lion's cage in a visiting carnival and three people had disappeared into the lion's jaws before the police had brought the depredations to a halt. Then there was the one about someone throwing a hand grenade into a Campfire Girls League get-together. That story ran for eight issues, with elaborate interviews. It was followed by a picture of Mr. Flagg receiving an award from some editors' guild for outstanding human-interest coverage.

I ran all the way home that night, trembling with a terrific exhilarating excitement. I paced my room all night, chain-smoking one cigarette after another. I began to feel for the first time the genuine thrill and excitement of newspaper work. My temples throbbed with an intoxication that was almost unbearable. There had never been a kidnapping or a drowning. Or a mad bomber. Perhaps Mr. Flagg might permit me to suggest one of these the next time.

I couldn't stand it. From sheer exhilaration I fell asleep.

And then several weeks later another lull set in. We sat in the office. Mr. Flagg appeared more deeply concerned than at any other time. But I was busy writing what I believed would certainly be an exciting lead.

"Gerber," he said wearily, "we've come to another impasse." He was getting old, losing his imaginative vigor. The hit-and-run story hadn't been as successful as he'd hoped.

"I'm working on something now, sir," I said.

"Good. Let me see it when you're done."

Then it was finished. I rose. Upon this day I was becoming a newspaperman. I could feel it. I brought the lead over to him. There in good, bold, black letters was my proposed lead: AWARD-WINNING EDITOR FOUND SLAIN IN OFFICE. As he whirled around I brought the paperweight down on his head, again . . . and again . . .

MICHAEL ZUROY

Never Trust an Ancestor

It was practically an inquisition. Eastern Chemicals, Inc., did not lightly select new employees for its ten stories of administrative offices in a Manhattan skyscraper. Drew Whitney had already filled out numerous application forms. He had undergone three grueling interviews. He now opened yet another form headed: ADDITIONAL PERSONAL INFORMATION, CONFIDENTIAL.

Flipping through it as he sat at one of the small bare desks for job applicants set along a wall in Eastern's personnel office, he had trouble keeping a sneer from his coldly handsome features. Screwball stuff.

Big corporations these days, Whitney reflected, sometimes nosed into a man's personal background to the point of foolishness. This questionnaire was about as bad as they came. Probably doped out by the psychologists and the bright personnel boys to, in some way, help set up an overall picture of a man and determine what niches he might fit. Whitney understood the purpose all right, but to him it was still piddling hogwash. "Have you ever owned a sports car?" He was applying for an accountant's job. What kind of a question was that?

Are you familiar with fine wines? Do you know any dentists socially? the questions went on. This was from outer space, Whitney was thinking. If married, list schools attended by your wife. Is your wife's hair color natural? Do you skin-dive? Is there a history of baldness in your family? Brother!

Forcing patience, Whitney began filling out the form. Objecting would only get him out the door and he wanted to work for Eastern. This was a deliberate, considered choice. Eastern Chemicals had what he wanted—standing, wealth, power, opportunity. It was in a firm like this that he'd decided to make his big push. A sardonic expression touched his lips. If they could see into his mind he'd lose his welcome here, fast. He'd thought out his methods while gaining experience in smaller firms. They were ruthless methods, but he meant to be a big man while he was still young. He meant to climb to power, no matter how many throats he had to cut. There was something in him that needed power and money.

Whitney wrote his answers neatly, knowing better than to let his handwriting betray impatience. They'd be watching for that, the bright boys, the psychologists. In sober figures, he put down his age, 26, although Eastern already had that information. Have you ever been arrested? the form inquired at another point. Whitney wrote, "No."

Father's occupation? Without pride, Whitney wrote, "Waiter." At least he didn't have to tell them what kind of third-rate joints the old man had worked until he died, or about the seamy life he'd given his family. The kind of a life, Whitney thought, he was going to put far behind him, forever . . .

Do you know of any criminal record against your father? Whitney blinked at that one. He wrote, "No."

Your mother? Whitney blinked again. It wasn't his parents who were applying for this job. He answered, "No."

Do you know of any criminal records against your grandfathers, paternal and maternal? Your grandmothers?

Whitney stared at the form. This was over the line. This was too senseless and nosy even for Eastern Chemicals. He had a fleeting temptation to write in, "None of your damned business!" but while he hesitated he realized that from one of the nearby glassed-in cubicles he was being watched by the coldly appraising eyes of Mr. Johnson, the personnel man handling his application. Whitney knew that a show of annoyance would mean a mark against him. He knew he'd made a good impression so far. Tall, personable, respectful, he was aware that one of his assets was that he appeared the potential executive type favored by large corporations. Without further hesitation, he answered "No" to the question. He completed the form and handed it to Mr. Johnson with a calculated smile, pleasant but not obviously ingratiating. He spent the rest of the afternoon taking an I.Q. test, then went home to await the results.

Some days later, he was called back to Eastern's offices. He was to have a final interview with the president of the corporation. "The president himself?" Whitney said, surprised that he rated this. He was only being considered for a minor accounting job.

"President Mitchell personally passes on all administrative applicants, regardless of grade," Mr. Johnson explained aloofly.

President Mitchell's office was at the top of Eastern's tier, on the thirty-seventh floor of the skyscraper. The room was spacious, deep-carpeted, mellow with dark wood, heavy with the air of tradition. One wall was covered by an impressive mural depicting Eastern's mines and plants. On another wall were several portraits in oils of gloomy and severe-looking people who seemed to resemble Mitchell. A bank of low-silled windows afforded a spectacular panorama of the city and the river beyond, unobstructed by any other nearby tall buildings.

Whitney drew a quick, excited breath. Here was the pinnacle, the stronghold of power. He wanted this place for himself. Someday he might have it.

President Mitchell was a massive, powerful man whose shoulders bulged like a lumberjack's inside his expensive suit. Still under sixty, his voice was forceful, eyes uncompromising pits under looming brows. An overwhelming personality, but Whitney did not feel intimidated. He met the scrutiny guilelessly, while deep within himself the thought snuggled that Mitchell's throat, too, could be cut.

At last, Mitchell grunted. "You seem the right type."

"Thank you, sir."

"We're fussy, yes," Mitchell said. "A company can be ruined by its employees. We don't want anybody here who doesn't fit our picture. Above all, we insist upon high moral character. Did that grandparent question surprise you?"

"Well—a bit, sir," Whitney admitted cautiously.

"My own idea, that," Mitchell rumbled. "Based on a theory that hasn't failed me yet. I believe in heredity. Crooks breed crooks."

"Yes, sir," said Whitney, knowing when to agree. President Mitchell's stare brooked no contradiction.

"Blood will tell," Mitchell said.

"Yes, sir."

"For your job level, we check the grandparents. The higher the job level and the trust we have to place in an employee, the further back we check his ancestry. If an individual has a marked criminal heritage, no matter how far back, it will come out in him sooner or later. We can't take any chances on that sort."

"Yes, sir," Whitney said, incredulous at the idea, not venturing to comment that nobody could have a model ancestry.

As though divining his thought, Mitchell said. "Oh, we're realistic, we don't expect perfection. We use a crime-time ratio system that passes the great majority of our employees, but determines the worst risks. An unsatisfactory ancestry rating closes the more responsible positions to an employee. Serious ancestral crimes—such as murder—carry the most weight, naturally. Do you have enough faith in your heritage to work for us, young man?"

"I'm willing to trust my ancestors, sir," Whitney said without hesitation, knowing that it was the right answer. His thoughts were contemptuous. The personnel boys in big companies were sappy enough. When the big wheel butted in with his pet ideas it could be downright idiotic. Nothing to worry about once you were in. He was sure you couldn't run a company that way. Mitchell, himself, had just said that most employees passed. Besides, how much could be dug up about anybody's ancestry, especially as it got more ancient? He didn't know very much about his own grandparents, for instance.

Again, as though understanding Whitney's thought, President Mitchell said, "Our investigators are expert and thorough. An individual's knowledge of his own ancestry is unreliable, so we do not depend on it. Our agents operate all over the world. The past is obscure, certainly, but each generation back double in number; if they lose one trail, they switch to another. They seldom fail. They are, in effect, detectives who work in the past. Understand?"

"Yes, sir."

Mitchell raised a thick finger. "This may be a new idea to you. It may seem harsh. I am satisfied that it works. Some of our key executives were cleared as far back as the eleventh century A.D. They've proved to be men of the highest integrity. Blood tells, right?"

"Right, sir," agreed Whitney, feeling somewhat dazed.

"Well," said Mitchell briskly, "our check of your grandparents bore out your statements. They're cleared. This will suffice for your present job level. You may report back to the personnel office."

Which, Whitney realized, meant that he had the job. He smiled.

Drew Whitney spent the next few months marking time, becoming familiar with the company and his job, preparing for his first ruthless move. Not for him the slow merit promotions, the crawling advance in seniority which might, in thirty years, bring him a minor executive post. He'd doped it all out. The fast way was to eliminate whoever blocked the road. It was a matter of watching for opportunities, creating them if necessary. Whitney found himself chuckling. Let Eastern putter around with the past and Mitchell's stuffy ancestor theories. Something was going to happen in the near future which they'd never understand.

The department he was in was Equipment Inventory. Whitney's first objective was to become head of this department. There were fourteen people with more seniority between him and his goal, all jockeying for position, while the incumbent head seemed to be settled for years to come, a usual situation in a large firm. Everybody wanted to climb, but nobody had the guts or the brains to do what he was going to do.

Whitney picked Ed Thorpe as the most suitable victim. Thorpe, a slight man with hair that curled around a bald spot, had been with Eastern for twelve years and was one of the hopefuls for department head, when it became open. Whitney cultivated Thorpe. He turned on the charm, so that soon they were joking amiably together, engaging in serious discussions, lunching with each other. The friendship ripened gradually to the point where they began getting together with the wives on occasional evenings. Whitney even brought Thorpe's three curly-headed youngsters little presents, earning the name Uncle Drew. Oh, a great guy the Thorpes obviously considered Drew Whitney, with his clean-cut looks and sincere manner.

Naturally, when Whitney began to ask casual questions about Thorpe's work, Thorpe was glad to explain. When the questions grew sharper, Thorpe showed no annoyance. Why not teach a friend a few things? Young Whitney couldn't be a competitor, he was too far behind in seniority. At home, and in the office, Thorpe taught Whitney the fine points of his work, transferred to him the essence of what he'd learned in twelve years at Eastern. "Hope this helps you, someday," Thorpe smiled.

"Oh, it will, Eddie," Whitney smiled back. "It will."

Once the brain-picking stage was over, Whitney gave thought to working out the next step. Tax time was approaching. This could be useful. Whitney began looking through certain folders from the files, referring to some of the entry books that were amassed in this accounting division. No one paid any particular attention. He worked here, he was doing his job, the records were open to him.

Whitney felt confident he would get away with what he was planning, simply because it was unthinkable. There were things that just weren't done in offices. There was a line that few, even the worse back-biters, would think of stepping over. He was going to step over that line. Because he had the guts.

From a current file of penciled tax work-sheets awaiting posting to the permanent ledger, he chose several entitled ALLOWANCE FOR DEPRECIABLE EQUIPMENT. They had been prepared by Ed Thorpe and carried his signature. They also bore the O.K. of Lee Southerfield, who had checked Thorpe's work.

From among the crowded entries, he picked out one which read, "Owens-Hookworth Ore-Pulverizer Unit, Model G-48, Serial Number 879904R—$7,423.00." Deftly, he erased the figures which represented Thorpe's calculated depreciation allowance and substituted a figure of $9,898.00. He chose four more items scattered through the work-sheets and altered those figures upward too. So meticulously did he make the changes and imitate Thorpe's figures that when he was done, Thorpe himself could not have detected the tampering.

He waited patiently some weeks until after the tax returns were in and all entries posted to the permanent ledger. Then he approached Mr. Bobak, the department head. His manner was that of one performing a reluctant duty.

"A serious tax error? An over-deduction for depreciation?" Bobak's round face was incredulous.

"Yes, sir," Whitney said. "Internal Revenue's sure to spot it. If we don't amend it first, it's liable to hurt us with them in the future."

Bobak's blue eyes had turned frigid and unblinking. They plainly conveyed his opinion of this young upstart. "Thanks for the warning," he said. "So, out of all the experts we got here, you were the one to find it out, hey?"

"Well," said Whitney diffidently, "I noted the figures in the ledger. They didn't look right to me. I computed the items according to our years-digit method. The figures were incorrect."

"A genius," Bobak murmured tiredly. "So who did the original accounting on this?"

"Uh . . . Ed Thorpe," Whitney answered with a nice show of hesitation.

"Yes." Bobak leaned back in his chair. "Look. Thorpe's been with us twelve years. He knows his job. Southerfield does the checking in that section. Another top-notcher. I'll go by them. We can't spend all our time re-checking complicated figures. This is very conscientious of you, young fellow, but I think you're speaking from inexperience."

Whitney left, outwardly subdued. In fact, he was quite satisfied. So much the better that Bobak hadn't risen to the bait at once, the shock would be all the greater when it came. Internal Revenue would see to that. But Internal Revenue was slow. However, they could be safely accelerated. They did not reveal their informants. Whitney posted a note to the Treasury Department.

Within a week, two polite men with briefcases visited Eastern Chemicals, Inc., and spent some time going over the books in Bobak's department. As one of the results of this visit, Bobak emerged red-faced from what was apparently a severe chewing-out by his superiors. He, in turn, chewed out Thorpe and Southerfield. "Don't know how I made those errors," Thorped muttered. "Don't understand at all."

To Whitney, Bobak said privately, "Eastern doesn't like spots on the record, especially with the tax people. I don't know why in hell I didn't listen to you, it would've been less damaging then. You seem to be a sharp young man. No one else caught this. Thorpe seems to be slipping . . . and if I can't trust Southerfield . . . look, Whitney, I'm going to try you out on more responsible work . . ."

"Thank you, sir," Whitney said gratefully, reflecting that the next throat to be cut would be Bobak's.

Thorpe's chances for the department head slot were gone. So were Southerfield's. And Bobak's status had been weakened. Eastern Chemicals was not tolerant of major blunders in any of their departments.

Whitney applied himself to his work during the next few months. He knew that he was sharp enough, that much was true. He'd picked Thorpe's brains. He had no difficulty applying what he'd learned. And he'd turned the charm on Bobak, he was high in his favor, acting as his watch-dog. He made a practice of looking for the inevitable small errors in other people's work and exposing them to Bobak. Inexorably, he was taking over an increasing share of Ed Thorpe's responsibilities. Thorpe had the seniority, but his title was losing much of its meaning. Whitney now had only a distant politeness for Thorpe. He had served his purpose.

Eventually, Whitney received official promotion. The day before this happened, however, a messenger from Personnel dropped a sealed envelope on his desk. Inside he found papers headed, CONFIDENTIAL ANCESTRY REPORT— EMPLOYEE'S COPY. "Congratulations!" it said. "Your ancestry has passed further examination. You are cleared for this promotion."

Whitney had almost forgotten about President Mitchell's pet project. He read the report, impressed despite himself with its thoroughness. He'd never known this about his ancestors. Four generations back, a Stafford Whitney had operated a sawmill in Turnbull, Missouri. There had been a Silas Whitney, intrepid Indian fighter. Barbara Sherman, who later married Colin Whitney, trader, had, as a girl, been noted in the town of Amesworth, Pennsylvania, for her skill with the needle.

They dug hard enough, reflected Whitney with contempt. Let them, as long as they dug only in the past. The future concerned him.

He continued to work diligently, often putting in extra hours on his own. He was the first to arrive, the last to leave. He was creating the picture of a dedicated, dependable, and highly capable company man, and he knew that the picture was in time noted by S. D. Simpson, head of the division and Bobak's superior.

Meanwhile, he continued to deftly snipe away at the others in his department. Thorpe and Southerfield, who had been the two strong contenders for department head, were now out of the running. The others in the department were not serious executive possibilities, but Whitney was taking no chances. He never relented from undermining them, trustingly backed up by Bobak.

He let another year go by, to build up more seniority and solidify his status. Then he went after Bobak.

His plan was simple, but he considered it safe, because again it was unthinkable, something that wasn't done. Again, he was willing to step over the line.

He managed a private talk with the white-clad cafeteria man who brought up their orders during coffee break. He showed the man a bill which made his eyes narrow in greed. "Just some office fun," Whitney smiled. "You know. But you've got to keep your mouth shut or you might get us both in a little trouble. Everybody might not understand."

The man nodded slowly, but still with a shade of doubt. "Oh, sure, I know you guys kid around sometimes up there. But I don't wanna take any chances. You sure those pills are harmless?"

"For Pete's sake," Whitney said with a show of impatience, "I'm letting you buy them yourself, what more do you want? They couldn't harm a baby. Ask the druggist. All you got to do is slip a couple into Bobak's coffee order when I tell you to. But if you'd rather forget about . . ."

The man reached for the money, convinced.

Shortly afterward, some time past one of the coffee breaks, the office astounded to see Mr. Bobak sound asleep in his chair. The sleeping pills were working very well.

Gradually, Bobak slumped to his desk, pillowed his head comfortably on his arms and began a piercing, regular snoring. For the benefit of the others, Whitney tried to shake him awake, but Bobak was too deep in sleep to respond. Later, Whitney was gratified to observe S. D. Simpson looking in disgustedly through the glass partition at the slumbering Bobak. Bobak awoke in a couple of hours, horror-stricken when he realized what he'd been doing.

A couple of weeks later, the same performance was repeated. "Don't know what got into me," Bobak muttered, aghast. "I don't usually feel sleepy during the day . . ."

Whitney was not surprised to find himself in S. D. Simpson's office one afternoon. "Of course, you're on the young side," Simpson told him, "and not as long in experience as some of the others, but, by George, we're convinced you're the most capable man in the department. And we're afraid Bobak's losing his grip. That tax trouble in his department last year . . . and when a man keeps falling asleep at his work . . ."

Again, another confidential ancestry report appeared on Whitney's desk. With some curiosity, Whitney noted that one of his forebears had been a naval officer under Drake. Well, well. There was a physician, a magistrate, a couple of clergymen. Another line showed blacksmiths, cobblers, other artisans, still in England. A few minor indiscretions had been noted, but the sum total was a satisfactory rating. Cleared for promotion to a department head.

Bobak was removed to an obscure niche. "Too bad, Bobak," Whitney told him, having shed his respectful tone. "This is as much a surprise to me as it is to you. But you've still got your seniority. You've still got a pension to look forward to."

Whitney invested two more years in consolidating his position, presenting the ideas of underlings as his own if they had merit, running his department with a strict and efficient hand, calculating every move toward impressing the big wheels. He didn't mind doing a little waiting now; he was in the executive class. His next step could be a big one.

When at last he moved up again, it was to bypass three high-level executives, including S. D. Simpson himself. A bit of blackmail could be useful.

While he waited, Whitney had had a firm of private detectives secretly snooping for indiscretions in the lives of Eastern's top officials. They couldn't all be angels, Whitney had reasoned. He'd struck pay dirt in the case of the Comptroller, Van Shilder. There had been a liaison between Van Shilder and a certain blonde model. Van Shilder had boosted Whitney up the line to avoid a scandal that would have ruined his reputation and his domestic serenity.

He was getting closer to the inner circle now. He disposed of the next man in his path in short order. Whitney had built up a rumor mill, a private corps of spies and toadies, to which he consigned the reputation of R. J. Fredericks. Rumors soon spread all over Eastern that Fredericks was an alcoholic, that he was given to placing bets on the horses with bookies, that he was accepting under-the-table kick-backs from Eastern's vendors, that he was selling out Eastern trade secrets to competitors. There were no open charges, nothing that Fredericks could defend himself against, only rumors, but the rumors kept coming to the ears of the top echelon, until at last, disquieted, unwilling to run risks, they removed Fredericks to a harmless sinecure. Whitney moved up again.

Barely thirty years old now, he was in line for a Vice-Presidency in the huge Eastern Chemicals Corporation. A most amazing advancement. He was regarded as one of the brightest young men in the industry, a man who undoubtedly must have remarkable executive ability to rise so fast.

With his promotions, further ancestry checks had been run, of course, far back into previous centuries, but had given no trouble. Whitney had anticipated none—that far back in the past, how much could be learned? And how much could it count?

He was somewhat surprised when President Mitchell, meeting him in the corridor, placed a hand on his shoulder and, with a relaxing of his features that might have been a smile, rumbled, "Ah, Whitney."

"Yes, sir?" Whitney said respectfully. Beyond some occasional routine contact, Mitchell had had little to do with him. Mitchell was a remote, unbending figure, inhabiting a world of forbidding dignity penetrated only by Vice-Presidents, members of the Board, and others of equal importance.

"I've read your latest ancestry report," President Mitchell said. "An interesting point—in the thirteenth century, your ancestors lived in Wicklington, Cheshire, in old England. So did mine."

"Really, sir? Then they must have known each other."

"Precisely," said Mitchell, in a kindly tone. He chuckled. "In a way, that makes us old acquaintances, doesn't it?" He took Whitney's arm, walked him along the corridor, chatting cordially about thirteenth-century life in Wicklington.

While Whitney responded to the huge man in the proper tones of respect, interest and geniality, he was thinking that here was his ultimate target. This was the man who held the position he wanted above all. This was the most important throat he was going to cut. The king is dead, long live . . . President Drew Whitney of Eastern Chemicals, Inc. It would have a fine sound.

During Whitney's other operations, he had also steadily been gathering data on Mitchell, seeking out his weaknesses. This ancestry business was one of the weaknesses. Whitney had discovered that it was not popular among the other high-level company officials, considered little more than one of those eccentricities to which men of great achievement and power were entitled. Mitchell sometimes delivered talks on heredity to his officials. "Heredity is not a dead record," he would say. "The past lives in us. We follow the patterns of our ancestors, we are to a degree responsible for their actions . . ." Whitney had detected notes of weary boredom in the polite agreement of the other executives. There was no doubt that the ancestor policy would be thrown out when Mitchell was out of office—meanwhile, it was a chink in Mitchell's armor, possibly it could be useful in some ways to help discredit the man with the Board of Directors when the time came.

But Whitney was not ready for Mitchell yet. He needed a Vice-Presidency first. He needed the job of his immediate superior, Vice-President F. Griswold.

And Griswold proved to be the most difficult obstruction he'd yet faced. Griswold was comparatively young and vigorous; there seemed little chance that he would retire in less than fifteen or twenty years. He was efficient, capable, sharp, powerful. He was strongly entrenched—his reputation was top-drawer. Blackmail was out of the question. Whitney's agents had been unable to get anything on him. Whitney felt that it would be dangerous to repeat any of his previous tactics, and against this man it would be futile. Griswold was too highly placed and impervious.

Griswold was blocking the road.

Whitney debated a long time before he reached his decision. He was willing to do the unthinkable, he was willing to step over the line, but this far? He would prefer some other way. It was a serious, risky act he was contemplating, the kind of thing which belonged in some other incredible, unreal world. Yet, would not its very improbability be its strongest point?

And against Griswold there seemed no other way. He wanted the Vice-Presidency badly, he needed it, like his right arm.

Whitney then made up his mind.

Once this was done, he acted with his usual thorough-going resolution and efficiency. During his investigations he moved cautiously and warily until he was sure that he had found the right man. "I'll pay top money," he told the man, "but I want a perfect job. Not just an injury. Injured people can recover."

The thin man looked at him from under light, almost invisible eyebrows. "I got a rep, mister," he said softly. "When I go after a guy, he's through. Quit worryin'."

The office was shocked by the news of the tragic accident. Vice-President Griswold had been struck down and killed by a hit-run driver. They had not been able to trace the car.

Another ancestry report reached Whitney's desk. Whitney had stepped into the Vice-Presidency. Sorrowfully, he stated: "It is with deep regret that I take over poor Frank Griswold's duties. These are painful circumstances under which to accept the honor of a Vice-Presidency. I shall try to respect Griswold's memory by doing the best job I can."

Actually, Whitney did have faint misgivings about what he had done, brief feelings of guilt. They soon vanished. He was almost there . . . Nothing must stand in his way. Nothing. He'd see to that.

In the third week of his Vice-Presidency, while he was still savoring the change in his status, the prestige, the new deference accorded him, he was summoned to President Mitchell's office. He walked into the room expecting that this would be an executive consultation on high-level affairs. He was not prepared for the grimness in the big man's face. He saw that they were alone. He closed the door behind him, hearing the automatic click of the snap lock.

"Sit down," Mitchell grunted. Whitney took a chair. Mitchell went to the bank of windows that looked out upon the vast panorama of the city, flung open a couple and took a deep breath. "This air-conditioning's all right," Mitchell said, "but I like to get some real air in here every day." Whitney waited. Mitchell returned to his desk, extracted a folder from his drawer and opened it. His heavy brows drew together. His deep-set eyes regarded Whitney so steadily that the younger man's glance flicked away uncomfortably for an instant, registering again the heavy dignity of the room, the mural, the oil portraits of a few of Mitchell's forebears. "Got some new information here," Mitchell said at last. "It came late. Our investigators in England just turned it up in the old vaults at Wicklington, Cheshire. It concerns your ancestry, Whitney. Belongs with your last report, by rights."

"My ancestry?" This was the furthest thing from Whitney's thoughts.

"That's right. It's a deathbed confession by an ancestor of yours, Garth Whitney, fletcher of Wicklington. It's dated August 12, 1173. Almost eight hundred years ago. Now listen."

Mitchell read:

" 'Synce I, Garth Whitney, did knowe that Baker Mitchell was a man of muche welthe, I did hie me to his abode on this darke nighte and did spie thru the window that he was alone and did knock uponne his dore and he did comen and openne. Then did I smite with a cudgel uponne his hed agen and agen and he did dye. I did find muche store of gold inne his cotage and I did flee and hyde the gold, so that when muche hue and tumulte was afterwards raysed, none did wot it was I who had donne this. So did I lyve out my dayes in Wicklington and later have gude use of the gold, and none did suspecte, but nowe I lye on my dying bed, I wishet that the treuthe be knowne.' "

There was a silence. "It appears," said President Mitchell at last, "that you have murder in your heritage, Whitney."

Whitney did not allow the stir of concern to show in his face or voice. He knew how seriously Mitchell took this stuff; it had to be minimized. He said lightly, "Sorry to hear that, but I disown the old boy. My other ancestors averaged out all right, didn't they?"

Mitchell's severe expression didn't change. "Did you note the name of the man your ancestor murdered? Mitchell, the baker. My own ancestor."

It struck Whitney. He stared incredulously at Mitchell. Of all people, why did old Garth have to pick on a Mitchell? He forced a smile. "But that happened in the twelfth century, sir. Surely, you don't hold that deed against *me*."

"Well," Mitchell said, not returning the smile, "as you know, I hold that we're all in some degree responsible for our ancestors' actions. However, I don't wish personal bias to enter into company affairs. The main point here is that the murder drops your ancestry rating below that required of a Vice-President. You'll have to give up that position."

"You'd take away my office because of this?"

"According to our present rating system, yes. You're still qualified to hold certain limited lower positions. Sorry, Whitney."

A wave of bitterness swept through Whitney. To have come so far, to have risked so much . . . and to have it snatched away because of the asinine theories of this man . . . For an instant he considered fighting, lodging a complaint with the Board of Directors, trying to rally other company officials to his support. Then he knew that it would be hopeless. Mitchell was unassailable right now. Eastern Chemicals had achieved much of its greatness under his leadership. Like many other strong men, he could afford a few eccentricities. No, he couldn't get Mitchell now, he needed more time, another couple of years.

Desperately, feeling that it was futile, Whitney said, "But this is ancient history. How about the present? How about my own record? You'll admit that it's topnotch. I've given my best efforts to Eastern. Doesn't that count?"

Mitchell rose, went to the windows and looked out. At last, he said slowly, "It carries weight, yes. As I say, you're still qualified for some responsibility. But, as for a Vice-Presidency, I'm afraid . . ."

It was while Mitchell was talking that the thought came to Whitney. The man was no more than a step or two away, back toward him. The window was open, the sill low, ankle height. One firm push would do it. He'd say it had been an accident. Who could prove otherwise? Mitchell's habit of breathing deeply in front of the open window was known. The man might have tripped or had a dizzy spell, he was getting along in years—

He'd destroy the report on Mitchell's desk. With Mitchell gone, nobody would concern themselves with ancestry reports anyhow. The whole foolish business would be thrown out; from the Directors on down, there was no real sympathy for the thing. He'd retain his Vice-Presidency; might even have a chance at the vacant Presidency sooner than he'd expected.

Whitney rose silently. Yes, he was willing to go this far. He'd already done so with Griswold. The decision was easy this time. One quick push would give him everything he wanted.

Whitney took a step and lunged at Mitchell's back.

He hadn't thought the big man could hear him or move so fast.

He found his arms imprisoned in a crushing grip, Mitchell's deep-set eyes locked with his own. He tried to struggle. It was useless. The man was too powerful.

"Murder me, would you?" Mitchell said quietly. "I thought you might try that. Proves my point, doesn't it? There's murder in your heritage. Blood will tell."

"Let go of me," Whitney said.

"In a moment," Mitchell said. His eyes held the detached contempt of a judge's regarding a vicious criminal. "The law's practically helpless against you right now, it can't punish you much for what you tried to do to me. Let you go free and in time you'll succeed in murdering someone, if it suits your purposes. And there's another small consideration. Garth Whitney never paid the penalty for his crime. Eh?" For an instant longer the two men's eyes remained locked. Then Mitchell said, "Well, over you go, my lad," as he heaved Whitney out the window.

EDWARD D. HOCH

Another War

But that was in another war," Mason argued, pausing to light his cigar. "You simply can't compare the use of tanks in North Africa with that in Korea. The terrain was different, the weather conditions . . ."

Roderick Care shuffled his feet against the carpet and stared at the younger man. "I'm not running down what you fellows did in Korea—don't misunderstand me! I'm only pointing out that given the right circumstances a massed armored attack can be both impressive and effective."

Mason leaned back in his chair, enjoying himself for all the surface disagreement. Care, ten years his senior, was the sort of man with whom he liked to argue. "I don't know," he said with just a hint of a smile. "If they're all like you, I don't know that I'd be too welcome in the AWB."

Roderick Care, a graying man with a spreading paunch, and no sense of humor, leaped to the defensive. "Come, now! You can't be serious! The AWB is the finest bunch of guys you'd ever want to meet. They accepted me, and I'm British! That must prove something right there. We're not the American Legion or the VFW or the Catholic War Vets, you know. We're strictly social, just a bunch of fellows out for a good time. We like to get away from the wife and children for a few days occasionally and do some hunting or fishing, or just drink beer and talk about our service days."

"The others have plenty of social activities," Mason argued. "In fact I dropped out of a veterans' group once because they were a bit too social. Dinners and dances and all the rest."

"But those things are with the wife! I know you like to get away with the boys once in a while. Everybody does. Hell, how many other veterans' organizations have a hunting lodge like our place in River Forks?"

Mason was ready for that one. "The Khakis have a lodge not too far from there."

"The Khakis! Would you rather belong to the Khakis or the American War Buddies—buddy?"

"Neither group excites me too much, to be perfectly frank about it," Mason told him.

Care spread his hands in a pleading gesture. "At least come to one of our meetings, see what it's all about. What harm can that do?"

More to put an end to the discussion than because he really wanted to go, Mason finally agreed. He'd expected an evening of reminiscing when he agreed to dine with Roderick Care, but he'd hardly foreseen the sort of high-pressure sales talk to which he'd been subjected. As he drove home through the warm autumn night he reflected that he had now committed himself to next week's meeting whether he liked it or not. Well, at least he could tell that to the man from the Khakis who kept phoning him.

"Nice dinner, dear?" Maria asked him as he came in from the garage. "He didn't try to sell you any insurance, did he?"

"No, we talked about North Africa and Korea, and tank warfare and stuff."

She'd put the children to bed and was in the process of finishing the dinner dishes. He sat at the kitchen table smoking a cigarette and watching her, ever amazed that she could still manage to look as youthful as when he'd married her twelve years ago. "Well, I'm glad you didn't buy anything," she told him. "Both our children are going to need new shoes soon, and we still have the color TV to pay off."

"He wants me to come to the next AWB meeting."

"The *what*?"

"You know. The American War Buddies."

"You're not going, are you?"

"Why?"

"Well, it's just that you've always been sort of cynical about veterans' groups."

"Well, maybe this one's different. Or maybe it's a sign of middle age that I suddenly want to talk about my days as a tank commander in Korea."

"You were never a commander!"

"I was for a day, after Scotty got killed. I told you about that."

She sighed and went back to the dishes. "I should think when fellows come back from the wars they'd just want to forget about all the killing, not go on being reminded of it at monthly meetings."

"Oh, they talk about other things, Maria. In fact, Care said it was mostly a social group. They have a hunting lodge up in River Forks."

"That figures!"

He found himself growing a bit annoyed at her attitude. "Hell, I usually go hunting once or twice every year anyway. If they've got a lodge I might as well use it."

"Do whatever you want," she said.

He grunted and started reading the evening paper, looking for some newsy item with which to change the subject.

The following week's meeting of the American War Buddies was about what he'd expected. It was held in a big private dining room at the Newton Hotel, a room which also served the needs of the Lions' Club and the County Republican Committee. A large American flag hung from the wall behind the speaker's table, and several of the members wore ribbon-bedecked campaign hats.

A man named Crowder, who walked with a stiff-legged limp, conducted the meeting, running through routine matters and the preparations for the autumn reopening of the lodge at River Forks. Peering out from beneath bushy black eyebrows, he reminded Mason of a movie-version communist at a cell meeting in the Thirties.

After the surprisingly brief meeting, he walked over to greet Mason personally. "Pleasure to have you here, Mr. Mason. I'm Crowder, this year's president of AWB. Roderick Care tells me you're thinking of joining."

"Only thinking right now."

Crowder offered him a cigarette, shifting weight onto his good leg. "This is the best time of the year to join. There's the lodge, and the Christmas party, and then the big national convention in the spring. Frankly, Mason, we're looking for young blood—Korea and after. Too many of our members are left over from wars that everyone's forgotten. You could go high in the organization right now—maybe even a national office on the executive committee."

"I'm not looking for more work," Mason told him. "Besides, you look young enough to have been in Korea yourself." His eyes dropped unconsciously to the stiff leg.

"I was over there, right at the end of things. But not a tank commander like you."

"I came out without a scratch," Mason said. "I have great respect for those who didn't."

Crowder gave a short, husky laugh. "This leg? Foolish hunting accident two years ago. Shot myself in the kneecap."

"Oh." Mason felt a gentle hand on his shoulder and turned to see Roderick Care beaming at him. He had another man in tow, a white-haired man with a small and gentle face.

"Mason, this is Dr. Fathion, one of our most respected members. He was a major during the South Pacific campaign."

"Pleased to meet you, Doctor," Mason said.

"A pleasure, Mr. Mason. I trust you've been won over by our president?"

"I'm considering it," Mason replied with a smile.

Roderick Care motioned toward the back of the room, where the hotel waitresses were preparing to serve coffee and cake. "Let's discuss it over some coffee. Or would you rather go down to the bar?"

"Coffee's fine."

It was good coffee, and Mason found himself beginning to like these men who clustered around him.

"Tell us about Korea," Crowder said. "I never saw much action over there myself."

"Except with the girls," Care said, muffling an explosion of laughter. "Crowder here is quite the lover."

"You will be joining us at the lodge, won't you?" Crowder asked Mason. "You *do* hunt?"

"A little." He turned to the doctor. "How about you, Dr. Fathion? You do much hunting?"

The doctor shook his head, slightly horrified. "I never fire a gun. Never even fired one in the army. But I go along for the opening of the season. I'm a great poker player, and we usually get a few nice games going."

"It must have been tough going through the South Pacific without firing a shot."

The little doctor shrugged. "Oh, they made us fire at a few training targets, but in battle I was always too busy with the wounded. Field hospital, behind the lines. One day I operated on fifty-five wounded men. I was ready to drop by nightfall."

Mason liked the doctor, and he liked the others too, to varying degrees. After the coffee he joined them at the hotel bar for a quick drink, and found himself signing a membership application with no resistance at all.

Maria was waiting up for him when he got home. "It's pretty late," she said. "I thought you'd be home by ten."

"We had coffee and then I stopped with them for a drink."

"You joined, didn't you?" she asked, making it into something like an accusation.

"Well, hell, yes I did! That's no crime! They only meet once a month and for a few social gatherings. If I get tired of it I just won't go."

"All right," she sighed. "I didn't mean to sound like a shrew."

He mumbled something and went out to the kitchen for a glass of milk.

"So now I'm an AWB wife. Do they have a ladies' auxiliary or something?"

"I'll ask," he replied, not certain that she wasn't continuing to needle him.

"That means you'll be going hunting with them, I suppose."

"Just the first day. I'll only be away one night. Or two at most."

In the morning she was her usual cheerful self, and his membership in the AWB was not mentioned again.

About a week later he received a call at work from a lawyer he knew slightly, a member of the Khakis. "Have you thought any more about joining us, Mason, boy?"

"Sorry, Cliff. I've signed up with the AWB."

"Oh. Sorry to hear that."

"They seemed like a nice bunch of fellows."

"Well . . . yes. But that sort of puts us on opposite sides of the fence."

Mason chuckled into the phone. "Not really, Cliff. I'll still throw some legal business your way. How about lunch one of these days?"

Cliff seemed to hedge at that. "Um, let's make it after Thanksgiving, huh? I'm getting into my busy season."

"Fine. I'll be talking to you." He hung up, wondering if he had made the right choice. But Cliff had told him very little about the Khakis, really, and had never invited him to one of their monthly meetings.

He went back to the pile of work on his desk and promptly forgot about it.

A few days before the opening of hunting season, Roderick Care phoned him. "Monday's the big day—just thought I'd call to remind you. A group of us are driving up to the lodge Sunday night, just to be there at dawn when the deer start running. You might as well come along."

Mason hesitated only a moment. "All right," he agreed.

"What kind of rifle do you have?" Care asked.

"I've got two—a Remington and an old Italian army gun I don't use much any more."

"Better bring them both. Somebody might be able to use one."

"All right."

"I'll pick up Dr. Fathion and then swing by for you around six. It's a three-hour drive."

Mason was ready on Sunday evening, and he stepped into the brisk night air as soon as Care's auto pulled up in front. He wasn't too anxious for the men to come in and face Maria's cool indifference to the trip.

Dr. Fathion was in the back, and Mason rode in front, feeling good for the first time in days. "Put these with the others," he said, passing over the two gun cases.

The doctor accepted them. "You should get rid of that red hat," he suggested as they got under way.

Mason fingered the fluorescent material. "This? Hell, I don't want to get shot for a deer," He glanced into the back seat at the other cased rifle. "Mind if I look at yours, Care? Not loaded, is it?"

"No, no. Go ahead!"

Mason leaned over the seat and unzipped the case. "A carbine? Semi-automatic? I thought they were illegal in this state."

Roderick Care smiled. "The deer never said they were illegal."

They drove for a long time in silence, with both Care and the doctor reluctant to join in any conversation about their common interests. Mason mentioned North Africa and the South Pacific and finally Korea without getting a rise out of either man.

It had been dark for more than two hours by the time they turned off the main highway, and there was another hour's trip over a rutted mountain road before they finally reached the hunting lodge at River Forks. Three other cars had gotten there ahead of them, and a dozen men were already inside, playing poker and drinking beer.

Crowder limped over to greet them, startling Mason with his costume of green-and-brown camouflage. "That's a heck of a thing to wear when you're hunting," Mason said.

"I probably won't go out with this knee anyway."

The lodge was large enough to sleep a score or more men. There were three big bedrooms with an array of cots, plus a kitchen, indoor toilet, and central living room where others could sleep. It was a pleasant place, though it seemed to Mason that none of the men were very relaxed.

Mason chatted with the various men and examined an AWB banner that he hadn't seen before. He ended up in a card game with Care and Crowder and the doctor, and won five dollars. He drank a few beers, talked guns with Care for a time, and finally caught a few hours' sleep on one of the cots. None of the others seemed interested in sleep, and he awakened around three-thirty in the morning to hear Crowder sending one of the men out of the lodge on some mission.

Mason felt around for his fluorescent cap but it was gone. While he slept someone had substituted a dark brown one with ear flaps that was a size too large. He got up and joined the others, yawning, noticing for the first time that none of them wore any brightly colored garment.

"Where are the cars?" he asked, glancing out the window.

Care walked over to stand beside him. "We have a garage around back. They'll be safe there."

"What? Say, who was that who just went out?"

"Schlitzer. He's just looking around."

"It's a couple of hours till daylight."

Dr. Fathion was making coffee, and passing the steaming cups around at random. Mason drank, feeling an odd sort of tension building in his gut. It was almost the way he'd felt in Korea.

Then something about the windows caught his eye, something he hadn't noticed before. He walked over to feel the folded shutters, then turned to Roderick Care. "Since when do you need steel shutters on a hunting—"

The crack of the rifle shot was very close, off in the woods somewhere but very close. Instantly, Crowder was on his feet shouting orders. Two men grabbed their rifles and hurried outside, while a third picked up the AWB banner and went out the door behind them, planting it in the soft earth with a firm hand.

"What *is* it?" Mason shouted to Care. "What in hell's happening?"

The answer came through the door. The two hunters were back already, carrying the fallen Schlitzer. He was bleeding from a wound in the stomach.

"On the table," Dr. Fathion shouted, slipping his arms into a white plastic jacket that had a large red cross on front and back. "Get my instruments. Quickly, men!"

Crowder was issuing orders as the others grabbed for their rifles. Someone shoved Mason's into his hands. Then he was facing Crowder as the lame man spoke quickly. "It's a sneak attack by the Khakis," he said, talking in an officer's monotone. "Two hours before the official start. Somebody get those shutters closed."

As soon as he had spoken, one window shattered under the ripple of gunfire. Roderick Care pulled Mason down along the wall. "We're in for it this year," he said. "It's another Pearl Harbor!"

"You mean this happens—"

Care was hugging the wall, edging toward the window with his carbine. "Last year we were lucky—only two wounded. I suppose we were due."

"But this is madness!"

"No more so than any war." Care lifted his head to the window and fired a quick burst with his carbine. "Didn't you ever wonder why so many people get shot on the first day of hunting season?"

ALICE SCANLAN REACH

Sparrow on a String

Harry Fortune woke up one Saturday morning in May with one thought in mind. He was going to kill Eddie.

Eddie was Harry's fifty-five-year-old sister, Edith, who couldn't have been more appropriately nicknamed when you took into account her masculine swagger, shingled gray hair, voice the timbre of a bullfrog's, and the unmistakable mustache looming over her thin, mean upper lip.

Harry hated her. He couldn't remember a day in his life when he hadn't loathed the sight and sound of Eddie. His earliest memory—he couldn't have been more than five or six—was of an afternoon when she discovered a small, drab, obviously injured sparrow floundering in some tall weeds. Fascinated, Harry watched as Eddie fashioned a cage of boards and chicken wire, made a nest of twigs and grass, and then commanded him to fetch a handful of sunflower seeds, a worm or two, and a shallow tin pan of water.

"Now," Eddie had said, as she settled the sparrow inside the cage and secured the wire, "you just tend to our little birdie real good and maybe we can cure what ails him."

Dutifully, Harry did as he was told. After a week or so, the injury—whatever its nature—seemed to heal and the sparrow began to chirp and hop around its cage.

"And now," Eddie said one day, "we'll see if our birdie can fly." Laughing, she opened the cage. The sparrow hopped out, spread its wings and soared skyward for a moment or two, then suddenly faltered and fluttered to the ground. It took Harry almost another moment to realize why: Eddie had tied a long—but not too long—string to one of the sparrow's legs. Still laughing, she reeled the bird in as she would a hooked fish, and placed it back in the cage, leaving the string tied.

Despite Harry's cries of protest and pleading, which gained him nothing but a sore bottom, Eddie repeated the torture day after day; tantalized the sparrow with a brief taste of freedom, and then relentlessly pulled it back into the cage. So it was almost with a sense of relief that Harry went to water and feed the sparrow one morning and found that in its frantic efforts to free itself from the string it had strangled. Harry wept. Maybe it was then that, subconsciously, he began to think of himself as another helpless sparrow tied to Eddie's cruel string . . .

When, at eighteen, Harry enlisted in the Navy, he promised himself that he would never lay eyes on his sister again, but a German submarine smashed Harry's promise and Harry as well. After spending a year in a veterans' hospital, he finally hobbled home; back to the old frame farmhouse which still squatted in gloomy solitude some fifteen miles from town.

Once there, Eddie saw to it that he didn't "baby himself," as she put it, that he pitched in to help her raise a few scrawny chickens and vegetables, and that each month he endorsed over to her his disability check.

Things wouldn't be so bad, so lonesome, Harry often reflected dismally, if they just had a TV set. But whenever he ventured this suggestion aloud, Eddie would explode. "Ain't hardly enough money to put food in our mouths and you want a TV! If you weren't such a no-account bumbler you'd know how to fix the radio!"

Harry always subsided after such an exchange. He *had* tried, time and again, to fix the old pre-war radio, but his efforts were always, in the end, futile. Sometimes it squawked to life, then quickly lapsed into dead silence.

The only day of the week that could bring a straightening of Harry's thin shoulders and an anticipatory gleam of excitement to his pale blue eyes was on Saturdays. After supper Eddie would hoist her bulk into their battered truck and wait impatiently for Harry to climb in beside her. Their destination was always the same: the nearest farmhouse seven miles down the road, the home of Sheriff Jess Snell, his wife, Ida, and an assortment of offspring. Then, having deposited his passenger, Harry would gun the truck's engine and head for town and the Easy Rest Tavern where invariably the first person to greet him as he crossed the threshold was—the sheriff.

"Well, here he comes, right on time," Jess would boom out to the general amusement of all. "Henpecked Harry himself!" Whereupon, for the next ten minutes or so, Harry was joshed mercilessly about himself and his sister.

Harry didn't mind. He was too grateful for the warmth of the cozy tavern, the companionship of menfolk, and the sound of their laughter, even if it was at his own expense. He always just smiled, sat down at the bar, and listened to the voices around him while he sipped a couple of beers until it was time to pick up Eddie. And so it went, week after week, year after year, with not a single variation.

Harry knew the exact day and hour when he decided that the only way to get rid of Eddie was to get rid of her. It was shortly after the miracle happened; when Eddie got the letter from Cousin Lucy who lived in Ridgeway, ninety miles away. Playing her usual cat-and-mouse game, Eddie didn't immediately reveal its contents, but kept a sly, smug look on her face for almost a week before she finally mentioned it.

"Cousin Lucy wants me to come for a visit," she announced importantly as she plopped a plate of lukewarm beans in front of Harry.

"Reckon so." Harry swallowed a forkful of beans.

"Course I'd only be gone a week or two. Maybe three."

"Uh-huh."

"Maybe we could get a TV—on time—to keep you company."

Abruptly, Harry shoved his plate away and got to his feet.

Eddie's marble-size eyes widened with surprise. "Ain't you gonna finish your supper?"

"Had enough." Harry opened the kitchen door and, unseeingly, limped out to the far pasture. It wasn't the first time that Eddie had held out a half-promise of pleasure, a half-hope of freedom. She knew very well how much he longed for a little privacy, a little comfort, a little peace. She knew!

But what she didn't know, Harry told himself with a great sense of satisfaction, was that this time she wasn't fooling him one bit. She didn't know that less then twenty-four hours after the arrival of Lucy's letter, Harry had discovered its hiding place and read it. Cousin Lucy had made no mention of a visit. Indeed, all she wanted from Eddie was a "a bit of cash to tide us over"—a request which would most certainly be ignored.

Harry paused in his aimless wandering and threw himself down among the gently waving wands of grass. How he wished that Lucy really *had* invited Eddie for a visit! How he wished that Eddie would go away not for just one, two, or three weeks, but for good! The grass smelled fresh and sweet, and for a long time Harry lay there smelling the sweetness and staring up at the stars . . .

When he picked up Eddie at the Snells the following Saturday, she'd barely settled herself beside him before she started her taunts.

"Ida says I should pack up and visit Lucy, and I've about made up my mind to do just that."

Harry glanced at her out of the corner of his eye and saw the familiar sly smile on her face. He knew she was deriving enormous pleasure out of spinning her fictitious tale to Ida. At the same time, she thought he'd swallowed her lie; that he really believed she was going to set him free. And then, like the sparrow on a string . . .

Lying sleepless that night, Harry had only one thought in his head, the same thought he'd had ever since that night in the pasture: how to get rid of Eddie. He finally fell into exhausted sleep still wondering how, how . . .

Then another miracle happened on the following Saturday as he walked into the Easy Rest Tavern.

"Hey, Harry," Jess boomed. "Ida says you're gonna lose Eddie for a spell. Now ain't that a shame?" The Easy Rest patrons exploded into laughter. "How you aim to spend your spare time?" Jess prodded. This time the laughter was interspersed with acid words of advice and deprecating jibes about Harry's physical prowess.

Harry barely heard them. He had a wild thought that set his heart to hammering and caused him to spill some of his beer. He knew *how*!

When the laughter subsided and his hands stopped shaking, Harry swallowed the last of his beer, got up, and walked out to the truck. He drove out of town until he reached a deserted stretch of road where he pulled over to the side and cut the truck's motor. Sitting there in the darkness, he worked out every detail. He decided to wait one week—no, two—just to make sure that Eddie would continue to play her vicious game, keep on telling her lies.

Eddie was in a rage when he pulled up at the Snells. When she finally lapsed into silence, after railing at him for keeping her waiting, Harry decided to risk a question.

"You and Ida talk anymore about you visiting Cousin Lucy?"

"Sure did," Eddie snapped. "Told her I might take off any day now."

Any day now! Harry almost smiled.

The following Saturday at the Easy Rest, Jess roared at him from across the room. "Guess you're almost a free man, huh, Harry? Ida says Eddie's gonna take off any day now."

"Yup," Harry replied, calmly sipping his beer. "Any day now."

He was right on time that night to pick up Eddie. She settled herself in the truck and for a few moments neither brother nor sister spoke. Finally Harry broke the silence.

"Ran into Jess at the Easy Rest," he remarked in an offhand manner. "He said you told Ida you were aiming to take off any day now."

Eddie snorted. "Your ears going bad like the rest of you? I've told you a hundred times that I was going to visit Lucy."

"Yeah," Harry nodded. "You told me, but I didn't know you'd told Ida."

"Told you that too! And I told Ida again tonight."

"You did?"

"Course I did."

"Then you really mean it?"

"Now why . . ." A sly smile played around the corners of her mouth. ". . . *Why* would I say a thing like that if I didn't mean it?"

Harry's heart sang. He drove the truck into the old barn, picked up the heavy hammer he'd hidden under the driver's seat, and followed Eddie into the house.

"Guess you'll be mighty sorry to see me go," Eddie said smugly as she turned her back to him to hang her coat and hat on a peg in the darkened hallway. "Guess you'll be sorry—"

Harry swung the hammer and cut her off. He swung it again and again and cut her off permanently. Then he methodically went to work, and as he worked, he whistled. It was almost dawn before he was finished; until there wasn't a trace of his toil and Eddie lay safe and sound at the bottom of the old abandoned well in the far pasture.

When Harry walked into the Easy Rest the next Saturday, he didn't wait for Jess Snell's usual raucous greeting, "Eddie finally took off for Ridgeway," he announced as he signaled for his customary beer.

"That so?" Jess whistled. "Never thought the old girl would make it. Or your old truck."

"Truck?" Harry shook his head. "I put her on the six-fifteen bus last Wednesday. Her and two suitcases." He *had*, in fact, packed most of Eddie's belongings, and they now shared her final resting place

There was a sudden unaccustomed silence in the room, but Harry was too engrossed in his own happy thoughts to notice.

"You put Eddie on the bus?" Jess said slowly. "Last Wednesday?"

"Yup."

"You're sure?"

"Sure, I'm sure!" Harry grinned. "And the first thing I'm going to do with my vet check is buy me a TV." Another happy thought struck him. "Come to think of it, maybe I'll get one of those fancy combinations—TV, radio, and hi-fi."

The silence in the room persisted. Only vaguely was Harry aware that Jess was standing next to him.

"Guess your old radio is on the blink again, huh, Harry?" Jess said.

Harry chuckled. "Hasn't been a squawk out of the old box for at least six months."

"Then you wouldn't have any way of knowing."

Harry turned to him, puzzled. "Knowing? Knowing what?"

"That there's a strike on," Jess said heavily. "That there ain't been a bus in or out of here since last *Sunday*." He placed a firm, sheriff-like hand on Harry's shoulder. "Now, if Eddie's really gone, Harry, suppose you tell me where. Where, Harry?"

Harry stared at him, openmouthed and speechless, and somehow the only words he could think of were: *sparrow on a string . . .*

CLAYTON MATTHEWS

The Missing Tattoo

The carnie night was a kaleidoscope of psychedelic colors and a riot of sound, the whoosh of the rides, the braying voices of concession-joint men and sideshow barkers, and over and under it all the merry tinkle of the merry-go-round calliope.

Bernie Mather, the front talker for the Ten-in-One freak show, was just beginning his bally, beating on a gong to attract attention, his voice pouring into the hand mike. "Hi, lookee, hi, lookee! Gather down close, folks, for a free show. Hi, lookee, this is where the freaks are!"

I stood on the edge of the gathering crowd before the freak show bally platform. It was going to be a big tip. Montana's Wonder Shows was playing at a fair, and the crowds were satisfactorily large along the midway.

A passing carnie tapped me on the shoulder. "Hi, Patch. I see you're still with it."

"Yeah, I'm still with it."

That's me—Patch. Real name, Dave Cole, but to everybody on the Montana carnival I was Patch. To a carnie, a patch is exactly what the name implies. A fixer, the guy who greases the local fuzz, if grease is needed, to allow the games to operate openly and to permit the broads in the girlie shows to strip down to the buff. Oddly enough, considering the insular carnie world's dislike of any and all fuzz, I also operated as a sort of law on the lot, keeping the peace, seeing that the game agents didn't get too greedy, arbitrating disputes, whatever. In short, a carnie patch is a troubleshooter. In some ways I had more power around the carnie than Tex Montana, the owner, who paid my salary.

In fact, Kay Foster, the cook-tent cashier, had once accused me of just that. "You know why you stay a carnie, Dave, when you could probably set up a private law practice somewhere? You like the power you have here. Big frog in a little puddle."

Kay and I had a mild thing going, and she hated carnie life. I had practiced law briefly some years back, had run into a spot of trouble, not enough to get me disbarred but close to it.

Anyway, Kay thought I should marry her, quit the carnie and return to being a townie. I was willing to marry her, but wasn't yet prepared for the other. I resented the frog-in-the-puddle crack. I enjoyed the life of a carnie, and the job I had. It had its compensations.

I noticed that Bernie had spotted me in the crowd. He winked and turned with a flourish of his cane.

"All right, folks, I'm going to bring out the freaks now, give you a free sample of what you will see inside for the small price of an admission ticket!"

The freak show had ten acts. For each pitch Bernie brought out three freaks, usually different ones. Those that were mobile, that is. Sally, the Fat Lady, for instance, weighed in the neighborhood of seven hundred pounds, and it would have taken a hoist to get her onto the bally platform.

This time Bernie brought out Sam, the Anatomical Marvel, Dirk, the Sword Swallower, and May, the Tattooed Lady. Some freaks are natural born that way, others are gimmicked. The Anatomical Marvel was natural, the Sword Swallower gimmicked, and May would have to be placed somewhere in between. I had been with Montana's Wonder Shows for three seasons and had made myself familiar with all the carnies, the Ten-in-One freaks included, but I was still fascinated by May's tattoos. Bernie, who'd been a freak show operator for twenty years, once told me she had the most thoroughly tattooed body he'd ever seen. Bernie was also the inside talker during each performance, so May was right under his nose, in a manner of speaking.

May was thirty, give or take, and had a lovely face. That was all you could see of her on the bally platform. She wore a long robe covering her from neck to toe. I'd seen her on exhibition inside any number of times, wearing briefs and a halter. The rest of her, every visible inch, was covered with marvelously designed tattoos, like a painting you have to study a long time to get its full meaning. Religious sketches, hunting scenes, profiles of famous men, the American flag, and across her abdomen sailed a two-masted schooner, which she could cause to pitch and toss with contortions of her stomach.

Wise old Bernie only tantalized with May now, flicking at the folds of her robe with the tip of his cane and giving the crowd a teasing peek at a leg tattooed up out of sight.

As I walked away, Bernie had already turned away from May and was pointing at double-jointed Sam, the Anatomical Marvel, who also knew just how much exposure a bally called for. He waggled each ear in a different direction and held one hand straight out while he rotated each finger separately.

It was close to midnight now, and the crowd was beginning to thin out as I strolled to the cook tent. The people remaining were mostly clotted around the show tents as the talkers did their last bally of the night.

The cook tent was beginning to fill up as some carnies had already packed it in for the night. At the cash register Kay was busy, so I flipped a hand at her and went on back for coffee and a midnight sandwich.

I took my time, having a second cup of coffee, waiting for all the shows and rides to close down, so I could prowl the midway and see that it was buttoned up for the night. It wasn't my job to do guard duty—we had two night men for that—but I liked to check things out for myself.

Soon, everything was closed but the cook tent. Many of the carnies lived in house trailers or tents on the lot and could cook there, but most of them came to the cook tent to lie about their night's grosses. I was about to get up and start my tour of inspection when I saw a man I recognized as a canvasman from the Ten-in-One hurrying toward my table. "Patch, Bernie needs you right away!"

I stood up. "What's the trouble?"

"It's May. She's dead!"

"Dead?"

"Murdered, looks like!"

I remembered where I was and glanced around, but it was too late. Those close to me had fallen silent, and I knew they'd overheard. The word would spread like a tent blaze. I waved the canvasman quiet and hustled him out.

We hurried toward the Ten-in-One, feet crunching in the fresh wood shavings already spread along the midway for tomorrow's crowds. The midway was deserted now, all the lights off except a string of bulbs down the center. The concession tent flaps were down, like greedy mouths satiated and closed, and the rides were still, like monsters of various shapes and sizes slumbering under their night hoods.

Bernie was waiting for me in front of the show tent. A slender, dapper man of indeterminate age, he leaned against the ticket box, a glowing pipe stuck in a face as narrow as an ax blade.

"What's happened, Bernie? Somebody kill May?" I asked.

"I can't see what else," he said in his raspy voice. "We turned a small tip for the last show and May said she had to . . . Well, she had something to do, so I told her to go ahead, the marks wouldn't miss one tattooed lady. After we sloughed it for the night, I went back to her trailer. The lights were on, but she didn't answer my knock. I found the door wasn't locked, so I opened it and went in. May was lying there, a knife in her back."

"Was the knife from Dirk's trunk?"

Bernie looked startled, at least as startled as he ever looked. "You know, I never thought of that, but it could be, it just could be."

I was silent for a moment, thinking. Before becoming a sword swallower, Dirk had had a knife-throwing act and May, before she'd been tattooed, had been his assistant. Knife-throwing acts are old hat, not much in demand anymore, so Dirk stopped throwing knives and started swallowing them, and May got tattooed. What was giving me pause for thought was a memory surfacing. Dirk and May had also once had a thing going, a romance that had dissolved when May met Vernon Raines, who talked her into becoming a tattooed lady. Vernon was a charmer and a crook. Not a crook in the carnie sense of a flat-joint operator, but a heist artist, a man with a gun. He had used the carnie as a cover-up, committing townie crimes, such as holding up banks. We hadn't known that, of course—Tex Montana wouldn't have stood for it. Last season, however, Vernon had held up a bank in a town called Midfork, killing a guard, and got away with a hundred grand. He was caught before he could spend any of it. That was when we learned Vernon had a record. Because of that record, and his killing the bank guard, he got life, with no possibility of parole.

The money was never found.

"Well . . ." I sighed heavily. "I guess we'd better go have a look."

We started around the tent to where May's trailer was parked. Bernie said nothing about my calling the police. I would have to do that eventually, of course, but the carnies wouldn't call them on their own initiative if the midway was stacked knee-deep with corpses.

As we rounded the corner of the tent and came in sight of the Ten-in-One freaks clustered before the trailer, Bernie stopped me with a hand on my arm. "Before you go in there, Patch, there's something you should know . . ." He hesitated.

"Well?"

"It's kind of a queer thing . . . and I've seen some queer things in my years of carnying."

"What's the queer thing? Get on with it, man!"

"One of May's tattoos is missing."

"What?" I gaped at him. "*What's* missing?"

"Somebody peeled a piece of skin off her back, about two inches square."

I closed my mouth with a snort and began plowing my way through the gathered carnies. The trailer lights were on, and I opened the door and stepped inside. May lay face down on the floor in the living area, still in the halter and shorts she'd worn for the shows. The brown handle of a long knife protruded from her back just below the left shoulder blade, and lower down on her back, just as Bernie had said, a piece of skin, roughly two inches square was missing.

There was very little blood, only a little oozing, which meant she had been dead, the heart had stopped pumping, when the skin had been cut away.

Bernie stepped inside, and I asked him, "What tattoo is missing?"

"How the hell should I know? With all the tattoos May had, how can I tell which one is missing?"

"I don't suppose any pictures were ever taken of her tattoos?"

"None that I know of."

"Somebody should know what one is missing. Vernon maybe—he had her tattooed, but he's in jail."

"Not anymore he ain't."

I stared at him. "What do you mean?"

"He escaped sometime last night. Didn't you know?"

"No, I didn't know!" I snarled. "How did *you* know?"

"May told me," Bernie said calmly. "She said Vernon called here, wanted to see her. That's what she was so upset about."

"Did he show up?"

"He could have, but I didn't see him."

"He could have killed her, too! I don't suppose it occurred to you to tell the police an escaped con was on his way here?"

Bernie just looked at me.

"All right! Sorry I asked. You could have told *me*, at least."

He shrugged. "I didn't think it was any of my business."

"It figures," I muttered, then sighed. "I hope you don't mind too much if I call the police now, but I'd like to talk to Dirk first. I didn't see him outside."

"I imagine he's in his tent getting bombed. You know he still had a thing for May and the stupid broad told him that Vernon was out."

"Seems everybody knew Vernon was out but me."

"No reason for you to know, Patch. Who'd have thought he would kill her? What reason did he have?"

"*If* he did," I muttered, walking out of the trailer.

Neither of us put it into words, but I knew the same thought had to be in Bernie's mind. Obviously May had been killed for the two-by-two tattoo, and if Vernon had killed her, it could only be for one reason. The tattoo was a map of where the bank loot was hidden. That was ironic in a way. For over a year May had been walking around, on exhibition before thousands of people, with directions on her back where to find a hundred grand, except nobody could have recognized it as such. Yet, if Vernon had killed her, why would he do it for that reason? To save splitting the loot with her?

I told Bernie to stay behind and keep everyone out of the trailer. He was filling his pipe from a cavernous leather tobacco pouch as I left him.

Dirk's tent was up the line about thirty yards. Dirk had been hitting the booze, all right. I could smell it when I pushed the tent flap back and went in. I fumbled overhead for the light cord.

When the light came on, Dirk, lying fully clothed on the cot, stirred and sat up, which meant he couldn't be too drunk. He threw an arm up to shield his eyes from the light and said blearily, "Huh? What is it?"

Dirk was in my age bracket, around forty. Nobody knew his real name. Around a carnie, you don't ask that question. He was over six feet, thin as a board, with an emaciated look. As a part of the act he swallowed a lighted neon tube—you could see it through the outer wall of his stomach. It was pretty weird, watching that tube of light travel down inside his skinny frame.

"Oh . . . it's you, Patch." He blinked at me. "What's up?"

I decided to use shock treatment.

"May's dead, Dirk. Murdered."

"May's what . . . ?" He started away from the cot, staggered and almost fell. "Murdered?"

I snapped the questions at him. "Were you in May's trailer tonight, Dirk?"

"No . . . Of course not. Right after my last turn I came in here for a drink or two. May left earlier."

"Were you still in love with her?"

"No . . . Well, yes, but May . . . The marriage was over, Patch, you knew that."

I should explain that a carnie "marriage" is often without benefit of license or clergy and could last anywhere from a week up to a lifetime. A carnie doesn't consider this as illegal or immoral. It it works, who's hurt? If it doesn't work, it's much less trouble to dissolve, one or both parties deciding it's over. Carnies did this long before the hippies did, proving there's little that's new. But understand, many carnie marriages, probably the majority, *are* legal in every sense of the word.

"Did you know Vernon was on his way here to see May?"

Dirk hesitated a moment before replying. "Yes, May told me."

"Did you see him tonight?"

"No . . ." He took a step toward me. "Did Vernon kill her?"

"I don't know. Did *you*?"

He literally staggered, reeling as from a blow. "I wouldn't kill May, Patch!"

"Let's see your knife case, Dirk."

"Why?"

"She was killed with a knife, a throwing knife."

"And you're thinking—?"

"Dirk, let's see it!"

"Okay, okay!"

Dirk pulled a trunk from under his cot, from which he took a special case, flat like an attaché case and slightly larger. He put it on the cot and opened it.

I stepped closer. The case, lined in velvet, held two rows of knives in graduated sizes and shapes, all fitted into niches in the velvet and held in place by leather straps. There were twenty . . . No, eighteen. Two were missing.

Dirk gasped. "Two are gone!"

"And I know where one is. In May's back."

"Patch, I swear . . ."

How long since you've looked in the case?"

"Oh, weeks, I guess. I open it now and then to clean and polish them, keep them from rusting."

"Were any missing the last time you looked?"

"No, they were all there."

"All right, Dirk. Don't suddenly decide to take off. It's time I got the law in on this thing."

"I'm not going anywhere, Patch," he said steadily.

I went up the midway to the office wagon. Tex Montana, a huge man of sixty-odd, flamboyant in his cowboy garb, boots, Stetson, and the rest, was waiting for me. The nearest Tex had ever been to either Texas or Montana was western Missouri, when his carnie played a fair date there once. I briefed him on the situation, and he agreed I should call the town fuzz.

We were in Iowa, high corn country, and I expected a hick. Consequently, I was surprised by my first look at Sheriff Ray Tomlin. He wore a conservative suit, dark tie and white shirt—all business, with no manure on his shoes. It wasn't long before he showed the usual townie wariness toward, and distrust of, carnies. Then, when he learned that the murder victim was a tattooed female member of a freak show, with a piece of tattooed skin missing . . .

I was sure I could read his thoughts: *Who cares if one carnie freak killed another? Why put myself out? Two more days and they'll be gone from my bailiwick.* Then his second thought, when I'd told him about Dirk and Vernon: *An escaped convict and a sword swallower, either one could have done it and who cares which one lands in jail?*

Naturally his first choice would be Vernon. The capture of an escaped con, a murderer as well, could gain him a headline or two—but Vernon wasn't available, so Dirk would have to do.

After May's body was taken away, and the technicians had left, Sheriff Tomlin settled down to questioning a sullen Dirk. I eased out of the Ten-in-One tent, lit a cigar and strolled the midway, deep in thought.

The midway was totally deserted now. The only light, aside from the single overhead, came from the cook tent up front. I paused in front of the House of Mirrors. I was uneasy over the second knife missing from Dirk's case. Yet, if Vernon had been on the lot, had killed May, he'd be long gone by this time.

I dropped the cigar butt into the damp shavings and ground it out under my toe. Abruptly the front of the Glass House behind me blazed with light, the clown heads on each side of the entrance opening and closing enormous, hinged mouths, idiotic, recorded laughter pouring from them. A Glass House, ours called the House of Mirrors, is a structure of complicated glass corridors through which a paying customer wanders trying to find a way out. What he thinks are doors turn out to be mirrors, and vice versa. Most carnivals have one, for even though Glass Houses are usually a losing proposition, they are as traditional as Ferris wheels and merry-go-rounds.

I squinted against the glare of light, peering into the glittering mirrors. A wanderer in the glass maze is reflected again and again and can be seen as he blunders nose-first into mirror after mirror, providing a hilarious and free spectator sport.

Now I saw, somewhere in the center of the maze, what seemed to be the figure of a man in a kneeling position, as though in prayer. If you're familiar with the maze, you can walk all the way through and out again without faltering. I'd never mastered it. I was as much without a sense of direction inside as any mark. I thought of calling out, but I knew I couldn't be heard over the insane laughter, and I didn't know where the switches were.

With a sigh I tentatively stepped inside the House of Mirrors and was immediately lost in the glass maze. I stumbled and blundered, bumping my nose against solid glass until it began to throb like a sore tooth, and all the while I could see the crouching figure, now behind me, now ahead, never any closer. All the while, the canned laughter issuing from the speakers hidden in the hinged clown mouths assailed my ears until I wanted to scream.

After an eternity I made the right choice and stood beside the kneeling figure. I squatted and touched a finger to the back of the neck. Cold as ice. At the pressure of my finger the figure slowly toppled, falling on its side. It was Vernon Raines, his darkly handsome face contorted in death.

I had found Dirk's other missing knife.

Both of Vernon's hands were wrapped tightly around the knife handle, which was driven to the hilt just below the rib cage. Blood was thick and dark on the floor. From the position in which he'd been kneeling, he could have fallen on the knife, or committed suicide. He was in the typical hara-kiri position. Except Vernon wasn't Oriental, and I wouldn't have thought . . .

I frisked him quickly. I didn't find the strip of skin from May's back. I went through his pockets a second time, looking for signs of dried blood and finding none.

Without warning the canned laughter shut off. I jumped to my feet, shocked by a sudden silence that was almost painful.

Then a voice came over the loudspeakers. "Patch, is that you in there? We can see you . . ."

I couldn't see out, of course. I nodded several times.

"All right, stay there. We'll be right in." It was Bernie's voice.

It took them only a few minutes to reach me—Bernie, Sheriff Tomlin, and two of his men. There wasn't room enough for all of us in the small corridor formed by the mirrors, and the two deputies were stacked up around the turn. Their images were repeated endlessly in the mirrors, and I had the smothering sensation of being surrounded.

Bernie said, "We heard the laughter and wondered . . ." He stopped, staring at the body. "It's Vernon. Is he dead?"

"He's dead."

Sheriff Tomlin said alertly, "Vernon Raines? The escaped convict?"

I nodded. "None other, Sheriff."

"That seems to be it then," the sheriff said with satisfaction. "He came back, killed the woman, then killed himself."

I started to comment, then changed my mind and said instead, "It's too close in here. Let's go outside."

The sheriff turned to one of his men and told him to get the medical examiner back. The man started out and crashed face-on into a mirror. He retreated, cursing and rubbing his nose. Bernie took the lead and guided us out. I drew a grateful gulp of fresh air and busied myself lighting a cigar.

I felt the sheriff's hard stare. "Like I said inside, that seems to wrap it up."

I sighed heavily. "It leaves a lot of questions that way, Sheriff."

"Such as?"

"Such as, why did he kill May?"

"Jealousy. She was playing around with this other guy, this knife swallower."

"That was long over, as I understand it. And it was long over with Vernon and May, too. At least as far as she was concerned. It was over when she learned Vernon was a bank robber."

"But she was still keeping in touch with him. Otherwise how did he know where to find her so quickly, the way you carnies jump from town to town, week after week?"

"That's easy. The carnie bible."

He stared. "The carnie bible?"

"The magazine, *Amusement Business*. It lists show dates and locations of all carnivals. All carnies read it religiously, even one in prison like Vernon."

The sheriff subsided, grumbling.

I went on, "Why did Vernon kill himself, *if* he did, in about the hardest way possible?"

"How should I know? Remorse, any number of reasons."

"And what happened to the piece of skin from May's back?"

"I don't think anybody can answer that one." He snorted laughter. "Maybe one of your carnie freaks is a cannibal."

It wasn't at all funny, but I let it pass. "I think I know what happened to it."

"Do you, now? Well, I'd be right interested in hearing." His slow voice dropped sarcasm.

"That square of skin is some sort of map showing where Vernon hid the loot from the Midfork bank holdup. He was going to prison for the rest of his life, but he wanted a permanent map showing where the loot was hidden in case he ever managed to escape."

"So? He came back and killed her for it."

"He doesn't have it on him. I happened to look for the thing."

"What right did you . . . All right, you didn't find it. So?"

"So, somebody, knowing Vernon had escaped and was on his way here for May and the map, killed May, peeled the skin off, then waylaid Vernon and killed him as well. That's why *two* knives were taken from Dirk's case instead of one. Two murders were planned all along. Now the murderer has a clear path to the hundred grand."

"*Who's* got a clear path? Do you know?"

"I think so, yeah. Bernie?"

Bernie, standing beside me and silent all the while, jumped. "Yes, Patch. What is it?"

"What did you do with the tattoo, Bernie?"

"Me . . . ? You're out of your mind, Patch!"

"Not the way I've got it figured." I dropped the cigar butt and ground it out. "You told me you didn't know what tattoo was missing. I don't believe that. You'd know if a freak in the Ten-in-One had so much as a hangnail. And with May right under your nose day after day . . . You knew, Bernie. You may not have known what it meant at first, but you found out. Either May told you or you guessed. It's possible May knew what the tattoo meant and told you. She was conscientious that way and figured she could trust you. You were biding your time, probably until we played Midfork this year, but suddenly you couldn't wait any longer. With Vernon out of the pen and on his way here, you had to act . . ."

One thing about Sheriff Tomlin, his reflexes were good. As Bernie broke away at a dead run, the sheriff tackled him and brought him down not twenty yards away.

They found the tattoo rolled up in Bernie's tobacco pouch, with tobacco shreds stuck to it.

The sheriff showed me the tattoo. At first glance it appeared to be a beautifully detailed pastoral scene, a clutch of farm buildings, a grove of trees and a pasture with grazing animals. Closer inspection disclosed faint figures etched in. They could only be longitude and latitude markings. Beside one tiny tree was an x, so small as to be almost invisible to the naked eye. I returned it to Sheriff Tomlin. "I hope you find the loot."

"We'll find it, never fear," he said grimly.

I stood and watched them take a stubbornly silent Bernie away, the deputies towing him along between them up the deserted midway. It appeared everyone was bedded down now, but I knew this wasn't true. They were watching from various points. One carnie—I doubted I would ever know which one—had turned on the lights in the House of Mirrors so I would find Vernon's body. They would never have told the fuzz, but they wanted me to know.

Now, as the sounds of the siren died away in the distance, the midway was silent and peaceful, at long last buttoned up for the night. I sighed and started up the midway to the office wagon. I knew Tex Montana would be waiting for my report.

I learned later that Bernie finally confessed to both murders and was convicted.

When we played the Midfork Fair a few weeks later, I asked around. They had found the bank loot buried at the base of a tree on a farm a few miles outside of town, exactly where the tattoo had indicated.

PATRICIA MATTHEWS

The Fall of Dr. Scourby

Ms. Gladys Grumly, stout thighs pistoning powerfully, left hand sliding along the banister, purposefully pounded her way up the cement stairs of the Administration Building Tower. Her eyes fixed straight ahead, she climbed close to the left side of the stairs. She was more than a little afraid of heights, and if she walked to the right, the terrifying vortex formed by the spiral staircase seemed to suck her eyes downward, until her mind crashed against the cold, hard square of concrete at the bottom.

Breathing deeply—good for the lungs—she approached the landing of the seventh floor. As she paused a moment to get her breath, she became aware of a sound from above her. She raised her eyes to a blur of motion. Before her nearsighted gaze could register what she was seeing, something plummeted past her line of vision. It took a moment for her mind to identify the "something" as a human body. As her mind registered this fact, it also registered the sound of a heavy object hitting the cement square, seven floors below.

Ms. Grumly prided herself on the fact that she was a strong, healthy woman, who had never fainted in her life. Ms. Grumly fainted now.

It was 1:15 P.M. Mark Cassidy, chief investigator for the campus police at State University, looked at the report in front of him and sighed wearily. He pulled out his desk drawer and rummaged for cigarettes, before he remembered that he had quit the nasty habit. He slammed the drawer shut, and took a roll of candy out of his pocket. Putting one of the candies in his mouth, he pulled the report toward him: a motorcycle stolen from Lot B; obscene words on the walls of the men's room in the Science Building; a doodle-dasher in the library, and some minor vandalism at the Martin Hall escalator—a usual day's activities.

He became conscious of the sharp sting of heartburn in the pit of his stomach. He should not have had the enchiladas at the cafeteria; or maybe, as his doctor had suggested, it was the job. There were certainly enough aggravations to ruin a man's digestion.

The door to his office slammed back loudly, and he looked up as Sue Collins, the desk clerk, burst in and then stood white-faced in his doorway, as if unable to go farther. She opened her mouth, but it was a moment before the words came out.

"Mr. Cassidy! Mr. Cassidy! Someone has . . . Someone is . . ."

Cassidy got up from his desk quickly and pushed past the girl, who now seemed incapable of movement as well as coherent speech.

As he entered the other room, he saw the rest of the staff hovering over and around a stout, pained-looking woman, who seemed familiar to him.

Sergeant Walters stepped forward. "This is Miss Grumly, Mark. She works in Accounting. She was returning from lunch, going up the tower stairs, when she saw a man fall from the eighth-floor landing."

Cassidy felt his gut tighten. He was already moving toward the door, giving orders. "Walters, get a blanket and come with me. Sue, you and Margaret stay with Miss Grumly. Don't let her leave until I talk with her."

Cassidy had seen more than a few dead bodies in his time, but that had been a few years back. Campus police work had left him strangely unprepared for the sight of this one. With something of an effort, he made himself look at the body professionally. The body was male, Caucasian, with thinning brown hair worn just past collar length, and bushy sideburns. He was wearing cream-colored pants, a white shirt with Mexican-designed trim, brown sandals and red socks. The man had landed on his back, and Cassidy recognized Dr. Daniel Scourby, head of the Drama Department.

Suddenly Cassidy became conscious that a vast, cumulative whisper was coming down from above him, like the susurration in a giant seashell. Looking up, he could see tier upon tier of white faces peering over the banisters of the stairway as it coiled up to the eighth floor.

"Put the blanket over him," he said to Walters. The other man lifted the blanket and gingerly placed it over the body.

Lt. Leo Moreno, of Homicide, sat on the edge of Cassidy's desk as if he belonged there. He was a stocky man, with a smooth, tanned face, and sharp, blue eyes. "Hi, Cassidy. Your chief tells me that you've got a little trouble here. I understand that one of your profs took a dive from the eighth floor of the stairwell."

Cassidy nodded. "That's about it."

"Jumped, fell, or pushed?"

Cassidy sighed. "I don't know yet, Leo. I was just going to talk to the only witness."

"Want us to take over? You know, this is a little different than somebody ripping off a bicycle, or demonstrating in the dean's office."

Cassidy tried to keep his voice calm. "I know that, Leo. After all, I do have some experience with this type of thing. You never seem to remember, but I spent ten years on a city police force."

"Yeah. I do keep forgetting that. Well, suit yourself. But if you find you can't handle it, don't forget to give us a call. We're pretty busy right now, but we can always find time to help out a brother officer."

Cassidy watched Moreno leave the room. He sure had the needle out. Cassidy knew that the city police had a patronizing view of the campus force. There *had* been a time when campus police were little more than traffic cops and guards, but now they had a real force, and men with good backgrounds in law enforcement who were authorized to handle any crime that occurred on campus, and Cassidy, as investigator, was involved in almost all of them.

Cassidy hesitated a moment. He was anxious to talk to the witness, Gladys Grumly, but maybe he should talk to his chief first.

Chief Baker was a big man, heavy-shouldered and crag-faced. He looked up from his desk as Cassidy entered the room.

"Oh, hello, Cassidy. I heard that you've been talking to Moreno. That son-of-a-gun is like a genie, the way he pops up. I still don't know how he found out about this thing so fast."

"The lieutenant has good connections," Cassidy said, "but listen, I want first crack at this. I know this case is a little bigger than the ones that usually come up on campus, and I know Homicide will start putting pressure on us if the case isn't tied up quickly, but first give me a couple of days on my own. All right?"

Baker looked at him and shrugged. "All right, Cassidy. You're a good man. Take your best shot."

Cassidy left his office to question Ms. Grumly.

She was determined to be a good witness. Cassidy could tell by the determined look in her eye, and the controlled set of her face. Only a slight tic in her right eyelid, and the pulse throbbing in her sturdy throat, indicated her nervousness.

Cassidy leaned toward her, trying for the right blend of respect and solicitude. "Now, Miss Grumly, I know it's difficult for you to talk about what has happened, but—"

"*Ms.* Grumly, if you please, Mr. Cassidy." Ms. Grumly's tone was cool, and so were her eyes.

"Of course," Cassidy said smoothly. "Ms. Grumly. Now, we need your help. As the only witness, your testimony is very important."

Ms. Grumly's stern expression softened a bit.

"I will do my duty," she said.

"Good. Now, tell me just what you saw and heard before Dr. Scourby fell."

"I was just coming to the seventh-floor landing. I stopped for a moment to rest, and as I stopped, I heard this funny sound above me."

"A funny sound? Just what kind of a sound was it?"

A frown creased Ms. Grumly's ample forehead. "Why, just a sound, a noise."

"Think about it. What was it like?"

Ms. Grumly's gaze turned inward. "Well, it sounded a little like a cough, or a grunt. I'm sorry to be so vague, but it was not a sound I am accustomed to hearing."

"And after you heard the sound?"

"I looked up to see where it came from. I saw something on the eighth-floor landing; a movement."

"A movement?"

Ms. Grumly's wide cheeks pinked. "I don't see very well without my glasses, Mr. Cassidy. All I could see was what appeared to be two people moving about on the landing, and as I looked up, one of them went over the railing."

Her face went pale at the memory, and for an instant she lost her composure. Cassidy realized he could get nothing more from her at the moment.

"Thank you, Ms. Grumly. You've been a big help. If you remember anything else, about the sound you heard, for instance, let me know at once, will you?"

She nodded, and the color began to come back into her face.

"Oh, there is one thing more. How did you happen to be using the stairs instead of the elevator?"

She looked at him with great disdain. "I always take the stairs. Exercise! If more people around here used the stairs, and their legs, they'd be in much better condition."

Not Scourby, Cassidy thought wryly, and she must have read his mind, because her face flushed a dark and unbecoming red.

Dr. Daniel Scourby, Cassidy soon discovered, had not been the best-liked member of the drama faculty. A flamboyant and volatile man, long on temperament, and short on good manners, he managed to alienate most of his colleagues and a good number of his students with his egotism and cruelty. Despite these traits, however, he had been quite a man with the ladies, and was well known on campus for his numerous love affairs.

Cassidy learned that Dr. Scourby had been in the accounting office on the eighth floor shortly before his death. He had gone there to pick up a travel check. The check had not been ready, and with his usual patience and charm, he had caused a scene. His visit to the accounting office was well remembered. Elsie Smith, who had waited on him and borne the brunt of his anger, verified that he left the office at 1:00 P.M. She remembered the time, because he had kept her fifteen minutes past her lunch break.

Ms. Grumly had seen Scourby fall at about 1:10 P.M. Cassidy was unable to turn up anyone who had seen Scourby during those last ten minutes. Too, Cassidy wondered why Scourby had taken the stairs. He thought about the eighth-floor landing. He had found nothing there to help him, no physical clues that might show him what had happened there. The railing was sturdy, and approximately waist-high. Scourby was not a tall man, but he was heavy-bodied and broad-shouldered. It would not be an easy job to force a man of his size and weight over the railing.

Cassidy sighed. There simply was no physical evidence to go on. On the other hand, he had more than enough suspects. Almost everyone on campus had disliked Scourby, and more than a few people actively hated the man.

Cassidy was acutely conscious of the passage of time. He could almost feel Moreno leaning over his shoulder, waiting for him to admit that he couldn't get it all together. Well, damn Moreno! He *would* get it together.

He ran his mind down the list of people who might have the best reason to hate Scourby. Cassidy had determined that Scourby had two ex-wives, but they were both remarried, and lived out of state. There were no children, and evidently no other living relatives. That pretty much ruled out his family.

From what Cassidy had been able to learn, the man had few friends outside of the campus community. Like many academicians, the main thrust of his life seemed to revolve around the campus. Despite his general unpopularity, he was very active in the life of the university in general, and in his own department in particular.

Since the incident had occurred on campus, it seemed logical to Cassidy that whoever had been with Scourby on that landing was also from the campus. It also seemed logical that the most likely suspects were in Scourby's own department: Dr. Linus Martin, the man whom Scourby had climbed over in his race for the chairmanship of the department; Ben Aldon, student, actor, who had publicly stated that he hated Scourby's guts because of a coed's suicide and would like to see him hanged from a certain portion of his anatomy; Melissa Jackson, student, actress, part-time student assistant. It was general knowledge that she'd had an affair with Scourby. It had ended badly, and she had taken it hard. There must be others, too, who hated Scourby, but whose reasons were not public knowledge.

Cassidy sat in the fifth row of the darkened theater, his eyes fixed on the two young people on stage. The young man was tall, athletic-looking, and ruggedly handsome. The girl was also tall, and very beautiful.

Ben Aldon and Melissa Jackson were starring in the Drama Department production of *Picnic*, which was being directed by Linus Martin. The kids were good.

A slight figure entered stage right. Cassidy knew this was Jimmie Breen, Scourby's girl Friday in the drama office. Cassidy had not been able to find out how she felt about Scourby. From all accounts, she did her job well, and stood up under Scourby's little attacks of sadism with commendable aplomb. She was an excellent actress. Cassidy, who usually attended all of the drama productions with his girlfriend Maryann, had seen her in many other productions. She was a thin, childlike girl, with pale androgynous features.

Thinking of the other productions he had attended made Cassidy think of Maryann. If Scourby hadn't gotten himself killed, Cassidy would be with her right now, in her comfortable apartment, having a nice cold bourbon, and a good warm meal, and a little comfort, instead of here, in a stuffy theater, in the dark.

Ben Aldon was his first target during a break. Aldon's young face was flushed, and his eyes were hot.

"Yes!" he said. "I hated Scourby, and I had good reason. Cindy Purdom was one sweet kid, before he got his hands on her. Scourby messed up her mind with pot and fast talk. Told her he would make her a big star. Of course I resented his taking her away from me, but that wasn't the reason I hated him. I hated him because when he had used her, he threw her out. She was never the same after that. It was only a month later that she took the pills. Yeah, I felt like wasting him, but I didn't, and I have an alibi. I was with Melissa. Neither of us has classes on Tuesday afternoons, and we were over at her pad going over our lines until about 3:00 P.M."

Cassidy looked at him mildly. "I don't suppose you have any other witnesses. Someone at the apartment house who saw you together?"

Aldon looked back at him sullenly, but his eyes were uneasy.

"No, at least I don't think so. You check it out. You're the cop!"

"I will, son, I will."

Aldon muttered something under his breath and moved away. Cassidy sighed. If the regular police got little respect from today's youth, a campus policeman got less.

Melissa Jackson corroborated Aldon's story. She admitted that she still hated Scourby, and was glad that he was dead, but she had been with Ben Aldon at the time, and under the circumstances he had described.

Cassidy looked at her appraisingly. She was a big girl; tall, lithe, and strong. Was she strong enough to have pushed Scourby over the stair railing?

After talking to Melissa, Cassidy talked with Dr. Linus Martin, a tall, narrow-shouldered man, with pale, defenseless-looking eyes. He rubbed at them wearily as he talked to Cassidy.

"Sure, I hated Scourby. I and several dozen other people. But kill him? He's done enough to me without my letting him drive me to murder. I was in my office from 12:00 noon until 1:30 P.M. Jimmie Breen, the drama secretary, can verify that. We've been having some rather late rehearsals, and I was bushed."

Cassidy talked last with Jimmie Breen. Her large, waif's eyes looked much too big for her narrow little face.

"Yes, Dr. Martin was in his office from 12:00 noon until about 1:00 P.M. and I was in the office until 2:00 P.M. No, I don't think anyone else saw me. At least I didn't see anyone myself. It was pretty quiet around here during the middle of the day."

Cassidy studied her child's face. "How did you feel toward Dr. Scourby, Jimmie?"

She lowered her eyelids, but her face did not change expression.

"Like everyone else, I suppose. He wasn't a very likable man. He was hard to work for; a real male chauvinist. Then, after what he did to Cindy . . . We were roommates, you know, Cindy and I. After what happened to her, I could never feel friendly toward him."

"Why did you stay in this job?" Cassidy asked gently.

She shrugged her narrow shoulders. "I have to work to get through college. This job is convenient, being right here in the department. I could put up with Scourby. I just didn't let him get to me."

Cassidy resisted a desire to pat her shoulder. As he left, he was thinking that Scourby had certainly gotten to someone, and that someone had in turn, really gotten to him.

Cassidy returned to the office. Only young Thompson was there; the rest of the night shift were out making rounds. Cassidy waved a weary greeting to Thompson, and went into his inner office.

He picked up the coffeepot and shook it. There was some left, but it smelled strong and stale. He decided that, at the very least, he deserved some fresh coffee. He cleaned the pot and filled it with fresh water. It had been a long day, and his mind was growing sluggish with fatigue.

The faces of the people to whom he had talked kept passing before his mind's eye like the faces in a police lineup. Any one of them had sufficient motive, and none of them had an ironclad alibi. If only Ms. Grumly had been wearing her glasses . . . If only she could better describe that strange sound heard on the landing above her . . .

The thought of that sound tantalized Cassidy. He could do nothing now about Ms. Grumly's nearsightedness, but if he could discover what the sound was, or who had made it, he might be on his way to Scourby's murderer.

He unwrapped the sandwich he had purchased from the vending machine, and poured a cup of the fresh coffee. He really ought to relax for a moment. His mind was going over the same things again and again.

He reached over and turned on the small television set that he kept on the corner of his desk.

There wasn't anything decent on. It was summer, and all that was playing, even during prime time, was reruns. He switched through an ancient variety show, an even older mystery, a Japanese Western, with lots of violence and bad dubbing, and a space opera. He moved his fingers to turn off the set, then switched around the dial once again as he suddenly realized what he had just seen and heard. He watched the program he had turned to for several minutes, tapping his fingers thoughtfully on the arm of his chair. Again he turned off the set. He had a plan.

The Personnel Office was closed, but Cassidy simply let himself in. He knew where the faculty records were kept, and it did not take him long to locate Dr. Linus Martin's file. He read the material thoroughly, replaced the file, then called the Records Office.

Mrs. McIntosh, the assistant registrar, was none too happy when Cassidy arrived at her office a short time later.

"You just caught me," she snapped. "I was about to go home. Been working late every night. This quarter system is murder."

"I won't be long," Cassidy soothed. "I need to see the schedules of classes for three students: Ben Aldon, Jimmie Breen, and Melissa Jackson."

Mrs. McIntosh grumbled, but she brought the records quickly enough, and sat watching Cassidy as he went over each of them carefully.

When he was finished, he smiled at her. "Thanks."

"Well, I hope that you found what you were looking for."

He smiled again. "I think maybe I did."

He waited until Mrs. McIntosh had locked the office, then left the Administration Building and headed back toward the theater.

He had looked at four sets of records, including Dr. Martin's. Only one of them had the information for which he had been looking. Alone, it didn't mean a thing. Just a hunch, but maybe, just maybe, he could use that hunch as leverage.

The light was still on in the theater, and when he went inside, he saw that rehearsals were still going on. Both Ben Aldon and Melissa looked tired, and Linus Martin, sitting in the back of the theater, looked up wearily as Cassidy came in.

"Almost through," he said softly. "Along about this stage of the game, you begin wondering how it will ever come together, but it does. It does. Do you want to ask more questions? If you do, I warn you that we are all too tired to make sense."

Cassidy shook his head. "No more questions. At least not tonight. I'm just going to nose around a little."

Martin nodded tiredly, and slumped back into his seat. On stage, the two young people had finished their scene. Cassidy walked through the door at the side of the stage, and made his way over the ropes and props to the back.

Jimmie Breen was there, busily painting a portion of a picket fence. She turned at the sound of Cassidy's footsteps.

"You're working late tonight, Jimmie."

She looked up at him seriously. "So are you, Mr. Cassidy. But I guess there's no law against that, for either of us."

"None at all. Jimmie, I wonder if you would come with me to Dr. Scourby's office?"

She looked at him warily.

"Why?"

"I'll tell you when we get there."

She put down the paintbrush, wiped her hands on her jeans, and turned toward him. Cassidy turned his back to her and began leading the way toward Scourby's office. When he had gone about ten feet, he whirled, as quickly as he could, raised his arm, and lunged toward the girl.

He had a vision of round, startled eyes, a white face, and then a good picture of the ceiling, as he landed hard on his back, dazed but intact.

He could hear the sound of running footsteps, and the sound of the girl's ragged breathing, but before that, he had heard something else—the sound for which he had been listening; a funny sound, like a cough, or a grunt, or a judo *kiai*; the sound made as part of a judo move . . .

It was hard to hate her for it, Cassidy decided. Sitting there in the chair in his office, she looked more like a war orphan than a murderess.

"How did you know it was me?" she asked softly.

"I didn't know for sure. We have a witness who heard a strange sound, a sound that could have been a *kiai*. I checked Dr. Martin's, Melissa's, Ben's and your records. Yours were the only ones that showed any experience in the martial arts—two years of judo classes."

She shook her head. "I didn't mean to do it. I mean, I didn't plan it. After Cindy, I promised myself that I would get even with him some way. But I didn't plan it. It just happened."

She looked up, her dark eyes wide. Her hands fumbled in her lap like two lost things.

"Cindy and I were . . . We were very close. He just the same as killed her, you know."

Cassidy said softly, "What happened? What happened today, Jimmie?"

She swallowed, and made an attempt to focus on his questions. "He asked me to call about his travel check. Accounting said that it wasn't ready. He gave me a bad time about that, as if it were my fault. He said he was going over there himself, and straighten things out.

"After he left, I found the papers on his desk. He hadn't submitted them, and that's why the check wasn't ready. I thought I had better get them over to the accounting office before he tore the place apart . . ."

"So you left the office, and went to the Administration Building."

"Yes. I was in a hurry, so I went around back of the cafeteria. I didn't meet anyone I recognized. I took the elevator up to the eighth floor, but I was too late. Dr. Scourby was already coming out of the accounting office. He started swearing at me, and suddenly I just couldn't handle it. I ran for the stairs, but he followed me. I ran down the steps to the first landing and turned. He was coming down the steps toward me. All I could think of was how much I hated him. He kept on coming toward me and I . . ."

In one fluid motion, she rose from the chair and twisted her upper body as she lifted her right shoulder. Cassidy had a vivid mental picture of Scourby pitching over her shoulder into the stairwell.

There was a long silence, broken finally by the sound of a strident, feminine voice in the outer office, then the sound of Walters' baritone attempting to override it.

Walters opened the door and stuck his head in. "It's Ms. Grumly, Cassidy. She says she's got to talk to you."

Cassidy looked at Jimmie. Then he reached over and patted her shoulder.

In the outer office, Ms. Grumly stood, pink-cheeked and glowing with self-satisfaction.

"I told him that you said to contact you if I thought of anything else, and I have," she said triumphantly. "That sound, the sound I heard on the landing? Well, tonight, I was watching an old movie on television . . ."

Cassidy sighed wearily as his stomach twinged painfully.

STEPHEN WASYLYK

The Loose End

The tall, baggy-suited, black-haired kid carrying the lightweight briefcase was making too many trips in the automatic elevators to be up to anything legitimate, especially since he was Nipsy Turko, a small-time thief with a long record of losing.

The only person in a position to notice or pay much attention was me, Mark Stedd, a one-armed ex-detective operating a newsstand in the lobby of the building where the elevators were located, and to tell the truth I don't know why I bothered.

The only reason I was inhabiting that cramped hole behind the newsstand was as a personal favor to Manny, an old friend who at the moment was living it up in Florida. Manny's request had been heartily seconded as good rehabilitation by the doctors' who had removed what remained of my left arm after the psycho with the shotgun had ripped it to shreds three months before.

I moved out from the cramped hole behind the newsstand to keep an eye on the jack-in-the-box movements of Nipsy. That hole was tailored to fit Manny, six inches shorter and fifty pounds lighter than I, even without a left arm, and I was happy to get out of it.

At the lobby doors I glanced at my watch. Within five minutes the building would begin to empty for lunch and Nipsy could get lost in the crowd. At the other end of the empty lobby glass doors revealed the writing counters of the bank on the first floor of the adjacent building. Friend Nipsy suddenly barged out of an elevator, walked through to the bank, stopped at one of the writing counters, and dropped his briefcase at his feet. Then the lunch crowd hit and the lobby filled rapidly.

I began to push my way forward, almost reaching the doors, when a short, older type with a narrow face hurried through the bank, stopped alongside the kid, busied himself for a moment, then took the kid's briefcase, while the kid picked up the one Narrow Face had brought. Narrow Face, another loser in Nipsy's class named Slow Harry Fisher, went out the far bank door in a hurry, and the kid headed back through the glass doors, angling for the nearest elevator. I caught his eye above the crowd and Nipsy, stony-faced, paused for a moment, then stepped into the elevator, pushed a button, and the doors slammed in my face.

Now I heard the wailing of police sirens, which sighed to a halt outside the bank. I reached out and caught the nearest arm. An attractive dark-haired woman, on her way to lunch, turned, looked at me with narrowed eyes.

"Take it easy." I grinned at her. "I'd like you to go out there and bring back a policeman, any policeman. Will you do it?"

I'd always gotten along pretty well with women and this one turned out to be no exception. Her face softened, she smiled, nodded, and headed out through the bank, surprising me because local citizens weren't noted for their willingness to become involved in police business.

She brought back one of the older patrolmen, a sensible type named Tompkins.

"Mark," he said, "glad to see you up and around."

I nodded at the crowd outside the bank. "What goes?"

"Someone took the jewelry store next door."

"I think I saw your man switch briefcases. Even if you pick him up, I don't think you'll find the jewels on him. They're somewhere upstairs with a kid named Nipsy Turko."

"You sure?"

"I'm not sure of anything. I'm telling you what I saw and think. Who's in charge?"

Tompkins shrugged. "Barnes, probably. Your friend here collared me before I had a chance to find out."

"Then let's get Barnes in here and let him worry about it."

Tompkins moved. "I'll get him."

I shook my head. "No, thanks. Nipsy is big enough to handle a one-arm like me if he comes down while you're gone. My battling days are over. I'd rather you took the bank end of the lobby while I stay here. We'll let our beautiful friend get Barnes." I turned to the woman. "What's your name, beautiful friend?"

"Diane Waverly."

"Look, Miss Waverly, will you go to the jewelry store, find the officer in charge, tell him we have some information concerning the robbery, and bring him in here?"

She looked at me coolly. "Shall I lead him by the nose or the hand?"

I watched her walk away and grinned at Tompkins. "If I were Barnes, I'd follow her just to follow her."

Tompkins grinned back. "Why do you think I came?"

We separated and waited. The lobby was still crowded and I hoped Nipsy wouldn't show. It would be no big chore for him to come down and take off before Tompkins or I could get to him through all those people.

The woman brought Barnes more quickly than I anticipated. Cold-eyed and dapper, Barnes looked more like an advertising executive than a detective-lieutenant, but he was smart. Younger than I, he was a loner, cool and hard, and had moved up through the ranks fast, acquiring a reputation I'd always felt was a little inflated. I never did like him very much.

"Mark, you look good."

Smooth, I thought admiringly. I know how I looked after three months in that hospital, but he stands there telling me I look good and sounding as if he meant it.

"Joe," I told him, "I might have something for you here. You have a make on the guy who knocked off the store?"

He shook his head. "Small build, thin face, middle-aged; that's all I have."

"How does Slow Harry Fisher sound?"

"Slow Harry taking a jewelry store? By himself?" Barnes looked at me in amazement.

"Description fits, doesn't it?"

"Sure, but it fits a lot of other guys too."

"How many other guys come running into a bank, switch briefcases with a loser like Nipsy Turko just a minute or two after the robbery, and take off in the noonday crowd like he just welshed on a big bet?"

"You saw this?"

"Joe," I said patiently, "losing your left arm doesn't affect your eyesight. Naturally, I saw it. I also saw Nipsy take off with the briefcase, hit one of the elevators here, and disappear upstairs. So far as I know he's still up there, unless he knows a way out that doesn't come through this lobby, and all this after Nipsy spent a half hour riding each elevator in the building before he met Slow Harry."

"Slow Harry and Nipsy, there's a combination for you. They'd be in over their heads taking a corner candy store."

"How much did they get?"

"Maybe about two hundred grand in cut and uncut stones, nothing mounted."

"No sense standing here gabbing about it. You going to look for Nipsy?"

"I guess I'll have to. I'll put an all-points out on Slow Harry, too. If you saw it, you saw it, although I still don't believe it."

In no time at all there was a uniform at each entrance, one in each elevator, and the superintendent was explaining the building to Barnes.

It was also no time at all before they brought Nipsy down. The trouble was, Nipsy no longer carried the briefcase. Barnes looked at me and I nodded, laughing to myself. Since Nipsy no longer had the briefcase, he'd passed it off or stashed it somewhere. Now Barnes had to go look for it.

Standing alongside the newsstand, my beautiful friend asked, "What's going on? As official messenger, don't you think I'm entitled to know?"

I explained the situation. "Just putting two and two together," I nodded toward Barnes, "it appears we've come up with zero."

Two policeman led Nipsy away as Barnes came up. "Well, he knows his constitutional rights. Not saying a word. I'm booking him on the basis of what you saw but unless we find that briefcase we don't have a thing."

"Then find the briefcase."

His eyebrows went up. "You're a real bundle of joy. Fourteen floors, who knows how many closets, rooms, rest rooms, offices and people. It will take us all afternoon."

I grinned. "I'll make a deal with you. For ten percent of the take, I'll search the building for you. Payable only if I find it, of course. I tell you the kid took the briefcase up. It hasn't come down yet."

Barnes shook his head. "I still don't get it. Two losers like Nipsy Turko and Slow Harry Fisher, who couldn't plan their way out of a subway concourse even by reading the signs, coming up with something like this. Ordinarily, if either got his hands on two hundred grand worth of anything, he'd be moving in a straight line so fast he'd be a blur. But not this time. They take it slow and easy like a couple of pros. One hits the store during the noonday rush, passes the stuff to the other, who ditches it so that if they get picked up they're both clean. Someone set this up for them. The question is who? Someone from this building?"

"I doubt it," I said. "Nothing here except corporation offices, lawyers, advertising agencies, insurance companies, that sort of thing. I'd guess it would be someone from outside. This is a public building. Anyone can walk in. The only thing you can do is find the briefcase before he does."

Barnes scratched his ear and shrugged. "Well, I don't have any better ideas. Might as well follow yours." He lined up the super and a half-dozen men and gave them their instructions. With a man at each end of the lobby, no briefcase would leave that building without being examined.

I remembered Diane. "If you were on your way to lunch, I'm sorry I held you up. What's your boss going to say? Anything I can do to help?"

She half-smiled. "I won't have any trouble. My boss is away and I'm pretty much on my own. How about you? What were you going to do for lunch?"

"Never gave it a thought."

"Suppose I bring something back for you?"

"Would you mind? Just coffee will do."

"On one condition. You look tired. Get behind that counter and get some rest."

"Lady, you have a deal."

I gratefully sank onto the stool Manny kept behind the counter. Things were quieter now in the lobby, most of the building crowd back from lunch. I could imagine Barnes' men working their way down, office by office, floor by floor, looking for that briefcase.

Twelve years of my life had been spent in situations like this and now they were gone with nothing but a small pension to show for it. I smiled grimly. I could have been dead, but all I lost was an arm. I didn't intend to stop living because of it. There were plenty of ways for a one-armed man with twelve years of police experience to get along. All it would take would be a little thought and some hard work. One thing was sure, I wasn't giving up on Mark Stedd.

Glancing up, for the second time that day I saw a man taller than myself. This one, a complete contrast to Nipsy, was expensively dressed, well built and distinguished looking in a dissipated sort of way, and carrying a briefcase. He motioned imperiously at Barnes, spoke to him for a few minutes, then paced back and forth impatiently until an elevator appeared.

A soft voice said, "Here's your coffee."

I looked up at Diane. "Beautiful friend, you look more beautiful than ever."

"You didn't say how you like it, so I guessed black, one sugar."

"Someone told you," I lied. Actually I liked plenty of cream and sugar.

She smiled. "Nope. You just look the type."

I used my thumb to pry up the lid of the plastic container, rotating the cup slowly as I gradually worked it loose. I noticed she didn't offer to help and liked her for it. The lid gave with a sudden pop.

"You two have anything more to contribute?" Barnes asked, leaning against the counter.

"Not a thing, Joe. Who was the big guy with the briefcase?"

"He's the poor victim," Barnes said dryly. "The owner of the jewelry store. Going up to see his insurance company to report the loss. Doesn't waste any time, does he?"

"Looks more the type to get on the phone and yell for his insurance man to come to him, especially for a couple of hundred thousand dollars."

"They won't pay until we tell them the jewels are gone," said Barnes. "No sense rushing."

"Those jewels aren't gone," I said. "They're somewhere in this building." I grinned to myself. Why not give Barnes something to think about? "How's this for a theory? He's your outside man. He hires the two to rob the store, has the kid plant the jewels here in the building right next door, comes in supposedly to see his insurance company, files his claim and picks up the jewels at the same time. That way he doesn't lose a stone, yet collects the insurance. Be pretty safe. You'd never check his briefcase. Even if you did, you wouldn't know if any stones he had in there were the stolen ones or not. Be a nice way to get out of money trouble if he's been living it up too much, and he sure looks like he has."

Barnes looked down into the coffee cup. "You could be right, but what are you drinking? It has to be more than coffee to come up with a wild one like that."

"Okay." I grinned. "Put a man on him or don't. From now on come up with your own theories."

I finished my coffee and flipped the cup at the wastebasket behind the counter. It missed and I muttered under my breath.

As I picked it up, I turned it over in my fingers and the idea came, went, came again and I grinned. Why not? I moved past the woman, motioning Barnes to come with me, headed toward the elevators, and punched the call button. One of the elevators hit the lobby floor and opened its doors. I stepped inside, looked up, and found what I was looking for, the usual service door in the ceiling. I reached up and pushed. The door moved. With two good arms, I could have thrown the door open, grasped the edge and taken a look at the elevator roof.

Barnes looked at me strangely and whistled softly. I gave him credit for catching on quickly.

"Now you know what Nipsy was doing in the elevators," I told him. "Each of these service doors has a catch that needs a half turn with a screwdriver or coin before it can be opened. Not knowing which elevator he would get after the switch, Nipsy took no chances. He opened them all. Probably pushed the briefcase up through the door the minute the elevator was empty. Want to bet that briefcase isn't riding on the roof of one of these elevators?"

"No bet, Mark." Barnes motioned to one of the men in the lobby. "See if there is anything up there."

The detective leaped up, poked his head through the opening, then dropped down.

"Nothing but grease and dirt," he reported.

The fifth one had the briefcase resting on the roof.

"Get it down," Barnes ordered.

"No, hold it, Joe," I said slowly. "There's no hurry. Nipsy left it here for some reason. As you said, if *he* was supposed to keep the ice, he'd have kept going through the lobby. He left it here for someone. Why not play it cool and see what happens?"

Barnes stroked his chin. "Why not? With someone on the roof of the elevator and a couple of plainclothesmen at the lobby doors, I can wait to see if someone picks it up."

I grinned. "Good luck. I think I'll go sell some papers. That's what Manny's paying me for."

Diane was still waiting.

"Sold any papers for me?"

"Not even a magazine."

"Manny better not spend too much in Florida. At this rate, he'll be broke when he gets back."

She laughed. "Is the action over now?"

"All except the grand finale. Barnes will take care of it from here on."

"In that case, I'd better get back to work. I've enjoyed every minute."

"I owe you one coffee. Settle for a dinner tomorrow night?"

"Now that's what I call a fair offer. Accepted."

"Fine. I'll be waiting for you here."

I watched her swinging hips move away—regretfully. I wouldn't be here tomorrow night. By then, I'd be well on my way out of the country.

The lobby was practically empty now. I told Barnes I was going to the men's washroom on the second floor. Once there, I removed the jewels from the paper towel dispenser where Nipsy had left them for me, locked myself in one of the stalls, and carefully began to stow them in the pocketed belt I was wearing under my shirt.

Two hundred thousand dollars; little enough payment for my left arm, and quite adequate payment for the three weeks it took me to plan the operation, talk Manny into taking his vacation, and browbeat Nipsy and Slow Harry into pulling the job for a small fee. They couldn't refuse since I had plenty on both that the syndicate boys would like to know. Besides, they were safe enough. The only thing the police had on Nipsy was my testimony and I wouldn't be around; as for Slow Harry, they'd have only a simple eyewitness account and no substantial evidence.

Two hundred thousand dollars. I laughed. I owed the department this little job for passing me up for promotion twice and for sending me into that house with a rookie partner who froze instead of firing when the psycho swung the shotgun my way. If I hadn't moved fast, he would have nailed me dead center instead of catching my arm.

Too bad Barnes hadn't bought that story about the jewelry store owner. It would have been good for a big laugh. The only touchy part of the operation was when he wanted to bring the briefcase down. For a quick moment, until I talked him out of it, I regretted showing him where it was. I had expected him to figure it out himself, especially after telling him about Nipsy riding the elevators before the switch, but he didn't pick it up. As I thought, he wasn't as smart as they said he was, so I had to hurry things along.

I had long relished the thought of walking out with those jewels around my waist while somebody guarded that empty briefcase on the elevator roof and I didn't want to be cheated out of it.

Sure, I could have set it up in a half-dozen other ways a lot safer, but this was the way I wanted it—right under their noses—and Bright Boy Barnes getting the assignment was the cake's icing.

I carefully checked the belt to make sure it didn't bulge, buttoned my shirt and coat, unlocked the stall and stepped out into the washroom.

Arms folded, Barnes was leaning against a wash basin, looking at me with his cold eyes. "You going to make trouble, Mark? We don't want to hurt you. We know that arm isn't quite healed yet."

I could have killed him, not because I was caught, but because he had absolutely no business being there. With two good arms . . . But I didn't have two good arms.

"No trouble, Joe."

We walked out of the washroom and took the elevator to the lobby.

"Search him," Barnes told one of his men. He found the belt with no trouble.

"You want to know why, Mark?" he asked gently.

I nodded, although I really didn't care. All I could think of was the two hundred thousand dollars in that belt the detective was holding, the two hundred thousand that really was mine.

"The odds," Barnes said. "I figured the odds of you being here in the lobby, of seeing the kid Nipsy, of seeing the briefcase switch, of knowing where to look for the briefcase. The odds were tremendous, Mark. You always were a hard-luck cop, a good man to have around but no big brain, yet you were always one step ahead of me today and that just didn't figure. The percentages say I should have been one step ahead of you. As far as I was concerned, until the whole thing was wrapped up, you were a loose end and I never liked loose ends. Watching you was just something I had to do."

I'd given him a neatly wrapped package that any sensible man would have bought with no questions asked. All he had to do was watch that briefcase. It was the right thing to do, the logical thing to do, but here he was babbling about odds, percentages, loose ends.

I started to laugh. *Some* detective. And they passed *me* over twice for promotion.

FRANK SISK

That So-Called Laugh

Captain Thomas McFate, the man in charge, turned from the swimming pool and came back to the patio. Again he looked down at the body which lolled in a redwood lounge chair and was obviously clothed in nothing but the terrycloth robe.

A purple bubble above the right eye marked the bullet's point of entry and a little cloud of gnats behind the left ear indicated where it had come out. Big blue-winged flies were exploring the toes of the bare feet. McFate leaned over a half-filled glass of tepid liquid on the redwood table beside the chair—gin and tonic, about an hour old. An ashtray contained a self-consumed cigarette, a cylinder of gray. It was then that he noticed the powder-blue envelope protruding from the pocket of the robe.

Crumpled, as if it had been shoved into the pocket with undue force, the envelope was addressed in a somewhat immature feminine hand to *Norman Markham*. There was no further address and the flap was not sealed. Inside were several pages of powder-blue paper compactly covered with lines of writing that sometimes formed a grammatical sentence.

"Dear Norm," read McFate, "even knowing it's useless I am still fool enough to give you one more chance, a showdown, whether it's me or Michele, only I want you to look me right in the eye this time and say it with your own lips and not thru some third party. And if it's Michele as it seems to of been these last few lousy months, well then it's curtains for me, Norm, and this time I mean it so help me.

"I've suffered enough in the name of 'love' to be an old decrepit hag, Norm, and here tomorrow I'm going to be just 24 years of age if I live that long. Maybe you'll be able to check it out in the obits, my real age.

"I'm penning these words by your swimming pool, the same pool that once upon a time was going to be ours. Remember? If you can force your mind back a million years maybe you can remember and how you used to tell me I was the brightest star on your horizon. It must of been at least a million years ago because I was young enough then to believe every word you said. I was going on 22, Norm.

"Don't laugh. I know these are mere words on paper and you are 10 miles away at the studio but I half expect you to laugh as if you were right here looking over my shoulder. Like you had ESP or that Yoga thing. And I can't stand that so-called laugh again, Norm.

"Funny how I once thought that laugh was the freakiest thing, good freaky I mean, and I used to admire how you spooned it out on a bad shooting day to the actors and prop men and the sourballs behind the cameras but I was only a script girl then and I couldn't tell a mask from a pancake job, hardly. Then you gave me those three lines to say in that western pilot, the floperoo of the TV season, and I got to know the laugh better, the off-duty side, and the way it could cut a girl's heart to ribbons as easy as any knife.

"You employed it the day you pulled the rug out from under our wedding plans. Remember? Friday nite Sept. 29th, a day I won't ever forget, never. We were supposed to drive to Vegas and have dinner on the way but when I arrived at the office you were leaving with two two-suiters and a flight ticket to New York, a big-money emergency, and when I asked how long you'd be gone you said 'Long enough, Sara, just long enough,' and then you made with that so-called laugh which you might as well have throwed a glass of ice water in my face.

"What was it supposed to mean, what was I suppose to figure?

"Well, I found out later the hard way, didn't I, Norm, when you came back a week later with that so-called redhead, a third lead in a second-rate musical from summer stock, and you didn't so much as give me a buzz and probably wouldn't have looked me up at all if I hadn't taken that overdose of sleeping pills. So then you came to the hospital with flowers and a smooth story how the redhead was simply a new face for the variety pilot and I believed you hook, line and sinker until the next time . . ."

"What is it, Skipper—a love letter?"

McFate glanced at the man who had just wandered through the French windows. "I'd classify it more a suicide letter, Sergeant."

The sergeant looked at the body. "Suicide? You must be kidding, Skipper."

" . . . it was that slinky dame you picked up on location in Mexicali," McFate resumed reading. "I warned you it was she or me, this life wasn't big enough for both of us, but you came on with that laugh of yours. Even when I told you I'd kill myself you gave me the laugh again. 'Have a big sleep,' you said. Well, I almost did, Norm, and you know it. If that extra hadn't left his bike in the garage and come to get it when he did, I'd have slept forever on the front seat of the car with the gas purring out of the pipe.

"The story of my life, one imported witch after another, and this time it's a so-called Frenchy but this time I got a peculiar feeling it's a little different. This time you're talking marriage again, like you did with me long long ago, and though I don't believe you have any real 'follow-thru' in your makeup, I never the less have to confront you with the $64 question. Are you serious about Michele or not? If the answer is yes then, Norm, I am really going to kill myself and no near misses this time, no pills, no gas pipe, no razors on the wrists. This time I got a gun with bullets in it—that cute little 2-shot derringer you gave me in an ivory case, so that I could defend myself from all the wolves but you. Ha ha. And I'm going to make you a witness, Norm, like it or not, because if it's Michele instead of me I'm going to stand right in front of you and pull the trigger so that you'll remember this moment the rest of your life, what you done to an honest girl whose worst fault was loving you. And I don't think you will laugh this off in a hurry, Norm, wait and see. Always your Sara."

"If it's suicide, Skipper," the sergeant was saying, "where the hell's the gun?"

McFate put the letter in his pocket. "A girl named Sara took it with her, one of the deceased's girlfriends."

"You mean this guy Markham shot himself and some girlfriend swipes the gun?"

"Not exactly, Sergeant. The girl intended to shoot herself but Markham laughed at her. Notice there's still a slight smile of sarcasm on the face."

MARGARET B. MARON

A Very Special Talent

"**B**ut he used to hit me," Angela explained, rubbing her shoulder in memory of past bruises. "What else could I do?"

"You could have divorced him," I said firmly.

"He wouldn't let me. You know what the grounds for divorce were in this state then. Don't you care that he beat me?"

Of course it enraged me that that brute had hit my lovely, fragile-looking wife, even if it had been before I'd met her. "Nevertheless," I said, "it's the principle of the thing. It just isn't done."

"It was his own fault," she insisted. "I told him it was dangerous to have the radio that close to the bathtub when he'd been drinking, but that was like waving a red flag at a bull. He would have done it then or died."

She giggled suddenly, remembering that he had, indeed, died.

I was appalled. What does a man do when, after seven blissful years of marriage and two lovely children, he discovers that his adorable little fluff of a wife is a cold-blooded murderess who goes around killing people who aren't nice to her?

"I am *not* a cold-blooded murderess," Angela flared indignantly, "and I would never, *never* kill anyone who wasn't nasty to a whole lot of other people, too."

At this point the back screen door banged and Sandy, my five-year-old replica right down to a cowlick of red hair and a faceful of freckles, burst into the room and angrily demanded, "What's the matter with you guys? Can't you hear Matt crying? Georgie hit him and he's all bloody!"

Angela whirled and followed Sandy from the room at a trot, with me just behind them.

Four-year-old Matt sat sobbing on the back doorstep. Blood trickled from a split on his lower lip onto his white T-shirt while Sandy's best friend, Chris Coffey, awkwardly patted his shoulder.

One of the things I love about Angela is her absolute cool whenever one of the boys is hurt. I tend to panic at the sight of their blood, but she remains calm and utterly soothing.

She swooped Matt up in her arms, assessed the damage and cheerfully assured him that he wouldn't need stitches. In the kitchen, she applied a cold cloth to his swollen lip and soon had him tentatively smiling again.

The screen door banged again and Jill Coffey, our next-door neighbor and Angela's closest friend, came charging in. "That Georgie! I saw it all! Matt hadn't done a thing to him and Georgie just hauled off and socked him!"

"Yeah, Dad," Sandy chimed in. "He won't let us swing, and it's our jungle vine. Chris and me, we built it."

Matt started to cry again, Jill raged on, Angela began to shoot sparks, and Sandy's shrill indignation pierced the chaotic din.

"Hold it!" I shouted. "One at a time."

With many interruptions, a coherent story finally emerged.

When our development was built, the creek which used to cut through our back yards had been diverted, leaving an eight-foot gully overhung with huge old willows which the developers had mercifully spared. With so much of the area bulldozed into sterility, the gully lured kids from blocks around.

Depending on the degree of danger, various stretches of it attracted different age groups: the pre-adolescents usually congregated a block away, where the banks were somewhat steeper and the old creek rocks larger and more jagged. In the section between our house and the Coffeys', the bank was more of a gentle grassy slope and there were fewer rocks, so the pre-school set usually played there.

It seemed that Sandy and his cronies had tied a clothesline rope to one of the overhanging willow branches and had been playing Tarzan, swinging out over the gully as if on jungle vines, experiencing a thrill of danger more imaginary than real. Then Georgie Watson had come along and, as usual, destroyed their fun by taking over the rope swing and hitting Matt.

An overweight nine-year-old, Georgie was a classic neighborhood bully, afraid of boys his own age and a terror to everyone under six. No neighborhood gathering was complete without a twenty-minute discussion of Georgie's latest bit of maliciousness and a psychological dissection of his motives which usually ended with, "Well, what can you expect, with parents like that?"

I suppose every suburban neighborhood has its one obnoxious family; it seems to be written into the building code. At any rate, the Watsons were ours: loud, vulgar, self-righteous, and completely heedless of anyone else's rights and desires.

They gave boisterous mid-week parties which broke up noisily at one in the morning, or they would come roaring home at two from a Saturday night on the town and Mr. Watson would lean on the horn to bring the baby-sitter out.

After such a riotous night, you'd think the man would have the decency to sleep in on Sunday morning nursing a king-size hangover, but no. There he'd be, seven o'clock the next morning, cranking what must be the world's noisiest lawn mower and carrying on a shouted conversation with Mrs. Watson in the upstairs bedroom.

Mrs. Watson was just as bad. Georgie had been born after they had given up all hope of having children and she doted on him. Though quick enough to complain when any boy Georgie's age or older picked on him, she was completely blind to his faults.

If confronted by an angry parent and bleeding child, Mrs. Watson would look the enraged mother straight in the eye and say blandly, "Georgie said he didn't do it and I find Georgie to be very truthful. Besides, he *never* provokes a fight."

"That kid is a menace to the neighborhood!" Angela fumed, after the three boys had settled down in front of the TV with a pitcher of lemonade.

We had moved out to our screened back porch and Angela was still so angry that her paring knife sliced with wicked precision as she frenched the string beans for dinner.

"But the doctors must love him," Jill said wryly. "Five days into summer vacation and he's drawn blood at least four times that I know of."

She stopped helping Angela with the beans and ticked off the incidents on her fingers. "Dot's boy had to have three stitches after Georgie threw a rock at him; he pushed little Nancy Smith onto a broken bottle; my Chris got a cut on his chin when Georgie tripped him yesterday, and now your Matt. How we'll get through this summer without having all our kids put in the hospital, I don't know."

"Somebody ought to do something about him," Angela said, giving me a meaningful look.

"Not me," I protested. "The last time I complained to Watson about Georgie, he waved a monkey wrench in my face and told me adults ought to let kids fight it out among themselves."

"I know!" Jill exclaimed brightly. "Let's hire a couple of twelve-year-olds to beat him up!"

"The Watsons would sue," said Angela glumly.

"Maybe they'll send him to camp or something this year," I offered hopefully.

"Not a chance," Angela said. "Mrs. Watson couldn't be separated from him that long."

She finished the beans, wiped the paring knife on the seat of her denim shorts, then gazed out through the early evening twilight toward the gully, absentmindedly thwacking the handle of the knife on the palm of her hand.

"Think positively," she said suddenly. "Maybe Georgie did us a favor just now."

Jill and I looked at each other blankly.

"Maybe that rope isn't safe to swing on," she said.

"But it's good and strong, Mrs. Barrett," Chris volunteered from the doorway. Their program over, the three boys had drifted out to the porch.

"Yeah, Mom," Sandy added. "I tied it with a square knot, just like Dad showed me."

"He did," echoed Matt with all the assurance of one who hadn't even mastered a granny knot yet.

Angela grinned at him and tousled his hair, a gesture he hated. "Just the same, I'd feel better if your father and I took a look at it."

So out we all went, across the already dew-dampened grass to the gully, and while I examined the rope for signs of fraying, Angela swung her lithe hundred pounds up into the willow tree with catlike grace. Naturally, Matt and Sandy are the envy of their peers with a mother who thinks nothing of dropping her work and her dignity to shinny up a tree for a tangled kite or to a clamber onto a roof to get a ball lodged in the rain gutters.

"It seems strong enough," I said. "What about the knot, Angela?" Between the leaves and the fading light, I could barely see her.

She poked her neat little pointed face through the willow leaves. "I really don't think it's safe, Alex. Could you pick up a stronger rope?"

She dropped to the ground, barely panting with the exertion. "It's a fine knot," she said to Sandy, "but the rope *is* old. Dad'll get you another tomorrow; but until he does, I want your solemn promise that you won't swing on it or let any of your friends swing on it."

"That goes for you, too, Chris," Jill said.

"Well it doesn't go for me!" sneered a juvenile voice.

We whirled, and there was dear old Georgie, cocky in the security of knowing that we were too civilized to smack the impertinence off his face.

"Oh, yes, it does," Angela contradicted coldly. "If it isn't strong enough to hold the little ones, it isn't strong enough to hold you."

Georgie flushed at this allusion to his weight. It seemed to be his only sensitive spot. "You're not my mother," he yelled, "and I don't have to mind you!"

I took a step toward him, my civility rapidly retreating before a barbarous desire to flatten him, but Angela restrained me.

"It's dangerous, Georgie, so you'll have to stay off of it," she said, and took the end of the rope and tossed it up into the tree.

"I can still get it," Georgie taunted, but he showed no inclination to do so, with me blocking his path.

At that moment, Mrs. Watson called him in for the evening, Jill suddenly remembered that she'd forgotten to take a steak out of the freezer and headed for home with Chris, while Angela, Sandy and I gave Matt a head start before racing to our own back door.

The prospect of a long summer spent coping with Georgie Watson, together with the usual mayhem of feeding, tubbing and bedding our two young acrobats, blotted out the interrupted conversation I'd been having with Angela until we were in bed ourselves. I remembered it with a jolt.

"Didn't the police suspect anything?" I asked in the semidarkness of our bedroom.

"The police were very sympathetic and nice," Angela murmured sleepily. "They could see he had locked the bathroom door himself. Actually, all I had done was balance the radio too close to the edge of the shelf and hope for the best." As if that ended it, she rolled over and put the pillow over her head.

"Oh, no, you don't!" I muttered, lifting the pillow, for I had just recalled something else. "What about 'The Perfect Example'?"

"Sh!" she whispered. "You'll wake the boys."

"Well, *did* you?" I whispered hoarsely.

In that city neighborhood where we had spent our first two years of marriage, home had been a second-floor walkup in a converted brown-stone. Its age, dinginess and general state of deterioration were somewhat ameliorated by the low rent and large, relatively soundproof rooms, and it attracted several other young couples.

We were all blithely green at life and marriage, determined to succeed in both, and that old house would have exuded happiness had it not been for the constantly disapproving eye of our landlady.

She lived on the third floor of the house, and every time the outer vestibule door opened she would appear on the landing, lean over the wobbly old mahogany railing and peer down the marble stairwell, hoping to catch someone sneaking in a forbidden pet or leaving a shopping cart in the vestibule.

She bullied her husband, tyrannized her three timorous daughters, and took a malicious delight in stirring up animosity among her tenants. "I don't care what that snip in 2-D says," she would confide to her innocent victim, "I think your clothes are very ladylike."

It was only after you had lived in the house a couple of months that you realized she was putting lies in your mouth, too. It was like an initiation to a fraternity, that first two months. Afterward, you would laugh with the more experienced tenants and compare the lies as they recalled, with amusing mimicry, how they knew by your icy expression exactly when she had slandered them to you.

She was such a perfect example of everything the young wives never wanted to become that we all called her "The Perfect Example" behind her back.

It was bad enough when she pitted couple against couple, but it stopped being funny when she managed to slip her knifed tongue into a shaky marriage, as happened twice while we lived there. The first marriage probably would have crumbled anyhow, but the second was a couple of teen-agers deeply in love but handicapped by parental opposition and the sheer inexperience of youth.

When she discovered what was happening, Angela broke the rule of silence and tried to make them understand how "The Perfect Example" was destroying them, but it was too late. The girl went home to her parents and the boy stormed off to California.

Never had I seen Angela so blazingly angry. "She's like a big fat spider, leaning on that railing, watching us flies walk in and out, spinning her web for the defenseless midges!" she raged, almost in tears. "Why aren't there laws against people like that?"

So it had seemed like divine vengeance when, two days later, the decrepit mahogany railing had finally pulled loose from the wall and collapsed under her weight, and "The Perfect Example" had plummeted to the marble tiles of the vestibule three floors below. As soon as the police had declared her death a regrettable accident, her husband had put the house up for sale and happily removed himself and the three dazed daughters back to the corn fields of his native Kansas.

"What about 'The Perfect Example'?" I repeated, shaking Angela.

"Oh, Alex," she pleaded, "it's after midnight."

"I want to know."

"She *knew* the house was old, but she was too miserly to spend a cent in repairs. That rail would have collapsed sooner or later—you heard the police say that—and I just helped it along a bit. And don't forget that I told her it wasn't safe to lean against all the time."

"That was sporting of you," I said bitterly. "Just because you warned those two—that *is* all, isn't it?—you think that justifies everything!

"Tell me something, Angela—*Angela!* Boy, your parents had some sense of humor when they named *you!*—how do you see yourself? As an avenging angel or Little Mary Sunshine scattering rays of joy through oppressed lives?"

"I'll tell you how I see myself, Alex Barrett," she said in exasperation, propping herself up on one slim elbow. "I see myself as the very tired mother of two boys who are going to be awake and wanting their breakfasts in about five or six hours! I see myself as the wife of a man who wants to hash over every petty little incident that happened *years* ago when I am exhausted!"

She fell back upon the bed and plopped the pillow over her head again. I didn't think it prudent to take it off a second time; she might decide to tell me it wasn't safe.

"Petty little incident," indeed!

The night was broken by restless dreams in which I defended Angela before massed benches of irate judges and policemen who demanded adequate reasons why she should not be taken out and hanged. They were unmoved when I argued that she was a perfect wife and tender mother, and it only seemed to infuriate them when I added that she in no way *looked* like a murderess. Through it all, a hooded hangman with a frayed clothesline rope looped around his shoulders swung back and forth on the chandelier chanting, "We're going to give her the rope! The rope! We're going to give her the rope! The rope!"

Shreds of the dream clung to me all day. I couldn't rid myself of a feeling of apprehension, and when I stopped at a hardware store after work to buy Sandy's new rope, it seemed as if I were somehow adding to Angela's guilt.

As I drove into the carport late that afternoon, I saw Sandy rummaging in the toolshed. "I got your Tarzan rope for you," I called.

"Thanks, Dad," he said, dragging out an old tarp, "but we're going to play army men. Can me and Chris and Matt have this for a tent in the gully?"

"O.K., but aren't you afraid Georgie will tear it down?"

"Oh, we don't have to worry about *him* anymore," Sandy said cheerfully, and disappeared around the corner of the house before I could find my voice.

Oh, no, I thought, and roared, "*Angela!*" as I tore into the house, nearly ripping the screen from its hinges. No answer.

"Surely Sandy would have thought it worth mentioning if the police had carted his mother off to jail," I jittered to myself, trying to look at the situation coolly. "Angela!"

Then I heard her voice: "Alex! I'm over here at Jill's. Come on over," she called.

"Hi, Alex!" Jill caroled as I pushed open their screen. "We're sort of celebrating. Want a drink?"

Women! Were they all so cold-blooded that they could murder a child, obnoxious as that child had been, without turning a hair? I sank down on the porch glider, unable to speak for the moment.

"Poor dear," said Angela solicitously. "Did you have a bad day? You look so drained."

"What happended to Georgie?" I demanded, glaring at Angela.

"Didn't Sandy tell you?" asked Jill as she handed me the tall cool drink that I so desperately needed. "He was swinging on the boys' Tarzan rope and it broke with him. He fractured both legs, one in two places," she added with satisfaction.

"He wasn't killed?" I croaked weakly.

"Of course not, Alex," said Angela. "How could he have been? There weren't any rocks under the rope and that stretch of gully is mostly grass."

"I hate to seem ghoulish," Jill said, "but it really does make the summer for us. By the time he gets out of those casts and off his crutches, school will be open again."

She grinned at Angela. "I just can't believe it! A whole summer without Georgie Watson beating up every little kid in sight!"

"Just a lucky break for everyone," I murmured sarcastically. There was no point in asking if the break had occurred up by the knot which Angela had examined last night.

"Well, it is," Jill insisted stoutly. "And as I told Mrs. Watson, it was his own fault. Angela very specifically warned him not to swing on that old rope till you could get a stronger one."

"Angela's very thoughtful that way," I observed.

At least she had the grace to blush.

The next day, a Saturday, even I was forced to admit that if it were any indication, it was going to be a very relaxed summer. The boys peacefully slaughtered the bad guys all day in the gully without once running in to us with tearful tales of Georgie's latest tyranny.

After all, I thought as I watched an afternoon baseball game undisturbed, maybe a summer of enforced solitude will be good for Georgie's character.

When I awoke early Sunday morning, my subconscious had completed the job of rationalizing the situation: don't some wives occasionally bring unusual talents to their marriage? If a woman loves to tinker with machinery, is it wrong to let her clean the carburetor on the family car? If she wants to paint the house herself, take up tailoring as a hobby, or learn how to fix the plumbing—if, in short, her oddball talents add to the comfort and serenity of her family—should her husband make an issue of it if it doesn't get out of hand?

That settled, I turned over in bed and began drifting off to sleep again when the loud spluttering roar of a lawn mower exploded on the morning quiet. I shot up in bed, examined the clock, and groaned: 7:02 A.M.!

I buried my head under a pillow, but the racket rose in volume. There was no way to escape it.

Sighing, I leaned over and kissed Angela's bare shoulder. "M-m?" she murmured drowsily.

"Angela," I whispered, "do you suppose you could give Mr. Watson a reason why it isn't safe to mow his lawn before nine A.M.?"

BETTY REN WRIGHT

The Joker

The tiny microphone just fit into a hollow in the low terrace wall. Harry stepped back and told himself, with a kind of anguish, that there was no danger of its being noticed. Anyone concerned about eavesdroppers would be looking toward the door into the house, not at the wall with its forty-foot drop to the sea.

He stared over the wall into the deep, foaming pool that had undercut the cliff and polished the walls of the cove to unmarred smoothness. He was terrified by water—Greta was, too—but the lashing of the waves suited his mood tonight. There was the same uneasy surge beneath the surface, the same sudden furious thrusts. The water reflected a Harry that no one—except perhaps Greta—had ever seen.

He really had to smile a little at the idea of Greta and his secret self. He had hidden his fear of the water by building a house overhanging the sea. He had hidden his fear of being deserted, of being left all alone in an indifferent world, by marrying the kind of woman who would be desired and pursued by other men always.

It was an interesting trick, he thought. One of his best. And if Greta, more perceptive than most people, had recognized her limited role and resented it, he couldn't help that. Confidence, trust, frankness were expensive toys for a privileged few. He had learned to get along without them.

He shivered, and called himself a fool for being nervous. After all, no one would suspect him of malice in putting the tape recorder on the terrace. His jokes had never been vicious. This time it would appear that for once he had been caught in his own trap. People would talk about it for a long time and pity him, and though he regretted the pity he relished the talk. There were other ways in which he might have killed Greta (he'd use one of them if this didn't work out tonight), but in none of them would her friends have seen her so clearly for what she really was. That was important. He hated her now, with the same shattering intensity with which he had wanted her five years ago.

The doorbell rang.

"I'll get it." Harry stood at the French doors and watched her come down the last few stairs and cross to the foyer. She was small, straight, auburn, like a fall candle, and tonight she would make all the cameo-skinned, elegant females at the party wish they had been born with red hair and freckles. He could be quite objective about her now—could marvel at what no longer belonged to him—had apparently *never* belonged to him. (And that was the bad part—the wound that was not going to heal. She had been Peter Buckley's girl before their marriage; for the last six months she had been seeing him regularly again. The two facts invalidated all that had happened between.)

It was, predictably, Peter Buckley arriving first. Harry greeted him too loudly, toned it down, fixed him a drink, and went back to the door to meet the next arrivals. During the hour that followed he welcomed at least twenty more people, asked them how their work was going, whether their vacations had been exciting, how they liked their new houses, cars, and spouses. He showed first-time guests around—the fireplace made with not-quite-genuine fossils, the mirror that took your picture when you turned on the light over it, the mounted muskie that inflated while he described what a fight it had taken to land it. He mixed a great many drinks, told a great many stories. And all of this it seemed he accomplished without once taking his eyes from Greta and Peter. Every word they spoke to each other, every casual gesture, every smile was in some curious way a symptom of the disease that was destroying him. He felt like an invalid making bright conversation while at the same time he took his own pulse and found it dangerously irregular.

When Greta and Peter finally went out on the terrace together, closing the door behind them, he was actually relieved. If they had *not* wanted to be alone, it would have proved nothing except that they were inclined to caution now, when caution was ridiculous. Harry thought of the overheard, whispered phone calls in which she had arranged to meet Peter, the times he had seen them driving together—the bitter afternoon when, coming home early along the shore road, he had seen them driving up from Buckley's beach cottage. Greta was supposed to be in the city that afternoon; when he asked her, she described in detail where she had eaten, whom she had seen, the antique sale at which, not surprisingly, she had seen nothing worth buying.

"—so marvelous," a voice streamed in his ear. "Like living in an eagle's nest. You two must adore the water!"

"Adore looking at it," Harry corrected with a smile. It was Joe Herman's wife—a shrill, peevish kind of woman who embodied all the things Greta was not. Ugly, he thought, still smiling at her—ugly, malicious, domineering, and loyal. She might treat poor old Joe like dirt but nobody else had better try it.

June Herman's face turned red, as though some unexpected acumen let her read the thoughts behind his smile. "A man with a wife who looks like Greta *ought* to keep her in an eagle's nest," she said viciously. Harry turned, looking for an explanation for her anger, and saw Joe talking to Greta with obvious enjoyment.

The party dragged by, like a hundred others before it. He had been careful to add a few of the ingredients his guests had learned to expect: one of the "gelatin" molds on the buffet was made of rubber; the woman in the painting over the fireplace smiled at people who stopped to admire her; the new bearskin rug growled when Joe Herman stooped to pat its head. "Marvelous," everyone said when they finally left, and he knew exactly what they were thinking. *Good old corny old Harry—he'll never change.* Not one of them knew he existed apart from his jokes.

Peter Buckley and the Hermans were the last to leave. "Thank goodness," Greta said when the door closed behind them. Harry looked at her sharply, but her expression was as innocent as her tone. She yawned and, as if on cue, crossed to the terrace door and went out into the silver light. He followed. As he crossed the room he seemed to leave his state of fevered alertness and enter into a kind of dull automatism. He did not have to think about what was going to happen next. It was set, inevitable.

"I'm tired," Greta said. Her face was very white. The yellow dress was subdued fire against the darkness of the sea. Far below her the water lashed against the foot of the cliff.

"You had a terrible time tonight," she said when he walked over beside her. "Why do you bother with jokes when you're feeling this lousy? Why don't you tell me what's worrying you?"

She had the knack, he thought. She should have gone on the stage; it was wonderful the way she delivered those small lines. *Tell the little woman all about it,* he thought savagely, aping the sense if not the tone of her plea. He moved a few steps along the wall, picked up the microphone, and waited until she looked at him.

"What's that?"

"Another joke," he said and waited again, but she didn't seem to recognize what he held. "It's the microphone of the tape recorder," he said carefully. "I had it set up out here to get an hour or two of private-type conversations. Ought to be good for some laughs."

Awareness came slowly, just as he had imagined it would, in the long, painful night-hours of planning. And now, it was *her* voice that was careful, controlled, as she asked, "You had it—out here?"

He nodded.

She took it well, considering the depth of the pit that had suddenly opened up before her. "You ought to be ashamed of yourself," she said. "Funny jokes are one thing, but that—that's cheap and ugly."

He pretended to be startled. "You have a pretty poor opinion of our friends," he said. "What do you think we're going to hear, for heaven's sake? A lot of small talk about how pretty the ocean is in the moonlight and isn't it a dull party and wouldn't you think that joker would get tired of his little games after a while . . . that's all it'll be. We can play it at the next party if things are slow . . ." Without looking at her he lifted the tape recorder from behind the column of greenery in the corner and set it on the wall. "Sit down," he said. "Might as well listen to it before we go to bed."

She moved then, gliding along the wall so swiftly that he had only a fraction of a second to get ready. Her hands were on the tape recorder, pushing wildly, when he caught her around the hips and lifted her over the wall. One moment he was thrusting her away from him into space; the next his hands were empty. Her scream was cut short when she hit the water.

He had tried to prepare himself for the moments right afterward. Horror was what he expected, and it came, a wild trembling, a violent nausea as he stared down into the water. Doubt, fear, remorse because now he was a murderer and would know himself to be one forever. But he hadn't expected the overwhelming loneliness which, when it struck, drove every other feeling out of him. With his own hands he had done it, had rendered himself alone in a world that thought he was a very funny man indeed. She was the only one who hadn't laughed.

Later he thought that he might have followed her over the wall in that moment, might have ended it right then, if the doorbell hadn't rung. After the third or fourth ring he recognized the sound. And he knew he had to go ahead with the plan.

When he opened the door Joe Herman stepped inside, pulling his wife behind him. "Damn tire," he snarled and grabbed the telephone in the entry. "That's the second one this week—I don't even have a spare . . . " He looked at Harry more closely. "What's the matter—too much party? You oughtta cut out all that cute stuff."

"Call the police," Harry said. "Call somebody. Greta just jumped off the terrace. She's killed herself."

He didn't have to pretend the sobs that shook him when he actually said the words.

The Hermans stared. "Look, funny boy," Joe said, but something apparently convinced him it was not a joke, for he ran across to the terrace and his wife followed him.

"The cliff walls are smooth as marble for a hundred yards around the cove," Harry said harshly from the terrace door. He watched them stare over the edge, seeing the churning blackness himself though he didn't leave the lighted living room. "That was one of the reasons we built here—privacy, no beach parties, nobody peeking in the windows."

He went back to the phone and called the police himself. When he was through the Hermans were behind him, their faces white and curiously hungry as they struggled to believe the worst. "You—you *wouldn't* joke about a thing like this," Joe said uncertainly. "I don't believe you would. But why would Greta—do that?"

Harry saw then that they were the right people to have here when the police came. They both knew him as The Joker; Joe had been involved in several of the best. They would believe the picture of the clown and the joke that backfired. They would want to believe it, would want the police to believe it. They would feel, in a way they would not even admit to themselves, that he had it coming.

"I don't understand it myself," he said simply. "We were just talking—you know, after-the-party talk. I mentioned that I had had the tape recorder turned on out on the terrace this evening. She looked strange—kind of sick—I asked her if she was feeling all right—she said yes, but then she started to cry and when I switched on the re-wind she started to moan and then she ran across the terrace and just—jumped."

They looked at him.

"Poor kid," Joe said. "I wonder why . . ."

"What about the tape recorder?" June asked eagerly. "Why don't you play it now and see if there was something on it that might have upset her?"

He knew he didn't have to let them hear the tape. June Herman knew the whole story already, or thought she did; he had watched her eyes widen when he mentioned the recorder, had seen the eager twitching of lips as she tasted the story she would have to tell.

"Greta never had anything to hide," he said stiffly. "That's a lousy thing to say."

Joe shook his head and his wife made a small, protesting sound. "Of course not," she said soothingly. "But just the same, Harry, you ought to listen to the tape before the police come. You just ought to."

He thought it over, then shrugged as if he were too tired to argue. The recorder was still out on the terrace; he got it quickly and brought it back in. He knew he was taking a chance, but not a big one; there had been no doubt that Greta had not wanted him to hear the tape. And June Herman was the right one, the absolutely right one, to hear the whole story.

He pushed the re-wind button and waited, while the tape whirred innocently to the other spool. Then the room was full of the sound of waves. Loneliness came back as he listened; he was powerless before it, though he reminded himself that he had lost nothing, that he couldn't lose something he had never really had. Still he strained to hear Greta's voice, wanting the sound of it once more, regardless of the words it spoke.

Joe Herman leaned forward and turned up the volume of the recorder. There was the sound of footsteps on stone and then a giggle. Harry didn't recognize the voice but he could tell June was cataloging this, too, for future investigation. There followed a long pause with nothing but the splash of waves, and then, suddenly and sweetly, there was Greta's voice.

"It's more than a joke now, Petey," she said. "He hasn't trusted me from the very first, and lately we've been farther apart than ever. At first it just seemed as if it would be fun to turn the tables on him—once. Now it's much more. At first I had no intention of frightening him—now I feel as if shock is the only thing that might bring him back . . ."

"You're wonderful," Peter said. "I think I've mentioned that before. When are you going to do it?"

The Hermans frowned, trying hard to follow the conversation. As the tape whirled on, their faces seemed to move farther away, leaving Harry alone on a small island surrounded by Greta's voice.

"Soon," the voice said. "I'm not quite sure how I'll do it, but I can tell you this, Petey—I'll plan it so he think's he's lost me. For a minute or two or maybe more he's going to face up to how much he needs me—he's going to value me as a person and not just as part of his pretty little stage set here on the cliff. I want him to wish to heaven he had one more chance to make our marriage work. I want him to know exactly what it's like to love someone terribly, as I love him, and not be able to reach him . . ." She took a deep breath. "And I do thank you, Petey, for making it possible."

The entry door opened. Joe saw it first; with a real effort he tore his eyes from the tape recorder and got up clumsily. "It's the police—" he said and then suddenly stopped.

Harry did not move. In the mirror over the couch he could see two figures neatly framed in gold, a picture to carry with him the rest of his life. Here the tall policeman, puzzled, frowning, and there, just beside him, the small, freckled, red-headed girl in a drenched yellow dress. They had come together in the darkness behind them; the policeman would have seen her somewhere on the beach beyond the smooth walls of the cove, walking slowly across the sand, trying to believe the thing that had happened.

Well, he thought, *I certainly found out what she wanted me to.* And then he began to laugh, because somebody's joke had backfired, and if he didn't laugh now he was going to cry. He laughed for himself, for the wife he had had, and for Peter Buckley who must have spent a good share of the last six months teaching Greta how to swim. He was still laughing when the policeman put the handcuffs on him and led him out of the house.

HELEN NIELSEN

The Very Hard Sell

The call came over the loudspeaker above the used car lot at 3:00 P.M.

"Mr. Cornell, you're wanted on the telephone. Mr. Cornell, telephone—please."

It was a godsend, Cornell felt. Mr. Garcy was in a bad mood and so somebody had to take a beating. Here of late that somebody always seemed to be him. It wasn't fair and Garcy knew it. There were slack periods in the auto market when nothing moved. Sales were down in the new car show room, too. What was he supposed to do—hypnotize the customers? The woman hadn't wanted the blue Olds; she didn't like blue. Even Jack Richards, who was almost twenty years younger than Glenn Cornell and who always wore a perky little bow tie that charmed the feminine trade, couldn't sell a blue car to a woman who didn't like blue no matter how good a buy it was.

"Mr. Cornell, you're wanted on the telephone . . ."

Cornell took advantage of the chance to break away from Garcy and made it to the office before the girl on the switchboard could finish her second call. The voice on the telephone was masculine—young, definite.

"Is this Garcy Motors on Sutter Street? Mr. Cornell? You had a black Cadillac on the used car lot a few days ago—a '57 sedan. I think it had a card on it—$3750. Yes, that's the one I mean. Is it still there? It is? Good. I'm coming by to look it over as soon as I get off work. If it runs as good as it looks, you've got a sale."

"It does," Cornell insisted. "It handles like a new car and carries a new car guarantee. What time will you be in? 5:30? Fine, I'll have her warmed up and ready. Say, what's your name so I'll know you? Berra? Okay, Mr. Berra, I'll see you at 5:30."

When Mr. Berra hung up, Glenn dropped the telephone in the cradle. He raised his head and found himself eye level with the salesmen's rating chart Mr. Garcy always kept in plain sight. There had been six names on the chart, but the last two had lines drawn through them. Mr. Garcy never erased a name when he let a man go. He left it there, cancelled out by a chalk line, as a grim reminder of what could happen to anyone whose sales dropped too low. The name just above the last chalk line was Glenn Cornell. He turned around and saw Mr. Garcy standing in the doorway.

"A customer of mine," Cornell said with forced brightness. "He's been looking at the black Caddy. I'm taking him out on a demonstration ride at 5:30."

It wasn't much of a lie. Cornell had never laid eyes on Mr. Berra; but Garcy didn't know that, and it was worth stretching the story a bit to see the way his expression altered from surprise to near disappointment and then to one of the leers he used for a smile.

"Good man!" Garcy said. "He's really interested. Sell him, Cornell. Don't let him get away. He's on the hook. All you have to do is reel him in."

It was more than a pep talk; it was an order. Cornell vowed then and there that he'd sell the black Caddy to Mr. Berra if it was the last thing he did.

Exactly one week later, at a few minutes before 11:00 P.M., a patrol car answering a neighborhood complaint found a black Cadillac parked in an alley behind a lumber yard, about two miles across town from Garcy Motors. A man was slumped over the steering wheel, his chin pressing down on the horn rim and the horn, according to the complainant, had been sounding for nearly an hour. The first officer out of the patrol car opened the right front door of the Cadillac.

"Hey, mister," he called above the din of the horn, "this is no way to sleep off a drunk. You're keeping people awake." And then he paused and leaned forward, sniffing at the interior of the sedan. "Bring your flash over here!" he shouted to his companion. "I think this car's full of fumes!"

The second officer appeared at his shoulder and inhaled deeply.

"Not gas," he said. "Smells more like burnt alfalfa."

But when the light from the flash caught the man slumped over the steering wheel, both officers fell silent. He wasn't drunk; he was dead. Glenn Cornell would never sell anything to anyone after what the .45 slug had done to the right side of his head.

Hazel Cornell was a nice-looking woman in spite of the grief in her eyes. Twenty years ago, Police Detective Sommers decided, she must have been the prettiest bride of the season. Now she was a widow. She didn't cry—praise heaven for that! There were dark shadows under her eyes and a tightness about her mouth; otherwise, she might have been a typical housewife who had donned her best cotton dress and a small hat with blue flowers on the brim that was usually worn only to church, and come down to report a mischievous neighborhood child, or some other minor disturbance.

But Police Detective Sommers handled homicide cases.

"I know what I told the police officers last night," she said, "and I know how it all looks. But I knew my husband, too. It isn't true what was printed in the papers this morning. Glenn didn't kill himself. He was a religious man. He wouldn't take his life."

Her voice was low but firm, the inner tension held in careful check. Sommers glanced down at the Cornell file open on his desk. All of her statements of the previous night were there.

"But Mrs. Cornell," he remonstrated, "you admitted that your husband had been depressed and in ill health."

"Not really ill health," she said. "His cough had been bothering him some.

Glenn had bronchitis when he was a child. Ever so often, his cough came back. It was nothing new. He wouldn't have killed himself for that."

"But you also said that he was worried about the prospective customer for the car he was trying to sell. He'd been working on the deal all week without getting a definite answer. He came home for dinner last night and refused to eat."

"He had a headache," she explained.

"He went to his room for about ten minutes and then came out again, saying that he was going to meet Mr. Berra and—" Sommers glanced down at the report again "—put an end to the indecision."

"'I've got him on the hook,' he told me. 'All I have to do is reel him in.'"

"Ten minutes," Sommers repeated, ignoring the interpolation. "Now, Mrs. Cornell, didn't you identify the gun found on the seat beside your husband's body as his own gun, which, you stated, was kept in his bureau drawer?"

"Yes, but Glenn—"

"And the ballistic test has proved that your husband was killed by a bullet fired from that gun."

"But Glenn didn't fire the gun!"

She wasn't excited, she was adamant. She hadn't come alone. Sprawled in the chair beside her, a teen-age youth stirred restlessly at her words.

"Mom, I wish you wouldn't get so worked up," he said.

"I'm not worked up, Andy," she replied quietly. "I'm merely telling this officer the truth. Your father didn't commit suicide."

It wasn't going to be easy to talk her out of such conviction. She was a firm woman. She must have been a devoted wife, and must be a good mother, an uncomplicated personality who was still in a state of semi-shock from learning that such an evil as violent death could happen in her orderly life.

Sommers tried again. "Mrs. Cornell," he said, "do you realize what your statement means? If your husband didn't commit suicide, he must have been murdered. Do you know anyone who might have wanted to murder your husband?"

"Oh, no. Glenn had no enemies."

"And yet you insist that he was murdered."

"It might have been a hold-up. He was driving that expensive car. Someone might have thought he had money."

She was grasping at straws, illusory straws.

"But you identified Mr. Cornell's personal effects at the morgue," he reminded. "His wallet, containing $17, his key case, his cough drops—"

"That cough of his," she said. "He was never without them."

"—his wrist watch and his wedding ring. Nothing was taken. Men have been murdered for much less than $17, Mrs. Cornell, but your husband wasn't one of them."

"Then it must have been a madman," she said. "One of those crazed fiends we read about."

If she wasn't going to change her mind, Sommers could at least take the out offered him.

"It might have been," he admitted.

"Or Mr. Berra. Have you found Mr. Berra?"

Her eyes were accusing him across the desk. But Sommers had never seen a clearer case of self-inflicted death. There had been no indication of a struggle in the car. He'd gone there himself as soon as the patrol car radioed in. No struggle, obviously. And there were no fingerprints on the gun except Glenn Cornell's. He opened his mouth to answer, but Andy beat him to it.

"Mom," he pleaded, "the police know what they're doing. Leave it be."

"No, they don't know. Not when they tell the reporters that your father committed suicide. They should at least talk to Mr. Berra."

She stood up, a small, determined woman without tears.

"Glenn Cornell did not kill himself," she said.

She turned and left the office, and Andy scrambled to his feet to follow. He hesitated in front of the desk.

"Don't mind my mother," he said. "She's all upset, you see. She just can't believe it."

He was a good-looking kid, ruddy-faced, short pale blond hair, broad shoulders encased in a school sweater with a huge S over his chest.

"But you can believe it, is that it?" Sommers asked.

"Sure, I understand. A man's confidence can go. His pride. I mean, maybe this customer he was trying to sell cracked wise, or maybe old Garcy was riding him too hard. Some bosses are like that. As soon as they smell chicken, they're like a wolf sniffing blood."

"Chicken?" Sommers echoed. "Are you trying to tell me that you think your father was chicken?"

Andy Cornell flushed red up to his close-cropped hair.

"Look, I didn't mean— Well, anyhow, I know he could be pushed around."

"How old are you, Andy?"

"Sixteen."

"And nobody pushes you around, do they?" Sommers asked.

"I'll say they don't."

Sommers' eyes held the boy for a few seconds and then dismissed him. Andy went out, but long after he'd gone Sommers stared after him. At least the boy had inadvertently explained what was behind his mother's refusal to face the obvious. "Chicken," he repeated to himself. It wasn't much of an obituary. He could at least talk to Mr. Berra.

A row of red and white pennants dangled listlessly above the used car lot of Garcy Motors on Sutter Street, limp reminders of a sale that wasn't being patronized. Inside the showroom office, Mr. Garcy showed a similar lack of enthusiasm for his inquisitive caller. He'd already had to cope with a couple of reporters. Suicide. That was a bad subject to fool around with. Morbid. Could give a place a bad name.

"To be honest with you, Officer," he said, "and I am honest with everyone, I wasn't too surprised when the police called me down last night to identify

Cornell's body and my Cadillac. Not surprised that he'd killed himself, I mean. The man was on the down grade—not up to par at all. A few years ago he topped the list on that sales chart month after month, slack season and heavy; but lately he'd lost his drive. Brought his problems to work with him. That's bad. When a man can't leave his problems at home, he's bound to hit the skids."

"Problems? What problems?"

"Any problems. We all have them, don't we? Family problems, health problems, money problems; but we learn to keep them out of our work. Not Cornell. Excuses, always excuses. His boy stayed out too late at night so he couldn't get any sleep. His boy was getting in with a bad crowd at high school. He didn't want his boy going wrong. I tell you, Officer, if Glenn Cornell had had five or six kids he'd have been alive today. He'd have had to give up worrying long ago."

Sommers thought of Andy Cornell—tall, blond, handsome.

"His son hasn't been in trouble, has he?"

"Andy? Of course not. Good kid, Andy. Wish I had a son just like him. My luck—four girls. But Cornell worried just the same. Maybe it was physical. He had headaches a lot—took pills all the time, and always had trouble with his throat. Never smoked. But he'd been with me for nearly eleven years, and I hate to let a man go."

Garcy's eyes inadvertently strayed to the chart on the wall. Sommers' followed. "Moroni, Taber—" he read aloud. "What does the chalk line indicate, Mr. Garcy?"

Garcy scowled. "I can't carry dead weight. I've got a business to run."

Sommers nodded.

"Cornell," he added, reading the next name above the discharged salesmen. Silence filled in for the things nobody said. "So you think he was sufficiently depressed to have committed suicide."

"Depressed, unstable—use whatever term you want to use, Officer. The fact is still the same. He did kill himself, didn't he?"

Of course he'd killed himself. Nothing had ever been more obvious, and yet Sommers, irritated by one derisive word, had to keep asking questions.

"What about Mr. Berra?" he queried. "Did you talk to him?"

Garcy's expression changed from bridled impatience to momentary bewilderment.

"Who?" he asked.

"Berra. Cornell's customer for the Cadillac. Mrs. Cornell has told us that her husband had taken the death car from the lot in order to close a deal with a Mr. Berra."

Garcy met Sommers' gaze with unblinking eyes.

"I don't think there was a Mr. Berra," he said. "I'm serious, Officer. I know, I told your men the same story Mrs. Cornell told them last night; but I've had time to think it over, and I'm convinced the whole thing was a fabrication. I'll tell you why I think it. It began last Friday—a week ago yesterday. Cornell had muffed what should have been a sure sale—that was just before noon. I had a luncheon date at my club and had to leave, but I told him I wanted to have a talk with him when I returned. He was in trouble, and he knew it. It was almost three o'clock before I got back. I'd no more than gone out to the lot to speak with Cornell—he was in charge of the used car sales—than a call came over the loudspeaker for Mr. Cornell to go to the telephone. I followed him back to the office and got there in time to hear him making an appointment with a Mr. Berra to demonstrate the black Caddy at 5:30."

"Didn't Berra show?" Sommers asked.

"He did not. At about 5:15 there was another call. I usually go home at 5, but I was staying around to see how Cornell would handle this sale. The second call was from Berra again. He couldn't make it down to the lot in time, but if Cornell would drive over to a service station at the corner of Third and Fremont he could pick him up and demonstrate the car from there. It sounded all right, so I let him go."

"When did he come back?"

"I don't know," Garcy said. "I went on home. In the morning, the Caddy was back on the lot, but Cornell told me he had a sure sale just as soon as Mr. Berra raised the cash. I got after him about pushing for a low down payment, but he said Berra didn't want to finance—that he only did business on a cash basis and would have the money in a few days. I didn't think much about it at the time, but now, thinking back, I realize that Cornell was acting strange even then."

"Strange?" Sommers echoed. "In what way?"

"I don't know exactly. He didn't seem to want to talk about Berra, except to assure me that he was sold on the car and would raise the money. Usually the salesmen chew the fat a little about their clients, brag on how they handle them, or even have a few anecdotes; but Cornell was like a clam. I even tried to pump him. I asked him if Berra worked at the service station where he'd picked him up. He said no, he didn't think so, and that was all I got out of him. Three days later—no, four, Tuesday, it was. Last Tuesday I asked him if he'd heard from Berra and told him to get on the ball and not let the customer get cold. That afternoon he took the Caddy and said he was going to drive over to Berra's house. He came back about half an hour later saying that nobody was home and he'd try again."

"And did he?"

"I don't know. I only know that on Thursday—day before yesterday—Mr. Berra called back. This time he said that he'd raised the money. His mother, who lived in Pasadena, was putting up the full amount on the condition Cornell would drive him over to her house and let her inspect the car first. I thought then that it sounded fishy, but a $3750 cash sale isn't something you toss in the waste basket, and I trusted Cornell. I told him to go ahead, but to—"

Garcy hesitated and a little color came up in his face.

"But what?" Sommers prodded.

"I was only kidding, of course."

"But what, Mr. Garcy?"

"But not to come back until he'd closed the deal."

The silence in the shop was broken only by the distant sound of voices in the back lot garage.

"And did he come back?" Sommers asked.

"No. He called in yesterday morning and said he'd run into a little difficulty, but would get it straightened out before the day was over. He still had the Caddy with him." Garcy's face was no longer red; it was chalk white. "Damn it, it was only a figure of speech! I didn't mean for the man to blow out his brains!"

Sommers let Mr. Garcy indulge in his anguish without interruption. The well-adjusted machinery of his own mind was tabulating and arranging certain facts. All of them led him to one question.

"Mr. Garcy," he said, "you've just told me that this man, Berra, telephoned Cornell here at the office three different times, and yet you started out by saying that you didn't think the man existed. How do you account for that?"

"Timing," Garcy responded, grateful for a change of thought. "I got to thinking about it this morning. Cornell got that first call just after I'd started dressing him down for fluffing the other sale—at a time when he knew I'd be talking to him because I'd told him as much before I went to lunch. And then there's the way he dragged out this deal for a whole week, all the time insisting the car was as good as sold. I think he'd already flipped, Officer. I think he'd so lost his confidence that he rigged up Mr. Berra out of his imagination and fixed it with some friend to make the calls just to make it look good. I never saw the man. Nobody on the premises saw him, and Cornell never told us anything about him. The switchboard girl heard his voice—a young man, she says. Maybe it was his son. But I still think Mr. Berra doesn't exist."

Garcy could be right, but something stuck in Sommers' mind. No, not his mind; his senses. The senses absorbed and retained in an instant what the mind needed time to analyze. Some small thing. He scowled over the nagging thought of it.

"You say that Cornell took the car to Berra's house," he said. "Did he tell you where the house was?"

"No, he didn't. He said it wasn't far, and he was back in half an hour."

"Could he have jotted down the address somewhere—in his sales book, for instance?"

Garcy shrugged.

"You can look through his desk if you want to. Believe me, if I could locate this Berra I'd have a few questions for him myself. Do you know how many miles Cornell put on that Caddy last week? Nearly two hundred. I checked the mileage down at the police garage last night. I have to keep an eye on that kind of thing. Some of the young salesmen like to take a late model out on their dates at night and eat up the fuel. Little things like that can wipe out a businessman's profits. It only takes one leak to sink a ship, if it's neglected long enough."

Sommers ignored the lecture and went to work on Cornell's desk. There was ample evidence of other customers—names, addresses and telephone numbers, but nothing concerning Mr. Berra.

"You see," Garcy told him. "He made up this customer out of the whole cloth. It's tragic when a man's so weak he has to resort to lies to keep up a front."

Chicken. Garcy's vocabulary was thirty years removed from Andy Cornell's, but they were saying the same thing. For Sommers, it was just another goad to keep looking.

"Third and Fremont," he mused aloud.

"What's that?" Garcy asked.

"The location of the gas station where Cornell was to meet Berra."

"Oh, sure. That's what he said. Look, Officer—" Garcy's words stopped Sommers at the door. "If you want to go on looking for Mr. Berra, that's your business. Selling cars is mine. I'd like to get that Caddy back on the lot in time for the Sunday display."

"I'll have it cleaned up and brought over to you, Mr. Garcy," Sommers answered. "In the meantime, there's something you can do to jack up your sales force and keep them on their toes."

"Yes? What's that?"

"Draw a line through Cornell's name," he said. "On that chart."

According to the lettering on the canopy, the manager of the service station at the corner of Third and Fremont was a man named Max Fuller. It was a busy intersection and several minutes elapsed before Detective Sommers could command Fuller's attention. Even then it was hardly undivided. They stepped inside the office, but Fuller kept a wary eye on his assistant.

"New kid on the pumps," he explained. "Have to watch 'em the first few days. Police, isn't it? What's on your mind? Selling tickets to something?"

Sommers wasn't selling tickets to anything. He explained what was on his mind, and, as he did so, Fuller forgot about his pumps.

"Berra?" he echoed, at the sound of the name. "Say, what's this guy done, anyway?"

It was an interesting response.

"What do you mean?" Sommers asked.

"Well, there was a fellow in here yesterday asking for the same man. Wanted to know if anyone of that name worked here, or if I knew where he could find him. I told him I'd never heard of the name, so he described him to me. A young fellow, he said. Twenty, maybe, but no more. Swarthy skin, dark hair and eyes, expensive-looking clothes. The description didn't ring any bells, so he goes on to tell me a story about having picked up this Berra here at my station nearly a week ago. Craziest thing I ever heard."

"Crazy," Sommers echoed. "In what way?"

"In every way. The way he picked up Berra. He drove over to the side of the building, see, so as not to block off my pumps. He cut the motor, figuring he'd have to come inside the office to find the person he was supposed to meet; but before he could get out of the car, the door of the men's room opened and Berra came out of it—running, he said, with his head ducked down. Berra pulled open the car door, asked if he was Mr. Cornell—"

"Cornell?" Sommers repeated.

"That's the name of the fellow who came in here yesterday asking about Berra. Cornell said he was, and so Berra got into the car. 'Okay,' he says, 'let's go.' Cornell is a car salesman, you see. The fellow who came running out of the rest room had called him about buying a black Cadillac—"

Max Fuller's voice broke abruptly. He'd been cleaning his hands on a wipe cloth as he talked. When he dropped it on the desk, his eyes caught the front page of the morning paper that had been staring up at him all this time. One story had a black headline: Auto Salesman Suicide Victim. He followed the story for a few lines and then looked up, puzzled.

"Why, that's the guy," he said. "The same one who was in here yesterday."

"The same one," Sommers agreed. "Tell me, did you see the man Cornell described—the day he was supposed to have come running out of the men's room?"

"No, sir, I didn't. Late in the afternoon—this was at 5:30, he said—things are really jumping around here. People coming home from work, you know. I don't have a chance to watch anything but the pump meters. To tell you the truth, I don't even remember Cornell driving in, but he sure could have without me noticing. You can see for yourself. There's plenty of area out there for a man to park a car clear of the pumps."

Sommers moved back to the doorway. Fuller was right. It must have been thirty feet from the station office to the edge of the lot—an inner edge where a two-story commercial building rose up like a tall, windowless wall. A man could park his car clear of the pump area and not be noticed by anyone during the rush hours. By the same token, a man coming out of the rest room, which was in the rear end of the station building, would have been shielded from view.

"And you keep the rest rooms locked, I suppose," Sommers said.

"Have to," Fuller answered. "Company orders. Sure wish I didn't. Those darned rooms give me more trouble than the rest of the business put together. I could write a book!"

"Mind if I look at it?"

"Go ahead. I've got to get back to my customers. If I can be of any help, let me know. I doubt it though. I couldn't help Cornell. He left here saying he was going to the other station."

Sommers had started to leave. He paused outside the doorway.

"The other station?" he echoed.

"The other service station," Fuller explained. "The one down at Eighth and California. He told me that was where he left Berra after demonstrating the car. He sure seemed anxious to find that guy Berra. Crazy story, isn't it? Stories, when they're crazy like that, they stick in your mind."

It was a crazy story. Sommers wondered how Garcy would have reacted to the tale he'd just heard. Would he still believe Berra didn't exist, or would he point out what was still an annoying fact: that nobody except the dead man had seen Berra? He went around the building and proceeded to inspect the men's room. It was exceptionally clean. The company could give the management a seal of approval for cleanliness. There wasn't a thing out of order or out of place. Not a thing. The waste basket was in full view, the towel dispenser was filled, there wasn't so much as a leaky faucet or a dripping plumbing pipe. And there was no apparent evidence of Berra's having been in the room a week ago. Sommers made a careful inspection of the lavatory. It was an inexpensive casting with a hollow rim. He ran an exploratory finger along the under edge until it touched something unfamiliar. He squatted on his heels and examined the area by the flame of his cigarette lighter. There was a lump of something that looked a little like hardened chewing gum, but that scraped off on his fingernail into slivers of lead. Solder. Liquid solder. There were fragments of several lumps of it dotting the underside of the fixture. He didn't scrape off any more of it. He snapped off the lighter and stood up.

What did it mean? Chewing gum he would have understood, but not liquid solder. He left the rest room and went back to his car. For a few moments he sat parked in view of the spot where Cornell must have parked a week before his death. The door of the rest room was in full view. If it had been ajar when Cornell arrived, it would have been an easy matter for anyone waiting inside to see and recognize a specific model that had been requested to call for him. A very special form of taxi service—but to where? Max Fuller had told him. Another service station at the corner of Eighth and California.

The station at Eighth and California was an independent—not so modern or so clean as the one Sommers had just visited, but twice as busy. The reason for that was the garage about twenty-five yards behind the pump area. It was there that Sommers located a stout, balding man in overalls whose name was Donnegan, and who owned the business. Like Max Fuller, Donnegan had a story to tell. Cornell had been in the previous day inquiring after the same party—a man named Berra.

"I don't know anybody by that name, let alone employ him," Donnegan explained. "All I've got on the payroll are relatives. I don't say they work, mind you, but they're on the payroll. Might as well be. I feed them anyway."

"What did Cornell say about Berra?" Sommers asked.

"Just what I told you," Donnegan said. "Asked if I knew him. Told me how he looked—young, dark, well dressed. Said he'd dropped him off here a week ago after taking him for a demonstration ride in the '57 Cad Cornell was driving. Berra wanted to buy it, he said. Made him promise not to sell it to anyone else. Said he was going to meet his father here and put the bite on him."

"Here?" Sommers echoed.

"Yeah. That's a good one, isn't it? The car salesman fell for it, too. You'd think those guys would get used to deadbeats playing them for suckers. Still, for a commission I guess a man will go a long way."

"Two hundred miles," Sommers said.

"How's that?"

Sommers didn't bother to explain, but it was hardly more than half a mile from Fuller's garage to Donnegan's. Allowing for a demonstration ride, there were still a lot of miles to account for to reach that two hundred total Garcy had complained about.

"Did Cornell tell you anything else?" he asked. "Did he mention where he was going when he left here?"

"No, he didn't say anything about that," Donnegan answered, "but he did tell me one peculiar thing. He said this fellow Berra, when he got out of the Cad to meet his father here, ducked his head and ran for the men's room. 'Maybe he was carsick,' I cracked, but Cornell didn't laugh. He seemed worried or puzzled. Maybe that's a better word—puzzled."

It was a good word because Sommers was puzzled, too. Something was beginning to take shape, some vague pattern—but of what? The man Garcy had insisted didn't exist was becoming more real. A young man—a young voice on the telephone. A perturbed salesman retracing his route a week after he'd first taken it, and a day after Berra's second call. He wouldn't have gone to those lengths to search for someone he'd put up to concocting a prospective sale in order to get him off the hook with Garcy. Sommers had one more thing to do before leaving Donnegan's station, and after he'd inspected the men's room he was even more puzzled. On the underside of the lavatory he found several lumps of hardened liquid solder. There was a pattern, all right, but he needed more pieces before it could be meaningful.

Assuming that Mr. Berra did exist—why had he used Cornell for a chauffeur, and where else had they gone? Cornell had told his employer that he'd driven out to Berra's home, but that Berra wasn't in. Unless this was an outright lie, Berra must have given an address. It hadn't been in Cornell's desk, but there was a possibility that he'd jotted it down on a scrap of paper in his wallet. Sommers returned to headquarters and examined the dead man's effects. Nothing. A trail that had started out so promisingly had come to a dead end. There was only one other place to look.

Downstairs in the garage, Mr. Garcy's well-traveled Cadillac was ready to be returned to its owner. Cornell had been very neat with his dying. The upholstery wasn't bloodstained and the bullet had lodged in his skull, thereby saving the door's glass. Properly advertised, the car would make a quick sale to some morbid individual. Sommers wasn't morbid; he was determined.

The instant he opened the door of the Cadillac, he was again aware of that sense of something known, but not recognized. He'd done this very thing not more than twelve hours ago—opened the door of the death car, to which he'd been summoned, and peered into the front seat. Was it something seen? No. Only Cornell and the gun that had fallen to the floorboards at his feet had been seen. But something smelled—yes, that was it: a pungent, smoky odor as if something had been burned. He opened the glove compartment. Nothing to explain the odor there—no oily rags or singed material of any kind; only one detailed price ticket from Garcy Motors and one city map.

One city map. Sommers was excited the instant he drew it out into the light. It was a new map, but it had been marked with a red pencil. Crosses, small red crosses at various locations. The more he studied the locations, the more interesting they became. One cross was at the corner of Third and Fremont; one at Eighth and California. There were three others at widely separated locations: two on corners and one in the middle of the block. Add the distances together and double for round trips and a good piece was gone out of the missing two hundred miles. Now, he had three more chances to locate the elusive Mr. Berra.

Sommers pocketed the map and closed the glove compartment. The car was ready to roll now—cleaned, vacuumed, the ashtrays pushed in. Ashtrays. Now there was something to be seen. Last night the ashtray on the instrument panel had been open. Sommers yanked it out and examined the contents, overlooked in the cleaning of the car, perhaps, because someone had pushed the ashtrays in. Glenn Cornell didn't smoke because of his delicate throat, and Garcy Motors would surely be more careful of a display model than to leave an ashtray full of stubs still faintly smelling of the weedy scent Sommers remembered from the previous night. And these were not standard cigarette stubs either; this was marijuana.

The pieces of the pattern were gathering fast. Sommers turned the contents of the ashtray over to the lab for analysis and got set for a tour of the city. There were three locations on the map to be identified. The first turned out to be a small independent grocery located across the street from a high school—the Charles Steinmetz High School. Sommers noted the name of the school with interest. He didn't linger at the grocery. Strolling in for pack of cigarettes was enough to show him there was no one working inside answering the description of Mr. Berra. He didn't expect there would be. The second location on the map was even more interesting—an herb and health food shop operated by an oriental who, if not inscrutable, was at least self-possessed. Sommers didn't know what he was going to do with the wheat-germ flour he bought, but he did know the pattern was beginning to form a most interesting picture.

The third red cross on the map was in the middle of the block on a residential street, where aging bungalows were being replaced by modern multiple-unit apartments. Without a house number, it would have been difficult to learn just what the third cross indicated except for the pattern in Sommers' mind. A man who didn't want to be found wouldn't give a correct address; he would give, if possible, an address where nobody lived. Vacant lots were the rule in such cases, but in this instance there was something even better. A house about to be moved stood like an empty shell with uncurtained windows and a collection of advertising throwaways cluttering the lawn and the front porch. *Nobody was home.* This is what Cornell had reported back to Mr. Garcy after calling on Berra. Nobody, certainly, was at home here. Sommers parked the car and began to examine the property for some sign of ownership.

At a casual glance, the building might have been only temporarily vacant; closer inspection showed the wreckers had already been at the porch foundations. Several brick pillars were in ruins and the brick fireplace just around the corner of the house was half-demolished. It was there that Sommers discovered the man with a wheelbarrow. The man looked up, surprised, a brick in each hand. These he promptly added to the growing pile on the wheelbarrow. When Sommers showed his badge, the man grinned.

"It's okay, Officer," he said. "I've got Mr. Peterson's permission to take these bricks. It's his house. We were neighbors for years. 'Go ahead, take 'em when they move the building,' he said. 'Finish your patio.' I don't know why I bother, to tell you the truth. One of these days, one of the buyers is going to offer me a price I can't resist and they'll be hauling my house away."

"Where's Mr. Peterson?"

"Gone to Carmel. Retired. Suppose that's where I'll be going someday."

"How long has it been since Mr. Peterson moved away?"

"From here, you mean? Oh, he hasn't lived in this old house for seven or eight years. Rented it out. The last tenants left about three weeks ago. Glad to see 'em go, too. Most people in this world are fine—just fine. All nationalities, all races. But once in a while you run across some bad neighbors. This Berrini family—"

"Berrini?" Sommers echoed.

"That's right. Not a family, really. Couldn't blame the mother so much. She was a widow who had to work. Three young girls in elementary school to support, and two sons who should have been a help and never thought of anything but hot-rods and flashy clothes. The older one—Bruno—even served time at one of those juvenile delinquent work farms a few years ago. I don't know about Joe. He's still in high school."

"How about Bruno?" Sommers prodded. "How old is he now? What sort of looking fellow is he?"

The man with the wheelbarrow stared at him thoughtfully.

"Is Bruno in trouble again?" he asked. "He must be in trouble again. A man was here yesterday asking those very same questions. I don't think he was a police officer though. He was driving a big car, a big black Cadillac."

Cornell again. A trail that had started with a trip to Third and Fremont was almost completed. Only one more location was needed to fill in the gap that stretched between an abandoned dwelling and an alley behind a lumber company.

"Bruno's a nice enough looking young fellow," the man was saying. "About twenty, I'd say, and a real flashy dresser. I don't know where he gets his money."

"I think I do," Sommers said grimly. "Do you know the Berrinis' new address?"

"Couldn't tell you that, Officer, but I suppose the Post Office people could. Wherever they moved, they have to get mail."

"That they do," Sommers said. "I've got something for Bruno Berrini myself—special delivery."

It was a very neat plan. Back at headquarters, Sommers conferred with Lieutenant Graves of Narcotics, and the little red crosses on the map found in the glove compartment took on significance.

"The way it looks to me," Sommers said, "the car salesman, Cornell, marked this map himself. Berrini—or Berra, as he called himself—would have been more careful. Cornell was used—that much must have been obvious to him yesterday morning when he called Garcy and said that he'd run into difficulty with the sale, but would have it straightened out before the day was over."

Graves nodded agreement.

"The used-car routine is a new switch," he admitted. "We haven't run into it before. Berrini couldn't use his own car; if we spotted those delivery stations and watched them, it could be traced to him. The way he ducked his head and ran in and out of the rest rooms indicates how afraid he was of being seen. This scheme beats the stolen-car method where there's always a resulting investigation that might lead to an arrest. Who would think of reporting a reluctant car buyer to the police?"

"Exactly," Sommers said. "Cornell didn't even dare report him to his employer. Imagine his feelings when he realized he'd been tricked into chauffeuring a marijuana peddler on his rounds. He must have spent that last day of his life retracing the places to which the elusive Mr. Berra had caused him to drive: the station at the corner of Third and Fremont, the station at Eighth and California—that was the first day's route. Then he repeated the second trip: to the grocery store across from the high school and to the health food shop, checking the map as he went. By this time he knew what those locations meant. Berrini made one mistake. Maybe he was just too cocky, but on that second drive he smoked some of his own product. Cornell didn't smoke at all, and the fumes must have bothered his throat; in any event, something happened to draw his attention to the stubs I found in that ashtray."

Graves had listened intently; now he asked, "Why—?"

"Because Cornell was shot with his own gun, a gun usually kept in his room. He went home, according to what his wife said, just long enough to have gone into his room and taken the gun. By that time, he must have located Berrini. He told his wife that he was going out to meet Berra and 'put an end to the indecision.'"

"'I've got him on the hook,' he told me. 'All I have to do is reel him in.'"

Mrs. Cornell's words intruded in Sommers' mind. They fit into the pattern too.

"A man doesn't go home to get his gun," he added, "if he's only going out to sell a car. The going was rough for Cornell, but not that rough."

"That's one thing I don't understand," Graves remarked. "Granting that you're right and that Cornell did realize that he'd been used to deliver marijuana to the supply points on this map, why did he go after Berra himself? Why didn't he go to the police?"

There were alternative reasons. There was the possibility of attempted blackmail—that was the obvious one. Cornell had needed that sale badly enough to cling to it all week. He had enough on Berra to make him buy the car.

There was also the possibility of anticipating a reward if he nailed a marijuana peddler; Cornell could have used a reward. But to know why a man does anything, it is necessary to know something about the man himself; and everything Sommers had learned about Glenn Cornell suggested that he was a good citizen and a conscientious father. He was risking his life when he went after Berrini. He must have known that a hopped-up person was capable of anything. The only reason a man like Cornell would do such a thing was the kind of reason that stood tall and broad-shouldered in a high school jersey with a big S on the chest. S for Steinmetz.

Graves listened to that possibility spelled out, and then asked, "Do you think Cornell's son is mixed up in this?"

"It isn't what I think that matters," Sommers said. "It's what Cornell feared. I'm going to do a little checking at Steinmetz. Right now, I'd be willing to give odds that Andy Cornell and Joe Berrini are pals and that Glenn Cornell knew about it and worried about it. I'm not looking into a crystal ball when I say that, either. The man who called Garcy Motors asked for Cornell by name. If Bruno Berrini's kid brother pals around with Andy Cornell, chances are he knew Andy's father was a salesman at Garcy's. He might even have known that he was easygoing—'he could be pushed around' was the way Andy put it. I think that's your answer, Lieutenant. I think Cornell took his gun and went after Berrini on his own because he was afraid police action might hurt his son. Guilt can rub off on the innocent, too, especially when the innocent is an adolescent with more bravado than brains."

At least it was a reason, and there had to be a reason—even as there had to be a reason for the lumps of solder on the undersides of the two rest-room lavatories.

"You may be right," Graves said. "It shouldn't be too difficult to find out what happened last night. We know the deposit points for the marijuana—all we have to do is watch. Berrini's used them before, the multiplicity of the soldering lumps indicate that some kind of packet or container has been hidden under the lavatories more than once, and he'll use them again. Cornell's dead—a published suicide. What does he have to fear?"

Sommers was thoughtful. Lieutenant Graves' job seemed simple; his wasn't so easy.

"He may use the car salesman method of transportation again," he suggested. "You've got to admit, it's a good one. If it hadn't been for Cornell's curiosity and that marked map, we'd never have traced the black Caddy to him."

"And Berrini knows nothing of the map," Graves added.

"Of course not. He'd have destroyed it if he'd known. Lieutenant, I've got a request to make of your department. I want you to contact the used-car dealers in this area and alert them to Berra's pitch. Chances are he'll be going through this same routine within the week."

"Within the week?" Graves echoed.

"It's the football season," Sommers said. "What's a logical place to peddle marijuana—particularly marijuana that's been delivered to the pushers before Saturday?"

Graves grinned.

"You've been nosing around in my detail," he said. "You know we've been getting reports from the football games."

"It's a report from a used-car dealer that I'm interested in," Sommers said. "You want Berrini for passing narcotics—that's an easy job. I want him for something that's going to take a little doing. I'm going out now and take some instructions in how to sell an automobile."

"You?" Graves asked.

"Who else, Lieutenant? I'm the man who wants Berrini for murder."

Bruno Berrini was watched. Before the day was over, his new residence had been located in a stucco duplex within a few blocks of the house about to be moved. The school office was closed over the weekend, but on Monday it was learned that Joe Berrini, the younger brother, was a junior at Steinmetz High and a classmate of Andy Cornell. The two boys were seen together in the schoolyard on the day after Glenn Cornell's funeral, which was on Tuesday. It was the same day when Lieutenant Graves reported on the results of notifying the local used-car dealers of Berrini's routine. He'd wasted no time in trying his trick again. He used his own product, and that gave him more daring than sense. This time it was a salesman named Hamilton from Economy Motors who had the same story to tell that Sommers had already pieced out of interviews with Max Fuller and the man named Donnegan. A man who called himself Mr. Baron had telephoned in on the previous Friday and inquired about a '58 Buick displayed on the lot. Told it was still there, he expressed great interest and asked that a salesman pick him up for a demonstration ride at a service station on the corner of Third and Fremont. From there on the story was the same. Baron's peculiar conduct had puzzled the salesman, but customers could be peculiar.

"Friday," Sommers mused. "That's the same day he used Cornell the first time. I was right. He works on a schedule. He should call back about the Buick on Thursday. He had to divide these trips up. No salesman would fall for making four stops on a trip. He'd be suspicious."

"So Berrini divides his distribution points into two parts and services them a week apart," Graves concluded.

They were right. On Thursday, Hamilton called in to report that Mr. Baron had decided to buy the Buick, but had to get the money—the full amount—from his mother, who insisted on seeing what he was buying before writing the check. Sommers and Graves went out to the lot together. By that time, Mr. Baron had called back to say he couldn't make it in, but would meet Mr. Hamilton in front of his home. The address given was the empty house.

Sommers got into the Buick.

"I'll be behind you," Graves told him. "Berrini will have the stuff on him, but I don't want to take him until he's made his deliveries. I want the receivers as well as the distributor."

"I want more than that," Sommers said. "I want a murderer."

He picked up Berrini in front of the house that still looked as if somebody had just washed the curtains and forgotten to pick up the throwaways from the porch. Berrini was a man of habit. He'd worked out a means of transportation to his delivery spots, but he wasn't prepared for a stranger behind the steering wheel. He balked at the curb.

"Where's Mr. Hamilton?" he demanded.

A young, dark, good-looking kid in a very sharp tweed jacket and slacks. He might have been all slicked up to go paying court to his girl, but Sommers knew a killer could look like an angel.

"Sick," he answered, trying to sound convincing. "He asked me to take his place."

Berrini hesitated. Was the word "cop" written all over Sommers' face, putting the lie to his story? If it was, he should be reaching for the holster under his coat. He didn't. He let the weight of the gun lean against his ribs, while Berrini's suspicious eyes passed judgment. The eyes were a little glassy. He was about ready to make that almost inevitable switch from reefers to something more potent. His judgment wasn't good. Almost a week had passed since Cornell's death, and there had been no public notice of anything but obvious suicide. Berrini felt safe. He crawled into the front seat and gave an address. He said very little during the half hour that passed before Sommers pulled up before a ranch-style home in one of the better districts. This was supposed to be where Berrini's mother lived. He waited for the story and it came.

"I don't see her car in the driveway," he said. "She must have gone to a little store a few blocks down the street. She buys a lot of this health food stuff. Let's drive down and see."

"Maybe you should ring the bell," Sommers suggested. "She might have left the car in the garage."

"She never leaves the car in the garage—never! She's at this store—I'll bet ten dollars. Just a few blocks—"

It was a thin story, but to a commission-hungry salesman eager for a cash sale it would have been convincing. Sommers listened to the directions and then proceeded to the herb shop. He pulled up to the curb and parked about half a block ahead of the unmarked car in which Lieutenant Graves was waiting. Berrini went inside alone. Through the front window, Sommers observed him in earnest conversation with the proprietor, after which they went into the back room for a few moments. When Berrini came back into view, Sommers knew the first delivery had been completed; but the lieutenant wouldn't make his move until they had proceeded on the delivery route. That was the agreement between them. Berrini's supply points were the lieutenant's concern, but Berrini belonged to Sommers.

Berrini returned to the Buick with another story.

"She was in here a little while ago," he reported, "but they were out of what she wanted. The clerk sent her to another store. If you don't mind driving a little farther, we'll catch her there. This car's what I've been looking for."

So a man with a lagging sales record and a family to support would go along with the pitch. He'd come this far; he had to keep riding that sale. Sommers was beginning to get the feel of the part he was playing. Be pleasant, be nice, keep smiling. Pretend you don't know the next stop is a small independent market across the street from the Steinmetz High School. He glanced in the rear-view mirror as the Buick edged away from the curb. Lieutenant Graves was sliding across the seat to get out of the unmarked sedan. Within minutes, he'd have relieved the herb shop proprietor of his latest consignment. So far, everything was working out according to plan.

It was almost dark when they reached the store. The schoolyard was deserted and the streets empty. Berrini went inside and Sommers, as he had done before, watched from the Buick. Five minutes passed, ten minutes, fifteen. Nobody else went into the store or came out of the store. Little independents didn't do a volume business, particularly not at an hour when housewives were already preparing the dinners their families were waiting to devour. Twenty minutes. Sommers crawled out of the Buick and scanned the street behind him. Something must have delayed Graves back at the herb store; there was no sign of his sedan. By this time Sommers knew what Glenn Cornell had learned at the end of his long drive. Berrini, Berra, Baron—whatever he called himself—wasn't coming back. This was the end of the line. Thanks for the ride, sucker, but I don't need you any more. Sommers gave the lieutenant five more minutes and then went into the store alone.

The balding proprietor was adamant. The gentleman must be mistaken. A dark young man in a tweed jacket? Here, in this store? Nobody had come into the store in almost an hour. Business was slow; it was closing time.

"I don't think so," Sommers said. "I think it's opening time."

He pulled his badge from his pocket and thrust it under the man's startled eyes.

"Open!" he ordered. "Where's Bruno Berrini?"

The man's face reddened. "Who?" he stammered.

"Bruno Berrini. He's in trouble—big trouble. You don't want to cover for a killer, do you?"

It was one thing to peddle marijuana to high-school students, one thing to twist young lives so that they might never be whole again; but it was something entirely different to face a detective from Homicide and risk your own sweet freedom. One wild glance toward the rear of the store and Sommers had his answer.

"What's back there?" he demanded.

"Only the stockroom," the man protested. "Nothing else!"

There was only one reason for the man to scream the words. Sommers wouldn't listen to him, but Berrini would. There was no time to waste. The stockroom was dark, but beyond it a ribbon of light showed beneath a closed door. As Sommers moved toward it, the light disappeared. Now there was only a door—vague in the shadows—and behind it a man who knew why Glenn Cornell had died with his chin on the horn rim of a Cadillac he hadn't sold.

"Berrini!"

Sommers fired the word at the silence and dropped back against the wall beside the door.

He waited a few seconds and then—

"I'll give you to the count of three to come out, Berrini. If you don't want twice the trouble you've got now, you'll come quietly. We know you killed Glenn Cornell. We found a nice, clear print you forgot to wipe off his gun. One—two—"

It was a lie. There hadn't been a print on Cornell's gun that hadn't matched Cornell's own; but Sommers got no farther with his threat. The first interruption was an undistinguishable oath, and then the walls seemed to split open with the sound of gunfire. But Berrini wasn't shooting at the door. Berrini wasn't shooting at all. Sommers discovered that when he jerked open the door and let the fading finger of light from the front of the store stretch to the place where Berrini crouched with his arms folded over his face as if they could stop the .45 leveled at the back of his head from splitting open his skull.

"Drop the gun!" Sommers ordered. "Drop it on the floor!"

For about five seconds Berrini's life expectancy hovered at zero and then the barrel of the .45 drooped, lowered, and finally fell to the floor.

"Okay, kick it this way," Sommers said.

The gun slid across the floor. Not until it was safely under his foot, did Sommers draw an easy breath. It was no small thing to have talked down the hatred blazing in the eyes of a tall, blond kid with a big S on his sweater.

Back at headquarters, Bruno Berrini made his confession. He hadn't meant to kill Cornell. Cornell had sought him out and insisted on one more demonstration ride. Not until they were under way did he reveal his knowledge of his brother Joe's use of him and demand information about his brother's association with Andy. They quarreled then, and Cornell pulled his gun. It was self-defense, Berrini insisted. It was an accident. A guy has a right to defend himself, doesn't he? So the gun went off while he was struggling for it and killed a guy. It was self-defense. That was the story he would take into court, and whether or not he succeeded in selling it to a jury wasn't in Sommers' department. What was in his department, in his office, in fact, was a kid with a story to tell.

Andy Cornell was shaken and subdued.

"It was a crack Joe Berrini made the day after my father's funeral that made me suspicious," he admitted. "He was trying to be nice, I guess. 'Your old man had to have a lot of guts to put a .45 to his head,' he said. I got to thinking about it later. I even looked through all the old newspapers to make sure, but nobody had mentioned that my dad's gun was a .45. I didn't know it myself until the police returned the gun to my mother and I got hold of it. Dad would never let me near it. Too many kids got killed playing with empty guns, he always said. But it was a .45 all right, and how did Joe know that unless he knew a lot more? Then I got to thinking about this Mr. Berra and how much the name sounded like Berrini.

"I knew my dad didn't like me hanging around with Joe because of his brother's record. I didn't see what that had to do with Joe, but it had worried him and so I got to thinking that maybe he'd had a fight with Bruno, or something. I knew Bruno was mixed up in what was going on at the grocery store across from the school. Kids know more about that kind of thing than cops, I guess. I just kept watching and waiting for my chance to talk to Bruno, which happened to be today."

"A talk with Bruno," Sommers repeated, "at the point of a gun." He was scowling when he said it. The kid might have been killed, taking that gun away from Bruno. "Haven't you Cornells ever heard of going to the police?" he demanded.

Andy ducked his head. It was time for a lecture on the folly of a citizen taking the law into his own hands; but Andy Cornell suddenly wilted, as if the excitement of his search for Bruno was all that had held back the grief of his father's death and now that barrier was gone. He would be remembering the warnings his father had given him about the Berrinis and picking up that burden, too. The kid had too much hard living ahead of him to be handicapped by additional crosses of guilt.

"Well, there's one thing I'll have to hand to you," Sommers admitted, having decided to forego the lecture. "You're not it any more than your father was."

Andy looked up, puzzled.

"What's that?" he asked.

"Chicken," Sommers said.

RON GOULART

The Tin Ear

It was a bad day to be ransacked, a yellow, smoggy, eighty-five-degree morning. John Easy tossed his denim sport coat over his desk chair and scratched the place where his shoulder holster chafed him. Beyond his office windows he could see limp palm trees, and sports cars flickering. Easy hunched his wide shoulders and cracked his knuckles. "How about Ad?" he asked his secretary. It was after ten and his partner hadn't yet called in today.

"He's still down in San Amaro, I guess," said Naida Sim, fanning herself with an empty file folder. "On the Shubert case, I suppose."

Easy frowned and unstrapped his gun. "This damn thing," he said.

"I thought you and Mr. Faber were going to get a burglar alarm in?"

"We got you the electric typewriter instead." He wiped perspiration from his forehead and squatted down. Spilled all across the gray rug were file folders, letters, envelopes, tape spools. "Wonder what they took."

"Something pretty important, I suppose," said Naida. She was a pretty blonde girl, slender and freckled. Her hair had no curl today.

Easy sniffed. "What's that smell?"

"Cinders in the air. Another fire over in the valley."

"Why did I leave the San Francisco police and come down here to L.A.?" Easy complained.

"I guess because they busted you after you were supposed to have taken that bribe," said Naida, kneeling down beside him.

Unbuttoning his top shirt button, Easy said, "Well, let's get this stuff gathered up and try to figure who swiped what."

The phone rang and Naida popped up to answer it. "Faber and Easy, Detective Service." She blinked. "He's right here, I guess."

To Easy, she said, "It's a Lieutenant Disney of the San Amaro police."

The phone was damp. "Yeah?" said Easy.

"This is Lieutenant Bryan K. Disney. We found your partner down here."

"Found him how?" asked Easy, inhaling sharply. "And where?"

"Dead. Shot twice with a .38, it looks like. In a place down the beach called Retirement Cove."

"What is Retirement Cove?"

"New senior citizens' beach town being built. Not finished yet and nobody living there. Workman found the body about two hours ago, spread-eagled on a badminton court."

"Damn," said Easy, grimacing at their secretary.

"What was he working on?"

Easy answered, "Nothing. He was taking a few days off. Vacation. He was a latent beach bum and liked to get the sun." A silver sports car flashed by and the glare made Easy duck.

Naida had started to cry. "I guess Ad's hurt."

"He's dead," said Easy. "Do you want to see me for anything, Lieutenant Disney?"

"You might come down and talk to me today sometime, yeah," said the policeman. "Anything you can say now? Enemies, affairs, that kind of thing?"

"Ad led a blameless life," said Easy. "But I'll think about it."

"My office is across the street from the equestrian statue of General Grant. See you."

Easy cradled the phone and wiped his palms on his thighs. "Well," he said. He sat down in his swivel chair.

"Why didn't you tell them Mr. Faber had been watching Mrs. Shubert for a week and a half?"

"I don't know," said Easy. "I've got a habit of not confiding in the police. Anyway, I want to check some things out myself." He strapped his gun back on.

"Maybe he found out something big," suggested the girl.

"I doubt it," said Easy. "Ad had a tin ear most of the time. If he heard anything important he wouldn't have known it probably."

"He was your partner."

"That doesn't mean he was an exceptional operative. We were probably going to bust up this partnership in another few months anyway."

Naida wiped her eyes. "I hate to have anybody I know get killed."

Easy looked past her at the bright morning. "I'll go down to San Amaro now. Clean up the office and let me know what's gone."

"Does this rummaging here tie in with what happened to Mr. Faber?"

"Maybe," said Easy, shrugging into his coat. "If Ad's reports on the Shubert case are missing it might mean something."

"Shall I close the office?"

"Why?"

"I imagined we might go into mourning for a day."

"Nope. Ad didn't have any family. That means we have to see him buried. We can't afford to lose a day. A client might walk in any minute."

"I guess you're not very sentimental."

"No," said Easy, walking out into the hot morning.

The real estate cottage looked down on a white stretch of beach. The San Amaro afternoon was relatively mild. Easy rested his arms on the half open Dutch doors and called in, "Mr. Majors?"

There was a purple-haired secretary, old and wide, sitting at the nearest desk and a thin blond man of about forty at the further desk. "Yes," the man said, half rising.

A phone rang and the secretary caught it. "Mr. MacQuarrie for you, Mr. Majors."

"I'll call him later," said Majors, walking out of the shadows toward the unmoving Easy. "Did you want to come in?"

"Out here would be better," said Easy. "This is what they call a delicate situation."

Majors had on a golf sweater, tweed slacks. He had a nice outdoor tan. "Who are you?"

"John Easy. Until today my outfit was called Faber and Easy."

"You're trying to sell me something, Mr. Easy?"

"Maybe," said Easy. "Protection and security. It all depends. Right now I want to find out who killed my partner."

Majors smiled, his lips pursing. "This is a very cryptic sales pitch."

"I'll be direct," said Easy. "You're Norm Majors, aren't you?"

"Of course. So?"

"For the past three months, from what I've been able to put together from the reports and tapes my partner turned in, you've been having an affair with a Mrs. Nita Shubert. We've been on the case a couple of weeks. That is, Ad Faber was down here at the request of our client, Mr. Shubert. Okay?"

Majors opened his mouth and studied Easy. He reached back and felt for a low rustic bench that fronted the cottage. "I didn't know," he said, letting himself sit.

"Didn't know what?"

"That we were watched." He straightened. "Tapes, did you say? That's illegal, isn't it?"

"So's adultery. I'm not here to chat on ethics, Majors. I wanted to see you."

"Why?"

"To ask you," said Easy, "if you killed Ad Faber."

Majors coughed. "No, Easy, no. No. I didn't."

"Did you ever see him? Know about him?"

"I told you I didn't."

"You were with Mrs. Shubert yesterday."

"No," said Majors. "Not at all yesterday. Nita said she couldn't get free yesterday." He put his knuckles against his cheek. "Wait. Your partner must be the one who was found down at Retirement Cove. A friend of mine is selling that and called me."

"That's right," said Easy. "I drove by it a while ago. It's not too far from the beach house Mrs. Shubert is renting for your meetings."

Majors rose up. "Shubert is aware of us?"

"For a week."

"Then what did you mean about protection?"

"The police don't know about you as yet. You might mention that to Nita Shubert."

"This sounds like blackmail," said Majors.

Easy shrugged and headed back for his car.

Easy called his secretary from a phone booth in a drugstore near the San Amaro town square. A few seconds after he'd stepped into the booth a teenage singing group appeared on a platform next to the soda fountain. They were singing about surf riding now as the place filled up with a sun-bleached after-school crowd.

"Are you in a saloon?" Naida asked.

"A soda fountain. What's happening there?"

"Did you see Lieutenant Disney yet?"

"I'm en route." A silver blonde in an orange shift jumped up on the entertainment platform. A big sign over the fountain said Grand Opening. All the guitars were amplified. "What's missing?"

"Nothing at all," said Naida. "I double-checked. But listen . . ."

"Any new business?"

"A man called you a couple of times but wouldn't say who he was. But listen . . ."

"Okay, what?"

"A final report came in from Mr. Faber. Mailed late yesterday in San Amaro."

"Well, tell me what he said."

"I'm trying. No tape this time. He said that Mrs. Shubert met somebody new yesterday. He listened in and got the feeling this was somebody she hadn't seen for a while. No names. He couldn't catch any name for the man. But the man mentioned money, a lot of it. And he wanted Mrs. Shubert to leave with him but she said no."

"Leave with him?" He had the impression the phone booth was gently rocking.

"To Mexico."

"This new guy came to the beach place she uses to meet Majors?"

"Yes," said Naida. "Is there some kind of political rally going on where you are?"

"It's a musical event. How hot is it in L.A.?"

"I guess about 92," answered his secretary. "Are you going to Lieutenant Disney?"

"Soon," said Easy, and hung up. He worked his way out of the thick crowd of teenagers. Until now, thirty-four hadn't seemed that old. Suddenly he felt his years.

Lieutenant Disney was almost too short to be a cop. He smoked cigarette-sized cigars and kept his hat, an almost brimless checked thing, on indoors. The walls of his humid office were papered with what looked to be long out-of-date wanted posters. He didn't tell Easy much, and Easy didn't tell him anything. Their interview lasted twenty-five minutes.

Kevin Shubert, Easy's client, made his money in some way that allowed him to be home daytimes. He talked to Easy beside a glass-enclosed swimming pool. The grounds around the big low Moorish house were almost sufficient to let the place be called an estate.

"I'm in perfect health," Shubert said. He was tall and about fifty, with his balding head crewcut. "You'd think all this anguish Nita heaps on me would make me ill."

"Maybe you'll collapse unexpectedly," said Easy.

"Does the murder of your partner tie in with Nita and her lover?" Shubert asked him.

Easy was sitting at an awkward angle in a striped canvas chair. "Probably."

"Do the police know about us?"

"Not by way of me. But they could find out," said Easy. "You told me you'd been married how long?"

"Nearly two years. My second marriage. Nita's first."

"You met her where?"

"In San Francisco," said his client, making a flapping motion with his thin elbows. "Your old haunt."

"Something I'm trying to place. Something about the pictures of Mrs. Shubert you showed me. What was her name then?"

"Halpern. Nita Halpern."

"There was some bank scandal, wasn't there?"

The skin of Shubert's pale lips was dry. He moistened it with his tongue. "Well, yes. She was secretary to a bank official who vanished, a man named Robert L. Brasil. Three hundred thousand dollars vanished along with him. You may have seen Nita's photo in the press. Nothing was ever laid at her door, however. That was three years ago."

"I wonder," said Easy. "Is your wife around?"

"For a change, yes. She's in her studio. Nita paints a little."

"I'd like to talk to her."

"Listen, Easy," said Shubert, rising, "I'd like no more scandal to touch my wife. I appreciate your keeping things to yourself so far. What will it cost for you to continue silent?"

"You've already paid us," said Easy. "I'd like to see Mrs. Shubert alone," he added peremptorily.

"I assumed as much."

Large on the canvas was a faithfully rendered box of wheat cereal. Nita Shubert was rangy and dark, angular in yellow stretch pants and a shaggy yellow pullover. The small pitchfork wrinkles at her eyes indicated she was about thirty-five. "You've fouled things up, Mr. Easy," she said, putting a white-tipped brush aside. "You and your late partner. I don't even think it's legal to eavesdrop the way you apparently were."

"When did you first realize you were being watched?" Easy asked her.

"Kevin told me just a short time ago, when the death of your partner became known."

"Ad," said Easy. "That's Ad Faber, my partner, was given to being heavy-handed at times. I think he gave himself away yesterday somehow; yesterday, when you didn't see Majors at the beach house."

The woman didn't reply. She slowly squeezed earth-colored paint onto her palette.

"Ad had a tin ear," said Easy. "But sometimes he could tumble to what he was hearing. I think he heard something yesterday, and finally figured out what it might mean."

"I was with Norm Majors yesterday," said Nita Shubert. "No matter what you might believe."

"Ad must have gone back to your beach house last night, after he'd sent his last report off to me. Somebody spotted him and got worried."

"Yes?"

"Probably your ex-boss," said Easy. "Robert L. Brasil."

Her head gave a negative jerk. "He vanished three years ago."

"I want," said Easy, "to be clear on one thing. I haven't told the police any of this. For a consideration, nobody has to find out about Brasil."

"Nobody will find out anything," said the woman. "He's long gone."

"If he wants to stay vanished," said Easy, "he might think about as little as $20,000."

Nita Shubert turned her back on him.

"I noticed a motel down near your beach house, the Mermaid Terrace. I'll stay there tonight if anyone wants me." He studied the painting. "You spelled wheat wrong."

"Perhaps I wanted to," she said. Easy nodded and left.

Easy got the call at a little after nine. A muffled male voice told him to be at the #3 lifeguard station on the beach in a half hour.

The night was warm and overcast. The lifeguard station was down the silent empty beach, near a closed soft-drink stand. Easy found it early, but there was someone sitting up in the lifeguard chair.

The dark water glowed faintly, fluttering silently.

"Brasil?" Easy called to the figure on the tall-legged chair.

The shadow of the protecting beach umbrella hid the upper half of the man. He was wearing a dark coat, hands in the pockets. "I didn't know we were being watched and listened to," he said. His voice had a touch of chest cold in it. "I picked a bad time to come out of the woodwork."

"My partner bumped into you?"

"I had planned to spend the night in the beach house. He came poking around, not too covertly, and offered to keep quiet for a fee. He had figured out that I wasn't anxious to be found here in California."

"You shot him, huh?"

"Yes," said Brasil.

"Then drove up to L.A. to see if he'd turned in anything to the office."

"I'm cautious, and I don't like paying money out needlessly, Easy."

"I figured you didn't go in for payoffs," said Easy. He lunged and caught the man's legs, and jerked him from his perch. Brasil's head hit the lowest rung of the chair as he fell.

Brasil rolled and grabbed out a pistol from his coat pocket.

Easy dived sideways, got out his own .38.

Brasil's first shot went up and tore the umbrella into tatters.

Easy planted himself and fired twice. Brasil twisted up until he was almost standing and then fell. He died face down in the sand.

Easy put his gun away. He still didn't know what the man looked like.

His secretary said, "Iced tea," and put a paper cup on his desk.

The office was cleaned up now, and the sunlight on the street was not too glaring. Easy drank tea and leaned back in his chair. "You really weren't planning to blackmail anybody, were you?" Naida asked.

"Wasn't I?"

"No, you were just setting yourself up as a decoy to lure somebody out into the open, I guess."

"Run over to the delicatessen and get me a sandwich. No chicken."

"I think you really are sentimental," said the girl. "You actually do care about Mr. Faber and you wanted to avenge him. Right?"

"And don't take any of those dill pickles they give away."

"I guess you're not a bad person at all," said Naida, leaving the room.

Easy sighed and closed his eyes.

CHARLOTTE EDWARDS

The Time Before the Crime

One day in June, James J. MacClinton swung his two-year-old, medium-priced, inconspicuously colored sedan slantwise into the parking place before the post office. He pulled himself out from behind the wheel, and yanked gently at the back of his inconspicuously checked jacket.

Irma always said he looked neat as a pin, except that when he drove he let his jacket ride up into wrinkles.

He walked briskly across the sidewalk and up the nine broad steps to the double post office doors. He held one of them for a girl coming out with her arms loaded. Baby. Package. Basket. He let it shut slowly, his head swiveled to watch her descent.

Then he went through the door, changing the swivel to a slight shake.

Sometimes James J. MacClinton thought he would never get used to the way people got themselves up in California. You take a morning like this one now. Sunny and clear for a change and not yet hot. You'd think people shopping down in the center of town would have a little pride about the way they looked. Not girdles for the ladies, maybe, and ties for the men, gloves and all that. But at least neat skirts and shoes with heels. Or a sport shirt that didn't look slept in.

Take that one now. Faded, dirty-looking pedal pushers. Flapping flat slippers. Pin curls like metal worms all over her head. Oh well.

Irma wasn't like that, thank heaven. Irma had brought a lot of her Eastern ways and Eastern culture with her. Eight years of Western breeziness, heat and don't-give-a-darn hadn't been able to rub her sloppy.

James J. MacClinton fingered through the keycase in his hand for the long slim one which unlocked his post office box.

He liked having a post office box, even if when he had first got it, Irma had thought it was silly.

"The mailman comes every morning, James," she said, frowning a little, buttering a tiny fragment of toast torn off precisely from the perfectly browned whole. "I'll admit it's well after you're off for the day. But, my goodness, the mail's right on the desk when you get home."

He nodded, and swallowed the last of his coffee.

"I know that." He touched his lips with the linen napkin, fresh every morning and more power to Irma. "It's just that with a box I can check before I head for the city."

She smiled at him, the no-matter-how-old-you-are-you're-still-just-a-boy smile.

"Very well," she said sweetly.

It was as if she gave him permission. Well, of course, in a way she did.

There was always a lot of mail addressed to Irma. She was consistent about keeping in touch with her girlhood friends, and the few relatives (none of them close, thank goodness) who resided back East. She was also a great one for birthday cards, anniversaries and such.

You don't put out without getting back. And so, almost every morning when he opened the box, most of the stuff in it was for Irma.

James J. MacClinton very carefully sorted out all of Irma's mail and put it back in the box. Irma would pick it up, using her own key, when she went out to shop for groceries. Sometimes, if none of his customers wanted to see him before eleven, James took the mail back home to her. Even took the time to listen to a letter or two. But usually, he left it where it was.

His correspondence mostly came in long envelopes, cheerfully edged in the red and blue rickrack denoting Air Mail. The ones with glass windows held his expense checks from the home office each Friday, and twice monthly his salary and commission checks. The others were manila and big and square and sometimes quite fat.

He always felt a small leap of his heart when they were fat. These contained his sales invoices. It was a little like Christmas, opening them and looking them over, counting out what he could depend on next month. There were even surprises sometimes. Sales in remote areas he'd considered dead territory. These gave him a real lift.

He didn't exactly explain it to himself. But the post office box, and looking at those invoices in the car, cashing the checks himself, gave him a sense of freedom. Yes, of manhood. A feeling he hadn't known before he rented the little metal square with its impersonal number on the front.

Irma never opened his mail. She was far too honorable for that. But she did have a way of hovering over him while he slit the flaps, and reading the figures over his shoulder. A mite too much of a shared experience, he sometimes thought.

Then, too, she was quicker with numbers than he was. She added them up in a flash, while he liked to take his time and maybe be surprised a little at the second toting.

This June morning there wasn't a thing from the home office, not a thing, although he expected some news about the new product they said would be out soon. Just two cards for him, and a long white envelope. No rickrack. He felt a momentary drop in his morning spirits. His walk out of the double doors and down the nine broad steps and across the sidewalk wasn't quite so sprightly.

He got into the car, remembering again to smooth his jacket behind him, pushed the ignition key into its slot and sat back.

There was an advertisement from the place where he'd bought his car. They had some hangovers, greatly reduced and brand new.

Card number two informed him that his favorite men's shop was having a clearance sale of spring suits. That might be a good idea. Something dark, plain and really classy-looking, that didn't wrinkle. If Irma thought they could afford it.

The envelope was white, long, heavy and official-looking. He picked it up, back first, and turned it over slowly. There was a busy day ahead of him. He ought to get going, now that the first early rush was cleared from the freeway.

But he turned the envelope over slowly, savoring this quiet moment, this time alone, unknown and anonymous in the front seat of his car. Passers-by would see a man reading mail, perhaps important mail which would change the structure of his life, or of many lives. How would they know the difference?

He glanced at himself in the rear view mirror. He looked serious, sure and important. It was a thing that always surprised him a little. The dignity about the way he walked. The way his dark hair lay neatly on his skull. The arrogant nose and the heavy black eyebrows.

He didn't feel dignified inside. Nor arrogant. He felt meek, most of the time, and often apologetic. Something about the years of his life, maybe in childhood, maybe in the struggle since then. Something about the war and being a G.I. instead of an officer, the starting again afterward in a lowly position and having to prove himself every step of the way. Maybe the fact that he was already married and too old to take advantage of the higher education offered by the G.I. Bill. Maybe one of these, maybe all, kept him feeling young and insecure despite his forty years.

Or maybe it was Irma. Bless her. She was so sure in every direction. As she should be, product of the best schools and all sorts of luxuries before her parents were killed.

He studied his name, typed on the front of the envelope.

James J. MacClinton
1848 Sandarwood Place
Franklyn City, California

In the upper left-hand corner there was a return address.

Superior Court of Los Angeles County, it read.

James' heart began to do a nervous tattoo in his chest and his breath turned quick and shallow.

That was a hangover from his childhood. His mother had had such a respect, almost a fear, of the law that she had transmitted it right into his blood. Never so much as a traffic ticket. Not many men his age could possibly present a record like that. Even in the Army, no matter what live-dangerously attitudes the other men had, he never broke a rule.

His fingers didn't shake as he tore open the envelope, not slowly and neatly, leaving quick ragged edges instead. But they wanted to. They did what he told them only because he kept assuring himself, over and over, that he had done nothing wrong, and therefore this communication could pose no threat to him.

He unfolded the paper and smoothed it out against the steering wheel. He began to read, carefully, making himself absorb each word.

With the final sentence a long breath oozed out of James J. MacClinton, as if it had been retarded through all of the typed phrases. He folded the sheet neatly, turned the ignition key, started the motor and backed the car away from the post office. He rode at a legal limit up the main street to the freeway ingress, stayed in the slow lane and headed toward the city.

The plan for the day's work which had been so carefully laid in his mind blew out of it. The words of the letter kept spelling themselves before his eyes.

Well, now, what do you know?

Strange, of course, when you came to think of it, that in all his forty years he had never before been called for jury duty. Next August or after, they said.

Well, it could be arranged, of course. They paid you for that sort of thing. Not much, probably. But something for your time. In a job like his he could work extra hard before the time they might call him, and day and night afterward if necessary. There would be no hardship.

Maybe it would be one of those things where the trial went on and on and the jury had to stay at a hotel and be locked up at night or some such.

He could just see Irma's face in that case. She didn't like it one bit if he was late getting home. She certainly wouldn't care for having her husband shut up day and night with a bunch of strangers. Women among them, of course.

They called lots of women nowadays. Seemed as if any time you picked up the paper and read about a trial, it was always a jury of ten women and two men. Maybe because the men had regular jobs and asked to be excused.

James decided that he wouldn't ask to be excused. Not for all the tea in China. It would be a real thing to sit up there and listen to the judge, and two lawyers, and the clerk or whatever he was who asked, "Do you swear to tell the truth, the whole truth and nothing but the truth, so help you God?"

It would be something now, to say, "I do."

You don't get to swear to the words you're about to say very often. It gives them a certain importance that words don't usually have, even if they're the gospel truth. You don't get a chance to promise anything very often, as a matter of fact. The vow to defend your country when you go into the service. The promise to love, honor and cherish your wife, when you stand before a preacher.

He laughed suddenly, aloud and at himself.

Who the devil was going to swear to tell the truth? That was a witness, wasn't it? Or the defendant? James didn't have any idea how a jury was sworn in. Something about no prejudice and how do you feel about this and that, and have you read of the case and formed any preconceived ideas. That was about it.

Just the same, he thought, it will be quite a thing to be inside a courtroom, seeing all the workings. Who knows, they might even make him the foreman of the jury. He'd sit at the end of a long table and keep things in order and try to think of arguments for any holdouts. It would be a nice change.

He reached forward to the glove compartment, carefully steering with one hand, and brought out his little brown notebook. He flipped the pages to the next to last, balancing the book on the steering wheel, and glanced down quickly. Yep. Sorban's first.

He headed the car off the freeway at the civic center and drove comfortably, careful of stop lights, over four crowded blocks and down two. He pulled up into the parking space beside the shop and got out. He reached over for his brief-case, saw the letter, tucked it into his pocket, and pulled himself, loaded, out of the car. He locked it deliberately and walked, with a new kind of briskness, a new kind of sureness, into the store.

By golly, he thought, it's something to be an American. To be picked at random to sit in judgment up there, all important and one out of many, on your fellow man.

He opened the door, nodded to the nearest salesman, and watched Mr. Sorban come toward him.

First thing he's going to do, he thought, is chew me out because the new equipment hasn't come through.

He forestalled it.

"Say, Mr. Sorban," he said, without preface, "how does it feel to be on jury duty? You ever do it?"

Sorban was short, round, and full to the skin of himself.

"You think I'm a sucker, Jim?" he asked heartily. "All you got to do is be busy. You'll get out of it."

"Don't know as I want to get out of it," James said. "Seems to me it might be—well, an interesting experience."

Sorban grinned. He had a weird grin which did something to his eyes. Nothing pleasant, either.

"Now you may have a point there." He scratched the bald circle on the top of his head. "Depends on the trial. You get a nice juicy one—"

James found himself changing the subject. "About that shipment," he jumped in, surprised at his boldness. "That new equipment, Sorban, is going to be worth waiting for. And I'm sorry, but it looks as if you'll just have to wait for it."

Sorban backed up two steps and blinked his eyes three times. His face was a jigsaw trying to decide which piece of emotion fitted it. He wiggled his mouth, and finally let a short sentence escape.

"All right," he said, pacifyingly. "All right. I'll wait, Jim. I'll wait for it."

When James J. MacClinton walked out of the store, the briskness of earlier morning was nothing compared to his step. Downright jaunty, it was, and he knew it.

He sat in the car for a moment before heading for the next customer. He smiled to himself, and shook his head a little and was tickled pink. Not only had he stalled old Sorban, by golly. But there was an extra order for three more machines in the briefcase.

First time he'd ever felt superior to any of his customers. Gave you an advantage, feeling superior.

He took the white envelope out of his pocket and tucked it up on the dashboard where he could see it on the way to the next store.

Sometimes, he thought, it doesn't take much. Just a guy who doesn't see what a privilege it is to sit on a jury—and all of a sudden you know you're better and smarter and surer than he is.

Frank Savrano woke up. He groaned. He didn't want to. His head hurt, his back ached, and the room smelled dirty and hot. He could hear the kids whining through the thin wall that separated the dark little bedroom from the dark little kitchen, and the flap of Pica's slippers as she moved around seemed to slap against his eyes.

Dirty, dirty, dirty. Everything hot and dirty. And summer was worse than any other time. And the filthy vino didn't help it at all. Because you always had to come home. You always came home. They wouldn't let you sleep it off in a cool black park somewhere. You lie down to rest and forget the dirt and the heat and let the vino beat itself out of your veins. And a cop comes, like he smelled where you were. So you might as well come home. And it's worse here than anywhere else. And it all happens over again.

He heard the squeak of the bedroom door and buried his dark curly head deeper in the sweat-soaked pillow.

"Frank," she called softly.

He could see with his eyes closed how she looked, standing in the doorway, leaning around the edge, as nervous and afraid as her voice. Pin curls, pedal pushers, and a bad cook.

"You awake, Frank?"

He grunted. Like the park, they wouldn't let you alone. All you wanted was to find a way to be alone.

"What else?" he asked roughly.

It is not a good thing for a wife to be afraid of her husband. Whatever there is in the husband that makes her afraid grows stronger and bigger and more sure of itself. More—more demanding. Just because she knows this fear, no matter how she has learned it.

It is not easy to be kind to a woman who fears you. And the more you are not kind, the more afraid she is, the more something inside of you, under the dirt, the sweat, the vino, aches and cries because of this fright.

He opened his dark eyes, shining, even now, even with the red in the whites shining pure and dazzled between the long black lashes. He watched her swing the door wider and walk hesitantly toward him. As if his tone, though rough, could have been worse. As his words could have been. And had been.

Pica said, "Yesterday, in the mail, this slip comes. It says a package is at the post office."

He looked at her. No pin curls, by the grace. And a dress. A red and white dress with a full skirt. Her hair combed out, long and thick, to the soft, tan shoulders.

"So?"

There was a smile on her lips, tentative and asking—and lipstick over them, bright and brave.

"So!"

She twirled slowly before him.

He could say it, if he would. Looking at her he thought it.

You are a pretty girl, Pica. Three kids, bang, bang, bang, and a huddled nasty little house, and five years with me, and you're a pretty girl, Pica. Still a pretty girl. He could say it, if he would.

But still—he couldn't.

They get afraid like this and you say the nice, sweet thing that lies so deep inside, and they melt. A wife like Pica, she melts. She kisses and smiles and sings with the work, and gets the dirt from the house. She maybe even cooks a little better, like at first, like the first of the marrying, before any kids, before the garage did any firing. She sings and is happy and forgets about the vino and the meanness.

Then—bang! Along they come. Always, like coming home, the meanness and the vino return. Nobody knows, least of all Frank Savrano, if the vino brings the meanness or the meanness brings the vino. But they come. That he knows. For sure. For certain. For all the years since he was a boy.

So, the one good and decent thing you can do is keep it steady. It makes sense to be steady mean. Let Pica melt and grow happy and think it is different, that it will be for good, better and nice—then when the meanness comes it is worse. It is the bottom and no more sureness.

Pop used to say, "You get used to batting your head with a stone after a lot of bats."

Let her get used to meanness, then.

"And the money? Where'd you get it?"

He sat up slowly, trying not to feel the pains shooting up his neck into his forehead and out his eyeballs. "Who give you money to buy such a fancy dress? And why?"

She stopped twirling. She stood very still, her hands clutching the edges of the full, bright skirt, like a good little girl in another age, about to make a curtsy.

She swallowed. He could see the swallow travel all the way from under her round chin down the column of her throat, hard, as if it had a square shape and was a solid thing.

"It is nothing that takes money," she said after the swallow was hidden in her breast somewhere. "I told you of the slip. The package at the post office. From Mama." She bowed her head toward the bright color. "For my birthday."

Frank stood up. Pica moved a little backward. They held positions, staring at each other.

It was so. He remembered June.

He remembered June before they were married. The boss at the garage liked him plenty. Liked the way he ran to serve the customers and grinned at them and talked them into a quart of oil, or a grease job. The boss liked the way he slid under the cars and found out what was the matter.

It was good the June before they married. It was a time with no anger jumping at him from any place at all. It was Korea over with, the hunger and the pain, the cold, the killing.

It was, that June, buying a box of candy with roses painted on the top, and a perfume, pale pale green in a tender bottle, and a card of paper lace. It was writing, "To Pica, on her seventeenth birthday, from her friend, Frank Savrano."

He moved toward Pica suddenly, that June after Korea and before marriage suddenly returning full and strong inside him. Stronger than any meanness and any vino.

Pica's eyes went wide. Her tanned face went white. Her skirt whirled as she turned and ran from him. The back door slammed. The kids began to cry.

Frank slumped back on the bed. He doubled over on himself, his elbows on his knotted knees. He ground his fists into his aching eyes. A crazy thing happened. His fists turned wet. Warm wet, and salt wet.

After a while he got up and pulled his pants over his shorts and tightened the wide belt around his waist. He went into the bathroom and slapped cold water against his face. He shaved carefully and brushed his teeth, roughly and for a long time. He rubbed tiger wax into his curls and combed through them until they lay down a little.

There were two shirts in the closet. Pica ironed. She couldn't cook, but she ironed good. He picked the green one with the brown plaid, and walked out into the kitchen.

He stood for a moment in the center of the kitchen, getting his bearings, letting the shave, the combing, the brushing, the clean shirt put a feeling into him.

Pica stepped through the doorway. "I will get your breakfast," she said. She moved toward the stove.

Pedal pushers, flats. Only the long, thick, black, combed hair was different without its pin curls. Only the hair remembered the pretty girl in the red and white dress with the full skirt.

"No breakfast," Frank said. "I'm going out."

She will ask me where, he thought. She always tries not to. She always asks. This time she didn't. She moved her shoulders up and down and turned toward the doorway.

"You—you want to know where I am going?" Frank found himself asking. "You want to check up on me?"

She stopped, but she didn't turn. The back of her heavy hair fanned out and sidewise as she shook her head.

A little seed of anger popped its shell. Not a very big one, though. Not with the clean shirt and the idea.

"I am going to see the old boss," Frank said. His words drowned the seed's pop. They sounded good in his ears.

Pica's whole body swirled and fanned as her hair had.

There was in her eyes the thing that Frank hated more than all else. The thing that kept him from saying she was a pretty girl. Or any other gentle thing.

In her eyes was the hope, the wild, terrible, loving hope.

Frank began to yell, forced, compelled, propelled, by the eyes and the pop-pop-pop inside of him.

"But do not plan," he yelled. "Do not get foolish and think there is anything better for us. He fired me once, remember? He always said, 'Savrano, boy, you're the best mechanic I ever had—but—but—"

The words the boss had said roosted on the bursting anger, each one fire-hot.

A lousy ten bucks. On a Saturday night and no dough and the boys stopping by. A lousy ten bucks. When there was forty, seventy, almost a hundred more in the till. Only ten. Only enough for a bottle of vino and to get into the game. Put it back Sunday. Or Monday, sure.

"Nobody's got the right to talk to me like that," Frank yelled, there in the kitchen, at Pica, white and frightened, reading it on his face. There on a June day, again living an October Monday morning. "Nobody's going to call Frank Savrano a thief. Not and live, he ain't."

The slam of the door behind him told him that he was out of doors. He did not feel his walking until he was halfway downtown, halfway to the corner where the big garage, all white and trimmed with red, like Pica's dress in reverse, caught the best and largest trade in the city. He stopped so sharply somebody bumped him from behind. He glared at the man who muttered an apology and circled around him.

Go to the boss, would he? Frank Savrano go to the boss and eat humble pie? "Mr. Michaels, I'm sorry I was a naughty bad boy. I promise to be good now. Please, please, Mr. Michaels, let me play in your yard again."

Hah!

Back there, way back there, you have a fight with some kid, what do you do? Go say sorry? Say, "Your yard's bigger. I like it here enough to let you tell me off?" Hell, no. You double fists every time you see the boy, and spit at his feet and keep him scared.

Keep 'em all scared. Twelve, fourteen, eighteen, now twenty-three, Frank Savrano backs down for nobody. You hear? Nobody. You hear, Mr. Michaels? You hear, Pica? Birthday, not birthday, no crawling.

He crossed the street slantwise and walked down the block away from Michaels' garage. He walked for a long time. Finally the heat began to go out of the sun and the breeze from the far ocean sniveled into the city and dried the sweat on his green and brown plaid shirt.

The streets are full of bars, of men leaning against dirty doorways, standing in uneven clusters in the middle of the sidewalk, one man, even so early, lying with his head snapped up, turtlewise, against a building.

Frank walked into one of the places. He went to the bar and ordered a drink. He sent it down, unadorned and bitter, into his mouth and throat and chest. He slapped the quarter on the bar and walked out slowly, comforted and cool. He stopped at a liquor store halfway down the block and bought a bottle of wine. He forced it, a lumpy bulk, into his pants pocket.

When he reached the park, he sauntered, dreaming and slow, looking up at the trees, and brightly around at the remaining playing children, the families having picnic suppers, a stray brown dog nuzzling his way from path to trees.

There was a quiet place, way back from all the people, in the thickest of the trees, there was a quiet place. You could sit there on the grass that was cooler than sun-touched grass, and lean your back against a tree that was nubbled, but somehow fitted your shoulders. You could wait awhile, a good long while, until the dark came, with the whiskey in you holding you steady through the moments of waiting.

Then, with the dark you could take out the bottle and let the red warm stuff slide, a little at a time, into you, into your blood and your heart.

When it was all gone, late, late and night because you knew how to make it last, you could lie down and rest and forget the dirt and the heat.

For a while you could. For a while. Because you always had to come home.

And it's worse there than anywhere else. And it all happens over again.

Scare them. Scare them all.

James J. MacClinton stood before Irma. "Do I look all right?" he asked. He tried to make it sound like a joke. But he found that he really wanted to know.

Irma blew a fragment of dust off the coffee table. She whisked a quick scan in his direction and nodded slightly.

"All right. As always. If you were as successful as you look, things would be—"

"I have to go down to this place, you see," he interrupted quickly. "I have to fill out things. Then, Sorban says, they give you a mark." He laughed happily.

Irma walked away from him toward the dining room.

"Where are you going?" he asked.

Her back was very neat in the crisp cotton dress. Her hair was twisted in a figure-eight at the back of her head. One thing, Irma had pretty hair.

Once, when they were first married, she let it down around her face, and she became different. So different. It did something wonderful and fearful to him to see all that soft tan hair, loose and silky for his fingers.

He moved his mind sharply away. It only made her seem different. Didn't change her at all, of course. Only disgusted her that he should react the way he did. At night, ever since, she had plaited it in tight, long braids.

Oh, well. A long time ago. A long dream ago.

"I'm going to wash the dishes," she said, not turning. "I don't like them to stand beyond nine o'clock. Just because you have no plans this morning doesn't mean that mine should be disrupted."

"Irma," he found himself crying. "This thing—"

She turned then. She had the patient look on her face.

"Oh, for pity's sake, James," she said. Not cross. Never cross. Just the way she'd talk to a child, if they had one, who tried her patience and demanded more than she had to give. "You've gone over every word, every phrase, every bit of that jury duty business for the last week. What's so magnificent about being called?"

Well, what was? he asked himself. Sorban didn't see it, Irma didn't see it. Why try to share it, then?

This feeling of power, long before the day. The clear pictures that came to him

in the night. Of himself as foreman. Of the lawyers, arguing, defending, prosecuting. All for him. And the other eleven, of course. Of the judge, sitting there,
pompous and a big shot. Yet with his hands tied in many ways. Tied by James J.
MacClinton. By the ideas, beliefs, judgment, of James J. MacClinton.

He could see it all. He could almost hear it.

The only thing he couldn't see, though, no matter how hard he tried to picture
it, was the face and figure of the man on trial. He couldn't see him at the table
with the lawyer. He couldn't see him raising his hand to testify in his own behalf.
He couldn't see him sitting down in the chair, hanging his head. Or maybe lifting
it arrogantly.

Oh, well. Oh, well.

"I'm off, Irma," he said. It sounded bright. It forgave her careful patience,
colored as it was by his fascinating thoughts.

He followed her to the kitchen and kissed her cheek. "I'll go right on into the
city," he promised. "I'll work harder than ever because I'm getting such a slow
start. Maybe I'll even be a little late."

Irma ran the hot water hard into the sink. She sprinkled soap over it.

"You'd better not be," she said, reaching for the silverware. "I've got liver and
bacon and you know it won't take a bit of standing."

Then, as he stood there beside her, with the quiet of her voice ringing in his
ears, James J. MacClinton had quite a shocking thought.

Irma wasn't a very nice person. She really wasn't. Despite the schools and the
fine background. It was sacrilege. Like saying heaven didn't exist. He pushed the
thought away.

From the first time he met her, way back there during the Second World War,
at the U.S.O. place, there had been a looking-up inside of him about Irma. On a
pedestal, like they always say. The way she was, all tidy and fastened together.
The way she spoke, knowing what was right at once and with no quibbling. The
way she took hold of their lives. And the house. Why—there was nobody like
Irma.

Caught by the mental declaration, the quick affirmation to deny the sense of
guilt, he took her firm shoulders in his hands, swung her around and kissed her
on the mouth.

"There," he said definitely.

He walked out of the kitchen door.

Irma's voice, tinged with surprise, followed him through the half-open casement window above the sink.

"You'd better wipe that lipstick off your mouth," she called. "You'll look a
fool filling out all those important papers with smears like that."

There was no reason to be surprised at the number of people. But he was. At
the door a woman sat and handed him papers and took his letter away from
him.

She said, "To your right." James followed her directions.

It was a big room, filled with tables that were so close together that he could hardly pull out a chair. The chairs were so tight that he felt as if the fat woman on one side of him and the foreign man on the other were breathing a steam bath in his direction.

Somebody ought to open a window, he thought. He looked toward the street. The windows were all open. It didn't help a bit.

He settled himself to the papers.

There were all sorts of words. Tricky, too. They meant almost the same thing, but not quite. He took his time. Not using the pencil until he had figured it out in his mind, gone over it, and was sure.

He was meticulous about the law problem, figuring out the phraseology. People came and went, jostling his chair. But it was like the times in school. The times when he really had prepared his lesson and wanted to make a good showing. He lost himself in doing it.

When it was finished, he read it all over carefully. It looked fine. Nothing was changed, not even a comma was erased. It looked, he thought proudly, like the work of an orderly mind. A man who could sort facts, weigh them, juggle them, and come up with a logical result.

He pushed back his own chair the scant three inches the seat behind him would allow and edged his way up the narrow aisle to the first desk. He smiled at the woman who sat there.

She glanced at the pages quickly. James knew a sudden disappointment that she didn't read them. She placed a sheet of cardboard, like a child's stencil cut-out with variously shaped rectangles, over each sheet.

She smiled warmly and looked up at him.

"But this is very good," she whispered, leaning forward a little. Then louder, "You wouldn't do anything to overthrow the government of the United States, would you?"

James backed up a step. "Good night, no," he said. It came out loud and shocked.

She nodded again. "Of course not. We just have to ask, that's all." She pushed his papers toward him. "Mr. Ford is over at the next desk. You just wait your turn."

There were only two people ahead of him. Both women.

Women, James J. MacClinton thought, are somehow, very slowly and subtly, dominating the whole nation. He didn't like the idea. Exploring it, he found abruptly that the two women were gone, and that Mr. Ford had extended his hand for the papers.

As he gave them to him, James felt a pucker of worry around the edges of his mind. What if the answers weren't right, after all?

But Mr. Ford, as quick or quicker than the woman at the other desk, looked over the papers, used a stencil, and picked up a red crayon.

With it he wrote a big fat A on the first sheet. Wrote it so big, by golly, that it covered the page from top to bottom.

"You'll certainly be able to serve, won't you?" Mr. Ford asked happily. "Man like you—we could use."

James stood very tall. "It will be a pleasure and a privilege."

Mr. Ford nodded cheerfully. "You're a salesman," he offered. "You'll find out plenty interesting about the characters in a trial."

"It should be fascinating to discover how the criminal mind works," James said, making it sound scholarly.

Mr. Ford looked at him again. "Yes—well—yes, of course," he said absently. He smiled in the same way, and reached around James to hold out his hand for another set of papers.

James J. MacClinton walked, as proudly as a kid with a good report card, out of the building.

Everything went well that day. Everything. People cooperated. There was a letter at the post office saying the new products were ready for shipment. It was as good a day as James had ever known.

He was riding slowly from the post office toward home, when the thought came to him.

While I am going about my work, he thought, filling out those papers, going home to Irma, getting up in the morning, going to bed at night, waiting to be called for jury duty, something parallel is happening somewhere around here.

In the city, in the country, maybe even in this town, there is another man. Right now he is going about his business, too. Maybe even upright and sober and honest. But before I receive my summons to jury duty, before I sit up there in judgment, he will commit the crime I am to judge. He can't have committed it yet, because they don't call you for quite a long time.

Maybe the crime isn't even in his mind yet. Hasn't even entered his head. Maybe he's never done anything wrong. Maybe he doesn't know that he's going to rob. Or—or rape. Cheat. Or murder.

Murder.

It was a very exciting sort of thing to think. Quite out of the ordinary run of James J. MacClinton's meditations. It stirred him up inside. As much as the letter from the Superior Court had. Only in a different way. Quite different.

It made him look at Irma in a changed way, even.

When he walked in and she asked, "Well, how did the big doings go?" he just smiled and said, "Quite well, thank you. Is the liver ready?"

That night he studied the newspaper very carefully. He read every account of violence and misdemeanor. There seemed to be a great many of them, even in a town this size.

He decided that in the morning, before he left for the city, he would buy the city papers. At least one of them. After he got the mail he would sit quietly in the car and read the paper straight through.

If you were going to be a jury member, perhaps a foreman, it behooved you to be informed about the sorts of criminalities which went on in the world.

There might even be some books at the library. Of course there would be. Research. About crimes of various kinds. What made them happen. What forced them to come to mind. How they worked out. What the court did about them.

It would make an interesting hobby. Indeed it would. It would clarify the face of the man accused, climbing into the chair, to face the twelve people.

What sort of a thing, James J. MacClinton wondered, all through dinner, through the writing of his reports, through his shower and his teeth-brushing and his preparing for bed, what sort of thing would this unknown man do?

Frank Savrano had no money for vino. He knew that by the end of June. Glad to see June go. That month was the worst. July was hotter, but June was worst. In June, even with the most vino bought and drunk and the farthest place in the park, it was like walking with a black ghost in the mind. "To Pica, on her seventeenth birthday, from her friend, Frank Savrano."

July then, no black ghosts. No white. No vino. No nothing.

Oh yes, something. Three days working for a contractor picking up lumber.

"Here." He stomped into the house and threw the money before Pica. "Make chili. Make eggs and milk for the kids."

That was bad. The money on the table. The way Pica ran to him and held him, still sweaty from the picking up in the beating sun. How she loved him and put the baby in his lap.

July was a week helping out in a gas station in the next town. Hitchhiking the fourteen miles at night. Driven home by friendly truckers—and by one other thing. By trying to spend no money so he could throw the bills on the table.

Saturday night of that July week it was good to put the money there.

Pica made a fine pizza pie. Recipe from a book, she said. The kids laughed at the table and made silly jokes. Pica rustled around, proud, important. Frank sat back, full, and no anger anywhere.

Then the knock came.

Three of them, three of the boys and a game going in the back room of Casetti's.

All held still in the kitchen, kids, baby, Pica. Frank stood in the dead breathless center of a tornado, the place where no air moves.

"You comin'?" Pedro asked.

"You afraid of the old woman?" Jose grinned. His grin foamed over at Pica.

"Or maybe you got other plans—at home, eh?" Dommy put in. His eyes had the same story in them as Jose's grin.

Frank stood still. He could feel the slip and skid of the cards in his hands. Better, he could feel the slip and skid of the vino down his dry throat.

He flipped one arm toward Pica. "The dough," he demanded.

Pica's eyes fluttered. He wasn't looking at her, but he knew how they fluttered. Not her eyelids. Not her eyelashes. But the shades of brown in her eyes, rippling from light to dark with many things.

"Frank," she begged, a whisper, no more. "Please," she begged.

Let it come up then, the anger held for many nights and many days. For the sweating in the sun and the lumber. For the strange gas station and the strange boss who didn't know how good Frank Savrano was with cars, how skillful his hands. And didn't care. Wanting only a boy. A come-here, go-there somebody to do odds and ends while the regular man was on his vacation.

"The dough," he yelled. Oh, the familiar voice, the loud hard man voice. The angry voice. "What do you think I worked like a pig all week for? To sit watching you wash the dishes? To hear the kids squeal and whine? The dough!"

He turned. He pushed Pica, hard, toward the cupboard. It felt fine to push her. Fine for the three standing there, to show them here was a man.

He stood close behind her, waiting for her trembling fingers to clutch the money, to hand it to him. Sure, sure, he could reach for himself. But it smoothed the soul of the anger and proved to the three standing there that here was Frank, to be reckoned with, and Pica to do his bidding.

He moved back one step and snapped his fingers against her shoulder, sharp and stinging.

"Hurry it up," he cried. "I ain't got all night."

The three in the doorway made a restless sound.

Frank raised his hand to slap against Pica's shoulder. It was in the air, ready to flail, when she turned sharply, the money dangling from her own hand. Flat against her face his fingers landed. The smooth skin pinked and welted in four thin lines.

Pica, Frank thought. Pica. Stop this in me. Take it from me. Let it not be those behind me and the money for vino.

It was a new asking. It hurt. It strangled.

It died without saying.

He grabbed the money from her limp hand, swung around and shot across the kitchen, plunging through the three men, truly like the tornado in crazy movement. He ran down the walk, down to the sidewalk, down to Dommy's car and slammed his way into the back seat. He heard them, far away, oh, very far, pace after him, climb in. He heard Dommy grind the jalopy's motor into loudness, felt the jerk as it pulled into the street.

"Guess you showed her, eh?" Dommy slung over his shoulder.

Beside him Jose playfully knuckled into Frank's arm.

"No wonder she don't look at nobody else. She don't dare. She get killed, man, she get killed slow."

"Shut up," Frank dimly heard himself scream. "Shut up and keep shut, or more than Pica gets hurt tonight."

For a moment it was quiet in the car. Dommy's eyes met Frank's in the rear view mirror. Jose pulled away toward the window. Pedro put one arm on the back of the front seat and stared at Frank, studying him.

What did they say, alone, about him? Did they say, "That Frank Savrano, man, he's crazy! Keep away"? Did they see the whiteness in him? Know the seed pop? The atomic anger?

"Okay, buster, okay," Pedro said at last quietly. "We gonna play cards at Casetti's. We ain't lookin' for no fight."

"Better not," Frank muttered sullenly. "Better not."

Casetti's back room was hot with July and the naked overhead light and the many men crowded around the table.

Frank pushed his way in.

Somewhere, down inside of him with Pica's face, there was an itch of hope.

Almost hope. With so much money and not much vino, perhaps this would be the night to double the dough. To make it three times as much. To go home and pull it from all pockets. Like the magician in the circus that time Pop was sober and took him to see. Under the arms, even, money pulled out. From behind the collar and out of the cuffs.

The anger slowly, slowly, tucked in upon itself.

"Vino," Frank called. "Vino—and deal me in."

The first glass of vino was like no other glass. Not ever. It cooled the hot days of picking up wood, and dimmed the voice of the strange boss. It loosened and eased the muscles of Frank's throat, and warmed the cold place he couldn't touch with mind or finger.

Heat then, and silky cards with bright colors, and voices. Smoke then, and grumbles or grins. And hours going by in the red sweetness of vino and friends.

When it was over, Frank Savrano found himself walking slowly down a dark street. Behind him, far behind somewhere, he knew there were many dark streets and that he had been walking them for a long time. Since when? Since the money was all gone. The week of hitchhiking all gone. The time of throwing the money on the table all gone.

This time, his feet said, pacing steadily to somewhere, this time, not the park for sleeping. Not home because of no place else. This time, his feet rhythmed, we get money. Lots of money.

Down two blocks and over five. All quiet. All asleep. Stores pricked by a back night light. But on the corner, Michaels' big white and red gasoline station.

Down there, see, Frank? Way down there. It waits with a welcome.

Not the welcome it used to have. Early every morning, remember? The pavement to wash down. The grease racks to clean. The tools all in place in the repair department. Everything ship-shape.

"Good morning, Frank," Mr. Michaels always said. "Best-looking station in town since you came here, boy."

Boy, boy, always boy. It sounded good, though, in the early morning. Like Pop calling down the field. "Boy!" Pop used to call. "Supper, boy."

Mr. Michaels always said, "I've got plans for you, boy. Those hands of yours. Someday we'll buy the lot next door, you know? We'll put in a full service place. And you, Frank—well, you'll be in charge. You like that idea?"

Walking in the darkest hour of the night, toward the corner up there, the banished welcoming place, Frank Savrano could not remember what he had said back to Mr. Michaels. It was a long time ago, that October.

Ten lousy bucks, he remembered instead. Ten lousy bucks, he walked in time to.

His hand went into his pocket and the switch knife was there. Why it was or where it came from he didn't actually know. He could see it on the table, glittering and pushed toward him at some time of the game. Some winning time, and in the place of money.

There should be anger now, he thought. There should be the feeling like in the kitchen, when was it? When wasn't it? There should be meanness, like with Pica. Because the switch knife is in my hand. The station pulls nearer with my steps.

Whoever is there, Mr. Michaels, or another boy built big with Mr. Michaels' promises, watch out. Watch out. Ten lousy bucks.

He stood still in the shadows beyond the station. The lights radiated out to the corner. In the little glass house a figure sat before a desk, feet up, chin on chest.

The echoes of the vino put a wavering film in front of Frank's eyes. The station, the pumps, the grease racks, the glass cage, the figure, all were under water, shimmering and under clear water.

In the darkest place of the dark then, blacker even than the hidden part of the park, Frank Savrano stood lonesome and lost. Lonesome without the anger, lost without it. He shook his head back and forth, waiting for its stir.

Pica, he said inside, in one half hour I shall be home. I shall wake you, if you are sleeping. Are you sleeping? Or does it hurt too much, the face and the melting and knowing that the melting should never have been?

When you are awake, we will go. You. Me. The kids. We will go fast, before they find the figure in the glass house. Before they wonder. We will go very far and fast and with money to move on.

Thief, Mr. Michaels said. He put it on me. The word. Thief. So I am. He said it. He made me thief.

Frank moved slowly from dark to dark, around the back of the station. He slipped neatly into the grease room. He lifted his head for a moment and let the gasoline smell, the grease, the oil spilled from the shiny round cans, climb sweetly up into his nostrils. Funny thing, it was so sharp at last against the back of his eyeballs that tears spurted on his lower lids.

He listened, head tipped, waiting. At once then, and clearly, he knew why the anger was gone. He knew why he waited. Even why the tears.

This was the thing he had forgotten in the summer of the time before the marrying. This was the thing, that despite all of the anger, had not come. The thing learned in Korea. Beyond all anger.

He took it to himself again, reaching out for it, welcoming it as the gas station used to welcome him in the morning. Knowing that it was the reason why the station welcomed him this middle of the night. So different, in such a different way. But welcome.

With the knowing, his hand slid, working for itself, down into the pocket of his trousers and clutched around the switch knife and pushed the clasp and felt the sharp cool tongue spit out. With the knowing came the wild stir. He moved silently through the doorway.

"Mr. Michaels," he called softly, insistently, to the figure. "Mr. Michaels."

The figure stirred, stretched, eyes still closed. Then it straightened, and Mr. Michaels looked at him. Clear. Close.

He opened his mouth.

Say it, Frank begged him silently. Say thief.

He waited for the word. He waited for the word to start the moment of the slump. The moment of the strange, strange joy.

Mr. Michaels looked surprised, startled. Not yet scared. Not yet smart enough to be afraid.

"Frank Savrano," Mr. Michaels asked quietly, "what are you doing here?"

All through the rest of June and into July and most of the month, James J. MacClinton could see, when he thought of it, that he was getting on Irma's nerves.

He was sorry about it. When he thought of it. It was a new thing. All this time the patience had stayed in Irma's voice, while she talked to him as if he were a child who tried her. Then, beginning with the day of the big fat red A on the examination papers, the patience had begun to slip.

When he wasn't busy thinking of other things, he tried to figure out what irked her so. Then, at last, he tried to ask her outright.

"Don't you feel well, dear?" he asked her one hot night when they were getting ready for bed. "You seem so—well—"

She stood before the mirror, her quick hands braiding that tan hair, pulling it tight and squeezed.

Something symbolic there, James thought. Hair all loose and relaxed and giving, if she'd let it be. But she pulls it tight and scrimps it firm, and allows it only measly and controlled freedom.

My, he thought proudly, so much has happened to me inside. There was a time, and not very long ago, either, when I would never have had an idea like that. It's the books, of course. Strange, you can't even read about the psychology of crime without picking up a lot of psychology of other things.

"So—what?" Irma snapped.

She had a rubber band in her mouth, ready to flip and twirl around the thin, ragged shreds of the bottom of the braid.

He grinned to himself. Snappish, with a rubber band. Pretty cute, that.

"And what are you smiling at?" The band was around her hair now. It gave her a chance to tighten her lips.

"I was just thinking of something I read," he said placatingly. "And I asked you a question first."

She snorted, as much a snort as her delicacy and her Eastern culture would allow her.

"I feel perfectly well," she said definitely. "I think you're the one who ought to see a doctor."

He smoothed down the jacket of his pajamas. They felt good against his skin. Everything physical and mental lately—these months of summer since he'd signed up for jury duty, since he had found all of the books in the library, and his mind had stirred away from sales and customers, and, yes, from Irma—felt close and alive. Even clean sheets, like the ones he now eased his body down against.

"I never felt better in my life," he said. He yawned widely. The night air, beginning to cool after the warm day, seemed to have a flavor in his mouth and a bubble in his lungs.

It was that way with colors, too. Everything looked brighter. The cars on the freeway, new and old. The palm trees. The shining equipment in the customers' offices. The pedal pushers, even, of the pin-curled young girls.

Strange. Everything but Irma. She was fading away to a dun color, even with her pale pink lipstick on.

He turned his head to watch her climb into bed. It stood to reason. She didn't look all greased up like most women, just as she didn't look all painted up daytimes like they did. She looked like a scrubbed little girl, with her tight braids and her soap-shiny nose. A good, good little girl. A goody good. Little Goody Two Shoes. He smiled again.

Irma said, not looking at him, "I wasn't talking about your physical well-being. That, I'm sure, is all right. Certainly you haven't killed yourself with work this past six weeks or so."

"Irma," he said, surprised to find himself saying it, "you should have married somebody else."

She looked at him then, quickly and with narrowed eyes. "Now what do you mean by that?"

He shrugged. "Exactly what I say. There's more to this marrying business than meets the eye."

It would be a fine time for Irma to cry a little. He'd never seen her cry. As a matter of fact, he added mentally, he'd never seen her any particular way. Emotionally, that is.

"Actually," Irma said, thinking about it calmly, "we are very much alike, you and I. I recognized it almost at once. Oh, of course, you haven't had some of the—education advantages—"

James J. MacClinton found himself chuckling. "I'm getting them," he said. "Slowly but surely."

Irma sniffed. It was dainty, but, like her snort, it said what it meant to. "If you mean all those detective books—"

He sat up quickly. "Now you see here," he stated, "those are not detective stories—"

"So you keep telling me."

"Those are case histories—most of them, in fact—" His mind went off.

They worked out those cases very smoothly, really. You could sort of start out with the man, maybe way back in his childhood, before he knew what was going to hit him. You could, well, in a way, live with him growing up. See the idea planted like a seed. Watch it grow in the dark moldy earth inside of him. And then see it erupt—dazzling and shocking, like a deadly flower bursting into bloom. Into violence. Into murder most foul.

Irma's voice lost its softness. That's the way it had been lately. Out of kilter.

"There you go again," she cried. "That's what I mean. It's an obsession. I think you ought to see a doctor about the way you drift off—"

He brought himself back. He didn't, after all, have to ask Irma why she was losing her patience with him. Suddenly he knew. It was a simple psychological fact, really.

He had always looked up to her, let her make decisions. He had been—he'd been hers. But since he got interested in this research to fit him for jury duty, she felt she was losing him. She was, by golly, that was it—she was jealous of his mind when it went away from her. When she couldn't control it.

Now, that was a thought he would have to explore later. Apparently, in his natural-born humility, implanted at birth, nurtured by his mother, increased by his war experiences, or lack of them, he'd been letting Irma do his thinking for him.

And she resented it when he walked where she could not lead.

He said, "Let's get back to this being alike, my dear. In what ways, would you say?"

Irma eased her face back to normal. "Well," she continued slowly, "we like a pattern. We like to know where we stand. At the bank. In our budget. In our routine. The things we do and don't do."

He saw it very clearly, listening to her. It was a pattern, all right. Quite a small one. Up, breakfast, post office, city, home, dinner, reports, TV. Once in a while dinner out at a modest restaurant. Very few friends.

He wondered about that. Irma was so meticulous about those birthday cards and anniversary cards. But when it came to people coming in and out, or inviting them—it was a rare time. Usually business, too.

"Dull, isn't it?" he heard himself say.

He heard her gasp.

Well, if Irma should cry, or lose her temper, it would be breaking the pattern with a smash, all right. Just as his absorption in the crime books was breaking it.

"As a matter of fact, Irma," he went on quietly, "you're pretty dull yourself, you know."

That ought to do it. He lay there, and somewhere inside of him James J. MacClinton shook for his rudeness. Or, like the morning when his hands tore open the envelope from the Superior Court, he wanted to shake for it. But somehow he managed not to.

"Well, I never—I never—" Irma began thickly.

Then she broke off, reached for the light, switched it off and rolled over on her side.

James lay still beside her. He waited for her body to quiver a little. He had always been very nice to Irma, really. It must have been a shock, that sentence.

He waited with the nicest clean feeling inside of him. It was better, oh much, than the time he'd walked out of Sorban's office, feeling superior for almost the first time in his life.

If he could just make Irma cry. If he could prove to her, and to himself, that whatever he said was important to her. Important enough to break down the barriers and free the soft tan hair—and everything else inside of her. If he could know that the pattern could splinter because she cared enough for him to be hurt by what he said. If he could only know that.

It would be the easiest way. It certainly would. Because if it didn't work, he would have to try some other way.

What did the psychology books call it? Compulsion. That was it. He, James J. MacClinton, red A juror at some near time now, knew a real honest-to-goodness compulsion.

He just had to break the pattern of their lives, somehow. He had to get under Irma's skin and break her down and prove to her that she had married a person. A man. Not a boy. Not a child. A thinking man.

He lay very quiet, listening intently.

A little broken sob, perhaps? A heaving of the shoulders?

It would be so wonderful, really. He could reach over and touch the warm tears on her cheeks and put his mouth down on hers. Then he could pull those damned rubber bands off the bottom of those damned tight braids, and unwind all that beautiful hair, and hold her close and unwind her—and himself—

The sound came. It came in a little spurt.

It was a gentle snore. Irma lay beside him, snoring a blister of air from her puckered lips.

James shook then. He shook so hard that he had to double his fists to give himself strength enough to pull out of his side of the bed.

He reached for his robe and went, barefooted and silent, out of the door and downstairs to the living room. He stood for a minute in the middle of the room and the shaking was like the time he had pneumonia when he was ten. First his bones would rattle, and then he would be ravished with heat.

The heat came, too. When it ebbed away, he felt very weak and tired.

He went to the big chair, turned on the reading lamp, and reached to the coffee table where the books were piled up. He shuffled through them, slowly beginning to feel better. Finally he pulled out one volume. He sat studying the white imbedded letters on the cover for a long time.

"Wife Killers of History," they read.

He grinned at last, freely amused.

One of the other books on the table somewhere held a line telling the need for reading this book right now. Something about vicarious satisfaction, and all men's controlled and hidden urge to kill the thing they loved.

Oh well.

He settled down to his reading. The calm began to work its way all through him.

Under the calm, under the words he was putting into his mind from the printed page, ran the familiar repeated thought. Somewhere, perhaps there is a man like these in the book. Ready to murder. Tonight? Tomorrow?

Very soon, now. Because as soon as he does, James thought, I'll be called to jury duty—and it's meant to be.

It's a pattern. A lot stronger than the pattern in this house. We're bound to meet, this man and I. When the time is right.

He read until his eyes began to close. Then he went to the closet and brought out Irma's afghan. He settled himself comfortably on the davenport, turned off the light, and stared through the squares of the casement window into the night which was only a little darker than this room.

It was a pattern, all right. Funny thing, though. No matter how hard he tried, he just couldn't seem to imagine what the guy looked like.

Frank Savrano ran quickly, lightly, clinging to the dark places, crossing the streets in the blackest spots. He ran toward home.

All of the vino had drained from him. His breath was short and jumbled in his ears. He ran, block after dark block, away from the brilliance of the gas station. Away from the grease rack and the figure in the little glass cage.

The trees hung limp over him, weary and still without a night's breeze to stir them. Limp, in this latest hour of the night, the short shocking time before dawn, when all moved sluggishly, heart and sleeping mind and brain.

He padded around the side of his house. His poor miserable house which was a thin roof only over the head of Pica. A thin wall only between the kids and the slash of the world.

No more. Thicker walls. Thicker roof. Food for all. Different now. From right this minute. Different. With money. With a padding.

He turned the knob. It twisted easily in his hand. With the door shut the kitchen turned to a muffled black, thick against his eyes. He stood still for a moment. Call her? Should he cry "Pica" into the dark and rouse her to come to him?

No. Instead he would go to her. Softly. He would kneel beside the thin flat bed and touch her awake. Then he would tell her, the two of them whispering. Not waking the kids to questions and excitement until it had to be.

The old linoleum creaked. It tried to snare his feet. He lifted them high and put them down delicately. He felt his way through to the bedroom, his hands and arms jutted before him. He touched the iron bottom of the bed, and followed his searching fingers until he came to the top. He knelt, reaching slowly, exultation in him, a glow, a strange glow like none before, toward a warm tan shoulder.

Then he remembered the money and pulled his hand back. He reached into his pocket and touched the bills. Reassured, he stretched his hand once more toward his wife.

His questing fingers met the roughness of the old blanket, the unflattened contour of the pillow. The bed was empty.

He jumped to his feet and ran to the door to switch on the sharp overhead bulb. The bed was empty. Pica was not lying there, awake or asleep, worn from tears or bright with smiling. Pica was not in the bed, in the room.

He raced across the narrow hall to the other bedroom. Once more he slammed on the light. The kids' bed was empty. Where there should have been three dark curly heads there was only the blankness.

Of all the things which had screamed inside Frank Savrano, anger and killing, and the strange sweet June before the marrying, this thing made the loudest crying.

It carried from his bowels a knife sharper than any switch blade, rasping and slashing and tearing, through his stomach, through his heart, through his throat, to imbed itself in the top of his head.

"Pica," he yelled. He ran from room to room. "Pica. Pica. Pica."

Nowhere. Nowhere. Pica was nowhere.

He stood on the lopsided gray porch and watched across the weeds the slow rise of the sun. Morning. Pica.

At last he ran to the house next door. It was a long time of pounding before anybody answered.

"Pica," he yelled at the man who stood there. "Where is Pica? Where are the kids?"

The man was bigger than Frank, broader. Surer, too. Never had he spoken to Frank in the years of living beside him.

"Your wife's vamoosed," he said. He smiled, as if it were a happy thing. "She come over here, bawling and carrying the baby with the little ones dragging on her skirt. My old woman—" he signaled a fat thumb toward the inside of the house "—my old woman give her ten dollars and a cup of coffee and dried her tears."

Frank cried, "Where? Where?"

The man looked bigger than ever. "You punk," he said slowly. "You dirty rotten punk. You're no good yourself, so you gotta prove somethin' by hurtin' the only people who think you ain't a punk. I got no use."

Frank let the words roll around him.

"Where?" he cried again. "Tell me where. I gotta find her. I gotta hurry. Where?"

The man looked as if he wanted to slug him. One fat ham of a hand drew back a little. Then he sighed, shrugged, and shook his head.

"What difference?" he asked mournfully. "She went to her mother's on the bus."

He turned around quickly and walked into the house. The door slammed, slapping echoes.

The running began again then.

The day lifted itself from the edge of the sky, and yawned from gray to blue. The trees stretched their limpness to movement, and shook themselves in the new breeze.

Frank Savrano ran along the sidewalks, not hiding in the shadows, not finding any shadows, as he had before. He ran boldly and wildly, down the streets beginning to move and stir with the day. He crossed the corners slantwise, the quickest way. He did not know if anyone looked at him.

In his feet this time there was only one word, one name. It tore him and pushed him, and gave him breath when there should no longer be breath.

At the bus station he yanked into the pocket and pulled out the bills. He grabbed one and shot it under the wicket. He named the town where Pica's mother lived. He picked up the ticket and raced toward the buses.

He leaned against the building then, weakness all through him. He did not know how long till the bus would turn the corner. It did not matter how long. The bus would come. The bus had to come.

After an uncounted time, when his breath was smooth except for the way his heart shook it, the right bus pulled up before him.

Twenty-five miles of city and country ran together before his eyes. There could have been a policeman beside him and he would not have known. There could have been ten bottles of vino beside him and he would not have cared.

Miles ran out and time ran out and the bus was a centipede with a hundred sore feet crawling over sharp stones. The bus was a snail inching its way across a wet sidewalk. The bus was a jail, each window barred with steel.

One thing only did he hold clearly in his conscious mind. The name of the town. When the driver called it, he pushed roughly through the aisle and tossed himself down the steps and onto the highway.

He ran again. The country lane was there, screaming at him from the opposite side of the town. He answered its scream with the pain inside of him. And ran. And ran.

The house was old, but clean. No weeds. Set back from the road. A clean, good place Pica came from before that June of the marrying. A clean, good place, with a fat good bed, and food on the table and trees around. A rosary and the Bible in the living room. A cross above her bed.

He leaned on the door for a minute, once he reached it. The sweat rolled down from his hair like hot rain. Then he grabbed what he could of his breath and knocked, keeping it weak and gentle, on the door.

Pica's mother answered it almost at once. She stood there, small, dark, sharp in her nose and eyes. She stood there, like her daughter grown older. But not afraid. Never afraid, because she had known, and still knew, a thin good clean man for husband.

"Go away," she cried, clearly, full of hate, full of sickness at the sight of him. "Go away and do not come back. Don't ever come back. Or Papa, old as he is, will thrash you before the police manage to get here in answer to the call I will make."

"Please," Frank said, the word strange on his twisting mouth. "Pica. Please." She began to shut the door. He pushed against it. Not roughly. But strongly.

"You have hurt her enough. Your kids got to have a chance—"

The door gave way, and she gave way. Frank was in the room, off balance from the pushing. In the clean good decent room.

There was Pica. There she was. She stood in the middle of the room, no color at all about her, except the dark of her eyes and the black of her hair. Painted by ink on white paper.

"Pica," he cried. He hurried toward her, his arms out.

Pica backed away, flinging an arm before her face. To protect herself, save herself from blows. From the meanness. The meanness she knew for sure now, and would not melt against.

"Pica," Frank cried again.

He reached her. He went, all in one motion, his arms around her waist, slipping and sliding to the floor on his knees. He hid his face against her ankles.

"Do not leave me," he sobbed. "Do not go. I love you, Pica. I love you."

No sound then in the room but the sound he had never heard before. The sound of a man crying. A man who could no longer spit on anybody. Who could scare nobody. Who knew, instead, himself, the spit and the scare. Deeply and at last.

Slowly, slowly, with a whispered little rustle under the noise of the sobs, Pica slid down to rest beside him on the floor. Slowly, her arms touched his shoulders. Her hands moved to his head and made a cup and pulled it against her.

Rocking and holding, rocking and holding.

From a great distance, muffled and hiccoughed, Frank heard his words begin to come. The thing he had to tell her. The thing he had run through the night for.

"I went there. To the station. I stood there in the dark. And Mr. Michaels, he slept. I called him. He woke and looked at me. In my hand, Pica, in my pocket, there was a knife with the switch blade. In my heart, in my soul, Pica, there was the killing, like in Korea."

Her hands loosened, then tightened. The rocking stopped, and then started up again.

"He opened his eyes and looked at me. He said, 'Frank Savrano, what are you doing here?' He got up. Easy he got up and sure and not afraid of me. He—he put out his hand, Pica.

"'Frank,' he said, 'I'm glad to see you. Boy,' he said, 'I've been getting up my courage to come over to your place. I think about you, Frank. I think of the good you did around here. The way you whistled. How hard you worked. I think, I can forgive one mistake, I think.'"

The sobs worked themselves out with the words, the wonderful unbelievable words. Frank took his hands from Pica's ankles, to cover her own hands on his head. He took them and brought them around and held them tight against his chest. Then he lifted his head and looked at her.

"In the night, Pica," he said slowly, "while I stood there waiting to rob—and to kill, maybe, Mr. Michaels said he was sorry. He said I was a good boy and he guessed he always knew it. He said, 'Tomorrow you come back to me, Frank. We work hard together. Maybe we have that repair shop someday sooner than you think.' He said that to me, Pica."

He waited a moment, thinking about it. "Then he gave me money to begin. I ran home. You were gone."

Frank shook his head. Tears sprayed out from the corners of his eyes. He did not notice them. He saw only the tears on Pica's cheeks and the colors, shifting and sliding, in the brown of her eyes.

"Pica," he whispered, "if there could be the melting one more time. The hoping once again. I promise—I know—never again, never, never, in the whole of my life, will there be the meanness. Never again this anger. This I know. Pica, I will be so good. In the name of God, Pica, I swear it, I will never hurt you again."

Because of the way the words came out, soft and needing to, and real, Frank knew they were true.

Knew they could always be true.

The look on her face began and it was morning rising from the dark time. It spread in light and sweetness. It spread and was so bright Frank could not stand its glitter. He put his head onto her shoulder.

Pica held him and rocked him, there on the floor of the good clean house of her decent parents. Held him and rocked him. After a while she began to hum.

Pica's mother said, softly, as if not to break anything with her voice, "I go make coffee."

As she passed the two kneeling figures she touched her hands against the tight-held heads.

It was a blessing.

Sometime in the night, perhaps because of the discomfort of the couch, James J. MacClinton came widely, startlingly awake. He lay for a moment, knowing that it was close to dawn because it was so dark; then he sat up.

He did this without benefit of pillows to lean on, or elbows. Up square and straight. He felt light, in a very queer way. As if he had been ill and was now better, and tasted every sensation of improving health. He stood, stretched tall, and there was no yawn in him.

He began to walk back and forth across the unlighted room.

It would come soon, now. He felt it. The real summons for jury duty. In just a little while he would be called.

He would sit in a room and there would be many others from whom to choose. But they would look at his dignity, his new sureness, his fine solid appearance, and they would select him.

They would ask him the questions and he would answer them. Firmly. Definitely. In a voice that showed he knew exactly what he was about. They would see his arrogant nose, his heavy eyebrows, hear his decisive tones, feel the knowledge of his research and ability. And they would select him.

The bubbles of excitement began to stir in his chest again. He turned on the light. He walked by the coffee table and patted the books gently, smiling a little, feeling himself put the smile on his face.

He began to hunt for a cigarette. There was none in the little cloisonné jar which Irma treasured above all other possessions. There was none down behind the cushions of the chairs or the davenport.

He opened the desk.

It was probably a hopeless wish. Irma thought smoking was messy. She deplored ashes as women with children deplore muddy footprints on a freshly waxed kitchen floor. She deplored a great many things, now that he thought of it.

He sat down on the little chair before the desk.

Really, it was a good thing he hadn't thought of it before, he decided ruefully. All the years until this summer he had knuckled under to Irma and her ideas and foibles. He had accepted her own valuation of him. A poor clod, really. That was it. Heaven help Irma if she had married somebody else. By this time she would be deserted—or dead.

He grinned. Never should have read *Wife Killers of History* just before going to bed, looked like.

He sat still, staring at his hands.

Suddenly, as quickly as wakefulness had come, a depression began to fill his mind and slip down through all of his body. It took away completely the good feeling he had known over the past few weeks, the unexplained joy of being rude to Irma, the strength of his mind, studying and analyzing and making a place for itself.

He pulled a pad toward him and began to scribble on it.

"There is a reason for everything. Ergo there is a reason for this fog of misery which has so quickly descended on me. The reason is—"

He stopped, his eyes focused dully on the sharp point of the pencil. "It is," he continued, and it was almost like automatic writing, the words coming out shaggy and run-together and not at all like his usual neat hand, "that somehow, all at once, I can see what freedom means. What being a man means. What it would have been like if I had never married Irma. Never married a woman who will not let her hair, or her heart, flow unbound."

He stared at the words. They ran together with more than his carelessness. They ran together with the great sad sense of truth that was in him.

His eyes stopped focusing. His mind came to a point. From now on, it said, with great decision and sureness, I am master in my own home. Never again will Irma lean over my shoulder and add up figures before I can. Never again will she talk to me in that sick and patient tone. I shall do as I like from now on.

The words sounded very good in his mind.

They did nothing much to lift the depression, though.

It would be so much better, his thoughts went on, without his volition, as the writing had done, if he were really free.

Really free.

A small apartment somewhere in the city. So that never again would he have to get up and beat those freeways. There, and back home. Never again would he have to be home on time because Irma was cooking liver. Nor explain where he had been if he was fifteen minutes late.

He could eat out after his last call, sitting in some snug, small restaurant with a book in front of him. He could go to some of the night classes at the college, if he liked. He could bowl any number of nights he desired. And meet some men and make some friends.

He could invite people in for drinks before dinner. Irma deplored liquor, too. And later, when he had tasted the aloneness, the learning, the singular freedom, to the full, he could look at other women.

Other women.

You get out of the habit, if you stay a boy and don't become a man. It's as if a wife like Irma were always traveling with you. Even on your calls. Always and forever peering over your shoulder. Saying, "No." Saying, "Don't you dare." Plucking at your sleeve. Holding you back.

So when did you look at a woman last? Except the pedal-pusher type on the street? When did you talk to a soft, happy-voiced girl? Or see the look of respect in an older woman's face?

Not for a long time. Not for a very long time.

Not ever.

So, it isn't enough then, James J. MacClinton, to be master in your own house, is it? You want more than that.

You want to be master of an empty place. You want to fill that place with exactly the furniture you like. The books you like. The music you like. The men friends you choose.

And last, oh lovely last, you want to fill it with the women you like. Loose-haired, joyous women, who know better than to plait a tight braid of their love, and keep it ragged and thin with a rubber band.

Absently, absorbed in the struggling ideas, his hands of their own accord filtered through the slots of the desk, feeling for cigarettes. They found none.

They pulled, instead, two clean white envelopes from one pigeon hole. They laid the envelopes neatly, side by side, on the gleaming mahogany surface.

"There," they seemed to say to James. "Take a look. See what we found."

One envelope had a pure stamp in the right-hand corner. A stamp as yet unsullied by lines and use.

The other stamp, James noted slowly, was canceled.

There was no reason for his heart to beat so loudly. No reason at all for the roaring in his ears. He hadn't allowed his eyes to fall on the addresses, had he?

Yet he knew that one was typewritten. And that the other was methodically spaced in black handwriting.

He forced himself to read the typewritten address first.

"James J. MacClinton, 1848 Sandarwood Place, Franklyn City, California."

The typing looked familiar, recognized, very real.

His heart grabbed a quicker tempo. He turned his eyes slowly, suddenly blinded with headache, to the upper left-hand corner.

"Superior Court of Los Angeles County."

When had she picked it up? A later sorting? In with her letters? After he left for the city?

"I knew it, I knew it, I knew it," he heard himself whisper.

He tore open the already opened envelope, noting that it had been slit neatly, the way Irma slit all letters with her little ivory opener.

He took each word to himself slowly, letting it hit in joy against him.

It was the summons, all right. It was the clarion call he had been waiting for. It asked him to appear Friday morning. Wednesday, Thursday, three days from this dawning day.

He didn't savor the joy, though. The heavy thud of his heart, the thickness of the depression, wouldn't let him.

They told him that beside this envelope there was another one. With a pure stamp. With Irma's careful writing on it.

He picked up the second letter.

For a moment he was caught and held in an old habit. Irma never opened his mail. She was far too honorable for that. In return, of course, he never opened hers. Didn't even want to. Now he wanted to.

But first, the address.

"Superior Court of Los Angeles County." How black her ink was. How carefully she dotted her i's and crossed her t's.

He tore the envelope almost in half, savagely ripping it open.

"My husband," Irma had written, "is away on an extended business trip. Therefore, he will not be able to serve on jury duty as you have requested. He would also, I am sure, because we have discussed it, like me to request for him that he be excused from further calls at this time. His business requires much traveling. He has not been well. And absence from his work would wreak a very real hardship upon the pattern and the budget of our lives."

The pattern. The pattern.

After a long while James whispered to himself, "She shouldn't have done that. She had no right to do that to me."

He got up slowly, one letter dangling from each hand. He walked into the kitchen. There was an opened package of cigarettes on the window sill above the sink.

He set the letters down, as if they were fragile ceramics, and picked up the cigarettes. He lit one. He noticed that his hands were shaking. Not just wanting to shake. Moving up and down in a fine quick little arc that could not be controlled.

He ran water into the small coffee pot. He turned on the gas and stood watching it. He reached into the cupboard and brought out the coffee canister. He measured as carefully as his trembling hands would allow. He put the stem and strainer into the pot. He waited for it to boil, so that he might turn down the heat.

He didn't think. He didn't feel. He shook and dragged on his cigarette and watched the amber bubbles come at last into the bigger glass bubble of the percolator, and plop and sing, plop and sing.

When it was almost time he pulled a cup and saucer from the dish cupboard. He set them neatly down beside the stove. He turned the gas off and let the coffee stand a moment. Then he poured it, a silken steaming stream, into the thin cup.

He stood to drink it. It was scalding against his tongue. But he did not feel it. All of him, tongue, skin, throat, heart, body, spirit, seemed to be wrapped in a strange insulation, impervious and thick.

When he had finished the coffee he walked across the kitchen and read both of the letters again. Slowly. Word by word, until sentences stayed clear.

He shook his head and sighed.

Then he walked into the bedroom.

He did not turn on the light. Dawn was on its slow way through the drapes and there was an eerie, faintly luminous quality about the room.

Irma lay as he had left her. On her side, her braids splayed. Through her puckered lips a blister of air snored itself into the quiet. Over and over. Steady and unremitting.

James reached gently over Irma. He picked up his own unused pillow. He held it lightly, cradled in his hands. They had stopped shaking.

He moved the pillow, very slowly and definitely, down toward the source of the snore. He touched it against the goody good clean face. He leaned, suddenly, hard, all muscles and man, against the pillow, against the struggle.

When he lifted it, after an unknown time, the snore had stopped. The blister of air had broken. Permanently.

There was never such a quietness in the world.

In the middle of the hush, James reached down and slid the rubber bands off the snagged skinny ends of the braids. With easy, deft fingers he unbraided the long, thick hair. He ran his fingers through its looseness, its silken cleanness. He spread it out on the pillow, beautiful and wanton.

"Such a shame," he mourned softly. "Such a shame."

The shame of it was thick in his throat and the clustered tears in his eyes.

James turned and walked out of the room, shutting the door softly, as if not to awaken somebody.

In the living room he went to the chair before the coffee table. He sat down and reached forward to touch the books. The name of the top one stared insolently back at him.

Wednesday—Thursday—Friday. Friday morning.

Then it hit him. Hard. Blow after blow.

He could not serve on the jury. Not now. Not ever. Not on any jury.

He pushed his head forward into his hands and sobbed.

After a long time, when the sobs were thinning of themselves, way in the back of his mind another thought began to stir.

It would be something now, to say, "I do." You don't get to swear to the words you're about to say very often.

A long time ago, one morning in the car, when was it, he had heard those words in his mind. He had thought, It would be the real thing, to sit up there and listen to the judge, and two lawyers and the clerk or whatever he was who said, "Do you solemnly swear to tell the truth, the whole truth and nothing but the truth, so help you God?"

What else had he thought?

Pull it out now.

Remember, remember.

He had thought, Who the devil is going to get a chance to swear to tell the truth? That is the defendant, isn't it?

The defendant!

Excitement drifted into him, cool at first, then getting hotter, getting steaming, like the coffee in the pot.

Somewhere, his mind pulled out from its earlier thought, perhaps there is a man like these in the book. Ready to murder. Tonight? Tomorrow? Very soon, now.

And it's meant to be, he had thought. It's a pattern a lot stronger than the one in this house!

It's a pattern so big—so wild and big and inevitable—that the pattern in this house had to be smashed first. Completely and finally smashed.

He stood up on the strange great wave of stimulation. He walked with certainty across the room and picked up the phone. He dialed carefully.

While he listened to the bell ringing, he began to see a picture. A picture of a man accused. The heart, the center, the spotlight of the courtroom. The vibrant living source who had brought the court into session.

Abruptly he laughed aloud in the quiet house which had nobody in it but himself.

A voice answered him, tinny and metallic, on the phone.

"Police Department," the far voice said.

James stood very straight and assured, as a man who has studied crime and police procedures should.

"Homicide," he stated clearly into the phone.

He stared beyond the instrument. Straight, straight, into the mirror with the polished brass frame, touched now by a finger of the new day's sun. The picture came very clear then. Detailed and total.

He saw the face and figure of the man on trial. At the table with the lawyer. Lifting his hand to testify on his own behalf. Climbing, dignified and arrogant and sure, to the raised witness stand. Not hanging his head, though. Holding it proudly. To face twelve people.

A new voice came through the receiver. "Homicide," it snapped at him, already in a hurry.

James took a long, easy breath. "This is James J. MacClinton," he said steadily, "of 1848 Sandarwood Place. I would like to report a murder."

He lifted his head, tipped it slightly to bring out the strong chin, and smiled at himself in the mirror. Smiled at himself in complete recognition at last.

"We were bound to meet, this man and I. When the time was right."

On October 16, the jury called to sit at the trial of James J. MacClinton, Franklyn City, California, confessed wife-killer, consisted of, in alphabetical order:

> Anderson, Jane
> Cleater, Mrs. Frances
> Hargrove, John
> Kimmel, Eric
> Long, Mrs. Ellen
> Norton, Paul
> Oliver, Henry
> Otis, Katherine
> Park, Mrs. Dolly
> Reynolds, Eleanor
> Rostenheim, Martin
> Savrano, Frank

BARRY N. MALZBERG

After the Unfortunate Accident

After the unfortunate accident I find myself sitting in a large room, rows and rows of straight-back chairs and a movie-screen in front, set up flat against the wall. The room seems half-filled or a little more with people who I do not recognize, some of them slumped over in attitudes of catatonia or boredom, others smoking cigarettes and regarding the pictures running on the screen with varying degrees of interest. Still appalled by what has happened to me—until that moment I had never lost control of a car in my life—I concentrate upon the movies, trying to restore some sense of order.

The movies, it seems, are films of my own family when I was a boy; scenes I dimly recognize float before me and in jarring close-ups I see the face of my mother, my sister and myself, superimposed against backgrounds of the sea or heavy traffic, embarrassed grins against the facades of the various apartment buildings we occupied throughout the first twenty years of my life. Now and then my father appears in these scenes but only rarely; he did not trust anyone else to hold the camera and became embarrassed when placed before it.

The movies remind me how intensely boring I found not only my early years but the principle of the family home movie itself which in its ability to trap people in the smallest and least significant particles of their lives has always managed to cheapen emotion, deaden any sense of connection. I note for the first time how unpleasantly cramped the room is; how penetrating the cigarette odors, how disconcerting the whine of the projector as it ticks off from the booth behind me and I decide at this moment that I do not want to stay any longer; that I must try to leave this room but when I attempt to stand I find that I am rooted to the chair and this brings from me a squawl of terror which attracts attention all around and I find that as the movies grind on, I am being stared at by many people in the room. "Excuse me," I say, showing my palms, "I didn't mean to shout. It was only the circumstances—"

"You'll ruin everything," a fat man in front of me says, turning, glaring at me. "Just because you're new here is no reason to scream. Now attend to yourself and watch the pictures; you'll find some of these very interesting and in any case it's your life which is being shown so you could use a little respect."

"Don't be so rough on the boy," a woman beside me says. She is rather attractive although in no sexual fashion; perhaps *motherly* is the word I am seeking. "He is new here and it's always a bit of a shock for them. I remember how *you* were when you came in," she adds sharply and the fat man blushes, turns around toward the screen again, his shoulders hunched. "Don't worry about it," the woman says. "He's just nasty-tempered, like so many of them here. He died of a bad fall, I understand, and the suicides are always the most offensive. How did *you* die?" she says but with such concern and interest that I do not find the question offensive. "You're awfully young."

"I missed a curve in the rain in an old Dodge," I say, "and ran off the road. The last thing I remember is heading toward a tree so I guess I must have been killed instantly. I never lost control of a car before."

"Well," she says nodding, "it is always a shock. Still, you're perfectly comfortable here as you can see and the movies are fairly interesting so it wasn't that bad for you after all. You'll find that you're never hungry or thirsty or need to sleep so you can just watch the movies all the time so all in all it worked out pretty nicely. I was afraid of death like everyone but if I had known that it was this pleasant afterward I wouldn't have fought so hard; I would have had the operation and might even have been saved. Still," she says, shaking her head, "who's to say? The important thing is that after you've been here for a few days it will feel like forever. You'll be one of us."

I look back toward the screen where a shore scene is now playing; my sister and I are tossing a large beachball in the air and through layers of recollection, it comes back to me that it was at this very beach, possibly on this very afternoon, that I broke her nose with a cruelly thrown softball. My sister and I wave at the cameras, run toward them mischievously and then out of the scene. There is a slow pan, one of my father's amateur specialties, and then the scene switches to my mother in bathing-suit, lying on a raft, waving.

"This is horrible," I find myself saying to the woman, "I can't spend an eternity watching this stuff; I always hated it."

She says nothing, absorbed in the film. Desperately, I turn in my chair and look toward the projectionist's booth and at just that instant the projectionist is looking out, head and shoulders protruding, checking the audience while the film rolls. The projectionist—how could I have doubted it?—is my father. I have not seen him in five years.

"Dad!" I shriek impulsively, focusing his attention with a wave, and locking my gaze with his. "Dad, you've got to get me out of this!" Despite our years of separation I retain my ability to cut to the bone of all discussions with my father. "I can't spend eternity looking at family home movies; I hated them! You've got to get me out of this; there's been some mistake! This is hell!"

My father looks at me through layers of smoky darkness, his eyes shrouded and gives me a long, intense smile. "No, son," he says, waving at me before he disappears forever back into the booth, "you don't understand at all." His eyes twinkle with happiness; I remember how he loved to show the movies. "This is heaven."

PATRICK O'KEEFE

The Grateful Thief

Strolling forward along the promenade deck, Captain Brier saw Miriam Stroude emerge from the entrance hall and cross to a window of the glassed-in section. She paused there, staring down at the dazzling blue sea, as still as a mannequin in the white pleated dress he had admired across the dining saloon at breakfast time. He started toward her, returning the greetings of passengers who glanced up from their steamer chairs at his large, confidence-inspiring figure in whites, a kindly smile on his broad, rugged face, a seagoing roll to his walk.

On the previous afternoon the chief officer had invited Miss Stroude, who sat at his table, to take coffee with him and the captain at watchchanging time on the bridge. Captain Brier intended to repeat the invitation, in his own behalf, for that afternoon. As he neared the entrance hall, a young officer, wearing the gold stripe of an assistant purser on his epaulets, hurried out to his side.

"Will you come down to the office right away, sir," he said breathlessly. "Salmon just found Miss Coston murdered in her cabin."

Captain Brier hurried into the hall and down the wide staircase, the assistant purser at his heels. Salmon, a bedroom steward, stood beside the purser's office window, flushed with excitement. The captain glanced inside, snapped, "Where's the purser?"

"I think he went up to his cabin, sir, to wash up for lunch," replied the assistant.

"Tell him to come down to Miss Coston's cabin at once; the doctor, too. Not a word of this to anyone else."

The captain then followed the steward along the port passageway on the same deck, which at that late forenoon hour was deserted. Salmon opened the door of cabin 15, led the way in, and closed the door again. It was a double-berth room with a private bath and smelled of cosmetics. Captain Brier saw Miss Coston the moment he was far enough into the cabin to come within view of the bathroom doorway. She lay on her back across the threshold, eyes staring. She was a pretty woman, thirty perhaps, clad in a pink sleeveless dress. Her short blond hair was damp with blood, and a patch of the brown carpet on which it rested had turned dark.

The captain glanced up at the steward. "How did you happen to find her?"

"I was coming along the passageway, sir, on my way back to cabin 19. I'd just remembered I'd forgotten to fill the water bottle in there. The door of this cabin was swinging to the roll of the ship, like someone had gone in without latching it. I thought Miss Coston or maybe her roommate was in, so I came in to tell them about always latching their doors on ships. I found her like that. I shut the door quickly and beat it along to the purser's office."

Captain Brier studied Salmon's face as he was replying. The steward was middle-aged and fat under his spotless white jacket, making his first voyage in the *Truxillo*.

"Was there anyone else in the passageway?"

"No, sir, except for a little girl going into one of the rooms when I was heading for the purser's office."

Captain Brier glanced around the cabin. On the glass-topped dressing table stood an assortment of jars and bottles; dresses and blouses hung from hooks, and a plaid bathrobe was draped over a chair. There were no signs of a struggle.

Stepping over the body, the captain inspected the white-tiled bathroom. The door was hooked back, partly concealing half of the tub. In the washbowl, beneath a mirror, lay a wet face cloth stained red, undoubtedly blood. The bottom of the tub was still damp from that forenoon's cleaning by the steward; in the portion behind the door, it was smudged, as if someone had stood there in shoes.

Captain Brier returned to the cabin which, with the fan stopped, was hot and humid; Salmon had loosened the collar of his jacket. The captain stood gazing in thought through one of the two open portholes, which gave directly onto the sea. They provided a quick means of disposing of a murder weapon bearing fingerprints, though not an escape route. The arc of the cloudless horizon rose and fell to the gentle sway of the ship in the sparkling blue sea, the movement that, according to Salmon, had caused the unlatched door to swing and catch his attention. Plausible enough, mused the captain. Too plausible?

There was a sharp knock on the door and the purser hurried in, the doctor right behind him. The doctor had evidently come in haste from his cabin as two buttons on his coat were still unfastened. The purser had not stopped to put on his uniform jacket but had rushed down in shirt and white trousers. He was around thirty, but almost completely bald, and wore gold-rimmed spectacles on his thin face. He looked quickly at the body, then glanced away.

The doctor, stout and dignified, white-haired, displayed a shocked but professional calm. After making a cursory examination, he straightened up, red-faced and puffing.

"She was struck a heavy blow on the back of the head, possibly more than once, with a flat weapon of some kind—perhaps not heavy enough to have caused death. Death may have been due to shock."

Light footsteps sounded in the passageway, approaching the door. The captain motioned to Salmon but before the steward could reach for the bolt, a frowning young woman with fluffy dark hair pushed open the door. She was shapely in a yellow dress, and wore gold bangles dangling from both wrists.

"What on earth's keeping you, Fanny?" The young woman stopped on seeing the four men. The captain stepped past the others and took her by the arm. "Come in, Miss Keeling."

He led her wonderingly to a chair. As she sat down she saw her roommate and opened her mouth as if to scream. The captain grasped her gently by the shoulder. "Easy now, Miss Keeling." He motioned to Salmon to switch on the fan.

"Is she—dead?" she gasped.

"I'm deeply sorry to say that she is. She was found like that several minutes ago."

"I can't believe it! She left the bridge table to come down here for her cigarettes, a special brand of Turkish. I came down to see what was keeping her."

"Did Miss Coston suffer from heart trouble?" inquired the doctor.

Miss Keeling nodded. "Poor Fanny had a slight attack about a month ago." Miss Keeling's arm shot out, pointing at the body. "If you're trying to pass that off as a heart attack—" She jumped up and turned to the dressing table, snatched open the long top drawer.

"It's gone!" she shrieked. "The pearl necklace." She swung around.

"I laid it here last night. It was still there this morning when I got my lipstick out. Now it's gone."

"Apparently Miss Coston surprised a thief and was attacked," observed the captain.

Miss Keeling dropped back into the chair. "Poor Fanny!" she moaned. "She didn't want me to bring it along on the cruise. She said I was careless with jewelry. I got it out of the purser's safe to wear last night at the get-together dinner. I meant to put it back after breakfast. It's worth over ten thousand dollars."

"It's still on board," said the captain. "The murderer too. No one will be allowed to leave the ship until after the police have made a thorough investigation in Kingston tomorrow."

Miss Keeling moaned again. "I shouldn't have brought it along. Poor Fanny!"

"I'll arrange for you to be moved into another cabin," said the captain. He turned to Salmon. "Take Miss Keeling up to cabin 6 for the time being. Then report to the chief steward. I'll phone him from my office about transferring Miss Keeling. Don't spread word of this. I don't want passengers crowding down here."

Miss Keeling rose and followed the steward out. The captain then turned to the doctor and the purser. "Doc, wait here. I'll send the chief officer down to arrange with you about moving the body." To the purser he said, "Mr. Frabe, come up to my office with me. I'll need some information from you for making out the radiograms reporting the murder, names, room numbers."

On arriving with the purser at his office just abaft the bridge, Captain Brier telephoned instructions to the chief officer and the chief steward, and then sank into the leather-upholstered chair beside his desk.

"A fine thing to happen on the third day of the cruise!" he said grimly. "It'll not only cast a gloom over the ship, but cause her to be delayed tomorrow in Kingston—unless we can find out who did it before then."

"I think I have a pretty good idea who it was," said the purser. "I thought it better not to say anything in front of the others down in cabin 15, but not long before Salmon found Miss Coston, I saw Miriam Stroude sneaking out of cabin 15."

"Miriam Stroude! Sneaking out!"

"That's how it looked to me. I was standing just inside the doorway of cabin 11, returning a book I'd borrowed from John Granger." The purser grinned sheepishly. "O.K., so it was a book on the stock market. You won't think me so crazy when I make a killing. Besides, if I hadn't been interested in the stock market, I wouldn't have been there to see what I'm telling you about. Granger wasn't in his cabin, so I left the book on the table just inside the doorway. Another book lying on it caught my eye, on Speculation. I started to leaf through it when I heard someone out in the passageway. Holding the door open with my foot, I looked out casually and saw Miriam Stroude walking away from cabin 15. She had come out so quietly I wouldn't have heard her if I hadn't had the door open."

"Salmon said he found the door of cabin 15 swinging—unlatched."

"It's obvious why. She pulled it to so gently it didn't quite catch. The first good roll to that side opened it again."

"But Miriam Stroude! You're sure she came out of 15?"

"Absolutely." The purser took a handkerchief from his hip pocket and began wiping his spectacles. "It's hard to believe of her, I know; a good dancer, popular, chased by all the wolves. Have you noticed, though, she never lets herself be monopolized by one man? She circulates, keeps to herself a lot. That gives her plenty of freedom to slip off somewhere anytime she wishes. She's listed as a private secretary, but I've been wondering if she might be a high-class jewel thief. I was thinking of mentioning it to you. Now, after seeing her sneak out of cabin 15—" The purser shrugged.

"But murder!"

The purser put on his glasses. "Not intentional. Probably hit her from behind so as to get out without being recognized."

"Did she see you?"

"I don't think so. She was walking away in the other direction, toward her own cabin."

Captain Brier reached for the telephone beside his desk. "I'll send for her."

He telephoned the chief steward to send a bellboy in search of Miss Stroude with a request that she come with him to the captain's office. "Has word of the murder got around?" the captain asked.

"No, sir. Miss Keeling was too upset to say anything about it going up to cabin 6, and Salmon has kept his mouth shut. But it'll be all over the ship pretty soon, when the body is taken down below and my men start moving out Miss Keeling's things. The word gets around fast."

A few minutes later a sallow-faced boy ushered Miriam Stroude in from the sunny deck. She had an abundance of brown hair, tossed awry by the head breeze, and there was the scent of violets about her. She glanced curiously at the captain and then at the purser seated opposite him. The captain rose and led her to a chair; as he sat down again, he came straight to the point.

"Miss Stroude, would you mind telling me if you were in cabin 15 during the past twenty minutes or so?"

She hesitated, looked embarrassed. "I suppose it was cabin 15. I didn't notice. It was very stupid of me. I was in a daydream and opened the wrong door by mistake. They're so much alike. Someone apparently saw me and reported it. I'm really most sorry."

"Did you go far enough into the cabin to be able to see into the bathroom?"

"I must admit that I was well into the cabin before I realized I wasn't in my own."

"Did anyone else enter while you were in there?"

She shook her head. "No one." She paused, as if perplexed. "Is there something wrong?"

"Miss Stroude, shortly after you left cabin 15, Miss Coston was found brutally murdered in the bathroom doorway. Also, a valuable pearl necklace is missing."

Miriam Stroude looked stunned. "Then I'm being accused?"

"Not accused, merely questioned. Mr. Frabe saw you leaving Miss Coston's cabin. I wished to have his statement verified."

"Then if he saw me leaving, he must have seen Miss Coston go in immediately afterward." Miriam Stroude turned anxiously to the purser. "She came down the stairs from the lounge as I was going to my cabin. I stopped to speak to her. She hurried past me, saying she'd left her bridge game to get some cigarettes from her cabin and was in a hurry to get back."

The purser shook his head at the captain. "I didn't see Miss Coston. As I told you, I only looked out of cabin 11 for a second when I heard Miss Stroude sneak out of cabin 15."

"If you heard me sneak out, as you put it," said Miriam Stroude sharply, "you must surely have heard Miss Coston going in. I hardly think she sneaked into her own cabin."

The purser ignored her and addressed the captain. "I definitely did not hear Miss Coston go into her cabin."

"Miss Stroude," pursued the captain, "did anyone see you and Miss Coston in the passageway?"

"I really can't say. I didn't look back as Miss Coston hurried by me. I do know that there was no one in sight ahead of me."

"You went straight to your cabin?"

"Yes, I remained there a little while and then went up to the promenade deck."

The captain nodded. "I saw you come out of the entrance hall." He turned to the purser. "How soon after seeing Miss Stroude did you leave Mr. Granger's cabin?"

"Not more than a minute at the most, I'd say."

"In that time Miss Stroude could have reached her cabin and no longer been in sight. Miss Coston, too, could have reached her cabin and been out of sight. What about Salmon? Did you see him?"

"No, sir. There wasn't a soul in the passageway when I went along it to go up to my room. I was just getting ready to wash up for lunch when you sent for me. I didn't wait—came down just as I was."

"It would seem, then, that between the time you left the passageway and Salmon came into it, someone went into cabin 15, killed Miss Coston, stole the pearls and, so far as we know now, left unseen."

"The thief could have been in one of the adjoining cabins on either side," Miss Stroude said. There was desperation in her brown eyes. "He could have dodged into cabin 15 and out again in a short time."

"There's another possibility," said the captain. "The thief may have been in Miss Coston's cabin all along."

"Miss Stroude would have seen him," said the purser.

"Not if he were hiding behind the bathroom door."

"That's it!" cried Miriam Stroude. "The thief heard me coming and hid behind the bathroom door. Miss Coston caught him in there."

"Then why didn't I hear her go in," queried the purser, "if I heard Miss Stroude sneak out? It seems to me that Miss Coston went into her cabin just before I got to Mr. Granger's."

"I definitely passed her on way to my cabin," said Miriam Stroude. "She was not in hers when I entered it."

Captain Brier reflected that if Miriam Stroude knew that Miss Coston had left the bridge game to get cigarettes, she was presumably telling the truth. Another point in her favor was the fact that she was still wearing the attractive white pleated dress she had worn at breakfast. The captain glanced at his bald, bespectacled purser and wondered whether it was more than haste that had caused him to come down to cabin 15 without his jacket.

The captain suddenly rose. "I have a theory I'd like to try out. It shouldn't take long, so please remain here, Miss Stroude. You come along with me, Mr. Frabe. I'll need your help."

The captain and the purser went out by the door leading to the passageway running across the officers' quarters. The captain halted abreast the purser's cabin and opened the door. They went inside and the captain closed the door again. He glanced around. On the leather-cushioned settee was a white uniform jacket with only one epaulet in place; the other, together with brass buttons, lay beside it.

"Where's the jacket you were wearing when you saw Miss Stroude leaving cabin 15?"

The purser turned white. He gestured at the settee. "That's it. I was putting a fresh set of trimmings on it when you sent for me. I didn't stop to finish."

The captain stepped over to the clothes-locker door and opened it. Peering inside, he stooped and brought out a rolled-up white bundle. He unrolled it. It was a uniform jacket bare of epaulets and buttons; on the front were some red stains. The captain eyed the purser grimly.

"Where are the pearls, Mr. Frabe?"

His face now ghastly, the purser opened the top drawer of a brown filing cabinet, and from under a heap of forms he drew out a long, narrow manila envelope. He handed it to the captain. Captain Brier raised the flap and glanced inside, then looked up at the purser.

"Mr. Frabe, I'm confining you to your cabin until the police arrive on board tomorrow."

"Captain, please, give me a break." The purser eyed the captain piteously through his gold-rimmed glasses. "I didn't kill her. It was her heart. You heard what Doc said."

"I also heard Miss Keeling say her necklace was missing."

"I've taken heavy losses in the market. I'm in deep with loan sharks to cover margin calls. They threatened me if I didn't pay up soon."

"You tried to frame Miriam Stroude for Miss Coston's murder."

"It wouldn't have happened if it hadn't been for her," said the purser bitterly. "When I heard her coming, I thought it must be Salmon coming back to do something he'd forgotten. I'd left Miss Coston and Miss Keeling up at the bridge game. I took a chance and hopped behind the bathroom door. If he'd come in there, I'd have pretended I was checking for a leak reported in the cabin underneath, but it was Miss Stroude. She didn't wander in by mistake. She headed straight for the dressing table. I saw her go by, through the crack between the door hinges. I couldn't see her at the dressing table, but I could hear her. I heard her open the drawer. I heard her close it again and then hurry to the door and out. She's a high-class jewel thief. No doubt about it."

"Then why didn't she take the necklace?"

"She must have thought she heard someone coming. It wouldn't have washed to say she'd gone in by mistake if the pearls were found missing. I thought she'd beaten me to them, so I looked for something else worth taking. The pearls were still there. I'd just slipped them into my pocket when I heard someone coming again. There wasn't time to put them back into the drawer. I dodged behind the bathroom door again. It was Miss Coston."

The purser swept his hand miserably over his bald head. "She came into the bathroom. I panicked. I grabbed up the long-handled bath brush and hit her before she could look around and see me. I had to hit her twice."

"It's a pity you didn't do your panicking before you went into cabin 15," said the captain grimly.

"Captain," pleaded the purser, "don't let me down. No one will know. I'll throw my jacket overboard after dark. That's what I planned to do. No one saw the stains on it. I came up from cabin 15 with it folded over my arm, as though I'd left my office without bothering to put it on. Let that fancy jewel thief get out of it on her own. No one will suspect me. Even if I am suspected, I'd leave you out of it. I wouldn't let you down."

"Mr. Frabe, I feel very sorry for you, but I cannot help you."

Captain Brier then rolled up the jacket and went out with it tucked under his arm. He paused in thought for a few moments in the passageway before returning to his office. If the purser hadn't lied in saying that Miriam Stroude went to the dressing table drawer, she must, indeed, be a jewel thief. That would be something for the police to look into tomorrow. Meanwhile, it might not be amiss to question her himself about the drawer.

Captain Brier found Miriam Stroude seated as he had left her, permeating his office with the scent of violets. She glanced up hopefully. The captain tossed the jacket onto the top of a filing cabinet. Opening the top drawer of his desk, he slid the manila envelope into it and closed the drawer again. Then he dropped back into the swivel chair and met her intensely curious eyes.

"The pearl necklace," he said, nodding at the top drawer.

She looked startled. "Where did you find it?"

"In the purser's cabin."

"You mean—?" she stopped, as if too incredulous to finish.

"He was the man behind the bathroom door. There was a bloodstained face cloth in the washbowl. I surmised that the thief had got some blood on his hands; perhaps some had spurted on his face too, and maybe his clothing. Salmon's jacket was spotless, as is the white dress you've worn all forenoon. The purser was in shirtsleeves. That's his jacket rolled up, bloodstained. Trying to throw suspicion on you was a big mistake; it placed him near the cabin 15 around the time Miss Coston was murdered. I might not have suspected him otherwise."

Miriam Stroude took in a long breath. "Captain Brier," she said earnestly, "you certainly got me off a pretty nasty hook. I can't tell you how very grateful I am to you."

"Miss Stroude," asked the captain, watching her face, "why did you hold back the fact that you went to the dressing table drawer in cabin 15?"

"The purser told you," she replied awkwardly. "I'm sorry. I really should have mentioned it, but I didn't wish to appear even more stupid by admitting that I actually got so far as opening a drawer before discovering I was in the wrong cabin."

"It was very unwise of you to withhold it. The police would have forced that admission from you tomorrow, had they been obliged to find the murderer. It would have been most damning."

"I realize that now," Miriam Stroude admitted.

"I'm sorry I had to call you up here for questioning, Miss Stroude. Under the circumstances, I was obliged to do so. It was an unpleasant duty. I hope you'll understand."

She rose. "Please don't apologize for what my stupidity brought about." She glanced toward the top drawer of the captain's desk. "Miss Keeling is going to be so happy and relieved when you take the necklace down to her."

Captain Brier eyed his passenger for a moment before replying. "That's for the police to do tomorrow. I'll tell her, of course, that it's been recovered and is safe in my desk."

"She'll be very grateful to you, I'm sure."

Miriam Stroude then stepped out into the midday sunshine. As the odor of violets slowly faded from his office, Captain Brier remained standing, frowning at his thoughts. If Miriam Stroude is a jewel thief, she is also a good actress. Stupid? Or clever? That glance toward his desk drawer, and the remark that Miss Keeling would be happy to get the necklace back, may have been intended to learn the future disposition of the necklace. If she had really been frightened away in her first attempt to steal it, she might be considering a second attempt. And if she were so bold as to try to take it from his desk, he knew the time she was most likely to choose. It was well that he hadn't invited her to afternoon coffee.

Captain Brier had lunch served in his quarters, wishing to avoid a barrage of questions from excited passengers. The chief steward had telephoned that he was virtually under siege in his office down by the dining saloon. The captain spent most of the afternoon attending to the radiograms reporting the murder, and then reading over and signing papers and documents pertaining to the *Truxillo's* arrival on the following day at Kingston, her first Caribbean port of call. At about a quarter to four, he stepped out on deck and casually glanced aft along the boat deck. A number of passengers were sunning themselves in steamer chairs toward the after end; nearer to the bridge, close to the sign barring passengers from that section, stood Miriam Stroude, gazine seaward. She had changed into tan slacks, a loose flamboyant blouse, and, Captain Brier noted grimly, white canvas shoes with rubber soles.

He strolled toward the wing of the bridge and turned into the wheelhouse. The moment he was inside, he picked up speed. To the chief and second officers chatting by the percolating coffee pot, he said, "I'll be back in a few minutes," and then hurried through a doorway into the officers' quarters and along the passageway to his office. He crossed into his living room and stood to one side of the curtain screening the entrance.

Presently his office dimmed briefly as someone came in from the deck, momentarily blocking the sunlight; then followed the sound of the desk drawer being opened, the rustle of paper, the drawer being closed again. Captain Brier stepped from behind the curtain. Miriam Stroude, clutching a small leather handbag, was hastening toward the door to the deck. She halted, her face startled. "Another daydream, of course," said the captain. "The cabins are so much alike."

"You were expecting me."

The captain gave a wry smile. "Another theory of mine. The purser suspects you of being a jewel thief. He thinks something frightened you out of cabin 15 this forenoon. If true, then you were likely to try again, and you'd naturally choose the time I'd be absent for coffee."

"What do you intend to do now?"

"Call in the chief officer to be a witness to the opening of your handbag." Captain Brier strode past her toward the telephone beside his desk.

"Before you ring, Captain Brier, I suggest you look in your desk."

Captain Brier eyed his passenger curiously, then opened the top drawer of the desk. The long manila envelope still lay intact. He lifted its flap and glanced inside. "I'm curious about the flaw in my theory," he said.

"It was based on a wrong fact. The purser's suspicion about me is correct, but the necklace he gave you was a cheap string of mine which I happened to have along with me. It resembles Miss Keeling's except for the diamond clasp. I substituted it for hers. Having a perverted sense of humor, I enjoyed the vision of Miss Keeling discovering the switch, and then trying to convince all concerned that she wasn't introducing some new scheme for defrauding insurance companies and shipping lines.

"The purser complicated matters. Had it been left for the police to return the wrong necklace, Miss Keeling would have spotted the switch immediately. Miss Keeling undoubtedly would have accused you, and others would surely have had their doubts. I couldn't let that happen to you. So I switched the strings again."

"That was a very generous act," murmured Captain Brier.

"I had to express my gratitude in this way," she went on, "because I couldn't have gone to you with the truth without incriminating myself. I was forced to do so now to spare you the embarrassment of bringing a false charge against me.

"To spare you further embarrassment, I intend leaving your ship tomorrow in Kingston and flying back to New York. I want to thank you again now, Captain Brier. I have a police record, so you can imagine how slim my chances would have been if I'd been charged with the murder. I'll also take this opportunity to say good-bye to you."

Miriam Stroude then walked out into the late afternoon sunshine, and the fragrance of violets slowly faded from the office.

TALMAGE POWELL

The Inspiration

Juliano stirred on the soured straw ticking, the movement of his slender body provoking a creak from the hardness of the crude plank bed. A breeze filtered out of the warmth of the Mexican night through the cracks of the slab-and-sod lean-to. It was tainted with the smells of the nearby bullring, parched sand, horse sweat, the faintest suggestion of old and rotten blood.

Juliano stared into the darkness. The silence seemed to pulse. None of the usual small sounds came from the stable or bull pen, the pawing of a hoof, a whinny, the blowing of slobber. Even the gaunt coyotes in the desolate hills above San Carlo de las Piedras were ignoring the fullness of the moon.

Juliano squirmed to a half-sitting position, a premonition chilling him. He glanced at the lax form of Jose, his twin brother, beside him. *Burro,* his edgy mind formed the thought, *one could not look at you and guess that our sister is in trouble.*

His angry condemnation was followed by a quick barb of remorse. Jose loved Lista even as he did. It was only that, for all their alikeness, they were different. When time came to sleep, Jose slept.

Juliano got up and padded to the open doorway. Clothed in the coarse gray cotton pantaloons in which he both worked and slept, he was tall and very slender for his fourteen years. The moonlight lent a quality of brown satin to his bony, ridged chest, wiry arms, and an almost gaunt, broad-cheeked mestizo face that was shadowed under a mane of coarse, hacked-off black hair. His details added up to a look of a particular kind of hunger, the hunger one suspects in the sinewy puma that has survived every hardship.

His large, liquid black eyes searched his surroundings, the shadow of the stable against which the lean-to clung, the barren stretch of dusty earth between him and the bullring thirty yards away, the pens against the wooden wall of the arena where the bulls for Sunday's fight were black, lurking shadows.

Nothing moved, and the night was as silent as death. The scene was suddenly not good, as it had been three years ago when he and Jose arrived barefoot in San Carlo, papa's gift of twenty centavos easing the pain of papa's explanation that it was now time for their hungry mouths to leave his table.

San Carlo had seemed the jewel of cities to their young, goggling, peon eyes. The sun-baked buildings of board and dusty stucco were two, three, even four stories high. The narrow streets spilled their traffic into a broad plaza where pigeons flew from a towering stone monument and a man of great authority in a brown cotton uniform could make the cars stop by blowing his whistle.

Now, memories of the time before that first day came like a burro's kick, in sharp pictures. The mud-brick adobe on the rocky farm far back in the hills where one coaxed the straggly corn with a tireless hoe and water carried into the fields. A dung fire burning on the hearth. The pat-pat-pat of mama's hands making tortillas. The ill-tempered old goat with one broken horn. The treasured red hen that laid eggs with two yolks. The corn-husk doll Lista had played with about the time he and Jose were born . . .

Juliano went rigid in the lean-to doorway as a weak, gasping outcry came out of the night. A similar note of torment was surely what had awakened him.

He'd taken only a few jerky steps when he saw her, a slender, twisted form on the ground beyond the corner of the barn. He ran, and fell on his knees beside her. His mind whipped away from what his eyes saw. For a second he was about to faint. "Lista! My sister! Por Dios!"

The soft oval of her face was hot and wet with pain. The cascade of lustrous black hair was tangled about her cheeks and forehead. Her large dark eyes were sunken and filled with the sight of death.

Her full red lips parted. Her beautiful teeth gleamed. "Juliano . . . I knew I would reach you. Help me, Juliano, help me!"

She was trying to rise to an elbow, her other slender arm reaching toward him. He couldn't move, held by the sight of so much blood. It stained the cotton dress that clung to her slender, once-vibrant and youthful form. It had run glistening down her calves to dye the edges of the guarachas on her feet.

"Lista . . ." he said in a disembodied voice. "Lista . . ." Then he was gathering up the loose lightness of her, staggering toward the lean-to doorway, his hoarse shouts rustling the horses in their stalls and the great dark bulls in the pen. "Jose! Quickly! Wake up, you burro, and help me! Our sister, she is dying!"

Dr. Diego Sorolla de Luz stepped onto the front porch of the long, low, mud-brick building that housed the free clinic for the poor of San Carlo. He closed the screen door, squinting as he turned into the glare of the early morning sun.

He was a lean, swarthy man dressed in white ducks, smock, surgical cap. He looked for a moment at the backs of the two boys sitting on the farther end of the porch, their legs dangling. He drew a heavily reluctant breath and started toward them.

Juliano and Jose turned their heads toward the sounds of tired footsteps on gritty planking. They read the pity and sympathy in the doctor's face. Juliano paled a little. Otherwise, they reacted outwardly to their sister's death with the stoicism of their ancestors.

"I am sorry to be a doctor whose best was not good enough," he said.

"Gracias, Señor Doctor," both boys said. Juliano added, "We shall pay you when . . ."

"It is all paid, my young friend."

"How? Muno Figero hasn't been here, and no one else would bother."

The doctor wedged himself down between them, Jose on his right, Juliano on his left. "Muno Figero? The young torero? Was he the prospective father?"

Juliano nodded.

Jose leaned and spoke across the doctor's chest. "Shhh, Juliano! Lista asked us not to tell."

"Your sister mentioned her troubles?" the doctor asked.

"Lista and I were very close," Juliano said. "She always turned to me when the trouble was bad—even at the end. Not to mama, or papa, or Muno, who she loved. But to me . . ."

"Juliano," Jose said.

Juliano looked at his brother. "What does it matter now? It is right for the doctor to know." Juliano lifted his eyes to the man's. "She was not really a bad woman, Señor Doctor, even though she lived with a man not her husband."

"I'm sure of that. She was the loveliest of young women. I want you always to remember her that way."

"I shall remember her grief," Juliano said. "She was to have a baby, which Muno didn't want."

De Luz's hawkish face with its beaked nose became almost saturnine for an instant, the dark eyes angry and hooded. "I'm sure our torero will be in the clear." He didn't say the rest of it, the part that experience and medical knowledge had taught him. The girl, undoubtedly on her lover's insistence, had crept to some dark hole where some dirty-fingered old woman had used a sharpened stick or filthy hatpin to start the flow again, to abort the living thing in the womb. Then, when things had gone wrong, the old woman, thinking only of her own safety, had abandoned the girl. And the pain-wracked girl had somehow dragged herself to the one person on earth she believed in.

The doctor laid his hand on Juliano's shoulder, feeling the bony, wiry strength of it. "Don't brood, my young friend. It won't help—and she wouldn't want it."

"I try to tell him so," Jose said, "but he thinks of little else for two, three days, since Lista came and told us."

"Burro," Juliano said, "she needed to tell someone. Can't you understand?"

"Did she tell you she was planning an abortion?" the doctor asked.

"Abortion, Señor Doctor?"

"A way of doing away with the thing before it became a baby."

"She mentioned it."

"Did she say who, where, or how she planned to go about it?"

"She said Muno knew of such things. I begged her not to do it."

"I see." De Luz got up heavily. "The matter will of course be reported to the police, but I doubt that anything will come of it. The young man involved will doubtless exhibit a great shock, and one might as well try to run down an individual rat in the garbage heaps of San Carlo as to hope to nail the dirty-fingered old woman. Half the crones in town would take the assignment, for a price."

Juliano stood up on the edge of the porch. "Well, it will soon be forgotten. We are but peons."

The doctor looked at him quickly and started to say something, obviously in denial of the boy's wisdom-hard statement. Instead, he said, "There are details. Your papa will have to be notified. The funeral arrangements must be made. I will see to it."

"You are most kind," Juliano said.

Noontime came and went, and Juliano continued to sit in a dark silence on the bench in the city square. Jose grew increasingly alarmed at the change in his brother.

"Juliano, I'm hungry . . ."

"Then go and eat!"

"But you, Juliano . . ."

"Shut up, Jose," Juliano said. *Papa and mama*, he thought, *I meant for nothing like this to happen when I brought together Lista and Muno. I only meant good . . .*

Was it I who ignorantly started it all? Or was it a tale written by a finger in the sky?

They had squandered the twenty centavos, he and Jose, the first day in San Carlo, on cakes of brown sugar candy sold by sidewalk vendors from fly-specked glass showcases.

Their third day in the city, Juliano and Jose had met three others like themselves. The belly cramps were now urgent, and the others were wise in the ways of urban life.

The five spotted a well-dressed man staggering from a cantina. They followed him, invisible shadows on the dark street, and when the moment was right, they sprang on him, beat him down, and ripped the wallet from his pocket. They divided the fortune, forty-three pesos, in the sanctuary of an alley.

Later, bedded for the night in a culvert, Jose patted his comfortably rumbling stomach. "This is a good thing, I think."

"No," Juliano said, "it is a bad thing."

"Well, what are we to do?"

"We'll find work."

Jose grunted his disbelief and went to sleep. Juliano lay wakeful, feeling dirtied, remembering the sudden sober, pitiful look on the big, dumb animal's face when the young wolves had dragged him down.

The day after the robbery was a Sunday, and Juliano and Jose followed the crowds to the bullring. Juliano soaked in every detail, from the tinny trumpet announcing the processional of the costumed matadors to the dragging away of the last dead bull.

"Jose," Juliano said when it was all over, "we shall be toreros. It is the only way the likes of us can hope to be rich and famous."

"Not I," Jose said.

"You will follow where I lead." Juliano's voice left no room for compromise. "Come. We are going to see the manager of this place."

The impresario, located after asking directions of countless people, turned out to be a stooped, sallow man with incredible pouches under his eyes. "So you would go to work?"

"Sí, Señor."

"Doing what?"

"Anything for a start, Señor. Someday I will be a matador."

"You and a million others of your kind," the manager sneered. "Would you shovel manure from the stables?"

"Until our arms fell off, Señor."

"Mend the padding the horses wear? Sharpen the pikes the mounted picadores carry? Curry horses and tend the tame steers we use as Judas goats to lead the bulls into the pens when they're shipped in from the ranches?"

"Anything, Señor. Any work!"

"Well, muchacho, you challenge me. So I'll accept, because there is always work for willing hands who don't demand a fortune. But jump when you're told, mind you!"

"Forever, Señor!"

"And if I catch you stealing or loafing on the job, I'll cut off your ears and feed them to my dog."

"The dog will die of starvation," Juliano laughed.

"Where do you live, muchacho?"

"In a huge stone pipe that passes under a street."

"You'll catch your death in that. You can use the lean-to beside the stable."

"Gracias, Señor!"

After a hard day's work, Jose was always ready for his bean bowl and bed, but Juliano enjoyed the evening hours. As the sun set, he was a slender figure in the empty arena fighting imaginary bulls. His weapons were a ragged, cast-off cape, a wooden sword, a muleta made from a piece of sacking. He practiced everything he had seen and been told, and one evening when he turned in a series of veronicas the silence was broken by an "olé" and the clapping of a pair of hands. He looked up in surprise.

So it was that Juliano met Muno Figero, who would fight the next day and had come to the pens to see the bull he had drawn.

Muno was six years older, tall and slender, with devilish eyes and strong, square teeth flashing black and white in a V-shaped brown face. Already he was making a name for himself with his graceful and daring capework.

That season, whenever Muno was in San Carlo, Juliano was his dogged shadow. Muno enjoyed the adulation. He coached Juliano and took him sometimes to the cafes where toreros and their followers gathered to sip wine and talk. In these wonderful hours, Juliano soaked up the lore of the ring. He learned of Belmonte, who helped father modern bullfighting, of Procuna, refiner of the dead man's pass, of Perez, who fought the terrible bull Machin and was killed because a breeze brushed a corner of his cape and exposed him, of Saleri, who defamed the classic art with a cheap, spectacular trick, using a pole to vault over the bull's head. Saleri got his when he made the mistake of trying the trick twice on the same bull, finding the horns waiting when he descended the second time.

"Which proves," Muno remarked, "that the bull may be smarter than the man. They are quick to learn—and they never forget."

"Neither shall I," Juliano said.

The broadening of knowledge destroyed the illusion that San Carlo and its bullring were the center of everything. Indeed, there were dozens of such rings scattered all over Mexico in grubby little cities. Rings whose walls were of weathered clapboard and rusting tin signs exhorting one to *Tome Coca-Cola*, whose seats were tiers of unpainted planking worn smooth. Matadors fought in such rings at two points in their careers, if they weren't killed in between. They started here, young and eagerly confident. Or here they ended, old, scarred and bitter, gloomily fighting bulls they once would have ridiculed for the uncouth, bumpkin crowds they despised.

During this period, Juliano heard nothing from his family. It was the natural order of things. Each had his or her way to go; mama and papa on the farm and Lista with her husband, an old widower who came one day and gave papa ten pesos for permission to marry Lista, who was fifteen at the time.

Their faces all became affectionate memories; and then one afternoon Lista was waiting when Juliano and Jose returned to the lean-to. They had spent the afternoon spreading fresh sand in the arena. Their sweaty, parched, gritty discomfort vanished when they saw her standing beside the uncovered doorway, a pasteboard suitcase at her feet.

She held out her arms and ran to meet them. The three merged into a confusion of hugs, shouts, laughter. Then Juliano held her at arm's length. "What a fine woman is our elder sister, Jose!"

With rare vivacity, Jose laughed his pleasure. "But she isn't real, Juliano. She is too beautiful to be real."

The thought struck Juliano: "What of your husband, Lista?"

"He is dead," she said quietly. "He drank too much pulque in the village and fell from his horse and broke his neck."

Juliano closed the chapter in his mind without regret or sorrow. After all, the old man had had three wives.

"I had no place," Lista said, "so I came to you, Juliano."

He put an arm about her shoulders. "You did right. Tonight we go to the Cafe de los Toros and buy a bottle of wine to celebrate the reunion!"

She met Muno that night. After the old man, the dazzling, ardent young one aroused her love quickly.

Now she was dead.

Juliano raised his head slowly, aware of Jose fidgeting worriedly beside him. He looked about the plaza, at the cars in motion, the pigeons swooping from the stone monument. He felt the sun hot on his face and thought of the coldness of her in the clinic.

He uncoiled his lean body slowly, standing. Jose jumped from the bench beside him.

"Shall we eat, Juliano?"

Juliano gave him a long, baleful look. "No. We go to see Muno."

Muno was knotting a black string tie about the collar of a white silk shirt when the knock sounded on the door of the bed-sitting room of his cubbyhole kitchenette apartment.

With a final quick glance at his black-haired reflection, he turned from the bureau and crossed the room, picking his way through a small space crowded with sofa, chairs, table, the bureau, floor lamp, a wardrobe made of corrugated cardboard, and a wall bed that was still unmade.

He opened the door and stiffened slightly at the sight of the two boys in the sultry, dim hallway.

"Juliano, Jose . . ." he murmured. He stood aside and motioned them in, his face a shade lighter than normal. "Has something happened?" he asked, sensing that something had, indeed.

"She is dead, Muno," Juliano said.

"Oh." Muno drifted to the worn blue sofa and sat down slowly. He moved as if all of his joints were dry, the sockets grating. "Where is she?"

"At the clinic. The thing went badly, Muno. She won't have a baby. She bled to death."

Muno raised a hand and fingered sweat beads from under his eyes. "I'm sorry, Juliano. Truly, I am."

Juliano looked about the room, at the clothing tossed over a chair, the socks crumpled beside the bed, the bureau where her powder, lipstick and cologne lay as she had last touched them. "Yes, Muno, I suppose you are. She was beautiful and young, and gave you all of herself."

Muno bit his lips and moved his head numbly from side to side. "Do you hate me, Juliano?"

"Hate? No. I despise you!"

"You don't understand," Muno said. "A baby would have messed up everything, right when I'm on the edge of better things. Did you know that a famous manager has come all the way from Mexico City to watch me in the arena tomorrow?"

"I see." Juliano made a slight motion of his hand to Jose and they started toward the door.

Muno jerked himself upright from the sofa. "Juliano . . ."

Juliano pushed Jose into the hall, then stopped and turned in the doorway. Muno held out a hand. "Juliano, hatred will not bring her back."

Juliano stood and looked at him.

"Please, Juliano . . ." Muno said. "It is over, done. Nothing can change that."

"How quickly will you forget her, Muno?"

"Juliano . . ."

"Will you bring home another tomorrow night?"

Muno's face hardened. "Get out! Get out! You are a fool, like your sister. Get out, and don't come back!"

When the full moon was at zenith that night, Juliano nudged Jose awake.

Jose sat up on the straw ticking, rubbing his eyes with his knuckles and making gulping noises. "What is it, Juliano?"

"Come on, we are going across to the arena. It is as bright as day outside. I can't lay here."

Jose's hands fell limply from his face. "What? What is this?"

Juliano was already standing beside the bed, pulling his cotton blouse over his head and shoulders. "Muno Figero has drawn the bull called Santiago for tomorrow."

"Sí, but what has this . . ."

"I would try Muno's shoes," Juliano said. "I would test this bull. Now. In the arena. Will you help me chute the bull and work him back into the pen—or must I do it all by myself?"

Jose's eyes showed white with fear. "You are crazy, Juliano. You will kill yourself!"

"But I won't argue," Juliano said. "Are you coming to help me or not?"

Mumbling an incoherent prayer, Jose leaped out of bed.

Shortly, the bull Santiago took his first exploratory steps into the strange, new world of the arena when Juliano shouted to Jose to open the gate.

Limned in the moon glare in the center of the arena, Juliano watched the bull pause and paw the sand. He knew that Santiago had seen him and was taking a moment to size up the enemy, the situation. Santiago was a sleek, black Piedras Negras, almost nine hundred pounds with horns that swept dangerously outward and upward at the tips, a far better bull than was usually seen in San Carlo.

Afraid that his dry mouth and constricted throat had lost the power to speak, Juliano lifted his threadbare old cape with trembling hands. He stomped the sand. "Toro!" he said. "Toro!"

Santiago circled as if unaware of the two-legged creature's existence. Then the night exploded with the thunder of his hoofs.

Juliano choked back the urge to bleat and flee. Sweat burned his eyes. His hands were shaking the cape almost uncontrollably.

Santiago grew to monstrous size as the charge closed the distance. His eyes threw back red moonbeams. Juliano kept his gaze fastened on the needle-sharp horns. They dipped, hooking, and a flick of the cape changed their course by a scant degree.

Suddenly, the bull was past, and Juliano realized he was in one piece. He turned. Santiago was already wheeling, charging again. This time, it was less frightful. Juliano's heart ceased to be a choking mass in his throat.

Another pass, with the cape swirling. Then again, and again.

Juliano dared a laugh. He stomped his bare foot. "Toro!"

The seconds became minutes, and a thin haze of dust clouded the surface of the sand. Santiago turned, hooked, and the cape swept him safely past.

"Toro! Toro!" Juliano flaunted the cape. He turned the bull in half a dozen more passes, working toward the side of the arena. Santiago was beginning to lather. *It is enough,* Juliano decided, and he leaped behind the barricade.

Jose, who had watched it all from the safety of the wooden shelter, pounded Juliano on the shoulder. "You were one of them, Juliano! A real torero."

"I have practiced the cape many months." Juliano was out of breath and soaked with sweat. "Now we work Santiago into the chute, back into the pen so that no one will ever know he was in here tonight."

Jose shook his head, still dumbfounded. "My brother—and a real live bull."

"Perhaps I had not only much practice but the strongest of inspirations," Juliano said.

"Did you not feel alone and naked?"

"As naked as Belmonte must have felt." Juliano's eyes met his brother's. "When he was a boy, the Great One would swim a river on a bull ranch at night and fight the bulls alone, secretly. It is the way Belmonte learned. He was too young to know then that he was sending many matadors to their deaths. If he had only known . . ."

Juliano turned, craned, looking over the top of the barricade. Santiago claimed the center of the arena, head lifted, horns gleaming, forehoof pawing, challenging all comers.

"When they first face a man, they think he and the cape are one. So the cape distracts them," Juliano explained. "But the second time around—should there be one—the bull in his wisdom knows the truth. This is the reason great care is taken from the day of their birth to keep them from facing a cape, until they go into the arena. Nothing is more deadly than a cape-broken bull such as Muno Figero will face when he meets Santiago in the arena tomorrow."

Jose nodded in slow comprehension of truths his brother had learned while he, Jose, slept the evenings away.

"I think Muno Figero will not live to see Mexico City," Jose decided.

And for once Juliano was quite certain that his duller brother was right.

ROBERT COLBY

Death Is a Lonely Lover

Carl Koenig: I came apart like a toy watch when I read about Lorrie Proctor in the newspapers. They had just found her body—six months and thirteen days after it happened. Beside her in the grave was her pocketbook containing her keys, a driver's license, and other papers. She was wearing the same pale pink dress of that night when we were together for the last time, and now the rotted fragments of it covered a skeleton.

She was also wearing my engagement ring, an item which wouldn't bring five bucks at a pawnshop. Her killers didn't even bother to remove it. Try to picture that tarnished band wobbling around on one bony little finger.

When the news broke and I read that pathetic bit about the ring, I cried. Later, when I was calm and empty of all but the hate which had grown like an extra organ inside me, I knew it was time to kill—no, execute—the four people responsible for Lorrie's murder.

I had been ready a long time because that little voice in my head told me that Lorrie was dead. Yet did you ever hear of a judge passing sentence on a hunch? No, I had to wait until her death was a fact.

You might think I would go to the police. Listen, I *did* go to the police—right in the beginning, right after it happened. I was barely conscious from the beating I had taken, but the police thought I was drunk. They gave me a hard time. When I finally squeezed some oil of truth into those mechanical brains with which some cops come equipped, it was too late. They couldn't find clue one. Even when they had recovered her body and the stuff buried with her, they came up with exactly nothing.

I broke contact with the police after the first week and moved from the address I had given them without giving a forwarding. When I could see that there would never be any legal justice, I kept what I knew to myself and prepared my own justice in secret.

Lorrie had *six* killers, but the law was aware of only *two* and would condemn only two as guilty of the crime. Such is the blindness and stupidity of legal justice. Since I could not find the two who were wanted by the law, the other four had to die first.

There were two men and two women. I decided that the women should precede the men. The men should be made to suffer their loss as I had suffered the loss of Lorrie.

The women were Nancy Jarrett and Vera Wynn. I chose a night and phoned to see if Nancy were at home. She was. I faked a wrong number and hung up.

I had been over the route several times before and I had no trouble finding the house. It was a bright yellow Cape Cod sort of cottage off Wilshire in West L.A. Amber light jeweled its windows, and set against the darkness, it looked snug and inviting. It had a phony air of innocence and cheer.

I parked a ways beyond and cut the lights of my station wagon. My dog, a sleek Doberman and a trained man-killer, was in back. I gave him an affectionate pat and, more from habit than necessity, told him to stand guard. An order to such an animal is something like cocking a loaded gun, and much more reliable.

Carrying a package under my arm, I climbed out and walked toward the house. I was wearing dark slacks, a light blue jacket and a matching visored hat, plus a thin pair of gloves. Most people are gullible, and if you offer something for nothing, any half-baked uniform will seem official enough.

I stood at her door, but through a near window I could see she was huddled in an easy chair before the television, her stockinged feet propped up on an ottoman.

She was alone, but that wasn't news to me. Her husband, Bruce Jarrett, was a radio engineer. He worked half the night at the transmitter, a lonely little hut beside a signal tower which sprouted from the crest of a hill. It was a beautiful spot for what came later.

I rang the bell, saw her start, scramble into her shoes, approach. She opened the door to the extent of a chain-guard and peeped out.

"Yes?"

"Mrs. Jarrett?"

"Yes, it is."

"Package for you, ma'am. Special delivery."

"Oh, my! All right." She released the chain and swung the door wide.

She was a small woman in her late twenties with a wolf-whistle figure. She was rather pretty, I suppose, but I didn't really notice. She waited expectantly for me to offer the package.

"You'll have to sign," I said, tapping a printed slip tucked under the cord binding the box. "It's registered."

"Heavens, how important!" she sang.

"You got a pencil?" I asked, like I was bored with the whole routine. "Every other delivery I lose a pencil to some joker."

"Hold on," she answered. "I'll get you one."

She went away, into the living room. I sprang inside, eased the door shut behind me, just in time. She was returning with the pencil, coming a bit unglued when she found me standing there on the wrong side of the door.

She hesitated a few feet from me, her eyes searching my face for a danger signal. That was when I lifted a flap at the end of the box close to my body, reached in, and yanked the box free.

I thought her jaw would fall right off her face when she looked down the barrel of that sawed-off shotgun.

I said, "Do just as I tell you, Nancy. Otherwise, I might spread you all over the room."

She took a step backward. The pencil fell from her hand. "Who—who are you?" she asked in a kind of whisper.

"It'll come to you, Nancy, before long. I'll help you remember. Now go and draw the curtains—every one!"

She hesitated, moistened her lips, swallowed.

"Hurry, Nancy. Hurry!" I centered the barrel between her eyes. Watching me, fascinated, she backed, sidestepped. She closed a drape, then another, until it was done. Then I stepped into the living room.

"What do you want?" she asked. "I have a few dollars in my purse. Please take them and leave."

"Where do you keep your purse, Nancy?"

"In—in the bedroom."

"Well then, let's go and get it."

"No!" She shook her head violently. "I don't believe you. It isn't money you want at all."

"You're a real thinker, Nancy." She backed off as I moved toward her.

Suddenly she turned and ran. I danced after her, caught her in the kitchen. She was hurling herself at the back door. Her fingers swarmed all over it, like crazy worms, trying to find the bolt in the dark.

I slammed the side of her head with the gun barrel. She fell, whimpering.

"Oh, please," she moaned. "Please, what have I ever done to you?"

I told her. She was on the floor staring up at me and I was holding the muzzle of the shotgun a foot from her face. When I stopped talking, I squeezed the trigger.

After the sound died, I bent to look at her. She had no face—no face at all.

Del Wynn: I hadn't seen Bruce or Nancy Jarrett for nearly a month. Although Vera and I were close friends of the Jarretts, we had moved to the other side of town and it was inconvenient to get together as often as we did when we lived practically around the corner.

Still, in that dreadful state of shock, I don't imagine Bruce would have come running over to tell us that Nancy had just been murdered. Further, the news did not reach the papers until afternoon of the following day. However, I got the story about mid-morning from an entirely different source.

A couple of detectives came to see me at my office in Burbank. I was working as a PR man for an aircraft company and I had my own private cubbyhole.

After they had settled in chairs before my desk, Sergeant Newbold lighted a cigarette offered by his partner, Detective Ferguson, then told me abruptly that

Nancy Jarrett had been blasted to death with a shotgun charge which all but tore her head from her body.

I was extremely fond of Nancy and it took me a minute or so to recover my composure.

I could see that Newbold had more to say, but he waited patiently and made comforting sounds in a flat, cool voice which seemed as if it had long ago been drained of any emotion.

"Bad as it is, Mr. Wynn, I wish that were the end of it," he continued. "But I suppose you guessed we wouldn't be here unless there were additional details involving you. Also your wife."

"I'm afraid I don't understand," I said blankly.

"The killer left something behind," Newbold said, and passed me a small square of white paper which showed typed names and a few rusty splotches of blood. I studied the paper:

ORDER OF EXECUTION

Nancy Jarrett√

Vera Wynn

Bruce Jarrett

Del Wynn

My name and Vera's leaped out at me!

"As you see," Newbold said evenly, "Mrs. Jarrett's name has been checked off. The rest is obvious." He extended his hand and I gave him the list. "This paper was pinned to Nancy Jarrett's blouse," he went on as he folded the paper and tucked it into his wallet.

I said, "Why should anyone want to kill me, or my wife?"

"Why should anyone want to kill Nancy Jarrett?" Ferguson asked with a wry twist of his lips.

Newbold nodded agreement. "Do you know why, Mr. Wynn?"

"No," I said numbly.

"In any case, the killer planted that list to scare hell out of you people."

"Speaking for myself, it does just that." I sent him a weak smile.

"There's got to be a connection," Ferguson reasoned. "You're all linked to something. Any idea what it might be?"

"Not the least," I told him. "The Jarretts've been friends for a couple of years. We lived close by, got together about once a week. We played bridge or went to movies, night spots—things like that. Perfectly innocent stuff, never any trouble."

Newbold squashed his cigarette in my desk tray. "You belong to any mutual societies, clubs, lodges—any sort of organization in which you were all members?"

"None. Nothing like that."

"Maybe you all went to a party," said Ferguson, groping. "There was an argument, a fight. You four took sides against someone."

I shook my head. "Never. Listen, you've got a point, but you're moving in the wrong direction. Let me say from the beginning that, as a foursome, we didn't take sides against anyone. There were no fights, physical or verbal. We're all mild enough, certainly not belligerent, and we kept pretty much to ourselves."

Newbold shifted uncomfortably in his chair. "Can you think of a time when some guy made a pass at one of the wives, causing a public scene?"

"No."

"Or there was some, uh, private incident. When you men heard about it later, you took action."

"Absolutely not. That would make it easier to understand."

Newbold sighed. "Take your time, think about this from every angle, all the way back, inside and out. Examine anything that has a taint of friction. The smallest event is important."

We were silent for a space as I forced my mind to poke in every corner of the total relationship. "Sorry," I said, "there just isn't anything at all to work with. And believe me, I'm a lot more anxious to get at the truth than you boys could ever be."

"Then we've got a psycho on our hands," Newbold said firmly, "someone who merely imagines that he or she has been given a rough time by you people. True or not, it doesn't help. The end result is the same."

"We're just as dead, you mean."

"Exactly."

"You think he'll go through with it, Sergeant?"

"Nancy Jarrett was no bluff."

"Can't you stop it?"

"We can try to find him," Ferguson said. "That's the only sure way."

"Don't count on finding him too soon," Newbold warned.

"I want protection," I snapped. "My wife is next, you know. Can't you give us a guard or two?"

"I could do that, yes," Newbold answered. "For how long?"

"I don't know. Indefinitely. Until he's caught."

"Impossible. We don't have the manpower for a long period of guard duty. We get maybe half a dozen calls a week asking for protection, one reason or another, and turn them all down. Of course, this is a quite different case, the need is obvious. But after a couple of days or so we'd only have to call our men back."

"What good are the police, then?"

"How would you like to live without us?" His smile had an edge.

"Let me tell you something, Mr. Wynn," Ferguson said. "If a man is set and determined to kill you without fear of consequences, he'll get the job done, sooner or later. All he needs is patience, a suitable weapon, and a decent plan."

"Coming from a policeman, that's a lousy piece of information," I growled.

"At least it's honest," Newbold defended. "It's realistic."

"No, it's plain negative," I said bitterly. "Maybe we should give up and pin targets to our backs!"

"Not at all," replied Newbold calmly. "We're starting with rock-bottom truth.

Awareness is a kind of armor. President Kennedy was guarded by the FBI, the Secret Service, and about half the police force of Dallas. One man got to him. That's a sad fact, but the truth.

"We're only trying to show you that the best watchdogs guarding each one of you night and day is no guarantee of safety. We've got to do a lot more. We've got to hunt this killer down and put him away! And we'll be hard at it, that's a promise.

"Meanwhile, if you and your wife can afford to slip out of town undercover, fine. If not, take every precaution. Perhaps the best precaution is for you two to get together with Jarrett and come up with an answer. When and where did you make yourselves an enemy? Who and why?"

He passed me his card. "Just as soon as you can tell me that, call me. Day or night . . . "

Nothing worked in our favor. We couldn't afford the expense of leaving town and my job might not be there when I returned. More, Bruce Jarrett was no help at all. The poor guy was too broken to help us discover where or how we had made an enemy and didn't seem to care.

Vera made a big try, but together we couldn't pick up a single thread. I kept her locked in the house with a small automatic I had bought her, and she was not to open the door for anyone. I called five or six times a day to be certain she was all right.

Mornings I ducked into my car and raced to the office, then raced back. We had laid in a supply of staples and frozen goods. We never left the house after dark. Most of this was done for Vera's sake. I don't scare easily; I am only bothered by an enemy I can't see—who won't come out and fight in the open.

In the third week, at lunchtime on Valentine's Day, I phoned Vera from the office. She thanked me sweetly for my card and again mentioned the little bottle of perfume I had given her that morning. The mail had come just a minute before my call and she had received a heart-shaped box of chocolate-covered cherries from her brother in Pasadena.

Delighted, she opened the box as we talked and I heard her munching. Then she made a small gasping sound and there was a thud, as if the receiver had been dropped to the floor.

I drove wildly, with mindless abandon. A cop raced after me. He was a bright one and gave me a full-siren escort after I explained, but death and cyanide are only seconds apart. Vera was gone when I reached her.

Bruce Jarrett: Del Wynn just left. He made a special trip out to the transmitter this evening, and since mine is a one-man job with nothing much required but to log the meter readings and do an occasional bit of maintenance, we had time for a long talk.

When Vera Wynn was poisoned and I saw that Del was man enough to put aside his wretchedness and take a stand for doing something about the murders other than weeping behind locked doors, I was ashamed. I agreed to help him make a real effort to put the killer or killers of Nancy and Vera in the gas chamber. It would be a kind of ironic justice for Del, since cyanide is used to execute murderers under capital punishment in the state of California.

Because of the threat to my life, a special patrol of the area had been ordered. Working alone at the transmitter made me a very vulnerable target, so I kept the only door locked and made Del go around to a window where I could see him before I let him in.

We shook hands and I said, "Well, how are you bearing up?"

He didn't answer. Instead he went past me to a chair by the control board and sat down. I took my place behind the panel. Music was blaring from the monitor so I reached for the fader and lowered the gain.

"You look beat down," I said. "I suppose you're going through the same emotions—the lost feeling, the sleepless nights full of images and memories. I think it's the little things you remember that get to you when you lie there and—"

"Shut up!" he barked. "Please just keep it to yourself, will ya?"

"Well, now listen, Del, I was only trying to—"

"Sure, sure," he said, waving me off. "But that stuff is all downhill—nowhere. I have the same feelings, but I can't afford to indulge them right now. Let's cry later and get to work. O.K.?"

"Sorry," I said woundedly.

Ignoring me, he got up and paced a moment before he said, "I think we've got to try a new approach. We need tangible clues. It'll be a long process, but there's only one way to find them."

"How?"

"We'll start from the ground up—from the first day we four met. On paper we'll make a chronological list of every single occasion when we were all together. We'll put a label to each date. When that's done we'll go back again to the beginning and talk in the details, step by step."

"It might work," I said, "but it could take half the night."

"Got anything better to do? Then find a pencil and some paper."

It went much faster than we had expected. We had drawn up a timetable of events and had discussed the details of the first fourteen months in less than two hours—drawing a blank. Then the phone rang.

It was Lieutenant Thatcher of Homicide. I had met him only once; most of my dealings were with Sergeant Newbold and his partner. Thatcher was hot on the case, working with the night trick. He had the mug shot of a suspect he wanted me to identify. He was sending a Detective Murray Gladstone with it in about an hour.

I asked for the name of the suspect in the mug shot, but he said he was going to withhold the name and let *me* tell *him*. It would be more conclusive.

I shared the news with Del. He said Thatcher was probably groping in the dark and it was a long shot. We went on with the task.

Nothing developed until we reached a night in the summer of last year. This particular foursome was labeled: *Malibu for dinner at the Lockwoods'. Drinks at The Point, followed by drive along coast.*

We were about to discard this one also when Del said, "Wait a minute! We didn't just cap the night with a drive and then go home. Don't you remember? We pulled off the coast highway into a parking area by the beach. We sat looking down at the ocean and we made a big funny deal about necking like kids."

"So?"

"So there was one other car in there, about a hundred feet off to the right. I'm not sure, because it was dark and cloudy that night and I never did get the whole picture, but I think there were two, or maybe three men in the car—and a girl. The men had a fight and the girl screamed. Now do you remember?"

I nodded. "Sure, a bunch of drunks having a brawl. So what?"

"At the time, nothing much, though it did upset me. But now, in the light of all this, I think it's worth a close look."

It was. In fact, once the scene was dredged up from my memory with Del's prodding, I had the awful conviction that this was the moment of truth about the murders and about myself. I can only guess that some Freudian block kept the memory locked in that secret closet of the mind where we hide from ourselves—because, by an accident of circumstance, I had seen more of that fight than the others, and for reasons of my own, remained silent.

We were using my car that night and after I parked at the edge of a shallow cliff above the beach, I sat listening to the others jabbering a minute, then got out and went for a stroll. I was cold sober but I had been mixing my drinks on top of a heavy meal and I hoped to walk off a sneaky feeling that I was about to be sick.

I was returning when I heard a low moan, as of a man in pain, then scuffling sounds. It came from the area of the other car quite close behind me, and I turned to look.

Three men and a girl were caught dimly in the splay of lights from a passing car. One man had another on the ground at his feet and was booting his ribs viciously. He came to life, scrambled out of range, and struggled to his feet. The man brought him down again with a clubbing motion, though if there was something in his hand I couldn't see it because his massive back was to me.

The third man had a tight hold on the girl's wrist, their heads were turned to watch the beating. Suddenly the girl broke away and ran. The man who had been clutching her wrist chased and caught her. He gave her a wicked backhand across the face and she screamed. The scream drew the attention of the kicker and he went jogging toward them.

Farther removed, talking noisily among themselves, Del, Vera, and my wife had seen nothing, had heard nothing but the scream. Alarmed, they then climbed from the car to look. I hurried up to them. There was safety in numbers and I was afraid.

The men were powerfully built animals and there was about them and their actions an aura of savage brutality. I could almost feel the bones of my face splintering under the impact of cast-iron fists, my ribs kicked in at the point of a stone-hard toe. I detest all forms of violence, I can't bear pain, and I did not want to become involved.

On the other hand, Del Wynn was fearless and he welcomed a good fight. If I gave him the true picture, he would plow in with fists flying. What, then, could I do? Stand and watch? I would be naked before them, an exposed coward. Below the surface, Nancy would never understand or forgive.

"What's goin' on over there?" asked Del. He was straining to see in the gloom. Except when the lights of a passing car brought the figures out of darkness for a few seconds, they were mere shadows.

"Bunch of drunks," I said, "fighting over some cookie. Kid stuff."

"We heard a scream," said Nancy.

"The boy friend gave her a little slap," I belittled. "Probably she was flirting and he was jealous." For all I knew, that might be close. "Nothing to it. C'mon, let's hit the road."

"Maybe we ought to go over and teach them some manners," said Del, molding a fist in his palm.

"Nahh, I wouldn't hit some lousy staggering drunk. That's one thing I never do—punch a drunk."

Del sent me a probing glance but said nothing. He seemed about to turn away, but just then a car moving along the coast highway came out of the north and splashed the scene with light.

Two of the men stood facing the girl, one shaking a finger in her face. The third, the injured one, was climbing to his feet. As if to back my story, he swayed and looked very drunk as he faced us and waved in a loose, awkward signal for help. At the same time he shouted something at us. It came out garbled—again, as if he were drunk.

Now, as the car on the highway swirled past, he stumbled toward the two men and the girl and was lost in the darkness.

"That guy is in trouble," said Del. "I'm gonna find out what kind. You comin', Bruce?"

"Can't you see he's drunk?" Vera said. "Please, Del, leave it alone. I don't want you mixed up with a bunch of drunks brawling over some little tramp."

"She's right," I agreed. "None of our business anyway. Let's go!"

Ignoring us, Del moved off deliberately. He hadn't gone but a few steps when the car backed, circled, and rocketed away, racing without lights until it reached the highway.

That seemed the end of it, but when my car neared the exit, a narrow opening in a chain fence because a parking fee was collected during the day, a man rose up and weaved toward us. It was the man who had taken the beating. He was young, dark-haired, and slender. His clothes were torn and disordered, but there didn't seem to be a mark on him.

The very sight of this guy looming up suddenly to confront us was astonishing. When he vanished, we had all assumed that he had driven off with the others despite the fracas.

As I drew abreast of the man he grabbed the window frame and said something idiotic which sounded like, "Worry, worry." His eyes were wild and hugely dilated, there was a definite smell of whiskey on his breath.

He sagged and fell to the ground. I paused a few feet beyond him, waiting for a hole in traffic. The women wanted to take him along but he didn't look hurt and I was against it. Unexpectedly, Del backed me up. "Stoned out of his mind," he said. "Let'm sleep it off."

That settled it, we left him. The incident crept into my mind briefly the next day but there is nothing I can rationalize and forget so quickly as any situation which tends to accuse me. I never thought of it again.

Yet now that Del had revived the experience and I could see a possible connection to the nightmare of murder and threat which followed long after, I didn't hesitate. I told him exactly what happened and why I had kept silent.

He paced across the room, turned. "Don't you get it!" he cried. "One guy is holding the girl, the other is beating the man, kicking his ribs in. Was that a drunken brawl over a dame? Right now we've got every reason to damn well believe it wasn't!

"I'll spell it out for you. Two of those guys were probably there for just one reason—to rob the man and take his girl off somewhere to rape her. Then what? Chances are ten to one they were afraid to turn her loose, so they murdered her.

"The girl's husband, boy friend, or whatever, sees the four of us watching like it was some kind of sideshow. So he goes psycho. He tracks us down and takes his revenge."

"We're absolute strangers," I objected. "How does he find us?"

"Yeah, that part had me boxed, but it just came to me that the only possible answer is too simple. He got your license number and he made a point to remember it. From there he just followed his nose, that's all."

Something hard and accusing crept into Del's eyes. He moved toward me with his big jaw clenched and his fists balled. He stood poised above me.

"Two of us are dead and the other two might as well be dead," he hissed. "Why didn't you drive us all over a cliff that night, Bruce? We'd've been better off!"

For a moment I thought he might knock me out of the chair, but he turned abruptly and left without looking back. I heard his car thunder off and fade down the hill . . .

Carl Koenig: I read that Vera Wynn is very dead. Certain types of candy don't seem to agree with her. It was quite clever the way I did it. I injected each piece with a shot of poison from a hypodermic syringe, leaving an invisible hole.

I had spent weeks snooping secretly, linking the Wynns to the Jarretts and gathering information about each one of the four. Posing as an investigator for a credit bureau I asked a few guarded questions and got some useful answers. One fact led to another and I soon discovered that Vera had a brother who was a real estate agent in Pasadena. When I found out where he lived, I put his return address on the package of poisoned candy.

I'm still laughing.

A while ago I called Bruce Jarrett at the transmitter to set him up for the kill. I told him I was Lieutenant Thatcher of Homicide, a name I got from a news-paper report on Nancy Jarrett's execution. I told Jarrett I was sending Detective Murray Gladstone with a mug shot.

Gladstone is not a phony name, he's a real cop and was the first one to talk to me after they found out that I wasn't drunk; I had a fractured skull and a couple of busted ribs, to say nothing of a ruptured spleen. I was in and out of a coma then, and Gladstone didn't get through to me until after they had operated and I had recovered enough to make sense.

I didn't lie about the drinking. Sure, I had quite a few, but I wasn't drunk. I had at least half a dozen drinks with Lorrie that Friday night. We had a lot to celebrate. We were getting married the next weekend and that day I had sold the interest in a marine supply store which my father left me a few months back when he died.

I had been working as a clerk in the store and I was always broke. Now I had a few thousand and I was planning to buy out a boat rental business. Also, I could afford to get Lorrie a new ring, a real diamond, although she claimed to have a sentimental attachment to the old one and wouldn't part with it.

Then there was this little furnished house in Venice where we were going to live after we were married. Lorrie said it was "cute," but it was kinda shacky on the outside. I took it because it had a fenced yard and they didn't object to my Doberman, big and mean as he is. I had just signed the lease and paid a couple of months' rent in advance. Like I said, we had a lot to celebrate.

On the night I lost Lorrie I was living in two rooms over a garage south of Pico in Santa Monica. My station wagon had a bad battery and when I went to start it, the battery was dead. I phoned Lorrie and she picked me up in her sedan. I didn't want to take the dog in her car so I left him home. That was a fatal mistake. But for a dead battery, Lorrie might be alive today.

We were pretty well loaded and very gay when we pulled into this parking strip by the ocean. It was a cloudy, moonless night. Once in a while there would be a wash of headlights from the coast highway but otherwise it was a blackout. There was only one other car in the area, nosed in quite a ways from us—a comfortable distance, you might say.

I was behind the wheel. We had been talking it up and loving it up for about five minutes. Suddenly, my door was yanked open and something struck me across the side of the head. When I came to I was lying on the ground. A hand was exploring for my wallet, snatching it. I felt dizzy and disoriented. I waited for my head to clear.

A car passing on the highway showered us with a sidespray of light and I saw Lorrie standing by the sedan. This ape had his paw locked around her wrist and I knew what was up—I got the picture. I tried to rise but the other goon began to play football with my ribs. One of those kicks went wild and ruptured my spleen, but of course I didn't know it then.

I rolled out of range and made another try for my feet. I saw the blackjack whipping down but it was too late to duck. A hot poker stabbed my brain. I don't even remember falling. Distantly I heard Lorrie scream and I knew I had to hold on.

From that moment everything became distorted, as if seen under water. Somehow I was on my feet, balanced on a tightrope. Under the sweep of headlights I saw the two couples standing beside their car, gaping at me dumbly as I shouted and waved madly, beckoning for them to come and help me save Lorrie.

I couldn't believe it! They were wax dummies rooted in place. We were actors, and they were watching our poor performance with barely concealed yawns.

These soulless mechanical beings considered themselves mere bystanders who were above soiling themselves by becoming involved in a messy struggle to save a stranger from being robbed and beaten senseless while a frail, defenseless girl was mauled and taken off to be raped and murdered.

What was the matter with those two gutless, husky men? And why didn't their women run for the police? Why didn't *anyone* send for the police!

There was no time to wonder. Moving like a sailor on a heaving deck, I went toward Lorrie and the animals attacking her.

I heard her car being fired up and I ran. I made a dive onto the rear deck and clung to it. We shot to the exit and then one of those hoods leaned out and hammered my hand with his sap. I let go.

I don't remember standing, but there I was, squinting into headlights. The car with the two couples drew up beside me. I saw their blank faces, their eyes watching me curiously as I made a grab for the door.

"Lorrie, Lorrie," I said to the driver, my own voice sounding far away, submerged. "Help Lorrie!" He gazed at me with a sneer of contempt, of disdain. He drove on, braked at the highway, as I went down again. I looked up from the ground and saw the blonde woman, Vera Wynn, leaning out the window, staring back at me. There was an odd twist to her lips, as if she might burst out laughing at any moment.

The blonde and her friends were something out of a dream, a mocking, violent dream. A great surging hate mounted inside me. I despised these people and all the self-loving, coddled ones of their breed.

Exhaust fumes choked me. I glanced up and saw the lighted tag. I read the license and wrote it in giant neon on the front wall of my mind. As the car sped away I repeated it over and over until it became a permanent fixture in my memory.

Later, a patrol car, making a routine check, hauled me semi-conscious to the drunk tank of the county jail. My injuries were not visible, these cops said later. My thick hair hid a broken skull. I talked, looked, and smelled like a drunk. It was three days before I could tell a coherent story to Detective Gladstone, but by then the trail was cold.

Now, having borrowed Gladstone's name and dressed for the part, I drove up the winding road to the transmitter. A squad car, searchlight poking in dark corners, was circling the building. I went on by and when I returned it was gone. I wheeled in and parked.

I got out and brought the Doberman along on a leash. He hadn't been fed all day. At the last minute I had merely teased him with a few scraps of meat, allowing him a couple of morsels from the bowl, then removing it. He was in a savage mood.

I hammered the door with my fist. Jarrett came to the other side and asked in a nervous voice who it was. I told him I was Murray Gladstone from Homicide, but he wanted to look at me through the window.

I knew he wouldn't recognize me, so I went to the window and, keeping the dog out of sight, showed him a fake badge. He frowned, hesitated, then left to open the door.

"Sorry," he said, "but you can't be too careful."

He studied me. "Say, have you been on this case before? I'm sure we—"

Then he saw the animal coiled beside me, jaws gaping, fangs gleaming. The head was lifted sharply, the eyes impaling Jarrett with unblinking malice.

"Brought you a little friend," I told Jarrett, and planted my foot determinedly against the door.

I removed the leash and as Jarrett backed, the dog advanced with a deep soft growl. I closed the door behind me. Jarrett was darting looks over his shoulder for a weapon, a route of escape. A jazzy discord of sound filtered from a speaker, adding a touch of unreality.

The Doberman came to a halt and stood crouching, poised. I gave him an order: "Lorrie—says—kill!"

Jarrett had reached back to clutch a chair and was trying to raise it when the animal launched himself and fell upon him, attacking him in a snarling, snapping frenzy.

Jarrett moaned, cried out as his fingers circled the dog's neck, tightening desperately. Oblivious, the Doberman tore chunks from his face until he screamed and relaxed his grip. Then, with a snake-like thrust, the dog fanged his throat.

That was the end of him, but I allowed myself another full minute of delicious satisfaction before I called the dog off.

He turned instantly, trotted over, and stood waiting for praise, looking up with a crimson grin of expectancy.

Del Wynn: Sergeant Newbold phoned close to eleven P.M. to tell me that Bruce Jarrett has been murdered—literally torn apart, mutilated by some savage animal, probably a killer dog. Bruce was discovered soon after his death by the chief engineer, alerted when Bruce failed to answer a call from the studio.

Why, oh why, did I leave!

I had been trying to locate Newbold to tell him that Bruce and I were certain we had discovered the motive behind the murders, that we had information he could use to identify the killer and hunt him down. Newbold was out and the desk man said he would try to locate him by radio. I didn't make a big issue of the matter since I assumed that Bruce would make a full report to this Detective Murray Gladstone who was en route to see him at the transmitter.

Newbold was astonished. He informed me that Detective Gladstone had not been on the case for months. It didn't take a minute to guess that our "executioner" was the fake Murray Gladstone.

Newbold was excited about the beach parking lot affair last summer. He agreed that we had probably uncovered the truth. He had the man's name on file—Carl Koenig, a former marine supply store salesclerk who had vanished.

Koenig had been engaged to a Lorrie Proctor. She had been abducted after parking with Koenig by the ocean, her skeleton had recently been found in a grave beside a desert highway. Koenig had been terribly beaten defending her.

At this late date, with the whole bloody horror nearly at an end, plainclothes cops are being sent to stake out my apartment house to prevent my murder and arrest Koenig when he makes his move toward me, as he certainly will before many days have passed. Further, I will have an armed escort to and from work.

What a filthy joke! I want to tell them, "Listen, thanks a lot, boys, but aren't you just a bit too late?" Instead, I keep silent and wait sleeplessly with a gun at my elbow.

I am exhausted in body and spirit. I am indescribably depressed.

Carl Koenig: From the very first step of the plan I had an uncanny sense of timing and superb judgment. I never made a mistake. With three down and one to go, with the newscasters shouting about "an unparalleled manhunt in progress," I still had the same feeling of godlike power and invincibility.

The sluggish machinery of the law was finally in high gear and, following the execution of Jarrett, it came to me at once that I must not delay, that I must put the last of Lorrie's known murderers to death in the next hour or two. The police could be stampeded into action by the prodding of headlines and the politically inspired whippings of their dull masters.

I went back to the rented house in Venice where I had been living all these months. It was the same shacky little house which I had leased as a place for Lorrie and me after we were married. The house was rented at the last minute, on the very day Lorrie was murdered, and I had told no one about it.

I left the dog in the car because I figured he might come in handy. I went inside and took a used leather suitcase, bought for the occasion, from a closet. The case was filled with paper-wrapped pieces of scrap iron. Atop the suitcase I placed a gray overcoat and a gray felt hat.

I washed and checked my clothing for bloodstains. Then I adjusted shell-rimmed glasses to my face, a pair I used only for reading. They added a touch of age and dignity to my rather boyish features. The gray hat compounded the impression.

Folding the coat across my arm, I carried the suitcase out to the station wagon and drove off. I parked the wagon at an all-night gas station a block from Del Wynn's apartment house and gave the attendant a buck, warning him to keep away from the Doberman.

Next, I called a cab. When it came, I gave the driver Wynn's address. Apologizing for the short ride, I handed him the heavy suitcase and a five-dollar bill. He practically drooled all over me.

I saw the unmarked police car in the shadows across from the entrance. I was expecting it. What is more obvious than a couple of men slouched in the front seat of a car a few minutes before midnight? I knew there might be other cars nearby and other men around the building.

The coat over my arm, I climbed from the cab and asked the driver if he would carry my bag to the door of my apartment. After my generosity he could hardly refuse.

As we walked up the steps to the entrance I took a ring of keys from my pocket and examined them casually. Behind me I heard a car door slam and I knew that we were being followed.

Sure enough, as we waited for the self-service elevator, two hefty cool-eyed types joined us. One was older and had a wart on his cheek.

"Evening," I said.

They nodded but did not smile. "Been outta town?" Wartface asked me. He made it sound like a felony.

"New York," I answered. "You like cold, dirt, and noise, I'll sell it to you cheap."

"Yeah," said the cabbie, "know what ya mean. I come from Jersey."

The cops were wooden. "Haven't seen you around," the younger cop said as the elevator arrived and we stepped on. "Must be a new tenant."

"If you haven't seen me around, then you haven't *been* around," I said cheerfully. "I've been up in 4C nearly five years." I thumbed the four button.

"What's your name?" asked Wartface with a lift of his eyebrows.

"Benson. Charlie Benson." There was such a guy, he did live in 4C. I knew he spent the winter in New York and rarely returned until April. He lived across the hall from the Wynns.

"I guess *you* guys are the new tenants," I said with a chuckle as we jolt-stopped and the door flew open.

They didn't answer and I got off, the driver behind me, toting the bag with a grunt, the cops on his heels. We turned a bend in the corridor, all of us. I walked up to 4C and began to fumble with the keys. It was a tight spot and I was worried. The two cops had paused and stood watching a few feet away as the cabbie set my bag by the door.

Stalling, I said to him, "You've been most helpful, my friend, and I'd like to give you a little something extra."

He looked at me in amazement. "Nahh, that's all right, you already—"

"No, I insist!"

As I produced my wallet, I glanced up pointedly at the cops. "Did you fellas want something?" I said acidly. "Maybe you'd like to come in and have a drink."

Wartface approached me. He flipped his ID and badge in my face. "Police officers," he said. "Sorry, sir, but we're expecting a bit of trouble and we're checking everyone. We have men covering every possible entrance to the building."

"That's different," I said. "What's it all about?"

"Can't tell you that, sir. But I would suggest that you remain inside your apartment until morning. Good night, sir." He turned and, followed by his partner, went down the hall.

The cabbie was fascinated and wanted to make small-talk about the incident. I let him go on until the cops had time to leave the building. Then I gave him another couple of bucks and I said, "Sounds like there's gonna be shooting here. You better scoot outta the area on the double or you might get hurt."

He thanked me and hurried off. When he was out of sight I moved the suitcase across the hall and parked it beside Del Wynn's door. In my overcoat pocket I had some gadgets to open just about any door lock. Without a sound, I had this one open in less than a minute. It didn't surprise me to find a chain-guard fixed in place. I had a gadget for that too.

Bringing the case and overcoat with me, I slipped inside and closed the door silently. It was a dangerous moment because he might have been watching the door with a gun in his hand. As a matter of fact, he was. The gun wasn't in his hand, however. When I followed the sound of his snores, I found it on a table beside his chair. I stuck it in my pocket.

I glanced around. The drapes were open. I closed them softly. I went back and turned on the lamp by his chair. That didn't faze him in the least, so I shook him gently. His eyes flew open. He stared at me, then reached for the missing gun.

"Hello, Wynn," I said. "Remember me?"

He examined me without a sign of fear. "I don't remember you, but I know you must be Koenig."

I grinned.

"You're making a mistake," he said calmly. "You've made a terrible mistake from the beginning. We would've helped you save the girl if we had known the real situation. It looked like just another drunken brawl."

"I'm touched," I said. But I had a small stab of doubt. I couldn't let him con me, so I began to reach into my pocket.

I saw his hands tighten around the arms of the chair and when he leaped at me, I danced aside. He went sprawling and I gave him a few brutal kicks in the ribs. He groaned, but he was game—and agile. He did a roll, bounced to his feet, and went after me in almost the same motion.

He had a fist like a steel mallet. The first blow cost me three teeth. The second felt as if it had jarred my brain loose from my skull. I knew then that he could finish me in a matter of seconds. So I feinted, then booted him in the groin. When he doubled I reached for the sap in my hip pocket and clubbed him down.

After that, I simply kicked and stomped him to death.

"That's just the way it was," I told his corpse, and went out.

There was a problem: how to leave the building. I was a mess. Blood poured from my mouth and drenched my suit. The swelling at my temple threatened to close one eye. Even unmarked, they would certainly stop me.

I didn't bother with the elevator. I took the stairs, two at a time. I dashed through the lobby and out to the front steps. I stood there, shouting for help. The same two cops raced up to me. I heard the pounding of others coming.

"Upstairs," I said breathlessly, "in 4D. Man beating Del Wynn to death. Tried to stop it, but—"

Wartface gave me a wild-eyed look, "C'mon!" he cried, and a whole flock of cops took off like a covey of frightened birds.

I sat on the steps and mopped my face with a handkerchief. Then I got up and wandered down the street. Around the corner I broke into a run. I slowed at the gas station. Hiding my face, giving the attendant my back, I climbed into the wagon and drove away at a leisurely pace. It was over. I had lived for the one purpose and I was empty. There had been a vague plan to spend the rest of my life hunting down the animals who had done the actual killing, but right then I could not ignite a spark of interest.

As I braked beside what had once been my little "dream" house, I noticed a dim light in the living room. I could not remember leaving a light on, but I had gone out in a rush and it was quite possible. I wasn't disturbed.

I took the Doberman out to the back yard, then entered the house and went to the bathroom where I began to wash and patch my face. As I did this, a feeling of deep melancholy overcame me.

Hate is a kind of companion, and now that the rage was burned out, loneliness swallowed me.

I went toward the bedroom and froze in the doorway. Light from the hall revealed a woman stretched out on my bed. It was a king-sized affair and, curled up, she was lost in the center of it. She was asleep. At the foot of the bed there was a small black suitcase.

I flipped the light switch and abruptly she sat up.

It was Lorrie Proctor!

When I was able to believe it, I became hysterical. I went over and shook her violently by the shoulders.

"How could this happen!" I shouted. "What've you done to me?" I sobbed. "Why, Lorrie? Why, why, why!"

Lorrie Proctor: Carl was even more upset than I had expected, but when I was able to calm him a bit, I gave him the whole sordid story. It all had to do with my former husband, Buzz Proctor, whose name I continued to use, even after we were divorced. There were certain things I hadn't told Carl about Buzz: that I still had a big secret thing for him; that he was an ex-convict; that he wanted me back and was a violent type who usually took what he wanted.

Since Buzz could turn me on like crazy, I had gone along with him on a lot of borderline schemes. When he asked me to drive and play lookout while he and Rusty McGrath held up a certain bank, though, I said, No thanks—and good-bye! You didn't turn Buzz off that easily, so I had to bide my time and sneak away. I hid out in Vegas while getting a quick divorce which he didn't dare fight because I knew too much about him that I could use in a contest.

I met Carl after I moved to Santa Monica. He was as much in love with me as I was with Buzz. What I felt for Carl was deep and quiet and solid—good for me, but not exciting.

If you skip the hearts and flowers, that brings us to the summer night a week before Carl and I were to be married, the night we parked by the ocean.

Did you guess? Sure, it was Buzz and Rusty McGrath who pulled that sweet little caper. Buzz had been brooding. He wanted me back and he went all out to track me down. I didn't know it was Buzz kidnapping me until I saw him in the light from a passing car. He told me that if I made a fuss, he'd kill Carl on the spot.

I was taken to this old house in the Valley where Rusty's girl, Zelma, was waiting. She shoved me into a room, made me strip and grabbed all my clothing, "So you won't get any ideas about running away." But why did she force me to give her Carl's engagement ring? And what really happened to my pocketbook? She told me it was lost in the scuffle.

Late the next day, Buzz brought me a whole bunch of new clothes and the four of us took off for Mexico. Buzz gave me some ID papers to carry, including a tourist permit, all under the name of Alice Kemp. He said that if I behaved myself, Carl wouldn't get hurt.

We drove all the way to Guadalajara where Buzz rented a big house on the outskirts for a song. In a very short time he managed to turn me on again as if we had never been apart. I could easily have escaped and gone back to Carl, but I was never so happy, especially since Buzz and I were planning to remarry.

One day Buzz got careless and left his desk unlocked. Curious, I explored and found a metal box which contained quite a bit of cash and a clipping from an L.A. paper. It informed me that *my* body had been found in a shallow grave beside a desert highway. The extreme heat had "accelerated decomposition" and "I" was little more than a skeleton.

That thing in the grave could very well be a girl about my age and size whose name was Alice Kemp. I was carrying her papers and it seemed logical.

In the metal box there was also a policy on my life. I had taken it out while working for an insurance company, making Buzz beneficiary. Apparently Buzz had kept up the premiums in secret. Why? In the beginning did he plan to murder me? Then, for some reason, did he kill Alice Kemp and suddenly decide to use her corpse for my double?

A letter attached to the policy had been forwarded by one of Buzz's con friends. It stated that the insurance company wasn't going to pay off because, for one thing, the police had not yet made a positive identification of the corpse.

They were trying to locate my dentist so they could check my dental chart. Well, I had fine teeth and never went to a dentist in L.A. Years ago I had gone to a dentist in Philadelphia but he had died, and if my dental chart still existed the police would have a tough time tracing it.

I took some money from the box for a getaway and, while Buzz slept, I escaped on the next plane for L.A. I went to a hotel where I spent hours in my room trying to work up enough courage to get in touch with Carl. Once I had made up my mind, I couldn't find him. He had vanished.

In desperation I went over to "our" little house, the one Carl had leased for us to live in after we were married. I thought maybe someone had moved in there who would have a clue. The house was dark and empty but as I walked around to the back yard I was amazed to find the small green boat Carl had used for fishing set up on blocks; also the doghouse, and the big metal bowl from which he fed the Doberman.

When we rented the place, Carl had decided to keep an emergency key hidden on a hook inside the doghouse. I bent down and searched. The key was there! I opened the front door and went in. When I found Carl's clothes about, I returned to the hotel for my suitcase . . .

I was sure that Carl would forgive me, but as I neared the end of my confession his face became fixed in this odd expression and his eyes were, well, weird. His features were swollen and lopsided from some awful fight which he refused to explain, and I suppose this added to the impression.

I said, "Listen, I'll make it up to you and you'll forget. I know how you must've suffered; but I'm alive and it's as if nothing ever happened. Just a little water over the dam, that's all, darling.

"Ahh, I can see that you're upset and all closed up inside yourself. Well, here, come let me hold you, darling."

I held out my arms and Carl got up and came toward me.

Carl Koenig: I held on to her for a long time—my thumbs pressing, my hands closing tighter—and, when she was long dead, I couldn't seem to let go.

After that I don't remember much. As in a disembodied dream, I was suddenly at the police station and they were putting me in a cell. It took a couple of days, but they recorded the whole thing on tape.

They tell me now that I'm a crazy psychopath and they've got me locked up for life in the state hospital for the criminally insane.

Well, I'm not insane—not in the least! The real nuts are those who kill for no reason at all. What I did was perfectly justified. I simply executed some people who committed the worst possible crime when they murdered poor Lorrie Proctor.

Does that make me insane?

FLETCHER FLORA

The Witness Was a Lady

It was a Thursday morning when Corey McDown called me. I hadn't heard from Corey for a long time. Not directly. After he got to be a cop, we sort of drifted apart and lost contact with each other. I'm not exactly allergic to cops, you understand, but it usually turns out that we're incompatible.

Corey was a bright guy, and he'd moved up fast in the force. He was pretty young for a lieutenant in Homicide.

"Hello, Mark," he said. "Corey McDown here. Did I get you out of bed?"

"I don't have to get out of bed to answer the phone," I said. "How are you, Corey?"

"I've been worse," he said, "and I've been better. I wonder if you'd do me a favor."

"Do I owe you a favor?"

"Do this one for me, and I'll owe *you* one."

"You think I may need it?"

"You may, Mark. You never know."

"True. There have been times before. What's on your mind, Corey?"

"I hate long telephone conversations. Ask me over."

"Sure, Corey. Come on over."

"Give me thirty minutes."

He hung up, and so did I. It must be a big favor he wanted, I thought, to make him so accommodating. I had an uneasy feeling that it was related to something that I didn't want to think about, and I wished I could quit. I got out of bed and shaved and showered and dressed, which used up the thirty minutes. I had just finished when the door buzzer sounded, and I went out across the living room to the door and opened it.

"Right on time," I said. "Come on in."

He came in and tossed his hat into one chair and sat down in another. His hair was cut short, a thick brown stubble, and he looked trim and hard. Right now, leaning back and smiling, relaxed.

"You've got a nice place, Mark. You live well."

"Heels always live well. It's expected of them."

"You're not a heel, Mark. You're just a reasonably good guy with kinks."

"Thanks." I walked over to a table and lifted a glass. "You want some breakfast?"

"Out of a bottle?"

"Is there another place to get it?"

"I had mine out of a skillet. You go ahead."

I poured a double shot of bourbon and swallowed it fast. Then I went back and threw his hat on the floor and took its place. The double helped me feel as relaxed as he looked.

"Go on," I said. "Convince me."

"Don't rush me. I'm trying to think of the best approach."

"The best is the simplest. You want a favor. Tell me what it is."

"Let me ask you a question first. You seen Nora lately?"

"No. It's been forever. Why?"

"I thought you might have looked her up when Jack Kirby was murdered."

"I didn't."

"That's strange. Old friends and all, I mean. The least an old friend can do when an old friend's boy friend is killed is to offer sympathy and condolences and all that."

"My personal opinion is that congratulations were in order. I didn't think it would be in good taste to offer them."

He looked across at me, shaking his burr head and grinning. The grin got vocal and became a loud laugh.

"You see, Mark? All you've got are a few kinks. A real twenty-four carat heel like Jack Kirby offends your sensibilities."

"Go to hell."

"Sure, sure. Anything to oblige. What I'm leading up to is, this favor isn't really for me at all. Oh, incidentally it is, maybe, but mostly it's a favor for Nora."

"You sound like a man about to be devious, Corey."

"Not me, Mark. Whatever I may be that makes me different from you, I'm not devious. I haven't got the brains for it."

"O.K. Tell me the favor for Nora that's one for you incidentally."

"I'll tell you, but let's get the circumstances in focus. Did you read the news stories about Jack Kirby's murder?"

"Once over, lightly."

"In that case, you'll remember what the evidence indicated. He had an appointment with someone in his apartment. At least someone came to see him there, and this someone, whoever it was, killed him. Cracked his skull with a heavy cut-glass decanter, to be exact. This was all in the news stories, and it's all true. What wasn't in the stories, because we put the lid on it, is that someone pretty definitely knew who it was in the apartment with Kirby that night. That someone is Nora."

"How do you know?"

"Never mind how. We know."

"That won't do, Corey. You can't expect to clam up on the guy you're asking for a favor."

"All right. I'll tell you this much. The day of Kirby's murder, Nora told a friend that she was going to Kirby's apartment that night, but she couldn't go until late because Kirby was expecting someone earlier that she didn't want to meet. This friend is a woman whose testimony can be relied on. We're convinced of that."

"Didn't Nora mention the name of Kirby's expected guest?"

"No. No name. Just that it was someone she didn't want to meet there."

"Did you ask Nora?"

Corey looked down at his hands in his lap. He folded and unfolded the blunt fingers. On his face for a few seconds there was a sour expression as he recalled an experience that he hadn't liked and couldn't forget.

"We hauled her in and asked her over and over for a long while. She wouldn't say. She denied ever having told her friend that she knew."

"I wonder why. You'd think she'd want to help."

"Come off it, Mark. You know why as well as I do. Jack Kirby was a guy who associated with dangerous characters. One of these characters killed him, and he wouldn't think twice about killing a material witness. Either to keep her from talking or in revenge if she did. If he couldn't do it personally, he'd have it done for him. Today or tomorrow or next year. Nora's been associating with some dangerous characters herself, including Kirby. She knows how they operate, Mark. She won't talk because she's afraid."

"Well, Nora's not exactly a strong personality. She'll break eventually. Why don't you ask her again?"

"I wish I could."

"Why can't you? Like you said, she's a material witness. You can arrest her and hold her."

"I could if I could get hold of her." He looked down at his hands again, at the flexing fingers. His face was smooth and hard now, the sour expression dissolved. "I should have held her when I had her, but that was my mistake. A man makes lots of mistakes for old times' sake."

"Asking and giving favors, you mean. That sort of thing."

"Maybe. We'll see."

"Speaking of favors, where do I come in? If you think I know where Nora is, you're wrong."

"That's not the problem. I already know where she is."

"In that case, why don't you pick her up?"

"Because she's across the state line. You may know that we don't have any extradition agreement with our neighbor covering material witnesses."

"I didn't know, as a matter of fact. Thanks for telling me. It may come in handy. I don't seem to remember reading any of this about Nora in the papers."

"I told you. It wasn't there. We've kept the lid on it. The point is, we can't keep the lid on any longer. The story's going to break in the evening editions, and that's what worries me."

"I can see why. You won't look so good, letting a material witness slip away from you. Tough. You expect me to bleed, Corey?"

"It's not that. I'll survive a little criticism. It's Nora I'm worried about."

"Old times' sake again?"

"Call it what you like, but you can see her position. She's a constant and deadly threat to Jack Kirby's killer, whoever he is, and the moment the story breaks, the killer is going to know it. He'll also know where to find her."

"I see what you mean. The threat works two ways."

"That's it. And that's where you come in."

"Don't tell me. You want me to go and talk to her and convince her that she's got to come back and turn herself in for her own good."

"You're a smart guy, Mark. You always were."

"Sure. With kinks. To tell you the truth, I'm not quite convinced that this mysterious visitor of Kirby's is going to be so desperate as you imagine."

"You think he won't? Why?"

"Well, Nora knows he was supposed to be at Kirby's at a certain time. At the time Kirby was killed. So she knows. That's not absolute proof that he was actually there. Even if he was there, it's not proof that he did the killing. It's a lead, Corey, not a conviction."

"A lead's all we need. The visitor killed Kirby. We're certain of it. Once we know who he was, we'll find more evidence fast enough. We'll know what to look for, and how and where to find it."

"You haven't told me yet where Nora is."

"About a hundred miles from here. The first place I thought to check. The natural place for a woman to run when she's scared and in trouble."

"Home?"

"What used to be. Down on the farm."

"Regression, as the psychs say. You were sharp to think of that right off the bat, Corey. You're quite a psych yourself."

He got up suddenly and walked over to a pair of matched windows overlooking a small court in which, below, there was some green stuff growing.

He stood there looking out for a minute or more, and then he turned and walked back but did not sit down again.

"You and Nora were always close, Mark, back there when we were kids. Closer than ever Nora and I were. I used to hate you for that, but it doesn't matter any longer. It's one of the things I've gotten over. The point is, she'll be in danger. I believe that or I wouldn't be here. She wouldn't listen to me, but she might to you. Will you go talk to her?"

"Why should I?"

"Do you have to have the reasons spelled out?"

"I can't think of any."

"As a favor for me?"

"I don't want to obligate you."

"For Nora, then?"

"Nora wants me to leave her alone. She told me so."

"Not even to save her life?"

"Nora's a big girl now. She associates with dangerous characters and makes up her own mind."

He stood looking down at me, his face as bleak and empty as a department store floorwalker's. Turning away, he picked his hat off the floor and held it by the brim in his hands.

"I guess those kinks are bigger than I thought," he said.

He went over to the door and let himself out, and I kept on sitting in the chair, thinking about a time that he'd recalled. She used to ride into town to high school on the school bus, Nora did. Corey and I were town boys. We were snobbish with the country kids until we met Nora, who was a country kid, and then we weren't snobbish any more. She was slim and lovely and seemed to move with incredible grace in a kind of golden haze. She was so lovely, in fact, that she intimidated me for almost a full year before we finally got together on a picnic one Sunday afternoon. After that, I began to know Nora as she was—as a touchable and lusty little manipulator, almost amoral, who already had, even then, certain carefully conceived and directed ideas about what Nora wanted out of life. I didn't love her any the less, maybe more, but I resigned myself to the obvious truth that I was no more at most than a kind of privileged expedient.

After high school, Nora and Corey and I drifted at different times across the hundred miles to the city. At first we saw each other now and then, but later hardly at all. Corey became a cop. Thanks to luck and cards and certain contacts, I learned to live well without excessive effort. As for Nora—well, I had just refused to do her a favor at Corey's request, but there had been plenty of others to do her favors, as there always are with girls like her, and some of the favors came to five figures. Jack Kirby had not been the first. Maybe he would be the last.

I stood up and walked over to the windows and looked down into the court, down at the green stuff growing. I wasn't used to the radiance of day, and the light seemed intensely bright, and it hurt my eyes. My head ached, and I wondered if I could stand another double shot, or even a single, but I decided that I couldn't. Turning away from the windows, I walked back across the living room and into the soft and seductive dusk of the bedroom. I lay down on the unmade bed and tried to think with some kind of orderliness, and the thinking must have been therapeutic, for after a while I lost the headache, or became unaware of it.

Granted, I thought, that Nora knew the identity of Jack Kirby's visitor, who was also Jack Kirby's killer. Corey was convinced that she did, and Corey was a bright guy. Being a bright guy, it was funny how he could go so far wrong from a good start. It was funny, a real scream, but I didn't feel like laughing. Because she'd refused to talk, because she'd run and hid to escape the pressure that would certainly have broken her down, Corey assumed that she was afraid of the consequences of pointing a finger, the vengeance of a killer or a killer's hired hand, but it wasn't true. It couldn't be. She had run from the pressure, true, but she had kept her silence simply because she did not want Jack Kirby's visitor to be known. For old times' sake. It was touching, really, and I appreciated it.

I went over in my mind again with odd detachment, as if I were reviewing an experience of someone else, the way it had happened that I had killed Jack Kirby. I hadn't intended to, although it was a pleasure when I did, and all I'd actually intended when I went up to his apartment that night was to pay an overdue debt of a couple of grand.

I had lost the two grand to Kirby in a stud game that proved to be the beginning of a streak of bad luck. In the first place, to show how bad my luck was beginning to be, I lost the pot on three of a kind, which is pretty difficult to do in straight stud. In the second place, to show how fast bad luck can get worse in a streak, I didn't have the two grand. All I had to offer was an IOU with a twenty-four-hour deadline. The deadline passed, and I still didn't have the two grand. My intentions were good, but my luck kept on being bad. I got three extensions on the deadline, and then I had a couple of visitors. They came to my apartment about the middle of the afternoon, a few minutes after I'd gotten out of bed. I'd seen both of them around, and I knew the name of one of them, but the names didn't matter. It was a business call, not social. They were very polite in a businesslike way. Only one of them talked.

"Mr. Sanders," he said, "we're representing Mr. Jack Kirby in a little business matter."

"Times have been tough," I said.

"Mr. Kirby appreciates that, but he feels that he's been more than liberal."

"Thank Mr. Kirby for me."

"I'm afraid Mr. Kirby wants more than thanks. He wants to know if you're prepared to settle your obligation."

"How about a payment on account? Ten percent, say."

"Sorry. Mr. Kirby feels that the obligation should be settled in full. He's prepared to extend your time until eight o'clock tomorrow night. He expects you to call at his apartment at that hour with the full amount due and payable."

"Tell Mr. Kirby I'll give the matter my careful attention."

"Mr. Kirby wants us particularly to remind you of the urgency."

"Fine. Consider me reminded."

"Mr. Kirby wants us to remind you in a manner that you will remember."

This was the clue to go to work, apparently, for that's what they did. I wasn't very alert yet, it being several hours until dark, and I put up what might be called a sorry defense. In fact, I didn't put up any defense at all. The mute suddenly had me from behind in a combination hammerlock and stranglehold, and the talker, looking apologetic, belted me three times in the belly. At the door, leaving me doubled up on the floor, the talker stopped and looked back, an expression of compassion spreading among the pocks on his flat face.

"Sorry, Mr. Sanders," he said. "Nothing personal, you understand."

I wasn't able to acknowledge the apology with the good grace it deserved. After they were gone, I began to breathe again, and a little later I successfully stood up. The beating had been painful, but not crippling.

It was a break in a way, the beating was. It was the nadir of the streak, the worst of the bad luck, and now that things had got about as bad as they could get, they began immediately to get better. What I mean is, I took the ten percent I'd offered Kirby's hired goons and ran it through another game of stud and brought it out multiplied by twenty. A little better than four grand in paper with not an IOU in the bundle. By midnight I had in my possession, as the talking goon had said, the full amount due and payable.

The next night at eight, I was at Kirby's door. I rang the bell, and Kirby let me in. He was wearing most of a tux, the exception being a maroon smoking jacket with a black satin sash. I happen to have an aversion to satin sashes, on smoking jackets or anything else, and this put me in a bad humor. It made it more difficult than ever to be reasonable about the beating he had bought for me. Apparently I was wearing nothing to which he had a comparable aversion. His long, sallow face, divided under a long nose by a long, thin moustache, was perfectly amiable.

"Hello, Mark," he said. "Glad to see you."

"Even broke?" I said.

"Sorry." His face lost its amiability. "Poverty depresses me."

"Never mind. I'm not one of your huddled masses. I come loaded."

"Good." The amiability was back. "I was sure you could manage if you really tried."

I took the ready bundle from a pocket, two grand exactly, and handed it to him. He transferred it to a pocket of his offending jacket with hardly more than a glance, and this put me in a worse humor than I was already in, which was bad enough. I knew he would count the money the moment I was gone, and it would have been less annoying if he had counted it honestly in front of me.

"Now I'll have the IOU, if you don't mind," I said.

"Certainly, Mark." He took the paper out of the same pocket the money had gone into. "I hope you don't resent the little reminder I was forced to send you."

"Not at all. It was very courteous and regretful, and it only hit me where it doesn't show."

"I'm glad you understand. Will you have a drink before you leave?"

"Bourbon and water."

"Good. I'll have one with you."

He turned and walked over to a liquor cabinet and worked for a minute with a bottle and glasses. "I'm sorry I can't ask you to stay for more than one, but I'm expecting company."

"Company's nice if it's nice company."

"This is nice. Someone you once knew, I believe. Nora Erskine? Charming girl. Beautiful. She has a very warm nature. Very generous."

He came toward me with a glass in each hand, and I hit him in the mouth. Don't ask me why. Maybe a disciple of Freud could tell you, but I can't. He fell backward in a shower of bourbon and came up with a little gun in his hand, which seemed to indicate that he hadn't been quite so amiable and trusting as he'd appeared. The cut-glass decanter was there on a table beside me, and I picked it up and smashed it over his head, and he fell down dying and was dead in less than a minute.

Stripped to the bone, that was how I killed him. I tried to remember if I had touched anything besides the decanter and the outside of the door, and there seemed to be nothing, and so I wiped the neck of the decanter with my handkerchief and retrieved the two grand, which was no good to him, and left. I went home and thought about it, wondering if I should leave town incognito, but I decided that there was no need. The goons knew that I was supposed to be at Kirby's, of course, but the goons were old pros. They'd done a job and were through with it. They couldn't care less that Jack Kirby had got himself killed. As a matter of fact, if they made the logical deduction, I would probably go up immeasurably in their regard. The result of my thinking was the decision that it was unnecessary to take any precipitate action. I only needed to proceed with caution, as the signs beside the highways say, in the direction I was going.

But that was then, and now was different. Now I knew that Nora knew, and Nora was not an old pro, and Nora would surely someday tell. Maybe not now or soon, but someday, the day she couldn't stand the pressure any longer, and the passage of time would not help or save me, for there is no statute of limitations on murder, not even murder which might turn out to be, with luck and a good lawyer, of lesser degree than first. And there was always the solid possibility, of course, of that grim first.

I could see that I had come to the time of decision now, and I didn't want to face it. Like many another in the same predicament, I found a way to avoid it temporarily, if not permanently. In any case it was simple. I simply went to sleep.

When I awoke again, it was evening, but the hour of the day was the only thing that had changed, not me or the problem or anything that had to be considered and done or not done. I got up and washed my face in cold water and put on a tie and jacket and went downstairs onto the street. There was a newsstand on the corner, half a block away, and I went down there and bought an evening edition and carried it back to the apartment without looking at it. In the apartment, I poured another double shot and drank half of it and sat down and opened the newspaper, and there was the story on page one: Material Witness in Kirby Slaying Flees State. I read the story slowly, finishing the second shot of the double as I read, and it was reported about the way Corey had told it to me in the morning, how Nora was believed to know the identity of Kirby's visitor at the time of the murder, and how she had refused to talk, and how, finally, she had escaped into the next state, from which she could not be extradited. It was also reported in the story exactly where she had gone and now was, the home of her childhood not more than a hundred miles away, and this was what I needed in order to make the decision I had to make, and you can see why. Now that her location was no longer a secret shared by me and the police, Nora was in greater danger and, as a consequence, so was I. There was therefore no longer any reason for indecision or delay, although there was probably no reason to hurry either.

I sat there for quite a long while, and it began to get dark outside in the city streets, and the incandescents and fluorescents and neons came on to drive the darkness back. I finally became aware, via my stomach, that I hadn't eaten all day, and that I had better eat something before I took another drink, which I wanted, and so I went out and had a steak in a restaurant down the street a few blocks. After eating, I walked back and had a couple more drinks in the apartment, and then I went down and got my car out of the garage in the basement and drove across town to a place where they were having a stud game. I won five hundred skins in the game, the good streak still running in the wake of the bad streak, and at some point in the time it took to win that much money, my mind made itself up and I knew what I was going to do. I dropped out of the game about three o'clock in the morning, a little after, and it was almost four when I got home.

In the bedroom of the apartment, I changed into slacks, sport shirt and jacket, heavier shoes. From a shelf in the closet I got a leather case that contained a .30-.30 rifle. I had been very good with a rifle when I was younger. There was no reason to believe that I wasn't still almost as good. I assembled the rifle and checked it and took it apart again. I put the parts back into the case and half a dozen cartridges into my jacket pocket. I don't know why I took so many, for chances were long that a dozen would not be enough if one wasn't. Carrying the case, I went back downstairs to my car and drove out of town.

It took me about three hours driving slowly, to reach the town where I had grown up a hundred years or so ago, and I did not drive into it after reaching it. Instead, I drove around it on roads I remembered, and beyond it on another road until I saw ahead of me, quite a distance and on the left, the white house of the Erskines. It sat rather far back from the road at the end of a tree-lined drive, though not so far as memory had it, and it had once been considered the finest farm home in the county, if not the state. Now it did not seem one-half so grand, a different house than I had known before, as if the first had been razed and a second built in its place in an identical design, with identical detail, but on a reduced scale.

I turned off before I reached the house, along the side of a country square. The road descended slowly for a quarter of a mile to a steel and timber bridge across a shallow ravine. There had been water in the ravine in the spring, and there would be water again when the fall rains came, but now the bed was dry except for intermittent shallow pools caught in rock. After crossing the bridge, I pulled off the road on a narrow turning into high weeds and brush. Getting out of the car, carrying the rifle case, I climbed a barbed-wire fence and followed the course of the ravine through a stand of timber, mostly oaks and maples and elms, and across a wide expanse of pasture in which a herd of Holsteins were having breakfast. Pretty soon I left the ravine and cut across two fields at an angle and up a long rise into a grove of walnut trees on the crest. I stopped among the trees and assembled and loaded the rifle, and then I lay down and looked down the slope on the other side of the crest to the house where Nora was supposed to be. There was a stone terrace on this side of the house at the rear. On the terrace was a round table and several brightly striped canvas chairs. Wide glass doors led off the terrace into the house. No one was visible from where I lay under the walnut trees about fifty yards away.

After half an hour, I rolled over onto my back and lay looking up into the branches of the trees where the green walnuts hung, and I began to remember all the times I'd come here to gather the nuts when I was a kid, sometimes with Nora in the later years. We gathered them in burlap bags—gunny sacks, they were called—and later knocked the blackened husks off with a hammer. For a long time afterward, if we didn't wear gloves, our hands were stained with the juice of the husks, a stain like the stain of nicotine, and there was no way to get this stain off except to wear it off, and you could always tell the ones who had gathered walnuts late in the fall by the stain on their hands that wore on toward winter.

I could hear a cow bell jangling back in the pasture. I could hear a dog barking. I could hear the cawing of a crow above the fields, and I thought I could hear, closing my eyes, the slow beating of his black wings against the still air. Opening my eyes, I rolled over and looked down the slope again to the terrace, and there was Nora standing beside the table and looking up toward the walnut grove as if she could see me lying in its shadow. She was wearing a white blouse and brown shorts, and her face and arms and legs were golden in the morning light. Drawing the rifle up along my side into firing position, I had her heart in my sights in a second, and I had a notion that it was a golden heart pumping golden blood.

She must have stood there for a full minute without moving, maybe longer, and then she turned and walked across the terrace and through the glass doors into the house, and I lowered my face slowly into the sweet green grass. I could still hear the bell and the dog and the crow, and I could hear the voice of Corey McDown saying that Mark Sanders was just a guy with kinks.

After a while I stood up and went back across the fields to the ravine and along the ravine through the pasture and the woods to the car. Driving to the city, I thought about what I had better do, and where I had better go, and how long it would take to learn to live comfortably with a constant threat, and I decided, although there was probably no hurry, that I might as well get my affairs in order and get somewhere a long way off as soon as possible.

PAULINE C. SMITH

Scheme for Destruction

"Let's get this straight," said Cliff Condon. "This man hired you, every Saturday night, to run over him. Right?"

The prisoner twisted his mouth, contracting his neck inside his tight collar, and nodded. "Yeah. That's right. He'd lay down on the road. Then I'd back up the car and drive over him . . . straddle him and his camera," he added.

Relaxed against the cell bars, Condon watched George Phifer as he sat on the edge of the bunk, running the palms of his hands over his now soiled brown gabardines. His eyes looked scared—small, brown, dull eyes, squinting with worry.

"Then one night you didn't straddle him."

"I straddled him, all right, but he'd pulled in another car on me—a newer, lower model. It didn't clear."

Thoughtfully, Condon sucked the inside of his cheek. "Let's go back to the beginning," he suggested, referring to the typewritten copy of the statement in his hand. "You met him in a bar. Right?"

"Yeah. Out in the Valley. It's across the street from the rigging outfit where I work. Every evening when I'd knock off, I went over for a drink. One day, this yuk showed up."

"Maury Temple. That his name?"

"He never said. I don't think he did, anyway. When the cops told me who he was, it sounded familiar, so maybe he did tell me, after all."

"Well, a formal introduction wasn't necessary for the kind of proposition he handed you."

"He didn't hand it to me for a while. It took him a couple or three times before he gave me the pitch."

"He just asked you, bluntly, to run over him . . . ?"

Phifer ran his fingers delicately over a hairline scar stretching from his jaw to brow. "He gave me a lot of double talk about angle shots and stuff like that. Then he said he wanted to get a shot of a car going over a man. First thing I knew, I was runnin' over him."

Condon frowned, studying the prisoner. "Didn't you think that was kind of a funny thing to be doing?"

Phifer shrugged. "He wanted the picture. It was his money." He looked up. "He paid me twenty-five smackers a Saturday—and my dinner—and the drinks."

"Drinks?"

"Sure. After that first Saturday tryout, we did the Sunset Strip each time before we went on up to Mulholland Drive. This whatever-his-name-is didn't drink. He just talked and watched me lap it up."

"He did? What did he talk about?"

Phifer's laugh sounded like the yelp of an excited pup. "About me—and my dames. I give him a regular Kinsey Report."

"Hmm." Condon shifted his weight from one foot to the other, and moved to a more comfortable position.

"I think he was kind of a mama's boy, and got a bang out of what was goin' on that he couldn't do." Phifer's broad, scarred face worked with a thought he tried to make specific. "Like readin' a dirty book," he decided.

Condon's eyes were steady. "Could be."

"Well, that's it." Moving his head, Phifer loosened his collar. He stood. "Do you believe me? That other guy from the D.A.'s office didn't."

"That was the deputy. I know he didn't. I'm an investigator. I've got to gather what facts I can so the District Attorney can make some sort of plea."

"Well, I didn't kill the guy. He asked for it."

"I think he did," said Condon thoughtfully. "I really think he did."

Beckoning, he watched Phifer while he waited for the door to be unlocked.

The prisoner's face had become righteously indignant. "I don't see why it had to be me he asked. There were other guys on those bar stools."

Moving into the corridor without looking back, Condon conjectured, "Maybe you were picked before you got inside the bar. Maybe you were picked a long time ago."

The Los Angeles sun was bright behind the veil of smog. Sighing, Condon walked to a telephone booth. He asked for the District Attorney. "Tell him it's Condon," he said into the mouthpiece.

While he waited, he looked over the copy of the prisoner's statement in his hand. It was Maury Temple who held his interest. This Phifer character was run-of-the-mill stuff—a muscle man turning to suet, whose desires were basic, whose methods were direct, and whose every action was a simple equation.

Stooping, Condon answered the phone. "Well, I've finished talking to him," he reported, "and he hasn't changed his story any." He listened a moment. "Of course I think he's telling the truth," he said. "My theory is that, in the first place, he hasn't enough originality to make up a fairy tale—and, in the second place, it would need just that kind of unimaginative mind to enter into such a transaction in the first place."

Maury Temple had lived with his mother in the old section of town. After Condon had found the house, stepped to the porch, and rung the doorbell, he looked back at his parked car. It did little more than clear the curb. About enough space, estimated Condon, between the chassis and pavement for a horizontal man, if he were thin and his bones didn't protrude.

Enough for this woman, he thought, as the door opened. She was as tall as he, and angular. "Yes?" she questioned.

"Mrs. Temple?"

She inclined her head.

After explaining that he was from the District Attorney's office to investigate the death of her son, he was allowed to follow her through a dark hallway and on to the deep reds of the carpet in the living room.

"Of course," she assured him positively, "my son would never have had any relations with a man of that caliber. Not any." Her protruding teeth closed over the statement as if she had bitten off a length of thread. "The man is undoubtedly lying."

"Your son was a cameraman?"

"For World Wide. They make short features and special educational films." Her eyes were gray and cold as she said, "But he certainly wouldn't have done anything as dangerously stupid as to lie down in the middle of the street to photograph a car passing over him. They opened his camera and searched his film. He never took such a picture. The man is lying."

Condon looked around the room, at the old marble mantel, the porcelain globed lamps, and, finally, at the portrait on the library table.

"Is that your son?" The question was an opening only, for the pictured face was a replica of the woman's, as if it had been done in watercolor on damp paper so that the sharp lines were diffused. "He lived with you?"

"Of course. We were very close. He rarely left me alone even for an evening."

"How about the Saturday night his body was found?"

"He went back to the studio that night to do some work. He must have been on his way home."

"Yes, ma'am." Condon rubbed his jaw. "Now." Standing, he thrust his hands into his pockets, half turning from her. "I understand he was heavily insured. That he took out a recent additional policy."

Mrs. Temple stiffened.

"So heavily insured," persisted Condon, "that the insurance company is also doing some investigating with the thought in mind that his death might have been a devious method of suicide."

"They are mistaken." Mrs. Temple looked back at him with a set smile. "The last thing my son would think of would be to take his own life." She spread her well-kept hands, spacing them neatly. "Suicide, as a matter of fact, was a frequent subject for his disapproval." Again she placed her hands in her lap and folded them.

"Yes, ma'am."

"He termed it a short-sighted final act, without speculative opportunity to reconsider."

Condon pursed his lips. "He did a lot of protesting along those lines . . . ?"

"It was an interesting subject with him. He claimed that unless one can build from destruction itself, by an organized plan, that the act of destroying is a waste."

Condon fingered his lip thoughtfully. "That's an interesting concept. Your son, then, felt that suicide should be the beginning of a scheme which would carry to an inevitable conclusion?"

"My son had a well-integrated mind." Mrs. Temple stood and smoothed her dress. Condon moved toward the hallway. He looked back at her.

"He wasn't depressed, was he?"

Mrs. Temple's face turned blankly interrogative.

"Your son. Had anything been bothering him?"

She stared at Condon coldly. "What could have been bothering him? He enjoyed his work. He had a fine home. He needed no other woman . . . It is really very simple," she went on. "This person who is now in custody overpowered my son on that lonely road. He stole the car and killed my boy."

Condon walked down the porch steps, his eyes on the neighboring Verdugo Hills. Standing there a moment, he looked toward the garage at the end of the driveway, then he walked the concrete ribbon and pulled the doors. Placing his hand on the fender of the parked car, he leaned over to peer underneath. There was about as much allowance, between the chassis and the pavement, as his own. Enough to clear a prone man if he didn't hunch a shoulder or raise a knee. The new car, which had finally done the damage, was impounded. It would be, Condon was sure, a good two inches lower.

He closed the doors behind him, walked down the driveway, and slipped in behind his own wheel.

The smog had thinned out in the Valley and the sun slanted into Condon's eyes beneath the visor. He drove to San Fernando Road and parked by a drug store. Inside, he shut the door of the telephone booth behind him and dialed the District Attorney's number.

"Yes," he said into the telephone, "I'm out in Burbank now. Just saw Temple's mother." He listened a moment. "She gave me more information than she thought she did," he said. "Temple was playing Russian roulette . . . Russian roulette," he repeated, "R-u-s . . . O.K., so you heard me. Then I'll explain it. It's a game, a gamble where you place one live cartridge in the cylinder of a six-chamber revolver. You spin the cylinder and then place the muzzle of the gun against your forehead. You've one chance in six of being killed. Well. The bullet in the gun was Phifer. When Temple spun it that first Saturday and didn't get it, he narrowed his chances the second Saturday by pouring liquor down the driver's throat . . . Yes, that's what I said. But that didn't work, either. So, on the last Saturday, he made sure the bullet was fired by getting a low-slung car."

Tapping his foot, Condon listened to the words in his ear. "Because," he answered, "I learned a little of Temple's philosophy this afternoon. Now, if I can discover what his plan was, I'll understand why he did it."

Condon hung up.

World Wide was a small, specialized studio, located on the edge of Burbank, in the middle of a flat acreage between a trailer court and a metallizing company. It was enclosed with a brick wall, high enough to give it an air of exclusion.

Condon told the gateman who he was. "I want to talk to someone who worked with Maury Temple. Someone who knew him well."

"No one knew him well, mister." The gateman stepped into a stucco booth and made a phone call, then he stepped out again. "Go to office eleven," he instructed. "There's a fellow can maybe answer a couple of questions." He pointed down the studio street.

Condon had been on the Warner lots, and Universal, both times with the impression of visiting a Continental city gone mad. This place was more like a staid university with a few irrepressible freshmen not yet indoctrinated. He passed a number of quiet offices and one sound stage where they were shooting a couple of space men about to take off, and reached Number Eleven.

A man stood in the doorway, waiting for him.

"Hi," he said. "My name's Kalis. You're out here about Maury Temple?"

Condon nodded. As he walked into the office and sat down, he looked around at the shelves of canned film. Stills were thumbtacked to the walls. The place held a typewriter desk and a work table.

His host perched on the corner of the desk. "That was a funny deal about Maury Temple," he said. "What gives? Was it an accident—hit-and-run, or what?"

Condon shrugged. "From where Phifer sits, it was an accident. From where Temple lies, it was premeditated."

Kalis frowned in an effort to understand.

"But it was no hit-and-run," explained Condon. "Phifer drove the car to the police station right after it happened—belligerent and self-righteous, wondering how in hell he got himself into such a bind. He thought the cops would pat him on the head and send him home with a veracity medal. But the story was too screwy, and he'd left Temple lying out in the road with his head bashed in. You don't tell crazy stories and you don't leave dead bodies where you drop them—so they locked him up."

"But . . . "

"Look." Condon leaned forward, placing his hands on his knees. "If it doesn't make sense to you, you're not alone. It doesn't come through to the Police Department, either, or the insurance company . . . What do you know about Temple?"

"Well," hesitated Kalis, "not much." He gestured vaguely around the office. "This was his old stamping ground. I inherited it."

Condon pointed to the cans of film. "Are there any pictures of a car running over a man in there?"

An uncertain light of understanding flashed in Kalis' eyes, then receded to leave perplexity. He shook his head. "No. Why?"

"He said he was interested in getting a picture like that. He wanted a shot of a car as it ran over a man."

The light flashed again and stayed. "If we'd have needed anything like that, we could have dug a pit here on the lot for the cameraman to shoot from, or built a ramp for the car to roll on . . . "

"Yes," agreed Condon, "I assumed so."

"Is that what Maury was trying to do, then? Get a shot of a car passing over him?"

"That's what he said he was trying to do."

"But it wouldn't clear . . . " Kalis narrowed one eye in thought. "Or hardly, anyway."

"His new car didn't. The last one he bought."

Kalis' mouth fell open. "We kidded him about that dropped-down job. He wasn't much for flash and we asked him if he was going in for whistle bait. But Maury didn't kid good. We only tried it once before—when he was carrying the torch for Elsie . . . "

Slowly, Condon straightened. "Who's Elsie?"

"Elsie Peters." Kalis whistled. "Brother! Talk about still waters running deep. She was a one!"

The two actors in space suits passed the open doorway. They grinned through their glass helmets and raised their padded arms in salute.

"She worked in personnel here. Nice kid, if you like 'em scrubbed and pure. Maury did. First time I ever saw his forehead go damp over a woman."

Condon stared at the speaker, attempting to resketch his visual picture of Maury Temple. It wouldn't work.

"Maury fell for her like a ton of bricks . . . No," Kalis amended his statement, "like a dead fish, like a cold, dead fish. That guy was strictly protoplasm. But he was gone on Elsie, I guess, in his own way, and the rigger blew the thing wide open."

Condon drew in a deep breath of fresh air. "Rigger?" he asked.

"Yeah. We hired him to move and reset a structure out on the lot. Elsie signed him in, and I guess she broke out in spots the minute she was exposed to him." Kalis swung a leg from the desk, watching the sunlight splatter his shoe. "You know about simple girls and muscle men? Well, the simpler they are, the harder they fall for lusty goons. Her eyes felt his biceps—she was like a school teacher who suddenly gets a grown man for a pupil after having nothing more around than seven-year-old boys. Brother!" Kalis smiled weakly as he remembered.

"What was the rigger's name?"

Kalis shrugged. "We don't call 'em by name. They come in, do a job, and leave. It'll be on the books."

Condon nodded. "What did he look like?"

"A gorilla. With a scar on his face."

Condon relaxed.

"He was only here for a few days. It was long enough for him and Elsie to get the same idea, even if their viewpoints were different. She wouldn't know, of course, that he was an old hand at the game, and according to his rules, no holds were barred except legal ones."

Slowly, Condon shook his head.

"It hit Maury. Evidently his love was pretty warm down underneath his chilblains—or maybe it was pride." Kalis' forehead wrinkled with thought. "Maybe something else. I don't know. He was a deep one too. Anyway, all he did on the surface was let her go the rigger's way, and stick her picture in his desk drawer."

"Here?" asked Condon.

Kalis nodded. "I put all his things away when we found out what happened to him."

Condon stood. "Let me see them."

"Sure." Kalis swung off the desk and moved around to open a drawer. He laid out a notebook, a couple of keys, pencils, and a small framed photograph. "We put his professional equipment in a locker."

Condon picked up the picture and stared at inhibition in sepia. The girl's face was angular, with strength and passion and possessiveness overlaid by her youth and repression. Her upper lip was short, her teeth prominent. The picture in Condon's hand shook as he realized how much she looked like Mrs. Temple.

"No wonder Maury Temple fell in love with her," he said softly.

Kalis, watching over his shoulder, laughed with embarrassment. "Never could see her, myself. But then, she wasn't my type."

"What happened to her?"

"She killed herself."

Slowly, Condon laid the picture on the desk. "She did?"

"Sure. Like I told you. To the rigger, it was an interlude. To her, it was for keeps."

"Well . . . " Condon looked at the picture again, then he wandered around the office with his hands behind his back. He looked over the cans of film, stacked like wheels on the shelves, ready to go. He turned and stared at nothing. "It's no wonder," he said, half to himself, "that Temple's favorite subject was suicide."

Kalis looked puzzled. He thought a moment. "I never heard him even mention suicide."

Condon took a moment to let his eyes rest on the man. "Not to you," he said impatiently. "Why should he talk about it to you? It was his mother he talked to. And when he talked to his mother, he was talking to the girl."

Kalis moved back a step, scratching his head.

"How about the rigger? Did he meet Temple while he was here?"

"No reason to. One was a cameraman—the other was a laborer."

"Then Temple would be likely to know the rigger and where to get hold of him, but the rigger would never recognize Temple. Right?"

"Well, sure . . . " Kalis' face held a confused suspicion. He reassured himself by becoming bored, sullenly rolling Maury Temple's pencils across the desk.

Condon hunched his coat squarely on his shoulders. He listened to an orchestra tuning up across the lot. He watched a shadow form in the sunset at the doorway. "You've helped," he said to Kalis. "You've helped a lot."

Kalis stopped the pencil under his fingers and looked up, surprised. "You mean the D.A. can work up a plea with what I gave you?"

"Well," qualified Condon, "not exactly. I doubt if a jury would believe what I've got to give them. I doubt if even the District Attorney will believe it . . . But I do, and it's my job to find the truth. Look," he said abruptly, "would you do me a favor?"

"Well, yeah. What is it?" Kalis became cautiously alert.

"Would you go over to the Personnel Office and find out the name of that rigger?"

"Sure. Will do. It'll be a little minute. We'll have to check back."

"Take your time. I'll use your phone while you're gone."

"O.K. Just tell the operator you want an outside line."

"All right."

As Condon watched Kalis lope through the door, he picked up the phone and talked a moment. Then he sat back to wait for a free line. Finally he dialed his number.

Waiting, he formed the words of explanation in his mind, and shook his head. The District Attorney wasn't going to like this. He wanted an investigation to come out black like guilt or white like innocence—it gave him a middle, politic lane to plea.

"Condon," he announced into the phone.

The two space men passed the door, this time in slacks and plaid jackets. They looked informal without their space helmets, and as insignificant as the rest of the world.

"Well, I've got it tied up," said Condon into the mouthpiece, "but you won't like it." He settled back in the swivel chair. "First, I'll go along with my statement that Phifer was telling the truth. Second, I was right about Temple playing Russian roulette—and third," he took a deep breath. "Now I know why he did it . . . What?" He listened closely, frowning. "You're on the wrong track. Look. His death was his sacrifice for falling in love . . . the insurance his recompense for daring to think of marriage with a girl in his mother's image who fell short of the image of his mother . . . No, I will not repeat that. I'll come on into the office and explain it—with pictures." He glanced over at the portrait on the desk.

"Oh, him?" He thought a moment. "We can't get him off. It'll turn out just like it was planned. He'll pay for his crime of Elsie Peters' suicide rather than Maury Temple's murder." Condon hung up on the words which ticked along the wire.

He sat there, then, waiting for Kalis to bring back Phifer's name from the Personnel Department.

MARY BRAUND

To the Manner Born

He knew he was absurdly early, and was half surprised to find the doorkeeper in his cubbyhole just beyond the open stage door.

The man looked up from the *Evening News*, screwing his eyes against the light and the smoke from his cigarette. He rose from his cushioned chair to peer at him over the ledge. "Ain't nobody here yet," he said, his manner slightly truculent, then he gave a second look and put his knuckles to his forehead in a half salute.

"Oh, it's Mr. Masters, ain't it? You're a bit beforehand, sir." He leaned his elbows on the ledge and closed one eye in a knowing wink. "Got a touch of the old first-night nerves, then?"

Richard forced a smile. "I suppose so," he began, and was alarmed to find his voice higher than normal and definitely hoarse. He cleared his throat hastily. *Keep calm now.*

He realized this was the first time he had spoken to anyone for several hours, not since they had been sent home this morning after the last brief run-through of a couple of scenes. "Go home now," Joe Taylor, the producer, had said. "Go home and forget all about the bloody play until tonight."

Richard had gone back to his digs, but he had not forgotten about the play. He had lain on his bed, gazing at the ceiling, going over and over his lines, wondering again at his luck in getting this part, praying that he would not muff his chance. The tension had finally become too great, and he had escaped to the theater, arriving hours before he should have.

Richard stared back at the doorkeeper, trying to recall his name. Briggs, that was it. At least he could remember that. But his lines? What about his lines?

He cleared his throat again. "Thought I'd get changed in peace and quiet, before the place gets too crowded. Help me get into the feel of things, you know."

Briggs shook his head. "If you take my advice, and I've seen some new ones in my time, I'd go across the road to the Unicorn and get myself a little drop of the hard stuff. Just a drop, mind you." He turned his head to look at the wall clock.

"Though I reckon you're even too early for their opening time. Tell you what," he said, "I'll get the callboy to bring you along a nice cup of char as soon as he gets here. Shouldn't be long now."

"Thanks," Richard said, "but I don't drink tea. You couldn't make that a cup of coffee, could you?"

"Don't drink tea?" The astonishment was ill-disguised. "Oh, that's right," he said, shaking a nicotine-stained finger at Richard. "You're an American, aren't you? Don't sound like it, I must say."

Richard smiled, knowing this was a commendation. "They knocked that out of me at RADA."

Paul, in Elocution, had taken him in hand. "A touch of Albert Finney they'll stand nowadays, and you can get away with your Welsh or Irish, but Southern Yankee they'll never take." Richard had not tried to explain that Southern and Yankee were contradictions, or that in any case he was neither. He had merely been grateful for the smoothing of his vowels and the softening of the hard nasal tones that he had not been aware of in drama school back home.

Richard flipped a hand at Briggs and walked down the narrow, chilly corridor to the dressing rooms. No, he had not been sorry to slough off his American background. When the head of drama at the university back in the States, a tall, gentle, sad Englishman, had suggested that he try for a place at the Royal Academy of Dramatic Arts in London, he, Richard Masters, had leaped eagerly. He had always wanted to come to England. Eighteenth-century England—the wit, the elegance, and the beauty—that was what he had dreamed of in the flat world of the Midwest.

Now, here he was, in this eighteenth-century theater, the oldest theater in England, where Edmund Keane and Mrs. Siddons had played. The best repertory in the whole of England, and he, Richard Masters, was playing Joseph Surface in *The School for Scandal*. A lead, no less, in an eighteenth-century comedy of manners. He wanted, suddenly, to laugh aloud with delight.

His qualms were gone, just as he had hoped they might, and now he couldn't wait to change into his costume and get his makeup on. He wanted to be rid of his twentieth-century skin.

Thirty minutes later, he was gazing at himself in the mirror with satisfaction. The clothes became him, no doubt of that. Cream silk knee breeches and stockings, pale green waistcoat embroidered in gold, and a dark green velvet coat with gold buttons. The ruffles of the shirt stood up at his neck, fell around his wrists. A short, powdered wig covered his fair hair and the heels of his buckled shoes made him seem taller than his six feet.

The bright, shadowless mirror threw back the dazzling reflection, and it was no longer Richard Masters standing there, but Joseph Surface, Sheridan's "sentimental knave."

He paused for a moment, absorbed in his other self, the face pale without makeup in the over-bright glass; then with an abrupt movement he picked up the green cocked hat and the gold-knobbed cane and stepped out of the dressing room into the dimness of the corridor.

The theater and the stage were in darkness, but he moved easily out from the wings onto the set. The velvet curtains were raised and he stood in Lady Sneerwell's bedroom, looking out across the footlights, over the orchestra pit, to the rows and tiers of red plush seats, the gilt cherubs and carved draperies. His eyes carried up and up to the faint chandeliers and the invisible ceiling. He stood very still and the theater was very quiet. A strange, suffocating excitement caught at his throat, shortening his breath.

Then, as he watched, lights began to flicker, along the walls and behind the boxes, unsteady, shimmering, like candlelight. The crystal chandeliers glowed and fractured into a thousand glittering fragments and a distant buzz of voices grew louder, swelling, until the sound filled the theater and swept across the stage, breaking into distinct levels: laughter, male and female; snatches of conversation, the chink of bottle and glass; the clatter of feet. A glow filled the auditorium, a glow of silks and satins, of bare, soft shoulders and powdered wigs, of silver buckles and sword hilts, a hundred fluttering fans.

Richard stood dazzled, bemused.

The voices became more distinct. One was calling to him. His eyes swept the crowd, fastening on a small, dark figure in the stalls, an urchinlike boy, hair uncovered, the face pale, the eyes wide, the mouth a round circle. "'Ere," it was saying, "who are you? What you doing up there?"

"I am Joseph Surface."

The noise of the audience died and drifted away. The lights dimmed, the men and the women faded, through the walls, beyond the pit, out of the boxes.

"I am Joseph Surface," he repeated, his voice loud now in the stillness of the empty theater. He found himself gazing down at the white face of the callboy, the two of them alone in the dimness, a few wall sconces illuminating the vastness. His throat was dry, his voice cracked. "I am Richard Masters. I'm playing Surface tonight."

"Cor, mister, you half scared me for a moment," the boy said. "I thought you was a ghost, honest I did. You shouldn't be standing there like that, not in the dark, with your costume on and all that."

Richard had difficulty focusing his eyes. "I'm sorry," he said. "I didn't mean to frighten you. I was just getting . . ." he paused. "I was just getting the feel of things."

The boy continued to stare. "Are you the American as wanted coffee?"

Richard gripped the top of the gold-knobbed cane, the round end warm under his hot hand. "I guess I'm the American," he said, "and I certainly could do with that cup of coffee."

"I'll bring it to your dressing room in a minute or two. Won't take me a jiffy to make."

Richard returned unsteadily to the small, cramped dressing room. The atmosphere of this place was really getting to him. He felt uneasy, strangely languorous and weary, as though he had taken a long journey. When the coffee came, he drank it down in a couple of gulps. It was the best British instant, milky and tepid. It did nothing to shake his torpor. He had an overwhelming desire to sleep. He stretched himself on the hard, too-short couch and was deeply, heavily asleep as soon as he closed his eyes.

The Playhouse did not run to separate dressing rooms for each member of the company, and Richard was roused by the noisy arrival of Simon Montague, who tonight was playing Charles Surface in *The School for Scandal*.

"What, asleep already!" Simon yelled at Richard as he threw open the door. "You Yanks take the dictum of early to bed and early to rise to ridiculous lengths." The door slammed behind him. "When I was in that play on Broadway, the whole audience fell asleep at nine o'clock." He pulled off his jacket and slung it across his chair. "Do you suppose that had anything to do with our closing after ten days?"

Simon rumpled his black hair and thrust his face two inches away from the mirror. "I've got to get at least twenty years off this crumbling ruin before I can present myself to my adoring fans." The bright blue eyes slid away from his reflection and he looked back through the mirror at Richard, now struggling to sit upright. "You don't look too hot yourself. Better get some goop on your face to bring back the old healthy tinge."

Simon began to pull off his clothes. Tie, shirt and trousers followed each other in furious succession to a heap around the chair.

"You're very quiet, Yank. Getting the old sinking feeling, eh? Not surprising, I must say, throwing you in at the deep end like this. But you'll be all right, never fear. You seem to be born to this period junk. Two months out of RADA, all the way from the prairies, and you're wearing those frills as though you've been used to them all your natural. Give me Pinter any day, I say."

The chatter washed over Richard. He liked Simon, who had been a good friend to him since he had come to the Playhouse, helping him find the digs in a tall Georgian terrace high over the city, guiding him around the pubs, putting him wise to the political nuances of the company, cheering him on when Richard got the part of Joseph Surface. Richard knew that Simon was amused at the way he, the Yank, had gone overboard for history, but Simon had only helped to foster his interest. He had shown him out-of-the-way antique shops and bookshops, and had introduced him to the Georgian Museum, tucked away in a quiet back street of the town. Richard suspected that Simon might even have pushed his name forward for this part, being not without influence as a long-standing member of the company.

Now, however, he could not listen to what his friend was saying; his mind felt detached, distant, and quite automatically he sat down in front of the mirror, tucking the cloth around his neck to apply his makeup. He heard, and yet did not hear, the voice of the callboy coming down the corridor, banging on the doors: "First call, ladies and gents. First call."

The detachment lasted while Simon rambled on, through the second call; while Simon took his arm in an over-firm grip and led him to the wings; through the sound of the national anthem and the swish of the rising curtain; even through the first few minutes of the play. Then came his cue and he was walking forward onto the stage, and suddenly the world was right again, the colors clear and distinct, the people three-dimensional.

"My dear Lady Sneerwell, how do you do today? Mr. Snake, your most obedient."

He was a great success. Everyone said so. Simon thumped his back as he made his last exit. "Marvelous stuff, Yank. To the manner born, no less. It'll be the National Theater for you yet."

As he took his bow with Molly White, who played Lady Sneerwell, the applause rose, washing over them in comforting waves. "All for you, Richard dear," she whispered, as they bowed to each other. "You were terrific, absolutely terrific." She smiled dazzlingly at him as she swept low to the ground. Richard felt dizzy.

The producer, Joe Taylor, slapped him on the back with the script as they went backstage. "Great, Dicky old son, great! I had my doubts about an American in the part, but you didn't put a foot wrong. Not a trace of accent. How did you do it?"

He didn't know how he had done it. It had been so easy; no effort at all. The lines had come as though he had been speaking them all his life; every step, every movement had been so natural. To the manner born, that's what Simon had called it.

There was a lot of shouting and laughter backstage. People were wandering around in various forms of undress. Beer was produced and they sat in each other's dressing rooms talking theater, and Molly White nibbled his ear.

Gradually, the excitement wore off. Molly White didn't look so hot in her mini, her hair falling over her face. When the shouting was at its loudest and Simon was nuzzling Mrs. Candour in a corner, Richard slipped away, down the narrow corridor once more, a faint muzziness in his head that he supposed came from the beer and the cigarette smoke. Briggs was still in his sentry box by the stage door, the hands of the clock now pointing to midnight.

"They still at it, are they?" Briggs asked, inclining his head in the direction of the dressing rooms. "It's usually like this on the first night, I always have trouble clearing them out." He leaned on the door, chewing on a matchstick. "You going home now, Mr. Masters? First to come, first to go, eh? How did it go tonight, then?"

Richard made the effort to stop and talk to him. "Did you see the play?" he asked, aware that he was half hoping to hear more words of praise.

"Me? No, bless your life. I've been working at the Playhouse for twenty years and I ain't seen a performance here yet. I have to wait until the morning's paper to see how you've all done. First thing, when I retire, I'm going to go out and buy meself a season ticket. Well, good night, then," he said, raising his hand in the mock salute as he saw that Richard was stepping out to the street. "Bet you won't be so early tomorrow night, sir. The excitement will have worn off a bit."

Richard spent a restless night. The lines of the play kept coming back to him, his first entrance, the waves of laughter, the applause, the glare of the footlights. As he tossed and turned, the theater seemed so much more real than his narrow bed. Even when he reached over and switched on the light, springing the small impersonal room into focus, his wandering mind could not pull away from Sheridan's world. He fell, at last, into a deep sleep as dawn began to illuminate the corners of the window.

It was the middle of the morning before he went into the town, where he bought a local paper so that he could read the reviews over a cup of coffee. The café was cool and quiet. Apart from himself there were three flower-hatted ladies attacking cream cakes with every symptom of guilt, conversing among themselves and not sparing him a second glance. He turned to the center page of the paper.

Mr. Richard Masters, he read, *brings to the part of Joseph Surface a panache and a naturalness seldom seen in plays of this period. Mr. Masters, I understand, is an American. How is it that this young man can conjure up the eighteenth century in a way that I have never seen an English actor of his age and experience achieve?*

Very gratifying. Richard folded the paper, reached for his cup, and looked over to the three ladies. He felt they should be aware that there was a rising young actor in their midst.

They were not there.

The room had become thick with smoke, and at their table sat three men, talking and laughing loudly, cards in their hands, a jug of wine on the table, a pile of coins glinting on the dark wood. One of the men tipped back on his heavy, sturdy chair, throwing his head back with laughter, his hair tied behind with a ribbon. His feet, clad in black, silver-buckled shoes, crashed to the ground; his ankles neat in white silk stockings. The noise did not come just from that one corner. Richard turned his head stiffly. The room was crowded with other men, wearing cocked hats and silk coats, buckskin breeches and lace ruffles, some with swords clanking at their side, some smoking long, curved clay pipes. The place throbbed with masculine vitality.

A girl moved among them, buxom, her dress low on her bosom, one arm lifted high carrying a tray, curls drifting around her forehead and her ears, her hips swiveling to avoid searching hands. Her color was bright, her eyes sparkled. They met Richard's and her cheeks dimpled. "More coffee?" She smiled at him, a beauty spot high on one cheekbone.

Richard only stared at her.

"More coffee?" she asked again, leaning over him at his table until he felt suffocated with her heavy female perfume. The empty, cool café was back and there was this girl in a short skirt and a mole on her face offering him coffee from a glass pot, and there were three genteel English ladies murmuring in low voices at an adjacent table.

He had another cup of coffee, then two more. The girl said, "You've been looking at me ever so queer, like. Was there anything wrong?"

He paid for the coffee and assured her, "No, there was nothing wrong, absolutely nothing, but, well, do you happen to know how old this café is?"

Her thick lips pouted at him. "Oh, it's been here since the year dot—they say it's been a café as long as anyone can remember. Used to be a coffee shop, they called it, when men wore wigs and that sort of thing, you know."

After that, the day was a jumble. Richard eventually ate a very late lunch in a Wimpy bar, the nearest thing to an American hamburger stand that he knew of in town. Amid the chrome and stainless steel he felt safe from the past. He had, for a fleeting moment, a sudden and unexpected wave of homesickness, and he wondered if his pals still used Al's Drive-In out on the strip, where they would congregate on those bright, warm summer evenings that were so rare in this country, and where they would talk and laugh about the girls and drink endless bottles of cola. So long ago. Another world; another century.

He ended up lying on his bed in his digs, staring at the ceiling, until the first half-light of evening crept over the city and the isolation and the confusion of his thoughts drove him inexorably down to the theater.

Briggs greeted him at the stage door. "What, you here again so early, Mr. Masters? Well, it'll soon wear off, mark my words. Didn't seem to do you any harm last night, though." He waved his edition of the *Evening News* at Richard. "They do say you were grand in the part. Keep it up. I like to be proud of my young actors." He grinned and winked at Richard. "Keep it up, then," he called to the departing back.

There was this compulsion to get into his costume again, and once armored by the silks and the velvets, the doubts and the disorder melted away. Yet he could not rest quietly in the dressing room. He had to get out onto the stage again. Was it to find out if the spell of last evening could be repeated?

Once more he stood still and silent in the eighteenth-century room, gazing out over the empty theater. He didn't have to wait long.

Soon those ghostly lights flickered, and the ghostly figures thronged the ornate auditorium, and the distant voices swelled and roared until he, Joseph Surface, was the focus of a thousand eyes and the object of applause for a thousand hands. He smiled and bowed, his hat in his hand, his gold-knobbed cane in the other, one buckled foot stretched in front of the other, his powdered head almost touching a silken knee.

The applause rose and fell and faded to a single handclap and a jeering voice. "Bravo, Mr. Masters, bravo," and there was the callboy again, waving from the pit. "You didn't scare me tonight, Mr. Masters. I knew it was you up there, as soon as I came in. What you doing there, Mr. Masters? Practicing for your knighthood?"

Richard retreated from the stage with as much dignity as he could muster. Back in the dressing room, he carefully removed his velvet coat and his wig and, stretching out on the couch, slept once more that deep, dreamless sleep.

Simon crashed open the door. "Well, you made it, my friend. The Yanks have done it again. Your fans are queuing at the stage door for your autograph. They positively booed because I wasn't you." He waved some newspaper clippings in Richard's face. "Here, I've started your fame file for you."

With a flourish, Simon pinned the clippings on the diamond-patterned board between the mirrors. "You'll have to send these to the old folks back home. They'll be real proud of you in Mastersville, U.S.A."

There was the same struggle to get back to reality, the same impression that everyone was painted onto stage scenery until the moment came for him to walk onto the set, then as he spoke the familiar words: "My dear Lady Sneerwell, how do you do today?" the world fell back in place again. He was Joseph Surface, and again he was a triumph.

As he took his bow, he felt for an expectant moment that the twentieth-century audience might fade away; there was a brief moment when the lights started to flicker and the faint iridescent glow began to fill the theater, but it faded again before it could grow to substance. The curtain fell for the final time after their fifth bow and he was left feeling flat. As he cleaned off his makeup with cold cream, Richard dreaded the thought of an early return to the tossing and turning in his solitary room.

Simon saved him. "I can see you have a touch of the second-night blues," he said, as he unbuttoned his lace shirt. "I would suggest a little visit to the Unicorn. The landlord can be most solicitous on these occasions. Apart from which, he will usually offer the ladies and gentlemen of the Playhouse a free drink." He pulled on his trousers. "We are considered good for business, and he is always given a few tickets to the show. An admirable, advantageous arrangement, I would say, wouldn't you?"

Richard could only answer monosyllabically. He was very subdued as they crossed the cobbled street to the old pub. The Unicorn had been an ancient dockside inn, and still retained the flavor, though the water had long since been diverted a hundred yards away. Where ships had once moored, there was now a street of warehouses and brokers' offices.

The landlord greeted Simon enthusiastically and did, indeed, offer them a drink. He was coming to see the play the very next day, he told them. He had read the splendid notices that Mr. Masters had received. "It's a pleasure to welcome you to the Unicorn, sir," he said, raising his glass in a toast.

Richard had a whiskey. It tasted good, though the two small pieces of ice that the landlord had provided melted rapidly. There was this strange inability of the English to produce enough ice to make a decent drink. However, he had a second one and began to cheer up. He felt it was time that he confided in Simon about his haunting visions.

"Simon," he began, "I've had the weirdest—"

"Just a moment, old man," interrupted Simon, "I must visit the gent's. Be back in a minute."

As Richard swirled the amber liquid in his glass, waiting for Simon, he half knew what was going to happen. The long, smooth legs of the girls in their mini-skirts, the tweed jackets and the ties, the gleaming rows of bottles and glasses, the red handles of the beer pumps, all shimmered and faded. Vague, somehow menacing figures began to creep into the corners of Richard's mind. He stood, clutching his glass, waiting for them to fill out and become human, but they were farther off than usual. Then one figure emerged, clear in bright colors, and it was Charles Surface, elegant in a red silk coat, laughing, walking toward him.

"Charles!"

"What do you mean, *Charles?*" and it was Simon in a red sweater and gray trousers, laughing at him. "Come on, Richard, old dear, you've got that damned play too much on your mind." He picked up his beer. "What was that you were going to say to me?"

Richard stared into the blue eyes, the uncomplicated face. "Oh, nothing. Forget it." He couldn't explain it to Simon. He couldn't explain it to anyone, let alone to himself.

For the rest of the week he avoided going to the theater too early. He stayed in bed late in the mornings, ate his lunch in the Wimpy bar, spent his afternoons at the cinema. He made sure that he arrived at the theater with only enough time to change and make up, when the place was already alive with the rest of the cast, stagehands, and dressers.

The ghosts still hovered, but he managed to keep them in the past where they belonged.

Then, on Sunday, he ruined everything by accepting an invitation from Simon to visit his parents in Bath. They walked in the perfectly symmetrical, eighteenth-century crescents and squares and took tea in the pump rooms. Richard was lost. He gave up the fight and abandoned himself to his phantoms. Richard Masters became a twentieth-century ghost in the eighteenth century.

He found that he could conjure up the past at will, in the old bookshops, in the parks, best of all in the Georgian Museum. The attendant greeted him as an old friend when he wandered there in the afternoons, and would leave him to stand entranced in the bedrooms and the sitting rooms, peopling them with rustling silken ladies and bowing gentlemen. The streets came alive with horses and coaches and Richard would catch tantalizing glimpses of bright groups and crowds that vanished as he came too near them. There was a barrier through which he could not pass; none of these figures would speak with him, and he soon found that a twentieth-century voice caused them to melt away. Neither would they appear when he was with anyone else, so he took to avoiding company, trying to become more and more immersed in this beautiful world.

The play ran for another two weeks. Each evening, Richard arrived at the theater by five-thirty. He tried coming earlier, but Briggs was not there and the stage door was firmly shut against him. Briggs took him for granted now, grinning indulgently, waving him into the darkness and the enchantment of his very own audience. He even took to using snuff.

His Joseph Surface improved with every performance. It was more polished, more elegant, more authentic every evening. The audience and the company applauded him rapturously. He was acclaimed as the most promising young actor that the Playhouse had produced for a generation.

The only one who stood apart from the praise was Simon. He would catch Richard's eye in the mirror some evenings, and there was a worried expression in the light blue eyes.

"You're keeping very much to yourself these days," Simon eventually remarked. "You've changed, Richard. Got yourself a good bird?"

For a moment Richard hesitated, half wanting to tell Simon, then dismissed the thought of his understanding. He couldn't bear the idea of ridicule. He smiled and shook his head.

"Well, maybe you should," said Simon. "A nice healthy girl would take you out of yourself a bit. How about Molly? She's healthy, all right, and she fancies you. I recognize the old light in her eyes."

"Oh, Molly." Richard rejected the suggestion. "She's . . . she's too modern."

Simon raised his eyebrows. "You prefer her as Lady Sneerwell, eh? Well, I tell you, this is a better world than it was in Sheridan's day. It wasn't all that it's portrayed on the stage, you know."

The last two evenings of the play, Richard Masters played entirely to his own audience. They came to watch him, filling the stalls and the boxes, the circle and the gallery as they had done each evening before the performances, cheering and clapping, more exuberant, more extroverted than any twentieth-century audience. Richard was inspired. He was a shining star, filling the stage, lighting it up, leaving an emptiness behind whenever he made an exit.

When the curtain fell for the final time on the final evening, he stood on the dusty boards, dazed and disbelieving. It was over. Suddenly he felt very tired.

Everyone was laughing and congratulating him. Simon slapped him hard on the back, yelling: "Well, how does it feel to have finished with all that period stuff? What about getting your teeth into a bit of Pinter next?"

The blood roared in Richard's head. For a moment he felt his knees buckling under him. He leaned heavily on the gold-knobbed cane, staring with wide eyes at Simon. Was it all going to disappear with that final swish of the curtain? Could he ever perform in a modern play?

"A party! A party!" Several of the cast swept him along off the stage. "Must have a party! Over to the Unicorn. Everyone get changed. Come on, quick. A toast for Richard!"

He sat in the dressing room, shaken, an empty shell. He wanted to put his head down among the containers of makeup and weep. Had his lovely charming world gone forever? Was it all to be no more?

Simon ignored Richard's white face and trembling hands. He kept up the usual string of chatter and banter, and as Richard reluctantly divested himself of the velvet coat and silk waistcoat, he threw his other clothes across to him. "Hurry up, old dear. They are all waiting for you. It's a big night for you tonight."

Once out of his Joseph Surface costume, Richard began to feel more normal. He'd make out—he'd look back on this one day and ridicule himself. Enough of this nonsense. Life was here, it was the twentieth century and he, Richard Masters, must live life where he found it. He tried to convince himself.

The cast thronged and jostled him across to the Unicorn.

"Tonight it's the local brew for you," bellowed Simon. "Drink up and be merry."

The specialty of the house was draught cider, sweet and rough, very palatable, very intoxicating. Two pints of that, downed rather quickly, and the English veneer began to leave Richard. He could detect the hard, nasal twang creeping back into his words, but there was nothing that he wanted to do about it. He laughed at himself, a loud, brazen laugh, and when Molly White leaned her warm flank against him, he squeezed her hard, letting out a not too subdued cowboy whoop. Her hair tickled his nose and he rubbed his face against her head, closing his eyes.

There was a moment when Richard Masters teetered on the brink between the past and the present, then without warning the past rushed at him.

"Take care, my good sir. This low class of tavern is not for the likes of you."

The voice came, hoarse and tremulous, from behind his left shoulder. Richard lazily opened his eyes and he beheld, in the corner, a bundle of rags, animated by two reedlike arms protruding from in front, and a wasted, cadaverous face above. The mouth, completely devoid of teeth, split into the travesty of a smile. A foul oder assailed Richard from the open mouth and he tried to draw back, the weight of the girl against his side preventing him.

"Nay, sir, I am only a poor beggar. I'll do you no harm." The claw of a hand reached out for him, but did not quite reach. "But look around, kind sir. There are many here who would see you beaten and robbed and lying in the gutter." The fleshless hand gestured.

Richard slowly dragged his eyes from the wreck of a human being, with reluctant dread. The inn was a scene from Hogarth come to life. Bawds and beldams; drunken, lurching sailors with tarred hair; scarecrow figures in filthy rags; emaciated, crying children; a small soot-covered boy coughing into a dirty rag. A rancid smell of unwashed bodies and cheap gin pervaded the smoky, ill-lit tavern; screams and oaths filled the thick air. Richard was nauseated, disgusted. This was not the world he had come to know so well.

"Look over there, kind sir. Those are the sort of ruffians you must beware of."

The dirty fingernail pointed along the counter to two dark men dressed in black broadcloth, a heavy growth of beard on their thin faces, woolen caps pulled down to the level of their eyes, which turned hungrily and menacingly toward Richard.

"And those women," the hoarse voice whispered in Richard's ear. "All doxies, I warrant you. That one by your side, sir. What would a fine gentleman like you be doing with a woman like that?"

Richard stiffened and froze for a moment, then suddenly he seized the girl by the shoulders and whirled her around to face him. His mouth dropped with horror. More hag than girl. A dreadful painted face, pitted with smallpox scars, drunken, bleary, red-rimmed eyes, loose lips hanging open.

He flung her from him with a curse. He saw the two men in black start forward from the bar and he wheeled, pushing his way through the stinking crowd. Hands reached out to stop him, but he tore himself loose frantically. He must get out of this awful place. He scrabbled desperately at the door, then was running down the dark corridor to the main entrance.

He could hear cries and pounding footsteps behind him. Panic blinded him and he threw himself out through the front door, looking neither to the left nor right. He neither saw nor heard the rumble of the coach and the horses, and was only aware at the very last moment of the hot breath of the animals and the rearing hooves that came crashing down on his skull. A wheel caught him and flung him to the gutter, where he lay quiet and still.

Simon and Molly were a second or two after him, running down the corridor in pursuit, slow to react as he had cast Molly from him with that look of horror on his face. They reached the door just in time to see Richard run straight into the front wheels of the bus, then the sickening sight of his body thrown in the air to crash by the curb right in front of the theater. The bus screamed to a slewing halt yards down the road.

Briggs came rushing from his box at the stage door. "I saw it," he cried. "I saw it. Never gave the driver a chance." Then, "Oh, it's Mr. Masters!"

They knelt by the body in the road. Molly sobbed and Simon clutched the still warm hand, his face contorted. He reached out gently to straighten Richard's torn white shirt. As he pulled the cloth around the body, his hand paused. "Look at this." He stared disbelievingly. "Look at this!"

There, on the white shirt, black and startling, and quite plain in the lights from the Playhouse, were the unmistakable imprints of horses' hooves.

Briggs, gabbling from the pavement, said loudly, quite inconsequentially, "The bus came from over there, where the old stagecoach station used to be."

RICHARD O. LEWIS

Black Disaster

They came plodding up the hill, singly and in groups, their bobbing lights turning the snow to yellow in the pre-dawn darkness, their bodies casting long, wide shadows behind them. Some, their bodies black blobs against the snow, had not bothered to light their lights, for they were creatures of darkness and needed little light to guide them.

As usual, Mike Kovchec was among the first to arrive at the steamy mouth of the slope that led down at a steep angle into the maw of the black pit. Other early arrivals were loading themselves into a string of small cars that, at a signal to the engineer, would whisk them down to the bottom in a matter of seconds. They were talking and laughing, making ribald jokes.

Mike did not join them. Alone, he began picking his way down the slag-strewn slope, the carbide light at the front of his cap casting a yellow nimbus ahead of him and glinting occasionally from the twin pairs of narrow-gauge tracks along which cars would soon be shuttling up and down between the bottom of the mine and the top of the tall tipple.

He was a short, heavy man, somewhat shy and slow to make acquaintances. Although his hair was black, his face was a contrasting white, for his face never felt the rays of the sun through the long wintry months unless the sun chose to shine down through the smoke-filled sky on Sundays—which it seldom did. He was not unfriendly; it was just that he sometimes found difficulty in expressing himself and in understanding the rough talk and crude jokes of the others.

He did not miss companionship. He liked being alone with his thoughts, even as now, for his thoughts were generally pleasing to him. There was a tuneless whistle upon his lips as he trudged along, the blackness ahead of him retreating steadily before his light. Andy, his son, would be proud of him, just wait and see! Andy should go to high school next year, become educated! In this great new world anything was possible! Andy would wear a white collar, never work in the mines! Not that mining was not an honest job, but there were dangers . . .

Mike leaped quickly away from the rails to flatten himself against the ribbing of rough boards that held back the earthen sides of the tunnel as a distant rumbling reached his ears. The rumbling became a sudden roar as a string of cars came hurtling down, the men in them crouched low to keep their heads clear of the flashing roof beams, their lights flickering and guttering in the rush of air. Mike heard words shouted at him as cars clattered by, but the noise of iron wheels upon iron rails and the swish of air made them nearly unintelligible. He caught but one of them: "Squarehead!"

That would be Joe Spore or son. Neither missed a chance to ridicule him in some way before the other miners. He hoped he would not have trouble with them again today. They were greedy and quarrelsome, and could easily become dangerous.

Stepping away from the ribbing, Mike continued down the slope, careful to avoid the tail rope of jagged, frayed steel that lashed and writhed between the rails in the wake of the descending car. A single lash from that thin serpent could shatter an ankle beyond repair; and he must avoid injury at all cost, must not be laid off from work, not now. Schooling would take money—books, new clothing, things like that—and he must stand proud in Andy's eyes . . .

The string of cars, now empty, came roaring up. Seconds later, a loaded string went thundering and clattering down the other pair of tracks.

The sloping tunnel widened suddenly to become the flat, cavernlike bottom of the mine. Twin rails branched out in various directions among the black, oaken props that held the slate roof in place, each pair of rails finally becoming lost in the shadowy mouth of an entry.

Here, the full scent of the mine greeted Mike's nostrils—minute particles of coal dust in suspension, damp mustiness of mildewed props, ripe with decay, a miasma of smashed forest that had flourished live and green eons before the memory of man. It was a heady odor, an opiate. Some claimed that once the scent of the mine had clutched a man's senses, it held him prisoner to the black tunnels for the rest of his working days.

Chin thrust forward, head bent low to avoid the low roof, hands clasped behind him in typical coal-miner's crouch, Mike followed one of the tracks into the wide mouth of the mule barn that had been cut into the side of one entry. Here, the scent of the mine was compounded by the odor of mule droppings and of moldy corn and hay; pungent, but not offensive.

Mike entered the second stall and let a hand run lightly over the neck of the small black mule there. "Hi, Molly," he said, rubbing the hollows behind ears that had been worn to stubs by their continual contact with low roofs. Molly turned her head toward him in greeting, then quickly turned away again. Her eyes had not seen the light of day since the end of summer in some nearly forgotten pasture, and the glow from Mike's light tended to be blinding.

Mike unsnapped her halter rope and led her from the stall. "Steady, girl," he said, and Molly stood obediently, head bowed, while he took the padded collar from its peg, strapped it about her neck, and crossed the leather tugs over her back to keep them from dragging through the muck.

"We go to work, Molly," he said, picking up the hickory butt-stick with its tail chain and hook.

Molly needed no further instruction. She followed the pair of rails out of the barn, placing her feet daintily in the worn hollows between the ties, and stopped at the parting where the pit boss waited amid strings of empties.

One of the chores of the pit boss was to make certain that every miner got his just share of cars to load each day, no more, no less, no partiality shown. He held up six fingers in front of his light.

Mike nodded, went to the sixth car in one of the strings, and pulled its end coupling. Then he took the tugs from Molly's back, snapped them to each end of the butt-stick, and dropped the hook into the coupling slot of the lead car.

"Hi-yup!" he commanded, placing his right foot upon the narrow bumper of the car and hooking his elbow over the splintery boards of its front. Then, as Molly strained forward to bring the tail chain taut, he slid his left foot out along it for support, crouched low between mule and car, placed his left hand against Molly's rump, and ordered, "Gee!"

Molly swung sharply to the right, clattered the cars across open switches, and set her course between a pair of rails that led into the narrow blackness of an entry.

Old Davy waited at the mouth of the first room, his face indistinct and shadowy beneath the shielding glare of the light upon his cap. Probably the oldest worker in the mine, he had been born into it and had never known another way of life.

He pulled the coupling pin of the end car, and Mike helped him slue it across the switch and into the room that was a shambles of fallen props over a flood of coal that had been blasted out by the shots of the night before.

Old Davy set to work immediately with his heavy scoop shovel. Ten scoops, a bushel, three cents; twenty-five bushels, a ton, seventy-five cents; four tons a day, three dollars—more than twice as much money as he had been making just ten years ago! When the car was filled, he would top it off with chunks piled as high as the low roof would permit.

Mike did not tarry; there was work to be done, miners waiting. "Car!" he shouted at the next room.

Hank Staley's light bobbed out of the black depths. He was a tall man, and big. Never throughout the working day could he ever stand erect. He hurried from the room, crouched, careful of the low-hanging crossbeams. "I get 'im," he said, turning toward the end of the string.

"Hi-*yup!*" shouted Mike when he heard the return clink of the coupling bolt.

Here the entry began a sharp incline to a higher level where ancient, subterranean forces had shifted the rocky crust of the earth upward a full five feet. The muscles of Molly's rump rippled and corded beneath Mike's hand as she leaned heavier into her collar to trundle the remaining four cars slowly up the hill.

Two lights awaited him at the black mouth of the next room, shadowy figures behind them; Joe Spore and son.

"Car," said Mike, bringing Molly to a halt.

"We want two cars now," said Joe. He started back toward the end of the string.

Mike stepped from behind Molly and went back along the cars after him. "You take your turn like everybody else," he said.

"We are two," said Joe. "We take two cars!" He shook a fist.

"You are one," said Mike. "One man and helper. I tell you that before!"

"My son is a young man now!" Joe insisted. "Very strong!"

"He is still a boy! He should get good education!"

"I educate him to work like a man!" said Joe. "Like my father educated me!" He leaned over to uncouple the two end cars.

Mike shoved him roughly away, uncoupled the last car, and nudged it away from the others. "You get one-car turn!" he said, straightening up. "You want more, you go ask pit boss!"

He pulled himself angrily along the cars to the head of the string and mounted the bumper. Molly leaned into her collar, brought the tail chain taut, and set the cars into motion.

"We get more, you wait and see!" Joe was shouting after him. "Or you better look out! You may not work long!"

Since the Spores had come to work in the mine two weeks ago, they had given nothing but trouble—always wanting more than their share, ignoring the rights of others, hurling threats. The boy wasn't so bad, but he was a complete slave to his father's will, forced to follow in his father's footsteps.

When Mike stopped at the next room, he discovered he had only two cars left. That meant that one of the Spores had jerked a coupling pin on an extra car just as he had pulled away.

"Damn!"

He delivered the final car and began retracing his steps back toward the parting, carrying the butt-stick under one arm to keep it from clattering and banging over the ties at Molly's heels.

As he passed the Spores' room, he saw by their lights that they had the extra car.

Well, there was nothing he could do about it now. He wouldn't fight with them; he would just skip them on the next turn.

"Andy," he said, as if his son were present, "you will not work in the mines. Your father will make it all by himself."

At Hank's room, he picked up a loaded car left over from the day before and rode it the short distance back to the bottom.

Mike held up six fingers to the pit boss, and the pit boss nodded reluctantly. All in all, there were only eleven men working in the entry, and Mike was making a twelve-car turn. He would have to compensate on the next turn. A week ago, he had made the mistake of giving the Spores an extra car and had got reprimanded for it. He must not let it happen again. The spring layoff would come all too soon. Then there would be slack times, two or three months without work. He must stay out of trouble, not risk his job . . .

Mike delivered the last two cars of his second string to the two men who were working at the extreme end of the entry, forging the tunnel deeper and deeper into the black seam of coal so that more rooms could be opened in their wake.

They were lean men, work-hardened and tough, and their chores were many. They took up bottom or broke down roof where necessary to afford head room for mule and driver. They erected permanent beams across the roof, shored the ribs where shoring was necessary, laid new ties along the extension of corridor, spiked rails to them and, in separate cars, loaded out the shale, slate, sulphur balls, dirt, and other debris of their advancement, for there was no room for gob piles along their narrow tunnel. Naked to the waist, they toiled, breathing deeply, bodies wet and black, for no matter how much fresh air the giant fans sent down the air shaft into the mine, the air at the dead end of an entry was always hot, stale, and dust-laden. They got paid by tonnage of coal, plus footage of progress.

Mike picked up four loads on the way back to the parting, delivered them, and dropped the tail chain hook into a string of five empties fresh from the top. They were wet and snow-laden, which meant that another wintry storm had gripped the world above.

He dropped a car each for Old Davy and Hank, and whispered encouragement to Molly as she toiled up the grade. Two lights bobbed at the entrance of the Spores' room. They had heard him coming and were waiting for him.

"We want car!" shouted Joe Spore as the string went by without slowing.

"You got two cars!" shouted Mike. "Now you skip a turn!"

The younger Spore lunged suddenly ahead, clutched Molly's halter, and jerked her to a stop. The slackened tail chain hit the ties, and Mike quickly thrust a shoulder into Molly's rump, his body braced to absorb the momentum of the cars so they would not crash over her heels. To a mine mule, a broken leg meant sudden and ultimate dispatch with a sledgehammer.

"Let go that mule!" he warned.

Joe was already heading back toward the end of the string. Mike leaped after him, clutched him by the shoulder as he stooped to pull a coupling pin, and spun him away. "You do not get car!" he shouted.

"We need car!" said Joe, backing away. "We need money!"

"You take turn!" said Mike, starting toward the head of the string.

He heard the swift shuffle of footsteps behind him and wheeled about just in time to see the swinging scoop shovel in Joe's hands. It was coming directly toward his head. He reached out with both hands, caught the handle of the scoop near its iron blade, and went stumbling back against the cars. Then he twisted his arms and shoved. Joe went spinning back against the rib of the entry and fell heavily to a sitting position, the scoop clattering from his hands. "I get you!" he shouted, struggling to get his feet under him. "I get you! You square-head!"

"I do not fight with you," said Mike, standing over him, "unless I have to. *But you do not get extra car!*" He picked up the shovel and flung it angrily away into the darkness.

"I get you, squarehead! You wait and see!"

Mike stepped back a pace. "Hi-yup, Molly!" he called, and as the mule obediently began trundling the cars forward, he hooked a ride on the rear bumper of the last car as it clattered by.

After delivering the remaining empties, he continued on to the face of the entry. The men had a car loaded and waiting, piled high with jagged pieces of shale that extended out over sides and ends. "Bring a load of props next trip," called one of them as Mike hooked the car and mounted a bumper. Mike bobbed his light in acknowledgment as he went trundling away, sharp shale stabbing at his back from the laden car.

He picked up two more loads along the way, and another load was waiting for him at the mouth of the Spores' room. He shunted it out onto the main track and added it to the string. The lights of father and son were huddled together at the far end of the room. Neither had bothered to come forward to help with the car.

At the top of the downward slope, he placed a protecting hand against Molly's rump and stiffened his arm as the string began its descent. "Easy, Molly," he said, feeling the pressure of the cars build up behind him. "Easy, girl."

Halfway down the slope, Molly's mincing steps became a gingery dance as she gradually increased her pace, picking her way rapidly over the ties and into the flickering shadows ahead as the hand pressed harder and harder against her. Outrun the cars, but not too fast. Hold back at the same time.

Approaching the foot of the slope, the cars reached maximum speed, jolting and bouncing, tail chain swaying. It was then that Molly, without warning, leaped suddenly to the left and away from the rails. Mike, finding Molly's rump no longer against his hand and the chain whipped away from beneath his foot, went sprawling forward. He saw the long slab of slate across the track just a split second before he fell heavily over it on hands and knees, the cars roaring and pounding behind him.

Taking advantage of his own momentum, Mike rolled quickly away from between the rails just as the lead car smashed into the rock barrier and leaped halfway across it. Molly squealed once in pain and fright, and a slab of shale shot from the top of the stalled car to shatter itself on the rail at Mike's head.

He scrambled to a sitting position, clutched his right knee in both hands, and slowly tried to straighten out the leg.

A light appeared at Hank's room, just a few yards away. Then Hank came running up, crouched low, arms swinging before him. "You all right?"

Mike nodded. "Look to the mule," he said. Then he rolled up his trouser leg and inspected his knee in the glow of the light that lay at his side. The kneecap was red, dented, and filled with pain, but there were no deep lacerations. He picked up his cap and light and got slowly to his feet, placing most of his weight on his left leg.

Hank came forward, leading Molly. "A bad cut and a bruise or two," he said. "But nothing broken."

"Good," said Mike. He hobbled over to Molly and inspected the ragged cut where a flying piece of shale had struck her just above the hock. Then he looked at the slab of slate beneath the car and up at the low roof above. There was no fresh break in the roof. The slab could have got across the rails only if two people had carried it and placed it there.

Hank, too, had taken in the situation. "Them devils up there tried to get you," he said, sweeping his light toward the top of the grade.

Mike nodded. "They mad because they don't get extra car."

"Joe spends too much time in saloon," said Hank. "Always in debt. Bad example for the boy."

Mike hobbled around the derailed cars and up the incline toward the Spores' room. Lights vanished from the mouth of the room as he approached. Obviously, the two had been standing just inside the room, watching and listening. The two lights turned toward him as he entered.

"You did that!" accused Mike. "You could have crippled me, caused me to lose work. You might have killed mule."

"Clumsy squarehead," taunted Joe. "You should watch maybe where you are going."

"I tell you once more," Mike said, evenly, "and for very last time. While I drive mule in this entry, *you get no extras!*"

"We poor people," Joe said, stubbornly. "We need extras."

"You not get them."

Mike turned to retrace his steps from the room and keep the peace.

"Then maybe we get new mule driver for sure!" Joe shouted after him. "New mule driver tomorrow, maybe."

A report, of course, could be made to the pit boss, but Mike didn't want to do anything that might hint that he was incapable of handling his own job. Anyway, Andy would not want his father to run for help. Andy would be proud of a father who fought his own battles.

Hank, with the help of Old Davy, had the track cleared and two of the cars back on the rails by the time Mike returned. Together, they slued the other two cars into position and coupled them.

"You be careful," warned Hank. "They'll keep after you, try to break you one way or another."

Mike nodded and placed his arm over Molly's neck. "We both got bad legs," he said soothingly, "but we got to get work done." He hobbled along beside her as she set the cars into motion.

"You hurt?" the pit boss wanted to know as Mike came limping toward the parting.

Mike shook his head. "Just shook up a bit. Fall of slate."

The pit boss nodded his understanding. In spite of many safety measures, slate falls were not at all uncommon.

A mule driver brought in loads from another entry and hooked on to a string of empties. He scooped up a double handful of snow from one of the cars, squeezed it into a ball, and tossed it away into the darkness beyond his mule. "If this keeps up till quittin' time," he announced, "we'll be wadin' home through drifts hip deep!"

Mike was extra careful during the rest of the day. He still rode the tail chain, but each time he came to the brow of the hill he dismounted, shot a wooden sprag into one of the rear wheels of the end car, and then led Molly down the grade, his light piercing the shadows ahead, the spragged wheel squealing and grinding on the iron rail.

The Spores accepted their rightful turn in silence and gave him no further trouble.

Later, Mike seated himself on a battered powder keg just outside the mule barn, unhooked his light and placed it on the floor so that its glow shone away from his eyes, and took a sandwich from his lunch pail. All the miners had gone now. Some would be stopping at the saloon to wash the coal dust from their throats or to get a growler for home consumption. Others would already be seeking the tin tub of hot water by the kitchen stove where they could wash the black grime from their white bodies so far as possible.

There came an occasional grunt or sigh from the mules as they munched their corn, the squeal of an angry rat, and the intermittent drip-drip of water seeping down from various faults in the roof. Otherwise, the silence was as complete as the great darkness that pushed in around the little island of light.

To Mike, it was the best part of the day. Here he could ease his back against the rough planking, feel his muscles relax from their crouched position, and be alone with his own thoughts for a few restful moments before taking up his final task, the task of shot-firing.

The mine was a new one and had, as yet, but four working entries and less than fifty rooms, but it was expanding rapidly as new entries were being driven and old ones extended. By next year there would be more than a hundred rooms.

As he ate his sandwich, washing it down with leftover coffee from the bottom compartment of his lunch pail, Mike's thoughts, as usual, turned to Andy. Andy could be proud of a father who was both a mule driver and shot-fireman, a father strong enough to work at two jobs.

The miners, too, viewed the shot-firer with due respect. His was a dangerous job, and without him there would be no coal to load out the following morning, for rules of safety forbade all miners from touching off shots of their own during working hours. A windy shot—one that blew the tamping of coal dust from the drilled hole instead of exploding behind the coal itself—could easily ignite the resultant cloud of dust as if it were gunpowder. Once ignited, the cloud would hungrily suck in a dust-laden draft, expand, and go roaring down the entry and into the other entries, feeding itself as it went, charring and destroying everything in its path, and leaving an oxygenless void in its wake. Such explosions were few, yet the possibility was always present.

Mike tossed the crusty part of his sandwich to one side and took a final gulp of coffee from the pail. Well, the sooner he got at the job ahead, the quicker he would get home to Maria, a hot bath, supper, and, finally, bed.

He picked up the light and unscrewed its bottom section. In the resulting total darkness, he shook out the spent carbine, poured in fresh granules, spat upon them, heard them hiss, and quickly screwed the bottom back into place. He cupped his palm over the reflector an instant to accumulate gas, roweled the automatic lighter with the heel of his hand, and popped the light into a six-inch lance of flame.

His injured knee paining him at each step, he picked his way across the switch rails at the parting, and headed toward the entry in which he and Molly had toiled during the day. The last cars to be brought down from above showed fresh accumulations of snow, which meant that the storm had not abated with the approach of night.

As usual, Old Davy's room was neat and trim, props well-set and tightly capped, fresh rails extended, and refuse and dirt loaded out. Mike swept the 30-foot face of the room with his light and saw at a glance the three pieces of torn newspaper dangling there, each piece marking the location of a shot so that the shot-firer would not have to waste precious moments searching for dark fuses hanging from their black background or, worse still, fail to find one and leave a shot unfired.

Light in hand, Mike picked up the first of the three fuses, speared flame into its split end, and saw it sputter into immediate life. The second fuse gave him a bit of trouble, and he had to peel the split ends farther back to expose more of the powder within before it responded to the touch of the flame. He had no fear of the first shot going off before he finished the work at hand, for the diggers always left enough fuse footage to insure the firer two or three minutes of safety—just in case he needed it. Seconds later, the third fuse lit; he limped from the room and into the entry.

Four shots showed in Hank's room, and Mike touched them off in rapid succession.

Halfway up the grade where the slag of slate across the rails had tumbled him earlier that day, Mike felt new pains begin to stab at his knee, and he was forced to slow his pace. By the time he reached the top of the little hill, he heard the sudden *whoomph* of one of the shots in Old Davy's room. Then, seconds later, *whoomph-whoomph* as the other two went off almost simultaneously. From now on, those jarring, muffled sounds would follow him through the darkness from entry to entry until his task was completed.

The Spores' room was cluttered, as usual. Props reached from floor to roof in crazy, unstable angles, and the floor was littered with the dust and debris of the day's work. There was a haphazard gob pile beside one pillar, and from it protruded the neck of a pint flask. Either Joe had been bringing whiskey to the mine with him or he had simply used the bottle to carry water for his carbide light.

Mike limped over the strewn floor to the first of four shot-markers. The fuse that dangled from the black face was scarcely more than a foot in length, and the split in its end was much longer than necessary. Mike shook his head. Probably an eight-foot hole with four feet of blasting powder! Trying to move as much coal as possible with a single shot! Or trying to save a penny on fuse!

A touch of the light brought the fuse into instant life, and Mike took three crouching steps to the right to pick up the second fuse. It was properly split, but it failed to respond to the pencil of hot flame. The powder seemed moist, as if the fuse had been handled carelessly with sweaty fingers. Mike rolled the split ends farther back and tried again. Then he held the tongue of flame steadily in the split, burning and searing, until the powder finally began to sputter and hiss in an acceptable manner.

The end of the third fuse was blunt, unsplit. Mike fished from his pocket the sharp knife he always carried for such emergencies, opened it, and began to make the cut. The fuse was wet. He lopped off four inches of it and began to make a second cut.

It was then that alarming thoughts began to hammer suddenly at his brain. What if one of the Spores had deliberately set a shot fuse in that first hole, a fuse that reached back into the face only a foot or so instead of the customary three or four feet? Instead of the usual slow-acting powder that pushed the coal out in desirable chunks, what if there was rock-shattering dynamite in that hole that would send the coal flying in death-dealing splinters and shards?

Even as the thoughts went through his head, he was scrambling away from the face, trying to get to his feet. It was best not to take chances. He could stop and fire the remaining two shots on his return trip down the entry . . .

Mike felt, rather than heard, the sudden blast that rocked the room. A giant concussion of air staggered him, something slammed into the side of his head with stunning force, and he felt himself falling backward—down, down, as if into some deep, black pit that was filled with flying props and crashing slate.

Half-stunned, he tried to roll out of the pit, tried to push himself up, but something was wrong. Something was holding him down. The air was heavily laden with coal dust and the acrid odor of spent dynamite, and there was a feeble glow of light that formed a pale nimbus about him. He turned his head toward the source of the glow and saw his light lying on its side a few inches from his hand, the flame at the end of its tube reduced to a mere button of yellow. He reached out for it and felt a sudden pain stab through his left leg. Stark realization swept over him. He was pinned down, and the fuse of the second shot was burning its way into the face of coal.

He clutched up his light, clicked the water valve a notch or two farther open, shook the button of yellow into a white flame, and made a quick survey of his surroundings.

His left leg lay in a jagged pile of coal and rubble, across it was a fallen prop, and pressing down hard on the prop was a thick slab of slate. Another slab hung precariously down from the roof directly above him.

Mike didn't know if the blast had knocked him unconscious or not. His head pained. He couldn't remember, couldn't think straight. Even now, the fuse of that second shot could be sputtering just inches—seconds—from its explosive charge, a charge that could cut him to ribbons, engulf him in rubble, and bring more slate crashing down.

He placed his foot against the prop and pushed. The prop rocked back and forth, bringing stabbing jolts of pain to the leg beneath. Crouching his body closer, he placed his foot against the slate and gave a mighty shove that was strengthened by panic. The round prop acted as a roller, and the slab of slate went slithering away.

Freeing his leg quickly, he spun about to hands and knees and began scrambling over the debris away from the face. The second explosion hurled him from the mouth of the room and sent him sprawling across the rails in the entry.

The light flipped away from his fingers, went out, and a silent wave of total blackness swept over him.

Mike lay for a time where he had fallen, breathing heavily, wondering if he dared try to move. He finally rolled slowly to a sitting position and began patting the floor on either side, his fingers searching for the light, but even as he searched, he knew that the chance of finding it among the rubble was remote.

He slowly drew up his left leg and began exploring it with his fingers. His trousers and underwear were torn, wet, and slippery, and there was a long, jagged gash in the calf of his leg. He couldn't tell how bad the wound was, but his fingers told him that it was deep and bleeding. Bad enough!

Alone in the darkness, he felt beaten and depressed. Now he would lose work, lose money—something no miner could afford in the wintertime—and all because of the stupidity and greed of one man. Had Joe really tried to kill him? Or was he merely trying to make things so dangerous for him that he would finally knuckle under? Either way, Joe had accomplished one thing; he would have a different mule driver in the morning, maybe one that would be afraid of him.

Mike had no fear of any further physical danger. Even without a light, there was no chance of becoming lost. He could easily follow the rails back to the parting and to the slope that would lead him up into the world above.

But, no, he must not do that! Andy would not respect a father who ran away from the job before him. He must find the light, fire the rest of the shots. Otherwise, the miners would come to work in the morning and find no coal. A wasted day!

He began searching for the light again, crawling from side to side, exploring each jagged piece of coal with his fingers. Head throbbing and leg filled with pain, he finally rolled over to his stomach for a moment of rest. It was then that his nose picked up the tangy, unmistakable odor of gas escaping from the unlit tube of the carbide light. Somewhere directly ahead! Hands groping, he inched forward until his eager fingers finally clutched the object of their search. He swung to a sitting position, heeled the wheel of the flint lighter, and saw the white flame shatter the darkness about him.

His first thought was his wounded leg. He held the light close to it and peeled back the bloody and torn trousers and underwear. The wound was long, deep, jagged, and dirty, and blood was still oozing from it. He sat looking at it, wondering what he should do. There was a water hydrant back at the parting, back by the mule barn. He could go there and wash the wound; but if he went back now, he would merely have to retrace his steps to fire the remaining shots in the entry. Best to fire the shots first, then fix the leg before going on into the next entry.

He pulled himself up along the rough wall of the tunnel to a standing position and stood for a moment with eyes closed, waiting for the dizziness to leave his head and for a sense of balance to return. Finally, he tested his leg with the weight of his body. Excruciating pain stabbed him, but the leg held firm. He began hobbling forward along the littered rails. "Maybe we make 'im now, Andy," he whispered.

When he finally emerged from the entry and reached the mule barn, exhaustion had laid hold of him. He staggered to the hydrant and sat down on the wooden watering trough to rest. The muttering of the mules and their warm smell soothed him, and a darkness blacker than the pit itself began to creep over him. He felt himself drifting comfortably away into some sweet oblivion, an oblivion where there was no more work to be done, no pain, no waiting drifts of snow to flounder through. He struggled against the feeling and finally succeeded in shaking the sticky shadows from his brain. Then he bared his wound and extended his leg across the trough beneath the mouth of the hydrant. The water was cold and numbing, but it sent a refreshing tingle through his body that partially revived him from impending lethargy.

The wound was caked with dried blood mingled with coal dust, and new blood was seeping from it. He washed it as best he could, trying to think what he could use as a bandage, but there was no material available except feed sacks, burlap, and his own rough and dirty clothing. He would wait, think of something later on. There was work to be done, shots still to be fired in the rooms along the other entries . . .

It seemed hours before he finally succeeded in dragging himself back to the parting, his task completed. He sat down on a powder keg to rest, and exhaustion swept over him again in a great, smothering wave. He wanted nothing more than to lie down on the inviting floor and let deep, warm shadows engulf him. The miners would find him there in the morning, see to it that he got safely home . . .

He didn't know if he had drifted away into a half-sleep or not, but he found himself suddenly wide awake. Maria! She would be wondering about him, worrying. He was already late, later than he had ever been before. She would feel certain that some terrible tragedy had befallen him in the mine, or that he had got lost in the storm. She might awaken the neighbors, organize a search party. Or, worse still, she might come alone in search for him, come trudging through the storm.

He couldn't let either of those things happen. He would have to get home under his own power, somehow. He couldn't afford to be found helpless, unable to do his work. He would have to get home, get his leg looked after, get some sleep, and get back on the job in the morning. To be off work because of illness might even cost him his job!

He began coughing, and the scene about him began to grow dimmer. Were the dust clouds from the exploded shots catching up with him, or was something happening to his eyes? Whatever it was, he realized now that if he expected to get home, he would have to start while he still had strength enough left.

He cast his light toward the mouth of the slope. The incline seemed steeper than before, insurmountable, and even if he did succeed in staggering to the top, there were drifts of snow to be taken into consideration.

Yet he had to try. There was little else he could do. Andy would expect his father to make an effort, not lie down and shift responsibility to others.

He needed a crutch, something to lean on. He swept his light over the spidery rails of the entry. There was nothing there except a few piles of cumbersome props. Perhaps in the mule barn . . .

Thoughts of the mule barn brought a new idea creeping into his brain. The idea was hazy and rather mixed up, but the more he pondered it, the more promise it held.

Minutes later, he came stumbling from the barn, leading Molly by her halter. "Whoa-up, girl," he said. "Steady." Then he brought the powder keg to her side, mounted it, and forced his injured leg over her shaggy back. She tossed her head around to look inquiringly at him. This was something new to her, something quite beyond the normal call of duty.

The light dangling from his left hand, he circled her neck with his other arm and rested his cheek comfortably against her. He lay there a moment, waiting for the giddiness to clear from his head.

"Hi-yup!" he commanded, presently. Molly swung to the right, toward the entry in which she was accustomed to toil.

"Haw!" shouted Mike. "Haw! Hi-yup!"

Molly straightened her course to the left, entered the mouth of the slope, and began carefully picking her way up and over the unfamiliar pattern of ties that clutched at her feet.

Mike lay low upon her, keeping his head down and his body flat to avoid the rough beams of the roof.

The moist warmth of the mine slid slowly back and away, and crisper, colder air took its place. Then the air became cold, and the timbers and beams of the slope showed white and ghostly where the moisture from the mine had turned to hoarfrost upon them.

Mike, his head dangling against the side of Molly's neck, sensed rather than felt that she had ceased her forward motion. He cast the rays of his light ahead. A drift of white lay across their path, and more snow was whirling and eddying. Molly laid her stubby ears back and made a whimpering sound through her nose, and Mike felt the quick shudder that rippled through her body as she studied the unfamiliar world of white that lay before her.

"It will be all right, Molly," he promised her. "You will sleep with neighbor's cow in warm barn tonight. Hi-yup!"

Molly stepped obediently forward into the drift, head lowered, ears flattened, shod hooves seeking purchase in the alien substance that sought to mire her legs. She went gingerly ahead, step after step, eyes blinking against the white flakes that gyrated blindingly about her head.

Mike could see nothing now save the snow-filled nimbus of yellow that pressed in about him. He rose higher on Molly's back, swept his light about and finally hooked it into the shield of his cap—where the wind promptly guttered it and blew it out. Then there was only the whiteness of the drifts beneath, the blackness above, and the rush and whip of flakes upon his face.

Directly to his right and down in the little valley lay the hidden houses of the camp. All he had to do was to turn in that direction and keep going downhill until he could find their black hulks.

"Gee, Molly!" he commanded. "Gee, girl!" And then, as Molly turned sharply to the right, "Hi-yup, Molly! Hi-yup!"

Molly floundered ahead and went to her belly in a drift.

"Hi-yup, girl!" Mike encouraged. "Hi-yup! We make 'im yet! You see."

Molly struggled forward and found firmer footing, only to plunge knee-deep in another drift a few feet farther on.

Mike shielded his eyes with a hand and tried to get his bearings, but the swirling snow shut out everything except the immediate drifts beneath him, the drifts that pulled at Molly's trembling legs. He could not see the slope of the land. The undulation of drifts had hidden the contour beneath a rolling blanket of mystery. There was no up, no down, just billows of white that lost themselves in almost instant nothingness.

Molly stumbled, and Mike fell forward to her neck. He clung there with both arms while blackness and confusion hammered at his brain. "Steady, girl," he whispered. "Steady." Then complete lethargy swept over him, closing in upon him, severing mind from body. "Steady," he whispered again, and slid slowly from her back into a soft bed of oblivion.

Mike awakened to find himself engulfed in a bright blanket of white. It took a while for his eyes to adjust sufficiently to find that the whiteness about him was the clean, soft sheets of his own bed and the brilliant sunlight that streamed through a window. He hadn't seen sunlight for more than a month, and its glare hurt his eyes. He squinted and shifted his gaze upward. Maria was standing beside him, her dark, shy eyes filled with anxiety.

"You—you all right?"

Mike shifted his position tentatively. "Y-yes . . . I-I guess so."

"You have company," she whispered. "I bring him in."

She left, and a moment later the doorway was filled with the bulk of Big Matt Trimbull, mine superintendent. His face was square and lined and the hair at his temples, once red, was a rusty gray. He carried his great mackinaw coat and fur cap over one arm. "You feel a little better now?" he asked.

"Yes," Mike said, hurriedly. "I be back to work tomorrow. Right away!"

Big Matt sat down in a chair and let his coat and cap spill to the floor beside him. "I think not," he said. "Doc says you have a very bad leg, lost a lot of blood. You stay in bed. Rest. We have a man to take your place."

Mike nodded. Naturally, a new man would have to take over, take both his jobs . . .

"We found out this morning what happened to you last night," Big Matt went on. "The trace of dynamite in Joe Spore's room, the two unfired shots, your fuse knife lying on the floor, the blood. And Joe is no longer working for us. He is a dangerous man. Besides what he did to you, he might have caused an explosion, ruined the entire mine."

Mike was silent. He was thinking about the loss of his two jobs, wondering how long he would be without work.

"Some of the boys will stop in to see you tonight after work," said Big Matt. "They want to thank you. If you had not fired the shots last night, the mine could not have worked today."

Mike shifted his position to ease the pain that was gnawing at his leg and felt the great tiredness begin to steal over him again. "Andy like that," he said, a faint smile touching his lips. "Andy like that miners want to come see me."

Big Matt picked up his cap and coat and got to his feet. "Your wife and the neighbor men would never have found you last night in that snow drift," he said, "if it hadn't been for the mule standing over you, marking the spot where you fell."

"Molly is all right?"

Big Matt nodded. "She is taking the day off and has an extra measure of oats. I'll go now so you can rest and get back to work soon." He stood for a moment looking down at Mike, wondering how in the world the injured man could possibly have persuaded a stubborn mine mule to carry him up out of the mine on her back and through a wintry blast of wind and snow. "You certainly must have a way with mules," he said.

Mike grinned. "Maybe we understand each other," he said. "We both square-heads."

"Whatever it is," said Big Matt, "I'm going to need you. The entries will be worked all summer to enlarge the mine, and by next fall we'll need many new mules. You will break them, train them, and help build new cars. Work all summer."

Happiness mingled suddenly with the great tiredness that had settled over him, pushing him down. Mike felt his eyes begin to close as if of their own accord. "Andy will like that," he said, drowsily. "Andy will be proud that I work all summer." He scarcely finished the sentence before sleep claimed him, leaving a lingering smile upon his lips.

At the kitchen door, Big Matt shrugged into his great coat and began pulling on his heavy boots. "You feed him well, Mrs. Kovchec," he said. "And make him rest. He'll be well again in no time."

"Yes," Maria said, shyly, trying to hide her embarrassment. Never before in her entire life had such a great personage as a mine superintendent graced her home. He had made a special trip through the snow—and she had been too busy to tidy up the house.

Big Matt straightened up from his boots. "This Andy," he said, questioningly. "Mike spoke his name a couple of times."

Maria looked at the floor. "Andy is—" She hesitated. "I don't know how to say. Andy is—well, he is what makes Mike work hard, try always to be good man."

Big Matt nodded. "I understand," he said, covering her confusion.

"If he had lived, Andy would be nearly fourteen now . . ."

Big Matt retraced the trail he had made through the sun-sparkled drifts. Once he stopped, shook his head, and then continued on again. He, too, had once had a son. But it had been so very long ago . . .

HAL ELLSON

The Marrow of Justice

The coffin was a plain one, finished in the shop of Carlos Martinez, without frills, stark naked wood of soft pine. Harsh sunlight splintered off it as the men carried it through the miserable street, treading its dust, stones, and the scattered fire of tangerine peels withering in the heat.

It was a day of flame but, in this land of perpetual sun, not unseasonable. No more than death. The poor in their shacks and crumbling adobes knew its ghastly visits all too frequently. Funerals were commonplace and all of a kind. A plain pine box for the deceased, four men to carry it, and a small group of mourners following.

A vast crowd followed the coffin of Rosa Belmonte, the third young girl in the city to die by violation. Half-starved dogs with their ribs showing, children, toddlers, and beggars amidst the crowd lent it a pseudo air of carnival which was diluted by the somber faces of adults and a muffled silence under which anger awaited eruption.

The police felt it, a news photographer sighted it in his camera. Detective Fiala was aware of the same phenomenon, but unconcerned with the crowd as such. His eyes sought only one man—the murderer who, through guilt or morbid disposition, might be lurking here.

No face riveted his attention till he noticed the limousine, with the crowd breaking around it and the Chief of Police, José Santiago. He was sitting beside his chauffeur, face bloated and dark, tinted glasses concealing incongruous blue eyes that resembled twin stones and reflected the basic nature of the man.

Without the uniform he might be the one I'm looking for, Fiala thought, turning away and moving on with the sullen crowd that refused to acknowledge the naked violence of the sun.

The funeral went off without incident, the police were relieved, Chief Santiago satisfied. His chauffeur returned him to the Municipal building, the location of police headquarters.

As he entered his office with Captain Torres, the phone rang. He picked it up, listened, then dismissed Captain Torres with a wave of his hand. Frowning now, he spoke to his caller, Victor Quevedo, mayor of the city and the one who had "made" him. These two were friends of a sort, but the conversation that ensued between them now was strictly business.

The murder of Rosa Belmonte, with the killer not apprehended, as in both previous murders, had created grave criticism of the police which, in turn, reflected upon Quevedo, exposing him to the machinations of his political enemies. This was the gist of Quevedo's complaint along with his sharp demand that Santiago do something and do it fast.

"Do what?" Santiago said.

"Get the killer before midnight."

Astounded, Santiago hesitated, stuttered inanely, and finally managed to say, "But, Victor—"

Quevedo cut him off sharply. "I am being embarrassed, politically and otherwise," he snapped. "If you wish to continue as Chief of Police, find the killer. Don't, and you're finished."

Sweating profusely, Santiago dropped the phone and sat down. Slowly, with trembling hands, he lit a cigarette and dispersed a cloud of smoke. His thoughts were in chaos, dark face swollen to bursting. Slowly the agitation within him receded. Behind his tinted glasses his cold eyes lit up as a face focused in his mind.

He crushed his cigarette, arose, opened the door, called Captain Torres into the office, and gave him his orders. "Pick up Manuel Domingo for the murder of Rosa Belmonte."

Manuel Domingo's criminal activities were long known to the police—but murder? Captain Torres raised his brows in surprise.

"Are you sure you have the right man?" he asked.

"Are you doubting me, or my source of information?" Santiago wanted to know, asserting both the authority of his office and intimating that the phone call he'd received was the "voice" of a reliable informer.

Captain Torres flushed and retreated to the door. From there he said, "I'll pick up Manuel Domingo personally."

At nine that evening, a black sky threatened the city and the lacy jacarandas stirred to a faint errant wind from the mountains where yellow lightning ignited the empty heavens. Behind the Municipal building four bars faced the plaza, loud voices broke from each of them.

Saturday night was just beginning and musicians lolled on the plaza benches, barefoot boys shined shoes, hawked blood-red and dove-white roses on trays of cardboard, like everyone else, forgetting Rosa Belmonte.

It was on this scene that Captain Torres arrived with three of his men after an intensive and fruitless search of all the usual haunts of the criminal Manuel Domingo.

Captain Torres was convinced that Domingo had fled the city when chance directed his eyes to a bench where two shoeshine boys vied for the privilege of doing the shoes of Detective Fiala.

Granting them each a shoe, Fiala looked up to see the strapping, youthful Captain Torres and his three men confronting him.

The latter were innocuous fellows, Captain Torres an arrogant whelp, but hardly that now. He needed help and Fiala, whom he despised and who despised him, might provide the information he needed so badly.

"I am looking for Manuel Domingo," Torres announced. "Perhaps you know his whereabouts?"

With a derisive smile, Fiala nodded toward a bar directly across the street. "Manuel Domingo is in there. You're picking him up?"

"For the murder of Rosa Belmonte," Captain Torres replied and turned on his heels.

Fiala sat where he was. Half a minute later Manuel Domingo came through the door of the bar across the street, accompanied by Captain Torres and his three men. All five passed through the plaza and entered police headquarters.

Fiala, who had gone off duty early that day, lit a cigarette and shook his head. No matter what, Manuel Domingo's fate was sealed, the murder was solved. Tomorrow the newspapers would be filled with it.

In disgust, Fiala flicked his cigarette to the gutter and noticed the group of men who'd come from the bar across the street. Anger echoed in their voices; word spread quickly around the plaza: Manuel Domingo had been picked up for the murder of Rosa Belmonte. Manuel Domingo . . .

Under the black angry sky a crowd began to converge on police headquarters, but too late to give vent to its feelings, for the brief interrogation of Manuel Domingo was already completed. Guarded by police, he stepped to the sidewalk and was quickly ushered into a waiting car.

Into a second car stepped Chief of Police Santiago and Captain Torres. With an escort of ten motorcycle policemen, both cars roared off toward the scene of the crime, in the desert several miles from the city.

The cavalcade soon reached it, the glaring lights of cars and motorcycles focused on a tall yucca beside the road. At its foot Luis Espina, a gatherer of fiber obtained from a small spiny desert plant, had discovered the body of Rosa Belmonte.

As Manuel Domingo stepped from the car, his face took on a ghastly hue, perhaps because of the lights, perhaps out of fear now that he was at the scene of the crime. Whatever he felt, he said nothing: he appeared dazed.

A sharp command from Captain Torres sent the policemen into a wide semi-circle, with guns drawn to prevent an attempted escape. That done, Captain Torres walked to the edge of the road with Santiago and Manuel Domingo. There, on orders, he took up position, while the prisoner and Santiago proceeded to the foot of the yucca.

Once there, Manuel Domingo stopped and stood like a soldier ordered to attention. Headlights impaled him in a glaring crossfire. A sheer wall of black enveloped this luminous area. Now the brief interrogation which Santiago had conducted at headquarters continued. He was seen to gesture; his voice in an unintelligible murmur carried only to Captain Torres.

Manuel Domingo turned, spoke for the first time since stepping into the car. He was frightened, the terrible black sky threatened, he did not trust Santiago.

"Get me out of this," he said, "or else."

"Quiet, you fool. This is routine. You've been accused."

"Who accuses me? Name him."

"Shut up and listen."

Manuel Domingo came to attention again. His chest heaved, chin lifted, then suddenly he bolted in an attempt to escape. Calmly Santiago fired from the hip.

Domingo seemed to be running on air. The weight of his body carried him forward, then his legs buckled and he plunged forward to sprawl on the desert floor.

Moments later Santiago stood over him and fired another shot as the others closed in.

The black night enveloped the desolate scene as the cavalcade roared off toward the city. Santiago glanced at the clock on the dashboard and settled back. It was still early, the issue settled. The mayor no longer had reason to be embarrassed.

As Santiago smiled to himself, Captain Torres turned and said, "Officially, we know now that Manuel Domingo was guilty of murdering Rosa Belmonte, but—"

"You don't think he killed the girl?"

"Do you?"

"No."

"Then why did he run?"

"I told him we couldn't protect him from the mob, that if he ran, I'd cover him and let him escape because I knew he was innocent."

"But you shot him down."

Santiago put a cigarette to his lips. "I had no alternative," he answered, flicking his lighter, and the cavalcade moved on toward the lights of the city.

In the early morning the body of the murderer Manuel Domingo, naked but for a white sheet that covered the lower half of his body, lay on a long table beneath a tree in a small plaza near the center of the city for all to see and take warning. Flies came with the heat; the light brought crowds.

All through the day the people of the city filed past the dead man and at dusk he was taken away, mourned by none.

Here the matter would have ended, interred along with Manuel Domingo, but for Detective Fiala, who knew one thing beyond doubt: Domingo hadn't killed the girl. With the murderer still at large, on his own time, Fiala conducted an investigation which quickly proved fruitful. That done, he appeared at the Municipal building, asked to see Mayor Quevedo, and was informed that he was at lunch with several men of importance.

Obtaining the name of the restaurant, Fiala went there, seated himself at a table next to Quevedo's party, bowed, and, in a voice soft enough to elude the ears of the others, said, "If I may have a word. It's a matter of grave importance which concerns you."

Such was his manner that Quevedo quickly nodded. When he and his companions finished eating, he contrived an excuse for remaining behind and sat down at Fiala's table.

"Now," he said with some anxiety, "what is this matter of importance which concerns me?"

"I'm afraid it's much too important to discuss here."

"In that case, we'll go to my office."

Fiala nodded and both of them rose and went out the door. A few minutes later they faced each other across Quevedo's ornate hand-carved desk. Quevedo offered a cigarette. Fiala refused it and presented his case, bluntly informing him that the Chief of Police had murdered Rosa Belmonte.

"A very serious charge," Quevedo said, turning pale. "But can you prove it?"

Fiala nodded and described how he'd gone to see Luis Espina, the fiber-gatherer who'd discovered the body of the dead girl. With a series of tactful questions he'd finally gotten the old man to admit that he'd actually witnessed the murder.

"If this is true," Quevedo put in, "why didn't Espina come forward and say so?"

"He couldn't," Fiala replied, "because at the time of the murder he didn't recognize Santiago. All he knew was that the killer drove off in a blue and white Cadillac. That was significant. I continued to question him and he produced a vivid description of the driver, but not his identity. That came later when I pressed him.

"He then admitted that he'd watched the spectacle last night. The lights drew him from his house, and he saw Santiago gun down Manuel Domingo. That's when he recognized him as the murderer of Rosa Belmonte."

Quevedo nodded and said, "The word of a confused old man. His story won't hold water. Besides, Domingo admitted his guilt at the scene of the crime by attempting to escape."

"Admitted his guilt?" Fiala smiled and shook his head. "That was the one fact I knew from the beginning, that he wasn't guilty. You see, Manuel Domingo couldn't have killed Rosa Belmonte. He wasn't in the city that day. I know. I trailed him to San Rafael with the expectation of catching him in one of his activities, dealing in marijuana.

"He remained at a bar in San Rafael till evening, and his contact never appeared. Perhaps he knew I'd trailed him. At any rate, the deal didn't come off. At nine he headed back to the city. By that time Rosa Belmonte was dead."

At this point Quevedo was convinced of the truth of Fiala's charge, but one thing was unclear. "Why did Santiago pick Domingo for a victim?" he wanted to know.

Fiala smiled again and clarified the point. "One," he said, holding up a finger. "Domingo's reputation was bad; the charge appeared to suit his character. Two: Santiago and Domingo were partners. Domingo controlled the red-light district, with the help of Santiago. They quarreled over money. Santiago claimed that Domingo was holding out on him. He probably was, so Santiago found it doubly convenient to eliminate him."

Quevedo nodded. It was all clear now, too clear. He frowned and his face paled. If revealed, Santiago's terrible act would threaten his own position. Frightened, his eyes met Fiala's.

The detective had read his thoughts and understood his predicament. "Of course, Santiago should be brought to justice," he said, "but to arrest him would be embarrassing to you."

Badly shaken, Quevedo nodded, but he was still alert. Fiala's statement implied more than it said.

"What do you suggest?" Quevedo asked.

Fiala moistened his lower lip with his tongue. "Speak to Santiago," he answered. "Give him the facts."

"And if he denies them?"

"If he does, tell him he'll be placed under arrest. After that has taken place—" Here Fiala shrugged. "You cannot guarantee his safety from the mob. I think he'll understand."

"Understand what?"

"Call him and see."

Quevedo glanced at the phone and hesitated, giving Fiala the opportunity to rise from his chair. "I'm going for coffee. I'll be back," he said, and left Quevedo to deliver his terrible message.

Ten minutes later he returned to the mayor's office. Quevedo was still troubled. He said nothing. Fiala sat and reached for his cigarettes. At that moment the phone rang. Quevedo picked up the instrument, listened briefly, then placed the phone back on its cradle.

"Santiago just shot himself," he announced.

Having foreseen this, Fiala merely shrugged and said, "But of course. He had no alternative."

At this point, Quevedo saw Fiala in a new light. The fellow was devilishly clever and had saved him from his enemies. "I am in your debt," he said.

"Not at all," replied Fiala.

"Ah, but I am," Quevedo insisted. "Besides, I have no Police Chief now. Would you consider the office?"

Fiala grinned and, to the consternation of Quevedo, shook his head.

"But why not?" said Quevedo. "I don't understand. Think of what it means to be Chief of Police."

"In this city," Fiala replied, "it means to have much power, and power corrupts."

"It would corrupt you?" Quevedo asked.

"I'm made of flesh and blood. Perhaps it might, but I doubt it."

"Then why refuse?"

"Because the job doesn't interest me. It's as simple as that," Fiala answered, and rose from his chair to light a cigarette. With that, he walked to the door.

Still puzzled, Quevedo watched him, then said, "But you must want something. What do I owe you?"

His hand on the doorknob, Fiala turned. "Nothing," he answered. "Just be more careful when you pick the new Chief of Police."

IRVING SCHIFFER

Innocent Witness

The detective was waiting for her as she emerged from the office building at five o'clock. Suddenly in the midst of the homegoers he was standing before her, very tall, a young man with a surprisingly gentle voice and considerate manner.

"Hello, Julie," he said.

She was twenty, a dark-haired girl who worked as a secretary in the financial district of New York. She was one of many, not much different at first glance from the girls who sat at the desks around her, pretty enough, not very sophisticated, a girl everyone liked, accustomed to anonymity. She was, above all things, not used to being singled out by detectives; and she looked about self-consciously as the other girls passed, certain that some of them recognized Sergeant Ruderman from his visit to the office that morning.

"I wonder," he said, as if sensing her thoughts, "is there somewhere we can talk privately?"

She nodded gratefully. "Yes, there's a diner next door."

Bill's Diner was one of those trolley-shaped affairs with a long counter, a few booths, and very good food. They sat in a booth, Julie facing the rear, and he signaled for two coffees. She looked at the telephone booths and thought that perhaps, if she were going to be late for dinner, she ought to call her mother. He said nothing until after coffee had arrived.

"Julie—Miss Stevens—something has been bothering me all day. This morning, when I spoke to you in your office—"

"Yes?"

"I had the feeling you wanted to tell me something. About your boss, Mr. Turner, and his wife."

She shook her head. She sipped at the coffee so that she could look away from him.

"I told you everything, Sergeant Ruderman."

"Did you?" If he weren't a policeman, his easy tone of voice could be considered that of a friend, even a lover. He was a nice man, she thought, and he was probably very good at his job. "You know what I think," he said, smiling faintly over his steaming coffee mug. "I think you're a very confused girl. Maybe you've a misdirected sense of loyalty. Come to think of it, I like a person who's loyal."

She didn't fall into that trap. "I really can't think of anything I haven't told you," she insisted.

"About the Turners . . . they weren't getting along too well. Some of their friends have told us that. Did they have a blowup or a serious argument in the last few days?"

Julie shrugged. She could tell he didn't believe her, but he wasn't angry. He was an even-tempered man, and he was calm as he finished his coffee, looking at her all the while. Then suddenly he glanced at his watch and placed some change on the table for the waiter. He handed her a card.

"That's my number at the station. You can call at any hour." His grin was a pleasant surprise. "Just in case you find you have something to tell me, I mean. Now, will you kindly write *your* name and address on this other card?"

"My address?" she said warily.

"Sure. Have you ever had a date with a detective?"

She thought of his motives, of his job.

"Don't worry," he said. "You won't hear from me until *after* the case is closed. I don't mix business with pleasure. And I don't meet girls like you every day."

She liked him, there was no getting away from that. And the straightforward, almost vulnerable way he looked at her was convincing enough for any girl. She filled in the back of the card and handed it to him.

"You'll hear from me," he said. "Or maybe—who can tell?—maybe I'll hear from you first. Goodnight, Julie."

After he left, she barely moved. A woman walked past to enter one of the phone booths. Abstractedly, Julie watched the stranger's lips through the glass door and thought again that she ought to call her mother; but she couldn't move.

Yes, there was something. The detective was right. It was not only the problem between Mr. Turner and his wife. About that she had lied. It was something else. But *what*?

She sighed. It occurred to her that Sergeant Ruderman might even believe there had been something between *her* and Mr. Turner. Well, there hadn't been. Not really. Mary kept hinting that there was, but Mary was always carrying on . . . like yesterday morning at the office—Wednesday—just before Mrs. Turner called.

Mary was Mr. Cassidy's secretary. He was one of several vice-presidents at Empire Investment—married, an outrageous wolf. Sometimes it seemed as though Mary, blonde and vivacious, led him on—just a little. On Wednesday morning, there was a lot of flirtatious patter before Mr. Cassidy got past Julie's and Mary's adjacent desks to enter his own office.

"Sometimes I'm inclined to forget that he's married," Mary remarked, once his door had closed behind him.

"You're just a lot of big talk," said Julie.

"Oh, I don't know. Married men are just men who happen to be married. Don't be so naïve, Julie. All these vice-presidents with their private telephone lines . . . I'll bet it isn't all business they talk about behind those closed doors. And I'll bet if your Mr. Turner gave you a tumble, you wouldn't exactly fight him off. I can tell when a girl has a crush—Oops, get to work, here's your boss now . . ."

Mr. Turner was as unlike Mr. Cassidy as a man could be. In his middle thirties, the company's youngest vice-president, he was clean-cut, methodical, and one hundred percent business. He walked by the girls' desks quickly, offered a brusque good morning, then disappeared into his office.

"Well, I have to admit he's good-looking," Mary sighed. "But did you ever see his wife? Ten years older if she's a day. And she looks like something the cat dragged in."

"No, she doesn't," Julie objected.

"Yes, she does. And everyone here knows he married her strictly for her money. I remember when she was just another rich client—only six months ago—a born old maid if ever I saw one."

"I remember her very well," said Julie. "She was just an unhappy, lonely woman."

"Sure. But then handsome boy took over the account and—wham!—they get married. One of these days, you'll see, he'll quit working, retire for life . . . on her money, of course."

Julie's telephone rang. Saved by the bell, she thought, reaching for it. But it was quite a shock—speak of the devil—to learn who was calling. "Julie, this is Mrs. Turner."

"Oh, good morning. Just one moment, I'll tell Mr. Turner you're calling."

"No, no, no, Julie. I don't even want him to *know* I've called. I want to speak to *you*. Can we meet for lunch? I must have a talk with you."

"With me?" There was no mistaking the urgency in the woman's voice, Julie reflected. "Well, yes, of course, Mrs. Turner. What is it you want to speak to me a—?"

A burst of static interrupted the girl as the intercom box on her desk came to life. The signal light was on.

"Julie!" Mr. Turner's voice crackled.

For one eerie moment, Julie experienced an inexplicable panic. She stared at the intercom box and then at the telephone receiver in her hand, realizing that if Mrs. Turner spoke again her husband would hear. Quickly, Julie clamped her hand over the telephone mouthpiece. Then just as quickly she realized she had covered the wrong end to shut off Mrs. Turner's voice, and switched to cover the earpiece.

"Julie, will you bring me the file on Sloban Company," Richard Turner's voice directed.

"Yes, right away," said the girl.

She waited until he turned off the intercom, then spoke hurriedly into the telephone. "I have to go now."

"Yes, I heard," said the woman.

"I'll call you back in a few minutes," Julie promised. "I'd better use a telephone outside. Are you home, Mrs. Turner?"

"Yes. Please don't forget. I'll be waiting."

Mary's eyebrows were two question marks, but Julie had no time to explain. She moved to the filing cabinets behind the long line of typists' desks and quickly located the Sloban file. Feeling strangely conspiratorial, she pictured Mrs. Turner in her Washington Square apartment, an overweight, somehow pitiful woman, waiting for the return call. Her expression revealing none of these thoughts, Julie knocked on Mr. Turner's door.

As she came into his room, Richard Turner was speaking on his private telephone. His gray eyes barely flicked in his secretary's direction while he continued to charm his widowed client, Mrs. Sloban.

". . . Yes, Vera . . . I realize you don't want to take risks with the principal. Empire Investment wouldn't allow such recklessness. I mean, we'd certainly advise against it . . ."

Julie gazed at the sharp, handsome profile. As always, it did something to her equilibrium she preferred not to acknowledge. There were two telephones on his desk, one an extension of the phone on her desk, the other for "confidential" contact with clients. Julie could remember when Mrs. Turner was one of those clients, a lonely heiress, who rated long conversations as he was now indulging Mrs. Sloban. Marriage, thought Julie, as she placed the Sloban folder on his desk, can certainly cool a man's ardor . . . if there had been any ardor in the first place.

"Are you waiting for something?" He had broken off his conversation and was frowning at her irritably. "Well, as long as you're here—" He fingered the folder. "Are the reports in here up to date? I'm speaking to Mrs. Sloban now and I may have to prepare a detailed report tomorrow—."

Julie explained that there was some tallying of latest dividends to complete but she could bring the folder up to date by tomorrow morning. He interrupted with a weary gesture.

"Instead of daydreaming at my desk, Julie, if you paid more attention to your work—"

He tossed the folder on his desk, dismissing her.

A moment later, Julie emerged fuming from the inner office. Mary's gaze followed her to her desk. "Obviously he didn't offer you a raise in salary," she quipped.

"Mary, tell me, do I ever daydream on the job?"

"Is that what lover boy said?"

Julie opened her desk drawer and yanked out her handbag. "I must be a masochist to find something appealing in a man like that! If he asks for me, say I'm off daydreaming somewhere."

"You going down to call Mrs. Turner?"

Julie nodded. "I promised. She wants to meet me for lunch. Wouldn't you just bet she'll ask me to help her pick out a lovely surprise gift for her dear, dear husband? Arsenic—that's what I'll recommend!"

The elevator man was chatty and helped to cool Julie's temper as he brought her down five flights to the lobby. The counterman at Bill's Diner next door waved to her familiarly. Faith in human nature was momentarily restored. Julie slipped into one of the telephone booths in the rear of the diner and dialed Mrs. Turner's number.

They arranged to meet for lunch at 12:30, at a restaurant Julie was reasonably sure her employer was not likely to patronize. He was expected at a business lunch today anyway.

When Julie arrived at the meeting place, Mrs. Turner was already sipping a drink at the table, her gross features a portrait of determination and bitterness.

It was not long before Julie understood the reason for this grim countenance. No sooner had the waitress brought their order when Mrs. Turner clutched her companion's hands across the table.

"Julie, I want you to be honest with me. Don't be afraid of hurting me with the truth—"

"I'll try, Mrs. Turner, but what—?"

"Tell me, is my husband carrying on with another woman?"

The girl was too surprised even to deny having such knowledge. Mrs. Turner leaned forward tensely. "Julie, I *must* know. I'm leaving him anyway, don't you understand? But I must know who she is."

"Mrs. Turner, I really don't know anything about—"

"Yes, you do. You're his secretary. All of you at the office know who she is. Julie, I want to strike back. You can understand that. I want to disgrace both of them!"

"Did he tell you he was in love with some other woman?" Julie asked, aware of a guilty flush on her cheeks.

"*Love?* Richard doesn't love anybody. He uses people. He married me only for my money." The ugly woman smiled thinly. "But now he's angry at me—oh, how he raged last night!—because I won't transfer any of my money into his account. Transfer my money? What kind of fool does he think I am?

"Do you know what he said when I refused? He taunted me. He said he was going to find other women . . . beautiful women . . . to take his mind off his money troubles—"

"But, Mrs. Turner, he didn't say there already *was* another woman, did he? He only threatened . . ."

The older woman shook her head sagely. "You don't know Richard. He never threatens until he's sure of what he has. The bird in the hand philosophy. But I want to ruin it for both of them. I want to leave *him* before he's ready to leave *me*. Then he'll have nothing. And at the same time I want to create such a scandal that I'll ruin all his chances of marrying someone else. They won't even dare speak to each other after I'm through. Julie, who are his clients? The unattached women?"

She was quite alarmed. "I couldn't give you the names of clients."

Mrs. Turner leaned back with an appearance of defeat. She could sense Julie's determination, and her own wilted. "Oh well, I understand. Of course you can't. I suppose you've been as helpful as you can, and, don't worry, Julie, I won't tell him about our meeting. But tonight I'll tell him I'm through with him . . ." Again she smiled. "I'll *enjoy* telling him. It'll be interesting to see how he tries to convince me he didn't mean to threaten me, that he really loves me . . . Yes, it'll be quite a night."

At the office again, it was impossible to get any work done. Mr. Turner was still out with a client most of the afternoon, but Mary gave her no peace until she had told her everything that happened; and it was relief to share the incident with someone. It was an even greater relief when five o'clock came and she left the office to board the subway to the Bronx.

Not until she was at the dinner table that evening did Julie remember the Sloban account. Her mother was berating her kid sister for not doing her homework, for daydreaming . . . and Julie suddenly realized that in her distress this afternoon, she had forgotten to bring the Sloban folder up to date. The idea of facing Mr. Turner the next day with this oversight was a dreaded one, especially after his criticism this morning and considering the mood he would be in after tonight, after his wife . . .

It was barely seven o'clock, she noted. She could return to the office, bring home the folder to work on it, and have it finished before bedtime. Despite her mother's objections to her going out again, Julie slipped into her coat and dashed out of the house.

The night elevator man at her office building was almost asleep behind his desk. He recognized her and smiled sheepishly.

"Can you take me up and wait for me?" Julie asked, as she signed the register book. He shook his head and reached for his keys. "No, I have to be on duty down here. Just buzz the elevator when you're ready to come down."

He brought her up—the elevator seemed so noisy when the building was empty—and opened the office door with a master key, then returned to his post. Julie felt deserted. Whistling, she snapped on a central overhead light and walked across the empty floor to Mr. Turner's unlighted office.

The Sloban folder was still on his desk. The moment she reached for it, his telephone rang. Her hand jumped back.

The effect of the second loud ring in the darkened office was no less startling. Who could be calling on Mr. Turner's private telephone at this hour?

On the third ring she collected her wits and picked up the receiver.

"Hello . . ." she said.

"What? Who—who is this?"

It was Mr. Turner's voice.

Quickly overcoming her surprise, Julie identified herself. She explained her presence at the office. "Is it all right if I take the folder home to work on it?"

"Yes—yes—certainly. Are you leaving now?"

"Right away, Mr. Turner." She could picture his intense face and she had never before known such a sense of intimacy and aloneness with this man. Perhaps it was simply the fact that it was night. More than anything else, she wanted to prolong the conversation. "Was there anything you wanted, Mr. Turner? Was there anyone—"

"No, of course not." His laugh was short, forced. "I just dialed the wrong number. I was having a few drinks at a bar and got mixed up. Good night."

"Good night, Mr. Turner."

She hung up and stared at the telephone. It occurred to her to wonder if Mrs. Turner had already told her husband she was leaving him, disinheriting him, and the rest of what she had threatened. If so, she could understand very well why he was drinking. But why had he called the office—at this hour? Was someone supposed to be here? Had her own presence frightened that other person away? She could not really believe that he had dialed the wrong number.

Julie picked up the Sloban folder and walked out to the center of the floor. She half expected to find some person lurking behind one of the typists' desks. Whatever the explanation, her curiosity had to be satisfied. Why should she let him chase her home? She could do her work here, couldn't she? She sat at her own desk and opened the folder. She could finish posting the dividends in less than an hour . . .

Slightly more than an hour was required. With a sense of accomplishment she closed the folder and returned it to Mr. Turner's desk. At her own desk, she picked up her handbag and topcoat. Then she froze.

Like a shriek in the night, the telephone on Mr. Turner's desk rang . . . first once, then again and again . . .

She swung about to look at the frosted glass entrance door. At any moment, she knew, someone would come bursting through that door in answer to the imperative ringing. But no silhouette approached the glass. Stiffly, resisting the magnetism of the unanswered ringing, Julie made her way across the office floor. Looking back, she flicked off the lights, opened the door, then closed it behind her. Standing at the elevator, she heard the telephone ringing still, like a petulant child, calling her . . . calling someone. Finally, just before the elevator arrived, the ringing stopped.

In the morning, Mary listened to the previous night's events with wide-eyed astonishment. "You mean he called the office? Yipes, he sure *must* have been plastered! But you know, I can't imagine that man getting so plastered . . ."

Mr. Turner arrived only minutes late and seemed as self-possessed as ever. He appeared to have forgotten that yesterday existed. After a sharp "Good morning," he entered his office and closed the door behind him. At about 9:20, the intercom came to life on Julie's desk.

"Julie," he said, "will you get Mrs. Turner on the phone for me?"

"Mrs. Turner?"

Somehow she was startled to find that he could still be on speaking terms with his wife.

"Yes, Mrs. Turner. Didn't you hear me?"

What she did hear, just before he broke the connection, was a puzzling undercurrent of sound.

"That's strange . . ." she mused, turning to Mary.

"What is?"

Julie nodded toward the closed office. "He's calling somebody on his private phone. I could hear him dialing . . ."

"The other woman," said the blonde girl, snapping her fingers. "He wants her to listen while he talks to his wife, don't you see? Or maybe it's his lawyer. Maybe they'll make a tape recording—evidence for the divorce."

Julie was disgusted with herself for believing Mary even for a second. She picked up the telephone, asked the switchboard girl for an outside line, then dialed. Mrs. Turner's line was busy.

"Well, what did you expect?" Mary said. "She's busy talking to *her* lawyer."

Julie pressed the intercom buzzer and waited for him to switch it on.

"Yes, Julie . . ."

"Your wife's line is busy, Mr. Turner."

"Oh? All right, thank you."

"Shall I try her again in a few minutes?"

"No, don't bother. It's not very important . . ."

Julie was thoughtful as she slipped paper into her typewriter and began almost automatically to compose a monthly statement to a client. She wondered, as she often did when life gave her a glimpse of private lives, what her own future would be. Would she marry someone in all good faith only to learn one day that she hardly knew him at all? Could one trust one's feelings?

Absorbed, Julie did not even notice the two strangers approaching her desk. It was shortly before lunch time. She was typing, and then there was a man's overcoat sleeve and an open hand showing her a wallet with a police badge.

That was the first time she saw Sergeant Ruderman.

"I'm very sorry I startled you. I guess you didn't hear me over your typing. I asked if I could speak to Mr. Turner, please."

There was another detective with him, somewhat shorter, older. She looked from one to the other. Then she nodded decisively. "Will you come this way, please?"

She led them to Mr. Turner's office. She did not follow them inside. Somehow she knew why they were here.

When they emerged with Mr. Turner, she could almost feel what he was feeling. She had never seen him so pale.

"Julie, Mrs. Turner has had an accident. I'll be out—" He looked questioningly at the detectives. "I'll be out the rest of the day."

"An accident? Is it very serious?"

He nodded briefly.

"The maid found her—"

Sergeant Ruderman stepped closer. "I'll explain it to your secretary, Mr. Turner. You'd better go with Detective Wilson. I'll be along later."

When they had gone, he asked Julie to step into Mr. Turner's office. He closed the door and offered her a chair. She knew by the slight narrowing of his hazel eyes that he had somehow read her involuntary feeling of resentment when he, in turn, chose the chair behind the desk.

"Mrs. Turner is dead, isn't she?" Julie asked.

He merely inclined his head, watching her.

"How did it happen? When?"

He showed little expression.

"The maid let herself in around ten o'clock this morning. That's the time she comes in every day. She found Mrs. Turner in the bathtub. Evidently, she had struck her head and . . . You don't really want to hear the details, do you?"

Julie turned away. "No. Of course it *was* an accident, wasn't it?"

"That's the way it appears. Julie, you spoke to Mrs. Turner on the phone this morning, is that right?"

"I did not. Who told you that?"

"Mr. Turner did. He said you called her this morning."

"Yes, he asked me to. But I didn't speak to her. The line was busy at the time."

"I see. Yes—" The detective's lips quirked with spontaneous humor. "That is what he told us. What time did Mr. Turner arrive at the office, by the way?"

"Nine o'clock. A few minutes after nine perhaps."

"And what time did you call Mrs. Turner?"

"Nine-twenty, I think."

"And Mr. Turner did not leave the office since he arrived?"

She was pleased at having stumped the interrogator. "He was here all morning," she said loyally.

"Well, that's good." He too seemed pleased. "We've determined that she died somewhere around nine o'clock. Whether it was before nine or after nine . . . that's in question. However, none of the phones in her apartment were off the hook when we got there, or when the maid got there. And you say her line was busy at nine-twenty. So the probability is that she was alive at that time and had an accident a short while afterward."

He smiled as he walked Julie to the door. "I don't exactly apologize for taking you away from your work. It was a pleasure, I assure you." His expression became earnest. "I admit I did have a kind of feeling . . . Julie, what was their relationship? Were they getting along?"

She almost said it then, all that had happened. He seemed such an easy and trustworthy man to talk to. But she stopped herself. He noticed all these transitions, she was sure.

As he held open the door, his expression was one of doubt and puzzlement. She knew he did not believe her murmured answer that she knew nothing about the Turners . . .

That was why tonight he had waited for her outside the building and then brought her to Bill's Diner. Yet even he could not fathom how much she had learned in the last two days about that unhappy marriage. Mr. Turner, himself, was totally unaware that she had spoken to his wife and knew so much. Would anything be gained by offering this information? It would only hurt Mr. Turner.

Then why, she wondered, did she have this feeling of wanting to speak to Sergeant Ruderman again, to tell him . . .

"*Julie* . . ."

It was Mary. She had slipped into the very seat the detective had just vacated. "Well. don't look so surprised," she said, pouting. "I saw him meet you outside the building, so I waited. You know I can't resist the latest gossip. What did he tell you? What happened?"

"Nothing happened. He asked me again about the Turners and I still didn't tell him."

"Good!"

Julie stared at her.

"Good? Why do you say that?"

"Because what's the point of making extra trouble for poor Mr. Turner?"

She leaned forward confidentially. "Now, what about that detective? Did he ask you for a date?"

Julie's change in coloration answered her.

"I knew it . . . even by the way he looked at you in the office this morning. Much to my surprise, I envied you that look, gal. And the next time I try to tell you I'm not interested in that sentimental gush, and the next time I say that only money counts, and it makes no difference if your boy friend is married—well, if I ever say those things again after all that's happened, please don't believe me, will you . . ."

Julie put her hand over Mary's.

"I never believed you. One thing I almost believed, though, was that you and Mr. Turner . . . that you—"

"*Mr. Turner? Are you serious?*"

Julie shrugged.

"It would have explained so many things. But I know it's not true. Still, something—" She frowned as she stared beyond Mary at the empty telephone booths. Suddenly she snapped her fingers. "Mary, suppose he wasn't calling his lawyer, or some other woman?"

"Who?"

"Mr. Turner. Remember this morning, when I said he was calling somebody on his other telephone? Well, suppose he was ringing his *wife's* number? I'd get a busy signal if I tried to call it at the same time, wouldn't I?"

Mary was unsure. Julie walked to the counter and asked for change for a dollar bill, then entered one of the booths.

"I have to find out if it works," she said.

"Who are you going to call?" Mary wanted to know.

"I'll call Mr. Turner's house on this phone and let it ring," Julie explained. "Then I'll call the same number from the other booth and see if I get a busy signal."

She started to put a dime in the slot, then pulled her hand away.

"No, I can't call his house. He might answer. Or the police might still be there. Is anyone at your place, Mary?"

Her friend winced. "The whole family."

"They're in at my house too. We need a phone that won't answer. How about the office?"

Mary frowned. "That's true . . . but I think the switchboard automatically shifts a second call to another line. So that wouldn't be a good test. Why don't you call one of the private phones? Mr. Turner's phone doesn't go through the switchboard."

Julie had already dropped the dime in the slot. She dialed carefully. They could hear the buzz-click as the telephone rang at the other end. Suddenly Julie gasped. With a stunned expression, she slowly hung up the receiver.

"What's the matter?" Mary stepped into the booth. "Why did you hang up? I thought you were going to let it ring and then try calling the number on the other—"

Julie was shaking her head. "No, Mr. Turner already made the test . . . last night. That was why he called the office. Now I can understand why he was so shocked when I answered . . ."

"Then he *did* it? He *murdered* her? You mean, she was probably dead before he even came to work this morning?"

Julie shuddered. "It's unbelievable . . . that it could happen with people in your own office, people you see every day. Do you know what gives me the creeps, Mary? It's knowing that I saw *everything*. I was part of everything that happened. I was a witness to every part of it . . . but I didn't realize it at the time."

She reached into her handbag for the detective's card.

"He said I had a misdirected sense of loyalty. Sergeant Ruderman, I mean. I guess he was right." Julie dialed the number from the card. "Hello," she said into the mouthpiece, "is this the police station? Has Sergeant Ruderman arrived? He has? Yes, I'd like to speak to him . . ."

SAMUEL W. TAYLOR

We're Really Not That Kind of People

It was on a Sunday afternoon, I remembered, that Blackie was poisoned. I remembered that the morning had been cold, with a high fog, as it can be in the San Francisco Bay region even in mid-summer. Peggy and I had invited the deKadts over for a picnic barbecue, and the anticipation of the event was a big thing for our eight-year-old, Sue. Sue was disappointed as only an eight-year-old can be, at the prospect of having the barbecue inside. But then the fog burned off about noon, I remembered, and it was just right for the barbecue, not hot, not cold, the kind of a day on which we Californians like tourists to arrive. ("Nice day?" we say casually. "Hadn't noticed. It's like this all the time.")

Lucille and Carl deKadt were our neighbors across the grapestake fence to the south. They made a good pair; Carl was slow, plump, and easygoing, while Lucille was a slender, hard-driving redhead—pretty too, though personally I go more for a girl like Peggy, with a little more meat on the bones and a disposition that allows you to relax occasionally.

Carl and Lucille brought Herb Berry to the barbecue. Herb was Carl's cousin, down from Sacramento for the weekend. Herb was down pretty often, but not, I figured, to see Carl; Lucille was a terrific cook, and Herb was both a big guy with a hearty appetite and a bachelor.

After eating, I went across the grapestake fence for a game of horseshoes, Lucille and I standing Herb and Carl. We were tied at 12-all, when Sue came through the gate.

"Daddy, Blackie's sick," the child said. "Mommy wants you to come look at him."

"Okay, soon as we finish the game."

Lucille and I were leading, 18-16, when Peggy came to the fence. "George, I think you'd better come and look at Blackie." There was a quiet urgency to her voice; so I left without finishing the game.

Blackie was lying in his corner of the carport. He was a small dog, part poodle and part wirehair, ugly enough to be cute. He lay there panting, and every little while he would twitch and moan a little. He had been chewing his tongue.

When I got the dog down to the animal hospital on El Camino, the vet shook his head. "Nothing can be done. We'll make him comfortable."

We'd had Blackie since before Sue was born. I let out a long, weary sigh. "I'll stay," I said.

I didn't get home until past ten o'clock. When I came in, Peggy met my eye, then ducked her head. I began to swear, which is a man's impotent reaction to a woman's tears. "I'd just like to know who would do a trick like that!"

"No, George," Peggy said. "We don't want to know."

Maybe she was right; Peggy generally was. We didn't want to know who such people were. People like us didn't want to think such people existed. Blackie had been a friendly little dog; it had been impossible to keep him in shape, because everybody in the neighborhood fed him.

Next morning we told Sue that Blackie must have been hit by a car. Peggy and I decided we didn't want another dog; not for a while, anyhow, and particularly not if there was a poisoner in the neighborhood. Maybe, we thought, we'd get a kitten for Sue. A cat would take care of the gophers that kept making mounds in Peggy's flower beds.

Looking back, thinking about it as I lay awake nights, I figured that poisoning the dog was the first step in the plan to kill me. But if anyone had told me such a thing, at the time, I would have laughed in his face. Who, me? What had I ever done, to make somebody want to murder me? What could anyone conceivably gain by my death? It was preposterous. Things like that didn't happen to managers of the local units of Fit-All Shoe Stores. I wasn't chasing anybody else's wife. I didn't play the ponies or hit the bottle. I wasn't involved in the sort of things that can lead to violence, and I didn't even know the sort of people who were. George Granger, 1138 College Avenue, Woodside Heights, was just another guy in the row, having a nice wife and a healthy mortgage; one child and a nervous septic tank; paying on a car, furniture, refrigerator, power mower, insurance and dental bills; a couple of E bonds tucked away and gophers in the petunias—there were a thousand like me in Woodside Heights alone. People don't go around murdering average guys.

But what if it wasn't me at all, but Peggy who was the intended victim? Quiet, lovely Peggy—oh, but that was crazy. Of course it was crazy, and that's what kept me awake nights. Perhaps it was even Sue who was the intended victim. What insane person might be plotting the death of your wife or an eight-year-old child? I would lie there remembering every little detail, trying to pick out the significant thing that might help in meeting this situation.

I remembered that when I got home Saturday, Peggy told me that Lucille had finally got Carl started on painting their house. Lucille had been at him for a year or more about it, but easygoing Carl could be stubborn when it came to unnecessary exertion. He didn't get much done, Peggy said. Every time she looked across the grapestake fence, she'd see Carl taking his ease atop the ladder, leisurely smoking a cigarette while gently stirring the bucket of paint.

"Not a hair out of place, shoes shined, trousers pressed," Peggy said, laughing. "Lucille spent more energy keeping him at it than he put into the painting. She'll never change that guy. Why does she keep trying?"

Carl was a pretty good insurance man. He had an air of calm confidence, coupled with an utter lack of a sense of humor, which enabled him to deliver a fund of bromides and platitudes with sincerity. He didn't have much push, but

Lucille had enough for both of them; she kept a record of his calls, and saw to it that he made them.

"Lucille ought to get Herb to come down to help," I said, "or Carl can take all summer on that job."

"She said something's wrong with Herb's car. He's coming later on the bus."

Herb Berry arrived that evening, and Lucille drove in to the bus station in the VW to bring him out. "With Herb here, they'll finish the house tomorrow," Peggy said. Herb was a big guy who liked exercise, but didn't get much chance for it. Ten years ago or so he'd been a professional baseball player, and had spent a couple of seasons in the big leagues. Now he was in real estate in Sacramento.

Next morning they were at work before sunup. I heard them banging away with scaffolds and buckets while we were in bed, their voices clear and strident in the quiet of the morning. By the time we sat down to breakfast, they had painted almost the entire side of the house which faced us across the grapestake fence. Carl's blond hair was mussed now, and he was splattered with paint, trying to keep up with Herb and Lucille. She was on the scaffold with the two men, slapping on paint.

I was pouring coffee when Herb Berry let out a yell, and I looked up just as the tall man took a header off the scaffold with the main paint bucket in his hand. Lucille screamed. Then Herb stood up into view with paint on him from head to foot, and began laughing. At this point, I realized I'd poured coffee onto Peggy's clean tablecloth.

"On you it looks good!" I called out the window to Herb.

He climbed onto the scaffold and began rubbing himself on the side of the house, using his clothing and hair as a paint brush. Carl howled with laughter. Lucille told Carl to go downtown for some more paint—they carried it at the Plaza drugstore which would be open on Sunday—while she washed the paint out of Herb's hair.

A bit later Carl came over. "My VW won't start," he said. "Can I borrow your car to run downtown?"

I gave him the keys. "This will teach you to get one of those foreign jobs."

"But it never happened before; she just won't start."

He turned to the carport, and I went back to breakfast. I remembered that I picked up the coffee cup as he slammed the car door. I took a sip and was putting the cup down, when there was a big grunt and something shoved me. It was like being caught in an ocean breaker. The table was picked up and flung upside down across the room, and I remembered seeing the coffee maker narrowly miss Peggy's head as she fell backward. I was thrown against the stove with my heels higher than my head. Every window of the kitchen was blown out, the roof lifted so a rim of daylight showed around it, and the entire wall adjoining the carport was sprung inward. But for all that, Sue sat exactly where she had been, her spoon raised half to her mouth. An explosion can do freak things, and it had completely passed the child by.

My memory isn't too clear about the next few minutes. I was pretty groggy, and my ears rang. Peggy helped me up, and there was a line of blood beginning to run down her cheek (only a scratch; boy, were we lucky). From outside came shouts and running feet as the neighbors gathered. Then somebody began shaking the kitchen door, but the explosion had jammed it shut.

"Are you all right in there, George?" It was Bert Miles' round face and heavy shock of curly hair at the window. He was our neighbor on the other side.

"I guess so. How are you, Peggy?"

Peggy seemed very young at the moment. She was like the slim girl with the brown hair and the big gray eyes who sat beside me a full quarter in Psychology 61 (we were seated alphabetically; her name was Grove, mine Granger) before I scraped up enough courage to ask her for a date. "I'm all right," she said to Bert Miles. "And thank heavens Sue wasn't even—"

"They're okay in here," Bert Miles called. "George and Peggy and Sue."

"George and Peggy and Sue?" someone asked. "Then who was in the car when she blew up? Who got blasted to pieces?"

And then, from somewhere, I heard Lucille scream, "Carl!"

The casket was closed at the funeral. I guess there wasn't much left of the mortal remains of Carl deKadt. Mr. Wheeler of the sheriff's office, who investigated, had decided that a bundle of dynamite had been placed under the front seat, wired to the starter. Carl got in, slammed the door, inserted the key, turned it on to engage the starter, and had been killed instantly. At least he didn't suffer. Poor Carl. And but for chance, I thought, as they lowered his casket into the grave, there go I. It wasn't intended for him. Thank you, Carl, but why did it have to be?

This is the sort of thing that can interfere with your sleep. In another couple of hours we would have gone out to the car, Peggy, Sue, and I, all dressed up for Sunday school. Except that Lucille had finally gotten Carl started on the painting, except that Herb's car was in the garage and that Carl's VW wouldn't start, except that Herb had fallen off the scaffold with the paint so that Carl borrowed my Dodge to get some more . . .

On the way home from the funeral Peggy suddenly said, "That's why Blackie was poisoned. They got rid of the dog, so they could fix our car in the night while we slept."

I drove back rapidly, wondering about Sue, whom we'd left with a sitter. It was good to find the child all right.

This was something that had been planned ahead. No telling what would happen next.

The following day, Peggy went to town and got another dog, a small, excitable type of mutt such as Blackie had been. Sue was delighted with the new pet, particularly delighted that this was a dog we could have in the house. We had a reason for that. A dog in the house can't be poisoned at night.

Next day I got a letter at the store. It had been mailed locally. The envelope looked like something Sue might have done with scissors and paste, my name and address composed of printed letters and numbers cut from a newspaper. The note inside was the same sort of a paste-up. It said:

You were lucky. But next time it will be you and your wife and kid.

Mr. Wheeler of the sheriff's office said he doubted that another attempt would be made in the same manner. He was a lean man with four of his front teeth forming a bridge, and not too good a one. He had a habit of eating soda mint tablets and a passion for questions that might very well uncover a motive for someone wanting to kill me.

But I told him a dozen times, "There isn't any motive. It's a crazy person. Goofy. Nuts. An oddball character."

Mr. Wheeler kept saying he doubted it, and kept popping soda mint tablets into his mouth. "Give it some thought, Mr. Granger. This is not a crime of impulse. Someone has a very good reason.

Fathead! My estimate, at the moment, of Mr. Wheeler.

Have you ever had your picture on the front page and seen your name in a newspaper streamer? Have you been pointed out on the street, pestered by busy-bodies, avoided by people who don't want to get too close until the dust settles? Have you ever had the feeling of standing apart, thinking that this guy isn't you, can't be you, because he isn't that sort of a guy and just doesn't fit the part?

But it was real enough. Particularly at night, when you woke up.

The workmen were repairing the house. I had to deal with the insurance people about this and about getting another car. It was enough to interfere with anybody's sleep. And as I lay awake in the night, I thought back over every detail of what had happened, and back and back into the past trying to get hold of something that could have made it happen. Everybody has enemies, Mr. Wheeler had said. Everybody has something another person wants, or wanted. Everybody has hurt somebody.

Tom Stone? He had been my rival for Peggy, and it had been a pretty bitter competition. Tom had threatened to get me, if it was the last thing he ever did. But he'd also promised to wait for Peggy, and he'd married Alice Duke within six months. That was eleven years ago; Tom and Alice now had four kids.

Henry Traut had been assistant manager of the first Fit-All Store I worked in, and I'll never forget his sly grin the night he showed me how to beat the store. With two of us working together, he said, we could clean up. When I turned down the proposition, I knew he was out to get me. He turned in bad reports to the boss about me, yet somehow I couldn't bring myself to squeal on him. I was thinking of quitting, when Traut was caught with his hand in the till. He swore he'd get me for squealing on him, but that was a long time ago, back before I got married—in fact, I proposed to Peggy on the strength of getting Traut's job. Could a thing like that fester this long? I'd never seen Traut since he was fired.

At the local store, I'd finally had to lower the boom on one of the most respectable housewives in town, Lydia Primrose, whose husband was on the city council, because of shoplifting. I didn't see why I should outfit her family with free shoes. The thing was settled quietly, but certainly both she and her husband would be glad if I were dead.

There had been a few hassles at the service club, where I was chairman of the committee of admissions. In particular, I had kept Phil Buckwalter out of the club year after year, despite his prominence, wealth, influence, and driving desire to be a member, and despite charges that I was acting from personal spite and malice. The plain fact was that Buckwalter's place of business was a clip joint, something which I couldn't prove nor openly charge, but which made me keep him out of the club, one way or another.

Lying awake nights, if you put your mind to it, it's amazing to find how many toes you've stepped on. Slights, affronts, arguments, flareups. Things you quickly put from mind, until you're digging back through memory in search of someone who let it fester.

The fellow businessmen who dropped by to say hello, the members of the Main Street Improvement Association, the people who came to my church, the associates in the service club, the neighbors—they didn't know that every time I said hello I wondered, is this the one? The cashier of the lunch counter, the janitor of the building, my bookkeeper, assistant manager, clerks—some one of you is out to kill me and my family. Mr. Wheeler of the sheriff's office was trying to find out why. Hell, all I cared about was who. I'd find out why later.

I'd had a little hassle with the guy across the street, who had a habit of backing out of his driveway into mine, to make his turn into the narrow street easier. I didn't mind his backing into the driveway, but I did object to him missing it and running over my ivy; so Fred Lacey and I had had words. I'd run over the cat of a guy who used to live down the block, and that had caused words. Could it have grown with him, even though he'd moved away and I'd forgotten his name? And of course we hadn't spoken to Loris Neilsson, since he'd threatened to shoot Blackie for walking on his new lawn; but, then, nobody in the neighborhood spoke to Loris.

These things couldn't grow to premeditated murder. Or could they? From what I'd read, most people got killed over small things—a slight, an argument, loss of face, an affront, avarice over a few dollars. Looking at it that way, there might be many people plotting my death, including Peggy, who might do it for the insurance.

Peggy wasn't getting her sleep, either. Her face got drawn and her big gray eyes bigger. We'd tried to keep it from Sue, but once it hit the headlines she got it from her playmates. What was it like for her, knowing someone was plotting her death, or the death of her mother and father? Childhood is filled with terrors anyhow.

"George, I just don't know what to do," Peggy said, speaking quietly as we both lay awake in the night.

"I've put in for a transfer. It shouldn't be hard; a lot of managers are anxious to get a store in California."

"What will this do to your advancement?"

It wouldn't help it. "I don't think that's the important thing, right now."

She said, "You should withdraw that application. Really you—"

"Honey, I'm no hero. I just want to walk away from this."

"But here at least we are among people we know. And all the people here are thinking, wondering who's doing this."

"Sure—and one of them *knows*."

"And the police. They're working on it—the sheriff's office out here, the city police because you got the letter at the store in town, and now it's a Federal case because they used the mails. This is our protection, George, to be here where so many are helping. It's all we've got. We simply have to hold faith in it."

"Okay," I said. "I'll withdraw the application."

She was right. And, come right down to it, there was no such thing as running away from this.

We adapted, as best we could. I came home each day for lunch, just to check up, instead of eating in town. Sue no longer rode the school bus. Peggy took her to school and picked her up. I had my deer rifle loaded and ready, on the shelf of the entry hall closet. Sue, I noticed, no longer watched the horse operas, whodunits, and other shows of violence on TV which she had been so fascinated with just a week ago. I don't know whether it was because they were a pale comparison with the real thing, or whether the child was too edgy to want to be reminded of the real thing; a kid won't tell what's eating her.

When I arrived home for lunch Saturday, neighbors were milling about the house, everybody talking about the poisoned chocolates. "I told Peggy not to worry you over the phone," Lucille said. The newly widowed redhead looked bad. Lucille was the nervous type anyhow, who took everything big, and she'd been living on coffee and cigarettes for the six days since Carl had been killed. Tragedy had stalked her. Lucille's first husband had been killed in a car wreck; her second had been shot while deer hunting; and now Carl—all three killed accidentally. I felt awfully sorry for her, Carl dying with the bomb intended for me.

The neighbors filled me in about the chocolates, talking all at once. Peggy had been helping Lucille sort the contents of Lucille's house. There were things the moving van would take to Sacramento, where Herb Berry had gotten her a job in the office of the real estate outfit where he worked; there was stuff for the Goodwill truck; there were things that would go with the house, which Lucille had put up for sale; and there was just a lot of accumulated junk that had to be sorted out and hauled to the county dump.

The two women had taken a mid-morning break and were having a cup of coffee at my place when the mail arrived. There was a package addressed like the anonymous letter had been, a paste-up of printed characters cut from a newspaper. Lucille had warned Peggy not even to open it, fearing a bomb or something. She'd called Mr. Wheeler at the sheriff's office, who had come out and taken the package. Just before I got home for lunch, he'd phoned that it contained chocolates filled with lead arsenate, the stuff used to spray trees.

I phoned Wheeler myself, and he didn't seem too excited. "A clumsy attempt," he said professionally. This was all in the day's work for him. "The address being the same style as the poison pen note—and you should have seen those chocolates, all gooked up, the white powder spilling out of some of them—it wouldn't have fooled a baby."

"Great deduction," I said acidly. "But what if Peggy had been over to Lucille's, and Sue had opened the package? The kid would be dead by now!"

"There's no use shouting, Mr. Granger," he advised me.

Fatheads, incompetents, parasites on the public purse. I told him exactly what I thought of him and the entire sheriff's office, after, of course, I had hung up.

This was like life in the jungle. You never went downwind. You approached each thicket with the expectation that it might contain an ambush.

Trouble was, I wasn't used to the jungle. I didn't know how to survive in it.

Herb Berry arrived from Sacramento in the afternoon, to help Lucille with the packing. Since her house was torn up, they came over to our place for dinner. And he spent the night with us. It was good to have Herb around. He was a big guy, a former athlete, plenty husky and capable. He'd taken care of all the funeral arrangements and estate details for Lucille.

After Sue was in bed, I broke out a bottle and we relaxed. We all needed it. I took a couple too many, as a matter of fact, and it was wonderful to feel great and not to give a damn, even if it would mean a hangover in the morning. I hadn't realized that Herb could be such a clown when he got a snootful, and Lucille really let loose for once. She'd had her cry, and now she was breaking the tension with a laugh. When the redhead and the big ex-baseball player got into high gear, I laughed until my ribs hurt. Peggy didn't really enjoy the time we were having for ourselves, but then she never takes more than one drink. Personally, I was glad to see Lucille unwind after the tragedy. She'd been keyed up like a fiddle string, and I'd been afraid she'd snap.

Next morning I was over helping Lucille and Herb with the packing, when Peggy called from the grapestake fence. She and Sue were going to Sunday school, and she'd left the sprinkler on the petunias. Would I turn it off in fifteen minutes?

Okay, I told her. But I forgot the water until an hour or so later. Oh, well, it wouldn't hurt the petunias to get a good soaking.

While I was at the house, I decided to warm up the coffee from breakfast. I felt pretty rocky from the night before. I turned the gas on under the coffee, then looked for last night's paper, which I hadn't had a chance to read yet. Peggy never let papers lie around, and sure enough I found it in the wastebasket. I took it out, opened it, and a shower of paper bits fluttered to the floor like confetti. Somebody had been whacking at the paper with a pair of scissors. It looked like something a kid would do, just to be cutting, but I knew it wasn't Sue, and it wasn't just to be cutting.

The newspaper had been uncut at breakfast. I'd been hoping to look at it while Herb was shaving, but Lucille had come over just then. The paper hadn't been cut until after I went with Lucille and Herb to help with the packing. All at once I knew. Peggy had done it.

The last person in the world. The very last person. Peggy. Why? Insurance? A boy friend? What? Romance with the choir leader at church? Clandestine meetings at the supermarket, wandering down the aisles with their carts? Stolen kisses behind the door of the Sunday school classroom, assignations in the poison oak and redwoods of the hills? Oh, it was possible. Love will find a way. But it didn't fit Peggy, not at all.

Or did it?

What did I know about Peggy, really? What does any man know about his wife? She was sweet, she was lovely—okay, but so were wives who had affairs and laced the morning coffee of their husbands with arsenic. No husband would ever be poisoned, or done in by his wife's lover, if he suspected such a thing might happen.

There was a sudden hiss as the coffee pot boiled over. *Peggy.* I poured myself a cup. *Peggy.* Then as I took a mouthful of the scalding stuff, it woke me up. I put the newspaper in the wastebasket and went across the grapestake fence to help Lucille and Herb with the packing.

They were in the attic, sorting things. I worked downstairs. I was putting the pictures from the living room walls into a box when the doorbell rang. "Will you get it, George?" Lucille called from the attic.

"Okay." I went to the front door.

"Special delivery for Mr. Herbert Berry."

"I'll give it to him."

The letter was addressed with characters cut from a newspaper and pasted on the envelope. It had been mailed locally; the postmark was not an hour old. Peggy had mailed it, I knew, on the way to Sunday school. But why to Herb?

"Bring it up, will you, George?" Herb's voice asked from overhead. He'd heard, then: I'd have to give it to him. Well, why not? He didn't know about Peggy; only I knew.

I went into the back hall, up the stepladder and through the trapdoor into the attic. Herb and Lucille were over in a corner, sorting the contents of a trunk.

"Maybe the boss has sold that Gresham property," Herb said. His big hand reached for the envelope, then froze as he saw the way it was addressed. Lucille sucked in her breath sharply, plainly more high strung than ever. Slowly they looked at each other, their faces a dead white—Herb's beard black in contrast, Lucille's freckles standing out sharply.

Suddenly she snatched the envelope, ripped it open and unfolded the letter within. "It's a lie!" she cried.

Herb's voice was tightly hoarse. "Who sent it?"

"Peggy—who else?" Lucille said. So she knew. Soon it would be headlines for everybody to know—wife plots husband's death. "Peggy knew about us," Lucille was saying. "Carl was a trusting oaf. George here couldn't guess. Men are fools. But you can't trick a woman about something like that. If Peggy didn't know before, she could see it last night, when we drank too much," Lucille said to Herb. "She knows how we feel about each other."

I saw it then. The whole thing.

"Shut up, you fool!" Herb grabbed her shoulders, and I knew it wasn't the first time he'd laid his big paws on her. Herb Berry hadn't been making those weekend trips from Sacramento just for Lucille's cooking. Why had I been so blind? A real estate man's best time is the weekend; he does most of his business on Saturdays and Sundays.

"Keep your mouth shut!" Herb warned her.

"If she knows, *he* knows," Lucille snapped. "They're married." Angrily, she tossed the letter spinning to the floor.

I saw the message, pasted from newspaper letters: *Carl was her third husband. You're next, chump.*

"They cooked this up together!" Lucille shrieked at Herb.

Herb turned to me. I hadn't realized, really, what an enormous guy he was. He was a full head taller, and he would outweigh me by almost a hundred pounds.

"How about it, buster?" he asked me.

I could have told him everything, right then. Carl deKadt had been an insurance man, and an insurance man is always his own best customer. They'd killed him for the insurance. The bomb in the car never was intended for me. It was like the first letter and the poisoned chocolates, to make it appear that I was the intended victim, to make Carl's death seem merely an accident. Everything had been planned—Blackie's death, Herb falling off the scaffold, the VW that wouldn't start. The chocolates never were intended to harm us. The paste-up address was warning enough, and in addition they were clumsily prepared, the lead arsenate spilling out of them. And Lucille had been on deck when they were delivered, just in case.

It was all so clear, but, confronted with the big man, I said, "I don't know what you're talking about, Herb."

"They know," he said to her. It must have showed on my face. "I told you something would happen!" he yelled at her.

Lucille, who tipped the beam at 102, was the strong one now. "Okay, and what can they prove?" she told the big guy towering over her. "There are lots of things that people know that they don't talk about." She indicated me. "Remind him not to talk, Herb. Give him a lesson he won't forget in a hurry. Let him know we're playing for keeps."

It was somehow hard to believe even as I eased around among the boxes and trunks, ducked behind a stack of old newspapers, slipped to the sewing machine, sprang to the dress form, darted to the wood-burning stove, that Herb Berry was implacably pursuing me, his long arms spread wide, herding me toward a corner. Herb was a friend. My association with him had involved playing horseshoes, eating barbecued steaks, sharing tall drinks, spinning yarns. Just the night before we'd had a hilarious evening together over a bottle. He'd slept overnight as my guest. And now he was pursuing me, heading me back into a corner of the attic as I darted from one thing to another among the accumulated junk.

He had been a professional athlete, and he was relaxed now as an athlete is, waiting for his chance, while I spent myself rushing about. Peggy of course had no way of knowing that her little trick, done all on her own, would lead to this. All she had undoubtedly intended was getting a couple of murderers out of our hair. I tensed, knowing that when Herb made his move, it would count.

I wasn't going to be trapped in that corner. But when I made my break he was expecting it, and he lunged for me with that swift ease of the athlete. I knew I couldn't make that trapdoor. And then I did the sort of thing I used to do as a youngster, the last trick of a kid pursued by a bigger kid. I flung sideways to the floor, sticking out a leg to trip him.

His big foot kicked into my calf, and I thought my leg was broken. He yelled, then, a single hoarse shriek, as he sprawled toward the open trapdoor. I heard him crash into the stepladder below, and then hit the floor with a sodden thud. I crawled to the trapdoor. When I looked down from the rim, I just felt, judging from the way he was lying, that he must be dead.

Kneeling beside him was Mr. Wheeler of the sheriff's office, and I was also surprised to see the two uniformed men who were below in the hallway. "Lucky I wasn't climbing that ladder when he dived through," Mr. Wheeler said. He arose, and put a soda mint into his mouth. "That saves the state the expense of a trial for one of them." He looked up. "The woman's up there?"

"Yes," I said.

"What people won't do for money. You've got a smart wife, Mr. Granger. When she phoned this morning that the pair of them were in love, it straightened out my thinking. The whole thing came in focus—make us look at you while they walked away with the loot. Are you all right?"

"Yes, I'm okay," I said.

At least, I thought I was.

HAROLD Q. MASUR

Pocket Evidence

T here is a cynical little caveat which says: If you can't stand the time, don't commit the crime.

U.S. District Judge Edward Marcus Bolt failed to heed this injunction. He had committed a crime and when he was found out, the prospect of serving time in a federal penitentiary unhinged him completely. Tossed off the bench, disbarred, disgraced, disavowed by his colleagues, ego mutilated, deprived of his sumptuous young bride, all this was more than he could stomach—so the judge put the muzzle of a gun against his temple and squeezed one off.

It ended the judge's problems, but created some new ones for his widow, Laura Bolt. Tall, blonde, with innocent blue eyes and teeth perfectly capped for her career as a fashion model, she suspended her work when she married the judge but resumed it after his death. Now she sat alongside my desk, pale, apprehensive, tremulous.

"The man wants his money back," she told me.

"What money?"

"The money he claims he gave my husband."

"The fifty-thousand-dollar bribe?"

"I guess so. He called me on the telephone and said he'd paid Edward fifty thousand dollars to perform certain services and Edward failed to deliver." She gave me a look of forlorn appeal. "I came to you, Mr. Jordan, because you were Edward's lawyer and you were very helpful after his—er—accident."

I let the euphemism pass. I had indeed been Judge Bolt's lawyer—for maybe like about thirty minutes. At the time he retained me, he'd been presiding over the trial of Ira Madden, president of Amalgamated Mechanics.

Madden was charged by the government with embezzling one million dollars from the union treasury and although the indictment failed to state as much, they suspected he had squirreled it away under a numbered account in a Swiss bank.

Then, while still presenting its case, the Justice Department started an investigation of rumors that one of Madden's lackeys, a man named Floyd Oster, had reached the judge with a fifty-thousand-dollar bribe—and that exact sum was found taped under a fender of His Honor's car and identified by serial numbers as a recent withdrawal from one of Madden's accounts. In a panic, the judge got through to me with an SOS, summoning me to his home, but he must have been very close to the brink because he finished himself off before I got there.

It resulted in a mistrial. Now the government was preparing to bring Ira Madden back into court again. Floyd Oster, the bagman, was himself under indictment for bribery. There had been sundry other complications which I managed to straighten out for the widow. Now, apparently, she needed my help again.

I said, "Tell me exactly what happened, Mrs. Bolt."

She swallowed and drew a breath. "I got the call late last night. A man phoned and said, 'Listen to me, lady. I'm only going to say this once. We paid the judge fifty grand. He promised to help us on something, but he chickened out and shelved himself before he could deliver. We want our money back. Do you read me, Mrs. Bolt? Fifty grand. Have the cash ready day after tomorrow and we'll be in touch. Just stay away from the law or you'll wish you'd never been born.' "

"Bluster," I said. "Empty threats."

"No." Her voice rose on a hysterical note and she leaned forward, gripping the edge of my desk. "Something terrible happened on my way here to see you. I left my apartment and when I stepped off the curb to cross the street, a car suddenly started and came racing straight at me. I thought, this is it! They know I called you and they're punishing me. I'm going to be killed or maimed. I was paralyzed. I couldn't move. And then, at the very last instant, the car swerved and roared past me." Recollection drained her face, leaving it bone-white.

"Could you identify the driver?"

"I don't know; it happened so fast."

I brought her a newspaper clipping from one of my files. "Look at this picture. Does it resemble the man you saw?"

She studied it, brow crimped. "I—I'm not sure. Is it that man Floyd Oster?"

"The same. From what I know of this particular insect, he's our most logical target."

"Doesn't he know I haven't got the money, that the police are holding it as evidence?"

"He couldn't care less. He knows you have the judge's insurance."

She was on the verge of tears. "But they're not entitled to that. It's my only security."

She seemed unaware of her assets. With that superbly extravagant figure, she had all the security she would need for a long time to come. "Relax, Mrs. Bolt," I said. "It's in my hands now."

She managed a weak smile. "Would you need a retainer?"

I never refuse payment. She seemed eager to write a check, as though the transfer of money would guarantee success. After she left, I sat back and gave it some thought.

Floyd Oster, presently under indictment, was out on bail. His defense attorney, Edward Colson, was general counsel for Amalgamated Mechanics. Ordinarily, a man like Oster would never be able to afford the ticket for such high-priced legal talent. I could make a fair assumption that the union, under pressure from Ira Madden, was paying Colson's fee.

Coincidentally, Colson's office was three floors above my own, here at Rockefeller Center. I dialed his number and was told that he was at an arbitration hearing and would not be available until tomorrow. I saw no impropriety in bypassing Colson for a direct approach to Oster himself. Undoubtedly, Oster had instructions to keep his mouth zippered, but I was not interested in any dialogue with the man. I just wanted him to listen; admittedly, a quixotic approach.

The building was a converted brownstone, indistinguishable from its neighbors on Manhattan's west side. When I rang the bell, he called out guardedly for identification. Then he opened the door as far as the protective chain would allow. Floyd Oster, a carp-faced and sulfurous little brute, with a smile like a curved scimitar and just as lethal, was Ira Madden's right hand. He remembered me without pleasure from our last meeting.

"May I come in, Floyd?"

"No."

"I have something I want to say."

"Say it to my lawyer."

"If Ed Colson knew what you're up to, he'd walk away and you'd need a new attorney."

"Ed Colson works for the union. He does what he's told."

"Are you sure of that?"

"Say your piece and bug off."

"You never learn, do you, Floyd? Right now you're in a sling with the U.S. Attorney on a bribery charge. But that isn't enough. You're chasing after more grief, adding a count of extortion to your indictment. I'm telling you to stay away from Laura Bolt. One more threatening telephone call, another attempt at intimidation like that automobile caper this morning, and I promise you I'll blow the lid."

"You're talking Greek."

"That's a bad hand, Floyd. Throw it in. You know exactly what I mean. And I don't think you're acting on instructions from Ira Madden. With what he has stashed away, fifty grand would be peanuts. So this is your own private little operation. I'm telling you to drop it. Get off the lady's back. Because if anything happens to Mrs. Bolt, the roof will fall in."

It bothered him a lot. He called me a name and slammed the door.

So maybe he needed money. Maybe his common sense was canceled by greed. Whatever, the judge's widow was back on the phone late the next morning, agitated and close to panic. She'd had another call. The banks would be closed over the weekend, so Monday was her deadline, the voice asking her how she would like to attend my funeral just before her own, and reminding her of the automobile that almost sent her flying through the air like a rag doll.

I calmed her, broke the connection, marched out to the elevator, and rode it up three floors to Edward Colson's office. Oster's lawyer would have to read the riot act to him. Colson's secretary told me that he would be leaving for lunch in a few minutes, and without an appointment . . .

"Just tell him that Scott Jordan is here."

She looked doubtful, but spoke into her phone. In ten seconds Colson emerged, a tall, shambling pipe-smoking man with blunt features and a shock of brown hair. Edward Colson was a courtroom orator of the old school, somewhat flamboyant but tough, shrewd, and knowledgeable.

"Counselor," he said, voice resonant, both hands employed for the shake, "you promised to call me for lunch one day. Must have been a year ago at least. Come in." He took my elbow and steered me into his private office.

He had company—a spinster-type, thin and flat, early thirties, with mousy hair and soft spaniel eyes that seemed to spend most of their time worshiping at Colson's shrine.

He introduced us. "My fiancée, Lily Madden."

"Ira Madden's daughter?" I asked.

"Yes," she said. "Do you know my father?"

"Not personally."

"Lily and I became engaged last week," Colson said.

She raised a hand, proudly displaying a blue-white rock about five carats in size. It caught the midday light and sparkled. No financial burden on Colson, I thought. Easily affordable, considering the annual retainer he got from Amalgamated Mechanics. Still, Lily Madden was so obviously enamored she probably would have been satisfied with a zircon from the five-and-dime.

From time to time I had seen Colson squiring a few lovelies around town. He was a connoisseur. So why settle for someone as plain as Lily Madden? Insurance, probably; Colson relished the good life, and as Ira Madden's son-in-law, his position as general counsel for the union would be secure.

"Shot of brandy?" he asked.

"No, thanks. Could I talk to you in private for a moment?"

"We have a table reserved for lunch. How long do you need?"

"Ten minutes should do it."

"Lily, please. There are magazines in the reception room."

She smiled at him, eyes lingering on his face, and stepped out.

"Marvelous girl," he said.

"All these years a bachelor, Ed. And now you're taking the plunge?"

"It's time, isn't it? I'm not getting any younger."

He settled behind his desk and folded his hands. "What's on your mind, Counselor?"

"One of your clients. Floyd Oster."

He made a face. "I take the good with the bad. As a union official, I have to go to bat for him.

"Naturally. But you must be soaking the man unmercifully."

"How do you mean?"

"Oster got his neck way out, trying to raise some heavy sugar."

"Impossible. This defense isn't costing Oster dime-one. Amalgamated Mechanics is picking up the tab."

"Then he's involved in a little private enterprise, highly illegal. Or perhaps your future father-in-law is prodding him."

Colson's smile vanished. "What are you driving at, Jordan?"

I recited for him, chapter and verse. "You're Oster's lawyer. You know the background. That fifty grand he gave Judge Bolt—"

"Correction. One adverb short. *Allegedly gave* . . ."

"Do you doubt his guilt?"

"He carries a presumption of innocence."

"An eloquent phrase, Edward. But for Oster, a mere technicality. If Judge Bolt were still alive and testifying, the government would have no problem clapping your boy into the slammer for a couple of years."

"Maybe, maybe not."

"Nevertheless, somebody handed His Honor fifty grand cash money while Ira Madden was on trial for embezzling union funds. It was not a charitable donation. And who else needed favors from the judge, preferential treatment, a biased charge to the jury? Whatever, Floyd Oster is now trying to get his hands on it."

"What makes you so sure it's Oster?"

"Come off it, Ed. Everything points to the man. And the U.S. Attorney would dearly love to nail him. None of this is likely to help Ira Madden when he goes back into court."

Colson shook his head. "I can't believe Oster would be that stupid."

"If he had anything but a vacuum north of his sinuses he wouldn't be in all this trouble."

"You think he'll listen to me?"

"You're his lawyer."

"Where's my leverage?"

"He knows the value of your services. You can threaten to dump him."

"No, sir. That's exactly what I cannot do. But I'll bend the rules a little. I'll talk to him. Just remember, these union people sometimes ask my advice. They don't always take it."

"Maybe they've learned a lesson. Both Madden and Oster are facing a serious prosecution."

"Madden feels he can beat the rap."

"How? By bribing judges?"

"That was a piece of damned foolishness. I had no part in it."

"So they keep piling it on, adding extra counts to the indictment. On the next round, you're going to have one very careful jurist up there on the bench. Seems your clients are hell-bent on shooting down the record of acquittals."

Colson got to his feet. He walked over to the window and stood looking at me, his jaw set. "All right, Jordan. I'll have a session with Oster. I'll lay it out for him. I give you my solemn pledge that if—"

The buzzer stopped him. He went back to his desk and picked up the phone.

"Who? *Who?* Yes, put him on." He listened and I saw him go tense, sudden shock in his face. "Oh, no!" he said in a hushed whisper. "When did it happen? Yes, of course, I'll come right over." He rang off and looked up, his mouth stiff with restraint. "Ira Madden is dead."

I whistled softly. "How did it happen?"

"Car accident. Madden was behind the wheel, heading north on the FDR Drive. Lost control at the Forty-second Street exit and slammed into a concrete abutment. Too damned lazy to attach his seat belt and damned near impaled on the steering wheel."

"Driving alone?"

"No. Floyd Oster was with him."

"Hm. What were his injuries?"

"Broken wrist. Seems he threw his hand up to keep his face out of the windshield." Colson shook his head. "How am I going to break this to Lily? She loved the old tyrant."

What they needed was privacy. He was brooding uncertainly at the door as I walked through it, his face half-past-six on a stopped clock. I thought I knew what ailed him. There always are dissident factions within a union, angling to take over top management. A new team might sweep out all of Ira Madden's old henchmen, including union counsel Edward Colson.

Madden was given a splendid send-off: bronze casket, a cortege of retainers one-eighth of a mile long, and floral offerings more suitable for a wedding. I attended the last rites out of curiosity but derived no pleasure from the proceedings. Funerals are a pagan ritual relished only by morticians and enemies and possibly a few heirs of the deceased.

Lily Madden, chief mourner, sole surviving relative, shoulders stooped, face hidden behind a black veil, was managing to stay upright with the help of Ed Colson's strong right arm. Floyd Oster was not one of the pallbearers. His left wing, in a cast, was cradled by a sling around his neck, no identifiable expression on the carp face.

In unctuous tones, the presiding cleric chanted a litany of Ira Madden's sterling characteristics and accomplishments that would have astonished the deceased. The words brought convulsive sobs from Lily.

Mourners departed from graveside just before the final planting. I watched Ed Colson hand Lily into a limousine and then drop back for a brief colloquy with Floyd Oster. There was a snarl on Oster's face. Ultimately, Colson threw up his hands in frustration and joined his fiancée. Oster climbed into the following car.

When I got back to my apartment, I phoned Laura Bolt. Her answering service said she had gone away for the weekend. I thought, *Why not?* Manhattan is not unalloyed bliss during the furnace summers. I longed for a touch of respite myself. Two days fishing on a quiet mountain lake seemed like a good idea. So I packed essentials and ordered my car.

Then, heading toward the Henry Hudson Parkway, partly on impulse and partly because it was on my way, I decided to stop off for another crack at Floyd Oster.

I parked in front of the brownstone and rang his bell. No response. I kept my finger on the button and finally gave up. As I left the building, there he was, sauntering toward me, lugging a six-pack of beer. I blocked his path at the entrance. He fixed me with a cold, reptilian stare.

"Move it, Jordan. Get out of my way."

"Ah, Floyd," I said, "you don't listen. Not to me, not to your own lawyer. Stupid, greedy, bull-headed. Words can't penetrate that skull of yours, so I'll have to try something else."

"Yeah?" A twisted sneer. "Like what?"

"Like putting you behind bars. My personal project, Floyd. I'm going to bring you down. Ira Madden is no longer around to provide protection. Some new boys are going to take over the union. Colson will dump you, too. So you're all alone, Floyd. And if—"

I stopped, clued by a sudden flicker in his eyes, a slight shifting of weight. As the tip of Oster's heavy shoe shot upward, I swiveled, grabbing his ankle, and twisting his leg through a ninety-degree turn. It lifted him off the ground and when I let go, he fell heavily to the pavement, arms flailing. Oster landed on the poor broken wing and he whinnied like a horse in a burning barn.

I bent contritely to lend him a hand. He pulled away, frothing obscenities. He had the lexicon of a mule skinner.

"Now you just leave that poor injured man alone," a high-pitched voice snapped at me from behind.

She was small and wrinkled, frumpily dressed, with flour-white hair, stern-visaged, brandishing an umbrella. "Aren't you ashamed of yourself, a big man like you? Attacking Mr. Oster, him wounded and helpless." Her lips were so tightly compressed they were invisible. She threatened me with the umbrella. "Get away from him. Shoo! If you don't leave this instant, I'm going to make a citizen's arrest. Felonious assault."

I repressed a smile. This feisty little specimen would barely tip the scale at eighty pounds, and I didn't for a moment doubt that she was ready to put the arm on me and hustle me down to the local precinct.

I looked down at Oster. "Sorry about your wrist, Floyd. It was unavoidable. But from here on, no more dialogue." Then I turned quickly and went to my car and drove off. I stopped thinking about Oster when I crossed the George Washington Bridge and headed north on Route 17.

It turned out to be a profitable weekend. I caught six medium-sized trout. I skinned, boned, sautéed, and consumed them with vast relish. I went to bed early and got up early and I thought how pleasant it would be to spend one whole month engaged in these wholesome endeavors. On Monday morning, I drove back to the city.

A visitor was waiting for me in the lobby of my apartment building— Detective-Sergeant Wienick, unsmiling, barrel-shaped and balding. "Have a nice weekend, Counselor?" he inquired politely.

"A reception committee from the New York Police Department," I said. "Well, Sergeant, what cooks?"

"A drive in a city-owned vehicle. The lieutenant is waiting."

He meant Lt. John Nola of Homicide. The lieutenant sat in his office, swarthy, trim, precise, abrupt to the point of discourtesy, probably the best cop on the force. Although I had not been in touch with him recently, he dispensed with all amenities.

"You go away for the weekend, Counselor, how come you don't let your secretary know where you can be reached?"

"And be at the mercy of the telephone? No, sir."

"Maybe there's an emergency."

"Emergencies are for doctors, not lawyers." I lifted an eyebrow. "What's your problem, Lieutenant?"

"We both have a problem. Yours may be more serious than mine. All right, Wienick, let the lady have a look at him."

The sergeant stepped out and returned a moment later ushering a woman through the door, the little old lady with the umbrella. She stopped short, staring at me. She pointed a quivering finger and announced in a shrill voice, "That's him! That's the man! I saw him attack poor Mr. Oster. I saw him with my own eyes." She fell back a step. "He's dangerous. Don't let him get close to me. He shouldn't be allowed on the street."

"No doubt in your mind?" Nola asked.

"I have 20-20 vision, Lieutenant. They oughta bring back capital punishment. Prison is too good for—"

Nola cut her off. "See that the lady gets home, Sergeant."

Wienick took her arm and firmly nudged her through the door. Nola sat back and shook his head sadly.

"Don't tell me," I said. "Let me guess. Something happened to Oster."

"It did, indeed."

"The works?"

"Enough to put him in cold storage down at the old morgue."

"I can't say I'm grief-stricken, Lieutenant. Society will survive the loss. When did it happen?"

"Sunday afternoon."

"While I was up in the hills, fishing."

"Proof?"

"If necessary."

"Routine, Counselor. I insist."

"Then you'll have it. Fill me in, please. Who found the body?"

"Mrs. Scrimshaw."

"Who?"

"The old lady. Holly Scrimshaw."

"You're kidding."

"That's her name, Counselor." A smile flickered, meager and brief. "She thought she heard a shot and went down to investigate. Oster's door was open.

He was slumped in a chair, one bullet in his left temple; about 2:00 P.M. Mrs. Scrimshaw ran back to her room and phoned. We caught the squeal and were there in minutes. She told us about that fracas you had with Oster on Friday. She said you got into your car and she remembered the registration."

"Remarkable."

"She is, indeed. We couldn't reach you and figured you were away for the weekend. Enough. Let's bring it home. What happened between you and Oster?"

"It's a long story, Lieutenant."

"I'll make time for it. Talk."

I sighed and sat back and told him about Oster's attempt to extort money from the widow Bolt. He listened, eyes narrowed.

"Would that be the fifty thousand dollars allegedly paid to Judge Bolt for favorable rulings in the Madden embezzlement case?"

"The same."

"You're certain it was Oster?"

"Everything points to him."

"Why you? Why didn't she come to the police?"

"Because he warned her to stay away from the law, and the lady was terrified."

"So you saw Oster on Friday for the last time."

"Yes."

"You couldn't budge him and you decided to use a little muscle."

"You know better, Lieutenant. Violence is not my style. Oster ignored my first visit, and when I asked Ed Colson to intervene, Oster continued intractable. So on Friday I decided to give him one last chance."

"And then?"

"I intended to turn it over to the law."

"You're a big man, Counselor. Are you telling me that Oster tackled you with one arm in a sling?"

"Lieutenant, Floyd Oster was a savage little fiend. If his dropkick had landed I would have been out of business for weeks. Dumping him was purely defensive. He seldom lost an argument. Look what happened in the accident. It killed Madden and only fractured Oster's wrist."

Nola studied me for a long moment. Finally he reached a decision and said, "The accident did not kill Ira Madden."

I sat erect.

"*What?*"

"Madden was dead when his car hit the abutment. As a DOA, he was taken to the morgue. An attendant found medication in his pocket. Nitroglycerin tablets. You know what they're for?"

"Hardening of the arteries. Generally prescribed for arteriosclerosis."

"Correct. They also found an anticoagulant. Obviously Ira Madden had been a candidate for a heart attack. He was autopsied and the M.E. found a massive clot blocking one of the major heart arteries. The M.E. says it finished him off in the blink of an eyelash and that's why he lost control of the car."

"And Madden kept his condition a secret."

"Naturally. He didn't want his enemies at the union to know."

"Those vials containing his medication, was there a doctor's name on them?"

"A Dr. Lewis Bukantz."

"You questioned him?"

"He was reluctant to talk, but we got enough out of him to clear the picture. Madden had a history of hypertension, high blood pressure. He suffered his first attack a year ago. He refused hospitalization. Bukantz advised him to ask the government for a delay in bringing him to trial, claiming that stress and anxiety might exacerbate his condition."

I arched an eyebrow. "Exacerbate?"

"Nice word, no? I learned it from the doctor. It means to exaggerate or intensify the disease. Madden turned thumbs down."

"Of course. It would have required a motion by Madden's attorney, stating a reason for the application."

"So the doctor washed his hands of responsibility."

I shook my head. "Seems the law is a little screwy on this. Cardiac failure is presumably a private matter, not affecting the public. Except they ought to revoke the patient's license to drive a car. Because if a seizure hits the man on a crowded street, he might start mowing down innocent pedestrians."

"You got a point, Counselor. And it's happened in the past." He regarded me narrowly. "How are you on history?"

"Now, there's a staggering non sequitur, if I ever heard one. What history are you talking about? Modern? Medieval? Ancient?"

"Ancient."

"How far back?"

"896 B.C."

"Nine centuries before the birth of Christ. Not my specialty. I'm a Civil War buff. Why do you ask?"

"Here. Take a look." He handed me a small square of paper with fold creases. "We found this in Oster's wallet."

I saw, written in pencil: *#1–896 BC*. It rang no bell. It stirred no recollection. I looked up. "Why don't you check with some historian who specializes in the era?"

"I did. Professor Bernard Buchwald at Columbia. He tried to come up with something." Nola made a helpless gesture. "But who kept records in those days? A few hieroglyphics in caves, maybe. Nothing we could use."

"You think the date is significant?"

"Counselor, that paper was in Oster's wallet. The man was murdered. Can we afford to ignore it? All right. Now, let me test you again. Here's another." He produced a second slip of paper. "Also from Oster's wallet. The name of a man. Ever heard of him?"

I studied it intently, like one of Dr. Hermann Rorschach's inkblots. It read: *C H George, NAS*. No periods between the initials. I dug deep, but the name triggered no response.

"He's a stranger to me," I said. "I see the handwriting on this slip of paper is different from the other."

"Correct. The date is in Oster's hand; the name was written by Ira Madden. We compared them both with known specimens."

"C. H. George. Have you checked him out?"

"He's not listed in the telephone directory, all five boroughs. Query, Counselor: Do you know of any degree or title or government agency carrying the initials NAS?"

"None I can recall. But the pension fund of Amalgamated Mechanics, the alleged source of Ira Madden's loot, was heavily invested in the stock market. Some of those securities are probably unlisted and traded over the counter. Madden was in charge. So NAS could be an abbreviation for National Association of Security Dealers."

"If C. H. George was in business, wouldn't he list his name in the telephone book?"

"Of course. But which one? Suppose he has an office in Newark or Passaic or Jersey City or Hoboken or—take it from there."

Nola looked sour. "Or maybe one of a thousand other cities. Madden would have dealt with any clown who'd kick back a piece of the commissions."

"Why not call the NASD itself and ask if C. H. George is a member?"

Nola thumped his forehead and quickly reached for the phone and barked an order.

As he hung up, the door opened and Wienick was back. "Keep your hat on," Nola snapped. "Pick up Laura Bolt and bring her in."

"Now, wait just one little minute," I said. "Why bother the lady? Can't you leave her in peace?"

"Your fault, Counselor. You tell me Oster was trying to extort money from Mrs. Bolt. Oster suddenly becomes a corpse, so we have to sweat the lady to find out if she's clean."

"Then you'll do it in my presence. I'm her lawyer."

"And you'll advise her not to talk."

"Come off it, Lieutenant, Mrs. Bolt has nothing to hide. She was out of town when it happened."

"Convenient. All interested parties manage to leave town while a murder takes place."

"Not all, Lieutenant. Just Laura Bolt and myself. Somebody apparently stayed here to do the job."

"Yeah, I know. Or maybe somebody sneaked back long enough to point a gun."

"Laura Bolt never fired a gun in her life. She couldn't hit one of the walls from inside a room."

"You know that for a fact, Counselor?"

I grinned.

"No. May I have five minutes with the lady before you put her on the grill?"

"I'd rather not."

"Lieutenant, the U.S. Supreme Court gives every accused the right to remain silent until he consults an attorney. You've heard of privileged communications. Where's the privilege if I can't see her in private?"

"Aagh! Who the hell can argue with a lawyer? You may consult right here in my office."

"Is it bugged?"

"Do me a favor, Counselor. Kiss—"

"Don't say it, Lieutenant. It's not dignified. If—"

The buzzer signaled. He put the phone to his ear and listened, one eyebrow arching. "The man can't wait? All right, send him in." He hung up and looked at me. "Stay put. This should be interesting."

Nola's visitor was a thin, humorless, balding primate with computer eyes and a razor-slit mouth. He introduced himself in a flat, uninflected voice and presented credentials: Mr. Harry Prime, Frauds Division, Internal Revenue Service. What he wanted was a line on Floyd Oster. He'd been told that Lieutenant Nola was in charge of the homicide investigation.

"Was Oster due for a tax audit?" Nola asked.

"Nothing like that, Lieutenant. Oster contacted my department several days ago and started preliminary negotiations. He wanted information about an informer's fee."

Nola frowned. "Informer's fee?"

"Squealer's reward," I volunteered. "A tip to the gentlemen at IRS about someone's tax evasion and the government rewards the squealer with a percentage of the recovery, if any."

Mr. Harry Prime regarded me with distaste. "I don't believe I caught your name."

"Scott Jordan."

"Yes, I've heard of you. Well, for your information, sir, we prefer not to call it a 'squealer's reward.' 'Informer's fee' would be more appropriate. An individual who assists us in tracking down money that rightfully belongs to the government is a patriot performing his civic duty."

"Mr. Prime, any time Floyd Oster performed a civic duty for patriotic reasons should be declared a national holiday."

Nola spread his hands. "What exactly do you want from me, Mr. Prime?"

"Perhaps I'd better give you a little background, Lieutenant. When Floyd Oster got in touch with us, he said that he had valuable information about a tax evader. He did not identify the man, nor supply any information about where the illegal funds could be found. He did say the sum was considerable, in excess of one million dollars. He wanted to know what percentage of the recovery he could expect. At the conclusion of our talk he made an appointment to see me later this week. Well, you know what happened. Oster was killed, foreclosing further disclosures. The Internal Revenue Service would like to know whether your investigation has turned up anything that might help us."

"Not yet. We haven't been in the picture long enough."

"Can you tell us anything about his associates?"

"The only name that comes to mind is Ira Madden. But there is nothing in the record to indicate that he would double-cross his former employer. May I make a suggestion?"

"Please do."

"Oster was under indictment by the Justice Department. They've been investigating him for months. It seems likely that the U.S. Attorney for this district would have considerably more information about the man than I do."

"He's next on my list." Prime snapped his head around to eye me with sudden recollection. "Scott Jordan . . . Weren't you supposed to represent Judge Bolt on that bribery charge for which Oster was under indictment?"

"That's right."

"Do you know anything about this matter?"

"Not at the moment," I said. "But I have a client who's being questioned about the Oster homicide, so I have a special reason for digging around. If I come up with anything involving this tax evasion, would I not be in line for an informer's fee?"

He wore a look of pain. "Each case must stand on its own merits. You are an attorney, sir. An officer of the court."

"Except that I'm not on salary. I'm just a citizen trying to perform a civic duty. I've been shelling out to the government all my life. I wouldn't mind getting some of it back. Strictly legal, of course, according to your own rules. Now, don't con me, Mr. Prime. Will I be entitled to a cut?"

He had to clear an obstruction out of his throat. He spoke with difficulty, as though any payment would be coming out of his own pocket. "Mr. Jordan, if you provide us with information that materially assists the government in making a recovery, yes, you would be entitled to a fee."

"How much?"

"I do not think you would be disappointed."

"Ten percent?"

"In that neighborhood."

Ten percent of one million was a good neighborhood. I said, "Okay. I'll see what I can do."

He produced a card. "Call me at this number." He stood and shook hands with Nola. With me, he skipped the amenities. After he left, Nola gave me a searching look. "I know that expression, Counselor. It troubles me. You're onto something."

"Only a vague notion, Lieutenant. An unleavened theory."

"Maybe I can help."

"Later, maybe. After I work it out."

He nodded in resignation, knowing it would be futile to insist. The door opened and Sgt. Wienick was back again with an outraged Laura Bolt, bitterly complaining. I silenced her with an upraised palm.

"This handsome gentleman," I said, "is Lieutenant John Nola. He will allow us to use his office and he assures me the room is not bugged."

Nola stifled a comment and stalked out, tugging Wienick behind him. I asked Laura Bolt many questions and was not especially charmed by any of her answers. She had driven out to Montauk, the weekend guest of friends. They had also invited another guest, male, a bachelor, hopefully suitable as a companion for Laura. A doomed pairing; ten minutes after the introduction she loathed him. Early the next morning, apologizing to her friends, she drove back to the city.

So she was right here in town when Floyd Oster had bought it.

Yes, she'd heard about his death. No, she had not been near his apartment. Her reaction? No trace of grief; in fact, some elation. She had finished the weekend watching television. No calls from anyone.

Nola is going to love this, I realized. With the Anglo-Saxon presumption of innocence, he would need more than coincidence before he could even hold her as a material witness.

Finally I opened the door and beckoned. "She's all yours, Lieutenant."

His attitude during thirty minutes of probing was one of polite skepticism. In the end, he dismissed us, still dissatisfied. I knew that within the hour he would have a crew on the job, scouring Oster's neighborhood, displaying pictures of the shapely Mrs. Bolt. I put her into a cab.

Theories need a maturation period, time to ripen; so I eschewed taxis and walked, pondering all the way. Destination: main branch of the public library, second floor, a room devoted exclusively to finance and economics. Most of the room's inhabitants were bent over long tables, intently studying stock market reports, seeking that elusive opportunity to corral the easy buck with neither sweat nor toil.

I checked out a fat manual on foreign banks and offshore tax shelters. I dug deep and long, straining my eyesight, flipping pages, and eventually felt a stir of excitement. Something had caught my attention. I ran it down, checking and cross-checking until one logical assumption followed another.

Lt. Nola and I had been hasty and arbitrary in drawing conclusions. We had been dead wrong on two counts: 896 B.C. was not a date; and C H George was not a man.

My initial lead came from Mr. Harry Prime himself, informing us that Floyd Oster had queried Internal Revenue about an informer's fee. Why would Oster do that? Simple. He knew that someone had perpetrated a tax fraud. Who? Who else but Ira Madden, suspected of squirreling away embezzled union funds in Switzerland? Oster had been close to Madden, a loyal lackey; but Madden had died, and there is no profit in being loyal to a corpse.

Now he was dead, and the U.S. Attorney for the Southern District of New York probably felt no pain. He had enough current cases to keep him occupied well into the next millennium. Consequently, he was not sorry to wipe the slate clean on the indictments of Ira Madden for embezzlement and Floyd Oster for bribing a federal judge, consigning his files to dead storage.

Not so Lt. John Nola; a homicide had been committed in his bailiwick.

Murder is murder, even the liquidation of so rank a specimen as Floyd Oster.

The files also remained opened for Mr. Harry Prime of Internal Revenue. So long as he could see any possibility for nourishing the government's exchequer, he intended to hang right in there, proceeding against Madden's estate, if necessary. He'd learned that Ed Colson had been named in Madden's will as executor.

After leaving the library, I tried a form of mental isometrics, drawing on random fragments of memory, and I now felt that certain conclusions should be passed along to the authorities. Nola was not available, and when I called Harry Prime, he asked me to attend a conference at his office the next morning with Ed Colson and the lieutenant.

The Manhattan District Office of the IRS on Church Street is a building that never failed to make me uncomfortable. Prime sat behind his desk and fixed us each in turn with his vigilant tax-collector's eyes. "A preliminary statement," he said, "just to get the record straight. There are four men in this room. Each of us has a different goal. Lt. Nola wants to catch a murderer. I want the government to collect every penny that's coming to us from Ira Madden's estate. You, Mr. Colson, as Madden's executor, would like to preserve that estate intact. And Mr. Jordan is after a piece of the action."

"Correction," I said. "The money would be a peripheral bonus, welcome but not essential. My chief goal is to clear Laura Bolt of any suspicion of homicide."

Prime was skeptical. "But you would not refuse an informer's fee."

"Would you?"

He looked startled and changed the subject. "Mr. Colson, you were Madden's defense attorney. You were also Floyd Oster's lawyer. Did you know that Floyd Oster had been in touch with my office before he died, informing us that he had information about a tax fraud involving over one million dollars?"

Colson shook his head.

"I had no knowledge of that, Mr. Prime. Floyd Oster was into many things of which I was not aware."

"Well, sir, if a tax fraud had indeed been committed, and Oster was aware of it, can you guess the perpetrator's identity?"

"I am a lawyer. I prefer facts to guesses."

"Isn't it a fact that Ira Madden had been charged with embezzling funds from the Amalgamated pension fund?"

"He had been charged, yes. An indictment is not proof. He was a far distance from being convicted."

"Only his death prevented that."

"No, sir. A lack of evidence would have accomplished the same purpose."

"Well, Mr. Colson, we at Internal Revenue are convinced that Oster was referring to Ira Madden. Would you care to comment?"

"Not especially, Mr. Prime, but I will. Supposing for the sake of argument that Ira Madden had lived, that he'd been tried and convicted, that embezzled money was located, just where would Internal Revenue fit into the picture?"

"Madden failed to pay taxes on that money."

"You're way off base, Mr. Prime. Again, conceding nothing, what taxes are you talking about? That money, if stolen from the pension fund, belongs to the union, and as general counsel for Amalgamated Mechanics, I intend to see that any recovery goes right back into the union treasury. Internal Revenue is not entitled to one red cent."

Prime sat blinking, his jaw slack. Generally, in the presence of tax officials, most citizens are apprehensive, humble, apologetic, so any change in the pattern comes as a jolt. Harry Prime was suddenly at a loss for words, but Lt. Nola had a few.

"As Floyd Oster's attorney, Mr. Colson, you must have spoken to him on numerous occasions."

"In preparation for his bribery trial, yes. I'd like to make one thing clear, Lieutenant: I think Floyd Oster was a moral leper. Ordinarily I wouldn't permit an insect like Oster through the door of my office. The only reason I took his case was because he was employed by the union and Ira Madden requested it."

"We found a slip of paper on Oster's corpse, bearing the name C. H. George. Did he ever mention anyone by that name to you?"

Colson frowned. "I have no such recollection."

"The name was written in Ira Madden's hand. Did Madden ever mention a C. H. George?"

"No, sir. Who is he?"

"We don't know. It had the letters NAS after it."

"C. H. George is not the name of a man," I said.

Sudden silence; all eyes swiveling and focusing. Nola dipped his chin and said in a very soft voice, "Would you fill that in, if you please, Counselor."

"It's an address in the Bahamas, Lieutenant. Specifically on New Providence Island."

"Keep talking."

"As written, 'C H George' is a form of speedwriting. It means Caribe House, George Street, and the NAS stands for Nassau."

"Who lives there?"

"Nobody. It's the branch office of a Swiss bank with headquarters in Zurich."

"Now how in hell did you find that out?"

"You remember you also found a number in Floyd Oster's pocket: 896 B.C. At first we thought it was a date. Then, in the light of Mr. Prime's information about Oster's inquiry, it occurred to me that it might refer to a secret numbered account in a Swiss bank. So I checked a source book at the library, and among the banks listed was one with headquarters in Zurich—Banque Credit."

Nola caught it instantly. "Banque Credit. Initials, B.C."

"Precisely. 896 B.C. The number of an account at the Banque Credit. I chased it down and discovered that the bank had a branch office in Caribe House on George Street in Nassau. That tied it. The connection was too obvious to be considered a coincidence."

"And the number one before the 896, where does that fit?"

"It fits the number-one man at Amalgamated Mechanics, Ira Madden."

"And Oster dug it up?"

"You found the evidence in his pocket."

Prime snapped, "Nobody ever mentioned this to me."

"You're hearing it now," I told him. "And it would not surprise me if that account had only recently been transferred from the Zurich headquarters to an offshore branch in the Bahamas to make it more quickly and easily accessible."

"Why didn't Madden close it out altogether?" Prime demanded. "He must have known the government recently negotiated a treaty with Switzerland regarding information about illegal funds."

"My guess is that he was preparing to do that, and would have, if a heart attack hadn't finished him first."

Nola brooded at me. "So Madden was dead. Who else had a motive to kill Oster?"

"Seems to me you were all primed to nominate Laura Bolt."

"That's past history."

"Good. Because she wasn't the only victim. Floyd Oster was also putting the squeeze on someone else."

"Who?"

I pointed. "Our lawyer friend. Mr. Edward Colson."

Colson's chair skidded back and toppled over as he came to his feet. "What the hell are you talking about, Jordan?"

"I'm talking about blackmail. Extortion. Floyd Oster may have been an insect, but his brain was working just fine. He knew what you were after. He spotted your game before anyone else and he braced you for a cut of the profits."

"What are you trying to say?"

"I'm not trying. I'm saying it. Right out in front of witnesses. You were Ira Madden's personal attorney. You had drawn his will. You were the executor. You knew that he had left everything to Lily, and you knew about Madden's heart attack and that he might kick off at any time."

Colson's jaw rippled. "So?"

"So you went to work on the girl. You zeroed in. She never had a prayer. All that high-pressure, virile charm beamed at the poor, sad little pigeon. And she fell. Oh, how she fell! I saw her in your office, mesmerized and moonstruck. You planned on marrying the girl, and after that it would be a breeze conning her out of the estate. Especially that money in the Bahamas. One million tax-free dollars."

"Why in hell would I need Lily's money? I'm a successful lawyer."

"Try another hole, Colson. That one doesn't fit. You've limited yourself to one client for ten years—Amalgamated Mechanics, Madden's private fief. Now Madden is dead and when the opposition takes over you'll probably get axed. It's too late to start a new practice. So you were desperate. Everyone knows you're a big spender and couldn't stomach a change in style. So you were itching to get your hands on Madden's loot in that numbered account."

Perspiration bathed his face. "How would I know where he kept that money?"

"You knew because Madden told you—an essential step in passing the money on to his daughter. That's the drill, a fixed procedure in transferring secret accounts. The bank has been told the name of the depositor's beneficiary. When he dies, his lawyer must notify them and furnish an official death certificate, which allows them to transfer the account. In this case, to Lily Madden. But only for a short time, because ultimately you'd take control. Not a cent to Amalgamated Mechanics. And knowing all that, Oster wanted in, so he put the bite on you."

White lines framed Colson's mouth. "If he was blackmailing me, why would he go to the IRS?"

"To pressure you. So you would deal with him. That's why he had to be put on ice."

Colson flattened a hand against his chest. "Are you intimating that I killed Floyd Oster?"

"Not intimating. Accusing you outright. You knew Oster. You knew he would bleed you dry. There was no other way out. I called on the man myself. I know that he doesn't open his door for visitors. But he'd open the door for you, especially if he thought you were ready to talk business."

Colson turned away, facing Nola and Prime, arms spread wide in appeal, voice charged with sincerity.

"Something's happened to Jordan. He's gone soft between the ears. I'm a respected member of the bar. It's absurd to think I would kill a man for money."

"Money," I said. "The usual motive. In this case, one million bucks. Men have plundered and slaughtered for less. But you had still another motive, Colson. I think you were the moving force behind Oster's attempt to bribe Judge Bolt. You set it up. You've been around the courts a long time and you knew that Judge Bolt was vulnerable. And you were terrified that if Oster ever came to trial he might break and implicate you. That would be the end; complicity, conspiracy, disbarment, disgrace, prison. How does that grab you for motive?"

A dark vein bulged in a blue diagonal over his left eye. "You haven't got a shred of evidence."

"Maybe not. But you have, Colson. You're holding it now in your sweaty right hand. Oster was killed by a bullet through the head. So the killer fired a gun. The police will perform a nitrate test to determine if any gunpowder particles were blown back into the skin of your palm. And if the test is positive, how will you explain it? Target practice in your office?"

He lifted his hand and stared at it.

"And that isn't all," I said. "I don't think you had the time or the foresight to drop your weapon off the Staten Island ferry. They know how to look. They'll find it and make a ballistics check."

He transferred his gaze to me, his tongue rimming his mouth.

"You want more, Colson? Here it is. Lieutenant Nola will put an army into the field, locating witnesses to prove you were in Oster's neighborhood at the critical time. That's a heavily populated area. Somebody must have seen you coming or going."

He found his voice. It was gravelly and hoarse. "I'm leaving. I don't have to stand here and listen to this ranting maniac."

As he headed for the door at an awkward trot, Nola came up fast and blocked his way. "Not so fast, Counselor. We have a little business to transact at headquarters."

Ed Colson blinked, his eyes lost. Then he doubled over and got sick, right there in the Manhattan office of the Internal Revenue Service.

S.S. RAFFERTY

The Death Desk

Ive been bouncing around the newspaper trade for almost thirty years—layman in Buffalo, police beat in Chicago, wire editor in Baton Rouge. I've been in a lot of city rooms and must have filed five tons of copy but, like all reporters, I have one yarn that has never seen the light of print. Some reporters will tell you they didn't print a certain story because they couldn't prove it, even though they knew it to be true. In my case, it wasn't just a lack of proof; I couldn't even figure the damn thing out. Now that I have, it's too late to do anything about it. Even if I could, I wouldn't.

I didn't have to go far to observe the whole thing, because it happened right under my nose in the city room of the *Frankport Post-Union*, up in New England back in the early '30s.

The *Post-Union* was a morning and evening paper with separate editorial staffs for each edition. I worked the night shift on the rewrite desk, which wasn't bad when you considered that Ted McCoy, the managing editor, worked on the day side. Of course the day crew had a large circulation and got all the prestige, but I was too old a newshand to put up with McCoy's testy ways and daily tantrums; but try to explain that to young Bobby Hawks.

Poor Bobby had been slaving on the night obit desk for almost fourteen months and hadn't moved a quad's width toward advancement. Now, all young fellows starting out usually are assigned to write obituaries. It's good training in using the five W's properly and learning the paper's stylebook. However, fourteen months on obits was unheard of—it was cruel and inhuman punishment.

The kid brought it on himself, though. Bobby's problem was not seeded in incompetence; contrarily, he was the best obit man the *Post-Union* had ever had.

His career had been crippled by his own enthusiasm and deferred by his initiative. He was imprisoned, seemingly forever, in a job he performed too willingly, too well.

Even the location of the obit desk, tucked away in a far corner of the city room, symbolized Bobby's isolation from the other men who handled hard, front-page news. In the cynical and sarcastic minds of the night crew, Bobby was a joke. While the rest of us worked from 6 P.M. through 2 A.M., McCoy had assigned Bobby to the "trick shift." All of us knew the "trick" was to stay awake from four in the afternoon till four the next morning. It made little sense to keep the kid there for two hours after the morning paper had been put to bed. Even if a late story came in, Bobby couldn't do much about it anyway, except leave it for the daymen when they came in at seven to work up the afternoon editions.

. "You know what that kid's trouble is?" Cal Slocum, a sportswriter, asked one night when we were drinking our dinner break in a "speak" about two blocks from the paper. "He's too naive."

"I don't know, Cal," I said. "I know what you mean—the conscientious thing—but there's something about that young guy that's, well, foreboding. I covered an execution once in Louisiana and the guy had the same kind of ice-blue eyes, the same intentness on the task at hand."

"Look of the doomed, huh?"

"No, I meant the hangman. Same kind of eyes."

"Probably gets that way from all the undertakers he talks to. You know they send him Christmas presents."

"Why not, Cal? For the first time in ten years the obits come out with the right ages and addresses—a definite improvement."

"Sure, but McCoy knows that too. The kid's stuck."

Well, if he was stuck, he was making the most of it. A few weeks later, I learned that Bobby had written several articles for a funeral directors' trade journal. I managed to get hold of one and was surprised to learn that he could write rather well. The subject, "The Obituary, Your Best Public Relations Tool," was a little bizarre, but showed crafty inventiveness. I know now just how inventive Bobby really had been.

I decided to play Dutch uncle when Fred Norris, the night editor, came down sick and took a leave of absence. I took over the night slot in the interim, but that didn't allow me to elevate Bobby to straight news. I didn't want McCoy on my neck. I did have a talk with Bobby, however.

"You ought to quit, Bobby," I told him on my way home one night. "Not right away, but make some plans. I know several people who have their own slots on papers around the country. I'll write them and see if they have any openings."

"Thanks just the same, Mr. Bowers, but I've got to make it here. I grew up in this town, I grew up reading this paper. I think it can be better. Thanks anyway, I'll remember this." He looked up from his typewriter, those cold blue eyes staring off somewhere else as if planning a dream.

Three days later I came in to work to find a message waiting from Ted McCoy. I reported to his office a little tremulous and a bit excited. I was thinking that maybe Fred Norris had died and I was getting his job. I should have checked with Bobby. Although Fred wasn't exactly kicking, he was alive, and McCoy was in a rage.

"Did you print this?" he snorted, tossing the morning edition's obituary page onto the desk in front of me. I read it quickly:

MRS. JAMES BERNOIT

Mrs. Mary Bernoit, 70, wife of James Bernoit of 215 Spring Street, died last night in St. Helena's Hospital. She had been a patient there since March 10. Funeral services will be announced.

I breathed a sigh of relief. Bobby had not let me down. The style and form were correct. "Yes, I edited this."

"Then where the devil is the rest of it, survivors, affiliations? It's half an obit."

"Well, that's all Hawks could get from the hospital."

"The hospital! Didn't he get this from an undertaker?"

"No, sir. You see, Hawks had an idea that we shouldn't wait for an undertaker to give us information. He just calls the hospitals and picks up the latest deaths."

The smile on McCoy's face eased my tension, and for a moment I had a glimpse of hope for Bobby.

"Now that's what I call running an obit desk." McCoy was beaming. "Tell that kid he's doing a great job."

"Well, Mr. McCoy, since you brought it up, don't you think a bit of reward is in order? Maybe I can start breaking him in on the county desk. You know, he really can write."

The grin and the beam went behind a cloud of rumbling anger. "Are you nuts? Are you out of your ever-lovin' mind? I finally have someone on that desk who does a good job, and you want to take him off. For ten years, I've had phone calls from irate families because we'd left out the fact that some joker was a Mason or an Elk or a Grand Exhausted Rooster. I used to get mail canceling subscriptions, but I don't get them anymore, and that's the way it's going to stay. I swear the only thing some people read in this town are the obits."

Well, that was the end of that, and I urged Bobby again to take my offer of looking around for him. He refused.

We started to slip into early winter and with it, the specter of influenza. Bobby was busy from the moment he set foot in the city room until I put the paper to bed. During that time, he had published another article for an undertakers' trade journal: "The Chig Beetle, Nature's Undertaker." It would never be confused with dynamite journalism, but it did show an ability to make a story out of nothing—absolutely nothing.

In a sense, this seemed to be Bobby's long suit. He could work within rigid confinements and still succeed. I have always admired people who can whip something up out of the materials at hand, like an inventive short-order cook. The only problem was that short-order cooks never become great chefs, nor do hack writers become great editors, even if they do sign their work "R. Southgate Hawks."

By midwinter, I thought I noticed a change in Bobby. At first, I analyzed it as occupational ennui, because he spoke very little and went about his business mechanically. Yet it was more than psychological.

"It's his stupid getup," Cal Slocum said, laughing at my lack of observation. "You're so busy you haven't noticed it. The dark suit, the black tie and piped vest. Do you know he wears a homburg on the street?"

"So the kid's conservative."

"The boob is dressing like a mortician, and he gives me the creeps. Have you talked to him lately? He gives you this low, soft monotone, like he's very sorry for everything. You ought to have a talk with him."

I never got the chance. At ten the next morning, I was roused from sleep by McCoy's telephone snarl. "Get down here!" I got down there.

Ted McCoy was more confused than angry when he handed me the typed copy:

CHARLES DONOVAN

Charles Donovan, 67, of 75 Cottonwood Road, a retired railway clerk, died at 8:15 this morning in St. Luke's Hospital after a long illness. He is survived by his wife, the former Mary Herrig, and a son, George. Funeral arrangements will be announced.

"Well?" I asked him.

"Well? What do you mean 'well'? We found this in the hold-over copy box this morning. Everyone thought it missed yesterday's afternoon edition, but when a rewrite man finally got through to the hospital at 9:30, we found out that Donovan had died *this* morning—an hour and a half ago. How could Hawks write an obit at 4 A.M. about a man who didn't die until five hours later?"

I told him I didn't know and he told me to "get Hawks the hell down here." I called and he got the hell down there.

"Where did you dig up that outfit?" McCoy commented on Bobby's attire in surprise.

"I'm sorry, sir, but on my salary, it's about the best I can do."

"Looks like you're going to bury someone." He said it offhand and then caught himself. He checked his pause and picked up the Donovan announcement.

"Would you mind explaining this, Hawks? Where did you get this information?"

"From a Mr. Demos. Nick Demos, I think he said. I assumed it was the Demos Funeral Home."

"To my knowledge, Hawks, there is no Demos Funeral Home in this entire city."

"Maybe it was from the suburbs, sir. Is there anything wrong? Is the copy incorrect?"

"Oh, it's correct, all right. Charles Donovan died this morning at 8:15, hours after this copy was written—that's what's wrong."

"I'm sorry about the error, sir. Mr. Demos said at 8:12. I took an editorial liberty and rounded it out."

"I'm not talking about a three-minute error, you idiot. I'm talking about a story written before the man died. What are you, a clairvoyant or something?"

"No, sir, at least not to my knowledge. I simply answered the phone and took down the facts. I'm pleased they were right, sir."

McCoy looked at him with confusion and then dismissed him after telling him to take his dumb homburg off in the office.

At least three weeks had passed when McCoy again summoned Bobby and myself from slumber.

"Hawks," he said, holding up another piece of copy paper, the one Bobby had put in the "hold" box earlier that morning, "this is insane. How in the world could you have known that R. J. Riggs was going to die this afternoon and write an obit ahead of time?"

"You have every reason to be angry, Mr. McCoy. I know the guidebook is quite explicit about getting the time of death right, but Mr. Demos wasn't quite sure and it was very late. I'll watch it in the future."

"Watch it, my foot. I'll tell you something, Hawks. After the Donovan obit, I had a reporter check with the State Licensing Bureau. There is no mortician practicing under the name of Demos. In fact, there is no Nick Demos listed in the city directory or the phone book or voter registration lists or anywhere else. What does this guy say when he calls?"

"Well, Mr. McCoy, it's hard to say. After working eleven or twelve hours a day, I get kind of fuzzy. When the phone rings, and I answer it, there isn't anyone on the line right away. There's a lot of electrical sounds, clicks and things, like a connection is being made. Then Mr. Demos comes on and says, 'I have one for you, my boy.' I'll tell you, Mr. McCoy, he has the deepest voice I've ever heard, and yet it's quite soothing. Well, then he just gives me the dope and I type it up. He doesn't say anything else, except, 'I'll be speaking with you again.'"

McCoy sent him back to work, and the next day had the phone at Bobby's desk changed to a new extension number. During the rest of the winter, Bobby placed three predeath obits in the hold box, but there were no more conferences with McCoy. The rumors spread throughout the building, and before spring not one soul would go within five feet of his desk. Lou, the counterman at the Diamond Luncheonette, asked him to please let him send the coffee up gratis rather than drink it in the restaurant. He continued to wear his mortician's outfit, with the addition of spats and a red carnation in his lapel.

By mid-June, Bobby's isolation was tantamount to Coventry. Then it happened. McCoy didn't call us in the morning this time. He was waiting for me when I came to work.

"Get Hawks and come to my office," he said in an agitated tone that was far from anger. Ted McCoy was visibly nervous. When we showed up at his office door, he motioned us in. His face was drawn and ashen, his words thick and slippery.

"Hawks," he said, taking a paper from his pocket, "when did this come in?"

Bobby looked at the copy:

(Date to come)

THEOPOLIS MACOPOLIS

Theopolis Macopolis, 56, . . .

"I should have tossed this away, sir. It was careless of me. I know you like desks kept neat."

"Don't play games with me, Hawks. This was found on your desk this morning. What did Mr. Demos say?"

"Well, he came on and said, 'I have another one for you. His name is Theopolis Macopolis,' and then something happened to the connection and the line went dead. I just put in 'date to come' in case he called back when I wasn't here."

"Do you know who Theopolis Macopolis is?"

"No, sir, I don't. Sounds Greek."

McCoy lowered his head solemnly. "Hawks, I am Theopolis Macopolis."

"But, sir, your name is Ted McCoy, or Theodore McCoy."

"I changed it years ago. There isn't a soul in this world, not even my wife, who knows my real name. Heaven help me, Hawks, didn't he say anything else? Mr. Demos, I mean."

"Not another word, except—"

"Except what? Look, son, you can tell me. I'm a pretty tough guy after thirty years in this business. I can take it, son."

"Well, he said, er . . . that the party was 56 years of age."

"And I'm 56. He didn't say anything about next Tuesday, did he? I'm supposed to fly to Chicago next Tuesday. No, he wouldn't do that, would he? He only tells you hours in advance, doesn't he?" He tugged his tie open and unbuttoned the neck of his shirt.

"Well, sir, Mr. McCoy, sir, I can see that this has upset you and I'm sorry. Now, he did say he was going to call back, didn't he? Maybe he will tonight."

McCoy winced at the word "tonight."

"Now that I really think of it, Mr. McCoy, it couldn't be you," Bobby went on.

"How do you know that, son?"

"Because if it were a person of your importance, he would have called the city desk, not me. It stands to reason that—"

McCoy gave us a weak smile. "That's right. No, wait a minute. There was no one here except you when the call came in. He had to talk to you, he always talks to you. Look, I don't want you here tonight. Take it off. In fact, you're starting on the day crew tomorrow morning. I need an assistant anyway, and you might as well learn from the best. Now go home and take it easy. And stop wearing those dumb clothes. Go down to the cashier now and draw an advance on your new salary. I'll call them."

Well, if Bobby's stock went up, mine went down. Fred Norris recovered and came back as night editor, so I called a few friends around the business and finally landed a Sunday feature writer's berth with a Jersey paper. I continued to follow Bobby's career via the "People and Places" column in *Printer's Ink*, and I have to admit I envied him. In his first year under McCoy's tutelage, he became the youngest city editor in the country. Then there was the Pulitzer for "best makeup" and two years later, "best reporting under a deadline." That was followed by the announcement that R. Southgate Hawks, on the death of Ted McCoy, had been made managing editor of the *Frankport Post-Union* and a director of its parent, the Post Communications Company.

I was telling a fellow scribe named Todd about Bobby's meteoric rise in journalism one Saturday night when we were waiting for the final page proofs to come up from Composing.

"It was a trick, plain and simple," Todd said. "He probably got McCoy's real name from his birth record. You can change your name, but the records remain the same."

"Oh, I figured it that way too. But how do you explain predicting the time of death?"

"Luck."

"Five times? And a couple of them almost to the minute?"

"Wait a minute. Who did obits on the day side?"

I thought about it for a few minutes. "A girl. College kid. Carol something."

"And she came in earlier than the rest of the day crew, right? So they dream up a scheme. She gets the deaths after they occur and she puts the copy in the holdover box rather than sending it through the city desk."

"That's possible. I never thought of that."

"And I'll go you one better. I'll bet this Carol is either sitting in a top job at the *Post-Union* right now or she's married to R. Southgate Hawks."

It was a good theory, but it didn't hold water when I finally got back to Frankport. One thing I can say for Bobby, he always keeps a promise. Back when I told him I would try to get him a job on another paper, he said, "I'll remember this," and he did. He sent me a letter offering the night editorship and a healthy raise. I jumped at it.

I was on the old job for two weeks and was surprised to see so many new faces in the city room. In fact, none of the old night hands were still there. Bobby had made the paper into a dynamic news machine that kept me busy and happy.

In the old days under McCoy, editors and subeditors were serfs. However, Bobby's regime gave us new status. We were even invited to a Christmas reception at the Hawks home, and I looked forward to it because I hadn't seen Bobby since I arrived. He now lived in a rarefied atmosphere of mergers with other papers and the management of three radio stations in the state.

I drove out to the Christmas reception with Millie Hogan, editor of the women's page. She had been lured away from a New York sheet and considered our boss in the same category as gods and saints. I gave a low whistle as we turned into the long drive that arced in front of the Hawkses' Tudor mansion. "He's come a long way from the obit desk," I said.

"Who?" Millie looked confused. "Mr. Hawks? R. Southgate Hawks actually worked the obit desk?"

"Not only worked it, he lived at it for fourteen months. And I was the guy who was going to get *him* a new job."

"You'll have to tell me about that," Millie said as I turned the car over to a parking attendant and we entered the main hall of the house.

The reception line was moving slowly, and I had a chance to get a good look at him. Seven years hadn't changed him much. He was more mature and expensively dressed, but he still exuded that same intent manner, that inner ability to make do with the things at hand. The short-order cook had indeed become a master chef.

Millie whispered that the woman to Bobby's right was his wife.

"Hey, is her name Carol?"

"No, Martha."

Well, that exploded that theory. Mrs. Hawks wasn't the type of woman you would expect a rising media czar to marry. She was a plain woman, in dress and in features. There was a sense of calm control about her, and when I shook her hand, I was impressed by its firmness. Bobby, or rather Mr. Hawks, asked me how things were going on the night side.

"Well, it's a lot different than the old days," I said jokingly, but he didn't laugh.

Once through the line, I joined Millie at the eggnog bowl.

"What did you say to Mr. Hawks?" she asked me between sips. "He looked a little angry."

I mumbled an "I don't know" but I had an idea. "Martha Hawks looks a little out of place, doesn't she?"

"It's got to be true love, let me tell you. I'm relatively new in town, but they tell me that he gave up a passel of beauties when the late Mr. McCoy made him city editor. He was considered the catch in this town."

"Did she ever work on the paper? I don't remember her."

"No, I did an interview with her last year. Nothing extraordinary. Born upstate and came here about ten years ago. She was a nurse at St. Luke's for a time."

I have never brought up Bobby's tenure on the obit desk to anyone again. I like my job. As for how they did it, I have convinced myself that she simply asked doctors the prognosis on terminal cases and then took a rough, professional calculation on the time of death. Of course, there is the alternative which I won't allow myself to think about.

Yet every Christmas, when I go to that reception and shake hands with Mrs. Hawks, the awesome thought creeps into my mind. Those strong fingers, cold and firm, the arms lean and sinewy . . . a pillow . . . a weakened, terminal patient . . . I always dismiss the idea immediately. That is, until I shake hands with R. Southgate Hawks and look into those determined blue eyes—the eyes of a man who can make the most of a limited situation.

AL NUSSBAUM

A Left-Handed Profession

He was a big red-faced man with a nose that was too large and eyes that were too small, and I never heard a grown man whine so much. He sat in the bar, surrounded by flunkies, and didn't shut up for a moment. To hear him tell it, and no one in the lounge of the Buena Vista Casino heard much else that afternoon, he hadn't made a nickel's profit in years. Taxes had left him with nothing.

He might have convinced the Internal Revenue Service, but he didn't convince me. His English leather shoes, hand-tailored suit and wafer-thin wristwatch all said he was a liar. So did the large diamond he wore on the little finger of his right hand—the hand he gestured with—and the thick roll of currency he carried.

From where I sat with my back to the wall, I had a good view of the bar and the entrance. I watched Benny Krotz nervously make his way across the casino floor, past the crap tables, blackjack dealers and roulette wheels. He paused in the entrance for a moment, blinking his eyes rapidly to adjust them to the reduced illumination. When he spotted me, he came over and dropped lightly into the seat beside me. Benny was a gambler who believed in flying saucers and luck, but he'd never seen either one. A loser if I'd ever seen one, not that my white hair and conservative clothes made me look like a world-beater.

I nodded toward the bigmouth at the bar. "Is that the mark?" I asked.

Benny hesitated, afraid of giving away the only thing he had to sell. Finally he acknowledged, "Yeah, that's the guy. How'd ya make him so fast?" His expression was glum.

"I'd have to be deaf, blind and have a cold to miss him," I said quietly.

"A cold?"

"Even if I couldn't hear him or see him, his smell would give him away." I allowed myself a brief smile. "He smells like money."

Benny brightened. "He looks good to ya, huh?"

"He looks almost perfect. He's a liar who lives well, so he's probably dishonest and greedy. There's no better target for a con game. There's only one trouble."

"One trouble?" Benny echoed.

"Uh-huh—this town is crawling with hustlers. If I can spot that guy in less time than it takes to light a cigarette, others have done it too. He's probably been

521

propositioned more times than the chorus line at Radio City Music Hall. And, considering the type of person he is, he's probably already fallen for more than one con game and is extra cautious now. That's right, isn't it?"

"Yeah," Benny admitted. "That's right. He's been burned."

"Badly?"

"Yeah, pretty bad. He's been taken in card games, crap games and a bunch o' con games, already."

I finished my drink and signaled for the waitress. When she had taken our order and left, I turned back to Benny. "What kind of con games?" I asked.

"All the usual—phony stock, underwater real estate, cheap stolen goods that turned out to be perfectly legitimate factory rejects. And Red Harris took him for twenty thousand about six months ago with a counterfeit money swindle. Red gave him fifty brand-new twenties, telling him they were samples of the stuff he had for sale. He let him try them out all over town, then sold him a wrapped-up telephone book and made a nineteen-grand profit."

I laughed and looked over to where the mark was sitting. "That must have hurt his pride," I said. "How about his wallet? What kind of shape is that in?"

"Good shape. Very good shape. That's Big Jim Thompson, the drilling contractor. He has about half a hundred rigs working throughout the Southwest, and he gets paid whether they hit anything or not."

"That's fine," I said, smiling again. "It would ruin my Robin Hood image to take money from a poor man."

The waitress brought our drinks and I paid for them while Benny fumbled politely in his empty pockets. Because my money clip was already out, I removed three $100 bills and passed them to Benny. "For your help," I said.

"You're satisfied with him?" Benny asked, snatching up the money. He couldn't conceal his surprise. "He's gonna be mighty cautious."

I shrugged. "I don't think that will be a problem. Can you introduce us?"

"Yeah, sure." Benny started to push his chair back. "What's your name? For the introduction?"

Benny had been recommended to me as a source of information. Since he was in the business of selling what he knew about people, I hadn't given him any more about me than he needed to know, which was nothing. I had been in the game too long to make that kind of mistake. Now I gave him a name. "William Henk," I said, but I didn't move to get up. "There's no hurry, Benny. Finish your drink, then we'll go over."

Benny could have had ten more drinks; it wouldn't have mattered. Big Jim Thompson was firmly ensconced at the bar. He was still holding court over his followers when we walked over to them a few minutes later, and he gave every impression of being there for hours to come. He glanced contemptuously at Benny, then he noticed me and his small eyes narrowed. "Mr. Thompson," Benny said, "my friend William Henk wants to meetcha."

Thompson swung around on his stool, but he didn't extend his hand, and I didn't offer mine. "Why?" he challenged.

"Because I've been hearing a lot about you," I said.

"What have you been hearing?"

"That you're a real sucker for a con game," I answered, and Benny looked as though someone had just kicked him in the stomach.

Thompson's face started to go from red to purple. "What business is it of yours?"

"I might have a deal for you."

"*Might* have?" Thompson snorted disdainfully.

"OK, *will* have. Tomorrow. Meet me here at this time and I'll tell you about it."

"What makes you think I'll be interested in any deal of yours?"

"It will give you a chance to get even for your losses. Maybe get a little ahead. You'd like that, right?"

"So why wait till tomorrow?"

I nodded pleasantly at all his friends. "The audience is too big, and I have someone waiting for me. There's no rush. This is no con game," I said, then turned on my heel and walked away. I could feel their eyes on me, but I didn't look back. I had sunk the hook into Thompson. Now I could reel him in—carefully.

I bought a stack of out-of-town newspapers, then drove back toward the hotel where I was staying. I made a lot of unnecessary turns to be sure I wasn't being followed and put the rented car in a lot a block away. I could hear the shower running when I opened the door of the suite, and my wife Margie's soft voice floated out to me. She was singing an old folk song, but she'd forgotten most of the words.

I slipped out of my suit coat, kicked off my shoes, and sprawled across the bed with the newspapers. I read all the crime news I can find. Doctors read medical journals; I study newspapers. Both of us are keeping abreast of the changes in our professions.

Margie came out of the bathroom wrapped in a yellow robe. Her long chestnut hair was freshly brushed and shiny. She sat on the edge of the bed and kissed me. "Anything new in the papers?" she asked.

I married Margie because she was beautiful and young, and made me feel young too. Later I noticed I had received a bonus—no one ever looked at me when we were together.

"Not much," I answered. "A couple of bank robberies in New York City—amateurs; a jewel robbery in Miami that has the police excited; and the Los Angeles cops are still hunting for the four men who held up the armored car three days ago."

"Do you think they'll catch them?"

"Probably. Men who have to make their livings with guns in their fists will never win any prize for brains," I said.

Margie stood up and started to unpack more of our clothes. I stopped her. "Don't bother," I said. "We won't be here as long as I figured. I've found a live one."

"Are you going to tell me about it?"

"When it's over. I'm still working it out in my head."

The next afternoon, Thompson was waiting for me in the lounge of the Buena Vista Casino when I arrived. He was alone and seemed smaller. He was one of those people who needs an audience before he can come alive.

"What've ya got to sell?" he asked, bypassing all small-talk preliminaries.

"Counterfeit," I answered, handing him a single bill.

Thompson stood up without another word and headed for the entrance. I followed him across the casino floor, and into the coffee shop. There were a couple of customers at the counter, but that was all. Thompson went to the last booth along the wall and sat down, waving away a waitress who started toward him. I took the seat opposite his and waited.

He pulled a ten-power jeweler's loupe out of his pocket, screwed it into his right eye, and examined the $50 bill I had given him. I knew he was studying the portrait of Grant, the scrollwork along the borders, and the sharpness of the points on the treasury seal—and he was finding everything perfect.

"You must think I'm a real fool," he said with a nasty smile. "This ain't counterfeit."

"You don't think so, huh?" I handed him another $50 bill. "What about this?"

He was a little faster this time, but his verdict was the same. "It's real."

"And this one?"

A look, a feel, a snap. "Good as gold."

"Nope." I shook my head. "Counterfeit."

He pointed a blunt finger at the center of my chest. "Listen, punk, I know genuine money when I see it. Whatever you're planning ain't gonna work, so forget it."

"You can be sure of one thing."

"What's that?"

I gave him a nasty smile. "I won't try to sell you a twenty-thousand-dollar telephone book."

His jaw tightened.

"Instead," I continued, "I'm going to give you the chance of a lifetime. Those bills *are* counterfeit. In fact, these samples have one major flaw that the rest of my stock doesn't have."

I took the three bills out of his hand and lined them up on the table between us. Then I added three more fifties to the row. "Unlike genuine currency," I told him, "all six of these bills have the same serial numbers."

Thompson's eyes jerked back to the bills, and he snatched up two of them. He held them up to the light and studied them, frowning. After that he compared two more and sat staring at the six identical Federal Reserve notes.

"Do you still think they're real?" I taunted.

"I've never seen anything like this," he said in an awed tone. "These bills are perfect."

"*Almost* perfect," I corrected. "But I'll deliver brand-new, absolutely perfect bills."

He started to scoop up the money from the table, but I put my hand over his. "Where do you think you're going with that?" I asked.

He gestured toward the gaming tables. "Out into the casino to test some of this."

"Not without paying for it first. I don't give free samples, mister. I don't have to. I've got the best queer there is, and I get fifty cents on the dollar for *every* dollar. That three hundred will cost you one-fifty."

"That's pretty steep for counterfeit, isn't it?"

"You said yourself, you've never seen anything like it. I've been in business for five years and not one bill has ever been questioned, let alone detected. It's not every day you get a chance to double your money."

Thompson gave me a hundred and fifty from the roll he carried, then took my six identical bills into the casino. I ordered a cup of coffee and a hamburger, and settled down to wait for him. I was drinking my second cup of coffee when he returned.

He looked a little stunned by his success. "Not one dealer so much as blinked an eye. I've had 'em look closer at good money," he said.

I didn't have to give him any more of my sales pitch. He was selling himself. I sat back and sipped my coffee.

He didn't keep me waiting long. "Tell ya what, I'll take twenty-five thousand worth."

I shook my head.

"That too much?" he asked.

"Too little. You've seen the last samples you ever will. From now on I sell nothing smaller than hundred-thousand-dollar lots."

He did some mental arithmetic. "That's fifty thousand to me, right?"

"No. The hundred thousand is what *you* pay. In exchange, I give you two hundred thousand in crisp, new tens, twenties and fifties. Each bill with a *different* serial number."

He didn't say anything right away. I gave him two full minutes to think about it, then slid out of the booth and stood up. "Hell, I thought you were big time," I said disdainfully, then started to walk away.

Thompson called me back, as I knew he would. He was as predictable as a fixed race. "OK," he said. "You've got a deal, but you better not be planning a rip-off."

"How can there be a rip-off? You're going to examine every bill before you pay me, and you can bring all the help you think you'll need. And I'm not worried about being hijacked by you because I'll tell some friends who it is I'll be doing business with. If anything happened to me, you wouldn't be hard to find."

"So we understand each other," he said. "OK, when can we complete the deal?"

"The sooner the better," I said. "The sooner the better."

Four hours later, Margie and I were on our way out of town with Thompson's hundred grand. We were in the rented car because I figured we'd better leave before there was any chance of Thompson getting wise to how I'd tricked him.

"You're really something," Margie said, hugging my arm while I drove. "When you bought the loot from the armored car robbery in Los Angeles, you paid ten cents on the dollar because all the money was new and the numbers had been recorded. You said it was so hot you'd be lucky to get fifteen to twenty cents on the dollar, and then only after you located the right buyer."

"That's what I thought until I met Thompson."

"Didn't he know the money was stolen?"

"No. He thought it was counterfeit. I showed him six perfect fifties, all with the same serial numbers." I told her what had happened in the coffee shop.

"Where did you get counterfeit money?" she demanded.

"I didn't. It was good. Part of the armored car loot, in fact."

"You must think I'm stupid," Margie said. "I know good money doesn't have the same serial numbers."

I stopped for a traffic light, then got the car rolling again after it changed. "It does if you take half a dozen consecutively numbered bills and erase the last digit."

Margie's mouth opened in surprise. "You can do that? You can erase the numbers?"

"Easier than you'd think, and without leaving a trace, either."

We rode in silence for a few minutes, then Margie said, "Why didn't you erase the first digit on all the bills? That way they'd all be good to spend and you'd have gotten one hundred cents on the dollar." She was smart as well as beautiful.

"Because the risk of detection was very slight with only six bills, but some smart teller would surely have noticed if I'd tried to change the numbers on every bill. Then it would have been you and I back there, trying to explain where we got the money, instead of Big Jim Thompson."

THEODORE MATHIESON

Second Spring

Maud Gullick was only eighteen on the spring morning in 1932 when she bludgeoned her mother and father to death over their breakfast.

According to the police report, Maud had calmly gone down to her father's basement workshop—the Gullicks lived at the top of a set of three flats in the San Francisco Richmond District—had picked up one of her father's hammers, and carried it back up, concealed under her bathrobe. Entering the kitchen, she called the attention of her parents to a roofing operation going on across the street. She hit her father first at the base of the skull, then her mother in the left temple. One blow was sufficient for each, for Maud was a big girl, six feet one, and weighed almost two hundred pounds. Afterward she called the police, but by the time they arrived, she had lost control of herself, and they could make little of her story. Later she refused to tell them anything.

Neighbors had given the police some information, but not enough to explain the murders. Old Man Gullick was in his fifties, a carpenter by trade, who'd been out of work most of the winter. He'd been married before, and Maud was the child of his first wife, now dead. The second Mrs. Gullick was ten or twelve years younger than Gullick, but didn't look it. A small, perpetually harried bird type, with a malicious tongue, she talked incessantly against her stepdaughter.

"Maud's as lazy and stubborn as a jackass," Mrs. Gullick used to say in the interims when she and her neighbors were on speaking terms. "Been tryin' to get her to go to business school after she graduates from high school, so she can get a decent job and support herself. It isn't as if she's goin' to attract the men, looking the way she does. But she won't listen. Just shrugs those big humpy shoulders of hers, and then goes on mooning over the movies and listening to those crazy records of hers."

Neighbors living directly under the Gullicks reported that they would hear screams and thumps now and then from overhead, but they could never make out what the fuss was about. They'd seen Maud going off to school occasionally with suspicious welts across her cheek, and once with a blackened eye.

Maud had a black eye the day the police jailed her for the murders.

When Joe Barnes, my city editor, heard about the black eye, he shook his finger at me and said, "Every other paper in town is calling the Gullick kid an unnatural monster. Just to be different, Caxton, I'm assigning you to uncover a little justification for slugging her old man and old lady. You can't miss. You can always fall back on mental incompetence. By the look of her photograph, I'd say that might be your best bet. But see what you can pick up."

Barnes was right. Maud's photograph was just a pale image of the unprepossessing original which I visited on her second day in jail. Her face looked small, set on that tremendous hulk of body, and her pallid skin had a middle-aged, pouchy look. On the other hand, her hands and feet were small and feminine.

"Miss Gullick," I said politely, "I am a reporter from the *Express*. My editor sent me over to see if there isn't anything we can do to help you."

Maud looked at me sharply for a moment, then blinked as tears came to her eyes. I imagined the police and other reporters had given her a hard time; she didn't have much to charm them with.

"How do you mean—help?" she asked. "Why would you want to after what I've done?"

"Well, you must have had a very strong reason for doing what you did," I said. "Maybe if we knew what it was, and could tell the people, it would be easier for you later—at the trial."

"My father beat me. Often," she said after a pause.

"He gave you that black eye?"

"Yes."

"And is that why you—?"

She shook her head, started biting her nails, which were already bitten to the quick.

"I think it would really help you to tell the truth."

Again tears appeared in her eyes. "If the others had asked me like that, I would have told them."

I waited patiently, and finally it came.

"Poppa broke my victrola. Dropped it on the floor and smashed it. And then he took my Buzzy Bidell records and—and he put them in the stove. Oh, it was terrible. They turned all bubbly and melty, and I just—I couldn't help—"

"It was after he put your Buzzy Bidell records in the fire that you went down to the workshop?"

"Yes, after that—and after the things he said about Buzzy!"

It took a moment to get to me. "You—like Buzzy Bidell?"

Maud's eyes which a moment before had been a drab and hopeless gray began to soften and glow, transforming her face from the middle-aged look to one of rapt youthfulness.

"Oh, yes, I think Buzzy's real keen. There's never been anybody like him. When he sings I just get beside myself. I've seen every movie he ever made, and I have—had—all his records. But the police lady says she's going to get me another victrola and some of Buzzy's brand-new records—and, Mr. Reporter—could you take another picture of me for your paper?"

"I think it could be arranged. Why?"

"Well, I didn't like the ones they took when I first got here. I was upset, and well, maybe if you took another it would turn out better. I know I'm not pretty, but—who knows? *He* may even see it, and—"

"Who?"

"Why, Buzzy Bidell. After all, if my picture appears again in the paper, and he sees it, he might get interested in me, *and even come to see me.*" In a sudden rush of conspiratorial enthusiasm, Maud put her hand under the pillow on her cot and brought out a small brown pencil tablet.

"I'm keeping a daily diary of everything that happens to me here," she said in a whisper. "When I think I've got enough to interest Buzzy, I'm going to send it to him. He might really get interested in me then. Just to *talk* to him would make me feel so much better about *everything.*"

"Could you let me—read your diary?"

"Oh, no—nobody but Buzzy will ever read this."

"I see." Then a thought struck me. "Have you ever kept a diary before, Miss Gullick?"

"Oh, yes. I've kept one for the past year. It's home in my bureau drawer. I didn't get a chance to take it with me."

A sergeant came shortly after that and showed me out. I think word had got around that Maud had spilled a good deal more to me than she had to the police, because on the way out I was detoured into Brown of homicide.

"What did you find out?" he asked.

"Exactly what you'll find out if you'll treat her nice." I said it several times in several different ways. Brown didn't like it, but he had to let me go.

The Gullick flat was on Tenth Avenue, just off Lake. You'd think the tenants in the downstairs flat would have seen enough going and coming in the last couple of days to last them for a while, but no; there were tremors at front door curtains of both flats as I went upstairs. I didn't have to be sneaky about it either; my editor, Barnes, had arranged to get me a key from the downtown realtors.

As I closed the door firmly behind me, making sure the lock was set, the first thing I smelled was stale bacon. From that fatal breakfast? The shades were drawn on the solidly conventional furnishings in the front room; I glanced in at the kitchen and saw that somebody had cleaned up. At least the dishes were off the table, and there were no stains around that I could see. Maybe hammer victims didn't bleed much.

It wasn't difficult to find Maud's room; it was the one with the walls covered with glossy photos of Buzzy Bidell, and pieces of sheet music of songs he'd made popular. Maud was obviously a jig-saw puzzle fan, too, because a shelf by her day bed was filled with them. I saw one labeled *Down Lover's Lane*, another *Moonlight on the Swanee*; a third *Buzzy Bidell at the Piano*. A pile of movie magazines lay under the bed, and near a window stood a tabouret whose dust traces told me it once held Maud's phonograph.

Maud's diary was in the bottom drawer of her bureau, as she said, under some well-worn nightwear. It was the size of a cookbook and half as thick, with red, simulated-leather binding generously covered with greasy smudges. Maud was clearly a messy eater.

I opened the book at random, and read:

"*February 2nd.* I just found out that Buzzy's birthday and mine are the same!

April 22nd! Just think—somewhere I've read that astrologists consider people born on the same date as having a natural affinity for one another. As if I didn't know that already! I wish Buzzy knew it. I wish just that he knew I was alive."

I skipped a few pages and read:

"*March 1st*. The Junior Ball is tonight. Those high school boys are too green for me. I'll take a bath, go to bed early, read my magazines, and listen to my records . . .

"*March 15th*. Went to see Buzzy in *Love Me Tonight* at the Lyric. My God, he's *handsome*! There were times I just had to close my eyes because I couldn't stand the sweet pain of looking at him. There was a girl sitting next to me who started laughing right in the middle of one of Buzzy's songs, and I hit her in the ribs as hard as I could with my elbow. She yelled and the usher came, but I said I had the jerks. I said I had them often, so the girl moved, and I was glad. I can't stand these snotty people who pretend they don't like Buzzy Bidell.

"*March 22nd*. I just had the most wonderful idea! I learned from the last issue of SILVER SCREEN, that Buzzy collects novelty tie clips. I saw one at Bascom's last night. It's only $1.98 and it's a treble clef. I'll have engraved on the back of it—from Maud to Buzzy. I wonder how much they'll charge?

"*April 19th*. I sent the tie clip off tonight. I was so thrilled putting the package in the mailbox; it was just like slipping it into Buzzy's own hand! Of course I don't expect any answer. But wouldn't it be wonderful if he sent me a post card or a signed photograph?

"*April 30th*. Gladys has been nagging me all week about signing up for secretarial school after graduation. She said a lot of pukey things about my looks, but I know. She's just jealous because I'm younger than her. I just don't listen to her. (I know things she don't even guess about—about Buzzy and me and what *could* happen!) Gladys is even mean about Buzzy. Says she can't stand him, because she knows it makes me mad. Mad! My God, I could kill the people who don't know enough to like Buzzy. It's worse than saying they don't like *me*—I *just can't stand it*."

I'd read enough. I hid the book inside my overcoat under the arm, and pressing it close I went down the stairs past the twitching curtains and into the street.

The defense used that diary, and I think it saved Maud's life. That, and my articles based on it. Public opinion had been against her at first, because she was not as frank with the police or with her lawyer about her motive for killing her parents as she was with me. It wasn't that our birthdays coincided, either—mine is in June—but the fact that I always treated her gently and with a certain amount of respect as an individual. I don't think she ever had had much of that. I'm certain that nobody ever called her Miss Gullick before. She was used to insults and black eyes, of course; she had plenty of *those*.

But when Curry, her attorney, read selections from her diary at her sanity trial, she listened with tears running down her cheeks, and I could see the jury beginning to get thoughtful. After a protracted out-session, they recommended commitment, and Maud's future seemed settled.

I got a last interview with Maud while she was on her way to Napa, the state asylum. Crossing the ferry to Vallejo she sat between two plainclothesmen, and I sat opposite, my knees almost touching hers. We sat upstairs in the middle of the boat, although Maud had wanted to sit up front, outside. Her guards weren't going to have her jumping overboard before they got her to the asylum. I'm sure now she didn't have the faintest intention of doing so.

"Don't look so glum, Maud," I said softly, patting her hand. "Life in Napa won't be so bad. It's not like prison, you know. It's a beautiful place, and you'll be allowed a good deal of liberty."

Maud glanced sadly through the ferry boat windows at the tawny, bare hills of Richmond and the Carquinez straits.

"It's fall now. Come spring again, I won't be free. I won't be free ever again."

From her expression I knew she was thinking of Buzzy Bidell. That girl didn't give up easily.

"Well, you've got the radio, and records," I said. "Your little world isn't shut away from you."

She suddenly burst into tears. It was a while before she quieted down and spoke again.

"He didn't send me a single word," she said finally. "Even though he must have known I did it only for him!"

Six months later, Maud Gullick walked out of Napa State Hospital and disappeared as completely as if she'd never been. For over twenty-five years no trace of her was found.

I was one of the first to hear of her again.

It was April, 1957. Now literary editor for the *Los Angeles Gazette*, I was taking a much needed rest at Las Vegas, and sitting one evening in the Nevada Room watching a frenetic floor show, I was approached by a waiter who bent over and whispered in my ear.

"There is a gentleman who would like a word with you," he said. "He would like to join you at your table."

"Who is he?" I asked.

"His name is Bidell, sir. Buzzy Bidell."

For a moment the name stirred memories dully, then suddenly remembrance exploded like a big one on the Fourth of July. "Tell him to come over," I said.

Bidell could only have been in his late forties, but he looked sixty, with lines of dissipation scoring his eyes and mouth. Even his voice sounded old and tired.

"Mr. Caxton," he said, sitting down at my invitation. "They told me you were here—my friends. You see, I work at a night club down the street, the Adobe. You must come and catch my show."

"If I have time, I certainly will," I said, and asked Bidell to join me in a drink. He seemed pathetically grateful and ordered a Scotch.

"You see," he said, "I've been—out of show business the past few years. My voice went back on me there for a while, but now I'm in great shape again." I knew he'd taken the cure several times, and I doubted if his voice was in great shape again. "I'm making quite a serious comeback, you know, Mr. Caxton," he went on. "Even have written a book. Van Fleet is publishing it. Expecting the galley proofs any time now—tells about my road back."

I saw the light.

"I always enjoy reading books on comebacks," I said truthfully. "I'll look forward with pleasure to reading yours, Mr. Bidell."

"Oh, that'll be real George! I certainly would appreciate a favorable reading. Make a big difference, you know, to my future." He made a facile, juvenile gesture with his hands, and tried to flush youth back into his raddled features with a boyish smile. The attempt was pitiful.

"The finest experience has been to find that they haven't forgotten me—all those hundreds of thousands of fans of a few years ago.

"I still get letters from them. Look." He dug his hand into his coat pocket and brought up a fistful of envelopes, some of them suspiciously yellowed around the edges.

"Twenty-five years," he said, "and they haven't forgotten me. And here—" drawing one letter from an inside pocket. It looked new. "Got this one just the other day. Let me read it to you. 'Dear Mr. Bidell: This is the first letter I have written to you in a long, long time. I cannot say that I've thought of you often, just now and then, in a sweet, distant way. But now I have been thinking of you more lately. I cannot tell why. Perhaps it is because I heard you on the radio the other night and it brought back memories. Your voice still sounds wonderful to me. I have been buying all the reissues of your old records, too. Then I heard you were publishing a book about yourself. I certainly will be one of the first to read it. And I sometimes wonder if in this book you will ever mention the names of some of the girls who wrote to you years ago. I was one of them. I sent you birthday cards (your birthday is the same as mine!) and once I even sent you a birthday gift.

"'But I think maybe I did more for you than *any* of the others; if you could only know about this, maybe you would put me in your book, as part of your life. But I cannot tell you what I did except to say—I did it only for you.

"'Please, dear Mr. Bidell, dedicate one of your songs to me there in your club in Las Vegas some night. I won't hear it, I know, because you don't broadcast like you used to, but it'll make me happy just thinking about it.

"'The kindest, best, and most loving wishes . . .'"

Bidell looked up, his eyes revealing the charge which reading the letter aloud had given him.

"How did she sign it?" I asked, trying to keep my voice casual.

"Maud Milham, Roswell, New Mexico."

"When was it written?"

"I got it about a month ago. It's not dated."

I left then, after promising Bidell I would review his autobiography. In my hotel room I walked up and down for a long while, feeling for the first time in years the solar plexal excitement which the uncovering of a big lead always gave me. To find the whereabouts of the long-missing Maud Gullick! What a story that would make! I had the better part of a week to myself; I had planned to go north to Salt Lake City, to visit a former newspaper buddy; but it would be just as easy to head for Roswell.

I went out then and started looking up bus schedules.

I determined later that it was around the time I caught the bus south to Kingman, Arizona, at eleven fifteen the next morning, that Maud Gullick or Milham, as she signed herself now, was entering Dr. Eberle's office in Roswell.

Eberle, a wizened dapper little man with a memory like a tape recorder, showed Maud into his office and sat down behind his desk. It was the first time he had seen her, and he told me he was impressed with her buxom, matronly size, the pallor of her skin and her petulant, self-pitying expression.

"What can I do for you, Mrs.—ah—" he glanced at the card the nurse had had her fill in—"Milham?"

Maud's voice was sullen. "My husband—he made me come. He's waiting downstairs. I—well, I haven't been acting myself, he says, for about five or six months, and he insisted that I see a doctor."

"I see," Dr. Eberle said briskly. "What seems to be the trouble?"

"I'm—restless, and can't seem to sit still. I cry a lot. That makes Buck mad and he—he—" She began to sniffle.

"Well, now, suppose we begin at the beginning. How long have you been married?"

"Seventeen years. Buck and I have gotten along very well, until lately."

"Any children?"

"Two. A boy and a girl."

"Ages?"

"The girl is thirteen, the boy sixteen."

"Do you all get on well together?"

"We always have. I guess I haven't been myself lately."

"What exactly do you do that annoys your husband?"

"He says I just don't seem to keep my mind on things. Like getting supper or—things like that. It's just that living by the clock doesn't seem important. I can't see that it is, doctor; so long as a person is happy—"

"Are you happy then?"

"If they'd just leave me alone, I would be."

"What do you think about when you let time slip through your fingers, so to speak?"

"Oh, I have a lot to think about!" Doctor Eberle noticed that as she spoke her expression cleared, her voice became younger and almost timid, like that of a girl. "I read my magazines—"

"What sort of magazines?"

"Motion picture magazines."

"What else?"

"I—listen to my records."

"What kind of records?"

"Well, I've got a big collection of reissues of Buzzy Bidell's records." Maud looked at the doctor hopefully, as if she expected him to respond.

"Bidell—Bidell—isn't he one of the old-style crooners?"

"He's not old-style!" Maud flared up, her eyes getting a wild look. "That's what Jack—my boy—is always saying. 'Mom and her crummy Bidell records!'" Her voice became sharp, vicious. "I slap him across the face for that, and then when Buck finds out about it, he hits *me*."

Dr. Eberle cleared his throat and looked thoughtfully down at the card.

"Well, Mrs. Milham," he said at last, "what you're going through is not uncommon. How old are you?"

"Forty-three."

"There, you see. Some women pass through this stage younger, some later, but all of them pass through it sometime. It's a time of great physical change, and along with it there are often emotional symptoms. What actually happens is that you have a sort of second adolescence; a resurgence of the old interests that held you when you were eighteen or nineteen. I imagine that Buzzy Bidell, for instance, was a great favorite of yours around that age."

"Yes—he was."

"Some women who were interested in dancing in their teens, and who have been good, steady wives for a quarter of a century, suddenly want to become ballerinas; or authors, or painters. It takes many forms. Some want to start another family. But this stage, fortunately, is temporary, and you will pass through it. I will write out a prescription for you, and you must take it faithfully. Come back and see me in about two weeks, and tell me how you're getting on."

I figured the whole time chart out later. I was waiting to change buses in Kingman when Buck Milham took Maud home after a visit to the pharmacist and stood watching in the kitchen while she poured a glass of water and pretended to take one of the capsules the doctor had prescribed. Actually, she told me, she never took one of them. The only reason for her refusal, so far as I can see, was that *she didn't want to be cured of her daydream.*

"And now, for God's sake," Buck said after Maud apparently swallowed the capsule, "get that washing done this afternoon. You can't get in the back door, it's piled up so damned thick. Besides, I need some clean clothes, so my customers don't back away when I serve 'em. Do you hear? If that washing ain't done when I come home, I'll blacken your eye!"

Buck ran a bar in Roswell, and usually didn't open up until noon, so now he had his lunch of steak and french fries, which Maud cooked for him, and then he went to work. He usually had his suppers at the restaurant next to the bar, so he wouldn't get home until one or two the next morning.

First Maud went out to the back porch, where she looked drearily down at the dirty clothes and sighed. Then she piled the lunch dishes in the sink, and went upstairs to an attic storeroom which she had appropriated as a sort of extra bedroom for herself. There was an old cot close under the roof. Pictures cut from movie magazines were pasted against the bare board walls.

A portable record player with three speeds occupied the place of honor under a dormer window.

Maud put a Buzzy Bidell forty-five on the turntable, and as the Voice filled the attic she sat down at an old drop-leaf sewing machine which she used for a desk and started writing in a wireback tablet.

"Buck made me go to the doctor today," she wrote. "He's trying to get me to forget you again, Buzzy. Quiet is all I need, my dear, to imagine myself with you, but they will not let me have it. There are times when Marcia and Jack come screaming up here demanding to play their terrible records on my phonograph when they have one of their own, and Buck never stops them. He seems to enjoy seeing me miserable. I can keep the kids out when he's not here, because I'm strong enough. But I'm not stronger than Buck.

"But I have done something that will keep them all out. I had our neighbor next door, Mr. Custer, who does odd jobs, build me a strong door made of one-by-twelves, to put at the head of the stairs. He installed it yesterday, but I was clever enough not to ask him to put on the heavy bar to keep the others out. He thinks I just want it to keep the noise from coming up. He only charged me $7.50. I shall make the bar myself. So I can have the peace I want, dear Buzzy, and think of you as often as I wish . . ."

She turned off the record player, then, and went to work. She had her tools ready; the saw, the bit, the screwdriver, the hammer. She cut her bar from a two-by-four and bolted it to the door; to hold it firm when it was closed, she screwed a two-inch metal U-bar to the door frame. It took her a long time, because she was clumsy with the bit and the saw, and by the time she had finished and swept up the sawdust, she heard Marcia and Jack yelling in the back yard, on their way home from school. She heard the slam of the screen door and went downstairs at once. As usual, Jack, sullen and black-haired like his father, was the first to the bread and jam.

"I see you been layin' on your fat backside again," Jack said arrogantly, pointing to the washing. He always used expressions which he heard Buck use to her.

"Don't you talk like that, or I'll wash your mouth out with soap," Maud said.

"Oh, corn," Jack said, his cheeks stuffed with bread.

"Hi, Mom," Marcia said. She was a small, skinny blonde girl with her father's razor-sharp features. "I'll bet you *have* been listenin' to your ancient ol' dreamboat again!"

"How long is this gonna keep up?" Jack asked. "Pretty soon, we'll have to be gettin' our own supper. Dad might just as well throw you out in the middle of the street, for all the good you are around here!"

"Just leave me *alone!*" Maud shouted and fled into the front room. The children followed her, leaving a trail of stickiness on wall and door.

"Why don't you listen to a real singer," Jack said and turned on a popular rock-and-roll record on his portable phonograph.

"Stop, stop!" Maud cried and ran for the stairs.

The children followed her.

Buck broke tradition by coming home to supper, possibly to check on whether the washing had been done. When Maud saw him coming, she fled to the attic and Jack met his father at the front door with, "She didn't do the washing, Pop!"

Buck growled a swear word and tore up the stairs to the attic, only to thump his head hard in the dark against the closed wooden door. Then he began cursing in earnest.

"Shall I get the crowbar out in back, Pop?"

"Why in hell didn't you tell me she had put a door in here!" Buck yelled at him.

"You didn't give me time."

"Get me the crowbar!"

With the two children watching in anticipation, Buck beat the bar against the door, and pried and pried until it splintered open. Maud was cowering on the cot. Buck grabbed her roughly by the shoulders and practically dragged her down the stairs and into the kitchen.

"Now you're going to do that damned washing while I sit here and watch!" he yelled. The kids were delighted. This was better than T.V.

Maud began loading the washer as if she were doing it in her sleep while Buck made a running commentary on what he was going to do to her if she didn't pay attention to business from now on; how he was losing money right this minute, having to hire a man to take his place down at the bar; how she must be crazy hanging a useless door in the house without telling anybody.

Jack and Marcia watched their mother's somnambulistic activity until they got bored, then Jack poked his sister slyly and pointed upstairs. The children when quietly up to the attic and for a while picked curiously into the things. Finally Jack uncovered his mother's collection of records.

"This'll help Pop out," Jack said. "If she doesn't have all these records to play, she won't waste so much time, and might start doin' a little work around the place again."

Marcia nodded eagerly as Jack spread a newspaper on the floor and started breaking the records up into little bits and dropping them on the paper. Marcia helped too, and when they were finished, Jack picked up the paper and carried it like a sack downstairs and into the kitchen.

"Look, Pop," Jack said. "Now maybe Mom won't spend so much time listenin' any more."

The boy threw the paper down with a clatter, and the shards of chitinous record poured out on the red linoleum.

"Good boy," Buck said, touseling his son's hair.

Maud stopped her washing then to look.

I got into Roswell around nine the next morning, and the first thing I did was look up Milham in the phone book. There was only one. I got into a cab that was waiting at the station and gave him the Milham address.

It was only two or three blocks from the center of town, a two-story green frame house set on a flat, brownish lawn bordered by locust trees. I told the cab to wait as I went up the walk.

In a moment now I would know whether I had found Maud Gullick.

I knocked on the door and nobody answered. Three times, no answer. I walked along the verandah and tried to look in the windows, but the shades were drawn. I went back to the door and turned the knob. The door was unlocked, and I pushed and went inside. For a moment I could see nothing, except that I stood in a kind of hall with a stairway.

There was somebody standing on the stairs.

"What in the hell do you want?"

A needle-faced character with a red face stood there in a beacon robe watching me.

"Is this the home of Maud Milham?"

"This is my home—Buck Milham. What do you want?"

"Does Maud live here too?"

"Yeah, she's my wife."

"I'm—a friend of hers."

He looked at me as if he were considering throwing me out, then walked across the hall and flung open a door.

"G'wan in and sit down," he said. Then in a big voice he yelled upstairs. "Maud! Maud!"

As I went into the living room, I saw two children come curiously along the hall, a girl and a boy.

"Friend, you say? Where did you know Maud?" Buck had followed me into the room and stood by the door.

"San Francisco."

"Yeah? She never told me she was in Frisco."

"These your children?" I asked, to change the subject.

"Yeah, Boy's Jack, girl's Marcia. I didn't get your name."

"Caxton. I'm a newspaperman."

"Oh, yeah?" Buck became a fraction more amiable. "I run a bar here in town, the Cactus, on Main Street. It's just a block from the bus station; a lot of newspaper guys drop in there. Oh, here, Maud. A friend to see you. Mr. Caxton."

I recognized Maud Gullick, all right. And she knew me the moment she saw me, because her face paled and she put her hand out against the door frame to support herself.

"Hello, Mr. Caxton," she said distantly.

"Hello, Maud," I said. "I'm surprised to see you married and with a family and all. How long have you been married?"

"Seventeen years."

All of a sudden a feeling came over me that I had no right coming here. The past was past. If Maud could go away quietly and get married and raise a family and live her own life for seventeen years, what right had I—

"You never told me you lived in Frisco," Buck said to his wife.

"I never liked to talk about that," she said almost primly.

"We knew each other only a short while," I said, rising. "I just happened to be alone in Roswell, and remembered—" I edged toward the door. "It's good to catch a glimpse of old acquaintances again, you know." Buck was eyeing me suspiciously.

"Maud lent me five bucks when I was down and out," I said, putting my hand in my pocket. "I thought after all these years, it's earned a little interest." I handed a ten-dollar bill to Maud. Buck's suspicion cleared; he could understand that.

"That's all I wanted, just to clear my conscience," I said. I wanted to get out of there, away where I could think. Maud was eating me up with her eyes.

"Goodbye, Mr. Milham—good luck, Maud. Nice children you've got there."

I got the front door open and looked back as Maud spoke.

"Mr. Caxton," she said. "They broke my door down."

"Did they?" I said and laughed uncomprehendingly. "Well, have your husband buy you a new one!"

Buck laughed and the children laughed this time, and I left. I was glad I'd had the cab waiting. I told the driver to take me back to the bus station.

Now that I had found Maud Gullick living, it seemed, so normally, I didn't want to inform the authorities; I just wanted to keep hands off. At the same time, I wanted more time to think about it.

I bought a ticket to Lincoln, up in the mountains. I'd always wanted to see the territory Billy the Kid had battled around in, and I thought a couple of nights away from Roswell, but not too far from it, would clear my mind and I'd know what to do.

I spent a day seeing the jail where they locked up the Kid; I saw the bullet holes in the wall where the Kid shot at the Warden. I visited the Mascalero Indian Reservation, and that night at the hotel I couldn't go to sleep. Her last words to me went round and round in my mind: "They broke my door down— they broke my door down." It was like a discord in a piece of music that sounded pretty good otherwise.

The next day I took a bus back to Roswell. I got the full blow as I came out into the afternoon sunlight and saw the newspaper in the stands: WOMAN KILLS HUSBAND, TWO CHILDREN. Their pictures were on the front page, and I had no trouble recognizing them. In a daze I went to the nearest bar. I couldn't understand why the place should be locked up until I looked up and saw the painted lettering on the door: The Cactus.

I went over into the plaza in front of the courthouse and sat down and read the paper with a mind that didn't take in much.

Only one fact I got quite clear. Maud had used a hammer again.

When I got hold of myself, I went over to the jail where they were keeping Maud. I showed my press card, but they wouldn't let me in. She was too hot. I wired my editor in L.A. and told him to do what he could, that I'd be sleeping for the next forty-eight hours on the police blotter, and if he swung it, I'd give him a story that would scoop every other paper in the country. Somehow he did it, and the next morning they let me in to see her for five minutes.

Five minutes were enough.

"It was you," she said. "You helped me do it. They broke my door down. There was no place for me to go. And then you came and reminded me. On the ferry boat, remember? You said the hospital wouldn't be bad, that I'd be quiet and free. And I was. And now I want to go back where I can be alone with Buzzy and they won't break my door down."

I had my story.

ARTHUR PORGES

Bank Night

Page Hampton was thinking very hard about the massive vault a few yards from his desk. Since he was president of Security-American Bank, this might seem quite normal, but his thoughts were hardly orthodox. He wasn't worrying, as other bank presidents might have, about the safety of the steel-and-concrete box; rather, he yearned to loot it.

Aside from the intriguing fact that it usually held half a million dollars or more in currency, Hampton had to get in because he was, in a sense, already there—into the bank's funds for well over $800,000. Only a much bigger loss, carefully staged, could cover his own peculations.

Compared to the underpaid tellers and cashiers, he had no excuse. His salary was quite high. But his expenses were even higher. As a widower possessed of good looks, prestige and a most attractive personality, he indulged a taste for glossy, expensive girls. Defying the usual "image" expected of a banker, he drove a Jaguar. His conservatism in financial matters related to banking made this deviation practicable. People inferred that all his recklessness went into the car, leaving none for bad loans.

A property-albatross in the form of a $65,000 house he had bought on the bluff overlooking Spanish Cove also played a part in forcing Hampton's hand. It was, to begin with, more house than he could afford, but to make matters worse, the cliff had been ripped apart (as is usual in southern California) with no regard for natural slopes or preservation of the vital watershed. As a result, the rains turned the subsoil to jelly and many of the area's magnificent structures, designed by top architects, were sliding inexorably toward the edge of the bluff.

Thanks to Jefferson Reed, a distinguished engineer and early settler there, the slippage had been halted. By assessing all the property owners, Reed had installed freezing coils at several key points—a trick learned from dam-builders—thus solidifying the loose earth and arresting the water's shearing action. After the next wet season, more permanent measures would be taken, but for the present, the houses were safe, he had assured them.

This was a good long-range program. It had saved highly valuable property that would have brought peanuts on the open market a few weeks earlier, for who would have cared to own the finest home built by a master architect—even one with an incomparable view of the Pacific—when his equity was heading for the deep six?

On the other hand, the assessment had come at a bad time for Hampton, when he was already overextended financially. And his share of the electrical bill for the essential freezing coils was at least manslaughter, if not murder. All of which explains why he thought constantly about the vault and of the power of negative thinking.

Hampton had always been a schemer. He had finagled his way through a good college by outwitting the professors. Instead of studying the books, he had studied the teachers. It's an old trick, but it seldom fails when practiced by a sharp-eyed lad.

Having acquired a degree with a minimum of effort, Hampton then wangled his way into banking, making full use of his assets. His appearance was impeccable; his voice dripped warm honey; and his powers of perception were finely honed. No matter how his quarry zigzagged, Hampton swerved at the same angle, always agreeing with, and supporting the ego of, those who counted. Yet he did this in so manly and frank a manner that nobody ever thought him a yes-man or a toady. And so, at 43, he was president of a bank   and a criminal de facto, if not de jure.

Now, when a schemer like Hampton puts his wits to work on a problem, he usually solves it. But even the best operator doesn't often hit on a gimmick so clever that he can't quite believe others have overlooked it. When he conceived his foolproof plan, Hampton considered himself with a kind of awe: He could not only loot the vault, cover his embezzlement and clear almost half a million, but with any luck, he would not even be suspected. Better yet, no one would be suspected; it was highly probable, in fact, that no crime would be recorded officially anywhere.

There was one small problem still to be solved: he needed technical help—someone who knew about explosives. And that little obstacle vanished almost as soon as it appeared. Who else but Morrie? Morrison Ball, formerly a sergeant in a demolitions platoon, and now, still in the National Guard, which had an armory—containing explosives galore.

In Korea, the team of Hampton & Ball had done very well on the black market. If Hampton was a schemer, Ball was the perfect accomplice. A roughneck from Chicago's West Side, his estimate of the value of a human life was more in accord with Attila the Hun's than Albert Schweitzer's. And yet, oddly enough, Ball had a code of his own. Far from being bright, he was nonetheless fiercely loyal and did exactly as he was told, once he accepted a leader. When he was tagged in Korea and faced severe punishment, he refused to implicate Hampton, who, using his rank, pulled every wire he could to help clear his partner. Both got away clean, while some luckless natives and a few of the squarer GIs were credited with an operation far beyond their abilities.

To Ball, uncouth, illiterate, with the manners of a stockyard hog, the handsome, urbane, glib and ingenious Hampton was a demigod. And it was also true that the brains of the team was both good-natured and openhanded, in appreciation of his subordinate's useful qualities. Once back in the States, they had drifted apart, of couse, but now, Hampton felt, it was time to revive the team for some business at the old stand.

At the little bar well off the beaten track, Hampton met his accomplice-to-be and laid the whole plan on the line.

"There's bound to be about $300,000 in there," he told Ball, mentally dividing the true amount by two-plus. A hundred grand was plenty for Morrie, Hampton thought. Probably the horses would get it all, anyway.

"Now," he went on, "I'm in and out of the vault every day. I could take the money any Friday evening and skip. But where to? These days they can extradite you from anyplace. Besides, I like this country. I don't care to spend a fortune somewhere along the Amazon, where all a guy can buy is bananas and the nearest doctor is 3,000 miles north, where it's all solid bugs, crocs, man-eating fish and headhunters! Not for me!"

"Yeah," Ball said with surprising shrewdness, his muddy blue eyes glittering. "And that's too simple for you, ain't it? You'd rather go around a few corners."

"Could be," Hampton grinned. "Anyhow, I've got a whale of a plan. Hell, they may not *ever* be sure anything was stolen. My idea is this: Suppose there was an explosion—a really big one. Blow that vault wide open. And a fire, too. With some of that stuff—what's it called—thermite?"

Ball nodded slowly. "Betcher life. Aluminum powder and iron oxide. When it goes off, you got melted iron"—he pronounced it "eyerun"—"and that will burn damn near anything."

"Good. Maybe napalm, too. That should burn anything the thermite misses."

"How you gonna work it?"

"Easy. You make up some bombs. Not too big; flattish, if possible. But maybe one big one for the main job—say, shoebox-size. There are a lot of shelves and pigeonholes in the vault that aren't touched for days at a time. I'll put bombs all over the place in such spots. The big one right near the currency boxes. Can it set off the others, or do they need timers?"

Morrie reflected for several moments, his brow furrowed. "Been a long time," he apologized. "I don't do that stuff in the Guard nowadays. Yeah," he assured Hampton. "I can use primacord or something that will go off when the big one does; then that'll start the others—as long as everything's only a few feet apart." He gave his partner a puzzled stare. "They'll know the stuff was inside. How you gonna explain that?"

"The deposit boxes are in a sort of anteroom. Anybody could put a bomb in one of them. I can get keys to the empties and really load that room. My idea is to have so many big explosions in and near the vault that nobody will be able to say just *where* the real blast came from. We've got to wreck the place, but good. As to a general explanation. I have a whole file of crank letters. You just can't imagine, Morrie, how many creeps get mad at a bank. We bounce a check that's overdrawn by six cents and then charge the sucker three bucks for giving us trouble! That would make Little Nell kick a blind man."

"You mean Little Nell, that big blonde from Jay Street? She'd belt a blind man just for bein' in her way, an'—"

"Forget it," Hampton interrupted, his lips twitching. "Point is, some nut could get even with the bank by loading his deposit box with an explosive. Maybe one box won't account for the damage, but as I said, we're going to do so good a job, nobody will know *what* happened. Besides, there are cashiers who go in and out. They aren't well paid and I know at least two who are in hock up to their ears. If they knew how to get away with it, they'd beat me to the punch!"

"Well," Ball said. "you know I'm with you, regardless. Like old times, Page. And I can use some moolah. What's my cut?"

"Since it's my idea, I thought a third—one hundred grand—would be fair. How's it sound?"

"Wow-e-e-e-e!" Ball said softly. "Nothing chintzy about you, Page. I ain't arguin' one li'l bit!"

"Okay. Make up the bombs, but be damn careful. Choose an armory away from your own area. You can still pick locks, I suppose."

"You can say that again."

"After you get the stuff, remember: one shoebox-size, with a timer. An ordinary clock setup should do, but make it reliable. If the explosion doesn't come off, I'll have enough egg on my face for the biggest omelet in San Quentin. Eighteen to 24 hours should do it. I'll smuggle the packages into the vault during the week. Friday evening, before the guard and I lock it, I'll plant the one with the timer and set it. And when the big boom comes, I'll be away, out of reach, on a fishing trip for the whole weekend."

"When will you grab the dough?"

"At the last minute. I've been getting the guard used to running little errands for me just before closing. I'll send for something and clean out the vault in the twenty minutes that he's gone. Then we lock up. If I'm right, and your bombs really blast the place, they'll think all the paper money was destroyed, I'll leave plenty of bonds in case they expect ashes, but with a thermite fire I should think ashes wouldn't mean much. Best of all," he chuckled, "I have access to the denominational number lists. I'll see that they disappear."

"Won't that look phony?"

"It's a small risk. I figure some of the offices will be messed up, too. Say—" he paused a moment. "I could guarantee that. Make me *two* timed bombs. I'll set one where it will ruin a lot of records *outside* the vault. That'll confuse matters even more. That should make it look like a nut with a grudge, all right."

"How many people gonna get clobbered?"

"None," Hampton replied coolly. "The bank will be deserted. So will the neighborhood—in case any bricks fly. That area's dark on a Saturday night. It's a business district. By the way," he added, "we can't touch the money for a while. I might be watched. I'll put it in a safe place I've got picked out. You'll have yours in about a week. But I won't spend a penny of mine for about a year—if I can hold out. Then I'll resign or something, and go east."

"Why should they watch you?" Ball demanded. "You said—"

"Ah," Hampton interrupted. "We're not dealing with a lot of suetheads aged in brass, like in Seoul. The cops—and the Treasury boys and the insurance investigators—they're not stupid. When half a mil—er—all that money disappears in a mysterious fire, they'll have nasty suspicions. But they won't be able to prove a dime ever left the vault—I hope—and after a while they may begin to believe the currency got destroyed incidentally when some crackpot blew up the Security-American. I'm counting on some flooding, too. There's a big waterpipe somewhere in the wall—leads to the fancy fountain in the lobby. So make the bombs, Morrie-boy, and leave the planning to me. Then we ride in a private car on the Gravy Train for life."

"How much time I got, you say?"

"Well, I'd like to blow the place the weekend of the 25th. Monday's a holiday. So the bank will be closed Friday night, Saturday, Sunday—and Monday. I'm going fishing, where there isn't even a phone. I'll come home Monday evening and when I hear the news, I'll be astounded. By then, they might begin to suspect I've skipped. My return should make them ashamed of doubting good old Page. That'll work in my favor—a bit of reverse psychology.

"They'll hesitate to suspect me again. But the cops will watch everybody. That's their business. Looking for a big spender. They won't find one in *my* neighborhood! Not yet. All clear?" he asked, looking Ball in the eye. "The explosion should come Saturday morning, between 7 and 10 A.M. I'll have to set the timer no later than 6:30 P.M. on Friday—we're open until 6, you know. So it'll be a bit over 12 hours."

"That'll take two good, small clocks, workin' together," Ball said. "One starts the other after 12 hours. It's the safest way, although under 12 hours would be a lot easier."

"But are they dependable? They *have* to work—or we're up the creek."

"They'll work. Don't worry about that," Ball assured him, a note of disdain in his gruff voice. "Kid stuff to an old pro like me."

The following days crawled by as if mortally wounded. As the critical weekend approached, the bombs passed from Ball to Hampton and were carefully placed in the vault, deposit boxes, at the backs of desks in the outer office and even on the tops of filing cabinets.

On Friday, everything went as planned, almost too smoothly to be reassuring. Such luck violated the age-old Murphy's Law: If anything can go wrong, it will.

At 6:12, with everyone gone but the guard and himself, Hampton sent the man out for cigarettes and, while he was gone, looted the vault of roughly $572,000. The number lists had been destroyed an hour earlier. They were incomplete to begin with, but why take chances?

The guard returned, accepted a generous gratuity from his openhanded employer and together they closed the vault. Inside its padded box, the first clock was ticking. Hampton, keyed up to concert pitch, thought he could hear it, but obviously the guard wasn't that alert. Like so many of his kind, he was ancient, slow and arthritic; in an emergency he would be more dangerous to customers and himself than to a holdup gang.

Having done all that was humanly possible to avoid detection, Hampton went fishing—far up Garrapata Creek, where the country was rough and communications lacking. There he sweated out a long weekend, relieving the boredom with visions of large bills and petite girls.

Naturally, he didn't leave the money lying around the house. Some days earlier he had prepared a good cache down on the beach, well above the high-tide mark. There under a huge rock, in a waterproof box buried deep in the sand, were 50-odd pounds of currency. And there they would stay for at least a year; maybe longer. Ball's share, however, had been turned over to him on Friday night, with a warning to spend it cautiously, just in case some smart cop connected them. Not that this was likely; the two men had seen little of each other since Korea and their few recent meetings had been in spots where they ran little risk of being observed.

The drive back on Monday evening, in heavy holiday traffic, seemed to last forever. Finally, Hampton came within sight of the winding, unimproved road that led to Spanish Cove. He got a terrible shock when he turned into the road leading to the residential part of the bluff: There were red lanterns in profusion, wooden stands with reflectors—and a horde of curious sightseers.

His house had vanished. Reed's was gone, too; and Harrison's; and the towering Truman place. Everywhere the raw earth, a network of gullies and dark cavities, was exposed.

As he stood there, bug-eyed, trying to make sense of it, a voice exploded behind him.

"That you, Page? What a mess, eh?"

He whirled. It was George Palgrave, whose own house, a sprawling ranch-type, was also among the missing.

"What happened?" Hampton managed to ask.

"You don't know? Say-y-y—that's right. You were away over the weekend." He brightened at this chance to break such big news—even if bad—to a new audience. "We've had it, Page. The whole cliff's taken a tumble—slid like hot grease when the power stayed off for so long and Reed's freezing job broke up completely."

"B-but," Hampton stammered, "he told us over and over that the earth would stay frozen even if there was no power for 36 hours. Don't tell me you've been without longer?"

"I do tell you. That explosion at the bank—*your* bank. Say, you don't know about that, either—brother!"

"What about it?"

"It ruined the bank building, to begin with. But that wasn't our headache. You know the power station across the street? Well, the explosion—and it was a lulu—threw those generators right off their beds. People heard 'em whining like animals blocks away. That shut off the power—and you don't fix generators overnight. It's not like a break in the lines. Hey, where you going? Be careful!"

Heedless of life and limb, Hampton stumbled over craters and mounds to the edge of the cliff, where he looked down at the moon-bright surf. If no longer creamed over a beautiful beach. About half a million tons of rubble—one for each dollar—had entombed the stolen money.

But he was no crybaby. "Hell!" he told himself, "I'm clear on the embezzlement. I still have my job. The money at the bank will be replaced by Uncle Sam. The house was a white elephant, anyhow. And if I can't hit Morrie-boy for at least five grand, I've lost my touch."

He looked up at the stars, then at Palgrave, peering down at him anxiously.

"Where were you, anyway?" Palgrave asked.

"Supposed to be fishing," Hampton said. "Actually, it was business mixed with pleasure. Had a chance to make a pile—a real killing."

"What happened?"

He looked up at the stars, then fixed his eyes on his neighbor. "I tried too hard," he said coolly, "and blew it."

BRYCE WALTON

The Contagious Killer

I chased more wild leads all through another hot July day and got back to the squadroom late and depressed. The case was going badly for me, but I had done all I knew how to do. The pressure was starting to build up.

The air conditioning was out again. The squadroom was sticky and smelled like a stale cigar. A few other boys stopped typing reports and mumbled embarrassed greetings. Someone even said "Hi," then hesitated before adding "Lieutenant," as if it were an uncertain afterthought. I hung my jacket over the back of my chair, rolled up soggy shirtsleeves and checked the memo spike on my desk. Nothing, as usual, but negative reports; and a note to call my wife. My boy, Jamie, would forge into the act. He would ask, "Dad, how come you haven't solved the murders yet?"

I could tell him what I'd been telling the reporters for a week, that I expected a break in the case any minute now. But kids, especially Jamie, know you're lying as soon as you open your big mouth.

I called the Bureau of Criminal Identification to see if they had turned up any sex criminals we hadn't questioned yet. They had not. I called Miller to see if he'd finished another check-through of cab company trip sheets; always a chance some cabbie might remember some suspicious character in a vital pick-up or let-out area. Miller had nothing new. I called to see if the pictures sent to the girls' home towns, to firms they had worked for, to schools they had attended, had turned up anything. They had not. I called Morelli to see if any anonymous tips had come in worth investigating. None had. I called Hoppy to see if he'd turned up anything by dragging all the flophouses again. He had not.

Then I just sat there feeling that frightening sense of failure and helpless anger. The truth was, I had to admit, I had a "cold case." When women are killed on impulse by a psychopath, you have to get a strong lead on a suspect within twenty-four hours, or it ices up and you may be years nabbing a killer; or you never do. The killer isn't usually acquainted with his victim. Probably he's never seen her before, has no personal connection with her other than some sudden sick compulsion. That eliminates all ordinary motives or leads, and there's no other way to connect this sort of murderer with the victims than through eyewitnesses and/or very obvious clues left by the killer. My killer hadn't left witnesses or clues. All he'd left lying around were the parts of his two dismembered victims, two young pretty girls who had come to the city to live a more exciting and glamorous life, but who had gone bad; the sort you see walking along the honky-tonk streets looking for adventure.

I felt an itch along the back of my neck, about where the axe would fall. It was my first big murder case since being made lieutenant, and it would likely be my last. Not that I'd get fired or downgraded. I'd be shoved down the hall to the clerical department as a typewriter jockey or a public relations stooge. No thanks, I wouldn't care for that.

The phone rang and I had the sinking feeling even before I picked up the receiver that it was the Chief.

"Get up here on the double, McKenna," he said.

The Chief's air conditioner worked just fine, but that office felt like an airless mousetrap to me. Our Chief is a heavy, intense and practical fellow who has few ideals and is very conscious of politics. He doesn't waste time or words and he didn't waste them now. He said, "Someone else is being put on your case, McKenna."

I felt numb, and for a minute I couldn't say anything. Then I said, "Well, all right, I'll see you around." I turned and started to walk out.

"Don't be stupid, McKenna. Just wait and listen a minute."

I turned. "It won't do any good. I've done all that anyone can do."

The Chief twisted his hands nervously. He blinked at me uneasily. "Just cool down a minute, McKenna, and listen. I know you've done all anyone can do; at least, all that any ordinary mortals around this precinct can do. But this is something special—a sort of weird, way-out thing. And I want you to listen. First, get this clearly, McKenna. Bringing this other guy in isn't my idea. It's the D.A. He's crazy for a quick arrest and conviction. It's his business, it's political. Our business is to do what we're told, and to remember that the D.A. is the mayor's nephew. Okay?"

"Okay," I said.

"Ever hear of an ex-cop name of Steve Blackburn?"

I shook my head.

"You were transferred to this precinct after Blackburn left," the Chief said. "But he was a lieutenant here too, in homicide. One day he found himself in charge of a butcher murder case, three women and a psycho. A case much like yours, McKenna."

He hesitated and gave me a funny squinting look. "In fact, according to Blackburn, it *is* the same case. He's convinced the D.A. that it's the same killer making a comeback."

I didn't care to say anything. I waited.

Finally the Chief went on. "This means a lot to Blackburn. His case was about a year and a half ago, and his killer got away. The case froze over. Blackburn was hit hard. Seems he was wrapped up in this case. It was like a fever. He couldn't think of anything else. Month after month he refused to do anything but hunt this psycho. For over a year he devoted all of his time to this obsession. That's what it got to be—an obsession. He says he learned everything about the killer.

He studied pathological crime until it was running out of his ears. But the guy disappeared. He didn't kill again. Blackburn had learned so much about the psycho he had a trap laid for him, but the guy didn't kill again, so Blackburn lost him. Blackburn kept saying, 'If he'd only killed again I would have nabbed him.' Anyway, to tag a long story, Blackburn was so obsessed with this thing that when he lost it, he couldn't stand the gaff. He hit the bottle too much, and finally he had to leave the force. It was all an ugly business."

"Blackburn's being put in charge now?" I asked.

"No. The D.A. has brought him in as a special consultant," the Chief said. "After all, if it is the same killer, Blackburn's way ahead of us."

"But what if it isn't the same killer?" I said. "What if Blackburn is, like you say, obsessed? What if he just has to come back to try to prove something, make up for his failure?"

The Chief laced his fingers together and pretended he was having trouble pulling them apart. "Ours not to reason why, McKenna. The point is, officially you're still in charge. Blackburn's not on the force." The Chief took a deep breath. "Anyway, Blackburn is certain he's right. Know where he is now? He's cruising in a police car down on South Main where the killings occurred. He says the killer will strike again. Tonight!"

"Tonight," I said. My mouth suddenly felt dry.

"That's right," the Chief said. "You're to take a car down there. Meet Blackburn at the Third and Main parking lot at six-thirty."

The unmarked patrol car rolled into the parking lot at exactly six-thirty. I walked over. There was a hot haze of smog that stung my eyes. Blackburn had a dark lean face that looked out at me like a vulture's. He said in a quick nervous way, "You drive, McKenna. That's your name, isn't it?" I nodded and he slid away from under the wheel. "You drive now. I want to look and get the feel of it again." He turned and looked out the opened window of the cruiser. "It's like getting in the mood again, McKenna. You get the beat and feel of a killer, and this is his street. This is Joe's street. You know it is."

"Joe?" I said.

"About the only thing I didn't find out about him was his name," Blackburn said. "I call him Joe."

"Where to?" I asked.

"Just cruise slow. Up and down Main."

"How far up and down Main?" I asked. I turned out of the lot into the traffic.

"Between First and Eighth," Blackburn said. He wore a dark suit, a dark tie, and he had black thinning hair speckled with white. He was in his forties, but had a dried-out look and his skin was as tanned as leather. He kept his head out of the window most of the time and sniffed like a bloodhound.

"No hard feelings I hope," he said to me once.

I shrugged. "It doesn't matter."

"Sure, you resent me coming in, McKenna. Don't blame you, but I had to do it." His voice got low and tight. "But don't worry, you'll get the credit. All I want is Joe."

"That's the important thing," I said, with effort. "To get him—get him before he kills again."

"No," Blackburn said softly. "The most important thing is that you should never get filed away in the books as the guy who let a big one get away."

He paused. "I'm not here to prove anything, or get back at them. It's too late for that. All I want is to finish that job. I just want to get Joe. I want to finish it for good and go home."

"Where's home?" I asked.

"San Fernando. I have a little dairy ranch out there." He looked out the window as I cruised easily along the street, and the neon lights went on, and the all-night shooting galleries and hot dog stands and bars and strip-shows and all-night movie houses lit up. "Don't worry, McKenna," he said. "Whatever we do, you say you did it. This is strictly personal with me."

After another block, he touched my arm. "This is going to be a rough night probably. You have any questions before it starts?"

I thought awhile. "How do you know—I mean how can you be so sure it's the same guy?"

"What little they had about it in the papers added up," Blackburn said. "Then I dropped into the police lab and checked. All the other clues were the same, especially those police photos." Blackburn chuckled, but I couldn't say what kind of humor it was, if any. "The public likes gore, but the dirtiest sensational sheet in the country could never publish pictures like that."

"I guess not," I said, to continue the conversation. The memory of those cheap rooms where Joe had done his work was bad. I'd been broken in to all the sordid stuff by serving my time with the Black Maria squad, but those two murder rooms had been too raw for my taste. Even the memory of them made me queasy.

"Take the gin bottles," Blackburn said. "You found two empty gin bottles. Well, there always was. In my three cases there always were two empty gin bottles. It always took him about ten hours to do a job, and all the time he was locked in the room using his knife on them he would be taking nips of gin. In both of your cases there were two empty gin bottles, right?"

"Yes," I said.

"And didn't the autopsy show that in both your cases the entire operation covered about ten hours?"

"Give or take a few minutes," I said. Blackburn's eyes were brighter now, and his voice was edgy with excitement. It was a very warm night but I felt a chill go down my arms.

"Same brand too," Blackburn said. "King's?"

"That's right," I said. "King's Gin."

"I know him, you see, McKenna. And every one of his kills are the same. Every detail is the same. With these psychos, murder is a ritual. I've read about all there is on the subject. It's part of a cycle, a repetition syndrome, as the books say. Everything in the ritual must always be exactly the same. In some, the cycle is longer than others. But this pressure builds and builds, and finally they have to do it. A ritualistic act, McKenna, and each Jane is what they call a live fetish. Each Jane is the same Jane to this Joe, always about the same age and looks. And everything Joe does just before the murder and during it is a strict repetition. That's how I know."

"But how can you know he'll kill again? Here, tonight?"

"He has to kill three of them," Blackburn said, "always three. I didn't know that before, you see. I set a trap and waited, but he'd already filled his quota and he didn't turn up again. But now I know there has to be three, and I know how many days apart the jobs are spaced. "You've had two so far. There has to be a third. The time is tonight."

"You knew he would come back?" I said.

"Nobody could know that," Blackburn said, "but I knew he'd come back if he were able. Things can happen to a psycho. Sometimes they get better and don't need the ritual anymore. They have split personalities. They can be fairly respected guys in some community, maybe with a family. They get this psychotic pressure and they go off somewhere—usually to the same or a similar place—and get rid of the pressure. Then they go back home and are good members of the community until the urge seizes them again. It goes in a regular cycle, so I figured if he ever repeated again, it would be here." His voice had risen and now had the taut sound of a stretched wire. "I've waited and waited, McKenna, and I insisted that the D.A. let me have one more chance at butcher boy. I had to convince him. You think I'd miss this chance?"

"I don't think so," I answered.

"Pull in there behind the station wagon," he said. We got out and Blackburn took a deep breath as if he enjoyed the smell of South Main, the sour feverish smell of that wild street on a hot Saturday night. "Let's walk, McKenna."

We strolled past the dark doorways under cheap signs saying ROOMS $1.50 AND UP. About every other entrance went into a dim bar with juke music beating out over the street, and girls perched on bar stools looking out into the dusk like hungry owls.

We strolled on through a dizzy glare as more midway neon blazed on. We walked past the sparkling jukelights. Sirens whined. A screaming woman was dragged out of a doorway by two uniformed cops. A bearded man, barefoot, sat on a curb, laughing softly. The air was ripe with the smell of chili, pizza pies, and stale beer.

Then it turned damp and misty and a thin drizzle fell under the blinking neon. Blackburn led me back down the west side of skid row, past the recreation palace and the girlie shows.

Once he stopped and stood looking up silently into the mist. I looked up and realized with a shiver that it was one of the cheap rooming dives where the second killing I was investigating had occurred. "You see, there's always the liquor store within a few doors, and within one block there's always the monster show." He pointed.

At the corner I saw the marquee of the horror movie, and I heard Blackburn say in an odd, tight voice, "Come on, McKenna. We have to get the mood of it. We only have a few hours."

We stood in front of the all-night, two-bit movie house which specialized in a triple horror bill. The teasers out front were life-sized cardboard cutouts of monsters, each holding in his arms a scantily clad woman whose mouth was painted a bright red, always open and fixed in a silent scream. The huge cutouts seemed to be leering and offering these screaming women to the pedestrians walking by, some of whom seemed to be secretly wishing they could accept the monsters' offers.

Blackburn said in almost a whisper as he stood close to me, "Take a good look, McKenna. You'll start to get the feel of it and of him—I mean Joe. See, the monsters and their Janes all look pretty much the same too, in a way, just like it is for Joe, and every movie is a ritual killing someone experiences vicariously."

"You sure have thought about it a lot," I said.

"For years," Blackburn admitted. "Is there much difference between Joe and the rest of us? A difference only in degree, McKenna. Every guy who enjoys this movie feels like our boy Joe, a little. It isn't so hard to see what this pressure is that builds up in Joe. You can feel it and so can I, and everybody else who will let himself do it. And that's how you catch guys like Joe. You have to identify with them as much as possible. I'm going to catch Joe because I've thought and studied, and I can *be* Joe. I mean, I know enough about what makes him tick—"

"I get the point," I said quickly.

"Good, that's fine. I'm glad you're getting it, because if we work this through to the finish, you've got to get in the mood."

"I'm getting into it now," I said.

A wino jostled us. Blackburn gave him a disgusted shove and he fell flat in the gutter.

We kept looking at the gorilla-man, wolf-man, and tattered mummy handling those silently screaming women. Characters kept ambling along and stopping and looking, and some of them kept looking and moistening their lips. It occurred to me that any one of them might be Joe.

Blackburn had gotten change out of his pocket and was stepping toward the ticket-seller's booth. I grabbed his arm, and he turned around slowly and looked at me for a second as if he had never seen me before.

"What's up now?" I asked.

"We're going to see the show. This is where it starts."

"I saw these shows years back," I said.

"Not the way we're going to see them now, McKenna. This is the first step." He paused and rubbed the flat of his hand across his thin mouth. "You see, this is where Joe always goes—before he does it."

I had to take a deep breath. "How do you know that?"

"Ticket stubs. Didn't you find them, too, McKenna? In those rooms, there must have been ticket stubs, from this particular theater?"

I felt a drop of sweat run down the side of my face. "Yes, there were. But they couldn't mean anything. The ticket seller here, the usher and ticket taker admitted hundreds that afternoon. They couldn't recall anything, or anybody unusual. The tickets could have been anybody's. They just don't add up to anything, so I don't see how you can tell."

Blackburn gave me a thin smile. Under the neon in the dark mist, that smile looked like a twist of black wire. "Five murders, and in every room a ticket stub from a local horror movie is hardly coincidence, is it, McKenna? In fact, every one of those killings was in a room rented within a block of a house showing these creep pictures."

"So how do the creep pictures figure in it?" I asked.

"Gets Joe in the mood," Blackburn said softly. "You can see how that is, can't you? Forget everything else, the way I do, and try to think like Joe thinks. You sit in the dark and look at this and you're all alone, sort of secret-like in the dark, watching this stuff, and you identify with it and start getting stirred up. It's part of the ritual, sort of like those war dances the Indians used, to get themselves worked up and in the mood. Come on, let's go in, get in character."

He bought the tickets and we went into the lobby, which had a stale, suppressing smell of wine, stale smoke and beer, sweat; the smell of skid row bottled up on a wet summer night. We stood there and Blackburn was breathing quickly. He moved over toward the center aisle and looked down it. I heard growls and screams from the screen. Empty bottles rolled in the dark somewhere. A few guys were snoring, their heads propped up skillfully on their hands. Bums scrounged a nickel here and another nickel or two there, and came in here to get a little sleep. They knew enough, though, to keep their heads from wobbling so the usher and the cops wouldn't notice and give them a whack and kick them back out into the wet night.

"It's about the fifth row from the front, in the center," Blackburn said. "Those seats are empty. That's where Joe sits."

"You couldn't know that," I said, "what row and seat he sits in."

"Just about," Blackburn said. "'I worked it out very carefully with an optometrist—several of them in fact. I know how tall he is too, and his build and the color of his hair. I've run lab tests on all that, strands of his hair, his skin, which we find under the fingernails of the Janes, and this all adds up to—"

"But how can you tell where he would sit in a movie?"

"One of the Janes broke his glasses, McKenna. We found part of the broken lenses. Couldn't trace the manufacturer, but we went over the lenses and figured out the exact degree of astigmatism. You can figure just about exactly where he sits. But the important thing is the mood, McKenna, the feel of it."

An usher with slumped shoulders, pimples, and a greasy uniform jacket came up and said, "You got to keep your voices down."

Blackburn looked at him like he was something pinned to a board. "Get out of here, boy," he said. The usher blinked and said it again. I showed him my wallet with my identity as a police lieutenant, and my badge. The usher backed off and Blackburn gave him a push. "Get lost."

Blackburn looked at his watch, then at the screen. "I've checked the show times. Joe usually starts working on the Janes about two a.m. He goes right up to the room from the movie. He's already got the Jane up there, drunk, or already too hurt to get away. He watches the horror pix, gets himself worked up to just the right pitch, then walks straight out of here to the room and goes to work with his shark-killing knife. That's an odd one, isn't it? The shark-killing knife. I never figured out where he picked up one."

"How do you know it's a shark knife?" I asked.

"We figured the length, breadth, thickness of the blade, also the sharpness. Also I got an isotopic analysis of the steel from particles in the bone. It's a shark knife, all right. Let's sit down."

Another movie started. My eyes ached, from straining at the screen and from the smoke-filled air. The smell was bad, too. I kept imagining I was inhaling about ten million germs a second. Six horror movies had gone by. And it was hot in there, but I kept getting chills up and down my arms.

I wasn't discriminating by this time. The monsters all looked alike, and the women being dragged away to a hideous fate, their clothes mostly ripped off, screaming and screaming, all looked alike to me, and their screams sounded the same, all phony and unconvincing. But the shadowy faces around me were absorbed in it. They sat there, their eyes wide and sort of glazed in the reflecting light from the screen.

"I figure this is about it, maybe another twenty minutes or so. It's nearly one-thirty. That means Joe's big hypo scene has to be coming up in about twenty minutes. Just keep a straight face and wait. I'll give you the sign. I'll squeeze your arm."

"Then what do we do? If we grab him, what about the woman?"

"What does that mean?" Blackburn asked.

"I mean," I said, "that according to your theory, Joe's already got the woman up in the room. He's already done some work on her, or tied her up. She has to be waiting when he leaves the movie here, all worked up and in the mood for it. So what if he gets shot, or gets away, or just won't tell us where the woman is?"

Blackburn stared at me, his face pale in the light from the screen. I don't think he'd considered the woman at all until then. "Oh, yes, sure. Well, I'll give you the sign, and when he goes out of here we'll tail him."

I nodded. We waited. Then Joe came in.

Blackburn squeezed my arm, and I rolled my eyes a little and my headache went away. Joe stood at the end of the row on the aisle, and he wasn't anyone you would single out to be much different than the rest of us. I couldn't tell the color of his hair, nor see that he was wearing glasses until he turned his face toward me, but somehow I had the feeling I would have known anyway that it was Joe. Maybe I was in the mood by then. I'd seen enough monster stuff to last me a lifetime. I had the beat, the feel of it.

I watched Joe out of the corner of my eye as he moved in and sat down just to my right. Only one seat separated us. He leaned back and braced his knees against the back of the seat in front of him. He sighed. Later—I don't know how much later but it was the longest period of my life—he leaned tensely forward. He put his hands on the seat in front of him and his head moved. It kept moving back and forth, and I saw the light shining on his glasses.

Blackburn had timed it within a few minutes when Joe would get up and leave the theater. We followed him. He went into a liquor store. He bought, I knew, two fifths of King's Gin, and came out twisting the sack and hurrying through the mist. A raincoat flipped, and thinning hair and glasses glinted in the drizzle.

We followed him to a dark entranceway under a sign that said ROOMS $1.50 AND UP. He hesitated, then ducked in there. I had a raw edgy feeling and a nasty taste in my mouth as Blackburn opened the door and looked up the stairs. I could hear his sharp quick breathing. When he turned and grinned at me his eyes had a shine like dark glass.

"We're wasting time," I said.

"We have to give him a little time too," Blackburn whispered. His eyes glittered with excitement.

"Listen," I said, "there's a girl up there. God knows what's happening. We've got to get up there."

"We've got time," Blackburn said. "First the drinking, the gin, remember. He has to work up to it."

"We've got him now," I said. "Let's go up!"

"Easy," Blackburn said. "You want to break the mood?"

"What's the matter with you?" I asked. "Who cares now about mood?"

The night man at the fleabag's closet-sized lobby told us the man we described as Joe had rented 307. I followed Blackburn up there. He was moving fast, then he started taking his time again, going up the stairs like he was suddenly tired.

The third floor hall was like a yellow cave. It smelled of stale grease and disinfectant and cockroach powder. Blackburn stopped and bent down and stuck his ear carefully against the door of 307.

I heard glass clinking in there. I heard a grunt and a sigh, and something like a moan in there. I could feel the sweat running down my face. I released the spring clip of the holster under my jacket and got my .38 out into the open. I touched Blackburn on the shoulder. He didn't move.

"Let's go in," I said, very low.

He didn't look at me. His body was rigid. He didn't seem to be breathing. He had his ear tight to the door and he was staring.

I heard other sounds then. Something in my stomach seemed to turn completely over. "Let's go in now," I whispered. He held up one hand for me to be quiet. He didn't look up at me. I heard those sounds again. I dug my fingers into Blackburn's arm. It was supposed to be his show. But what was he doing just listening to it?

"Blackburn?" I said.

He didn't move. He just squatted there, listening, and I heard a quick excited wheeze in his breath.

"I'm going in," I said.

His hand came around and touched my wrist. It was cold. It shivered a little. He whispered, and his eyes were pleading. "McKenna, wait! Give him a few more minutes. You can see how it is—I mean after all this time—you have . . ."

I saw how it was all right. I felt a moment of real horror. I saw how it was in his eyes—that glint of excitement.

"He's going to kill her," I said.

He gripped my arm and his mouth turned hard. "What does it matter?" he whispered. "Know what I mean, McKenna? You know? I mean, listen, some little chippie who will end up on a slab anyway, what does it matter now? Think about it, you'll see. You just don't feel it enough to know."

I felt his cheekbone slide under my swinging fist. Then I hit the door with my shoulder. I hit it again. I could feel Blackburn's hands dragging at me, and I kicked him in the face to get him off me before I got a shark knife in my belly.

The girl was too drunk to care much about whatever had happened so far. Joe looked at me through his thick-lensed glasses in a weird way, as if I had interrupted a study period in a dormitory. Then he came at me with his ten-inch hunting knife. I shot him.

When I went back out to go downstairs to call, Blackburn was on his knees. He was looking into the room and saying over and over, "Joe, Joe"—as if he had lost his brother.

GARY BRANDNER

Bad Actor

Young would-be actors filled the waiting room of the Bowmar Talent
School. They paced the carpet or perched on the chairs, sizing up the competition. I walked through the crowd to the reception desk and gave the girl my
phony name.

"I'm Alan Dickens. I'd like to enroll in an acting course."

The girl smiled without really looking at me and answered in a voice like a
recorded message. "Fill out an application and leave it in this basket. You will be
called for an interview."

I took a blank form from a stack on her desk and went over to a table where a
couple of beach-boy types were struggling with their spelling. In this room full
of eager kids I felt about a hundred years old.

I had felt much younger the day before when I rang the doorbell at Frank
Legrand's house in San Gabriel, where the suburban greenery was a refreshing
change from my dull office.

Legrand himself answered the door. A narrow-shouldered man in his mid-
forties, he wore a dark business suit and a worried expression.

"Thank you for coming out, Dukane," he said. "I—I've never done business
with a private detective before."

"Not many people have," I told him.

After inviting me in, he got on with the business. "As I told you on the phone,
I want you to investigate this Bowmar Talent School."

"You said your wife and daughter were involved," I prompted.

"Yes. A month ago Tina, that's my daughter, acted a small part in her high
school play. A couple of nights later a man from this Bowmar outfit came to the
house and said he'd seen Tina's performance, and wanted to enroll her at the
talent school. I was against it, but Tina got all excited and Esther, my wife, said
it couldn't hurt to go down and talk to them. So the next day she and Tina drove
into Hollywood, and *both* signed up for acting lessons. The cost seemed way out
of line to me, and it sounded like those people had made some questionable
promises about putting Esther and Tina into the movies."

"If you think there's fraud involved you ought to get the police in on it." I lit a
cigarette and looked around for an ashtray.

Legrand jumped up and said, "Here, let me get you something." He left the room for a minute and came back with a china saucer. "You can use this. When Esther and I quit smoking she threw out all the ashtrays in the house so we wouldn't be tempted."

I took the saucer from him and dropped my burnt match into it.

He said, "I don't really have anything to go to the police with—just a feeling. Anyway, I don't care about prosecuting these people. The important thing to me is my wife and daughter. I don't want them to get their hopes built up and then be hurt."

Legrand's eyes strayed to a pair of silver-framed photographs on the mantel. One was a dark-haired woman with dramatic eyes. The other was a pretty teen-ager with a face unmarked by emotion or intelligence.

"What makes you suspect that the school isn't on the level?" I asked, tapping ashes into the saucer.

After a moment Legrand said, "Dukane, I love my wife and daughter. There is nothing I wouldn't do for them. But I know them both very well, and believe me, they are *not* and never will be actresses."

I had accepted a retainer then and gone home to prepare for my entry into show business.

Now I waited in the lobby of the Bowmar Talent School while the receptionist worked her way down through the completed forms to mine. Then I almost blew the cue by not reacting when she called my new name. When the girl repeated it, I came to and hurried up to the desk.

"Miss Kirby will talk to you," she said, indicating a tall female seemingly made of Styrofoam and vinyl.

I followed Miss Kirby through a short hallway with several doors opening off it, and into a small office with walls the color of cantaloupe. She sat down and I took a chair facing her.

"Well, Alan," she said, scanning my application form, "so you want to become an actor, I see."

"I hope so," I said bashfully.

Miss Kirby leaned toward me, and the shadow of a frown marked her plastic features. "I hope you won't take offense, but you *are* just a tiny bit, er, mature to be starting out on an acting career."

My face stretched into what I hoped was a boyish grin. "I suppose I am starting a little late, but I just decided last month to have a fling at it. If it doesn't work out, I can always go back to the bank."

"Bank?" Miss Kirby's interest picked up.

"My father owns a bank back home in Seattle. I'll have to take it over eventually, but in the meantime I'd like to try what I've always wanted to do— acting. Unless you think it would be a waste of time."

Her tiny frown erased itself. "You know, Alan, now that I look at you more closely, I think you're just the type the studios are looking for these days. There are plenty of handsome juveniles around, but rugged leading men are hard to find. Yes, you're definitely the Burt Lancaster–Kirk Douglas type."

I lowered my eyes modestly.

"Come along now and we'll get some pictures of you."

"You want pictures of me?"

"Right. To send around to the studios and agencies. You want to get your face known in the business as soon as possible."

"Oh, sure," I agreed.

Miss Kirby led me across the hall and into a room where a man with orange hair and a big nose sat gloomily smoking a cigarette behind a desk. Photographic equipment cluttered the room, which smelled faintly of developer.

"This is Lou Markey," Miss Kirby said as she left me. "He'll take good care of you."

"Have a seat," Markey said, studying me without enthusiasm.

I put on an eager look and returned his gaze. There was something familiar about the bright little eyes, the comical nose, and the orange hair of the photographer. He used the glowing stub of his cigarette to light another, then jammed the butt into an overflowing ashtray. He offered the pack to me, but I saw they were triple-filter menthols and declined.

"Your nose is going to give us trouble," Markey said.

"It's been broken a couple of times," I admitted.

"They can straighten it, I suppose, but it won't help us now with the photos."

"Sorry," I said.

Markey sighed wearily. "Don't worry. I can light you so it doesn't look too bad, and later I can hit it with an airbrush."

"That's good," I said, feeling foolishly relieved.

He stood up and walked around the desk. "Let's get you over here by the curtain first."

When I saw the up-and-down bouncing motion of his walk I knew why he was familiar.

I said, "Are you *Beano* Markey, by any chance?"

He smiled for the first time. "Thanks for the present tense. Most people ask if I used to be Beano Markey."

"It was the early fifties, wasn't it, when you made your movies?"

"That's when it was. I must have been in two dozen low-budget teen-age epics. I was the comical kid who always lost his pants at the prom."

"Do you do any acting now?"

"Not since my voice changed. Of course, the critics said I didn't do much acting then either, the ones who bothered to review those pictures. And they were right. I never could fake reactions that I didn't feel, so I was always playing myself—the comical, clumsy high school kid."

Markey sat me down in front of a dark curtain, told me to turn this way and that, look up, look down, while he snapped away with a small, expensive-looking camera and kept up a low-key conversation.

"You seem like a fairly intelligent guy," he said at one point. "Why do you want to be an actor?"

The question surprised me. "I don't know, I guess it seemed like it would be fun and exciting."

"Yeah, exciting," Markey said in a flat voice. "Let me tell you something—"

Whatever he was going to tell me was interrupted when the door burst open and a young man with a thousand-watt smile bounced in.

"Hello there," he said, "you must be Alan Dickens. I'm Rex Bowman, president of Bowmar. How are you coming, Lou?"

"I just got started," Markey grumbled.

"You can finish up later," Bowman said airily. Then he turned to me. "Miss Kirby has been telling me about you, Alan. Let's walk on down to my office and we'll lay out a program for you."

He hustled me out of the photographer's room and into a large office walled with pictures of show business celebrities. A mountain of a man with blond curls was just leaving as we entered. Bowman took a seat behind an acre of desk and pushed a legal form across the polished surface toward me.

"That's our standard contract," Bowman said. He lit a long greenish cigar and blew the smoke toward the ceiling where an air conditioner sucked it out.

I ran my eyes down the paragraphs of fine print and saw that the contract implied much, but promised little.

"What's this 'career assistance'?" I asked, pointing to a line near the bottom.

"We make every effort to launch our graduates into successful careers in movies and television," Bowman said smoothly. "And I don't mind telling you that my personal contacts in the industry are a big help in landing that first part."

"What contacts are those?" I asked, as innocently as I could.

He chuckled indulgently. "The names probably wouldn't mean anything to you, but I'm in constant touch with the men who run things in Hollywood from behind the scenes." He walked quickly to a pair of filing cabinets and slid out one of the top drawers. He dipped into a row of manila folders and drew out several 8-by-10 glossy photographs. "Now, these are a few of my graduates whom you're probably seeing a lot of on the screen these days."

The attractive young folks might or might not have looked like somebody on television. All the stars under thirty seemed to come equipped with the Standard Face.

Bowman stuffed the pictures back into the file drawer. "That will give you an idea of the help I give my people to get them in front of the camera."

It gave me no such idea, but I nodded and said nothing. So far, though Rex Bowman appeared pretty fast on his feet, he didn't seem to be breaking any laws.

He took a look at his jeweled wristwatch. "If you want to sign the contract, you can start right in with classes this morning."

"Fine," I said, "I'm anxious to get started. But if it's all right, I'd like to take the contract home tonight and read it over."

Bowman's eyes narrowed a millimeter. "Ordinarily we don't let a student into one of our classes without a contract. You can understand that."

"Well—" I began.

He dazzled me with a smile. "But I'll make an exception in your case. That's how positive I am that we are going to have a long and profitable association."

"I appreciate that," I said.

Bowman touched a button on his desk and the plastic Miss Kirby floated into the office.

"It's almost time for the morning break," he said, "but Miss Kirby will take you in to catch the last few minutes of theatrical speech class."

In the classroom some twenty students sat on floor cushions listening to a young man who was mumbling something unintelligible. I spotted Esther Legrand and her daughter Tina near the front of the group. Both wore flared jeans and tie-dyed shirts. Esther had a loop of beads around her neck, and Tina wore a hammered silver ankh. The kid looked pretty good, the mother would have looked better if she dressed her age. I carried a cushion up front and sat next to them.

For several minutes I listened to the mumbler without understanding a dozen words. To start a conversation with Esther Legrand, I said, "There's a guy who really needs speech lessons."

She gave me an icy look. "That," she said, "is our instructor."

With that conversation out of the way I returned my attention to Mushmouth. Just before I dozed off he must have adjourned the class because my fellow students began standing up and chattering among themselves.

I turned to try again with Esther Legrand, and found her staring back at the doorway where her daughter was in animated conversation with Rex Bowman. He looked over and gave us the big smile and started in our direction. Tina frowned as he walked away from her.

Bowman said, "Glad to see you're getting involved, Alan. It will be about twenty minutes until the next class. You're welcome to sit in."

"Thanks, I'd like to."

"Most of us go up the street to a coffee shop for the break. Would you like to come along?"

"No, thanks," I said. "I'll stay here and look around."

"We'll see you later, then."

When Bowman and the students had trooped out I wandered back into the office part of the building, trying to look inconspicuous. The lobby was still full of aspiring stars. Through the open door of the photography studio I could see Lou Markey arguing with a chubby blonde about which was her good side.

As soon as I had a chance I slipped into Rex Bowman's office. His desk was clean except for the ashtray filled with cigar stubs. I moved to the filing cabinets and started pulling out drawers. Other than the one he had opened for my benefit, they were empty.

A bookcase gave me nothing until I came to a file folder wedged in at the end. The papers inside concerned the financial aspects of Bowmar. I hadn't read very far when I heard the voices of the returning students.

I was heading back toward the classroom when Bowman came in. He answered my smile with an odd look, but said nothing.

According to a schedule pinned on the door, the next class was going to teach us how to walk. I wasn't too surprised to see that the instructor was my friend

Mumbles from Theatrical Speech. Before I had a chance to learn much about walking, the bruiser I'd seen leaving Bowman's office came to the door and waggled a finger at me. I walked back to see what he wanted.

"Mr. Bowman has a special class he wants you to take a look at," the big man said.

He led me down the hall toward the back of the building and held the door open while I walked into another room. At that instant I sensed that something was wrong—half a second too late.

The sap hit me high on the back of the neck, in just the right spot and with just enough force. Curly was an artist.

I landed hard on my hands and knees, and tried to shake the buzzing lights out of my head. The room was small and bare with nothing to look at except the blond giant standing spraddle-legged in front of me.

He said, "Mr. Bowman thinks you ought to have a special class in minding your own business."

As I tried to push myself up, he leaned forward and tapped the point of my shoulder with the sap. My right arm went dead and I kissed the floor.

Curly was enjoying himself. He grinned and laid the sap along the side of my jaw. Pain clanged through my head like a fire gong.

"This class is just for private snoopers, Mr. Dickens-Dukane." He leaned over to let me have one in the kidney.

Curly stopped talking then and just moved around me picking his spots. My head had never cleared from the effects of the first blow, and every time I tried to get into some kind of fighting position he would hit me with the sap, just hard enough to put me down again.

After a while Curly tired of the game. Or maybe I wasn't showing enough life anymore to make it interesting.

The last thing I remember was the big blond face saying, "Nightie-night, snooper. Don't come back." He swung the sap at my temple and the lights went out, suddenly and completely.

I awoke to a sound like the surf. Then the sound grew louder and I got a whiff of diesel exhaust. I opened my eyes to see I was parked on a dead-end street next to the Hollywood Freeway. My head and body felt like I'd rolled down a mountain, but nothing seemed to be broken and there were few visible bruises. My wallet and watch were still with me, but the Bowmar contract was gone from my pocket.

As I reached for the ignition I saw my registration slip had been rotated from the underside of the steering post where I kept it. Bowman must have got suspicious and sent the muscle man out to check my car.

I kicked the engine to life and drove painfully home to my apartment. From there I called a friend on the staff of *The Hollywood Reporter*. She did some checking for me and learned that nobody of importance in the entertainment industry had ever heard of Rex Bowman. He had been a member of the Screen Actors' Guild a few years back, but was dropped for nonpayment of dues.

With a glass of medicinal brandy within reach, I eased my aching frame into a hot tub to soak and think. It was questionable whether Bowman was breaking any laws at his talent school, but at least I had enough information to cause him some trouble with the state licensing board. Also, I had a personal grievance now. Tonight I would pay him a visit and persuade him to let the Legrand ladies down easy, and then we would discuss my bruises.

Rex Bowman's house, I found, was small by Bel Air standards, which means it had something less than twenty rooms. It was after ten o'clock and the streets were empty when I pulled to the curb behind a gray sedan.

I climbed out of my car and started up the walk. When I was halfway to the house the front door opened and a woman ran out. When she saw me the woman stopped, looking around as though for an escape route.

"Hello, Mrs. Legrand," I said.

She went past me with a rush, swinging at my head with something on the end of a silvery chain. I made no move to stop her. She ran awkwardly across the lawn to the sedan, jumped in, and drove off with a shriek of rubber. As I continued up the walk to the open door of Bowman's house I had a feeling I wouldn't like what I found inside.

I didn't.

Rex Bowman sat in the center of a furry white sofa, his head sagging forward as though he were examining the bullet hole in his bare chest where the silk robe gapped open. One hand rested on the back of the sofa while the other lay in his lap with a burnt-out cigar between the fingers.

In front of the sofa was a glass-topped coffee table bearing a heavy ceramic lighter, a clean ashtray, and today's edition of *Daily Variety*. A molded plastic chair was pulled up to face Bowman across the low table.

I went to the telephone and dialed Legrand's number. I told him he'd better get hold of a lawyer and get him out there tonight. Then I called the police.

When Sergeants Connor and Gaines from Homicide arrived I told them as much as I knew, including how I ran into Esther Legrand on her way out. They let me come along when they left for Legrand's house in San Gabriel.

Legrand's lawyer was there when we arrived. He stood protectively behind Esther's chair, advising her whether or not to answer the detectives' questions. Tina, who had been summoned home from a party in Beverly Hills, sulked on the couch next to her father.

Esther Legrand admitted being at Bowman's house, but she refused to say why. Her story was that she found the man dead on the sofa, then ran out the door and panicked when she saw me.

Legrand, in something like shock, said he had no idea his wife had gone to Bowman's place. She had told him she was going to a club meeting, and he spent the evening alone watching television.

While Sergeant Connor questioned the family, Gaines went out to check the gray sedan. In a little while he came in and called his partner aside for a conference. Gaines handed something to Connor, who came over and dangled it before Esther. It was the silver ankh I'd seen Tina wearing earlier.

"Do you recognize this, Mrs. Legrand?" Connor asked.

Esther turned to the attorney, who shook his head negatively.

The detective turned to me. "How about it, Dukane, is this what Mrs. Legrand swung at you when you met her coming out of the house?"

"It could have been," I said.

Connor returned to Esther. "It was found tucked under the driver's seat of your car."

"I don't know anything about it," she said in a monotone.

Tina spoke up then from the couch. "Oh, Mother, it's no use. They'll find out sooner or later." To Connor she said, "It's mine. I was at Rex Bowman's house tonight. I slipped away from the party and went there—it's only a five-minute drive. We were . . . in the bedroom when somebody came to the front door. Rex didn't want us to be found together, so he told me to go out the back way. While he slipped on a robe to answer the door, I gathered up my clothes and ran out. I must have dropped the ankh."

"Did you see who was at the door?" Connor asked.

"No."

"It wasn't me," Esther put in. She brushed aside the protests of her lawyer and went on. "Rex and I were . . ." here she forced herself to look at her husband, "having an affair. When I found out he was seeing Tina too, I went over to have it out with him. When I found Rex dead and Tina's ankh lying on the floor, I was afraid she had killed him. I picked up the ankh and ran out. I still had it in my hand when Dukane saw me."

Sitting motionless on the couch, Frank Legrand looked like he'd just taken a shot between the eyes with a poleax.

While the Legrand family talked themselves into deeper trouble, I got out of there. I wasn't helping anybody, and there were some unformed ideas in the back of my head that I wanted to pull up front and examine.

It was the middle of the morning, and I was on my third pot of coffee and the last of my cigarettes when I figured it out. All I had to do was prove it, and I thought I knew how.

I drove out to the Bowmar Talent School. The death of the boss hadn't slowed the operation. I found the lobby as full of applicants as the day before. I walked past the reception desk to the office area. Through her open door I saw the plastic Miss Kirby in worried conversation with the mumbling speech teacher. As I continued along the hall, the big blond sap expert rounded a corner in front of me. He put on a weak grin and stuck out his hand. "Hey, no hard feelings, Dukane. Okay?"

I hit him twice in the belly before he could tense his muscles. The big man's mouth flopped open and he turned the color of raw modeling clay. I stepped back and planted my feet for leverage, then let him have my best shot on the hinge of the jaw. His face jerked out of shape and he hit the floor like a felled oak.

"No hard feelings," I said.

Lou Markey looked up from behind the desk when I walked into Bowman's office. His hair was uncombed and his cheeks were sprinkled with orange stubble. The ever-present cigarette smoldered in his hand. It took him a moment to place my face.

"Oh, hello, Dickens. Were you looking for someone?"

"My name isn't Dickens," I said. "It's Dukane. I'm a private investigator."

"Are you here about Rex Bowman?" he asked.

"You know what happened last night?"

"I heard it on the radio early this morning," he said. "I thought I'd better come in and start getting our papers straightened out. There's a lot to be done."

"Does that include changing the name back to the Markey School of Acting?"

"How did you know that?"

"I ran across it in some of Bowman's papers. It looks like he kind of took over your operation."

Markey shrugged. "Rex knew how to make money, I didn't. The new name, Bowmar, was supposed to be a combination of his and mine, but most people thought it just came from Bowman."

"What was he going to do next, phase you out completely?"

Markey's forgotten cigarette singed his fingers and he jumped to light another. "It doesn't make any difference now, does it? As the surviving partner I'll take over the school."

When he had his lungs full of smoke I snapped, "Give me the gun, Markey."

"What gun?"

The words popped out immediately, but Markey's eyes flickered down and to his right.

I got to the desk drawer before he moved, and lifted out a .32 automatic that lay inside. Markey sagged back in the chair and aged ten years before my eyes.

"I didn't go there planning to kill Rex," he said. "But I couldn't let him push me out of my own school the way he planned. I hated what he turned it into, anyway. Sure, he made money, but all the lies he told the kids who came to us. I told him it was wrong to lead them on like that, but Rex wouldn't listen to me. He wouldn't give an inch." He blew his nose, then looked up at me. "Where did I slip up, Dukane? How did you tumble?"

"It was the way you left things in Bowman's living room after you shot him. Something was wrong, but I didn't pin it until this morning. Bowman was smoking a cigar when he was shot—it went out in his hand. Yet the big ashtray in front of him was empty. Wiped clean. It had to be the killer who cleaned it—not to get rid of Bowman's ashes, but his own. Neither Esther nor Tina Legrand is a smoker. Frank Legrand either, for that matter. But you light one after the other, a distinctive cigarette that would point straight to you."

He stared down at the desk top for a long time, then looked up with the ghost of the crooked smile that belonged to Beano Markey, the comical kid in the high school movies. He said, "You didn't really know I had the gun here, did you?"

"No," I admitted, "but I figured you came straight here, not even going home to shave."

"And you tricked me."

"I just counted on your honesty. You told me you never could fake reactions."

"The critics were right," Markey said. "I'm a bad actor."

MICHAEL BRETT

Free Advice, Incorporated

Charlton McArdie took his first step toward becoming a millionaire as the result of a woman who dialed a wrong telephone number.

The way it happened, Charlton and myself, I'm James Hamilton, were trying to muster strength to leave the office and go home—not that we'd done anything to make us tired, but you can get tired doing nothing. We were the eastern sales representatives for Cool-Cool, a new midwestern air-conditioning firm, and it was the coldest, dampest summer in twenty years. Most of the few shoppers purchased name brands. Those who had bought Cool-Cool called back to complain about breakdowns, excessive noise, overheating, short circuiting and exploding sets. A fan blowing across a chunk of ice would have been more efficient than a Cool-Cool air-conditioner.

Charlton and I had already decided to sever connections with the firm when our contracts terminated at the end of the month. However, since we were on straight salary, we came to the office every day and put in our time.

Frankly, the prospect of being without a job worried me more than it did Charlton. I've got a wife and a small house. Charlton, on the other hand, is single and lives in a fleabag hotel over on Forty-third Street. He keeps talking about how he's going to get a duplex apartment and a fancy girl friend someday.

Charlton does a lot of daydreaming.

He also spends his time doing newspaper crossword puzzles and commenting disparagingly on the columnists who give advice to the lovelorn, on health, on finance, on not getting old—on just about everything.

His attacks were usually preceded by an explosive horse-laugh which shattered the silence in the office. Then he'd say, "Now look at this. You'd never believe that people can be so naive. Here's a college girl, writes to this Miss Common Sense. She's a college girl who believes in free love. Sex is an important part of marriage and she wants to be the perfect wife when the time comes. So Miss Common Sense tells her, 'Insofar as sex is concerned, practice does not necessarily make perfect.' That's just common sense. Now she didn't need Miss Common Sense to tell her that. Isn't that so?"

So I said, "Sure."

"And take this one here, for instance," said Charlton. "Here's a gal who writes that her husband is overweight and how can she make him lose weight. So Miss

Common Sense gives her a diet to follow and tells her to broil his food instead of frying it. Then she says, 'Send for my booklet, How to Keep Hubby from Becoming Tubby.'

"Here's another one. Somebody writes in and wants to know if it's all right to neck. So Miss Common Sense says, 'I will be glad to help you with your problem. Send fifty cents in coin and a self-addressed envelope for my booklet, How to Cool It.' Did you hear anything as silly as all this business about people writing in and asking for advice?"

He walked over to the window.

"Now look down there. There's thousands of people and the one thing you can be sure of, each and every one of them needs advice. Don't you think so, Hamilton?"

I was a little tired of the way he kept attacking the newspaper columnists, so I said, "You're probably right, Charlton. Why don't you go into the advice business? With your attitude, you'd probably make a fortune."

"You're telling me," said Charlton, and he gave out a loud guffaw.

Of course I had no idea that he was going to take me seriously when the telephone rang just then, or I might not have said it.

Charlton got it and said, "Hello." Then he listened for a minute and said, "One moment, Mrs. Abernathy." He covered the mouthpiece and said, "You know what? This is a wrong number. I'm talking to some dame who thinks she's talking to her psychiatrist, a guy named Dr. Kazoola." He winked. "You told me to go into the advice business. O.K., I'm going to give her some." He uncovered the mouthpiece.

"Mrs. Abernathy, now what can we do for you, dear?" He listened, nodding sympathetically and repeating bits of what she was saying so I could follow the conversation. "I see, the pills haven't worked. You still haven't been able to sleep . . . Well, that's bad . . . Ummm . . . Your life is confused . . . I do understand . . . I want you to remember one thing. There is absolutely everything in life but a clear answer . . . Yes, of course I sympathize with you over your husband's peculiar behavior, but many men think they're Hollywood idols. People are people, Mrs. Abernathy. When it comes to people there aren't any cut-and-dried answers . . . I agree, the situation with your husband is deplorable."

I laughed and said, "Cut it out, Charlton."

He ignored me and went on. "What I want you to do, Mrs. Abernathy, is place yourself completely in my hands. You may not approve or agree with what I'm about to say, but that's beside the point. Remember, it's for your good, no matter how unorthodox it may sound to you. Actually, what it is is a famous Far East method which is based upon the theory of taking strength from within. A form of mysticism. To make it work, you have to accept the treatment without question. Through it you'll be able to gain insight into your own character. The first act of insight is to completely throw away all of the accepted methods of psychiatric treatment. Now, Mrs. Abernathy, when I say go, I want you to take the telephone receiver and move it in a circle around your head, all the while chanting, *ah-zo, ah-zo*." He coughed. "I know it must sound ridiculous, but please believe me, it has a definite function. Now *go!*"

Then he covered the mouthpiece again, looked at me and said, "Hamilton, she's doing it. She's waving the telephone around in the air."

I said, "What's with you, Charlton? You nuts, or something?"

"Not me. She's the one, waving that telephone around and chanting. All I'm doing is proving something. You told me to give advice, right?"

"Charlton, you're crazy. I was kidding."

"You think *I'm* crazy? *She's* waving a telephone."

"She's crazy too."

He glanced at his watch. "The way I figure it, in about three minutes her arm is going to get tired and then I'm going to give her another routine. The point I'm trying to make is that people will listen and believe almost anything as long as they think the advice they're getting is from a competent source."

He moved his hand off the mouthpiece and spoke to Mrs. Abernathy again. "All right, Mrs. Abernathy, you can stop the ah-zo. Now what I want you to do is walk around the block in sneakers." He paused, listening, "Yes, house slippers will do. When you've done that, I want you to take a hot bath, then I want you to drink eight ounces of Scotch and go right to bed. I guarantee that you'll sleep." A pause. "All right, since you don't drink, you can make it four ounces. You'll sleep wonderfully . . . Yes, tomorrow I want you to call me. Thank you very much, Mrs. Abernathy."

He hung up and looked at me thoughtfully.

"Do you know the last thing she said? She said, 'Thank you, Doctor. I'll send you a check.' How do you like that?"

I had to laugh. "Wonderful. She's going to send this Dr. Kazoola, whoever he is, a check for nothing, and tonight the poor woman is going to run around the block and fall into bed potted. You ought to be ashamed of yourself, Charlton."

"Ashamed nothing." He crossed the room mumbling to himself and came back again. "Mrs. Abernathy gave me an idea. How to get *rich*. We can both get rich. Think of what happened. I gave a woman advice over the telephone and she's going to send her doctor a check. Now what does that mean? Do you have any ideas?"

"It means she's paying for services rendered. So what?"

"That's true, but what's important is that she's sending him a check for advice."

"Listen, Charlton, I'm beginning to get a headache. What are you driving at?"

"I'm going into the business of giving advice. I've given it lots of thought and the potential is great."

"That's good. In what field do you intend to specialize, law, medicine, finance? What?"

He sat down behind his desk and closed his eyes. With his eyes closed he said, "Medicine and law are out. The Bar Association and the Medical Association would crack down on me. Finance would be O.K., though. I'll be a *stock market analyst*."

I thought he was losing his mind. "Charlton, we've been here for too long, business has been bad for too long."

He opened his eyes. "That's right. Time for a change. I'm tired of not doing business, of being in hock, of worrying where next month's rent is coming from, of not being able to buy a new car. I'm going to give people advice and they're going to pay me for it."

"Yeah, I'd like to see it. Tell me something, what qualifies you as a stock analyst?"

"Your trouble is that you're negative. I'm a financial expert because I say I am. I've been reading about some guy, the leading exponent of transcendental meditation. It's a theory which says that people can do anything if they really think about it and tell themselves they can. It's like self-hypnosis. O.K., I tell myself that I'm a stock expert and I am. It's as simple as that."

"That's fine. Why don't you announce that you're a brain surgeon—are you something merely because you say you are? Be sensible."

"I didn't say anything about being a brain surgeon, did I? All I want to do is give people financial advice. Think of the possibilities. Do you know anyone who doesn't need advice on one matter or another? Everybody wants advice. There are people who don't make a move without consulting their horoscopes, and if the signs aren't favorable they won't get out of bed, much less leave their homes. What does it mean? They're following advice. And what about the millions of dollars spent with public relations firms, promotional attorneys, financial advisors, crystal ball gazers, mediums, psychics, goonies, and loonies? Name it and you've got it—there's somebody to give advice."

I could see that I wasn't getting anywhere. "Granted, but why should people come to you? Who knows you? What makes you qualified?"

"Nothing. I have no qualifications, but the one thing I can do is give advice, and the way I'm going to advertise it we'll make a million dollars. The advice I give will be free."

I thought he was demented. "Free advice—you'll go broke."

"Wrong. We'll clean up. They'll just think the advice is free. Let me explain my plan. Let's assume a man buys a certain stock. O.K., then what happens?"

"It goes up or it goes down. He makes or he loses money."

"Very good. You're getting the idea. There are two things that can happen, and right off the bat as far as you're concerned, the odds you're working with are fifty-fifty. Now suppose you predict a winner. The guy who's got it is going to send you a small donation for putting him onto a good thing. Or suppose you tell a stockholder to sell off or to purchase additional stock. Without knowing anything about the stock, you're bound to come up with the right advice merely through the laws of chance and probability."

"That's all fine and good. Now what about the guy who follows your advice and comes up a loser?"

"You can't worry about him. There's a hundred guys selling books on how to beat the market. More guys go broke following the tips in those books than you can count. Let's face it. If the guys who were writing those books really had a surefire way of predicting the market, they wouldn't be writing books in the first place. They'd be wheeler-dealer speculators."

"What about collections? What makes you think that a guy, even if he makes money on your advice, is going to send you money?"

"The honor system," he said.

"That isn't business."

"Exactly. But if I were going to follow the rules of business, this gimmick wouldn't work." He looked at me. "Hamilton, all it costs us is the price of an advertisement and we're in business. What do you say?"

I doubted that anything would come of it, but I said yes anyway. We went to work on the ad immediately. He took it to a newspaper and I went home. I didn't say anything to my wife about it.

We'd taken a good-sized ad, a square, heavily outlined. FREE ADVICE, INCORPORATED. STOCK ANALYSTS; a phone number and address. I kept thinking that I'd simply thrown away my share of the advertisement's cost. I also thought about the idea catching on. The prospect was bewildering. I couldn't sleep.

After breakfast, I rushed off to the office. Charlton was already there. "Any calls?" I said.

He whooped with laughter. "It's eight o'clock. Give people time to read it."

At nine the phone rang. It was a man threatening to sue unless we took back a Cool-Cool air-conditioner he had purchased a month ago.

At eleven, when I was beginning to think that the advertisement was a washout, the phone rang. It was the first reply to our ad. Charlton took it and said, "Free Advice, Incorporated. Yes, ma'am, there's no charge for this. This is a public service function. We need your name and phone number for our files. We'll give you a reference number. We are not responsible for any information that we dispense. This is a non-profit organization. However, if you feel that our advice has benefited you in any way, your donation allowing us to continue will be appreciated."

He wrote down the information and then said, "All right, ma'am, what can we do for you?" He listened, interrupting from time to time. I could follow the drift of the conversation. "All right, you've got a thousand shares of Santa Maria Railroad stock. It's gone up five points during the past month and you want to know whether to sell. My advice to you is, sell and take your profits . . . No ma'am, it's against our policy to reveal the information we use. However, I will say this, Santa Maria is negotiating two hundred million dollars in new loans from banks and insurance companies to refinance millions of dollars in outstanding debts. My advice is to sell. Your number, incidentally, is B 28." He hung up.

I was stunned. "Is that true about Santa Maria Railroad?"

"How do I know?" he said. "It could be. Railroads are always negotiating loans. It really doesn't matter. The main thing is that I've told her something." He wrote B 28 next to her name and the advice he had given her.

I took the next call. It was from a man named Summerfield. After I'd taken down the necessary information and had assigned him a number and had gone through the policy spiel, he told me that he had five hundred shares of Northern Tractor, which he planned to sell, and then he was going to invest the money in a Florida land development company.

"What's the name of the company, Mr. Summerfield?" I asked.

"Flamingo Land Development Company."

"Flamingo Land Development Company?" I shouted. "Forget it."

"What is it?" he asked excitedly. "Do you know something?"

"Sell off the Northern Tractor, deposit the money in a bank, and then call me at the end of the month, Ask for Mr. Hamilton," I said, and ended our conversation.

Charlton looked at me incredulously. "What do you know about the Flamingo Land Development Company?"

"About as much as you know about Santa Maria Railroad," I said. "That isn't important, though. What counts is that Mr. Summerfield *thinks* I know something about it. That land could be under water."

"It certainly could," said Charlton. "It probably is."

There were fifty-four calls the first day. The second day brought an even heavier response to the ad. We became more scientific. In giving advice on a specific stock, we advised fifty percent of those who called to sell and the other half to buy additional stock. We kept records. We watched the progress of our stock tips for a month. In that period the last number assigned was B 5028. We had advised five thousand people. Charlton was right. Money began to roll in from the winners who were eagerly seeking new ways to make additional monies. We had a good thing going. Those who had followed our advice and made big money were generous in their donations. To them we were heroes. We forgot completely about the others who had followed our advice and lost. To them we were bums.

Some good had come from our advice.

We had advised prospective purchasers of an oil company stock to buy as much as they could. Drilling for oil, the company had hit a vast underground source of natural gas and the stock had skyrocketed. The stockholders had become wealthy.

The woman Charlton had advised to sell off her Santa Maria stock called, angrily. The stock had gone up ten points.

"Don't worry about it," Charlton told her. "I have inside information that the bottom is going to fall out."

The man I'd warned about Flamingo Land Development Company called. I'd saved his life's savings. It was an out-and-out land swindle. "I'm sending you a hundred dollars, so you can continue with your good work," he said.

At the end of two months we were making big money. Charlton moved out of his room into a six-room duplex, got a fancy girl friend and bought her minks and diamonds. And all around us people were becoming wealthy. We began to study the market and the more we studied it the less we knew.

Charlton kept going through the records, talking to himself. "Look at this B 336. Here's a guy I made a millionaire. He didn't know what to do and I was the guy who tipped him off. It's absurd, Hamilton. We're making people into millionaires and not doing it for ourselves. I knew this stock was going to rise. The trouble with us is that we're not smart enough to follow our own advice."

"What about the people who listened to us and lost their shirts?"

"What about them?" Charlton shouted. "You're being negative again. Try to look at the good we've done for the rest."

I could already see what he had in mind.

At the end of the week he told me that he knew of a stock selling at four and a half dollars that was going to go to fifty.

"How do you know?" I said.

"How do I know? I know, that's all."

I really believed he did, but I didn't want any part of it anyway. "What do we need it for, Charlton?" I said. "We're doing all right, the way things are going."

"I'm going into it with every cent I have," Charlton said. "It's going to hit and it's going to make me a millionaire."

"I'll sit back and watch," I said.

"Suit yourself, but I want to tell you something. This is something that happens once in a lifetime." He laughed. "The difference between us, Hamilton, is that a guy like you doesn't really have imagination. Two years from now you'll be back selling air-conditioners."

I went home and thought about it. I didn't sleep all night. Six months ago I had nothing, and today I had fifty thousand dollars in the bank. One thing was sure, no matter how scatterbrained his schemes had sounded, I hadn't lost anything by listening to him.

In the morning I withdrew my money from the bank without telling my wife, and Charlton and I bought fifty thousand dollars' worth of the new issue apiece.

That was on Monday. By Friday my investment was worth ten thousand and by the following Monday the stock had gone off the board. It had all been a swindle. Charlton was going to ask his girl friend to return the mink coat and some of the diamonds he'd bought her, but she'd heard about what had happened and had gone somewhere.

My wife left me.

Charlton went slightly mad. He came in on Wednesday and pointed a gun at me and said it was all my fault. If I hadn't invested with him he never would have gone in all by himself. "Look what you made me do," he said. "I'm going to kill you."

"Let's talk it over," I said. "Now put the gun down. Look, let's not lose our heads. We still have a good thing going for us. We made money. We can do it again."

"I don't know how," Charlton said doubtfully.

"Think positive, Charlton. We can do it."

He burst into unexpected laughter and put the gun down. "I must be losing my mind. What was I thinking of? Sure we can do it again."

We were both laughing so hard by then that we didn't see the little man who stepped into the office.

"Are you Free Advice, Incorporated?" he asked.

"That's us," said Charlton exuberantly.

"You told me to sell off my oil shares. I had three thousand shares at a dollar. Do you know what the price is now? Ninety-four dollars. You ruined me."

When he drew a gun and started firing, I took cover behind a desk. I could hear Charlton fall, and the gunman running away.

I got up, walked over to where Charlton lay dead, and unthinkingly picked up the gun that his murderer had used.

When people came running, that was the way they found me, with the gun in my hand.

Explaining it to the police was very difficult. They didn't believe there was a little man with a gun. They found Charlton's gun on the desk and they came up with the theory that Charlton and I had an argument and that I'd killed him.

When I asked permission to check through my records—we were up to B7800—on the chance that I might learn the identity of the man we'd misadvised, they sent me to a police psychiatrist, who had an overbearing manner until I described the scheme Charlton and I had used to found Free Advice, Inc. He thought I was crazy.

I believe he would have committed me to a mental institution if Charlton's killer hadn't come forward then and surrendered to the police.

I was released. As I was leaving the psychiatrist's office, he said, "I'm lucky. If I had known about Free Advice, Incorporated, I might have been tempted to call you. I own three hundred shares of something called Western Pump. What do you know about Western Pump?"

I'd never heard of Western Pump, but, I thought, why should I tell him that? "Buy as much as you can get," I said. "That one is going to go to the moon. It has great potential."

He leaned forward eagerly. "Do you really think so?"

I nodded and went out, wisely.

JAMES M. GILMORE

The Real Criminal

Except for the rare psychopath who kills for the pure pleasure of killing, and the equally rare professional killer who does it for money, murderers usually aren't the cold-blooded monsters they're cracked up to be.

Most of them are nice, normal, average folk, people like you and me, who ordinarily couldn't swat a fly or run over a cat without feeling a little squeamish.

You find that hard to believe? Look up the facts in any good book on criminology. You'll discover statistics prove the chances of a murderer ever committing a second murder are something like a million-to-one. Why? Because in many cases the victim was, in fact, the real criminal.

Take the case of George Winnard, or "Good old George" as his friends called him, before they heard he shot and killed Ray Barber.

George was everything you'd expect a good-old-George type to be; a ruddy, plump, good-natured man in his late thirties, always ready with a joke and an immense grin. He was absolutely faithful to his lovely, if somewhat flighty, wife, Ruth. His faithfulness, however, didn't stop him from playfully patting secretaries or making harmless passes at waitresses. He was the perfect father to his three sons. At least, he put up with their shaggy dog of undetermined origin, seven rabbits, and three pet turtles. He went to church every Sunday, ushered every fourth Sunday, and never, never fell asleep during the sermon. He worked half again as hard as most real estate salesmen, was a member of the Chamber of Commerce, the Kiwanis, and the Booster's Club. George was truly a big man, a man of stature, a man of heart.

Why then, you may ask, was he arrested for Ray Barber's murder?

It probably wouldn't have happened at all if George's boss, Mr. Walter P. Grimes, *the* Grimes of Grimes, Hackett and Pederson, hadn't called him into his office that sunny, warm Friday afternoon in May, a lazy spring day.

Mr. Grimes sat back in his big leather chair, put the tips of his arthritic fingers together, looked across his huge walnut desk at George and asked, "What do you think of Ray Barber?"

George grinned his immense grin and shrugged, "He's a good salesman. . . ."

"But not the best?"

"I didn't say that."

"That's the trouble with you, George," Mr. Grimes said with a fatherly smile.

"You can't see anything bad in anyone." The smile disappeared as he shuffled through some papers on his desk. "I just checked the salesmen's status reports. Barber hasn't made a sale or brought in a new listing in over a month."

"Everyone hits a slump."

Mr. Grimes shook his head. "It's more than a slump. I've had several complaints about him."

"Complaints?"

"From women prospects," Mr. Grimes said with a deep frown. "Seems he can't keep his hands off them. Now, George, you know we can't have things like that going on at Grimes, Hackett and Pederson. We're the most respectable real estate firm on the north side."

George nodded. "I'll talk to him," he said.

"Fire him. Now. Today."

"Fire Ray Barber? Me?"

"Yes, you. You're my office manager, aren't you?"

"But—"

"No buts. Fire him! He's crazy. I want him out of here for good by five o'clock. We're running a real estate office, not a home for maniacs!"

"But he's not—"

"Fire him!" Mr. Grimes shouted, pounding his desk.

"Yes, sir," George said, getting up to leave. "How much severance pay should I give him?"

"Not one red cent!"

It took George almost an hour to work up enough courage to call Ray Barber into his office.

Ray was a small, thin man with a small, thin moustache who had an annoying combination of tics and nervous quirks that gave him a look of constant agitation. He was the kind of a man you couldn't look in the eye for more than a few seconds without becoming nervous yourself.

After he sat down, George looked at the ceiling and, to sort of break the ice, said, "Nice day out, isn't it?"

The muscles of Ray's left cheek suddenly contracted and he pulled on his right ear lobe. Then his eyes narrowed, "Are you trying to say I should be out drumming up business? That I'm loafing?"

George grinned, a smaller than usual grin, and said, "Heck, no. I just think it's a nice day, that's all." He took two cigars out of his vest pocket and handed one across his desk to Ray.

He took it, nervously fumbled with the wrapper, and said, "Okay. It's a nice day." He put the cigar in his mouth and lit it. Then he blew out a puff of blue smoke and rolled the cigar between his fingers. "You're going to raise Cain with me for not making any sales lately, aren't you?" He made an annoying sucking noise through his teeth. "I saw you in there with Grimes. What'd you tell him about me?"

"Honestly, Ray, I didn't—"

"Don't give me any of that. What are you trying to do, get me canned?" His head jerked to one side, "Well, you try that, Georgie boy, and I'll get you."

"Now, wait a minute! I didn't have anything to do with this. It was all Mr. Grimes' idea."

"What was Grimes' idea?" Ray asked, drumming his fingers on the desk.

George decided he had better get it over with as quickly as possible. He took a deep breath and said, "You're fired."

The color drained from Ray's face. "So you finally got Grimes to do it—"

"I didn't."

"Who did then?"

"Do you want the truth?"

"Truth?" Ray laughed, a nervous, high-pitched laugh. "You don't know the meaning of the word. You've been lying about me for months, telling everyone I'm crazy. That's why I can't make any sales. Because you tell lies about me."

George was shocked. "Ray, believe me, I never—"

"No. You'd never do anything like that, would you? You're good old George, the all-American Boy Scout. Everyone likes and trusts you. That's how you get them. They trust you, and you lie about them. You stab them in the back with gossip. Well, I'm on to you, George. Maybe you can fool all the other suckers, but you can't fool me. You're the kind of a man that should be destroyed. You should be stamped on like a bug! And I'll do it, George. I'll do it if it's the last thing I ever do!"

George was shocked. He rose to his feet and asked, "Are you through?"

Ray seemed to calm down. "For the time being."

"Then I suggest you clean out your desk. Mr. Grimes wants you out of here by five o'clock."

Ray stood up. The muscles in his left cheek suddenly contracted again. "Okay. But you'll be hearing from me."

"I hope not."

"You will be," he said, taking a puff from the cigar. He tipped his hand toward George in a mock salute. "See you."

A week later, at the Booster Club luncheon, it began.

George was standing at the bar, sipping a bourbon and water, when Al Wright, another Grimes, Hackett and Pederson salesman, sidled up to him.

"What did you have against Ray Barber?" he asked.

"Me? Nothing," George said with a grin. "Mr. Grimes asked me to fire him and I did. That's all there is to it."

"That's not the way Ray tells it."

"No?"

Al lowered his voice. "Maybe I shouldn't tell you this, but he's been calling everyone in the office on the telephone. He claims you're off your rocker."

George laughed uneasily. "Me, nuts?"

"He says you fired him because you've got some kind of phobia about guys who wear moustaches."

"He's the nutty one. Why, my own father wore a moustache all his life."

Al smiled and asked, "How did you get along with your father?"

George shrugged. "Well, you know how it is—"

"Did you hate him?"

"Are you kidding?"

"No. I mean, maybe that's why you've got this phobia about moustaches."

George stared at him for a moment, then he said, "You're the nut."

Al laughed and gave him a jab in the ribs with his elbow. "That's right, George, everyone's nuts but you."

"Look. I told you I fired Ray because Mr. Grimes asked me to. That's all there is to it."

"Sure, sure," Al said. "I know. You'd really have to be crazy to fire a guy because you didn't like his moustache. Come on. Let's go in and eat."

The man who sat across the table from George and Al had a moustache just like Ray's. No matter how hard he tried, George couldn't keep his eyes off it. The man must have felt his eyes on him because, just before dessert was served, he asked, "Is there anything wrong with my moustache?"

George could feel the redness working up the back of his neck. "No, why?"

"You've been staring at it all through lunch. I thought it might be full of soup or something."

Al looked at George, and then looked at the man across the table. "He's got a phobia about moustaches."

"I told you, I haven't got a phobia about moustaches!"

"Then why were you staring at his moustache all through lunch?"

"I don't know. I was just staring at it, that's all." George wiped his mouth with his napkin and got up from his chair. "I'm sorry," he said. "I've got to get back to the office." It was a lie, of course, but anything was better than getting into a crazy argument with Al over a stupid moustache.

When George got back to the office, he found a small package wrapped in brown paper on his desk. He opened it and discovered it contained a false moustache. He looked for a card. There wasn't any. Then he checked the brown paper to see if there were a return address. The only thing he found was his name scrawled in a handwriting he didn't recognize. Anyone could have put it on his desk. He buzzed for his secretary. When she came in, he asked, "Do you know who put this package on my desk?"

"No, it was there when I got back from lunch."

"Well, get it out of here."

"What was in it?"

"A false moustache."

He wasn't quite sure, but he thought she had a strange smirk on her face as she picked it up. Ray must have called her too.

Late that afternoon, a couple from Detroit came in and asked to see a four-bedroom colonial. George had the floor duty at the time. He looked at the multiple listing and discovered there were five. They wanted to see them all.

Since they had to fly back to Detroit the next morning, George was out with them until almost ten-thirty. When he finally arrived home he was tired and hungry and not in the mood for jokes. But one was waiting for him.

As his wife, Ruth, served him warmed-over supper, she said, "You had the strangest phone call tonight."

"From who?"

"Whom," she corrected him."

"All right, dammit, from *whom?*"

"Ray Barber."

George almost choked. "What did that nut want?"

"He said to tell you he would never shave off his moustache. Why would he ever say a thing like that?"

"He thinks I fired him because I didn't like his moustache."

"Oh, George, you shouldn't have."

He looked at her blankly. "Shouldn't have done what?"

"Fired him because you didn't like his moustache."

"Look," he said, pointing at her with his fork, "I didn't say I fired him because I didn't like his moustache. I said, he *thinks* I did."

"Now, George, I know how you hate moustaches."

"What ever gave you a stupid idea like that?"

She smiled at him coyly. "Remember that New Year's Eve party we went to eleven years ago at the Fischers'?" She sighed. "And remember that tall, dark, handsome bachelor with the perfectly lovely moustache who kept flirting with me all night?"

"He was a short, skinny pipsqueak. And that stupid moustache of his made him look like Hitler!"

"Why, George, you're still jealous!" she squealed.

"Jealous!" he roared. "Not on your life!"

"Then why did you tell him you'd punch him in the nose if he didn't shave off his moustache?"

"Because I was drunk, that's why."

"You were jealous."

George's shoulders sagged. "All right. I was jealous. I hate all men with moustaches. I fired Ray Barber because I hated his stupid moustache. Are you satisfied now?"

"You shouldn't have," she clucked as she cleared away the dishes.

Everyone in George's dreams that night had a moustache.

Saturdays are always busy at a real estate office, so it wasn't unusual that George didn't notice the picture of his family that stood on his desk until just before closing. In fact, it wouldn't have been unusual if he hadn't noticed it at all, it had become such a fixture in his office. The only reason he did was that he was filling out an earnest money contract and he needed more room on his desk. He picked up the picture to move it and was dumbstruck. Every member of his family had grown a moustache! Then he looked again, closer, and found someone had drawn the moustaches on the glass over the picture with grease pencil. He buzzed his secretary.

"Miss Quinn, this has gone far enough!" he exclaimed the second she walked into his office.

Somewhat taken aback, she said, "I don't understand, Mr. Winnard."

"Look at this portrait of my family," he said, holding the picture within four inches of her face.

Her eyes opened wide and she giggled. "Why, they all have moustaches! Did you draw them?"

"No, I didn't draw them."

"Then who did?"

"That's what I was going to ask you."

"Don't look at me like that, Mr. Winnard. I didn't do it. I know all about your phobia—"

"I don't have a phobia about moustaches!" he yelled, slamming the picture down on his desk so hard the glass shattered.

"Mr. *Winnard!*" she shrieked, and she ran from his office in tears.

He sat down at his desk, and, as calmly as he could, tried to gather his thoughts. Suddenly, it all became perfectly clear. That crazy Ray Barber was trying to drive him crazy! Well, it wouldn't work. No, sir, it wouldn't work. He dialed Ray's number on the telephone.

Ray answered after the second ring.

"Ray," George said, slowly, trying to control the quaver in his voice, "if you tell one more person I fired you because I have a phobia about moustaches, I'll kill you. Do you understand? I'll beat your brains out with my own hands."

"Is that you, George?" Ray asked, calmly.

"Yes."

"George Winnard?"

"You know it's me. Now, do you understand what I just told you?"

"Of course, you said you'd kill me if I told anyone you fired me because you hated my moustache."

"I mean it, Ray, cut it out."

"Why don't you like my moustache, George?"

"Because I'm jealous, that's why!" George yelled into the receiver. Then he slammed it down.

That night, the Winnards gave a small, intimate dinner party for Mr. Grimes and his wife, Belle. It was the first time in almost six months that they had been to dinner, and George had been very careful with the guest list. It included a few select—if not close—friends, the kind that never drink or talk too much. Ruth had prepared a prime rib roast, laid out her best china and silver on her best lace tablecloth, and had even had Mr. Sandin, the somewhat effeminate but exclusive florist, arrange the centerpiece.

The party started out slowly, as all dinner parties do, but after two rounds of martinis and a few George's choicest mixed-company jokes, the guests began to warm up. Mr. Grimes told the men about the state of the real estate business, while Belle deplored the deplorable household help situation to the women. By the time dinner was served, it was beginning to look as if it would be a successful party. It probably would have been, too, if the doorbell hadn't rung while George was carving the prime ribs.

You can imagine his surprise when he opened the door and discovered two policemen standing on the front steps.

"Are you Mr. George Winnard?" one of them asked.

"Yes, of course," he answered nervously. Ever since he had been a little boy, just talking to a policeman had made him nervous. "Why? Is anything wrong?"

"Sorry, sir, the Captain said to bring you down to headquarters," the other one said in a low monotone.

"Now?" George asked. "Look, I'm having a dinner party. Whatever it is, can't it wait until tomorrow?"

"Sorry, sir, the Captain said now."

"What is it, dear?" Ruth called from the dining room.

"Nothing," George called back. "Just two police officers." Then he lowered his voice to a whisper. "I can't go now, don't you understand? My *boss* is here. How would it look if I were dragged out of the house by two policemen right in the middle of the prime ribs?"

"You should have thought about that before you did what you did," the first policeman said.

"But what *did* I do?"

"The Captain didn't say. He just said to bring you in for questioning."

Ruth came to the door. "What's this all about, dear? Are they selling tickets to the Policemen's Ball?"

"Sorry, ma'am," the second officer said, taking off his cap. "We have to take your husband down to headquarters for questioning."

"Whatever for?" she asked.

"They won't tell me," George said.

"Well, then I wouldn't go."

"But, ma'am, he has to," the first policeman said, taking George by the arm.

"O.K.," George said, pulling his arm free. "I'll go with you. Just don't make a scene."

"But what'll I tell the guests? What'll I ever tell Mr. and Mrs. Grimes?" Ruth gasped.

"Tell them anything," George said, resignedly, as he started down the front steps with the two policemen. When they reached the bottom, he turned and looked back at her. "Just don't tell them *why* I'm being taken to headquarters."

"But why are you?" she asked, on the verge of tears.

He gave a helpless shrug. "I don't know."

"Well, I just don't know how I'll ever explain it," she said, and she ran into the house.

Captain Watowski was a short, stocky, hairy man. He reminded George of a secret police interrogator he had seen in a movie once, except he hadn't worn a bushy red moustache like Captain Watowski's.

"What's this all about?" George demanded.

Captain Watowski pointed to a chair and said, "Sit down, Mr. Winnard." George did as he was told.

Captain Watowski lit a cigarette, then sat down on the edge of a table that had a tape recorder on it. He sat there smoking and staring at Geroge for a few minutes. Then he snuffed out the cigarette in a coffee can cover that doubled as an ash tray. He reached over and punched the "play" button on the tape machine. At first, George didn't recognize his own voice. Then, suddenly, he realized it was a recording of the conversation he'd had with Ray Barber on the telephone that afternoon.

When the tape was over, Captain Watowski punched the rewind button and said, "Tell me, Mr. Winnard, was that your voice?"

George shifted uneasily in his chair. "Yes, of course, but I didn't mean it the way it sounded."

"How did you mean it?"

"It was just a figure of speech. I mean, I didn't mean it when I said I'd kill him."

"Just what did you mean, Mr. Winnard?"

George thought for a moment. "Well, I meant I'd *kill* him." He stopped and thought again. "No, that's not what I meant." He grinned his most expansive grin.

"I'm glad you think it's funny, Mr. Winnard." Captain Watowski lit another cigarette. "But let me warn you right now, I wouldn't make a habit of threatening people's lives if I were you. It could get you into a great deal of trouble, Mr. Winnard."

"I don't make a habit of it," George said, lamely.

Captain Watowski ignored him. "Unfortunately, I can't do anything but warn you this time. The recording was made illegally by Mr. Barber, without your knowledge. But illegal or not, I don't want you ever to threaten his life again. Do we understand each other, Mr. Winnard?"

"Yes," George answered in a low whisper.

"Good," Captain Watowski said, taking a deep drag from his cigarette. He sat and stared at George again until he had smoked the cigarette down to the filter. Then he deposited it in the coffee can cover. "You may go now, Mr. Winnard."

"You mean, that's all?"

"That's all."

George stood up and started to the door.

"Just a minute, Mr. Winnard."

"What?"

"How do you like my moustache?"

"It's beautiful."

Captain Watowski smiled. "I'm glad you like it."

The fury began to build up inside George as soon as he was outside the police station. Somehow, Captain Watowski's moustache had had the same effect on him as a red flag waved before a bull. He lowered his head and charged blindly down the street in search of the nearest bar. He had to have a drink to calm him down, to bolster his demolished pride, to help him think.

Unfortunately, the two double shots of bourbon he gulped down at the Clover Leaf Bar did none of the three. His rational thinking process came to almost a complete halt. The only thing he could see through the blindness of his rage was a moustache. A thin moustache, Ray Barber's moustache. Barber's moustache. Barber . . . shave . . . razor! George laughed to himself. Why hadn't he thought of that before? He threw five dollars down on the bar and headed for the door. He had to find a drugstore.

Twenty minutes later he found himself standing in the hallway outside Ray Barber's apartment, a shiny, new straight-edge razor in his hand. He knocked on the apartment door. "I know you're in there, Barber!" he shouted. "Open up! I've got a present for you!"

The door opened and there was Ray Barber, the thin moustache on his upper lip, a .38 revolver in his hand. "Why, hello, George," he said, pleasantly. "I've been waiting for you."

"You know what this is?" George asked, holding up his new razor. "It's a straight-edge razor, that's what it is. And you know what I'm going to do with it? I'm going to shave off that stupid moustache of yours, that's what I'm going to do!"

Ray's mouth twitched into a smile and he pushed the gun under George's nose. "You know what this is, George? It's a .38 Smith and Wesson."

George looked at the gun under his nose and blinked stupidly, trying to focus his eyes on it.

"And do you know what I'm going to do with it?" Ray went on. "I'm going to destroy you, George."

George was suddenly jolted to his senses. "Are you crazy?" he asked.

"No, you are," Ray said with snigger. "Everyone knows you have a phobia about moustaches." He lowered the gun and pushed it into George's stomach. "Now, please, won't you come in?"

"What are you going to do?" George asked, dumbly, as he walked into Ray's apartment.

"Why, I just told you," Ray said, closing the door behind them. His left cheek twitched. "But first I must call the police." He picked up the phone, tucked the receiver under his chin and dialed the number with one hand while he held the gun on George with the other. "Captain Watowski, please." There was a short wait, then he said, "This is Ray Barber. I'm afraid your little talk with George Winnard didn't do any good. He's here now. I think he was going to kill me with a straight-edge razor." There was a short pause. "No, I have a gun on him right now. You'll be right over? Good. We'll be waiting for you." He put the phone down. "You know, George, I could kill you right now—"

"You *are* crazy."

Ray shook his head. "No, you are. Don't you realize that by now? You were crazy to fire me. I could have been the best salesman Grimes, Hacket, and Pederson ever had. But you lied about me. And why did you lie about me? Because you're crazy, George. You'd have to be crazy to lie about me." He laughed and his head jerked to one side.

"You planned this whole crazy thing," George said, helplessly.

"Of course," Ray said. "I couldn't be crazy and plan such a masterpiece, could I?" He made a sucking noise through his teeth. "Everyone knows about your moustache phobia, even the police. And you threatened to kill me. The police know that, too. They even gave me a permit to carry this gun, as protection."

"And now you're going to kill me?"

"Destroy you," Ray corrected. "Completely."

George blanched and his whole body began to shake uncontrollably. "You can't kill me. I have a wife and three children," he whined.

"Don't be melodramatic."

George fell to his knees. "Please don't kill me," he sobbed. "I'll talk to Mr. Grimes. I'll do anything. But please don't shoot me."

For a moment, the only sound besides George's sobbing was the wail of an approaching police siren. Then Ray said, "I didn't say I was going to shoot *you.*"

George stopped sobbing and looked up at him. "You're not going to shoot me?" he asked, hopefully.

Ray laughed. "No, I'm going to *destroy* you!" His mouth twitched again, and he suddenly turned the gun into his own stomach and pulled the trigger. The deafening blast knocked him backward off his feet. He groaned and slowly sat up. "Here, George, catch!" he gasped, throwing the gun at him.

George made an instinctive one-handed catch. "You crazy fool!" he exclaimed, springing to his feet. He rushed over to Ray and looked down at him writhing on the floor. "You poor, crazy fool!"

"I'm not crazy," Ray said in a hoarse, labored whisper. "Shooting you would have been too easy. Now you'll suffer for months. People will lie about you, the way you lied about me. And then they'll kill you, George, they'll kill you." He coughed, and then lay still.

There was only one thing left for George to do. He opened the straight-edge razor and shaved off Ray's moustache.

And that's the way the police found him, standing over Ray's body, the murder gun in one hand, a straight-edge razor in the other.

Of course, George was charged with murder and would have been found guilty, too, if he hadn't been adjudged insane.

You see, everyone knew he had this phobia about moustaches. . .

WILLIAM DOLAN

The Hard Sell

"Buy a murdered man's car?" Sam Bates' revulsion at the suggestion was oddly balanced by the magnetism the car held for him because he had known its former owner. He hesitated, polarized between the red station wagon and another parked alongside it in the used car lot. The cars were identical except that the second was blue and lacked the garish black racing stripe which ran the length of its red stablemate.

"The red wagon is yours for $300 less than I'll take for the blue baby, and it's a better car." Joe Parkman, owner and sole salesman of Hensonville's only used car lot, sensed Sam's fascination for the late Charlie Walsh's car. "I'll level with you, Sam," he went on, looking earnestly at his prospect as he warmed to his sales pitch, "the car's been hard to sell. Everybody in town knows it was Charlie Walsh's car and nobody'll buy it. They all come to look, but nobody wants it. They're all fools, because it's in top condition. Now I've had it too long and it's got to go."

Sam Bates circled the red car while Parkman talked, then slid his slim six-foot length behind the wheel.

"Fits you good, Sam," Parkman interposed before expertly resuming the identical spiel he had practiced for the past month on anyone showing serious interest in the car. "A couple days ago I decided to give a break to the first one of my regular old customers who came by and showed interest. If I got to take a licking I don't want if from no stranger. And here you are and there the car is, Sam, you're in luck."

Sam didn't have much money, but the price was good, no question of it. Although Sam had known Charlie Walsh, he hadn't liked him. Charlie, the flashy type, had been meticulous with his cars—clothes, cars, blondes, everything—a big ladies' man. He was a bachelor like Sam Bates, who tried to be something of a ladies' man himself but never had possessed Charlie's ability to score. Then two months ago Charlie had been found in the little Midwestern town's park slumped over the wheel of his red car, with red blood staining his new red tie. He'd been shot between the eyes by person or persons unknown. There had been a big splash in the local paper, and tired-looking detectives from out of town had tirelessly gone about Hensonville asking embarrassing questions, but after a time people seemed to lose interest, and conversation in the local saloons returned to normal subjects such as crops and women. Now here was Charlie Walsh's car for sale at Joe Parkman's used car lot.

Was a $300 reduction enough discount for the faint bloodstain still on the front seat despite Parkman's skill in the chemistry of used car preparation? Sam wondered, felt revulsion a second time, then thought sadly once again of his financial inadequacy. Sam, thirty-three years old, had a minor government job, secure enough, but short on pay even for a bachelor.

"Knock off another hundred and it's a deal," Sam said impulsively, unaware, until he spoke, of his intent to make an offer.

Once he had spoken, he became faintly aware of other reasons for wanting the car, ones that he only partly acknowledged even to himself. They concerned his dislike for Charlie Walsh, which had been more intense than he liked to admit. Charlie's death hadn't satisfied Sam's feeling. Now Charlie's car seemed to offer a chance for Sam to continue the rivalry in which Charlie had always dominated.

The rivalry had been over women and had begun when Charlie and Sam dated several of the same girls. In a town the size of Hensonville it was almost inevitable for two long-time bachelors, both girl-conscious. Twice they had competed actively for the same girl's favor, with Charlie coming off the victor each time. The last girl had been Helen Pringle, whom Sam had thought of marrying but for whom Charlie had had no such noble intention. Helen had hurriedly left town, and Helen's father, burly Ed Pringle, was known to have visited the flat over the grocery store in which Charlie Walsh had lived. Pringle had carried his bull whip inside, but he had come out again without having used it. Charlie had been a good talker.

Sam had accosted Charlie and told him what he thought of Charlie's treatment of Helen. Charlie had listened sneeringly for a few moments before throwing the hard right hand out of nowhere that had left Sam sitting dazedly on the pavement. When Sam had risen it was only to be knocked down again. It hadn't been much of a fight.

Several months had passed after the fight before Charlie was murdered, but Sam still had been one of the prime suspects. He had the motive, the police knew, but so did Ed Pringle and several other people in the area. A heel like Charlie manages to make plenty of enemies. He was heavily in debt to the bank, and was thought to have suffered large gambling losses to a racketeer who ran dice and card games in the city fifty miles from Hensonville.

Having seen Charlie's red car all the while it sat on Joe Parkman's lot, Sam had not approached it as a prospective buyer until today. Then, when he had kicked the tires the way any used car shopper does, he had felt a sense of mastery over Charlie Walsh. Unable to beat Charlie in life, he felt that somehow he could do it in death by controlling Charlie's possession. Sam kicked the tires a second time, harder. As he made his offer to buy the car his memories churned together—the humiliation of losing Helen to Charlie; the fight and the added humiliation of losing; Charlie's murder and still more humiliation while he was held at police headquarters as a murder suspect. Then came the thought of how he had felt when kicking the tires. Sam quizzically awaited the used car dealer's reaction to his offer.

Joe Parkman showed only a minimum of professional hesitation before accepting. The car was an unpleasant symbol of violence that he wanted gone. Before Sam had time to change his mind the papers were signed, Sam's license plates affixed front and rear, and the red station wagon with the black stripe moved hesitantly from the used car lot, its owner already feeling that somehow he had made a serious error.

Hensonville had only two bars. Sam drove the short distance from Parkman's lot to the first of them and drew up to the curb. He needed a drink. He also needed to make his purchase known, to sound out public opinion.

Comment was not long in coming. Another car pulled up to the curb and Ben Thorpe, pudgy cashier of the town bank, emerged. Sam stepped out of his car with his back toward Ben, but when he turned around, Ben's face turned gray and his jaw slacked.

"I thought you were Charlie Walsh, back from the grave!" Ben said.

Until that moment no one had ever commented on the physical resemblance of Sam Bates to the murdered Charlie Walsh, but now Sam felt the validity of the observation. In height and build he and Charlie could have been twins. The similarity even extended to the thick brown hair that Sam never succeeded in keeping combed for long. There it ended, physically. Sam's taste ran to the same loud clothes that Charlie had favored, though. Seen from the rear, emerging from Charlie Walsh's car, Sam Bates looked like a ghost.

With a self-conscious effort Sam passed off Ben Thorpe's remark lightly. "Got a real good buy," he said. "I'm not loaded like you bankers, you know. Besides," he leered with an attempt at humor, "I thought this buggy might make me a hit with the girls the way Charlie Walsh was."

"You won't get any local dame within fifty feet of that car," replied Ben. "Charlie Walsh got the last action in the wagon that this town will see." Ben's comment was casual, but his voice was strained. It was as though Sam's appearance with Charlie Walsh's car had suddenly thrown into focus a previously hazy picture. His identity with the murdered man was taking a turn which Sam had sensed but not foreseen.

"Have a drink on the First National," said Ben, changing the subject to relieve the tension as he and Sam entered the bar. "I'm here on official business for the boss and I never like to miss a chance to drink during working hours."

"I thought Mr. Grimes handled the outside work himself," said Sam, unconsciously using the formal "Mr." that everyone in Hensonville invariably applied in naming Frederick Grimes, president and practically the owner of the town's First National Bank. Hensonville was generally an informal town where everyone knew everyone else, but the town banker, its two doctors, and its four clergymen always were deferred to when named by its citizenry. Mr. Grimes was nearing fifty, tall and somewhat portly, known as "an imposing figure of a man." He was all the more imposing by virtue of being the town's only millionaire.

"Mr. Grimes has gone to visit his wife," Ben said.

Jane Grimes, some years younger than her husband, had gone east to care for her aged and ill father some four months ago, almost two months before Charlie Walsh was murdered. Mr. Grimes, who could afford it, frequently flew east to visit her, but Jane Grimes had not returned to Hensonville. She was afraid of airplanes, and the distance was too far for easy return by train or car.

Inside the bar Ben Thorpe ordered drinks for himself "and the new owner of Charlie Walsh's car." Comment on the purchase by the bartender and the two men at the bar was slight but unfavorable. The bartender, an affable man who deferred to his patrons, allowed to hearing that Joe Parkman had it priced way low.

Finding the atmosphere of the bar unfriendly, Sam soon left. As he self-consciously approached his new car he saw Tess Bowman, the postmaster's middle-aged and mouthy wife, staring tight-lipped at him across the dusty street. Sam defiantly took out his handkerchief and polished an imaginary spot off the fender before entering the car and starting it. He raced the engine loudly in neutral before driving off at a deliberately slower than normal speed.

"With Tess Bowman and the bartender at work there won't be anyone in town tomorrow who doesn't know I bought Charlie Walsh's car," Sam mused, his new feeling of defensiveness growing stronger within him. "Small-town hicks," he said to himself as he reached open country and trod hard on the gas pedal. The car ran beautifully. Not a rattle in it, not a scratch on the finish, and the interior was perfect except for one small brown stain on the front seat. Sam's right hand dropped to the stain and patted it.

When he entered the office the next morning, Sam felt a new distance from the eight other government workers whose hostile backs gave him a wordlessly negative greeting as he entered. By mid-morning the feeling was confirmed. There were three unmarried young women in the office, two of whom had shown signs of interest in bachelor Sam. One of the two he had dated occasionally. Today even the single girls avoided him. To be certain, he asked the girl he had dated to go out with him that Saturday. She flushed, hesitated, and stammered something about a previous date. In the afternoon Sam, who was a man of impulse, suddenly found himself asking the other two girls to go out. Both refused. The girl who had shown interest in him, but whom he had never dated, hurried from her desk to the ladies' room in tears moments after raising her somewhat plain face to his and saying simply, "I couldn't." The last of the trio, who had other amorous attachments, was more forceful. "To hell with you, Clyde," she said, and turned back to her typewriter, her faster and louder than normal clacking of the keys spelling out a message which Sam understood perfectly. Ben Thorpe had been right. The romantic qualities of Charlie Walsh's station wagon did not transfer to its new owner along with title to the car.

Shortly before quitting time Bob Hawkins, the boss, called Sam into his private office and closed the door. Hawkins was perhaps ten years older than Sam, a small man, rather officious. "Sam, you made a mistake buying that car," he began without prelude. "I know the price was right in dollars, but it still was a bad buy in this town. Everybody's talking about it," he went on somewhat lamely. "If I were you I'd get rid of it fast."

Sam had never liked Bob Hawkins. Sam's advancement in his job had been minimal, for which he blamed Hawkins. He did not take Hawkins' advice well, especially coming as it did after his rejection by the girls. "I don't like that truck you drive either, Bob," Sam said, referring to Hawkins' flashy convertible.

"Just trying to give you a friendly tip, Sam," Hawkins said in a tone of mild annoyance. "The big difference between your car and mine isn't one of make or model. Has it occurred to you that people in this town are going to start all over again to say you had something to do with Charlie Walsh's murder?"

There it was. Sam had to face it now. Before, he had only let it peek at him around the corners of his mind. He had thought hard of something else, such as his genuine need for a new car and what a good buy it really was. Before, when he had been a murder suspect along with all the others, Sam had felt a brief excitement. It had been a nightmare, of course, the whole business with Charlie Walsh, but the limelight of recognition by the town had also been thrilling. Even when suspicion moved away from him as the police chased other false leads, there had come the brief afterglow when the citizenry, one by one, had sought him out, shaken his hand and told him they knew all along that he was innocent.

Then the flame had grown quite cold. Sam had ceased to be of interest, but now that he owned Charlie's car things were back where they had been before. In the moment of his indignant reaction to his boss's question Sam felt something akin to a glow of pleasure.

"The idiots!" he exclaimed after a long moment. "The stupid small-town idiots!"

"That's precisely it, Sam," Hawkins said. "This is a small town. It recently had its first murder that anyone can remember, and that murder is unsolved. People were just beginning to forget it and now you've got them started again. Since you're the focal point of the conversation, it occurs to them to pin the murder on you. At lunch I heard the old rumor that you killed Charlie because he was beating your time with a girl."

"When the city detectives were in town they checked me out along with everybody else," Sam said heatedly. "They even gave me a lie-detector test. I passed."

"When a lie-detector test indicates guilt, everyone believes the test," Hawkins said. "When it indicates innocence, they say that lie-detector tests are inconclusive. Just the fact that you took a lie-detector test makes you fair game."

"Well, they can all go straight to the devil as far as I'm concerned," Sam said. "I'm damned if I'll knuckle under to a scuzzy bunch of hick-town gossips." He hushed the voice inside him which still whispered his additional reason, his lust for the thrill of living dangerously that identification with Charlie Walsh gave.

"Your funeral, Sam," Hawkins replied as Sam walked through his office door to the outer room where town public opinion in microcosm awaited him, embodied in the self-consciously silent forms of his co-workers.

Years before Sam had lived in another small town where a false rumor arose about a rather odd neighbor of his that the man was a drug addict. The man, when the rumor got back to him, planted the path from the sidewalk to his front door quickly with poppies, their bright orange petals calculated to suggest opium to the scandal-mongers. Sam had enjoyed the man's triumph when the gossip stopped as the small minds wre intellectually unable to cope with the wordless rebuff.

In the same spirit of defiance Sam next day entered a hardware store and asked to see some .38 caliber revolvers. Such a weapon had eliminated Charlie Walsh as his romantic competitor. The furrows deepened in the bald head of Jack Welley, the storekeeper, as he waved Sam toward his gun display. Welley's hand shook slightly when he handed Sam the gun. Sam flipped the gun open expertly, squinted knowingly into the chamber and said, "Sold."

A permit had to be obtained and the local police thereby informed of his purchase.

The paunchy desk sergeant said nothing until Sam placed his permit in his wallet and turned to leave the station, then, "How do you like your new car?" he asked.

"Fine," replied Sam. "Best car I ever owned. I expect to keep it for years."

"It used to be a real good girl catcher," said the policeman.

Sam led the sergeant on. "I figured maybe some of Charlie Walsh's good luck would rub off on me," he said. "The gun is to make sure I don't have his bad luck too." Sam returned his wallet to his hip pocket and carefully fastened the button before leaving.

Two days later the city detectives visited Sam at the house where he roomed. Ruth Caldwell, his landlady, called him from the foot of the stairs. "Visitors, Mr. Bates," she shrilled, her aged voice cracking nervously.

Sam had roomed with Ruth Caldwell for three years and never been called anything by her but Sam. Now her formality emphasized his new status in town as leading murder suspect. The gun purchase hadn't worked for Sam the way the poppies had for his former neighbor. Nobody appreciated what Sam considered the humor of its purchase two months after the murder. "Cover-up," they said. "Running scared," somebody commented. "He's a psychopathic nut who *wants* to get caught," said another. "It won't be long now before they arrest him for it," said the voice of the town, echoing back to Sam from the office, the diner, the bar. Nobody else had really said anything to him, except Mr. Grimes, the bank president, in refusing to accept the time sales contract that Sam had signed to finance his car.

"Joe Parkman should have sold that car out of town," Mr. Grimes had said when Sam called at his office to learn why his credit was no good. Mr. Grimes' lips had pursed as he looked at Sam with evident distaste. "If Parkman hadn't been so greedy he'd have wholesaled it at the auto auction in the city like he was supposed to do when he got it from Charlie Walsh's estate. I won't have anything to do with it, and if you've got any brains, young fellow, you'll get rid of it fast.

"I'll help you out there, Sam," Mr. Grimes had continued in a more kindly tone. "I'll get Joe Parkman to tear up the contract and take the car back. He sees his mistake now and he'll do it, all right."

Of course Sam had rejected the banker's offer, forcing Joe Parkman to handle the financing of the car personally. Sam's view of the situation was that he was engaged in open war against bigotry and he had no intention of knuckling under.

"Maybe it's because I haven't got a lot to lose," he told himself. "They can't fire me from my government job, and I don't have a family to worry about. Besides, if I give in now I'll look like a damned fool and I'll lose my self-respect as well."

So Sam went calmly down the stairs of his landlady's house and answered the policeman's questions in her sterile living room while she waited in the kitchen with her ear to the swinging door.

"No need for fancy electronic bugging devices in this town," said Sam loudly to the detectives as he saw the door to the kitchen move slightly. "All the people have big ears."

"Maybe we'd better finish this downtown," said one of the detectives. "Downtown" doubtless was a term that meant traveling a considerable distance in the city. In Hensonville it meant four blocks. The detectives had walked from the police station to Ruth Caldwell's. Now they accepted Sam's offer of a ride in his new red station wagon. At the police station they opened the file on their previous interrogation of Sam and proceeded to ask the same questions. They were even more thorough this time. They also repeated the lie-detector test.

Three hours passed before they looked at each other, shrugged, and told Sam he could go.

Despite the late hour several people were lounging about the street near the police station when Sam left. He noticed others parked in cars nearby, their curiosity thinly concealed by the closed doors of their automobiles. The wolves weren't howling for blood yet, but they had the scent. Sam followed his now-standard practice of racing his engine loudly in neutral before driving off slowly. "Idiots," he muttered bitterly to himself.

His landlady met him in the narrow front hall as he entered the house, her husky son standing behind her. He lived a few blocks away with his wife and family. His mother obviously had called him over for a special purpose.

"I'd like you to leave my house, Mr. Bates," she said without prelude.

"Tonight," added her son menacingly.

Sam opened his mouth to argue, hesitated, then changed his mind. "I'm paid up until the first of the month," he said mildly when he finally spoke. "I'll want some money back before I leave."

Ruth Caldwell sniffed in what she intended to be her most contemptuous manner, but she produced the worn black handbag that to Sam had long been her emblem of office as landlady. Now it also became to him her badge of outraged middle-class respectability. She counted out the proper amount. Sam took it wordlessly and mounted the stairs to his room with the deliberate slowness of movement that had become characteristic of him.

Packing was simple. A few trips between bedroom and car and Sam's belongings were stowed. As he drove away from the house he wondered where he was going. At best, there were few places for a bachelor to stay in Hensonville. At worst—Sam's present situation—he could think of none. Private homes like his ex-landlady's would be closed to him. He wouldn't risk humilation by trying any of them. The same thing applied to the one or two regular rooming houses in town. That left the two hotels.

Sam chose the lesser of the two.

Lew Brody, night clerk at the Hensonville Inn, carefully returned the paperback book he had been reading to the revolving wire bookstand, careful not to crease the cover as he did so. Then he looked up expectantly to the man with the suitcase coming through the hotel door, but appeared disturbed when he saw that the man was Sam Bates.

"I'll take a room for a few days, Lew," said Sam. "Make it one with a front view, please." The rear of the old hotel butted against railroad yards which intended to be noisy as well as dirty.

Lew Brody looked over his glasses and beyond the top of Sam's head. "I'm sorry, Sam, but without a reservation we can't let you have a room." Brody spoke evenly and with a trace of formality, as though he had rehearsed his words for the occasion.

Sam had feared rejection and did not yield without argument. He had frequently shot pool with Lew Brody in the hotel's decaying billiard room, coming by evenings when both he and Brody had time to kill. Brody wasn't a friend really, but he was more than just an acquaintance.

"Cut the nonsense, Lew," Sam said. "I know as well as you do that there's dust on most of the doorknobs in this big brick monstrosity. You told me yourself the bank only keeps it open for a tax loss."

"All right, I'll give it to you straight, Sam," Brody said, straightening his thin shoulders inside his threadbare suit and looking squarely into Sam's eyes. "Mr. Grimes, who *is* the bank, had Ben Thorpe call yesterday to tell me not to rent to you."

"Yesterday!" Sam was amazed. "I didn't have trouble with my landlady until tonight! How could they know yesterday that I'd be coming here for a room?"

"Apparently your landlady thought of putting you out as soon as you bought your new car," Brody replied, "and she told half of Hensonville. Shouldn't be surprised if there's a hex on you all over town. It looks to me as if you're going to have to sleep in your car, Sam. Good thing it's a station wagon," he added dryly.

Brody was reaching for his paperback novel as Sam walked thoughtfully back to his car.

"Sleep in it?" It was nearly one o'clock and Sam had no better idea.

He drove to the town park, which was large for the size of the town, thickly wooded with several narrow winding roads radiating from the pond in the center that the townspeople dignified by calling "the lake." Like parks everywhere this one was a favorite of young lovers. Evening traffic had fallen way off, though, since Charlie Walsh had been found dead in his car on one of the side roads.

Sam saw only one other car along the road he chose, but went well past it before easing over to a wide spot on the shoulder and cutting the engine. He piled the front seat with his worldly goods before letting down the rear seat to from a roomy deck area, then removed part of his clothing and pulled his winter topcoat over him as a blanket. He left the two front windows partly open, tiredly wondering how long it would be before insects would force him to close them.

Sam knew nothing more until he was awakened by sunlight well after dawn. Two flies were contending for possession of the end of his nose. He scratched several fresh mosquito bites, flexed away some of the stiffness in his back, and reflected that it hadn't been too bad a night. "But the coming nights will be better," he said to himself, thinking of the purchases necessary to minimal comfort in his portable bedroom. He had no intention of giving up. It was summer. There were no restrictions against camping out in the park. Boy Scout groups often did. There was a bathhouse down by the lake. Sam went there now to shave before going to work.

On his lunch hour Sam purchased a foam mattress to fit the rear of his station wagon, a sleeping bag, and mosquito netting to cover the windows of his rear doors so they could be left open. He also bought a telescoping rod that fitted behind the front seat on which he neatly arranged his clothes on coathangers. Sam decided against a portable stove and ice chest. He would continue to eat out.

Sam had not spent his third night in the park before everyone in town knew he slept there. When he noticed he was drawing the curious to drive past his parking spot, he calmly closed the magazine he had been reading in the long light of the summer evening and drove to a movie. That night he slept at a new location in the park, and each night thereafter he moved his bedroom. Soon people stopped treating his sleeping arrangement as a zoological display, and Sam began to feel that his housing problem was solved as long as the weather held. He hoped something would happen before winter.

Something did.

Sam had been sleeping in his car nearly a month and was beginning to worry about the sharp night air of approaching fall. The hostility of the town continued exactly as it had begun. There had been no violence, no open accusations. Sam had quietly been ostracized, and a kind of armed truce existed between him and the citizens of Hensonville. The town waited for its opportunity to pounce collectively upon Sam and publicly name him murderer. "Wait," they said. "It won't be long now."

Sam was in the car in the park one night about ten o'clock, listening to his transistor radio. He was unhappy with his situation. The recognition he had sought and received had all turned negative. Even the police worked hard at ignoring him. He would quit his job and leave town before he'd sell the car, he decided.

The oncoming car's headlights flashed full on Sam's car. Its brakes squealed slightly as the slow-moving vehicle stopped suddenly, then backed up and parked by Sam. A slender feminine figure leaped hurriedly from the car, ran to Sam's auto, then stopped and peered about the interior before speaking breathlessly.

"Oh, Charlie, darling, I was afraid you'd be here with someone else—another woman."

Sam sat rigid, speechless. The approach of the woman had surprised him. When she called him Charlie he was astonished. Everyone within a radius of fifty miles knew that Charlie was dead. Sam decided it must be a joke and true to his impulsive nature found himself going along with it. "Hi, doll," he said softly, as Charlie Walsh often had addressed women.

The slim figure pulled open the door on the passenger's side and threw herself into Sam's arms. The warm body pressed against him and Sam felt an avid mouth on his neck, his cheek, and finally coming to rest under his ear. *Some joke*, he thought as she held him tightly. When she spoke again he knew who she was.

"Charlie. I had to come back. I know what we promised, and I tried. Really, I tried! But five months was all I could take, Charlie." Her lips sought his hungrily. After a moment she mildly accused. "You've changed."

Sam thought of Charlie's reputation as a lover and by way of reply kissed her again. He had heard enough to make him want to hear more. The woman was Jane Grimes, wife of Hensonville's banker, Frederick Grimes!

Jane Grimes had never been involved in scandal, and she had left town two months before the murder. But what of her husband? Nobody had so much as considered the possibility. Now Sam Bates did. Frederick Grimes was near fifty and he had a young wife. Charlie Walsh had been a big operator, and he and Jane Grimes obviously had been lovers. Now, Jane Grimes had been deceived by a combination of circumstances—the superficial resemblance of Sam Bates to Charlie Walsh, Sam's possession of Charlie's red car, the park which must have been their trysting place, and darkness.

Sam caressed the back of Jane Grimes' neck, holding her head on his shoulder so she would not turn and see his face. "Tell me about it, doll," he whispered into her ear.

Jane sobbed and clutched Sam as she spoke, almost frenziedly articulating the thoughts that had wordlessly churned inside her for months. "He flew out to see me every week. He was looking for an Eastern bank to invest in, but he was terribly slow about it. He was in no hurry to leave Hensonville himself, but he made me promise not to come back or even to write to anyone here. I was so frightened of what he might do after he caught us. You know how angry he was, darling. I . . ."

Jane drew her head back and looked into Sam's eyes. Calmer now, she saw the man who was there where previously she had seen the man she wanted to see. Recoiling from Sam, she pushed her slim shoulders back against the door.

"Charlie Walsh is dead, Mrs. Grimes," Sam said softly, sensing that his best tactic was to offset the shock of her recognition of him with a greater one.

He saw her eyes go wide, their whites reflecting what little light there was in the murky car. She seemed frozen in place.

"I'm Sam Bates, Mrs. Grimes. I bought Charlie's car after he was murdered." Sam realized by her gasp that the word "murdered" piled additional shock upon that caused by the harsh enough "dead" which he had used previously.

Sam looked away as she began to cry softly, then reached for her hand and held it gently. Finally she spoke.

"He promised not to do anything if I left town and never came back." Her voice was steady but her tone was lifeless. She stared through the windshield of the red car and seemed to be talking to herself more than to Sam. "He always was good to my parents. My father hasn't been able to work for years and Frederick takes care of him and mother. I don't know what will happen to them now."

She stopped, sobbing again. Sam gave her his handkerchief in a wordless gesture of sympathy, his feeling for her tempered by his own memory of isolation from the town for two weeks past.

"Your husband made you promise not to write?" he asked.

"Yes," she sobbed. "There was no one I cared to write to here but—but Charlie." She broke down again as she mentioned the murdered man's name. "I always hated this town. We had no friends. My husband is a machine for making money. He built a big house and put me in it for an ornament. I stood it for five years and then—when Charlie . . ."

Sam now knew all that was necessary, except how Jane Grimes had come to find him in the park.

"I flew to the city and rented a car to drive to Hensonville," she told him. "I just had to see Charlie again, promise or no promise. I waited until after dark so no one would recognize me, and then I drove to his apartment. When I didn't see a light I drove around town looking for him. Not finding his red car on the streets, I thought he might be out here with another woman. I was certain of it when I saw the car here. This is one of the places we came together. It's where Frederick found us and we had that terrible row. I . . ." She fell into Sam's arms as she broke down this time. He held her gently for a long time until she was calm again.

She was the one to suggest going to see the sheriff. This surprised Sam, who had feared her reaction to the idea and had been trying to find the right words to tell her what the two of them had to do. He gave a sign of relief.

The moon was high but veiled by clouds as they drove slowly toward town. Sam hadn't raced his engine in neutral when he started the car this time. The defiance that had been his dominant characteristic for weeks was gone from him. There was no sense of triumph in anticipation of what was to come when they reached the sheriff's. Sam just felt terribly sorry for Jane Grimes. For her husband he felt nothing.

"Probably got rid of the murder weapon at once," Sheriff Tom Jackson said to Sam Bates and Jane Grimes, picking up the phone to call back the two city detectives who were working the case. The sheriff had quickly seen the import of the story told him by the couple who had come to his home and roused him from bed.

"The police knew you were innocent, Mr. Bates," one of the city detectives said to Sam hours later, near dawn, as the detectives, Sam, Jane, and Sheriff Jackson all sat around the sheriff's oilcloth-covered kitchen table with empty coffee cups and full ashtrays before them. "We never suspected Mr. Grimes though," he went on. "He must have done it, all right, but how are we going to prove it?"

Jane Grimes said little. She had cried herself out while in the car with Sam, and now she sat dry-eyed while Sam told the story. She showed no desire to help her husband.

Neither Sam nor Jane left the sheriff's house that day. They were detained there, under guard, while the sheriff and the two detectives quietly built their case against Frederick Grimes. Until they were ready to charge him, the police wanted Grimes to remain ignorant of his wife's presence in Hensonville.

Sam's car was seen outside of Sheriff Jackson's house that morning and his absence from work that day led immediately to the rumor of his arrest. By ten o'clock the rumor had flowed up and down the main street and into the bank. Grimes was not the first person who had asked Sheriff Jackson about it by the time the sheriff made his way to the bank just past noon. To his other question-ers the sheriff had refused comment. He wanted them to speculate and he wanted Grimes, in particular, to become anxious. Ostensibly the sheriff was at the bank to cash a travel voucher for the two out-of-town detectives, a normal occurrence. Actually he was there to offer Grimes the chance to put his head into the hangman's noose.

"Keep it under your hat, Mr. Grimes," said the sheriff. "We think we've got our man. We're keeping Sam Bates at my house instead of the station because we're not quite ready to charge him. He flunked the lie-detector test and we know he had the motive—Charlie Walsh was beating his time with Helen Pringle. We checked with a psychologist from the city, and he thinks Sam really bought Charlie's car because he subconsciously wants to get caught. What we need to wrap up the case is either the murder weapon or a confession—preferably both. Sam Bates isn't too smart, Mr. Grimes," the sheriff concluded, "and those city detectives are real good at sweating a man. We'll get him."

As the sheriff pushed the brass plate on the heavy bank door and went down the granite steps, Frederick Grimes watched him thoughtfully. Then he went to his private office and closed the door behind him. Grimes did not go out to lunch that day, but remained at his desk until the bank closed. Then he drove straight to the big house on the edge of town in which he had lived alone except for his housekeeper since his wife went east.

The two policemen watching his home from the woods behind it reported nothing over their walkie-talkies until past midnight.

At twelve-thirty the housekeeper's small car emerged from Grimes' big garage. Grimes, its sole occupant, drove away from town, the police making no effort to follow, knowing Grimes would watch to see if he were tailed. Instead, state police were alerted in Barton, the next town east.

Meanwhile, police watched the roads back into Hensonville.

Grimes never reached Barton, but turned off on a side road and circled back to Hensonville, the stakeout on the park road spotting him as he went by. The park had been deduced as virtually the only place Grimes could plant the murder weapon in incrimination of Sam Bates. The sheriff was already there waiting, and men were stationed along each of the spoke-like roads leading from the park's lake.

Grimes stopped along one of the side roads and for a time sat motionless in the car, listening. The only sound was the chirping of crickets. Then he quietly left the car and walked several yards from the road into the dark woods. When he returned, the beams of several strong flashlights struck him almost simultaneously. He held a small shovel in one gloved hand and a revolver in the other.

"Where were you going to plant it, Mr. Grimes?" asked Sheriff Jackson softly. "In the bushes near one of the places Sam Bates has been camping out?"

"I refuse to say anything until I've consulted my attorney," Grimes said calmly, and spoke not another word. He didn't have to. The sheriff's ruse had worked, and Charlie Walsh's murderer was on ice. The case was closed.

Sam Bates did not find his triumph enjoyable. The townspeople still turned silently away from him, although now for a different reason—their shame. Sam continued to drive the red station wagon around town, showing its black racing stripe like a flag of small-town bigotry. He asked no more local girls to go out in the car with him. He roomed now at the Hensonville Inn, where Brody gave him a special monthly rate. One evening Brody suggested that he and Sam shoot pool together, but Sam said no, he had a book he wanted to finish. Brody didn't ask again.

After a time Sam was offered a transfer and promotion to another government job, in the East, near the city to which Jane Grimes had returned to live with her parents.

Sam had thought often of Jane since the trial. Now as he prepared to drive East, camping out in his red station wagon along the way, he thought of her again, and patted the faded brown stain on the front seat beside him—for luck.

BOB BRISTOW

The Prosperous Judds

The partnership of Reuben and Isaac Judd had proved to be a profitable one. By word of mouth, that most reliable form of advertising, their fame had spread across the rolling hills of South Carolina. Their product was in great demand because Brother Reuben and Brother Isaac had agreed in the beginning to produce a quality drink—not too harsh to the taste, not too devastating to the liver.

"No bad liquor, Brother Isaac," Brother Reuben had said firmly the day they hauled the large drum behind a mule up the steep grade where the product was to be manufactured.

Pure water and good copper coils and a real quality corn and barley mash, the Brothers Judd agreed, were what made the old family recipe the most famous in the hills.

They began modestly. That first run two years before had been only thirty gallons, but they had distilled the drink with utmost care, a care born out of family pride, and the moment of critical evaluation came when the two of them, alone, tested the alcohol.

It was a moment of sweet discovery. The liquor was mild to the taste. It did not—as inferior moonshine did—burn like a hot sword all the way to the stomach. And once inside, the kick was a gradual flowing glow that crept to the nerves and kissed them to life. That first night of discovery had been a memorable time. Brother Reuben, deceived by the mildness of the taste, took too much and fell off the mountain, suffering three cracked ribs. Brother Isaac, intoxicated with joy, was overcome with a long-secreted love for the Widow Carrie Stiles, who lived near the town limits of Pinesboro, and narrowly missed being cut in half by the Widow's double-barreled bird gun.

But the following morning the brothers knew they had a winner. They passed around—to a select group of hill people who had indicated a liking for moonshine—some small samples. Within hours, orders began to whisper across the hills, reaching the whiskey still nestled below the great pines of the mountain.

Thus, one of a select few famous names was born in the rich tree-covered hills. And, as it is said biblically, the brothers prospered. Always seeking to perfect the product, they installed a stainless steel drum and drew water from the spring only after the rush waters of a rain had subsided and the stream had returned to its purest state.

Because the drink was superior, it was soon in great demand. The brothers asked—and got—a dear price for a gallon of the brew. They responded to prosperity by taking to wearing the most expensive overalls and brightly colored skirts.

Life was good. The Judd farm, located not uncomfortably far from the still, abounded with good, blooded Yorkshire hogs and prancing, fighting cocks.

This prosperity, as well as fame, aroused the interest of Sheriff's Deputy Satterberry. As is the custom in the region, a man elected sheriff once acquires essentially the permanence of a federal judge, at least as long as he does not tread too heavily on the interests of the constituency.

Sheriff Otis Tatum had been in office since the Brothers Judd were boys, but now, aging and becoming senile, he was little more than a figurehead. After his twelfth election, he had appointed his son-in-law to the position of deputy.

Deputy Satterberry, however, was a pretty man who grew bitterly resentful toward those who acquired a wealth he would not work for. His sagging mouth drew into a tight line when he observed the shiny brass buttons on the Judd brothers' new overalls. The clusters of hogs in the shade on the Judds' front porch brought him to a seething envy. After considerable effort, Deputy Satterberry had discovered the precise location of the Judd brothers' still.

And Deputy Satterberry's proposition, reduced to its essentials, amounted to a payoff, a kickback to the law, in exchange for unmolested operation of the business. In the infancy of the Judd brothers' partnership, such a proposal would have been met with severe mountain hostility and very well might have claimed lives. But prosperity had tempered the brothers, and it seemed the choice was to pay the immoral tariff or lose the business entirely. The brothers reluctantly agreed to the deputy's terms—to pay a small sum on each gallon of moonshine.

Before this capitulation of principle, they had considered taking the matter directly to Sheriff Tatum who had always been a forthright man and who would certainly find a shakedown unsavory. But the brothers took into consideration the fact that Sheriff Tatum's mind was not what it had once been, and they could not depend on his favorable reaction.

A further consideration was that Deputy Satterberry was, through marriage, in the Tatum family, and loyalty to the family was passionately observed in the Carolina hills. If the Sheriff heard of the shakedown on a clear-minded day, he might react unswervingly in favor of his daughter's man and, once committed, would be obliged to destroy the still.

So Brother Reuben and Brother Isaac agreed to pay fifty cents on the gallon for the protection of the law. In spite of the unpleasant aspects of the agreement, as well as Deputy Satterberry's habit of visiting the location of the still to inventory suspiciously the output and make certain he was receiving his cut on the volume, the partnership continued to prosper. Without fail, Deputy Satterberry asked for a complimentary half gallon of the liquor.

But there came a day when it appeared to Deputy Satterberry that the original shakedown had been so easy he could see no reason why the brothers might not be willing to pay one dollar per gallon.

This was too much. Brother Reuben, who was the acknowledged leader of the pair, sat scratching the stubble on his chin, his face screwed down in an angry grimace. He loosened his high-top shoes and slipped a foot free, examining the lines of dirt that had crept into the wrinkles of his sockless foot. Brother Reuben was a tall man, more than six feet, and thin as a railroad spike. His head was oblong, a shock of dark hair sweeping back toward his crown. When angry, his pale blue eyes grew intent and his voice lowered to a whisper. Most wise people took a step back when Brother Reuben spoke softly.

He moved a big toe thoughtfully and peered across the fire at Brother Isaac, his elder by six years, and began to take stock of their vulnerable position.

"We might move the still, Isaac, where he can't find it."

Brother Isaac, the heavier of the two, scratched his head. "He'd find it. We'd lose this good water." Brother Isaac gestured toward the flowing spring.

They were silent as the fire crackled in the pre-dawn light and the first blue jay began to flutter high in the pine above them.

In one electric moment the brothers' eyes met across the fire and held. And silently they examined the thought that had not needed words.

"It couldn't be just a *plain* killing. Not him bein' deputy and all," Reuben said.

A few feet away the clear water of the spring murmured down the hillside and the cool water condensed the liquid, drip . . . drip . . . as steadily the moonshine filled a waiting glass jar.

"That's a fact," Isaac agreed.

Reuben's face was torn with indecision. He looked around him, weighing the problem, cherishing the thing the two of them had made here on the hillside.

"It'd have to be like a accident," he said wisely.

Isaac nodded and shoved a fresh stick of kindling on the fire. "They's lots a accidents," he agreed pleasantly.

Reuben stood, knowing the problem was his. He turned his back to the fire to absorb some warmth and peered down the hillside through the narrow opening they had cut in the timber.

"He's comin' today," Reuben said to himself.

"He said he was," Isaac agreed behind him.

"That's a right steep hill," Reuben said.

He visualized the hated fat-bellied figure of the deputy laboring up the hillside later in the morning, his head bent down, his shoulders hunched against the grade.

"I got a idea," Reuben said softly.

It was ten, or very nearly, before Deputy Satterberry slammed the door of the sheriff's car on the road a quarter of a mile from the hill. The brothers thought they could hear it as they peered through a crack in the stubby forest. They took positions behind a wall of logs.

"We got to move all at once, Brother Isaac. A great push all at once when he gets close."

Brother Isaac's eyes slid as though oiled bearings as he scanned the hillside and his mouth drew into a faint smile. "Yessir . . . yessirree," he said.

The two of them, poised with crowbars, began to breathe more rapidly as the fat man suddenly appeared at the bottom of the hill.

"Allo up there," Deputy Satterberry shouted nasally.

Reuben and Isaac remained, as was their custom, very silent.

The deputy began to climb, slowly and with effort. When he was halfway up the grade, he paused and his belly moved accordion-like as he drew in great gulps of air. At last he let his head drop and began the final assault.

Reuben waited until the deputy was no more than thirty yards from the crest, dug his crowbar deep under the stack of logs, and with a silent signal from his eyes, gave the order to send them rolling down.

The brothers reacted together, hidden behind the large stack of timber, and suddenly an avalanche was roaring down on the deputy. There was time only for the deputy to jerk his head up at the sound and dive to his left. He reached the protection of a tree and cupped his head in his arms as the flood of timber cascaded past.

Knowing instinctively that the plan had failed by a mere matter of feet, Reuben provided the brothers cover by shouting a warning. Then they watched with sad hearts as the logs rolled harmlessly toward the bottom of the hill.

Deputy Satterberry came up screaming, holding his right foot where a log had cracked against his toes. The brothers were at the deputy's aid in a moment, lifting him up, examining him in feigned concern.

"I like to got killed by that damned pile of logs. You stacked them logs too close to the hill, Reuben. That's dangerous steep, that hill . . ."

"You all right?" Reuben asked.

"Like to tore my foot off," the deputy said. "Lucky they didn't!"

"They was too close to the hill, I guess," Isaac said sadly.

The deputy limped up the hill, sat on a log, and removed his low ankle shoes and his red socks. An ugly blue discoloration surrounded his big toe.

"That's too bad," Brother Reuben said softly, thinking about the failure.

The deputy massaged the toe with much sympathy, his jowls sagging sorrowfully. He asked for a measure of liquor to relieve the suffering. Brother Reuben poured from a fresh jar and the deputy sipped appreciatively.

"How many'd you run this week?" the deputy asked, managing to get his mind back on business and away from his foot.

"Isaac was sick. We only done fifty gallons."

The deputy frowned. The dark little pupils betrayed that mathematically this volume—translated to dollars in terms of protection—was smaller than he would have liked. He also betrayed a suspicion, born out of his own dishonest mind, that the figure was inaccurate. He slipped on his sock and limped to the small stack of boxes which contained the capped jars. There were four in each box. He made no tactful pretense that the inventory was motivated by anything but distrust.

An oily mass of unruly hair fell over his forehead as he irritably returned to the fire, removed his cap, and wiped the sweat from the brim. "That ain't very good," he said wearily.

"Well . . . it takes the two of us," Reuben said.

"You wouldn't hide out any jars on me. I'd be hard on you if you done that, Reuben. I just wouldn't abide that at all."

Reuben had more dignity than to reply. He reached into his overall pocket and drew out twenty-five dollars which he tossed with some distaste across to Satterberry. He saw the deputy surveying the money. The deputy began to smile, not touching the money at all.

"It's a *dollar* now," he reminded. "You forgot about that, Reuben."

"That's too much."

The deputy rocked back and forth on the log, his belly bulging over his lap almost obscenely. "That ain't even the question. The question is you will or you won't, and if you won't, I'll be up here before noon with ten men and this whole thing . . ." He signaled the ultimate result with a snap of his stubby fingers.

Reuben resentfully drew the billfold out and counted again. He tossed the money across the log and glowered. Before the deputy was satisfied, Reuben had fetched the customary additional bribe, a half gallon of the whiskey, and placed it at the feet of the lawman.

Satterberry picked up the money, his face glowing with victory, got up with his jug and limped away from the fire. He seemed to be looking at the scattered logs at the bottom of the hill.

"That'll be a lot of work, gettin' them logs back up here," he said. "A lot of work."

With that he retreated down the hillside, stepping over a log here and there, until he disappeared. They heard the roar of his car spring to life.

"Think he knows?" Brother Isaac asked.

"He loves hisself so much, he don't suspect anybody'd try to kill him," Reuben said. "Three steps closer and he'd never a made it," he observed, gazing down the hillside.

Brother Isaac came to his side. "What now?" he asked.

"We got to figure."

The idea came while hauling sugar on the back of the mule up toward the still.

"Brother Isaac . . . you know that bend in the creek where all them copperheads den?" Brother Isaac knew. "I been thinking the deputy might git hisself snake bit."

"He don't pass that way."

"That's right, but we might fix it so's they go *his* way. He wears them low-cut shoes, just right for a bite on the ankle . . ."

Brother Isaac stuck his thumbs in his overall straps, his face softening somewhat. "That's a fact," he said.

"He likes that sheriff's car all shined, and I remember he draws it in a shed behind the house so rain don't make mud of the dust. And shuts the doors good."

"There ain't no snakes in . . ." Brother Isaac hesitated as his mind functioned ahead of his words. He smiled, the whiskers matting together. "Why sure," he said.

Thus, the brothers hurriedly built a box with a hinged door and crept to the bend of the creek with forked sticks where they endured the hazards of catching several copperheads, whch they deposited in the box.

Very late that night, while the deputy slept in a deep sleep induced by their own whiskey, they crept to the shed by the light of a new moon, turned the latch, and emptied out the deadly cargo. They closed the door quietly and stole away unnoticed.

It was on the mountain two days later that a horn honked from the road. They recognized the signal of a faithful customer, and from Saturday Smith they learned what had happened.

"Deputy shot hisself," Saturday Smith told them after they appeared through the bushes with a gallon of whiskey.

"Shot hisself?" Isaac asked incredulously.

The brothers exchanged perplexed glances.

"Went in his grodge," Saturday Smith said, "and they was a swarm of snakes in there. Must a made a home when fall come on . . ."

"He got bit?" Reuben interjected.

"No. He liked to steppcd on one, but he seen it and drew out his gun fast. But he shot the side of the car by accident and the bullet glanced off and hit the meat of his leg. He ain't hurt bad, but it give him a scare. That'll hold him!"

"That's too bad," Reuben said with deep feeling.

"A fact," Isaac agreed.

Having delivered the whiskey, they retired to the still and contemplated silently.

"He's hard to kill, Brother Reuben," Isaac said, shaking his head.

"He is that," Reuben agreed.

"We'd best think on it."

The brothers fell into a brooding silence that lasted all through the rains that came during the week. The stream swelled and filled with sediment and chemicals from the heart of the mountain. Usually the brothers were cautious about the water after such a rain until the stream had time to settle and clear. But they were so obsessed with their problem that they ignored principle, and the mineral from the mountain infected the whiskey. The brothers ordinarily would have destroyed the moonshine. But the work was done, and they capped it in jars.

"We could put glass in his food," Isaac offered.

Reuben shook his head negatively and huddled under a dripping loblolly pine as the rains began to dissipate.

No solution had offered itself when Deputy Satterberry limped to the bottom of the hill that Thursday. They saw him pause cautiously to survey above before he began to climb. Apparently satisfied that no wall of timber was about to descend on him, he crept, more slowly this time, up the hill. He arrived at the fireside breathing with difficulty.

"Lot a rain," he said, peering about in a suspicious manner.

"Like to washed the still off the mountain," Reuben said.

"Sold much whiskey?"

"Roads was too muddy to haul it down. We just ran a batch is all."

"How many?"

"Little more than fifty," Reuben said. "It ain't no good."

The deputy limped to the stack of wet boxes and inventoried the stock. Satisfied, he returned to the log and sat, his leg stretched out stiffly in front of him.

"I had a spell of bad luck," he said, as though asking for sympathy.

"Heard you did."

"Hair trigger on that gun. Bullet come off the car and hit my leg. There was snakes . . ." His eyes widened. "Come in there for warmth, I figure."

"Rattlesnakes?" Reuben asked cleverly.

"Copperheads. I liked to stepped on one."

"They's mean," Isaac admitted sourly.

The deputy took out his billfold to receive the bribe, ignoring the courtesy that it should have been Reuben's turn to move first. It was a rude thing to do, to just draw the billfold out like that and wait.

Reuben pulled the money out of his overalls and counted out the proper amount, not even attempting to bargain. The deputy was pleased at this. He took the money and demanded his jug.

Reuben went to the stack and selected a jar from the bad run. Since the deputy wasn't paying, he could drink from the polluted creek run.

They watched the deputy go down the hill favoring the wounded leg.

"If a man ever died from feet and legs, we'd have got him," Isaac said.

"Brother Isaac," Reuben said softly, "we got to be direct. Next time . . . I got it figured now. Next time when he sets, you'll pull a long rifle out from behind the log and aim it on his heart. You won't have to shoot him. I'll hit him in the head with some kindling and we'll carry him off ten or twenty miles and drop him in the river. He'll show up near Savannah probably."

"Might be risky, Brother Reuben."

"Well, it might, but we ain't doin' no good just hurtin' his legs."

Thus it was agreed, after some minor refinements in the plan had been devised, that the next appearance of the deputy would be the last.

More of the seasonal fall rains hampered business. The truck which usually arrived to carry the load was not able to negotiate the muddy roads. By the next Thursday, the rains had decreased, and the brothers waited for Satterberry to make his appearance. He would use chains on the car and get it muddy, if necessary, to get his money.

The long rifle was secreted behind a log. A solid length of kindling had been carefully selected. At ten that morning the brothers waited tensely. But the deputy did not appear. At eleven in the afternoon they were genuinely disturbed, because the fearful tension engendered by the intended murder became more oppressive as time crept by. At sundown, they knew he was not coming. "You think he knew? You think maybe he's about to break up the still?" Isaac asked.

"I just rightly don't know," Reuben admitted.

Friday passed and the deputy did not appear. In fact, nobody appeared, not even the truck which usually carried the whiskey to market. And the roads had dried sufficiently for passage.

"They's somethin', Brother Reuben . . . they's somethin'."

On Saturday they could bear it no longer. The brothers dressed in clean overalls and went into the town of Pinesboro.

As they arrived that morning, they began to observe sharp looks of silent disapproval from the people on the streets. A wall of reserve isolated the brothers.

"I feel somethin', Brother Reuben."

Reuben nodded, studied the sheriff's car parked in front of the courthouse, the windows rolled up tightly.

"We'd best find out," he said.

They strolled to the pool hall at the end of Main Street. A brooding silence descended as they entered. Eyes examined them coldly. Reuben made his way to the counter where old Nate Toombs sold chewing tobacco and soda pop.

Nate was distantly related, having married a Judd some generations back. Nate could be trusted.

"Folks is quiet. Nate, why is they a silence against us?"

Nate lowered his voice, his white stubble of beard glistening in the light of the 100-watt bulb above his head. "It's about how Deputy Satterberry died."

The brothers exchanged glances, pleased at first; then moment by moment their faces became grave.

"He died?"

Nate bobbed his head soberly.

"How'd he die then?" Reuben asked.

Nate lowered his voice so much this time the brothers had to lean forward to hear. "On *your* whiskey."

It was a harsh thing to say, a stunning thing to say to men of the Judd reputation, but Nate accented the report with a jerk of his white head. The deputy, he explained, died suddenly and the hospital over at Hayesville cut him open and ran some tests and discovered that some deadly mineral was in his stomach.

"They found an unfinished jar of moonshine whiskey," Nate said, lowering his eyes, "and there was some deadly mineral in it."

Reuben swallowed hard. He turned to face the men grouped about the pool tables, most of them his friends, his customers. He protested in his mind, but declined to speak because he knew it would be of no avail. No avail at all.

A man had died drinking Judd whiskey, and that meant the end of more than the deputy, whom they had plotted to kill. Although the bad mineral had gotten into the whiskey by accident, a distrust had been born that would not be dispelled until an entire generation of hill people died, and then not easily.

Later, Brother Reuben said softly, "It couldn't last forever."

Brother Isaac nodded, sensing that what was being offered was born of difficult truth.

"And you got to admit we ain't left with wants. If we take care, we'll never need."

"A fact," Isaac admitted.

"And," Brother Reuben began to smile, "the way it turned out with the deputy, the way he died . . . it's kind of pretty, considering what he was."

Brother Isaac's face accepted this thoughtfully, and soon he responded to the pleasure of the thought. Then together they began to dismantle the still.

The blue jay in the loblolly pine watched after them awhile before fluttering to the ground by the vacated campfire. The jay cock sang out a farewell, a unique cry of laughter touched subtly with a note of bitterness.

ROBERT W. ALEXANDER

The Dead Indian

If someone should ask how I got into this fix, I'd say because of a dead phone, but strangely it is because I was a dead Indian that I might escape unscathed. The only flaw in my ingenious plan is trusting an actress. The police want me, a syndicate bookie wants me worked over or eliminated and, worse if possible, a certain disgruntled man of the underworld has specifically ordered my demise. I'm sure!

Except for the police charge, I'm innocent, even though I have the money. Before all that, I was just making a few bucks at a job, to get the right clothes and meet the right people. I'm an actor—well, I wanted to be an actor. I had a taste of it, my first and only part, just a few months ago.

I've heard it said that if a person will knock around Hollywood long enough, opportunity is bound to strike. Nobody mentioned disaster. Anyway, after bothering casting offices and agencies for a while, I happened to be in the Levine agency resting my feet when they got a hurry-up call for an actor.

Previously, my lack of experience had precluded employment. I had never been in a movie or on TV; in fact, I'd never even been in a high school play. Doris gave me the idea. She's a ravishing brunette who is ga-ga over actors. So I thought, O.K., if it's an actor she wants, I can emote with the best of them. All I needed was the chance, which is tough to come by.

Doris seemed offended when I told her. Her yen for actors didn't include me? One would think she tried to identify with actors to further her own career. Well, she's young. She'd have to fawn around me when I was a star. I didn't mind starting as a bit player, and I could learn. I mean, what yokel *couldn't* squint down the dusty trail and say, "They went that-a-way."

The man in the Levine office was desperate enough to dash out to his waiting room to survey us hopefuls. I couldn't believe he decided on me! I'm rather plain.

"How quick can you get to Mervin Studios?" he asked. "They need an Indian. You got a car?"

It wasn't exactly the role I was looking for, but I said, "I could take a cab."

"You got the fare?"

"Uhhh . . ." I hedged. He shuddered, clenched his jaw, and resignedly shook his head. I guess he knew that most of us would-be's are broke and barely get by on meager night jobs, to be able to sit around in agents' offices all day.

However, my face must have fit the part because he advanced me ten bucks, had me sign an agency contract for the part, and then sent me out to the street to await the taxi he'd phoned.

At the studio, a huge one, I handed the unimpressed guard my paper. He said, "Get a hustle on. Stage three."

"Where's it at?"

My question pained him. "About a half mile straight down, you'll see the arrow. They're on their fannies waiting for you! Ya should've been on time. They'll never hire you again."

"I just got the role . . ."

"Don't tell me your troubles. Move!"

If they were in such a fireball hurry they should have had a limousine waiting—a car, at least. It was a long way. I dog-trotted down the pavement, hoping to sight a movie star; but no luck. Oh, well, I was on my way. Doris would be shocked. Someday in the near future I'd let her come along when I'm chauffeured down this lane in style.

I found an arrow pointing to Stage 3, an immense building, and picked up speed. The door was at the far end and I raced up to it, yanked it open, and dashed in. The first words that greeted me were: "Who the hell opened the door?"

An angry man in an open-collared shirt flew around a prop blocking my view. "Didn't ya see the red light?" he screamed. There was more screaming with everybody seeming to yell, "Quiet!"

I was quiet. I handed him my credentials: my paper from the Levine agency. He snatched it from me.

"The Indian!" He eyed me suspiciously. "Ugh! Well, follow me, and don't make a sound! They're reshooting the scene you spoiled."

The sound stage was impressive. They had an outdoor desert real enough to watch for rattlesnakes. There was a stagecoach, horses, a pretty girl in a checked gingham dress, and a suave, blue-eyed cowboy who was obviously the leading man.

Everybody greeted my apologetic smile with black glares, except the pretty girl in gingham; she seemed to have a twinkle in her eyes. Then they all ignored me, and I stood beside the assistant director who held my paper and watched them shoot the scene. It was an interesting shot of the girl getting out of the stagecoach.

I'd always thought they laboriously redid scenes over and over to get perfection, but not this crew. As soon as they filmed the girl getting out of the coach, the large director in the chair yelled, "Print it," and then they hustled the camera up to her face for a close-up. I wandered up beside the director where I had a better view.

After he yelled, "Print it," for the close-up, he whirled to the assistant director and ordered, "Shoot the Indian."

The assistant director worriedly nodded and rushed toward me, but the director was furious for any delay and screamed in my ear, "Where's the Indian?"

"I'm the Indian," I said. He looked at me in horror. Then he roared out a string of unprintable words, right in front of the gingham girl, who stonily pretended not to hear. I blushed.

Perhaps the flush on my face made me look more like an Indian. There were curses and threats for not having the Indian ready, and excuses that the Indian actor ahead of me had suddenly taken ill, gotten drunk or something. Anyway, they broke for an early lunch to let me get into costume and makeup. I quickly learned why the Indian actor before me suddenly took ill.

The assistant director rushed me to the nearest men's room and helped me strip off my clothes. I thought they would have dressing rooms, but I later learned it was a low-budget picture, the whole movie to be shot in three days.

When I was stark bare, the assistant director handed me a buckskin G-string.

"It's cold in here," I told him.

"Will you hurry!" he roared. I assumed that assistant directors were allowed to yell at bit players, so I got into the buckskin and looked for the rest of my costume. There wasn't any!

"Now wait a minute," I complained. "There's a girl out there."

He grimaced. "Do you think an Indian would care? Now, what are you? An actor or a misfit?"

It was a case of misfit, believe me. I'm on the skinny side and the low-budget costume was loose. I showed him, and he scoffed.

"Don't worry, we'll pin it tighter after we smear on your war paint."

I shrugged. Anything for art; I wasn't going to blow my career.

He hustled me out of the lavatory and across the way to where a dainty man with white hair and cold hands applied a film of reddish mud over my torso.

The assistant director approved. Then the real shocker came when he said, "Shave his head."

"What!" I blurted. If it weren't for Doris' obsession for actors, I'd have walked off.

"Look," he argued, "did you ever see an Indian with sideburns?"

I shook my head. Frankly, I'd never seen a real Indian—not one in war paint. So he shot me the ultimatum. "The script calls for a shaven-head Indian. Do you want the part, or not?"

The makeup man clipped me clean and ran an electric shaver over my head. My reddish locks dropped to the floor; some hair stuck to the grease on my body and had to be picked off.

The director was ready for me when I got back. "What's your name?" he asked.

"Steve McKing," I said, using my stage name.

He looked like he might be sick, but he explained my part. "You're the dead Indian," he said. "You just lie down there and don't move." The assistant director placed a tomahawk in my hand and showed me where to sprawl out on my back.

I heard them clack the sound gizmo, and I kept my eyes closed. Nobody had bothered to explain the story or the plot of the picture to me. I figured I would have to pay to see it, to find out what it was about.

I heard the pretty girl in gingham pretend to get off the stagecoach again. I was lying right at her feet. Suddenly, I heard her gasp! I thought, *My god!* I opened my eyes to see if—

Everybody yelled at me for moving. All she had gasped about was at seeing a dead Indian. It was part of the story. So the second time I didn't flinch when she inhaled. I heard her say to the leading man, "I suppose you shot him?"

He said, "Yes'm, I did."

"But he's just a boy," she retorted.

"He'd'a split yer head with the tommyhawk," said he. "Don't trust 'em. Not even a dead one!" With that, he pushed his pointed boot into my ribs. I'd been having fits with a tickling hair in my nose, and when his boot touched near my armpit, their dead Indian jumped a foot.

I caught hell, of course, but they finally got the scene they wanted on the fourth try. That was all the use they had for me, but no one told me that. I stood around freezing until quitting time, when everybody suddenly took off and left me.

The makeup man had disappeared too, and I didn't have any way to get the greasepaint off. I couldn't even touch my clothes. I wandered around, looking, and finally the girl in gingham, who had changed to a chic mini-skirt, saw me outside the building asking passing workmen if they had any cold cream. She brought me a jar and told me where I could find a shower. Later, out at the gate, I found her waiting for some friend she had phoned to pick her up. She smiled at my nude head. I had a look at myself in a mirror, and I couldn't fault her for grinning.

"Hideous, huh?" I lamented.

"Oh, I don't know," she said, watching my eyes compare her to Doris. "You might get a lot of work with a bald head."

"Really?"

"Sure. Not many boys your age are bald. Might be smart to keep your head shaved. A lot of 'quickie' companies can't afford elaborate makeup."

"That's mighty nice of you to tell me. I'm fresh out of loot right now, but tomorrow when I get my check from the agency—"

"I'm spoken for," she smiled. I smiled back. I had figured she might be, a budding star and all. Another thing, I'm cursed with looking younger than I am. For some reason I look nine years younger than my twenty-six.

A Lincoln picked her up.

I didn't break the great news to Doris that I had worked in a picture until the next day. After I collected my check from the Levine agency, I dashed up to her apartment. She lives only a block from my one-room pad which has running water at the end of the hall. I hammered on her door and hoped it wouldn't be opened by her roommate. I was in luck. Doris opened the door, but her mouth sagged.

"My God!" she exhaled.

"Oh, this." I touched my skin head. "I was a dead Indian," I announced proudly, and waved my check.

"You're a dead duck! A plucked one, at that! If you think I'll be seen with you, you're nuts!"

I lost my temper. She was envious because I had gotten a part. All she had ever managed was propositions.

"You're jealous," I said.

She slammed the door in my face. Worse, my taunt prompted her to speak to Mr. Crenshaw, who hires and fires at the drive-in where I filled in on Saturday nights as a counterman. She's a carhop there.

Mr. Crenshaw took a look at my head and said, "Uh, uh. You're not working here. You'll give the customers indigestion." But I knew Doris got him to fire me. He doted on Doris with futile high hopes, and I told him, "With her you'll make nothing more than change," *after* he fired me, of course.

So, I was a dead Indian as far as Doris was concerned, and could have given up acting, except that I liked it. I kept shaving my head and making the rounds of the casting offices, and I bothered the guy at the Levine agency every other day or so. "We'll call you," he'd groan, but I knew to keep reminding him that I existed.

Naturally, I had to find new employment to make out, and that meant a night job so I could pursue my career in the daytime. My bald head was a deterrent. Finally, after I added a pair of horn-rims with plain glass lenses, I appeared the studious type—I said I was working my way through college—and I got a janitor's job in an office building, a kind of run-down building, but located near the center of town.

A fat man with a lot of phones on his desk sat in his office by himself and tipped me to burn personally all his scrap paper. He said he was in the brokerage business.

This Mr. Shelly was really a bookie—I knew it—and one night at about seven, when I was sweeping up his place, the phone rang and some guy named Miller wanted to put ten on a horse in the fifth at Santa Anita the next day. I said, "O.K.," and left a note for Mr. Shelly.

"Not on my desk top!" he stormed at me the next night. "Ya crazy?"

"Sorry, Mr. Shelly. Thought I was helping."

He calmed down after I assured him I knew he was a bookie. He lit a cigar and studied me.

"Tell you what, Steve," he said, using my stage name that I gave everybody. "I'm moving out of here. Like, right now. How'd you like a job? You like figures?"

"Passionately."

"Yeah, well, these are numbers, but you can spend the profits on your choice."

So there went my night work. I became an assistant bookie. Sam Shelly worked for a national syndicate, and the bookie business was no small operation. I was amazed. Sam knew a lot about horses, too. He personally booked some bets.

"Look at this," he said once. "Two hundred to win on Stella Fancy. She ain't got a chance." So he didn't write the bet in the book, nor did he relay it to the syndicate. The horse lost and he pocketed the whole two hundred.

Hm, thought I. So, when Sam Shelly was out one day and a sucker called and wagered ten to win on a hopeless long shot, I booked the bet. The damn horse won and I had to cough up three hundred dollars, my entire salary for three weeks. I had to admit it to Sam, because he personally took care of the payoffs.

"That's the way it is," he shrugged. "Take the risk, pay the penalty. But get this, Steve—not too often. And be careful who you book. The syndicate hears we're taking bets on our own, they'll break our heads."

He didn't have to worry about me doing it again.

Two weeks later, Sam happily announced we were moving again. "Hey, top spot, kiddo. How about that? The boys promoted me to luxury. Watch the type of bets we get now."

He was right. We rented a swank office on the Strip and handled what Sam said was lay-off money. In cash! Sometimes five and ten thousand dollars a bet. Sam raised my salary to two hundred a week and I was nearly tempted to give up acting.

Most of the time I was a runner. Any time the money in our safe reached fifty thousand. I took it in a locked satchel to a big hilltop home with a view of the ocean. I gave it to a Mr. Bozelli, a large bull-necked guy who was sort of uncouth, would be the word. He had dark eyes and bushy brows and all he ever did was glare at me.

"Hey, baldy," he said on my second trip. "Ya know better than to touch this." He slapped the briefcase I'd given him.

"Yes, sir," I assured him, removing my glasses and pretending to be duly alarmed. The alarm didn't take much effort, but I don't know why I pretended I couldn't see very well without the fake glasses—unless I was afraid to let him know I was ogling the blonde out by the pool. Her sunsuit wasn't much more than ribbon.

I knew the blonde. She was the star of that Grade Z Western. The Levine agency told me the producer hadn't been able to get it distributed.

Mr. Bozelli said, "I'll get you the receipt for Sam." He never counted the money I brought in my presence, but went into a private office. It usually took him eight minutes. With nothing else to do, I used to clock him. Today was different.

I tore out to the pool. When she looked up, I said, "Hi, there."

"Well, hello." She was surprised. I didn't want her telling Mr. Bozelli I shaved my head. He might think I was nuts, since he didn't seem to be the type who understood actors. He might even order Sam to fire me. I explained my position to Miss Vida Lamour, after she told me her name.

She laughed. "Don't worry, Mr. McKing. Your secret is safe."

"Thank you. Uh—do you know Mr. Bozelli very well?"

"Yes." She contemplated me with amusement, obviously thinking me years her junior.

"I'm twenty-six," I said.

"Oh?" She winked. "Come on."

"Honest, I just look young." She didn't believe me. I shrugged. "There'll be no joy in Mudville . . ."

She cocked her head. "The mighty Casey struck out? Is there more than the obvious connection?"

"Casey is my real name. Steve McKing is just for the stage."

"I sort of guessed." Her brown eyes were suddenly friendly with that light of encouragement a woman can give. I whipped my wallet from my pocket.

"Would you like to see my driver's license?"

"I believe your name is Casey."

"No! My age. I'm twenty-six." A horrible thought struck me. "Uh—you're not married to Mr. Bozelli?"

"No. He's my uncle. Are you working for him?"

"Not directly. I work for a man who works for him."

She smiled. "You don't look the type. However, Casey—"

"I'd, uh, prefer you call me Steve. I started out as Steve McKing and they might not understand."

"All right, Steve—"

We were suddenly interrupted by Mr. Bozelli. "Who the hell told you to come out here?" he demanded. He grabbed me by the arm and propelled me through the house and out to the front porch where he handed me the receipt. "Don't try that again," he threatened, without allowing me to explain.

I didn't tell Sam Shelly about Vida Lamour, but that afternoon, about an hour after I got back from Mr. Bozelli's, I heard Sam answer a phone. "You want who? Twenty-six?

"Hey! That's for me!" I yelled. I pushed the button and took the call on my line. "Miss Lamour?"

"Are you really twenty-six? You look eighteen."

"That's encouraging. Everybody used to say seventeen."

We chatted on a little bit, me kind of under pressure with Sam sitting there. I took the opportunity, when he was busy with a phone bet, to tell her I was going to let my hair grow. She didn't want me to.

"No, Steve. I called to see if you'd be interested in joining a theater group. We're casting a play."

Naturally, I was entirely interested, and at the tryout I won the minor part of a woman whose head was shaved by the Nazis. I was with Vida every night that week, and life was good. Then it happened. Sam Shelly caught the Hong Kong flu.

I was left in charge of the whole operation—and I was busy! I had to handle all the phone calls, and the rare cash bets that were brought to the office. One thing Sam always did with the huge cash bets was to notify the syndicate immediately. If some outfit was trying to score with a fixed race, the syndicate seemed to know, and would bet a like amount at the track to cover themselves.

There was one guy in particular who visited our office every now and then and placed some heavy bets, but Sam took care of him personally. He was a sharp dresser with slick black hair, but his piglike, expressionless eyes ruined his looks. He usually had a couple of his boys with him. He gave me the creeps, and I didn't cultivate his acquaintance.

He walked in during the second afternoon that I was alone. Both of his men were with him. He placed a briefcase on my desk and waited until I hung up a phone.

"There's ten G's on Fightin' Fool in the third at Santa Anita. Count it."

That took a while, of course, and personally accepting the wager shook me a little, too. I wasn't conscious of the time—post time, that is, and I mean *our* post time. The track had the race scheduled for 1:40 p.m. and that meant we wouldn't take any bets on the race after 1:10 p.m. Our rule was that we had to have a half-hour leeway on any bet over a thousand. I looked at the clock. It was five minutes after one, so The Greek—that's what Sam called him—had just made it.

I wrote him a receipt in a hurry, and didn't bother to answer the ringing phones. I had a number to call—but quick!—to tell them of the bet I had accepted. The Greek picked up his receipt for the bet with a stone face.

"If it wins, I'll be back at five to collect. O.K?"

"O.K.," I nodded. Sam had that kind of arrangement with him. So I watched him leave and then rapidly dialed our center control office.

My phone was dead! I had five ringing phones, and my private line to the head office was dead! Not even a buzz. I told myself, *Calm down, boy, use another phone*. I wildly grabbed the one nearest me. Some guy who called himself Chazz, an old customer, attempted to place five hundred on Fightin' Fool!

I told him he had a wrong number. The idiot argued with me and stoutly maintained that he recognized my voice. He demanded to speak to Sam.

"Sam's sick!" I shouted, and hung up the phone. I took time for a breath and then lifted the receiver again. He was still on the line, cursing a blue streak and yelling that he had paid a hundred dollars for the tip, and that I wasn't going to gyp him out of a bet.

I dropped that phone and picked up another one. Another imbecile wanted to place a bet and wouldn't get off the line. All I could do was take his bet: two hundred to win on Fightin' Fool!

When I finally got him off the line I called central control, but got a busy signal. Never had that happened before. I was getting sick from the knotting in my stomach. I called Sam at his apartment.

"I'm sick," he groaned.

"Sam, listen. The Greek was in. Bet ten thousand, and I can't get our office. The line's dead!"

"Ohhh, I'm dying..."

"Sam! Damn it! What'll I do? The line's dead!"

"Ohhh . . . jiggle it. It's a private one-way line. Sometimes it sticks. Don't bother me." He hung up.

Jiggle it? I shook the living daylights out of it. Then I dialed, and shook it again, and dialed.

Finally, Mac answered. That's all the name I had for him. I tried to sound calm.

"This is Steve calling for Sam. The Greek wants to bet ten thousand on Fightin' Fool in the third—"

"You know the rules. He's a minute past our post. That's final."

"You don't understand—"

"Tell him no!"

"The phone's been dead!"

"I've been sitting right here, buddy, and you got me loud and clear. Tell him we're laying off and can't handle any more."

He hung up on me!

I called Sam again, but he wouldn't answer. My hand began to feel clammy, and I noticed a decided tremble when I lit a cigarette. I debated calling Mac again and telling him how I happened to accept the bet. The syndicate might not kill me; accidents happen. I decided it was better I explain to the syndicate *before* the race was run, than to attempt an explanation afterward to The Greek.

I was reaching for the private phone when the guy who runs the elevator broke into the front office. He dashed inside to where I was.

"The vice squad!" he hollered. "I saw them come in the lobby, and I shot up here. They'll grab the other car. You got about two minutes!"

Sam paid the elevator gang a hundred a week to spot the police. They knew every man on the vice squad, and they earned a two-hundred-dollar bonus for tipping us.

We kept the bets on a roll of paper like adding machine tape. I grabbed that and the ten thousand I'd placed in our escape valise—that was all the cash I had taken in so far—and raced to the elevator with my savior.

He clanged the doors shut and we started down just seconds before the police in the next car came up. I grimaced, and the elevator boy, a guy about my age, grinned.

"Wonder who tipped them?"

"I've got a good idea," I said. Undoubtedly the customer, Chazz, was mad because I didn't take his bet. "I'll see that Sam pays you," I told him.

"Don't forget," he said. He let me off on the second floor. I knew the escape route. I walked innocently down the back stairs and whipped through a parking lot. Sam had a car staked out in the second lot down. The key was in it and I was out of there in nothing flat.

I drove a few miles and stopped at a drugstore. I locked the money in the trunk of the car and went in to use the phone booth. Where does time go? It was already 1:42 P.M. on the clock in the store. The syndicate would never understand my phoning about the accidental bet *after* the race was run!

Maybe the horse will lose, I hoped. Wow! If it did lose, I was rich. I might have to split with Sam to keep his mouth shut, but five thousand? Wow! I left the drugstore and raced back to the car. I let my hopes build as I drove. After all, there were other horses in the race, and the odds were real great in my favor that it would be O.K. Anything could happen. Why, just a few weeks ago, the jockey fell off Swordfish when the horse was the favorite.

Fightin' Fool won the third at Santa Anita! Not only did he win by four lengths, but he paid $14.20. That's over six to one, and the syndicate owed The Greek over seventy thousand dollars and didn't know it.

I wondered how they'd settle it.

Actually, I'm not in bad shape—especially financially. I'll miss Vida Lamour, of course, but not for any longer than I did Doris. Down here in San Diego, where I'm residing, I met a redhead by the impossible name of Mary Jones.

I'm letting my hair grow, and I discarded the useless glasses, and even Sam hadn't known that I didn't need them. The only person now in the know—that I'm not a bald-headed unfortunate—is Vida Lamour. That's her stage name. Her real name is Thelma Bozelli, a name I'll never forget.

I chanced a phone call to her, at the theater where we were doing the rehearsals for the play about the Nazis. I didn't go into details about the trouble I was in. I just told her that I wouldn't be able to participate in her play.

She seemed to understand. She just asked, "Where are you?"

I said, "San Francisco." Then I said, "I just called . . . well, not only to tell you I'm out of the play, but to ask you to keep your promise not to tell your uncle or *anybody* that I'm capable of growing hair."

"Oh? Are you letting your hair grow?" She laughed nicely too.

"Uh, yes. My jet-black hair is sprouting up."

"That's odd. You had fiery red hair before they cut it."

"You remember," I laughed with her. "I've, ahh . . . been coloring it a little."

"I see. Well, Steve McKing, don't fret. I wouldn't *dream* of telling about your disguise."

"It's not really a disguise," I said quickly. "It'll be me, and I'm sure hoping nobody will recognize me."

"If they do, you're a dead Indian," she said.

We both laughed again—I had to force mine—and then hung up. She's not a bad actress. I hope she doesn't think blood is thicker than the bond between bosom troupers, because if she reveals that I'm a redheaded boy of twenty-six who looks eighteen, I *am* a dead Indian.

AUGUST DERLETH

The China Cottage

"**M**y esteemed brother," said Solar Pons as I walked into our quarters one autumn morning for breakfast, "has a mind several times more perceptive than my own, but he has little patience with the processes of ratiocination. Though there is nothing to indicate it, it was certainly he who sent this packet of papers by special messenger well before you were awake."

He had pushed the breakfast dishes back, having barely touched the food Mrs. Johnson had prepared, and sat studying several pages of manuscript, beside which lay an ordinary calling card bearing the name Randolph Curwen, through which someone had scrawled an imperative question mark in red ink.

Observing the direction of my gaze, Pons went on. "The card was clipped to the papers. Curwen is, or perhaps I had better say 'was,' an expert on foreign affairs, and was known to be a consultant of the Foreign Office in cryptology. He was sixty-nine, a widower, and lived alone in Cadogan Place, Belgravia, little given to social affairs since the death of his wife nine years ago. There were no children, but he had the reputation of possessing a considerable estate."

"Is he dead, then?" I asked.

"I should not be surprised to learn that he is," said Pons. "I have had a look at the morning papers, but there is no word of him there. Some important discovery about Curwen has been made. These papers are photographs of some confidential correspondence between members of the German foreign office and that of Russia. They would appear to be singularly innocuous, and were probably sent to Curwen so he might examine them for any code."

"I assumed," said an icy voice from the threshold behind me, "that you would have come to the proper conclusion about this data. I came as soon as I could."

Bancroft Pons had come noiselessly into the room, which was no mean feat in view of his weight. His keen eyes were fixed unswervingly upon Pons, his austere face frozen into an impassive mask, which added to the impressiveness of his appearance.

"Sir Randolph?" asked Pons.

"Dead," said Bancroft. "We do not yet know how."

"The papers?"

"We have some reason to believe that a *rapprochement* between Germany and Russia is in the wind. We are naturally anxious to know what impends. We had recourse to Curwen, as one of the most skilled of our cryptologists. He was sent the papers by messenger at noon yesterday."

"I take it he was given the originals."

Bancroft nodded curtly. "Curwen always liked to work with the originals. You've had a chance to look them over."

"They do not seem to be in code," said Pons. "They appear to be only friendly correspondence between the foreign secretaries, though it is evident that some increase in trade is being contemplated."

"Curwen was to have telephoned me early this morning. When seven o'clock passed without a call from him, I put in a call. I could not get a reply. So we sent Danvers out. The house and the study were locked. Of course, Danvers had skeleton keys which enabled him to get in. He found Curwen dead in his chair at the table, the papers before him. The windows were all locked, though one was open to a locked screen. Danvers thought he detected a chemical odor of some kind; it suggested that someone might have photographed the papers. But you shall see Curwen. Nothing has been touched. I have a car below. It isn't far to Cadogan Place."

The house in Cadogan Place was austere in its appointments. It was now under heavy police guard; a constable stood on the street before the house, another at the door, and yet another at the door of the study, which was situated at one corner of the front of the house, one pair of windows looking out toward the street, the other into shrubbery-grown grounds to a low stone wall which separated the building from the adjacent property. The house was Georgian in architecture, and likewise in its furniture.

When the study door was unlocked, it revealed book-lined walls, the shelving broken only by windows and a fireplace. The walls framed what we had come to see—the great table in the center of the room, the still-lit lamp, the motionless form of Sir Randolph Curwen, collapsed in his armchair, arms dangling floor-ward, his head thrown back, his face twisted into an expression of agony. Beside him stood, as if also on guard, a man whom Bancroft Pons introduced as Hilary Danvers.

"Nothing has been disturbed, sir."

Bancroft nodded curtly and waved one arm toward the body. "Sir Randolph, Parker. Your division."

I went around immediately to examine the body. Sir Randolph had been a thin, almost gangling man. A gray moustache decorated his upper lip, and thin gray hair barely concealed his scalp. Pince-nez, one eyeglass broken, dangled from a black silk cord around his neck. He appeared to have died in convulsive agony, but there was certainly no visible wound on his body.

"Heart?" asked Pons.

When I shook my head, he left me to my examination and walked catlike around the room. He examined the windows, one after the other, tested the screen on the half-opened window to the grounds, and came to a pause at the fireplace, where he dropped to one knee.

"Something has been burned here," he said. "Part of the original material?"

Bancroft said peevishly, "A cursory examination suggests that someone burned papers with figures on them, as you can see. We'll collect the ashes and study them, never fear."

Pons rose and came around to the table. He stood to scrutinize it, touching nothing. Most of its top was spread with the papers from the Foreign Office; these were divided into two piles, with one sheet between them, this one evidently being the paper Curwen was reading when he was stricken. A pad of notepaper, free of any jottings, was at one side of this paper. The perimeter of the desk was covered by an assortment of items ending with a small white, rose-decorated cottage of china, with an open box of incense pastilles beside it. Curwen's chair had been pushed slightly back from the table and around to one side, as if he were making an attempt to rise before death overtook him.

"Well, Parker?" asked Pons impatiently.

"A seizure of some kind," I replied. "But I fear that only an autopsy can determine the cause of death precisely. If I had to guess, I'd say poison."

Pons looked at his brother. "You mentioned an odor on entrance."

"We believe the odor emanated from the incense burner," Mr. Danvers said.

"Ah, this," said Pons, his hand hovering over the china cottage. He gazed inquiringly at Danvers.

"We have tested for fingerprints, Mr. Pons. Only Sir Randolph's were found."

Pons lifted the cottage from its base, where, in a little cup, lay the remains of burned pastilles. He bent his face toward the cup and sniffed. He looked up with narrowed eyes, picked up the base of the china cottage, and thrust it at me. "What kind of scent might that be, Parker?"

I followed his example and sniffed. "Almond," I said. "They make these pastilles in all manner of scents."

Pons put the china cottage back together and picked up the box of pastilles. "Lilac," he said dryly.

"The room was locked, Mr. Pons," put in Danvers. "No one could possibly have got in, if you're suggesting that someone came and poisoned Sir Randolph."

"Child's play," muttered Bancroft impatiently. "What did he find in the papers that someone should want to kill him? Or burn his findings?"

"You're irritable today," said Pons. "There's nothing here to show that Curwen found anything in the papers."

"On the contrary, there is everything to suggest that somehow someone managed entrance into this room, killed Sir Randolph, and burned his notes."

"Why not take them along? If he were clever enough to enter and leave a locked room without a sign to betray him, he must certainly have known that something could be determined from the ashes. I believe the papers in the grate were burned by Sir Randolph himself. He tore off what was on his pad and what had accumulated in his wastebasket under the table, emptied the wastebasket into the fireplace, and set fire to the contents. The ashes are substantial. There is among them at least a page or two from the *Times,* no reason for burning which I could adduce on the part of a foreign agent. Yours is the Foreign Office approach, all intrigue and espionage."

"It is indeed," said Bancroft shortly.

Pons turned again to the china cottage. "If I may, I should like to take this back to Praed Street." He picked up also the box of pastilles. "And this."

Bancroft stared at him as if he were convinced that Pons had taken a leave of his senses.

"This is bone china," Pons said, with a hint of a smile at his lips. "Of Staffordshire origin, it dates, I should say, to the early nineteenth century. This china, though translucent, will tolerate a surprising amount of heat."

"Pray spare me this lecture," said Bancroft icily. "Take it."

Pons thanked him dryly, slipped the box of pastilles into his pocket, and handed the china cottage to me. "Handle it with care, Parker. We shall examine it at our leisure at 7B." He turned again to his brother. "Sir Randolph lived alone. Surely there were servants?"

"A Mrs. Claudia Melton came in to clean the house twice a week," said Bancroft. "And there was a man-servant by day, Will Davinson. He prepared Sir Randolph's meals and tended to the door. He has come in, if you wish to question him. If so, let us get about it at once."

Bancroft signalled to the constable who stood at the threshold, and he led us out of the room to the rear quarters. In a combination kitchen and breakfast room, there sat waiting a middle-aged man who, immediately on our entrance, clicked his heels together, standing like a ramrod.

"Mr. Davinson," said the constable, "Mr. Solar Pons would like to ask you some questions."

"At your service, sir."

"Pray sit down, Mr. Davinson."

Davinson regained his chair and sat waiting expectantly. His eyes were alert and conveyed the impression of youth the rest of his body belied.

"You were Sir Randolph's orderly in the war?" asked Pons abruptly.

"Yes, sir."

"You had reason then to know his habits very well?"

"Yes, sir."

"He seems to have been addicted to the burning of incense."

"He has burned it for as long as I've known him."

"You will have had occasion to ascertain how many pastilles a day he customarily burned."

"Sir, he released the fragrant smoke only when he retired to his study. This was usually in the evening. He seldom burned more than three in an evening, and commonly but two."

"His favorite scent?"

"Lilac. But he also had pastilles scented with rose, almond, thyme, and, I believe, lavender. He always had a good supply."

Pons took a turn down the room and back.

He stood for a few moments in silence, his eyes closed, his right hand pulling at his earlobe.

"Sir Randolph was a reclusive man?"

"He saw very few people."

"Whom did he see in the past fortnight?"

Davinson concentrated for a moment. "His niece, Miss Emily Curwen. She had come to London from her home in Edinburgh and came to call. That was perhaps a trifle over two weeks ago."

"No matter," said Pons. "Go on."

"Mr. Leonard Loveson of Loveson & Fitch in High Holborn. That was a business matter. Sir Randolph held a mortgage on their place of business."

"Sir Randolph held other such mortgages?"

"I was not in Sir Randolph's confidence, sir, but I believe he did."

"Go on, Mr. Davinson."

"Well, then there was a great-nephew, Ronald Lindall, the son of Miss Emily's sister, also from Edinburgh; he was at the house six days ago, paying a courtesy visit, I took it."

"Anyone else?"

"Yes," said Davinson hesitantly. "There was a legal gentleman two days ago, all fuss and feathers. They had words, but briefly. Sir Randolph soothed him and sent him off. I believe the matter concerned another of Sir Randolph's mortgages."

"He was a hard man?"

"No, sir. Quite the contrary. More than once he remitted interest due him— even cancelled it. And on one occasion he forgave a small mortgage. No, sir, he was far too easy a man to deal with. Some of them took advantage of him."

Pons took another turn around the room. "Of these people, which were familiar visitors?" he asked.

"Mr. Loveson."

"You had not seen Miss Emily before?"

"No, sir. Sir Randolph had spoken of her, but she had not visited at any time that I was in this house."

"You admitted her?"

"Yes, sir. Sir Randolph never answered the door. If I had gone, unless he had an appointment, he did not answer the door at all."

"Will you cast your mind back to Miss Emily's visit? How did she seem to you?"

"I don't follow you, Mr. Pons."

"Was she composed—sad, gay, what?"

"She seemed to be a trifle agitated, if I may say so. But that was when she left, Mr. Pons. When she came in she was very much a lady."

"She and her uncle had words?"

"I could not say." Davinson was suddenly prim.

"Mr. Lindall, now."

"He was a somewhat truculent young man, but apologetic about disturbing Sir Randolph. They had a pleasant visit. Sir Randolph showed him about the house and garden, and he took his leave."

"Mr. Loveson. Do you know, is the mortgage a large one, presuming it has not been settled?"

"I don't know, but I had the impression that it is quite large." Davinson swallowed and cleared his throat. "I must emphasize again, Mr. Pons, that while Sir Randolph did not take me into his confidence, I was able to come to certain conclusions about his affairs."

"One could hardly expect otherwise of a companion of such long standing."

Davinson inclined his head slightly as if modestly accepting faint praise.

"The gentlemen from the Foreign Office," Pons said then. "Did you admit them?"

"No, sir. They came after I had gone to my flat."

"You answered the telephone while you were here. Do you recall any appointment after your hours during the past two weeks?"

"The foreign gentleman, three nights ago."

"Did he leave his name?"

"No, sir. He asked to speak with Sir Randolph. He spoke in a German accent. Sir Randolph was in his study. I made the signal with the buzzer, and Sir Randolph took the call. I stayed on the wire just long enough to be sure the connection had been made."

"You heard their conversation?"

"Sir, only enough to know that Sir Randolph was very much surprised—I took it, agreeably. Afterward, he came out and instructed me to prepare some sandwiches and chill some wine. So I knew he expected someone to come in during the evening. I assumed it was the foreign gentleman."

Pons nodded. "Your leaving arrangements were by your choice, Mr. Davinson?"

"No, sir. That was the way Sir Randolph wished it. He never wanted to be valeted, didn't like it. But he needed someone to do the ordinary things in the house during the day."

"You have your own key?"

"Yes, Mr. Pons."

"Sir Randolph was secretive?"

"Only about his work. He was a gentleman who, I should say, preferred his own company to that of anyone else. He treated me very well. Indeed, if I may say so, I should not be surprised to find myself mentioned in his will. He hinted as much to me on several occasions, and that ought to be proof enough that he was not unnecessarily secretive."

"Thank you, Mr. Davinson. I may call on you again."

"I want to do anything I can to help, sir. I was very fond of Sir Randolph. We were, if I may say so, almost like step-brothers."

"Was that not an odd way of putting it?" asked Bancroft, when we were walking away from the kitchen. "One says, 'we were like brothers.' Step-brothers, indeed!"

"Probably not, for Davinson," said Pons. "I fancy it was his way of saying they were like brothers one step removed on the social scale, Sir Randolph being a step up, and he a step down."

Bancroft grunted explosively. "You've frittered away half an hour. To what conclusions have you come?"

"I daresay it's a trifle early to be certain of very much. I submit, however, that Sir Randolph was murdered by someone he had no reason to fear. He appears to have been a cautious man, one not given to carelessness in the matter of his relationship with the public."

"You have some ingenious theory about the murderer's entrance into and exit from the locked room, no doubt," said Bancroft testily.

"I should hardly call it that. Sir Randolph admitted him, and Sir Randolph saw him out, locking the doors after him. Until we have the autopsy report, we cannot know precisely how Sir Randolph was done to death."

"We are having the papers gone over once again."

"A waste of time. You Foreign Office people think in painfully conventional patterns. I submit the papers have nothing to do with it."

"Surely it is too much to believe that Sir Randolph's possession of these papers at the time of his death amounts only to coincidence?"

"It is indeed an outrageous coincidence," said Pons. "But I am forced to believe it."

"Is there anything more here?" asked Bancroft.

"If possible, I should like to have a copy of Sir Randolph's will sent to 7B without delay."

"It will be done."

Back at our quarters, Pons retired with the china cottage and the box of pastilles to the corner where he kept his chemicals, while I prepared to go out on my round. When I left 7B, he was in the process of breaking apart one of the scented pastilles; when I returned two hours later, he had broken them all apart and was just rising from his examination, his eyes dancing with the light of discovery.

"Sir Randolph came to his death by his own hand."

"Suicide!"

"I have not said so. No, one of the pastilles contained cyanide. It was prepared and placed among the pastilles in the box on the desk, unknown to him. Since he used not less than two pastilles a day and not more than three, and the box contains normally two dozen pastilles, we can assume the poisoned pastille was placed there not more than twelve days ago. From the ashes in the china cottage it is possible to determine that the cyanide was enclosed in inflammable wax, and this enclosed in the customary formula. Sir Randolph fell victim to a death trap which had been laid for him by someone who both knew his habits and had access to his study."

"I thought it poison. What was the motive?"

"It was certainly not the papers, as was evident the moment I concluded that the incense burner was the source of Sir Randolph's death. That faint odor of almond, you will remember, was indicative."

"His estate then?"

"We shall see. Only a few minutes before your return a copy of Sir Randolph's will arrived. I was about to examine it."

He crossed to the table, took up the sealed envelope lying there, and opened it. He stood for a few moments studying the paper he unfolded. "An admirably clear document," he murmured. "To his faithful servant, Will Davinson, twenty-five hundred pounds. To Miss Emily 'who is otherwise provided for,' the sum of five hundred pounds. To Mrs. Claudia Melton, two hundred pounds. The bulk of his estate distributed equally among five charitable institutions. All mortgages forgiven!"

"There is certainly not much in the way of motive there," I said.

"Murder has been commited for as little as ten pounds," said Pons. "And less. But hardly with such care and premeditation. I fancy the stake was considerably more than two or five hundred pounds."

"Davinson has motive and opportunity."

"He could hardly deny it," observed Pons with a crooked smile.

"He knew he was mentioned in the will. He told us as much."

"Rack up one point against his having planned Sir Randolph's death," said Pons.

"I recall your saying often that when all the impossible solutions have been eliminated, then whatever remains, however improbable, must be the truth." Parker continued, "Davinson spoke of a foreigner, a German, who visited Sir Randolph only a few days before his death."

"We have only Davinson's word for it," said Pons.

"If not the papers from the Foreign Office, we seem to be left with only Sir Randolph's estate for motive," I pointed out, with some asperity.

"His estate seems to be well accounted for."

"The mortgage holders!" I cried.

"I have thought of them. Even before I saw this document, I suggested that some inquiry be set afoot about them. But I venture to predict it will be disclosed that Sir Randolph did not hold many unpaid mortgages, and that the total sum involved is not as large as Davinson, for one, believed."

"The man Loveson?"

"I have not forgotten him. His will very probably turn out to be the largest outstanding mortgage. He may have had motive in addition to having opportunity. The probability, again, is remote, for it must surely have occurred to him, should any thought of killing Sir Randolph have crossed his mind, that his motive would be instantly perceived. Moreover, we have Davinson's word for Sir Randolph's lenience with his debtors, and this is given adequate support by the terms of Sir Randolph's will, forgiving his mortgages. No, there is something else here of which we have as yet no inkling, something that induced his murderer to go to great pains to prepare a deadly pastille, secrete it among those on the table during the time of his visit with Sir Randolph—or his secret entry into the house, if it were that—and then be safely away when his victim by chance selected the poisoned pastille for use. It was all very carefully premeditated; there was nothing impulsive about it. That is why, patently, the papers have nothing to do with the matter, for whoever put the pastille into the box did so well before even Sir Randolph knew that he would be sent the papers for examination. By the same process of deduction, the foreign visitor lacked motive—if there were such a visitor."

"And if not?"

"Then, I fear, we should have to put Davinson through it. But there is little reason to doubt Davinson's story. A foreign visitor to Sir Randolph is not unlikely. And Davinson does not seem to me to be capable of so elaborate a plan."

"Who then?"

"We must consider that Davinson was gone by night. Sir Randolph was alone. He could have given entry to anyone he pleased, regardless of what Davinson believes."

"Well, then, we get back to motive."

"Do we not?" So saying, Pons sank into a reverie, from which he stirred only to eat, with a preoccupied air, a lunch Mrs. Johnson sent up. He still sat, smoking pipe after pipe of his abominable shag, when at last I went to bed.

Pons' hand at my shoulder woke me while it was yet dark.

"Can you spare the day, Parker?" he asked, when I sat up. "We have just time to catch the four o'clock from King's Cross for Edinburgh."

"Edinburgh?" I queried, getting out of bed.

"I have an unyielding fancy to learn what the late Sir Randolph and his niece had words about. We lose a day traveling later. The four o'clock brings us into Edinburgh by one-thirty this afternoon. We shall have ample opportunity to make our enquiries of Miss Emily Curwen. You will have hours to sleep on the train."

"Miss Emily!" I cried. "For five hundred pounds? Preposterous!"

"Unlikely, perhaps, but hardly preposterous," retorted Pons. "Poison, after all, is primarily a woman's weapon, so she is a suspect."

Pons had already summoned a cab, which waited below. As soon as I had dressed and made arrangements for my locum tenens to call on my patients for the next two days, we were off for King's Cross station, which we reached just in time to catch the train for Scotland.

Once in our compartment and northward bound out of London, Pons sank again into cogitation, and I settled myself to resume the sleep Pons had interrupted.

When I woke in the late morning hours, Pons sat watching the lovely countryside flow by. We had crossed the Scottish border, and soon the familiar heights of Arthur's Seat, the Salisbury Crags, the Braid Hills and Corstorphine Hill would come into view. Here and there little pockets of ground mist still held to the hollows, but the sun shone, and the day promised to be fine.

The tranquil expression of Pons' face told me nothing.

"You cannot have been serious in suggesting that Miss Curwen poisoned her uncle," I said.

"I am not yet in a position to make that suggestion," replied Pons, turning away from the pane. "However, a curious chain of events offers itself for our consideration. There is nothing to show that Miss Emily visited her uncle at any time previous to her recent visit. Then she comes, they have words, she hurries off, distraught. Does not this suggest anything to you?"

"Obviously they quarreled."

"But what about? Two people who have not seen each other for many years, as far as we know, can hardly, on such short notice, have much to quarrel about."

"Unless there is a matter of long standing between them."

"Capital! Capital, Parker," said Pons, his eyes twinkling. "But what ancient disagreement could exist between uncle and niece?"

"A family estrangement?"

"There is always that possibility," conceded Pons. "However, Miss Emily would hardly have come, in that case, unannounced and without an invitation to do so."

"Perhaps, unknown to Davinson, she had been invited to come," I said.

"Perhaps. I am inclined to doubt it. Miss Emily yielded to the impulse to confront her uncle to ask some favor of him. His failure to grant it angered her and she rushed off."

"That is hardly consistent with the premeditation so evident in the careful preparation of a poisoned pastille," I couldn't help pointing out. As usual, it was superfluous.

"Granted, Parker. But there's nothing to prevent such premeditation in the event that the favor she asked her uncle were not granted."

"What could it have been that, failing its granting, only his death would serve her?" I protested. "If a matter of long standing, then, why not longer? No, Pons, it won't wash, it won't at all. I fear you have allowed your latent distrust of the sex to darken your view of Miss Emily Curwen."

Pons burst into hearty laughter.

"Where are we bound for? Do you know?"

"Miss Emily lives in her father's house on Northumberland Street, in the New Town. I took time yesterday to ascertain this and other facts. She and her sister were the only children of Sir Randolph's brother, Andrew. Her sister married unwisely, a man who squandered her considerable inheritance. Both the elder Lindalls are now dead, survived by an only son, Ronald, who is employed in a bookshop, on Torpichen Street. But here we are, drawing into Edinburgh."

Within the hour we stood on the stoop of the house on Northumberland Street. Pons rang the bell three times before the door was opened, only a little, and an inquiring face looked out at us there.

"Miss Emily Curwen?"

"Yes?"

"Mr. Solar Pons, of London, at your service. Dr. Parker and I have come about the matter of your uncle's death."

There was a moment of pungent silence. Then the door was opened wide, and Miss Curwen stood there, unmistakably shocked and surprised. "Uncle Randolph dead? I saw him within the month. The picture of health!" she cried. "But forgive me. Come in, gentlemen, do."

Miss Emily led the way to the drawing room of the old-fashioned house, which was certainly at one time the abode of wealth. She was a woman approaching fifty, with a good figure still, and betraying some evidence in the care she had taken with her chestnut hair and her cosmetics of trying to retain as much of a youthful aspect as possible.

"Pray sit down," she said. "Tell me of uncle's death. What happened? Was it an accident?"

"Perhaps, in a manner of speaking, it was," said Pons. "He was found dead in his study."

"Poor uncle!" she cried, unaffectedly.

She seemed unable to fix her eyes on either Pons or myself. Her hands were busy plucking at her dress, or lacing her fingers together, or carrying her fingers to her lips.

"Perhaps you did not know he left you five hundred pounds?"

"No, I did not." Then her eyes brightened quite suddenly. "Poor, dear uncle! He needn't have done that. Now that he's gone, I shall have it all!"

"Somewhat over a fortnight ago you called on your uncle, Miss Curwen."

"Yes, I did."

She grimaced.

"You found him well at that time?"

"I believe I have said as much, sir."

"You left him, upset. Was he unkind to you?"

"Sir, it was the old matter. Now it is resolved."

"Would you care to tell us about it?"

"Oh, there's no secret in it, I assure you. Everyone knows of it here in Edinburgh." She tossed her head and shrugged, pitying herself briefly. "Uncle Randolph was as hard a man as my father. My older sister, Cicely, made a very bad marriage in our father's eyes. He had settled her inheritance on her, and when he saw how Arthur wasted it, he made certain I could never do the same. So he put my inheritance, fifty thousand pounds, in trust, and made Uncle Randolph guardian of the trust. I could have only so much a year to live on, a pittance. But the world has changed, and everyone knows that it is not so easy to live on a restricted income as it was twenty-five years ago when my father died. But now all that's over. Now that Uncle Randolph's dead, what is mine comes to me free of his or anyone's control."

"You must have had assistance, Miss Curwen," said Pons sympathetically.

"Oh, yes. My nephew, my dear boy! He's all I have, gentlemen. He has cared for his old aunt quite as if I were his own mother. I've been very much alone here. What could I do, what society could I have, on so limited an income? Now all that is changed. I am sorry Uncle Randolph is dead, but I'm not sorry the restrictions on my inheritance are removed."

Pons' glance flickered about the room, which looked as if it had not quite emerged into the twentieth century. "A lovely room, Miss Curwen," he observed.

"My grandfather planned it. I hate it," she said simply. "I shall lose no time selling the house. Think of having fifty thousand pounds I might have had when I was in my twenties! Oh, Mr. Pons, how cruel it was! My father thought I'd do the same thing my sister did, even after I saw how it went with them."

"I see you, too, are given to the use of incense, Miss Curwen," said Pons, his gaze fastened to a china castle.

"Any scent will serve to diminish the mold and mildew, gentlemen."

"May I look at that incense burner?" persisted Pons.

"Please do."

Pons crossed to the mantel where the china castle rested, picked it up, and brought it back to his chair. It was an elaborate creation in bone china, featuring three lichen-covered turrets, and evidently three burners. Carnations adorned it, and a vine of green leaves, and morning glories. Its windows were outlined in soft brown.

"A Colebrook Dale marking on this Coalport castle identifies it as prior to 1850 in origin," said Pons.

Miss Curwen's eyebrows went up. "You're a collector, sir?"

"Only of life's oddities," said Pons. "But I have some interest in antiquities as well." He looked up. "And what scent do you favor, Miss Curwen?"

"Rose."

"One could have guessed that you would select so complimentary a fragrance, Miss Curwen."

Miss Curwen blushed prettily as Pons got up to return the china castle to the mantel, where he stood for a few moments with the opened box of pastilles in his hand, inhaling deeply the scent that emanated from it. He appeared to have some difficulty closing the box before he turned once more and came back to where he had been sitting. He did not sit down again. "I fear we have imposed upon you long enough, Miss Curwen," said Pons.

Miss Emily came to her feet. "I suppose you will take care of such legalities as there are, gentlemen?"

"I fancy Sir Randolph's legal representatives will do that in good time, Miss Curwen," said Pons.

"Oh! I thought . . . "

"I am sorry to have given you the wrong impression. I am a private inquiry agent, Miss Curwen. There is some question about the manner of your uncle's death; I am endeavoring to answer it."

She was obviously perplexed. "Well, there's nothing I can tell you about that. I know he was in what looked like perfect health when I last saw him."

She did not seem to have the slightest suspicion of Pon's objective, and walked us to the door, where she let us out. From the stoop, we could hear the chain being quietly slid back into place.

"I must hand it to you, Pons," I said. "There's motive for you."

"Poor woman! I'll wager she's dancing around by herself in celebration now," he said as we walked back down to the street. "There are pathetic people in this world to whom the possession of money is everything. They know little of life and nothing of how to live. Presumably Andrew Curwen was such a one; I fear Miss Emily may be another. One could live well on the income of fifty thousand pounds if one had a mind to, but Miss Emily preferred to pine and grieve and feel sorry for herself, a lonely, deluded woman. I shall be sorry to add to her loneliness, but perhaps her wealth will assuage her. But come, Parker, we have little time to lose. We must be off to the police. With luck, we shall be able to catch one of the night trains back to London."

Inspector Brian McGavick joined us when Pons explained his need. He was in plain-clothes, and looked considerably more like an actor than a member of the constabulary.

"I've heard about you, Mr. Pons," said McGavick. "This morning, on instructions from the Foreign Office. I am at your service."

"Inspector, you're in charge here. I have no authority. I shall expect you to take whatever action the events of the next hour or two call for." He outlined briefly the circumstances surrounding the murder of Sir Randolph Curwen. By the time he had finished we had arrived in Torpichen Street.

"Let us just park the car over here," said Pons, "and walk the rest of the way."

We got out of the police car and walked leisurely down the street to a little shop that bore the sign, *Laidlaw's Books*. There Pons turned in.

A stout little man clad almost formally, save for his plaid weskit, came hurrying up to wait on us.

"Just browsing, sir," said Pons.

The little man bowed and returned to resume his place on a stool at a high, old-fashioned desk in a far corner of the shop. The three of us began to examine the books in the stalls and on the shelves, following Pons' lead.

Pons soon settled down to a stall containing novels of Sir Walter Scott and Dickens, studying one volume after another with that annoying air of having the entire afternoon in which to do it.

In a quarter of an hour, the door of the shop opened to admit a handsome young man who walked directly back to the rear of the shop, removed his hat and ulster, and came briskly back to attend to us. Since Pons was nearest him, he walked directly up to Pons and engaged him in conversation I could not overhear until I drifted closer.

"There is merit in each," Pon was saying. "Scott for his unparalleled reconstruction of Scotland's past, Dickens for the remarkable range of his characters, however much some of them may seem caricatures. I think of establishing special shelves for each when I open my own shop."

"Ah, you're a bookman, sir? Where?"

"In London. I lack only a partner."

"I would like to be in London myself. What are your qualifications?"

"I need a young man, acquainted with books and authors, capable of putting a little capital into the business. Are you interested?"

"I might be."

Pons thrust forth his hand.

"Name's Holmes," he said.

"Lindall," said the young man, taking his hand.

"Capital?" said Pons.

"I expect to come into some."

"When?"

"Within the next few months."

"Ample time! Now tell me, Mr. Lindall, since I am in need of some other little service, do you know any chemistry? Ever studied it?"

"No, sir."

"I asked because I saw a chemist's shop next door. Perhaps you have a friend there who might make up a special prescription for me?"

"As a matter of fact, I do have. A young man named Ardley. Ask for him and say I gave you his name."

"Thank you, thank you. I am grateful. In delicate little matters like these, one cannot be too careful."

Lindall's interest quickened. He ran the tip of his tongue over his lips and asked, "What is the nature of the prescription, sir?"

Pons dipped his hand into his coat pocket, thrust it out before Lindall, and unfolded his fingers. "I need a little pastille like this—with cyanide at the center, to dispose of old men and middle-aged ladies."

Lindall's reaction was extraordinary. He threw up his hands as if to thrust Pons away, stumbled backward, and upset a stall of books. Books and Lindall together went crashing to the floor.

"Oh, I say! I say now!" called out the proprietor, getting off his stool.

"Inspector McGavick, arrest this man for the murder of Sir Randolph Curwen, and the planned murder of his aunt, Miss Emily Curwen," said Pons.

McGavick had already moved in on Lindall, and was pulling him to his feet.

"You will need this poisoned pastille, Inspector. I found it in a box of rose pastilles in Miss Emily's home. You should have no difficulty proving that this and the one that killed Sir Randolph were manufactured for Lindall at his direction." To Lindall, Pons added, "A pity you didn't ask after my Christian name, Mr. Lindall. Sherlock. A name I assume on those special occasions when I feel inordinately immodest."

In our compartment on the 10:15 express for London Pons answered the questions with which I pelted him.

"It was an elementary matter, Parker," he said, "confused by the coincidence of Sir Randolph's possession of the Foreign Office papers. The death trap had been laid for him well before anyone at all knew that he would see the papers in question. This motive eliminated, it became necessary to disclose another. Nobody appeared to dislike Sir Randolph, and it did not seem that any adequate motivation lay in the provisions of his will.

"We were left, then, with Miss Emily's curious visit, angrily terminated. She went to London to appeal to her uncle for an end to the trust. She came back and complained to her nephew—her 'dear boy' who is 'all' she has—her designated heir, as an examination of her will will certainly show. In a fortnight, familiarized with Sir Randolph's habits by Miss Emily, he paid him a visit on his own, managed to slip the poisoned pastille into his box, and was off to bide his time. He had had two made, one for his aunt, and felt safe in slipping the other into her box of pastilles. He might better have waited, but he had not counted on the death of Sir Randolph being taken for anything but a seizure of some kind. He underestimated the police, I fear, and greed pushed him too fast. 'The love of money,' Parker, is indeed 'the root of all evil.' "